For Mary-Anne – my L.H.W.

Jude Morgan was born and brought up in Peterborough on the edge of the Fens and was a student on the University of East Anglia MA Course in Creative Writing under Malcolm Bradbury and Angela Carter. He is now married and lives in Peterborough.

Praise for *The King's Touch*:

'Conjuring up in extensive detail the politics, fears and licentious behaviour of the Restoration court . . . Morgan is careful to challenge the preconceptions of his historical characters . . . His skill is in bringing to life Jemmy's understandings of the deceitful atmosphere swirling around him'   *The Times*

'[Jude Morgan] handles incredibly complicated political intrigues with great aplomb and [his] characters take on real flesh. Charles himself emerges so strongly as the complicated character he certainly was, and his relationship with his brother James is very skilfully portrayed . . . A remarkably smooth and satisfying read . . . Catches the atmosphere of the times without dodging the intensely serious background to all the sexual licence and scandal which is normally taken to characterise the era'   Margaret Forster

'If you love historical novels in the vein of Georgette Heyer and Dinah Lampitt then you won't be disappointed with Jude Morgan's latest novel . . . The story is vividly portrayed with lots of period colour . . . a gripping read'   *Devon Today*

'Elegantly crafted and a joy to read . . . an impressive debut – imaginative and skilfully told'   *Historical Novels Review*

The King's Touch

Jude Morgan

review

First published in 2002
by REVIEW

An imprint of Headline Book Publishing

First published in paperback in 2003

10 9 8 7 6 5 4 3 2

ISBN 0 7472 6758 8

Typeset in Dante by
Letterpart Limited, Reigate, Surrey

Printed and bound in Great Britain by
Clays Ltd, St Ives plc

HEADLINE BOOK PUBLISHING
A division of Hodder Headline
338 Euston Road
LONDON NW1 3BH

www.reviewbooks.co.uk
www.hodderheadline.com

BOOK ONE

ONE

I was a boy of seven when the gentleman came to see me, and first opened the door to my destiny.

Anne Hill let him into the house one evening when my mother was out. He came into my bedchamber with a smile, which faded from his face as he looked around him.

'No fire?'

'No money,' said Anne. 'Jemmy, say how d'ye do to the gentleman.'

I had wrapped myself in a blanket for warmth, and was sitting curled on the window seat, watching for my mother's return, and amusing myself by drawing pictures on the cold misted glass. Now I put aside the blanket and went forward to shake the gentleman's hand.

'Hello, Jemmy.' He looked at my clothes – much rumpled and patched, I dare say. 'I thought to see you abed, perhaps.'

'Oh, I am not tired,' I said.

I knew him: at least, I recognized his face. I had spent much of my time that winter with my nose pressed against the window watching the street, which was the greatest entertainment I knew. This gentleman I had seen several times lately, lingering about outside, looking up at the house. I had supposed him to be something to do with my mother, who drew all sorts of men to her.

'There's no regular hours in this place, sir,' said Anne. 'She'll keep him up all night if it suits her. T'other week she comes in with her beau past midnight, drunk as a bee, and roused the boy up to dance a jig on the table. *That* should give you a notion.'

I remembered. I had enjoyed it. My mother had kissed me and called me her clever darling, and Mr Howard, the beau, had tried to jig himself

3

and fallen on his backside, and we had all laughed. Later, though, I heard my mother weeping.

'I see,' the gentleman said. 'There is a girl also, I believe?'

'She's asleep in her mother's room. Sickly, poor mite.'

'But she is not . . . ?'

'No. No question of that. Whereas this one—'

'Yes. Oh, yes, the resemblance is remarkable.' The gentleman ruffled my hair and kneeled down to face me. His accent was Irish, soft and liquid, and his eyes most narrow and penetrating. 'Well, Jemmy, and how are you?'

I said that I was very well, and hoped he was the same. I was used to meeting gentlemen, and showing proper courtesy; though I had never known any take this peculiar interest in me.

'A very pretty way. Tell me, Jemmy, what instruction have you had?'

I heard Anne Hill give a snort. She started to say something, but the gentleman gestured her to silence. 'Let the boy speak, mistress.'

'I have sat a horse,' I said. 'And I learned to skate on the ice.' We were living that winter at The Hague in Holland, and at Christmas I had gone with my mother and her beau to the frozen shores of the lake, and skated till the sun went down. 'Also fencing – a little. I'll show you.'

I fetched a stick from the corner of the room – there was a little cache of what I thought of as my treasures, a ball, a penknife, a broken doll, and such – and demonstrated my childish versions of parry and riposte. The gentleman watched, and seemed to smile a little sorrowfully.

'That is excellent,' he said. 'And now, what of religion, Jemmy? Do you know your Bible?'

'That is the big book in the church,' I answered confidently.

'Only in church?'

'Well . . .' I thought hard: I wanted to please. 'Mr Van den Bos has one downstairs.' Our landlord was a tobacco-seller who, outside of the counting house, spent all his time bent over his Bible. Or nearly all: there were also the quarrels with my mother, over the rent, over her habits. She called him a Calvinist prig, which I did not understand – nor did I quite understand the name he had for her, though sometimes Anne Hill muttered it too when my mother had vexed her.

'But have you not read in the Bible yourself, Jemmy?' the gentleman asked me.

'Oh, no. I can't read, sir.' I believe I said this quite cheerfully. I must have thought it quite a special attainment, and hardly to be expected.

'But you know your letters a little, surely?' the gentleman said, with a glance at Anne Hill, who just raised one eyebrow; and bending down to the floorboards, where there was, I fear, plenty of dust, he wrote with his fingers what I now know to be A B C. 'You know what these are?'

I shook my head.

'She's never troubled with it, sir,' Anne Hill said. 'And as for me, I'm no scholard, and I have enough to do keeping them clean and fed and clad.'

'Can you count, Jemmy?' the gentleman said. He was frowning now.

'I can count to ten,' I replied, and did so.

'You do not know what comes after ten?'

'No . . . but I would like to.' I wanted to please; but I spoke truthfully.

Gently smiling, the gentleman told the numbers from eleven to twenty; and I recited them after him, and then again, unprompted. He seemed delighted at my quickness, but in fact I was most passionately interested. There was only so much diversion to be had from watching the street, and no one had taken this manner of trouble with me before.

'You would like to learn more, I dare say, Jemmy?' the gentleman said, getting to his feet.

'Oh, yes, sir.' I began to suppose that he was a tutor of some sort, though his dress was very much of the Cavalier fashion, and he wore a sword. 'If my mother was agreeable.'

Anne Hill snorted again. 'Trust me, sir, she'll never consent to it. I've been with her these ten years, and I know her better than anyone. She's gone down and down. This new beau of hers – it's common knowledge he has a wife. What does that say about her? She's never fished in them sorts of waters before. I could tell you worse. There's a midwife in this very town knows a thing or two. There'd be more brats than this, if she hadn't found ways of being rid.'

Though I did not wholly understand this, I knew that my mother was being harshly talked about. She often was. I felt I should defend her in front of this stranger, but all that came to mind was: 'She is very beautiful. My mother.'

'Ah?' The gentleman smiled again. 'Well, you are a good boy, Jemmy. And chivalrous.'

'She sings to me,' I went on. 'She sings me to sleep when I have nightmares.'

'You often have nightmares, Jemmy?'

I did, though I supposed it normal – as I supposed it normal that we had no settled home, and that sometimes there was no food even though my mother wore pearls and satin. But it was true that my mother would sing the nightmares away – cradlesongs from her native Wales, tender as the call of doves in deep woods. I have since tried to sing them to my own babes, but that haunting note eludes me.

'He's forever having the horrors. But no wonder,' Anne Hill said. 'The wonder is he's not crazed, or an idiot.'

The gentleman shook his head, saying 'Tut-tut'; then bent down and, looking very seriously in my face, said, 'Are you happy, Jemmy?'

'Oh, yes, sir,' I answered; and then to my own surprise and shame I burst out crying, I think because this too was quite new to me. I was used to my mother's gentlemen giving me sweetmeats and, as I gobbled them up, looking on and saying, 'Ah, you are happy now, eh, boy?' But this was different.

Anne fussed, scrubbing my face with a handkerchief. The gentleman stroked his beard thoughtfully.

'I think, indeed, I must speak to Mrs Barlow, and put the matter to her.'

'Huh! I wish you joy of that,' Anne said grimly. 'And just what is the matter to be? Will his father own him?'

'My father?' The word jolted me out of my tears.

'Yes, mistress, he will,' the gentleman said; and then, putting his hand on my shoulder, 'Yes, Jemmy, that is who I come from. Your father the King.'

TWO

It was thus that I found out who I was – who I am. It marked, as I have said, the threshold of my destiny.

And yet the identity of my father was no secret. It was often talked of: I had even seen him. To explain this, I must tell of my mother.

At that time she went under the name of Mrs Barlow. Where the 'Barlow' came from I know not: certainly 'Mrs' was meant to confer respectability, as she was a lone woman with children. But her true name was Lucy Walter.

That is a name that has been much besmirched. Well, I shall be honest about her, and you shall decide for yourself.

She was born at Roche Castle in Pembrokeshire, of good family – good inasmuch as they were well-connected and not poor. I know they were not happy. Her father and mother quarrelled ceaselessly and at last separated, and though she never spoke much of them, I recall her once saying to Anne Hill that no one could hurt each other like two people who had fallen out of love.

'No knives can cut so deep. It is butchery – slaughter,' she said. I fear she had found that out for herself.

While she grew up in a house of bitter division, the kingdom went the same way. Like wrangling spouses, King Charles I and the Parliament came at last to their bitter parting, and the country was torn by civil war. There was blood and fire across a land that for so long had counted itself blessed. One of the many places on which the hand of destruction fell was Roche Castle. Soldiers of the Parliament burned it to the ground, as the Walters were of the Royalist party, though fortunately it stood empty at the time. My mother was in London with her father, who had a town house at Covent Garden. Though he did not take up arms for the

King, he must have shared in the general wreck of Royalist fortunes, as the Parliament began to emerge victorious. Many people fled abroad in the wake of that defeat, dispossessed and despairing. Amongst them was my mother, who with her maid, Anne Hill, and a few pieces of luggage took ship for Holland when she was scarce seventeen years old.

She did not go as some gentleman's mistress. That story has been put about, and I know by whom. But the fact of the matter is she had a relative who was set up as a merchant at Rotterdam, and my mother went to stay with him: a sensible arrangement, with things as they were in England.

It is true that many of the exiled Cavaliers, as the Royalist party were called, were gathering in Holland, and there were women who sought them out, for advantage. Like many in that troublous time, my mother was wrenched from her normal habit, and found herself in a world shattered out of its old custom and ceremony. But when she met my father she was no whore. She always said that fate had impelled her to him. And as I was the physical result of that meeting, I am the last person in the world to dispute it.

Certainly I know about fate. In my own life it has moved beside me, quite as apparent and unmistakable as my shadow. Only now, as I write these words at the town of Gouda in the year of grace 1685, do I feel its absence. Suddenly in my thirty-sixth year I must decide where my fate lies. It may be in a grave or on a throne. It is partly to help me decide that I set down this narrative. Also so that a portion of the truth may survive: for if it is indeed in death that I shall find my fate, then it is my enemies who will have the ear of posterity.

It was at The Hague, the capital of the Dutch Republic, that my mother met my father. They were both then eighteen years old. If there is any person of that age steeped in prudence and discretion, I have yet to meet them, and my mother's nature was singularly impulsive and passionate. They fell headlong in love, and she was very soon with child. Love – I have no doubt of that. Even Anne Hill, who was the most sturdy and sceptical of countrywomen, and often severe on my mother, said she never saw such a doting couple.

There would never have been any question about it, had my father not been who he was. But he was a prince, and so, of course, my mother must have been a designing harlot, aiming for titles and wealth. The gossips should stop and consider, though, what sort of a prince he was just then.

He was the eldest son of King Charles I of England, Scotland and Ireland: he was heir to the throne, and next in a line of illustrious monarchs that had included Henry VIII, the maker of our Church, and glorious Elizabeth, who repulsed the Armada and wrote our name on history's page in letters of gold. And when he met my mother, he had one good suit of clothes, and scarcely a penny to his name.

For the Royalist cause was by then in such ruin as, I think, neither side could have conceived when that deplorable war began. The last troops had been defeated, and King Charles I himself was Parliament's prisoner. Guessing what might befall him, the King had already sent his son and heir abroad to safety – but a dismal and despairing safety it was for that young prince. His native country was closed to him, and he could only linger about the Courts of Europe, living upon their charity, or on credit, and helpless to intervene as the tragedy of England and his House played itself out.

This was the young man my mother fell in love with. He was very tall and well-shaped, but not handsome: too dark and swarthy for that, his long face at once gaunt and fleshy. My mother, on the other hand, was a great beauty. That in itself explains much about her, I think. Beauty can be a burden as well as a blessing, for this reason: it takes away responsibility. Instead of shaping your own life, you find beauty speaking for you; decisions already made, as if by a well-meaning but meddlesome guardian.

My father was at The Hague as a guest of his sister, the Princess Mary, who had been married as a girl to the Dutch Prince, William of Orange, and so was safe from the wreck that came upon her family in England. My mother was well enough received by Princess Mary, who was unhappy in her marriage and disliked by the Dutch, and whose one solace was the company of my father. Him she adored, and it may well be that she was kind to my mother simply for his sake, for in later years there was a sad change. But that winter, while I grew in her womb and she basked in my father's love, was, I fancy, my mother's happiest time. Strange then that it should be marked by an event that shook the ground beneath the feet of Europe's kings.

In England the men of the Parliament sealed their victory by placing

King Charles I on trial, and sentencing him to death.

That event was midwife to the birth of a different world – the world in which I have grown up and lived. I can only try to imagine the effect it had on men's minds at the time. Crowned heads had rolled before, certainly – but only at the behest of other crowned heads, in the battle for thrones, the jousts of power. This was different. This was the King's subjects who warred upon their anointed monarch, defeated him, and took on themselves the power to execute him. And most importantly, they decided to have done with kings altogether.

They killed the King on a scaffold outside the Palace of Whitehall on a cold January morning, before a great crowd. There have been many accounts of that scene: of the dignity with which he went to the block, a pale figure dressed all in black, his long chestnut locks tucked neatly into a cap so as not to impede the stroke of the axe. Before dying he spoke to the crowd, and declared himself the martyr of the people, and it is as a martyr that many still remember him, keeping his portrait like a holy relic. This man was my grandfather.

His exiled followers did not hear of his execution until a week later, for Parliament sealed the ports; but my mother always claimed that on the afternoon of that fateful day I had given a great kick within her womb, as if I felt the killing stroke. On that, of course, I cannot speak. But I may as well set down my belief that if my grandfather was a martyr, then it was because he chose to be. It need not have happened. He would be absolute, and he paid an absolute price.

The scene on that black-draped scaffold has branded itself upon the minds even of men who never saw it, yet just as dramatic, and of even greater import, was what happened behind the closed doors of the Parliament-house that day. Because there, in haste, they passed a measure declaring that this was to be the last King of England. It was forbidden to proclaim his son as his successor: that was all done with. Oliver Cromwell, who was soon to assume the leadership of those men, is supposed to have urged my grandfather's execution with the words: 'We will cut off his head with the crown upon it.' I doubt he said that: Cromwell has become twined about with as many myths as my grandfather. But that is what in effect they did. And so when the shocking news came to my father at The Hague, he burst into tears.

He wept for the death of his father, of course, as any man would. But

I think he must also have wept for himself. For suddenly he was a king with no kingdom, a leader with nowhere to go, and a provider with nothing to give. Charles II, of nowhere.

Less than three months later, at a secluded house in Rotterdam, I was born. Surely no child of a king ever entered the world so inauspiciously.

My father chose my name: James. Like many, I came to be called Jemmy. It is a measure of my insignificance as an infant that I had no proper surname. Even 'Barlow' was entirely notional. Perhaps, indeed, my life has been a search for a true name, and it is still not found.

I was placed with a wet nurse, but my earliest memories are not of her, nor of my mother. Anne Hill is the chief presence. It is her tough red hands that tie laces, shoo away the crawling wasp, and bathe the grazed knee. I hear her rich country voice, which I somehow associate with dough and yeast, as she grumbles about my dirty neck or the meat I have pushed to the side of my plate. She was full of old saws that to me had a sinister thrill. 'Shut your eyes, or you'll see the fairies,' she would admonish me when I was put to bed; and, if I was late stirring in the morning, 'There'll be sleep enough in the grave.' That always set me scrambling up.

Against this, my mother is only an occasional figure, a scented and jewelled remoteness. When she did notice me, and take me on her lap, she was gently affectionate, kissing and caressing me and calling me her treasure. But I was faintly alarmed; I even thought it must mean I was ill.

As for my father, he had parted from my mother while I was still a babe in arms. He had a duty to try to win back his kingdom – indeed, there was nothing else for him – and so he sailed to join the Scots. They had not recognized the new republican government in London, and were willing to crown my father and march on England with him, provided he submitted to their religious conditions. These were strict, and many of his advisers were against the expedition, saying he would be no more than the Scots' puppet. But he saw no other choice. The powers of Europe would not intervene for him, for all their fine words. He was just a houseless young man with the empty name of king.

I think there was no question of my mother's accompanying him. The Scots were fiercely puritanical in their morality: many of his lords were even forbidden to go with him to that godly kingdom because of their reputation for profaneness and loose living. He and my mother may have sworn fidelity at their parting, for all I know, but those were disordered and faithless times, and I believe my parents may even have begun to fall out before he left. Suffice it to say that while he was away in Scotland, my little sister, Mary, was born, and she was certainly not his child.

How did my mother feel, with a king for a lover, and her child a king's son? There have been plenty of voices to say that such was her ambition all along. Well, if it were consequence she was after, she did not get it, nor seem to know the way to court it. My father supplied her with money, as much as he could, but that was little enough. As for influencing policy, I know my mother no more thought of that than of climbing a steeple and learning to fly. It was love my mother wanted, always. That was her only greed.

She was proud, though, of her royal lover. She invoked his name freely when, as often happened, there was trouble with landlords and creditors; and at such times she would seize me tightly in her arms, thrust me under their noses, and ask them how they could be cruel to the King of England's own son. They were never, in my remembrance, much impressed. That is partly why, though I soon grew used to my mother talking of 'your father the King', I did not take much account of it. Also, I am afraid, there were the men. They came and went – indulged me, mostly; ignored me sometimes. The notion of a single, fixed person who was my father did not really occur to me.

There was one man who was around a lot – the father, I now know, of my little sister, Mary. His name was Lord Taaffe. He was very grand and jolly, with a booming voice, and he wore lace and lovelocks in the true Cavalier style – though his face, close to, was flushed and coarse, and he smelled of liquor; and he had a great smile that sometimes looked like a bite. He would often bring sweetmeats, and invite me to hunt through his pockets for them.

'Do you have them yet? Ah, not there, that's my purse, you rogue. Though there's little enough in it, God knows. There, you like those, eh? What a greedy wretch he is, Lucy!'

I suppose I was. But life was such that you grabbed what you could, before it was gone.

'Why, he grows more and more like his father.' Lord Taaffe held me by the shoulder, staring at me. 'Look at that face. The very spit of

Charles, by God. Well, well. No chance of getting him to own the little she-brat as well, I suppose?'

'You beast. Do you think he can't count?'

'Aye, aye, I see what you mean. Hey, well, if my dead sovereign can own a bastard, then so can I. And damn me, on the same woman: how's that for keeping the King's interests warm?'

'Don't – don't speak of him.'

'Cock's life, you're passionate today.' A rumble of laughter. 'I speak no ill of Charles, God knows. I fought for his cause, and I count myself a pretty good friend of his. And now we share even more—'

'Devil!' My mother struck out at him, while he laughed. I heard, but did not understand. It was usually so. If I did question my mother about things, she called it being teasey, and pushed me away; and so I lived pretty much in my own world, separate from hers, which was mysterious and dramatic. I often heard her call Lord Taaffe 'devil', but sometimes also 'angel'. That was at night, in the dark. Our lodgings changed so often that they have all melted into one in my memory, but I know they were never large, and commonly my bed was in a closet close to my mother's; and I would hear grunting and creaking, and her cries. I soon learned to take no heed of them; likewise when she and Anne Hill quarrelled. They would call each other dreadful names, and throw things, and my mother would tell her to pack her bag. But the bag was always unpacked later on.

And it was in that spirit, I think, that I took my mother's talk of this absent person, 'your father the King'. I was not so precocious as to see in her a wild and unstable fantasist. But I felt that my mother moved in a different reality from that of Anne Hill, who darned and scrubbed and counted coins, and myself and Mary, with our colics and night-terrors and simple hungers, and that it was not one that concerned me at all.

I know Lord Taaffe was with us when I first set eyes on my father. The place was the palace of the Louvre, in Paris, where Lord Taaffe took us in his coach. Here my father's mother, Queen Henrietta Maria, kept a threadbare court of exile. Of French royal birth, she had never been popular in England as Charles I's queen. Her Catholic religion and her high-handed temper were equally disliked; and when the Civil War came, the Parliament bore a particular hatred towards her, which she returned in full measure. Long before my grandfather's final defeat, she fled abroad, where she lived as a guest of her French kin, and continued to dispatch ill-timed advice to her husband across the sea, right up to the eve of his execution. There is no doubt that his death hit her hard, and that she mourned most sincerely, even desolately. But even among the most loyal there were murmurs that her influence was partly to blame for the disaster of the royal cause, and that she still sought to dictate as a widow as she had as a wife.

Henrietta Maria had her circle, however, who were devoted to her. Most importantly, she had in Paris an establishment, which was precisely what the exiles felt the lack of. Later I came to know those royal apartments of my grandmother's very well, but nothing remains of my first impression, on coming to the Louvre with my mother and Lord Taaffe, except for my cry of disgusted discovery on stepping into a puddle of urine in one of the cavernous corridors. Appropriate perhaps. The French royal family did not much care for that grimy old pile, which hoisted its turrets above the stinking vapours of its moat like a revenant of a barbaric past, and the suite of rooms where my grandmother lived on a meagre allowance were shabby, draughty and ill-lit. And so, again, I had no sense of living in an exalted sphere. It was just another lodging. And the young man who came with Lord Taaffe one evening to look at me, and to ask me how I did, was just another young man.

Or, not quite: for in truth I think I was a little afraid of him, because he did not look like the others. They were always peacocks, curled and ribboned and exquisite. This man's thick crow-black hair was cropped short, and he had on a plain brown coat, much worn and soiled. His dark eyes looked soberly into mine, with no suggestion of a smile. I do believe, indeed, that I supposed he was one of those Roundheads of whose terrible deeds I was always hearing. There could hardly be a greater irony.

There was reason, of course, for the extraordinary appearance of my father at that time, though I did not learn it till later. He had recently arrived in France, a ragged and exhaustive fugitive, after such an adventure as no king can ever have known. His alliance with the Scots had been a tangled and embittered one, but at last he had led a Scottish army into England, hoping to reclaim his throne – hoping above all to rally his lost kingdom to his side.

That did not happen. There were Englishmen aplenty who preferred a king to a commonwealth, but that did not mean they wanted an invasion of Scots, who were foreigners after all, to settle their affairs. But I believe it was a sheer weariness with fighting and bloodshed that counted for most. Under the Commonwealth the country was settled at last, after a decade of war. Folk could turn to tending their farms, plying their trades, making love, rearing children. They could scarcely be blamed if they chose not to hazard it all again, for what seemed a mighty lean chance. The Parliament's armies were toughened and well-supplied, while my father's ragtag following melted away the further south he marched. When at last they made their stand at Worcester, with the troops of Cromwell at the gates, there could be only one result.

Battles always grow fiercer with each telling, but it is well attested that the streets of Worcester ran with blood that day. My father fought till the end, and at last, as night fell, escaped through the last gate with a handful of men, his army destroyed, his hopes blasted, and his enemies in triumphant pursuit. He was now the quarry, and his kingdom the hunting ground. 'Wanted for treason: a tall black man two yards high', were the words on the posters put up by the vengeful Parliament, and they offered a thousand pounds' reward for his capture. And so began that six weeks' miracle in which, his hair cropped and his clothes exchanged for a countryman's drabs, my father made his way across the country, smuggled from house to house by brave well-wishers, sometimes wearied to death and half starved, even clinging to the topmost branches of an oak while Cromwell's soldiers beat the thickets below him; until at last he got a ship at Shoreham, sailing just before the pursuing soldiers rode into the town, and was set down on the coast of France in so wretched a condition that the innkeepers would not give him houseroom.

The fabulous tale of his escape was one he loved to tell in after years. But the gaunt face I saw that first time was not that of a man triumphant, or even relieved. It was the face of a man who had lost everything. I wonder if he saw, as he looked at me, the innocent untried boy he had lately been, and whether he could not bear it.

My other memory of that time is my mother weeping, late at night. I was not unused to that, but commonly the tears came in loud fits, quickly ended, usually by someone giving in. Indeed, being a child I quite understood them.

'She wants to have her cake and eat it,' grunted Anne Hill, when I asked what was wrong.

As usual, I did not understand and it was not thought necessary that I should. Hindsight, casting its sad light, shows a woman who believed in love as enchantment, something not subject to normal everyday laws. She loved my father passionately before he went away; I believe she loved him till the end of her days. But she could not be alone in his absence, and there was not only scandalous report but the evidence of his own eyes to show him that. His late experiences had been of a bitter and disillusioning sort: they must have changed him. He expected, I think, little good of human nature – and I am afraid in my mother his expectations were met.

And yet she wanted them to begin again. Foolish, light-minded: perhaps. But anyone who knows anything of love knows that it *is* an enchantment of a sort, and can survive great divisions. If in my father the flame had gone out, she did not give up hope of rekindling it. Yet Lord Taaffe remained a friend and trusted agent of my father's, in spite of what had happened. That should have shown her how complete was the cooling.

Henrietta Maria, at any rate, professed herself shocked by this strange ménage at her court, and it must have been soon after that that we moved on again, to a meagre lodging in Paris. I think economy more than morality was behind it. The Court of the exiles was miserably poor by then, and I know that when my father dined at his mother's table, he had to pay in coin for his meals, which were set down in an account book.

It was a hopeless time for them and their cause. It was made even bleaker when Oliver Cromwell was declared Lord Protector of England, a title which satisfied the powers of Europe and made him a sort of king without the crown. Who had need of Charles II, that curious young relic of a vanquished house, trailing about the continent looking for a welcome? And it was a similar wandering, rootless, empty existence that I pursued with my mother, though as I had known no other, it did not seem to me strange.

Apart from my little sister, Mary, I did not mix with other children. Such as I came across did not speak English, straggling about France and the Low Countries as we did. I grew used to seeing the world beyond our chamber windows, the succession of cobbled squares and timbered gable ends, as an alien element – just as if the people going about their business down there were mer-folk swimming at the bottom of the sea. I knew only the company of adults, and they were all Royalist exiles: people who had nothing left but time, and nothing to fill the time but vices. Instead of fresh air, I breathed wine fumes and tobacco smoke; instead of lessons, I listened to scabrous gossip and bloody talk of duels, and innocently learned an array of curse-words.

I remember coming out with one of these to my mother. Unusually, she was seeing me to bed. Anne Hill was poorly, and had been in bed herself all day, clutching a charcoal foot-warmer to her belly. I asked if Anne had the gripes in her stomach, as I had once when I gorged on underripe fruit. My mother said no. Then I asked if the pain was somewhere else, using a word I had often heard among my mother's associates.

She slapped my face hard. I was too shocked to cry. I just stared at her. She seemed to tower over me, flushed and beautiful and terrible, her scented bosom heaving.

'I should soap your mouth for using such a word.'

'But it's what they say.'

'Who? Who says such things to you?'

I wanted to say 'the men'. And to add that they did not say the words to me, I just heard them because no one took any notice whether I was there or not . . . But young as I was, something restrained me, some recognition that to say it would be to cross a threshold. Once across, I must see my mother differently. I must even confront my own unhappiness, my knowledge that my life was being wasted.

So I kept silent. But it was my mother who seemed, just then, to shrink and slump, as if the knowledge had borne down on her without my speaking. She quietly saw me to bed, and then sat and sang to me a while. By the light of the candle I saw her hand steal to her cheek and rest there, as if it were she who had been struck.

Later, dozing, I heard a man come into the next room. After a time there was laughter. I felt relieved. In my circumscribed world, my mother had something of the stature of a goddess, and we do not care to see our deity shrunken and humbled. But when I heard the man say that word, I crammed the pillow over my ears.

I do not think it was Lord Taaffe, but he was still often with us. It was he who brought money from my father – not that there was ever enough. He brought sweetmeats for me and for Mary, and sometimes gifts for my mother; but increasingly, they were offerings to repair a quarrel. There were more devils than angels, as time went on: another cooling. Occasionally he stirred himself to take an interest in me, and I remember that causing a great row.

To beguile the time, I invented games for myself and Mary. One day, when my mother was out and Anne Hill was snoring in a chair, we investigated my mother's dressing table. We festooned ourselves in her pearls and earrings, and gaudily painted our faces with the white lead and Spanish paper and henna we found there. We must have looked like little Indian savages. When my mother came home, with Lord Taaffe, she gasped at us, then laughed and laughed. She had to sit down and hold her side. I was pleased. But I saw a frown on Lord Taaffe's face.

'These monkey tricks are all very well, Lucy. But at his age – damn it, he should know more. He should know his letters, he should—'

'I know what you are saying.' The laugher was gone, as if wiped off a slate. My mother turned on him. 'God damn your soul, you would have him took away from me, wouldn't you? That's the shape of it.'

'It need not be exactly so, Lucy. But he is concerned about the boy. You know he would not wish him to live so. His future—'

'His future is no concern of yours.' My mother took her handkerchief and began with fierce jabbing strokes to wipe the paint from my face. It hurt, but I could tell from her face that she was not seeing me.

'He's a bright fellow,' Lord Taaffe persisted. ''Tis a shame—'

'Get out.' She seized the lead pot and hurled it at him. It struck him on the brow, and shattered on the wall behind. His face darkened, and for a moment I was afraid.

Then he spoke softly, half smiling. 'You think to get him back, Lucy, by means of the boy? Is that how the wind sits? And so you will deny the child, and stunt him, just so as you can gain Charles's attention? Well, well. I'm aware, my dear, that you know some whore's tricks, but that is a new one.'

She screamed at him to get out, her face contorted, and then fell down weeping. Mary and I hung about her, plucking at her skirts, but it was a long time before she moved or spoke.

Then she embraced us and, taking my chin in her hand, said: 'One day your father will be with us, and we shall all be together, and live in a palace with gold platters to eat off, and sleep in beds trimmed with silver and satin. Do you believe me, Jemmy?'

I nodded, because it was an agreeable daydream, and I wanted to comfort her.

France had come to terms with Cromwellian England, prudently considering her a better friend than enemy. That made the presence of the exiled King on French soil an embarrassment. My father had to go. That other refuge, the Court of his sister Mary of Orange, could not welcome him either, even though Mary now reigned alone. William of Orange had died very young of smallpox, just a few days before Mary gave birth to their only son: a sickly boy, and for a time not expected to live, but mightily important. He was the heir to the House of Orange, and the Dutch made much of him. Against Mary's wishes, he was christened William too. Above all he must be Dutch in his heart. They always suspected Mary of being more attached to her brother's cause, the royal House of Stuart, than to her adopted country, and feared she would drag them into its misfortunes; and with the Prince out of the way, they made sure she fell into line. She was not to receive her brother. So he and his vagabond Court had to wander about such free towns and petty princedoms as would let him in.

And now I understand my mother's wanderings, which began to take us to out-of-the-way places. She was pursuing my father – perhaps for money, but, I believe, it was somewhere in her mind that she could win him again. At Cologne I think she secured a meeting with him. Certainly it was after that she showed off a paper promising her a pension of four hundred pounds a year. Anne Hill sniffed. 'Show it to the butcher and the chandler,' she said.

My mother only laughed; but later there were high words. The pension was to be paid at Antwerp, for the simple reason that Antwerp was out of the way. But the notion of being put out of the way was tinder to my mother's fiery temper. Anne Hill, ever practical, was shouted down. My mother would go where she liked. And so when we moved on again, it was to The Hague, where there was more fashion and amusement and English company. Also, of course, there was Princess Mary of Orange, my father's sister. The lonely Princess received my mother quite graciously, had her to supper and cards. I think she preferred the company even of a scandalous Englishwoman to that of the Dutch, whom she called a set of sour-faced cheesemongers. For my mother, of course, it was a link to my father: I doubt she was any more calculating than that. She was a woman who lived from day to day. And one day brought a new lover, one she never called anything but angel, one she told Anne Hill was the most beautiful man she had ever met.

'Huh! I dare say his wife thought the same when she married him.'

'You don't understand, Anne. You understand nothing. How could you, with your fudgy face?' My mother was dreamily practising dance steps, while Anne mended Mary's last petticoat. 'Love is outside your ken.'

'Thank the Lord it is, then, when it turns sensible creatures into fools,' Anne said, her cheeks reddening. 'Not that you've ever had any sense to begin with. And that don't make him any less married.'

'In London these things are accepted. In London—'

'We aren't in London. And even if we were, they don't hold with that sort of goings-on there now, from what I hear. It's all changed. And no bad thing neither, if you ask me.'

'Come, Jemmy. I'll show you the steps of the galliard. So – and point your toe, so . . . You make me laugh, Anne. I fancy you would fit in, you know, with that set of gloomy Puritans. They have closed the theatres and taverns, not because they are immoral but because they give people pleasure – and that's you in a nutshell, is it not, Anne? Oh, yes, that's you – the pinafored Cromwell—'

'Don't tell me what I am.' Anne was often angry with my mother, but something in her voice made me look at her. Her face was scarlet, and her eyes glistened. 'The Princess will soon tell you what you are, when it gets round.'

'Why should it get round? It's nobody's business but my own – mine and Tom's.'

Anne stabbed her needlework, saying nothing.

My mother's new beau, Tom Howard, was Master of the Horse to Princess Mary. I liked him. He was not coarse like some of the others: he was handsome and soft-spoken, and I fancied I detected something brotherly in the glance of his pale blue eyes. He took me to the stables of The Hague palace, and showed me how to sit a horse; taught me the first rudiments of fencing; and with my mother we skated when winter froze the lake meadows and trimmed the Gothic pinnacles of the old city with white. And so my narrative catches up with itself – or almost.

My mother was off somewhere with Tom Howard when that strange gentleman came to see me in my cold chamber, and spoke of my father the King; but the carefree happiness of their liaison had soured somewhat by then. Princess Mary had got to hear of it, and was stern. Colonel Tom Howard was a married man. Her unsteady position with the Dutch, a pious people, would not be improved by scandal in her household. She would have nothing more to do with my mother. But when she came home that night, foggy-eyed with wine and loud in her talk, my mother gave Anne her own version.

'I know what it is. I've been thinking of it – it all falls into place. The Princess has a taking for Tom herself. It's well known she cannot fend for herself as a widow, and looks for a man. Her mother-in-law rides roughshod over her – they scarcely give her a say in the bringing-up of that measly boy of hers. And so she looks about her – of course! I've seen the gleam in her eye, for all she acts the prim miss. I'm treading on her toes, and that's why she treats me so shabbily, and blackens my name, and sees to it that I am shunned by all good company . . . I wonder I didn't think of it before. How monstrous funny!' She beckoned me over and covered me with moist kisses. 'Well, I'm glad my boy is so strong and handsome. He will grow up to be a most splendid and dashing man, and turn all the ladies' heads, will you not, Jemmy?'

I had no notion of what I would grow up to be. I must have supposed that this wandering life with my mother would simply go on indefinitely. But now I felt a change within me. 'Your father the King': the words of the stranger still buzzed in my head. I had a father; he was the King. In the giddy vortex that my poor mother made of life, I had never been able to grasp these simple facts. Now the gentleman had made them real.

Most exciting of all was the realization that my father had sent him to look me up, that my father was watching me from afar, even perhaps making plans for me. It was like shutters opening, light streaming in from new perspectives.

I kept trying to picture again that gaunt, crop-haired, rather forbidding man I had seen at the Louvre. But somehow the image did not tally with those words 'your father the King', and my childish fancy replaced it with one of its own – some regal and potent shape – I believe it was something like a lion. It is a measure also of how unripe and unformed my impressions were at this time that this England of which my father was King appeared to me quite a mythical land. I had been born in exile, of course, and had never been there, and I could only conceive it as something like the fairy countries of the tales Anne Hill would some-times tell me, full of goblins and curses. I supposed indeed that this England was a land that had been conquered by some terrible monsters called Roundheads, of whom the chief was a fell creature called Cromwell, and that they had cast out the rightful King along with his followers good and true. I am amused to find that there are sensible grown men who would call that an accurate description of our country's history during the Civil Wars.

Though I had never before kept secrets from my mother, I did not speak of the gentleman's visit. Something in Anne Hill's look bid me be silent; but besides that, I felt it belonged to me alone, like a special gift. It was my little sister who gave it away. Kissing her good night, my mother asked what she had been up to today, and Mary innocently said that a man had been here.

'What man?' My mother was alert at once.

'He spoke to Jemmy.'

I did not know what I would say. I could not lie about it. But it was Anne my mother turned to – turned on, rather.

'What man? Anne Hill, you beast, what have you been about? What man?'

Anne was evasive. 'Someone from the King's party, I fancy. I don't know. He called, and went away again – he hardly stopped a minute.'

There was a storm in my mother's face, but then she smothered it, and was curiously quiet. She fell to thinking. My mother was not a reflective woman: she lived life upon the pulses, and when she did think it afflicted her like a depression of the spirits. She went drooping to bed, and for the first time I wondered if I had done wrong.

She soon found out what man, however. The very next day, when Anne brought Mary and me back from a walk to the market, we found the gentleman seated in our parlour with my mother. He just nodded at me, with a twinkle in his eye, before Anne hurried me to my chamber.

Soon I heard my mother's voice raised in anger, but the gentleman's voice remained smooth and muted, even when he departed – forced out by my mother by the sound of it, with a great crash as she slammed the door after him.

His name, I afterwards discovered, was Daniel O'Neill. In the Civil War he had fought for the Royalist cause under Prince Rupert, and now in the exile he was a confidential agent for my father, entrusted with the most delicate missions. 'Infallible Subtle' was his nickname, and justified. In spite of being turned out of doors by my mother in her fury – and that was something that made strong men quail – he managed another interview with her that evening. Anne Hill, whom my mother was refusing to speak to, had been sent out of the house, and though I was meant to be in bed, I could not help but creep to the door and listen.

'. . . But it's *she* who has been tattling these tales. She is full of spite against me – why, I cannot think, for I treat her better than she deserves, and she will never get half so good a place. Truly, sir, I am shocked that you should pay heed to the scabby lies of a common servant.'

'But I fear, ma'am, this matter of Mr Howard is common knowledge—'

'Because she has made it so! She will say anything to blacken my reputation! It pleases her to have me in her power. Dear God, it is a crying shame that I should be so. But what am I to do? If I dismiss her, she will only go about spreading more lies. Sir, will you not help me to be free of her? It might be simply done. I have heard that while a person sleeps, you may thrust a bodkin-needle into their ear, and they are snuffed out without a sign, as if they died in their sleep . . .'

I could tell my mother had been drinking. Even so, this was wild talk, and O'Neill said so.

'And yet you have been a soldier in the wars, have you not? And killed your enemies in battle? Why then so shocked – because it is a woman who speaks?' My mother was magnificently scornful.

'It is the kind of talk, madam, that has helped to procure you this unenviable reputation at The Hague. You are very public here, Mrs Barlow. Not only the court of His Majesty's sister the Princess of Orange, but the presence of many of the exiled party make this city a centre of attention. You may be sure that the agents of Cromwell watch here as elsewhere. And they will seize on anything that may injure His

Majesty's own reputation, which is most vulnerable just now—'

'Pooh, Charles is a king: what can kings fear?' That was very characteristic of my mother. She was a royalist of a grand, ultimate, Cleopatra sort.

I seemed to hear a smile in the voice of O'Neill as he answered: 'His Majesty is a king, indeed, madam, but he has nothing but the name. I will not disguise how desperate are his straits. One meal a day from a pewter dish is his habitual dining. I have known him not taste meat for ten days together. His clothes are scarce fit to be seen. All his suite are in like case. And yet he must try to maintain his dignity, and preserve his royal claim in the eyes of the powers of Europe. Consider, then—'

'I don't have to consider, sir. I am the first woman Charles ever loved, and between us there is a – a sacred bond that can never be dissolved. I am the very last person in the world who would injure his reputation.'

I do believe my poor mother meant this with her whole heart. She spent a lot of time in front of her mirror, but she never did really see herself.

'As for that wretch Anne—'

'Let us,' O'Neill said swiftly, 'let us pass over that now, madam. I have a sum which I believe will satisfy her present complaining state, and dispose her to be more discreet. And I urge *you* to be discreet, Mrs Barlow, because it is not simply a matter of your maid's tales. What I have heard from two midwives of this town I will not repeat. I will only say that they do not hesitate to repeat it – and that the city magistrates have shown some restraint in not having you banished from The Hague altogether. Yet.'

My mother was silent then. My imagination supplied the heaving breast, the gnawing lips. Often she made them bleed without knowing it, and I had had many a kiss that left my face bloody. Though I did not understand what was meant about the midwives, some instinct brought to my mind the couple of times when my mother had been mysteriously ill, and I forbidden to enter her chamber.

'It is done most humiliatingly, Mrs Barlow – with drums beating, and a cryer proclaiming your infamy,' O'Neill said, soft but distinct.

'You would like to see that, I dare say.'

'If I did, I would not be warning you thus, madam.'

'From the goodness of your heart.'

'Oh, come, who ever does anything so? I act for His Majesty's interests. Which brings us to the matter of the boy . . .'

There was a stir. I hesitated, dreadfully torn, for I wanted to hear about myself, but feared being found listening at the door. But my mother must only have got up and moved restlessly about. When she spoke her voice was cold, though not composed. She never was composed.

'You spoke secretly to him, sir, that I know. You are trying to turn him against me, aren't you?'

'Even if I were, it is plain I would have no success, for he is most loyally devoted to you.'

'Good. Tell that to Charles, then. That is what you are doing, is it not? Spying for your master?'

'Yes, I suppose.' O'Neill sounded almost bored. 'He is concerned about the boy—'

'He need not be. You have said it yourself.'

'I have said he shows a true and loving nature. And if such were all that is needed in life, then . . . The fact is, he cannot read or write, madam, nor reckon figures, and I think he has no more religion than a street urchin. If you love him, you would surely wish to see him properly raised and taught. Mrs Barlow, this is no life for him. The King—'

'He wants to take Jemmy away from me. Why do you not say it, sir?'

'What he wants is what is best for Jemmy. Many boys of his age, you know, go away for instruction: the sons of noble houses are sent to be reared elsewhere . . .'

I should have realized that my presence at the door would not scape my mother's keen senses. Suddenly she was there, seizing me and caressing me with ferocious tenderness, dragging me before the surprised eyes of Daniel O'Neill.

'Let us ask him. You cannot object to that, surely, sir? Let us ask my son.' She kneeled and fixed me with a look. I could feel her hot breath on my face. 'What do you say, Jemmy? This man wants to take you away from me, never to see me again. It is because I am a bad mother to you, and make you unhappy. But you do not have to go; it is only if you want to. If you do, it will break my heart and I shall die. But still it is up to you. What do you say, Jemmy? Shall you go?'

Tears stood in her beautiful eyes. I think it is no matter of wonder that I was weeping in a moment, and clutching at her desperately. I sobbed that I did not want to leave her, that she must not die, and other such things, all most heartfelt. But I believe part of me was weeping for something else.

O'Neill said nothing. When at last he got to his feet, I became aware of him, and embarrassed by my tears. I looked askance, through the damp net of my mother's hair, and found an expression on that subtle gentleman's face I could not read. It might have been pity, or disgust – perhaps they are never far from one another. Then he raised a hand in farewell, and I think I cried all the more bitterly because I believed it was for ever.

THREE

Soon we moved on again. Though I was not surprised, I found myself asking where we were going, and why. My mother, unused to this, said it was typical of the sulky humour I bore just lately.

Her lover, Tom Howard, was coming with us. It was he who took me aside and said, 'You have heard of the kingdom of Spain, Jemmy?'

'Are we going there?'

'Well, not exactly to Spain. The Spanish Netherlands, which belongs to it. The Spaniards, you know, have got hold of great portions of the world, even across the ocean, where they dig up great piles of gold and silver and treasure, and bring them home. You will tell them by the little forked beards the men wear, and the cloak thrown over one shoulder; and the ladies wear farthingale skirts that stick out like wings.'

What he did not say, but what I soon discovered, was that my father was there too.

Cromwell's England, a doughty fighter, had fallen to war with Spain, and begun helping itself to those treasures across the ocean. My father and his advisers saw their opportunity: here at last was a potential ally. He went to Brussels and had talks with the Spanish governors there, persuading them that as they had a common enemy they had a common cause. So his fortunes at last seemed to take an upward turn. The Spanish agreed to support him. By the terms of the treaty they gave him money and soldiers, and he was allowed to establish a court at Bruges in the Spanish Netherlands, with the Channel coast near at hand. Here he issued a call to arms, gathering all the Royalist forces about him, with the ultimate aim of landing in England. In return, he would show favour to Spain once he had brought down Cromwell and gained his throne. It must have seemed that heaven was, if not smiling on him, then lifting its frown at last.

Most importantly, he was solvent, and could oblige those who relied on him for provision – reason enough for my mother to head towards him. That Tom Howard went with us suggests she was not hoping to recapture my father's affections – but that I don't know. My mother relied much on her natural magic, and it was not an entirely misplaced faith. Men did lose their reason around her. As for Tom Howard, he pressed for the move. If he had plans of his own, he did not reveal them yet.

It was a short journey into Spanish Flanders, and at first I was disappointed that this tidy flat country looked little different from neighbouring Holland. But I was excited to see Spanish cavalrymen go by, with their vivid sashes and burnished breast-armour, and later a troop of musketeers on the march – proud-looking men, fierce and well drilled. As boys do, I imagined myself on one of those magnificent horses, charging into battle – the leader, of course, with my men cheering me. I did not suppose it could ever happen.

We had a good lodging, which Tom Howard must have secured, at the house of an English merchant in Antwerp. Here we were joined by a man I had seen but seldom, and never much liked. He was Justus Walter, my mother's brother – my uncle, though I hardly thought of him in such terms, for he was supremely awkward around children, and would look at me and Mary as if we were farmyard animals that had somehow got indoors. He had studied law, and since the end of the Civil Wars had attached himself to the Royalist party in exile, acting as agent for such of them as still had business affairs to conduct. He had not my mother's good looks or charm, being spare and sharp-featured and unsmiling. When they were together in a room she quite extinguished him. But he was equipped for the world in a way she was not.

He came to Antwerp to bring my mother news of a death in their unloving family. He was still in touch with England, and there Mrs Elizabeth Walter, their mother and the grandmother I had never seen, had died some months since. Her affairs were in some disorder, but it seemed there might be legacies.

'I shall have that coach and four at last,' my mother said, dancing me round, 'and it shall be lined all with red velvet, my darling!' No more mourning than that – but they were not a happy family, as I have said, and those were harsh, disjointed times, when people snatched what they could from the ruins. I am afraid I rejoiced too, the more so when my uncle spoke of our going to England to see to the business. That would be the greatest of adventures.

My mother, though, put him off. She had come here seeking my father, and she did not propose going away without seeing him. She began to compose a letter, announcing her intention of visiting his court at Bruges, but before it could be sent, Lord Taaffe arrived at the house. My mother's coming had already been noticed, and Lord Taaffe brought a message from my father himself.

'Aye, he is coming here, Lucy,' Lord Taaffe said, sprawling in the best armchair, and tapping mud from the heel of his riding boot. 'But quite incognito, you understand. There are many in his council who don't like you and your doings, I'm afraid, my dear, and would have you kept quite away from His Majesty's person. I don't see why, for you have always amused me greatly . . . Ah, is that the little witling there?' he added, seeing my sister, Mary. 'Here, sweetheart, I have some silver shillings for you. Mind your ma don't take 'em, for she'll spend 'em on liquor.' Such was the extent of his paternal obligation.

'Oh, I know what they say about me, and no doubt they have quite poisoned Charles's mind against me,' my mother said. 'No matter. My enemies will be scattered, and they will lick the dust.' There was quite a vein of religion in my mother, and sometimes she fell on these biblical phrases.

'Will they now?' Lord Taaffe smiled his biting smile. 'Well, I believe you, my dear: you're capable of anything, I'm sure. Anyhow, that's how it must be, Lucy – discreet. His Majesty is a guest of the Spaniards, and he must comport himself with dignity. He does have the greatest care for you and the boy, and would see you well provided. However, that's for him to discuss tomorrow: I've said my piece.' Getting up, he glanced at Tom Howard, who kept quietly in the background, and gave one of his loud hard laughs at nothing. 'And so you are protecting the lady on her travels, are you, Howard? Very chivalrous. I'm sure His Majesty will commend you.'

'I am His Majesty's loyal servant,' Tom Howard said, in his gentle way, 'and I ask for nothing.'

'Indeed? Then you're the first I've ever met. Every man has his price, that's what they say – don't they, Jemmy? Why, how you've grown. You'll be as tall as your father, I think. But make sure you grow in there as well, boy,' – Lord Taaffe ruffled my hair, and rapped upon my skull – 'grow in there, else you'll not last in this naughty world.'

I took no heed of this. All I could think of for the rest of the day, and the sleepless night that followed, was that my father was coming: my father the King. It was hard to tell who was the more excited, me or my mother, who took tremendous pains with her dressing and painting. But I had a conviction in my heart, which no guilt could quell, that it was really me he was coming to see.

I watched for him from my window all morning. Our lodging was opposite one of the old guild-houses of the city, a gabled fantasy covered all over with curious carvings, which could not fail to draw my childish eye when I grew tired of the waiting; and so I almost missed him, for he came very discreetly. He was on horseback, attended by only one gentleman, who took care of the mounts when my father stepped nimbly down, and then he had hurried up the steps to the house and was in, almost before I knew it.

Escaping from Anne Hill – with whom my mother had come to an uneasy peace – I ran to the landing.

I found my mother had done the same, and had thrown herself into his arms – at least, her arms were about him, and he was holding her – whether to him or away from him, I could not tell.

'Well,' he said. 'Hello again, Jemmy.'

He was changed from the bleak crop-haired man whom I had seen after the flight from Worcester. He had on a good suit of velvet with a lace collar and embroidered leather gloves, and his hair had grown back into those long glossy black curls now so familiar to the world; and instead of the listless abstraction there had last been on his face, there was that acute penetrating look that I came to know well. It did not transfix you, or question or accuse you. Rather it seemed to reach right into the inner chamber of your being, and behold all that was there, tolerantly and without surprise. I lost my tongue.

'Do you remember me?' he said. Being very tall, he kneeled down and extended his hand for me to shake. 'It has been a good while. I remember more of you, perhaps. I held you as a baby – odsfish, that does not seem so very long ago, yet look at you now.'

I shook his hand, which was very large and firm. I felt a fool for my silence. But he only smiled and went on: 'Alas, I wish I could have seen more of your growing. But I have had a strange, hither-and-thither life of it in late years, and it can't be helped.'

'Oh, so have we!' I burst out – I suppose in some childish attempt at fellow feeling. I noticed how my mother was looking at us – bright, breathless, somehow suspicious.

'Yes,' my father said. 'And a pity we couldn't have all had that life together. But sometimes grown-up people do not agree, Jemmy, and are better living apart.'

He glanced then at my mother. But she, with the same unnaturally bright look, said only, 'You must be thirsty from your ride, Charles. Will you have some ale? That was always your draught after riding, I remember. When we were first at The Hague—'

'Thank you, Lucy, that would do very well. And I would like to have some talk with Jemmy here. If you are agreeable, Jemmy?'

She could not stop him, of course, and I am sure part of her wanted it, as I was the most tangible evidence of their union, and so held them together. Yet she could not keep still while he sat me down in our parlour, and genially asked me about my health, and what I had seen of this country, and how I liked it. For my part, I was struck by how much older he looked than the general run of my mother's men – much older than Tom Howard, who had made himself scarce that day. My father was then only in his twenty-sixth year, but there already seemed a world of experience in those heavy-lidded brown eyes, gaunt cheeks, and wry heavy lips.

'Well, I am glad to learn you take no physic, Jemmy. As a boy I always refused to take it, because it made me worse. I remember telling my old governor the same, and he left off, and was much better for it.'

'I had a wart,' I said, 'and Anne Hill made a poultice for it out of tansy and crushed snails gathered under a full moon.'

'Indeed?' He smiled, though I did not feel myself laughed at. 'What does the moon have to do with it, I wonder.'

'It sheds a vapour, of course,' my mother put in impatiently. 'But you must catch it right.'

'Well, it is all very strange. There is a most clever man at Danzig,

Jemmy, called Hevelius, who has built on the top of his house a great tube called a telescope, and through that he can see the moon almost as plain as you can see the spire of the cathedral. I have seen the drawings of it, printed in a great book. There are mountains and valleys there, and huge pits and plains, and jagged outcrops like terrible cliffs.'

'Oh – why can't I see that?'

'Because the moon is so far away. Everything you see depends on where you are looking from.'

'It sounds monstrous ugly,' put in my mother restlessly. 'Pray, Charles, don't fill his head with such things, for he will only have more nightmares.'

He was alert. 'You have nightmares, Jemmy?'

'Sometimes,' I said reluctantly: I did not want him to think me a milksop. 'Sir, I should like to see that book about the moon.'

'I would like you to see it. But, Jemmy, I think you cannot read.'

'Oh! I have been teaching him his letters just lately, have I not, Jemmy?' my mother put in quickly, with a significant look at me. 'We spend each morning with a hornbook, and he gets along very well. But come, Charles, drink your ale, and sit easy. Where is Anne? It's time for the children's walk. They must have their exercise every day, you know. I am firm on that.'

'Aye, aye,' my father said, with a regretful nod at me, 'you are right, Lucy: you and I have much to talk of. But I shall see you anon, Jemmy. Here.'

He brought sweet-heart cakes from his pocket. I was ravenous, for there had been no breakfast that day: all our housekeeping had gone on viands for a grand supper in the evening. I fell most bearishly upon the cakes, I dare say. When I looked up, my father was watching me with raised eyebrows.

'Hm,' he said, reaching into his other pocket. 'Fortunately I brought more – for I knew you would wish to share them with your little sister.'

It was a reproof, but gentle, of a kind I was not used to. I felt my shame, though it did not sting.

My mother bustled me out of the room. Her hands were damp with sweat. I went to find Anne, but she declared her intention of staying, 'In case,' she said, 'there's pothers and ructions.' I understood. My mother had smelled of wine, and Anne was used to sweeping up broken glass, mopping spills, and binding cuts at such times. Somehow, though, I felt she would not be needed today.

Most unusually, it was my uncle Justus, at his own suggestion, who took us out for our walk. This felt strange, for he stalked along as aloof and taciturn as ever and, unlike Anne Hill, did not tug at me and keep me from darting off to explore this or that. It was summer, and hot. The old city was full of glare and stink as well as beauty: Flemish maids tittuped across the dung-strewn cobbles, their white-capped faces plain and creamy and wholesome as the milk they carried in yoked pails; here and there a door stood open in the heat to reveal a gaberdined Jew murmuring over the tortoiseshell trays of a jeweller's stock, or an old woman spinning flax at her chattering wheel. Down by the river seagulls quarrelled over rotten fish-heads, and ragged seamen diced in the doorways of slop-shops. There were many of these, and beggar boys too, thrusting out spidery hands for coins. A treaty had closed the Scheldt to shipping and the port was sadly decayed. My uncle waved them away, hardly seeming to see them, but I could not help noticing, in a dingy alleyway, two such boys who were huddled together and laughing uproariously, as if they had hit upon the most delightful game. I took advantage of my unusual freedom to investigate.

When they saw me, they turned round and actually bared their teeth. What they said I could not understand, but I had seen what their game was. They were hanging a mongrel puppy. They had looped twine around its neck, and tied the other end to an iron stud halfway up the wall. Beneath the poor beast's feet they had set a heap of stones, which they were pulling away one by one, so that it scrabbled for purchase more frantically each time, whining most piteously.

At once I pushed them aside, and tried to free the pup. The twine was tightly knotted around the stud, so I had perforce to untie the noose around its neck, which cost me some sharp bites, the poor creature scarcely knowing its deliverer from its tormentors. But I got it free at last, and it went skittering away. All the time the boys were raining blows on me with fists and bare heels. When I turned, and saw their faces all vexed at being disappointed of their torture, I believe I gave a sort of roar, and fell upon them wildly, gnashing and flailing. I have, I know, a hasty and inflammable temper – legacy, I fear, of my mother – but that was the first time it betrayed me into violence. The fight is an alarming blank in my memory, hidden behind a red mist of fury. I know one of the boys slipped away, but the other was quite pinned beneath me when I was roused by my uncle's voice, crying out in shocked admonition, and his hands gripping my shoulders and trying to pull me off. Little as I was, it still took him some effort to prise me away. When he did, I saw that the boy's nose and mouth were bloody, and there were livid bruises around his throat. He was weeping, and went whimpering away with a hand to his ribs, while I stood looking after him in a sort of trance.

'What do you mean by it?' My uncle looked down with distaste at Mary, who was howling and clinging to his leg. 'See here – you have made your sister cry.'

I tried to comfort Mary, who was slow to be placated, while Uncle Justus looked as uncomfortable as if he had been given the charge of a pair of goblins. At last he urged us away.

'It is an unsavoury quarter hereabouts. I should have taken more care . . . Tsk, Jemmy, here's your cuff torn! What will your mother say?'

I could have told him that my mother did not notice such things. Instead I said: 'They were brutes. They were hanging a little dog and laughing and . . .' the red mist had still not cleared, 'I could have killed them!'

'Plainly so,' said my uncle fastidiously. ''Tis all very well, Jemmy, but you must consider, you know—'

'Consider what?' My knuckles were beginning to sting.

'Well . . . that you are the son of a king.'

'If I am the son of a king, then why . . . ?' I burst out uncontrollably, then could not go on. But what I must have meant was, why the patched shoes, the boozy men chucking my chin, the trunks hastily packed and hurried downstairs at night, the emptiness and futility . . . ? Perhaps also I raged and burned because in those ragged urchins, neglected and untaught and with no path open to them but vice, I saw something not far removed from myself.

And Uncle Justus, no fool, must have understood.

'You know, boy, your father is not the usual run of king, as it were,' he said. 'He has come upon desperate hard times, and all those with him. Such times have never been known before. It is a new world, and a very perplexing one.'

'Will he never get his kingdom?' I asked – quite seriously, as of one adult to another; and my uncle answered me in the same way.

'It has often seemed so. I have had some talk with the men of his council, and there has been great despair these past years, more even than they care to give out. Cromwell's rule has grown stronger, and so has the fear that he will take the crown and be king himself. Most of the powers of Europe are content to live with him, and there is small chance of any effective rising in England. But now at last, perhaps, with the Spaniards aiding your father – well, who knows? There may yet be another new world.' My uncle stopped and looked at me narrowly, almost as if seeing me for the first time. 'He is certainly taking a great interest in you, at any rate, now that he has a chance. I wonder . . .'

He sniffed, and shook his head, and did not say what he wondered. But he was thoughtful all the way home.

We children were to sup with my mother and father, and Anne Hill filled a tub and gave us both a scrubbing before the event. She clucked over my torn cuff and the blood on my hands, and only thinned her lips when I told her the blood was not my own. She had not been needed here, it seemed: there had been no quarrelling or crashing. It made her, in her dour country way, more suspicious.

As for me, I felt awkward about facing both my mother and father – not because of the fight, but the outburst afterwards. Somehow I had all the pangs of a traitor as I sat at the supper table, but a boy's appetite quelled them. There was pickled sturgeon and anchovies, lamprey pie, rabbits in onions, chicken and mutton – such fare as we seldom had. When my father gave me a glass of canary wine, I felt I was feasting with the gods. I did not mind when he asked me if I knew my Catechism, and when I did not, began patiently to teach it to me. Learning was new enough to me to be a pleasure. My only concern was that my mother would not like this, for it took a lot of time, and I feared her jealousy of his attention.

Yet my mother had a quiet glow about her, I saw with surprise. She had on a new necklace of many brilliant pearls, but it was not that. She was, for once, at ease. No great thing perhaps, but it seemed so to me; and whatever my father's faults – some have been exaggerated, and there are some the world does not know of – he always had this gift of creating ease wherever he was. It is not a negligible gift, and was in some ways a curse, for I believe that to him ease and harmony were like drink to other men: he felt sickly without them, and had to have them, sometimes at any price.

I know that I soon felt so easy at that supper table, that I spoke of my encounter with the beggar boys. My mother did not reproach me: she gloried in my spirit. But my father looked so long and pensively at me that I asked him if I had done wrong.

'Oh . . .' He stirred, and drank wine. 'Who is to say what is wrong and right in this world, Jemmy?'

I did not understand. 'But if you do something bad, you must be punished.'

'Ah, but who is to do the punishing? Someone who believes himself to be entirely in the right. Yet everyone differs about who is in the right.'

'When they cut off my grandfather's head,' I said, the wine loosening my tongue, 'that was wrong, wasn't it?'

'Jemmy!' my mother cried.

But my father only smiled. 'Mr Walter,' he said to my uncle, 'there is a lawyer here in the making, I think. He will catch me in my own net. I only mean, Jemmy, that it is a hard task setting the world to rights.'

Which was precisely, of course, what my father was expected to do. In my innocence, I supposed that courage was enough for that.

'When I was with the Scots, trying to win my throne,' my father said, 'Cromwell brought up an army to their borders, to fight them. There was a great battle at a place called Dunbar. Now the Scots are a very strict people, and believe you must be thoroughly good in all ways. They pray all day, and fast, and even wear sackcloth and ashes when they feel they have not been good. Before the battle, they examined their soldiers, and the ones they thought were not good – meaning wicked and sinful – they got rid of, and replaced them with proper religious men, the sons of church ministers and so on. And they lost the battle. Those men were very good – but for that purpose, very bad.' A hard, remembering look came over his face as he spoke of the Scots, and for a moment he seemed to forget I was there. Then he brightened. 'Still, don't trouble your head over that, Jemmy. Just make sure, if you ever pitch in like that again, that they have no hidden knives about them.'

'Oh, I don't think they could have. They hadn't even any pockets.'

This amused my father greatly. I viewed his laughter with wondering delight. It was my first experience of a simple truth about him. He loved to be amused, and to amuse him was to earn his love. We think of amusement as a trivial thing, and it is on those grounds that many have judged him harshly. But I believe for him it was the counterweight to universal despair. I think his mind, like the eyes of a blind man, saw blackness.

'Everyone has a hidden knife, Jemmy,' he said casually. 'Mr Walter, will you take some more of this wine?'

After supper my uncle withdrew, and Anne came to take us away to bed, but I begged to be allowed to stay up a while, and though I saw my mother's eyes flash, it was granted at my father's urging. Anne sat Mary and me down to a game of cards at the table, while my mother and father took seats at the window, open to the pleasant breeze of evening, and talked.

What measure of accord they had come to that day I could not tell, but though the talk was of serious matters, there was no heat in it. We had a very simple card game, so that Mary could join in, and I was able to give most of my attention to their words.

'O'Neill,' my father was saying, 'is a trusted agent, that is all. I cannot do everything myself, and so I rely on him for such reports.'

'And those reports have gone all about your council, no doubt, and fuelled their hate for me.'

'Who hates you?'

'Sir Edward Hyde, for one. He has always been against me.'

'That may be so. But Hyde is against a lot of things that I do. He reproaches me for dancing, for riding, for doing anything but attend to business. I dare say he is right. I am a lazy dissipated fellow, and he cannot help but berate me for it. He is, God help him, a truly loyal servant of the crown. He wore himself out as my father's adviser, trying to save him from himself, and will surely do the same with me. But he is a prig, you know: he does not like any women.'

'Even that woman you have at Bruges? Aye, you see, Charles, I am not the only one whose affairs are talked of.'

'Yes, her also. What would you have me say, Lucy? Do you expect me to be the saint you are not? No, no. We are too much alike in that.'

'In that, perhaps. Yet we differ greatly. Do you not see how unhappy I am without you?'

'Are you?' There was a pause, as if he digested this. 'What about Tom Howard?'

My mother made an impatient movement. 'It is a separate thing. Life – life is full of separate things.'

'Lucy. You know, you are the only one I don't understand. Everyone wants something from me. It is usually quite clear-cut and for their own betterment. Hyde wants to be my chief minister, and to run the kingdom neatly with lots of ribbon and sealing wax. My mother wants me to marry a French heiress of her choice, and keep me under her thumb. My brother James, I think, wants me to fall off a cliff so that he may have a chance at wearing this damned invisible crown. People want peerages and honours and favours . . . but what do *you* want, Lucy?'

'I want you.'

There was a silence. Anne Hill, scowling, tapped my nose and made me attend to the cards.

'Then,' my father said at last, 'you want the one thing I cannot give. I must – keep something, Lucy. Do you see? It's the only way I can live. I cannot help it.'

'Do you suppose I can help the way I am? Your spies tell you I have gone to the bad. But why do you think that is? It's because I lack you, Charles. Without you, this is all I can be.'

My mother's voice was not raised, but it throbbed deeply as if her very lifeblood had given tongue. But my father's was flat as he said: 'No. If it is so, then . . . I am sorry. But I cannot be decisive for another mortal in that way. It's a responsibility I won't take.'

'Are you afraid?' my mother said, and I found an echo of that in my own mind, though it was quickly gone.

'I speak of the real. We are all alone for ever, each and every one of us. We do best not to pretend otherwise.'

'Your father would grieve to hear you talk so.'

'You didn't know him,' my father said, a little snappishly. He drew a deep breath. 'I have the last letters he wrote to me from his prison. The ink is black yet, the paper still crisp. He will be dust long before them. A hard thought. And here's a harder one: if I think of him up in heaven, he seems no more remote to me than he did in life. His parting advice to me, by the by, was that it is better to be Charles the Good than Charles the Great. Impossible to be both, of course, in this world. But I don't want to be either. Do you know who I want to be? Charles the Long-lived.'

'Why, that's a poor glory to aim at.'

'Perhaps. But it's the one and only permanence there is.'

My mother did not answer that. Instead she came over to us and, stroking my hair, said to him, 'Charles, I think you and I should have a hand of cards together, as we used to do.'

'Let the children finish their game first.'

'Oh, they have played long enough. And it's time they slept,' my mother said, and I found the cards snatched from my hand. Anne surrendered hers with a dark look.

'Very well, but if you mean high stakes, I had better tell you I have only a few pistoles left in my purse. And you don't mean to game that necklace away already, I hope? It is meant as portable income, my dear.'

'No, no.' My mother urged me out of my chair. 'Let us sit down to a game for love, Charles, as we used to.'

And that, I must think, is what they did that night, in some sort. For my father stayed. I slept as sound as a church, and did not know it till the morning, when I ran into my mother's chamber, and found my father there in shirtsleeves with a bowl of water, shaving himself.

'Good morrow, Jemmy. How do you find yourself this morning?' he said easily. 'See how I am reduced. Will you believe that once upon a time I had half a dozen pages kneeling about me for every little thing I did? At dinner a food-taster, and next to him a cup-bearer, and next to him a napkin-bearer to dab my mouth every time I took a sip of wine. The curious thing is, I get along very well without them.'

He had a very strong beard, as befitted his dark southern complexion, and the bowl was full of black flecks.

'Sir,' I said with childish directness, 'are you going to stay with us?'

'I wish it could be so, Jemmy, for I have only just begun getting to know you. Alas, I must go. That does not mean, of course, that we shall not see any more of each other, my son. You understand, don't you?'

I understood – better, perhaps, than anyone guessed. My mother knew no persuasions but love, and so he had employed them; and I was the object. How I grasped this knowledge I do not know, unless it be that I had spent my life among people who manoeuvred and manipulated in this way, and breathed an air of bad faith. Yet his motive was to get hold of me, and certainly there was a tremulous rejoicing in amongst the terrible confusion of feelings that racked me, as I stood before my father that morning, rumpled and blinking from sleep, with my future in the balance.

And so there was no surprise for me in what followed. In a way I had already seen it. My mother came up, very brisk and bright. She had been out early marketing, which was a thing she never did, and when she gaily asked me what I would like for my breakfast, I hardly knew how to answer, because that too was unheard of. My father knew it, of course. He missed nothing. But he said, smiling, that we would all sit down to breakfast together; he only craved a word first.

He was still in shirtsleeves, and I remember, as he spoke, that I sat down on the bed, and took up his doublet that was lying there, and toyed with the ribbon points that went round the waist. I counted them: twenty-one. I had practised my counting to twenty diligently since Mr O'Neill had taught me. I believe it was as I sat on the bed that morning, listening to my mother and father talking for the last time, that I realized twenty-one must be what came next.

'It is time to think of Jemmy's future, Lucy.'

'Yes.' My mother was temperate, at first. 'Yes, that is one of the things we must think of.'

'I have in mind a good household, where he can be set to a good tutor, and brought up as – as befits my son.'

'Ah. And what of me?'

'Well, you may depend upon me for a good maintenance. I know it has been unreliable in the past, but now my affairs are somewhat more settled—'

'Why, you bastard. Oh, you double-dyed whoreson bastard.' I had heard my mother use such language often enough, and I don't know why I flinched just then. She had brought a posy of flowers from the market, and I flinched again as she hurtled them at the wall. One fluttered, broken, on to the coverlet of the bed. 'So this is what it was all about. This is what it comes to – all those pretty things you said last night, Charles—'

'I said no pretty things, Lucy. You must be mistaking me for one of the others.'

'Pah! You stand in judgement on me,' she exclaimed in fury, 'you of all people – when even your counsellors despair of you for a whoremaster—'

'Precisely why I don't stand in judgement. Neither of us, Lucy, has any right to get upon the high ropes. So let us leave off talking morals at each other, in God's name, for it's all a sham. The matter is, what's best for the boy. Come, you are no fool, nor blind: you know that's what brought me here.'

But even I could see that such an appeal missed my mother entirely. She thought with her heart. She has been called wanton and light-minded, but I fear her real trouble was that she was the most romantic creature that ever existed. The airy castles of hope she had been a-building were absurd, no doubt, yet I cannot but pity the destruction of them.

'I know you want to take him from me,' she said. 'It is a great spite in you, and I cannot think what I have done to deserve it. You loved me once, Charles, you loved me—'

'I don't deny it,' he said dully.

'Good, excellent. Perhaps then you can say why you have decided to hate me.'

'I don't hate you, Lucy. But maybe you would prefer it if I did, eh? For at least then the play is still on, and we can stay in costume and strike attitudes, instead of facing the plain light of day. But if you can't be reasonable for your own sake, then be reasonable for the boy's – your little girl too, though I have no say in her fate. Let me have the custody of him, and you may do as you please.'

'Never,' my mother said. 'You shall never have him.'

I counted the ribbons again, while the words seared my ears. Twenty, twenty-one.

'Why?' My father seemed to search for some other expression, but could only repeat that pure, rational question. 'Why, Lucy?'

My mother could have answered, of course, that she loved me too much to part with me. Things might have been different, perhaps, if she had: I might have been different; and our country's history also.

But she said, spitting the words out: 'Why? Because you want him, Charles. That's why.'

'Him, and not you. At long last you are truthful.'

I grasped the flower, and began to pull off the petals. Well, it was already broken. My father's shadow fell across me as he picked up his doublet and put it on.

'Jemmy, don't weep,' he said. I didn't realize I was, but he put a hand gently to my face, and his fingers came away wet.

'Don't touch him.' My mother pulled him bodily away; he nearly overbalanced. I looked up at the two of them wrangling, and expected that it was time for the broken glass and the blood.

But my father had no taste for that. He lifted away my mother's hands, rather as one might lift away a couple of clinging kittens. He quickly finished his dressing, and went downstairs, with my mother screaming after him. After a while I followed – I don't know why, for I had seen and heard enough.

Outside the house my father's gentleman was there with the horses, and my father was mounting up. A little crowd had gathered, for my mother was yelling things about him, gutter things that made them stare and laugh. It was because of this crowd that I was able to slip through and get near him, unseen by my mother. He had just gathered the reins when he saw me, down by his horse's flank. His frown lifted a little.

'Jemmy. God bless you, my boy.' He reached down and extended his gloved hand, and I took it; and then I felt his grip tighten. He did not pull me, he did not speak, but his eyes bored into mine, and I knew what he was saying. It would be the work of a moment: up on to the back of his mount, and he would ride off at speed, and so it would be done.

And, of course, I did not. I could only shake my head, and slowly withdraw my hand. He sat up, and nodded, gathering the reins again, and it seemed he wore a faint look of shame at having put me to the choice. But it cannot have been as great as the shame that filled me, knowing that I had wanted to go.

So, burning with that shame, I went to my mother after he had ridden away, and hugged and embraced her till I could not breathe, seeking expiation; and felt it was only what I deserved when she thrust me away and went weeping alone into the house.

FOUR

Shortly afterwards, we crossed the sea in a leaky fishing boat out of Ostend, and I came for the first time to England. This was the most significant of my travels, and not only in its dangers – though they were greater than I knew.

My mother country – so it was, but an unwelcoming mother I found it at first, having been prodigiously sick on the crossing, and then at Gravesend finding we must take to the water again, almost as soon as I had stamped my trembling legs on the dockside. Two wherries were engaged at once, to carry us upriver to London. My mother was impatient to complete the journey, and had not suffered in the least, being naturally sturdy. Mary, Anne Hill, my uncle Justus, and Tom Howard were all as sick as me. But such was my mother's mood since we left Antwerp that no one chose to challenge her. It was not merely bad temper, though there was plenty of that. There was a heightened and feverish aspect to her, which broke out sometimes, for example, in tremendous exulting over what she would do with her mother's legacy, and the figure she would cut in the world, and so on. She was, I think, very unhappy, though it would have taken a brave spirit to suggest it to her; and for my part, I found only a new coldness towards me, which coupled with a brooding dissatisfaction in my own heart, disinclined me to much affection. A sad alteration, for I believe I had as loving a disposition, even intemperately so, as any child ever born. But I kept thinking of my father, as she well knew, and in that there could only be poison.

So, an ill-assorted party, we came to the capital, and struggled ashore at a set of steep and slimy stairs above London Bridge; and it was from then, I think, that the spell of the city feel upon me, and excitement drove out my sickness. On the Continent I had seen places handsomer and more well-proportioned; never had I seen a place that made my heart beat so fast, and filled me with something akin to a promise, as if here at last life would unfold a shining secret that hitherto had been but dim shadowings. The river was one vast swarm of craft, so that I fancied a nimble man, leaping, could cross its whole span from bank to bank dry-shod. The crowd of buildings, roof upon roof, spire upon spire, was so great that I made myself dizzy turning about to look at them in astonishment, and in that astonishment it seemed only natural to me that there were quaint narrow houses standing all along London Bridge itself – as if in the press for room they had been elbowed out, and had had to take their station where they could. And then the people – so infinitely various in their aspect and business, and somehow more vivid, noisier, and even more frightening than I was used to. We went by hackney coach to the Strand, where my uncle Justus had bespoke lodgings, and though my mother was for having the leather blind pulled down, I had my way, and hung my head out all the way, pointing out the sights to Mary. Of course, I was as little informed as she, and could do no more than cry 'Look' at the ranks of painted and carved signboards, which, hanging often from upper storeys crazily leaning over the road-way, seemed likely at any moment to take off our coachman's head; at the herds of pigs and geese being driven through the streets, under the very windowsills of grand houses, and in peril of the iron-shod wheels of carts and drays jostling on all sides; at the little ancient churchyard, like a shored-up mound of mould, that protruded hideously over the street and appeared ready to spill its crumbling dead at the feet of passers-by; at the languid lady in a mask, carried in a red-lined sedan chair with a Negro page trotting along behind. The noise was prodigious, and so was the smoke and smuts and stink. But it was magnificently alive, and I understood now why this England, the fabled land of which the exiles were always talking, was so important.

And yet I did not understand why they spoke of it as they did – as a place fallen under a monstrous tyranny since the execution of my grandfather, Charles I, and the driving out of his heir. There were no ogres in sight, nor people slinking about as if in fear of them. Dress was chiefly dark and sober, but, having lived in Holland, where the tall-crowned hats and plain bands were common, I found nothing remarkable in that – and though I saw a couple of mounted troopers, they had to make their way in those crammed streets like everyone else. When we came to the coach-stand by Somerset House, in the Strand, my mother cried out in fury: 'Oh, the great maypole is gone! Those devils have cut it down!' But I had no notion of what a maypole was, and as for the obliteration of the playhouses, bear gardens, bordellos and low taverns that was the distinctive policy of Cromwell's rule, that was not immediately visible. But I fear that to a child such as I was, nothing that went on in those places would have appeared noteworthy in any case.

'Lucy, my dear,' my uncle said, 'remember, tongue betwixt teeth, if you please. When we are behind closed doors, then you may speak your mind.'

My mother was silent at once. I was surprised, for normally nothing was more likely to make her fire up. But the truth was, for all her bravado she came to England in some fear. The Government of Cromwell was still vigilant about Royalists returning from exile. That did not mean they could not come. Many, as the years passed and the royal cause came to seem lost, decided to make their peace with the new masters, and return home. The Duke of Buckingham, one of my father's oldest and closest friends, did just that about this time, and even married the daughter of one of Parliament's greatest generals. What Cromwell's agents were chiefly on the watch for were any who came to foment Royalist rebellion. But, of course, they were interested also in those who were intimately connected with my father, the King in exile, their shadowy enemy lurking over the sea. There, they were very interested indeed.

In that regard, my mother ran a great risk in coming to England. And when I say she was fearful, I give perhaps a wrong idea of her personal courage, which was always absolute. No, what she feared was endangering my father, by anything she might do or say if taken. And this was in spite of their last unhappy parting. I have been unsparing of my mother in this narrative, because I am trying to set down the truth. That is part of the truth too: that not for a moment did she think of selling or trading her knowledge of him.

She may have been fearful of what she might say under torture, of course – such were the notions of Protectorate England that went around the exiles. Already on the crossing she had warned me to say nothing of who I was, or who she was, if put to the question. When we climbed down from the hackney outside our lodgings, she put up her hood and bustled me inside, as if everyone going about their business in the street was a spy.

As for me, I found this exciting, simply because it reminded me of what I had heard of my father's flight after Worcester – the creeping about in disguise, the secret knock, the dread suspense. I was a boy, after all. And it was as a boy that I very soon found our adventure turning to disappointment. Our lodgings, above a barber's shop in the Strand, were comfortable enough. We lived well, for my uncle was quick to raise credit on the strength of my grandmother's legacies, while the will was being proved. I ate heartily, and was measured for a new suit of clothes by a tailor who was quietly ushered upstairs one afternoon, and whom I was strictly enjoined not to speak to beyond civility. But of London I saw no more than the view from the window. My uncle went out often, about the legal business, and Tom Howard made the occasional foray, but my mother would not stir, and neither could I nor Mary. Even Anne Hill complained at not being able to slip out for a cup of ale. My mother said she could not trust that busy tongue of hers. Meanwhile I chafed at what I felt as no better than imprisonment. The noise of the great city – compounded of bells, street sellers' cries, wheels and hoofs, boots and pattens a-clatter, a thousand voices tuned to a thousand fascinating tones – seemed to call out in mockery to me, as I lounged at the lattice. I fear that, like a tethered dog, I grew destructive. One evening I tore up the *Publick Intelligencer*, the official news-sheet, which my mother had been anxiously scanning in case her coming was rumoured in it. Being unable to read, I found no better use than making pellets of it. My mother boxed my ears, and I went to my bed and wept and sulked. Tom Howard, who was often kind, came and tried to soothe me, but I would not lift my face from the pillow. I remember him, after a moment's pause, ruffling my hair with a most gentle action, and then hearing him sigh, and his footsteps going away; and then, the knock at the street-door below.

It was no great thunderous knock that set the house shaking; there were no cries to open up in the name of the Protector. And yet somehow it sent a shiver through me, and I knew. I scrambled up from the bed, and looked around me for, I suppose, something to strike out with. Before I knew it, the soldiers were there, standing in the doorway.

At sight of their buff coats, helmets and swords, I was paralysed. I remember being conscious of having been crying, and hoping they would not see the tears and think they were on their account, but that was the limit of my courage. Then my mother stepped forward, with a third soldier at her elbow. She was talking angrily. She had given it out that she was the widow, and we the children, of a Dutch sea captain, and this she kept loudly reiterating, turning her flushed face to each of the soldiers in turn, and demanding to know what they meant by molesting us in this way. She was not a good actress, but plainly they had their orders anyway, and they paid no heed to her. One of them, bending close and looking at my face with interest, bid me take up my hat and come with them. My eyes sought my mother's.

'Aye, do it, Jacky,' she said, 'there's no help for it, for now. It's all a monstrous mistake, and will be resolved soon enough . . . What do you do there, sir? How dare you?'

One of the soldiers was rummaging in her room, and searching the bureau there. But true enough, there was no help for it, and soon they marched us downstairs. My mother carried Mary, who was a picture of terror. I followed with my uncle Justus, who, though pale, was composed. Then came Tom Howard, who was not, for I saw the hair sticking to his forehead with sweat. Knowing him for a swordsman, I fear I despised him a little that he did not draw his blade and have at our captors, though there were another two soldiers posted at the door, and it was such odds as no man could have prevailed against. Last came Anne Hill. Outside my mother said to her in a clenched voice, 'Well, wretch? And what have you to say for yourself?' But Anne Hill was whispering prayers and puffing and blowing, and I think my mother did not truly suspect her of betrayal. Indeed, as we were led down to the landing-place on the river below Somerset House, I heard her catch her breath, and murmur: 'The tailor. He looked a fanatic. Damn . . .'

The soldiers at once commandeered two boats, and we were sculled downstream, my mother sitting very proud and complaining bitterly to the waterman of her ill-usage. Once she demanded to know precisely where we were going, and though the soldiers only stared impassively at the river, I saw the waterman give me a look of odd, fearful compassion.

On our first coming to London by water, I had glimpsed the Tower, and had longed mightily to see more of that fabled place. We do well not to have our wishes granted. As our boats made the best of their way through the shipping below the Bridge, the grey-white turrets of the Tower melted into view. They seemed insubstantial at first, in the dusky gloaming, above the sharp etching of masts and rigging, but as we hove towards Tower Wharf, they took on massive form, and what had seemed misty space became tremendous masonry.

An iron gate was opened at an inlet of the waterside, and we passed in through dripping darkness ill-lit by torches, amongst a dank cold smell that brought to mind moss and blind frogs and worse things. Then we were ascending a set of stone stairs, and following a lofty passage, with the clank of the soldiers' trappings echoing all around us.

By now I think I had made up my mind that we were going to be killed. I was determined to be brave. When one of the soldiers unlocked a stout door, and ushered my mother and Mary and myself inside, I found myself closing my eyes and taking deep breaths. Opening them, I expected to see a dungeon, chains, spikes, a block . . . Instead I found we were in a room, decently furnished though very old and quaint, with low beams and a great warped oak table and even a bed with dusty hangings. There was a single small window, too high to see out of, but a candle was burning and the soldier handed my mother another before closing the door and turning the key.

We sat huddled together on the bed. I was bewildered. Did they mean to leave us here to starve, perhaps? When I suggested it, my mother bid me hush, as she was thinking. But my question was answered when a soldier came with a tray of bread and pickled meat and a pitcher of small beer. For once, though, I had no appetite. I wondered what had happened to Anne Hill, to my uncle and Tom Howard. I wondered how dark it would be in here when the candles were gone.

My mother was pacing up and down now, gnawing her lips. At last she stopped and seized my shoulders.

'Say nothing of your true father, Jemmy,' she told me. 'Pretend you know nothing of him. Your father was a sea captain, and he died years ago, and that's all.'

I nodded very solemnly: I understood. But I asked what the sea captain's name was, as I thought I might need to know. My mother frowned at me – it may be that she had not even thought of a name – and then turned at the sound of the lock again.

'Ma'am, I hope you are comfortable enough. I ordered no fire lit, the nights being so warm. I pray you, be seated.'

It was a gentleman, though his dress was soldierly, and his face was bluff and weathered beneath a fringe of grizzled hair. He took a chair, and sat with his elbows propped on his knees, studying us quite dispassionately.

'Who are you, sir?' my mother said, very high.

'Colonel Sir John Barkstead, ma'am, and Lieutenant of the Tower.'

'Very well, sir, then you are the very man. I want to know by what right I am confined here—'

'And you, ma'am, are, I think, Mrs Barlow,' he went on, as if she had never spoken, 'lately come to the Protectorate of England from Flanders, where there are a great many disaffected and malignant persons of Charles Stuart's party. And these are your children, of course.' Colonel Barkstead's eyes lingered on me. 'You have a pretty boy, Mrs Barlow.'

'I cannot conceive why you address me so. My name, sir—' my mother licked her lips – 'is Van Gelden. That is my married name, my husband being deceased. A Dutchman – he died at sea. These children are his remnant. I do not know how you can have come to make such a mistake, but it is a very ill one, and you may be sure I shall protest it to the highest authority—'

'The highest authority ordered your arrest, ma'am, so we may as well have done with that,' Colonel Barkstead said. 'Mrs Barlow, you need not fear. I ask only that you be frank. Now, how long have you been in England?'

'Three weeks. I came over from Flushing, where my late husband lived, to return to my home country. I thought only to live quietly, and bring up my babes on such means as my husband left me. You may imagine, then, how shocking it is to be taken up in this way. Your soldiers frightened my little girl half to death—'

'I am sorry for that, ma'am, but she looks well enough – and really it was a foolish action in you to come to London and expect to evade our attention. The treacherous attempts of Charles Stuart and his followers to overturn the security of our Commonwealth has meant we must constantly maintain the greatest vigilance.'

'Spies,' my mother said dismissively.

Colonel Barkstead shrugged, then drew out a handkerchief and sneezed loudly. 'Charles Stuart employs them upon his side, ma'am, as you surely know. Come, Mrs Barlow, we have searched your possessions, and your intimacy with that man is not in doubt. Among other things, there is a document bearing his signature, relating to a pension or some such.'

My mother, who had been striding about, came and sat down by me, taking my hand in hers.

'You speak of past matters, sir,' she said. 'I knew the— I knew Charles Stuart, when I was living on the Continent, certainly. But I have not seen him in years. It is not a crime, surely, to have clapped eyes on him?'

'No one is speaking of crimes, ma'am. But it is well known that you did a good deal more than clap eyes on him.' Again his eyes dwelled on me. 'The boy is the living image of his portraits. And it is common knowledge on the Continent that you have proclaimed him to be Charles Stuart's son. It has been your boast, I think.'

'That boy is dead,' my mother said quickly, squeezing my hand so hard that the blood ceased to flow to my fingers. 'I tell you, you speak of past matters. The boy you speak of died in infancy, and so it was all put behind me, and I married Captain Van . . .' I almost cried out at the pain in my hand as my mother hesitated. 'Van Gelden. This is his son. Now you see, sir, where you are going wrong, and I think you can have nothing more to ask me—'

'What was your purpose in coming to England?'

'Purpose? Why, to live privately in quiet with my children. Is that a crime in your horrid republic?'

I had now begun to tremble violently – not because of any special menace about the colonel's aspect, but rather perhaps the reverse. He was so very much at ease here, in the midst of all this vastness of echoing stone, and we were so very much prisoners. I could not forbear thinking that these were the men who had cut off my grandfather's head, and pursued my father to an inch of his life. I had never felt any consciousness of royalty in my own person – it was not likely I should, with my upbringing – but now I seemed to feel it like a glowing brand on my brow. And I was afraid.

Colonel Barkstead looked at me again, and a shadow of pity passed across his harsh face.

'You do not deny, then, ma'am,' he said, stirring, 'that you have been the kept woman of Charles Stuart?'

'I have never been *kept*,' my mother said spiritedly. 'You do me dishonour, and him, and our whole relation, to speak in that way.'

'The enmity of Charles Stuart to our state, the tyranny of his father, and the disorders that his line would bring back to our country,' the colonel rapped out, 'make it impossible to talk of *honour* in that way, ma'am.' He got up. 'We will talk more on the morrow.'

My mother threw a wild glance at the door, as if she thought of making a dash for it. 'You cannot mean to keep me here. Sir, you cannot do it—'

'We cannot do otherwise, Mrs Barlow; that you know.' The door boomed behind him.

He spoke truly, though I could not appreciate it then – could appreciate nothing, indeed, but my fear, and the fear of disheartening my mother by showing it to her. For we represented a great prize, even if one they did not quite know what to do with. First, of course, there was information about my father to be got, and to that end Colonel Barkstead questioned my mother again the next day, having her brought alone to his private office for the purpose. The questioning was thorough, but she was not ill-used. Though there have been barbarities aplenty in that place, detention and confinement were the worst we knew. The information cannot have been of much account: nothing, I am sure, that Cromwell's spies on the Continent had not already reported long ago. They were most efficient in that regard, whereas the Royalists, I fear, were the veriest bunglers. So much so that even my poor mother could be suspected of being one of their spies, though no person more unsuited to the task ever lived, and I am sure Colonel Barkstead very soon realized that whatever she had come to England for, it was not that.

There remained, of course, the use to which we could be put by our captors. That was what they must have been thinking about, while our imprisonment continued. Though my mother still raged, our treatment grew milder. After the first couple of days, Anne Hill was allowed to rejoin us – she had been examined too, of course – and we took our meals together, and were given access to a little paved walk at the foot of the tower, and allowed to go under escort to the chapel if we wished. We were allowed to see my uncle Justus and Tom Howard too – though there it was a parting visit, because they had been set at liberty. My uncle had a pass from the Council of State to travel freely, as in his supple way he had never actually undertaken any activities against the Cromwellian government. But in his examination he had echoed my mother's story, and going out he promised her to do all he could to secure her release. As for Tom Howard, it seemed he owed his liberty to his position in Princess Mary of Orange's Household, for the Government of England had no desire to get at cross with Holland just then. So he said; and he took his leave of my mother and of me with tears in his soft grey eyes, and swore we would soon all be together again.

As for me, I remained in a state of fearful suspense, which curiously had much to do with something Anne Hill told me when she rejoined us: that there were lions in the Tower. I was most horribly taken with this idea, and could not drive it from my mind. Of course, the Tower menagerie, then as now the favourite spectacle of every gaping visitor to London, was not housed near us, and the cages were quite secure. But at night I fancied I could hear the beasts roaring hungrily, and I think I pictured them as roaming free like house cats. And when on the fourth or fifth day I was taken aside by a soldier when returning with Anne and Mary from the paved walk, and ushered alone down a long dismal passage, I do believe it was in my mind that they were going to feed me to the lions. But though I shivered, I did not scream aloud. Such is the oddity of childhood, in which we can create the most horrific imaginings, and bear them.

I was taken into a long dark-panelled room – so long it was like a gallery, or another corridor. Near at hand was a table covered with papers. Colonel Barkstead sat there, with at his right hand a young man who looked like a secretary of some sort. Beyond, the long room ended in a broad leaded window, through which the summer sun was streaming, and another man was seated apart there. His back was to the light, and I could not distinguish his features. There were, at any rate, no lions. Colonel Barkstead got up and, civilly placing a high-backed chair for me, bid me climb up on it.

'Now, my boy, don't be afraid: I would only have a little talk with you, and then you shall go back to your mother. They call you Jemmy, I think?'

'Jacky,' I answered faintly, for that was the name I was to use. But the colonel only smiled a little, then drew out a handkerchief and sneezed.

'Forgive me, Jemmy. A most wretched tisick, it will not be shaken off . . . Jemmy, you know who your father is, do you not?'

'Yes,' I said.

'You have been often with him? Lately, perhaps?'

'He came to see me,' I said. Not 'he came to see us', for somehow, at that moment, I came to a resolution that I would speak only the truth. Perhaps I felt I was more likely to endanger my father if I tried to lie. Also, there was a certain defiance in me now. These were only men, after all – not lions.

'What manner of things does he talk to you of, Jemmy?'

After a moment's thought, I said: 'The moon. I remember he told me about the moon, and how you can see it close through a great tube.'

'Indeed. And where—'

Colonel Barkstead was arrested by a great sneeze, which made his eyes water. He looked so uncomfortable that I found myself saying: 'Do you take physic for your cold, sir?'

'I have been taking physic, my boy, yes,' he said wiping his eyes, 'but od rot it, I conceive it has made me worse.'

'That's what my father says. He says it is best not to take it.'

'Well, he may be in the right of it . . .' The colonel exchanged a rueful sort of glance with the secretary. The man by the window remained quite still: it was as if he were entirely disregarded. 'Jemmy, how do you address your father?'

'As my father,' I said, not understanding.

'But you do not generally live with him, do you?'

'No. But he is always going about and has much to do.'

'Why, do you suppose?'

'Because he is the King.'

'Is he? The King of where?'

'Of England.'

'But this is England. And he is not wanted here, you know. We do not have a king.' The colonel spoke in a tone of kindly explanation. 'People are wrong to call him a king, and he is wrong to call himself a king. See this, Jemmy.' He took from the secretary a document, and held it before me, his stubby finger pointing to the signature. 'You see what it says there?'

'I cannot read it,' I said, still resolute upon the truth, but with a newly burning shame at the admission.

'It says "Charles R". That means Charles Rex, or King, and it is a great fraud in him to sign himself thus. See, it is quite plain.'

'I cannot read.'

The colonel and the secretary looked at each other in surprise, and I saw the man at the window raise his head. All at once I felt – I know not what, an angry humiliation, a passionate desire to assert what these gentlemen were coolly taking to pieces. I burst out: 'I have not learned my letters, but I shall – my father has said so. And he is the King, because his father was; and if I have no learning, it is because we have had to live in such a poor way, going from place to place, and never settled – and that is all because of that Cromwell, who is a great monster and rebel, and he will go to the block some day too.'

Such my innocence. But I was full of hot sincerity as I trotted out these commonplace laments of the exiles, which I had heard from the cradle; and I was satisfied to see the colonel and the secretary taken aback. The secretary raised his eyebrows, and cast a glance back at the window, but the figure there seemed to shake his head slightly, and they turned their attention back to me.

'Those are your father's words, I think,' Colonel Barkstead said.

'No,' I said. 'He doesn't talk in that way.' Another truth, and a significant one, though they could hardly be blamed for not believing it.

'Tell me, young sir.' It was the man at the window who spoke, getting slowly to his feet. 'Tell me, is your father married to your mother?'

Thus, for the first time, that question that has been so crucial to my fate, and that of my country, was asked of me in the Tower, by a man whom I did not know and whose face I could not see.

'I don't know, sir,' I said. Strange to say, I had not considered the question, but then I had been brought up in a wild disordered world, without a standard for comparison – the standard whereby a man and a woman married, and brought up children, under one roof. As the gentleman came forward out of the light, I squinted up at him – not that he was very tall – and made out a large heavy-featured face, with most bleak, pale, unrestful eyes. They seemed to probe me to the very quick of my being. In that, at least, they were like my father's.

'The woman says that she is, my lord,' Colonel Barkstead said to him. 'But then she has altered her story a dozen times, and there is no telling where the truth may lie.'

The unknown gentleman came to within a pace of where I sat, and bent stiffly down, studying me. I had done well to be truthful, I thought, for if there was a lie in me I was sure those eyes would have found it out. They seemed raw and pained as if by their own honesty.

'There is no gainsaying the evidence of that face, at any rate,' he said. 'The boy is a very piece of him. There is nothing about a marriage in her papers, Colonel?'

'Nothing, my lord. This grant of a pension or maintenance is unequivocal enough, however. Five thousand livres a year for life, and more when it should please God to restore him to his kingdoms.'

The gentleman grunted and rose. Those pale eyes riddled me for a few more moments, then as if he had seen enough he turned away.

'Let the paper go to Bradshaw for his scrutiny. As for our young friend here . . . Well, the case is very doubtful. If he is the legitimate offspring – let us not say heir – then . . .'

A long pause followed. There was a brooding heaviness about the gentleman, which I felt weighing upon me, as if he gave it off like an emanation.

'Then, my lord?' the colonel prompted at last.

'Why, then his state is not much to be envied,' the gentleman said, turning with a shrug and a spectral smile. 'Let us do him the kindness of returning him, with his mother, whence he came. Not that that is a very great kindness, by all accounts. But there: his kin have sown, and so they must reap. That is not our affair.' He gave me a last look. 'It is a naughty world, young sir, do you know it?'

'I do, sir,' I answered. And somehow, in his uneasy presence, I did: I felt that I knew a lot of things.

He nodded, and then dismissed me from his attention completely. 'Secretary Thurloe has had a full report of your examinations, Colonel?'

'He has, my lord Protector.'

'Then I shall give you a warrant of release presently. Let them be escorted quite out of the country, and we shall have done.'

My lord Protector . . . I must beware of attributing to my childish self an understanding I did not possess. But I surely knew, as the soldier took me back to our quarters, that I had just been in the presence of Oliver Cromwell himself. And I must have reflected too, amidst my astonishment, that I had seen no horns or tail, and that I had come away with no scorches or brimstone about me.

Nor was that the end of revelation. Down the passage, a door stood ajar. Inside the room I saw Tom Howard. He was sitting with a captain, one booted foot up on the fender, his head thrown back to drink a cup of ale. It was at that moment he saw me. I lowered my eyes and went on, but I had seen enough to know he had never been a prisoner as we were. I never did get that new suit of clothes, but at least the tailor was innocent.

FIVE

Soldiers escorted us all the way to Gravesend, the next morning, and the master of the ship was given strict instructions to set us ashore in Flanders. We had to wait about for a tide, and my mother was all impatient indignation, especially when another passenger brought on board a new copy of the *Mercurius Politicus*, the official news-sheet of the Commonwealth. We were described in it, in terms that made her tear it up and trample it on the deck.

For the question of what use they could make of us had, of course, been happily solved. It was a simple matter of advertising the facts, together with their great magnanimity in setting us free. 'Charles Stuart's lady of pleasure, and the young heir', was our description, with much mocking allusion to my mother's dress and jewels and pension. This was what my father, 'that pious charitable Prince', spent his money on. It all discredited him very neatly. More ominous for his cause, though, was the fact that they could afford to be so generous with us. That was how secure Cromwell's rule was. It was plain even to me that this was no tottering blood-soaked land crying out for the healing touch of an exiled king. For all that I had been in the Tower and seen the great general in the flesh, I went on board ship feeling as insignificant as ever I had in my life, and I could not imagine returning.

My innocence had been clipped, however. Not only had I new and confusing ideas about this England of which I had heard so much, there was the matter of Tom Howard, who was returning to Flanders with us, apparently as gentle and devoted as ever. I had said nothing to my mother of what I had seen on that last day in the Tower. It was something she would not want to hear, and I shunned it for that reason. It is thus, I fear, that volatile people like my poor mother become their own worst enemies: those around them take to lying and disguise simply to buy peace. Tom Howard was unchanged to me. Perhaps he supposed me too young and ignorant to understand; perhaps he was simply watchful under those long lashes. I do not know how much he had been paid for betraying us to Cromwell's spies, nor how long he had been acting on their behalf, nor even where his true sympathies lay, for I think he intrigued on both sides. The times threw up such men. I resolved, at any rate, to guard my tongue when he was about, especially on the subject of my father. I noticed that my uncle Justus, who was to remain in London to see to the business of the will, was reserved towards Howard when he came to see us off, and may well have guessed, but even his brief imprisonment had chastened him, and he seemed relieved simply to part with us.

About one matter, though, I could not hold my peace. We were sailing at last, and I stood on deck with my mother. She was as exultant at leaving England as she had been at arriving. She threw into the water some of the Commonwealth pennies, which were minted without royal arms, and said good riddance, and pulled me to her in an embrace. It was long since she had shown me such warmth, and that emboldened me.

'Mother, were you married to my father?'

I felt her stiffen.

'Is that what they asked you?' she said, after a moment.

'Yes. I said I didn't know.'

There was a curiously hard, absent smile on her face. 'Why,' she said, 'who else should be his wife, Jemmy, but me?'

'Then that means . . .'

'It means nothing,' she said. 'Paper and bonds, names and forms – they mean nothing, Jemmy, compared with what is here.' She tapped her heart. 'That is what you must always remember, whatever happens.'

Nothing, however, seemed likely to happen. And when I tried to answer my own question about what it meant – whether, in fact, I was the true son of a king – I came to a curious blank in my feelings. I was, after all, still the same person. How dismally true that was, I realized when we arrived again in Flanders, and went on to take yet another temporary lodging, this time in Brussels.

My mother was still with Tom Howard, but the souring had begun.

There was drinking and quarrelling, and sometimes the laughter of other men at night. This period of my life went on for many months, and yet all that is salient in it is summed up in memory by a single image. It is winter: there is ice on the windowpanes of my little chamber, and I am huddled in bed with Mary for warmth. In the next room, my mother and Tom Howard are arguing – the final quarrel, though I am not to know that – and the shouting ends with such a shattering crash as even I am shocked to hear. I jump out of bed, and hurry in my nightshirt to see what has happened.

I find my mother sitting on the floor half naked, her legs bare and her bodice unlaced, showing her breasts. (Some desperate last attempt to entice her lover, my later self supposes.) There is a great red stain on the wall, shaped like a vast bat, that makes me cry out, thinking it blood. I hurry forward, but then there is a pain in my bare foot – a splinter of glass – and I see that the stain is from a bottle of port wine that has been thrown there with such force as to explode all about the room. I look at my mother's face.

'Where is he? Has he . . . ? Where has he gone?' she says, blinking; and then, panting in distress, 'Oh! He has left me – he did not stay, I could have – I could have explained all . . . Jemmy, Jemmy, go after him! Quick now, go after Tom, call him back, don't let him go! I can't – I can't stir, my darling—' here she sways, almost overbalances – 'oh, run after him, or your poor mother's heart will break . . .'

I go. Perhaps most of all I want to get away from the sight of her uncovered in that way. I run down the dark stairs. Our lodgings are at the top of a narrow old house that creaks like a ship, and I am out of breath when I get to the street-door. Just as I am, in my nightshirt, I run out into the street. There is snow on the ground, and my bare feet are numb in a moment. I can see no sign of Tom Howard; there is hardly anyone about. But I am just on the desperate point of trying to discern the prints of his boots in the snow, when an elderly woman puts her hand on my shoulder, and turns me about. Clucking her tongue, she looks in my face, talking in soothing French, and then points behind me, and I see that I have left my own trail in the whiteness – a dabbled signature of red, from my cut foot. The woman walks on, gripping my shoulder, and I begin to cry, perhaps because I feel in some dazed way that she is reprimanding me for not finding Tom Howard. But at last I gather what that word *maman* that she keeps repeating must mean, and I point to the door whence I came; and she takes me there, and knocks at it, wiping my face with her sleeve the while, until our landlord's slipshod maid answers. And cold and wretched as I am, I hardly want to go back in there. There is nothing else for it, but I am reluctant, and that reluctance is the vivid and horrible summation of the memory, for it is as clearly stained with shame as the snow where I left my bloody footprints.

Where was Anne Hill throughout this? She might have been anywhere, in truth, for she had grown unreliable. Such, I fear, is the power of an atmosphere of vices. Grumbling, sensible Anne did not go spectacularly to the bad. It was simply that her weakness for gossip over a cup of ale took hold of her, and she would often take herself off without explanation or apology. She might have said, with truth, that there were worse things. But in a way she was slowly washing her hands of my mother.

In her turn, my mother might well have said that her vices were not out of the common, in that place and time. My father was still gathering an army about him from his court at Bruges, but his Spanish allies seemed unable to make the decisive stroke against England that would open the way for him to make a landing, and the suspicion must have grown in the Royalist camp that it was just another delusive hope. In the meantime his ragtag forces had to be quartered about Flanders, where they earned a reputation with their Spanish hosts for plunder and disorder; and the reputation of his court at Bruges was little better. The long years of unsettled waiting, of tense idleness, had brought his followers to such a pitch that even their dissipations were mechanical. Dancing, gaming, drinking, whoring – my father's circle had long been reproached for these: now there was a rash of brawls and duels, with men butchering each other over a disputed hand of cards or the result of a tennis match. If the loyal, gracious, chivalrous Cavaliers of the exile had ever existed, they were being superseded by a new breed.

Such, at any rate, seemed the man with whom my mother became embroiled, some time after the parting with Tom Howard. I never knew this man's name, beyond 'Robbie', as he would style himself. He took no notice of me, but I found him dreadfully fascinating. He dressed extravagantly – cloak over one shoulder, ribboned lovelock,

ostrich-plumed hat, clouds of lace at knees and wrists, curled moustache over cherry lips – and seemed, indeed, to take it to the edge of
mockery. He had dirty nails, and a feral smell overlaid with rose-water.
His talk was wild and fantastical and obscene, and he made a terrible
toy of his sword, whipping it out to spear a crawling spider or slice the
head off a flower. I did not think well of my mother for being with
him, but she had a motive, as I discovered in the summer of my ninth
year.

Mary and I went marketing one morning with Anne Hill. Her
weakness coming over her, she stepped into an alehouse, telling us she
would not be long and warning us not to stray from the porch. We did,
of course: I had been at Brussels long enough now to know my way
about, and so we wandered about the Grand' Place, I pointing up to the
great gabled fronts of the merchants' houses, and making up stories
about the people who lived there. So I did not see Tom Howard until he
was right in front of us.

He was leading a saddle-horse out of an innyard. He stopped and
smiled, seeing us, and in spite of my memory of the Tower, he looked so
decent and friendly that I could not help but respond, and shake his
hand. He told me he was on an errand to my father's court from that of
the Princess of Orange, and asked after my health, and that of Mary;
and then, after a smiling hesitation, asked after my mother.

'She is very well, I thank you,' I said.

'Is she? Good. I hear of her, of course. Impossible not to. I suppose
she has different gentlemen to visit her now?'

I knew what he meant, of course. But I could not admit it publicly,
when even my inner private disloyalties pained me. Howard seemed to
understand, at any rate, for he did not press me. He gave us each a penny
– mine seemed to burn my palm – and took a gentle leave of us. And so
it might have ended. I had learned to keep my own counsel, but poor
Mary never did, and when we returned home later, she prattled at once
to my mother of having seen Tom Howard, and so it came out.

My mother was very passionate when she learned that her old lover
was in Brussels, and called him all sorts of sarcastical names. But I realize
now that what really inflamed her was knowing that he was on a mission
to my father's court. For, of course, she had a reason for keeping her
lodging close by. She did still have a few friends amongst the Royalists

gathered there, and there was always the pressing need for such money as my father could supply; but what really kept her there, I am sure, was simply his presence. There must still have been a belief that she could win him back, somewhere in her clouded mind. Perhaps, indeed, it was the only solid thing there. And so she must have pictured Tom Howard gaining access to my father, telling tales of her, turning him further against her . . . I can only guess at the train of her thoughts, but I know the result. I was even present when her scheme was hatched, though I was not lucid myself at the time. In a word, I was drunk. It was that same evening. The frightening gentleman who called himself Robbie came to supper, and for some sportive reason of his own took notice of me. He gave me a drink of brandy – mixed with sugar and lemon and water, to be sure, but it flew to my brain at once, much to his amusement. My mother weakly protested, but her mind was elsewhere, and so I sat in a hot stupor while Robbie did tricks with his sword, and told me tales (I know not whether they were true) of when he had sailed under my father's cousin Prince Rupert, who after the Royalist defeat had taken to privateering on the high seas.

'. . . Then there was a pirate captain, a Portugee, who kept a string of mulatto concubines. D'you know what they are, boy? I'll wager you do. Oh, they were beauties, each and every one, dusky as chocolate, and eager to the rut as a set of she-goats. But here's the choicest thing: being a sensible man, the Portugee preferred their silence to their clack, and had had their tongues cut out, and nailed to his cabin wall in a row. Ah, Robbie has seen some sights in his life, but none so curious as that little collection of trophies . . .'

I remember imagining those tongues most vividly, and knew I would have nightmares, and yet, foxed as I was, I wanted to hear more. But my mother kept angrily claiming his attention, and while I sat drowsing and thinking strange thoughts, it came to me in fragments that she was talking of Tom Howard.

'. . . But he used me shamefully, I tell you, and now he will probably make more mischief for me. I am surprised at the Princess keeping him in her service – but there, I have never known justice in this world—'

'That's because there ain't any, my dear. Not unless you make your own.'

'How can I do that? I am a poor weak creature, conspired against on all sides. My name is already blackened. I have been no saint, but if I were a man, my reputation would not be half so low.'

'Way of the world, my dear. But 'tis as I said – if a man's in your road, push him out of it. It can be done in a moment: you have only to say the word.'

'Oh, you are jesting.'

'I'm always jesting. That's how I live. It don't mean I'm all talk, my dear, not a bit of it. I've killed a man in jest before, and I'll do it again.' He flung his sword neatly down so that it stuck upright in the floorboards, and I watched it wagging and quivering in a queasy enchantment. 'Quick and quiet, if you like, like snuffing a candle. Say the word, Lucy.'

I did not hear my mother say the word, for just then the queasiness overcame the enchantment, and I stumbled away to be sick. And I do not know whether she ever did say the word. But Robbie, at any rate, acted as if she had. Very early the next morning – it cannot have been far off dawn – the house resounded with a furious knocking.

The Spanish soldiers who stood in the dimly lit hall looked magnificent, impassive, and terrifying. This time, I thought as I trembled on the stair, we would surely see dungeons and thumbscrews. But it was a harassed-looking official from the palace of the Spanish governor who was trying to communicate to my mother, in a motley of French and English, what their business was.

Tom Howard was not killed, but he had been wounded, his assailant pursuing him in the street that night, and driving a stiletto into his back. When Robbie had been taken up by the city guard, he had wasted no time in naming my mother. That should have been no surprise to her, given the sort of man he was – and indeed, she did not look surprised, as she stood in the hall in her shift, her white shoulders glowing, and spoke to the governor's official with a surprising calm. She looked, if anything, faintly triumphant. It was soon plain why.

'*Le roi*,' she kept saying. 'The King. The King of England. I am his wife, and that is his son. *Le roi – sa femme*. I can say nothing. You must refer the matter to him. He will wish to know.'

It may seem strange to speak of my pity for my mother at this time. Yet I can only see as pitiable the way she lurched from one crisis to another, with my father as her continual object, like a broken rudderless ship tacking and luffing in sight of a landfall that could never be reached. Whatever she meant to happen to Tom Howard – and of that I am not sure, and neither perhaps was she – the upshot was this scandal, and at once she changed course, trying to use it to her advantage: to capture my father's attention, to throw herself on his mercy. Certainly he could not ignore it, but if she had hoped to see him as a result, she was disappointed. It was Mr Daniel O'Neill that he sent, to meet privately with her in an apartment at the governor's palace.

I was there – because, of course, I was the link binding her to him – and I at least was glad to see Mr O'Neill again. He greeted me very agreeably. There was another man with him, a gentleman of the bedchamber to my father, whom he introduced as Mr Prodgers. I found this name funny, and though I dare not smile, Mr O'Neill in his subtle way seemed to discern it, and said with twinkling eyes, 'Aye, it's a curious name to bear, is it not? One you'll not forget, I should think, Jemmy. And look at that face – isn't he an ugly fellow?'

Mr Prodgers was rather handsome than otherwise, though plump, but he did not seem to mind his description, and before I could frame an answer Mr O'Neill said, 'Yes, you'd not forget that ugly face, I'll wager, Jemmy, if you saw it again. An excellent fellow, mind: your father always says so.'

Though I did not understand, I saw a look of suspicion on my mother's face. But then she passed immediately on to demanding to know what my father's message was, and what he intended to do for us.

'His Majesty desires you to know that he has the greatest concern for your welfare, and that of Jemmy. But he wishes that you would show the same concern, Mrs Barlow, for these wild, disgraceful courses of yours seem designed only for your own ruin.'

'Why should he care?' my mother said, suddenly listless. 'Why should he care what becomes of me?'

'That's neither here nor there, Mrs Barlow. We are here to talk of practical measures. First, the matter of the assault on Colonel Howard. His Majesty has undertaken to pacify the Spanish authorities, but this is on the most stringent condition that you have nothing further to do with him, or the man accused of the attack.'

'What should I want with such rogues?' said my mother, in her haughtiest way: she was listening.

'Second, it is His Majesty's desire that you quit your present abode, and reside at the house of Colonel Sir Arthur Slingsby. He is a good friend to His Majesty and his cause. He has a fine comfortable house here in Brussels, with a park at hand, and you will be well accommodated. Your maintenance will be paid there, and—'

'What of Jemmy?' my mother said sharply.

Mr O'Neill made an open-handed smiling gesture. 'Jemmy, of course, will live with you.'

'So,' my mother said, tossing her head, 'Charles no longer talks of tearing my son from my arms, then?'

'I was not aware he ever did speak in such terms of . . . his son,' Mr O'Neill said smoothly, with the barest pause. And I think it was then that I began to understand.

My mother did not. At any rate, she accepted my father's offer, disappointed though she was at not seeing him in person, and we moved to our lodging the very next day. It was, as Mr O'Neill said, a very fine house – one of those extravagant gabled places about which Mary and I would fantasize – and we had good bedrooms and our own little parlour, with our own maid to wait on us, which tickled Anne Hill greatly. Colonel Sir Arthur Slingsby was a big clumsy man, a little deaf, in whom bluff humour and a hasty temper seemed to contend. He had a library downstairs, to which, in spite of my confession that I could not read, he would often invite me. He would lay out maps and prints for me to look at, and often when I glanced up from them I would find him hovering over me in a curious perplexity, as if there were something he wanted to say but could not frame.

All in all I suppose we were pretty well placed. But it was a more retired manner of living than my mother was used to, and it was out of dullness, I think, that she took to gaming heavily. Sir Arthur Slingsby paid over her maintenance from my father, but that would not stretch to high stakes, and more than once I heard Anne Hill asking her where she got the money from.

I knew: I had once espied Sir Arthur Slingsby passing my mother a purse, and it jingled. I was almost sure he had a taking for her, if only from the way he watched her, and so I drew the usual conclusion. But it was not that. I discovered what it was, in a way that was farcical as only the most horrible things can be, one winter evening when Slingsby tried to have my mother arrested.

It was all swift, confusing, and even to me, who was used to uproar, terrifying. Slingsby sent his servant to ask my mother down to the library, where he desired a word in private. I think it was my mother's instincts, rather than her understanding, that alerted her: she insisted that Mary and I come down with her.

Very pale and clammy-looking, Sir Arthur Slingsby stood by the window. He pointed to two solid Flemings in dark cloaks, and said without preamble that they were bailiffs come to execute a distrain for debt.

'Prison,' he said, mopping his brow. 'There's no help for it – prison it must be.'

As far as I understood him, I thought he meant that he was going to prison, and I was sorry for him. Then one of the men took out a paper, reading from it in a mumble in which I caught the name 'Barlow'. With a great jerk I found myself pulled to my mother's side, and she held me there so fiercely I could hardly breathe.

'Why, you craven bastard. And I thought you a decent man – at last. What a fool I was. You cannot look me in the eye, sir, can you?'

It was true. Sweating, Slingsby said: 'The sum – the sum owing me is above a thousand livres, Mrs Barlow. You have not paid me, so I must needs have recourse to the law. These men are to take you to a public prison of this city, where you must be held as a debtor until a judgment is—'

'Don't you dare lay a hand on me!' my mother shouted at the bailiffs, who looked uneasily to Slingsby. Still she clutched me to her, with Mary roaring on the other side. She was a strong woman, and I could not have got free if I had wanted to.

'You must go with them, Mrs Barlow. You cannot flout the law. Let go of the boy – let go of the children. It will all be settled soon enough, and they will do very well here with me. Mrs Barlow—'

Dragging us along with her, my mother bolted. We were out in the street before I knew what was happening. She was screaming with all her might. It was a mild evening, and a busy quarter of the city, so there were people aplenty about in the streets: merchants and their wives taking the air, tradesmen and artisans retiring to the taverns for their pipes and beer, servants and prentice-boys bringing home suppers, the last street-sellers; and the appearance of my mother, beautiful, crying out in distress, clutching her babes, very soon attracted their attention. When the bailiffs came running after us, and actually seized hold of my mother by her arms, people stopped and stared. My mother, weeping, began to call out to them.

'Good people, see how I am treated! Help me, for pity's sake! I am a poor woman alone – unprotected – with my two innocents. See how I am abused . . .' She had picked up only a few words of Flemish, which she threw in with French and English, but the appeal in her looks and voice overcame language. Very soon people were pressing closer, and some called out to the bailiffs, saying they must be beasts.

I fear I was rather mortified by this attention: boys can be great prigs. Yet as I looked at the circle of faces, open-mouthed, curious, flushed with emotion, puckered with sympathy, and saw their number increasing as more people gathered, drawn as if obeying some mysterious and irresistible force, obscurely I felt something else, deep in my blood. To behold a mass of people swayed like this, their passions roused, their differences put aside, and to feel that you were responsible – that they were, in fact, *for you* – well, it was an utterly new excitement, and that thrill of discovery has never quite left me.

When the bailiffs would not let go of my mother, people began to curse them more roundly and call shame on them, and when they tried to force her forward, someone shied mud, which hit one of them in the face. There were jeers then, and I saw that the crowd ahead would not part to let them through. One stout old man was grimly brandishing a staff.

Then Slingsby appeared. Plainly he had had to resist an inclination to hide in his house; and it was in a rather shrill voice that he began to harangue the crowd.

'You must give way – come, this will not do. The lady is a debtor, and is placed under arrest. She owes me a great sum of money, and will not pay—'

'You never asked for it!' my mother cried. 'You advanced me money in good faith, and then without warning you turn these creatures on me!'

One of the bailiffs got more mud in his face, and gave my mother's arm a most savage jerk, and that made her howl. The other bailiff let go, looking alarmed. Slingsby stepped up on the back of a dogcart, and shouted to be heard.

'You do not know what this matter is about. I act on behalf of His Majesty King Charles of England. I am in the King's confidence, and . . . and . . .'

I suppose he meant this to give him authority, but it only stirred the crowd like a nest of bees. Some shrieked at him for a liar, some cursed the King, some said the King should be appealed to. When the mud turned to a hail of stones, the bailiffs gave up. They let go of my mother, and would have slipped away, but it was plain that some in the crowd would have pursued and beaten them. So, amidst great confusion, it was agreed between them and Slingsby that the matter must be referred to the governor, and so we walked to his palace with the crowd in a sort of triumphal procession. My mother's head was high. She had not set out to cause a mob-riot in the streets of Brussels, but she was well satisfied – and, indeed, I think no one else could have done it.

As for me, once the excitement had died, I was thrust into a turmoil of contrary feelings. It was the mention of my father, of course. I saw clearly now that he meant to get me away from my mother. It was to that end that he had placed us with Sir Arthur Slingsby. That was the reason for those uneasy looks in the library – and the reason Slingsby had had my mother seized for debt, and tried to separate me from her. The thought of being taken away from this life, and going to my father, awoke all the old guilty longing, yet at the same time I was hurt and perplexed to think that he would resort to such a violent scheme as this. And worst of all, multiplying my guilt a thousandfold, I knew that my mother had tumbled to it now. She fairly gripped me like a vice as we went along, not letting me draw away even to arm's length, and in that I read my future. She was never going to let me go now, ever. And I hated her for it, and hated myself for hating.

At the governor's palace the intendant listened, elaborately courteous in the old Spanish way. But he was deeply displeased: he had had to call out troopers with pikes before the crowd would disperse. Sir Arthur Slingsby, very blustery and awkward, agreed to withdraw his writ, but there was no question of our going back to his house. In the end another Englishman resident in Brussels, Lord Castlehaven, a peaceable man of retired habits, was summoned, and in some bewilderment consented to take us in that night – to oblige, as he said, his king.

That was not the end of the affair. At Lord Castlehaven's house a few days later, my mother was presented with a stiff letter from one of my father's counsellors. These incidents had put him in an embarrassing position with his Spanish hosts, and the letter, a copy of one sent to the governor, was full of grave reproaches. My mother read it out loud, pacing, spitting out the pompous phrases with great relish. ' "It will be a great charity to the child, and to the mother, if she shall now at length retire herself to such a way of living as may redeem in some measure the reproach her past ways have brought upon her" . . . Oh, excellent! I am to be put out of the way, am I? Let them try it. I am not beaten. I still have his first letters to me – I shall publish them. Let them talk of embarrassment then.'

My heart is torn as I remember this. For who could blame her – a woman used to admiration and excitement – if she resisted being shuffled out of the way, like an old maid to the almshouse? And yet she would go on using me – I knew it: dangling me between her and my father, now bait, now weapon. And so I spoke up, clearly, and said it for the first time.

'I want to go to my father. Please.'

My mother stopped in mid-flourish, the letter in her hand. There was a long stillness. Indeed, I never saw her so still – she was always a-prowl and a-twitch – and perhaps that was how I noticed the bones standing out in her throat. A change: she had always been well-fleshed.

'Well,' she said at last, 'you can go. But you know that if you do, I will die.'

I could not answer that. I could only run to my room, and bury my burning face in my pillows.

Perhaps a child of that age cannot really know despair. What I felt in the succeeding weeks was a sheer absence of hope. My mother watched me closely, like a prisoner. When she went out alone, which was seldom, she paid an old fierce woman to sit with us, not entirely trusting Anne Hill, and left instructions that no one was to be admitted to our apartments. As for our outings, they were curtailed. We were not to go out in the confusion of the streets. Only an enclosed meadow close behind Lord Castlehaven's house was permitted for our daily walk – and she always came with us. It was a pretty enough place, with a pond and an avenue of trees, but I came to look upon it too as a species of gaol. I never expected it to be the place where my life would begin its momentous alteration.

It was a spring morning, dewy and soft – uplifting, surely, to any spirit less crushed than mine, but I was merely rambling about in a sulky fashion, swiping at the grass with a stick. I had strayed a dozen yards or so from my mother, who was bickering with Anne Hill, and I took no notice of the gentleman who was exercising his horse nearby – until he came past me at a canter and clicked his tongue. I looked up.

He lifted the deep-brimmed hat that shielded his face, and said quietly: 'Good day, Jemmy.'

He was gone in a moment, but I knew him. It was Mr Prodgers, and at once I remembered the way Mr O'Neill had called attention to him. *You'd not forget that ugly face* . . . Now I recollected that I had often seen a gentleman exercising his horse there, at this time, and my heart began to beat faster, and my head whirled with surmise.

I said nothing of it to my mother.

The next morning – for which I could hardly wait – we walked in the meadow again. I tried, without making it obvious, to look out for the gentleman again, but I could not see him. I was just resigning myself to disappointment when Anne Hill, after complaining several times of a headache, groaned and fell down in a swoon.

'Anne! Whatever is it? Anne, speak, can't you?' my mother cried, kneeling by her. Anne only moaned, and groped feebly at the pocket where she kept her smelling salts.

They were not there, of course. Anne played her part well: the approach must have been made on one of her taproom visits, though I do not know how much she had been paid. Much, I hope, for she put up with a great deal; and I never saw her again after that day.

'Jemmy, run back to the house, and bring her smelling salts,' my mother said. She had her arm round Anne's neck, and was patting her hand. She was fond of her, in her way – and yes, she was kind too, in her way. Alas, it was in one of her kind moods that I left her.

I ran off towards the house. As I drew near, Mr Prodgers came out of the trees on his horse, and swept off his hat.

'Jemmy! You know me. Your father wants you to come with me. Now, while we may – up!'

I reached up, and he lifted me and put me on the saddle in front of him, and gathered the reins tight.

At the last, as we rode away, I heard my mother behind us, wailing and calling my name. God forgive me, I never looked back.

SIX

'You understand, Jemmy, that it was the only way,' my father said.

I was supping with him, at the house the Spanish had given him in Bruges. It was a most enchanting place, with its gabled buildings and rows of linden trees reflecting in the waterways, and the house was the handsomest I had ever been in. Enchantment, indeed, describes my state since Mr Prodgers had brought me here. It all seemed very much like a dream, and I had something of the dreamer's uncomprehending heaviness about me: I could only blink at my father and nod my head.

'Slingsby acted like a fool. I instructed him to get the custody of you by some quiet and careful means. Instead he goes at it like a bull at a gate. Thank God for men like Prodgers.' He studied me. He looked drawn and weary, his face deeply grooved from cheek to jaw, his dark eyes so shadowed they appeared bruised. But he had grown a curly moustache since I last saw him, which with the long black tresses gave a touch of the dandy – so altogether it was a most commanding, worldly, impressive, and even grim man whom I saw across the supper table. It made me tongue-tied.

'I see you are troubled about something,' he said. 'Come, Jemmy, don't be afraid: speak out.'

'I am only thinking . . . well, there is Mary. I know she is not my true sister but I shall miss her. And Mother . . .'

'Well, it would be unnatural if you did not. But I shall see that they are maintained, and comfortable. Trust me, Jemmy.'

I did. Yet to be truthful about my father, I must say that the word 'trust' seemed different when it came from his lips. It was as if he could not help but clothe it with irony. Perhaps even then he had learned always to mistrust. Learned – or decided. For it is my belief that life cannot close our hearts: we do that from choice.

Certainly he had reason at that time to feel disillusioned. He had been ten years in exile. He was deep in debt once more. That supper was a single dish of gamey meat, and the candles were not lit until it was full dark, because they were the last in the house. The men of his soldiery that I saw about the town were all but in rags, and of a starveling look. There was sickness in the camp, and it had lately taken away one of his closest friends, the Earl of Rochester, commander of his guards. He it was who had shared the dangers of my father's clandestine escape after Worcester, and the loss hit him hard. As for his prospects, they had quite lost the glow that the Spanish alliance had lent them. The Spaniards were making no headway in their war with Cromwell's England, which was now powerfully allied with France. It was as much as they could do to hold their own, and the project of aiding my father in a landing on English shores was in abeyance. His throne was further off than ever.

'And here all I can do is kick my heels,' he said. 'Even my brother James is fighting at the front. But Don Devil' – his nickname for the Spanish commander revealed how their relations had cooled – 'will not have me risk my royal neck. God knows why: I've little enough to lose. Well, I shall go to Antwerp as soon as I can afford to pay the coachman. Perhaps I may stir things up there. They say Yarmouth would open itself to us, if we can just ship a force across . . .' He grew absent, crumbling bread nervously in his long fingers, then came to himself and gave me a smile. 'Do you like dogs, Jemmy?'

'I think so, sir. I have never had one.'

'Really? Well, here's a pretty tale for you. One of my loyal friends in England – of whom I am told there are so many, you know, 'tis a wonder Cromwell ever won – sent me a gift. It was a pack of hounds. Quite a gift, was it not? The pity is I can hardly afford to feed them, nor can I pay the carriage for their return. So this generous gift has actually ended up making me poorer. I can't tell the poor fellow that, of course. Was there ever such a king?' he said laughing, and tossing the breadcrumbs in the air. I joined in, but I thought his laughter had a desperate sound to it.

'Sir,' I said on a sudden, 'shall I go to Antwerp with you?'

'No, my boy, not this time. Forgive me, I have scarcely spoke of your situation. Jemmy, I do not mean you to live with your mother any more, because it will be the ruin of you, and because there can never be peace between her and me while you do. It is simply the best thing for all. You understand this?'

'Yes, sir,' I said, a little shakily, for I still had a kind of ache when I thought of it, as if I had tumbled downstairs or been pummelled.

'That's well. So, you must have a home, and be set to schooling, for I know you have had no instruction, and I feel the reproach of it. I have no establishment suitable for you yet, and I may, God willing' – here he grimaced, in a way that somehow shocked me – 'soon be about this enterprise of invasion. What I have in mind for you is Paris. My mother – your grandmother, Jemmy, though I don't know if you recollect ever seeing her – is there, and will be good to you. And there is a gentleman there who is captain of her guards, and has his own establishment, and he and his wife are mighty fond of children – they have lately lost one of their own. His name is Crofts, and he shall stand guardian to you while you are schooled, and look after you as one of his own kin.'

My life had been so unsettled, that I was less perturbed by this than a child of nine would commonly be; but my father must have seen trouble in my face, for he went on: 'This does not mean I am any less your father, Jemmy, nor that I love you the less. I mean to have you by me as soon as it is fit. I am not likely to forget about you, I think. Odsfish, you are the prettiest spark I ever saw. What do those great eyes of yours see, eh? Ghosts and fairies? You might well be a changeling, indeed: you have my darkness, but none of my ugliness, thank heaven. Now come, let us be merry awhile, eh?'

And so we were. A lady joined us after supper, and a French fiddler – a threadbare fellow, whom my father treated with the greatest affability. By the light of the last candles, my father and the lady taught me how to dance the new dances, a sport I enjoyed greatly. The lady was very beautiful, and rather dreamy and quiet. She was his mistress, of course. I know now her name was Catherine Pegge, but she made no such noise in the world as my mother, and I saw her but little after that. I see us dancing, laughing, to that tripping music, in light that would burn out all too quickly, like figures in a seer's crystal, prophesying the world that was to come. And dazed as I was, perhaps even then I saw some things clearly. My father was with grace and kindness trying to keep my mind from dwelling on my mother. *Forget*, said his shrewd eyes; *forget* sang the fiddle. It worked, but I don't know if it was right. And then the lady: I knew even then she would not be the last. He could not keep faith.

Yet he must keep faith with me. Though my tongue was too shy, my heart begged it that night. I had torn my soul from its old lodgement, and placed it in his hands – and if he did not keep faith with me, I was surely lost.

SEVEN

Lord Crofts had only recently been ennobled by my father – the handing out of empty titles was one of the few kingly things he could do in his exile – and whether I came as part of the bargain I never knew. Certainly Lord Crofts seemed content enough at becoming my guardian. When he came to Bruges to fetch me, he exclaimed that I was the finest young spark he ever saw, and ruffled my hair, and said we should be excellent friends. And so we were, very soon. Carrying me away from Bruges in a coach, he pretended not to notice the tears I shed at parting with my father, so soon after our reunion, and kept up a flow of talk that was wild, entertaining, and often obscene.

That was nothing new to me, of course. For the same reasons, I was not shy of him. I was simply grateful that he plied me with no questions, all bewildered and smarting as I was. When my tears were dry, and I began to sit up and take notice of my surroundings, he continued very cheerful with me; spoke with esteem of my father, for whom he had been a gentleman of the bedchamber, and talked of the delights of Paris, whither we were bound.

The delights included wenching and gaming and other things unfit, I suppose, for my young ears. But that was Lord Crofts' way: nothing went very deep with him, and he undertook the charge of a young untaught boy in the same harum-scarum spirit. There was a livid scar upon his neck that came from a duel, and when we dined at an inn upon the road, and a serving-girl recoiled on seeing it, he laughed hugely, and invited her to kiss it, saying the new skin was uncommon sensitive. As for the other fellow, he said pointing to the birds roasting at the fire, he had spitted him like that capon; and he laughed again. And there was such good humour in him, that I laughed too – though there came to me a little sore thought of Tom Howard, stabbed in the dark, and that in turn brought thoughts of my mother. I could not help wondering what she was doing now, and whether she hated me for my desertion.

But Lord Crofts soon brisked me out of that. Once we were on the road again he began teaching me a song, with a refrain about 'Fair Kitty, maiden no more', and that made me forget my doubts. That was how it was with Lord Crofts: a restless man, he whisked through life as if time were scanty, and I was whisked along likewise, without a moment to draw a repining breath. He was a man who could not sit still without beating a tattoo with his feet, as if they itched to be off to the next diversion. It was the same, I fear, with his domestic life. His lady, who was no more than distantly kind to me, seemed not even to expect his fidelity. More than once I heard him vent his impatient temper on her, and he would get violently at cross with servants. But I never received more than the odd irritable word from him. That may have been because I was the son of his king, albeit a king without power, but I am sure besides that I gave very little trouble. Not that I had any particular goodness of disposition: it was just all new and wonderful to me.

Like most of the exiled Royalists, Lord Crofts was in a perpetual perplexity about money. All the same, he had taken a house in Paris close by the Louvre, and there I found such homely order as I had never known – mere matters of my own bedchamber, with a fire lit when it was cold, and meals at regular hours, and water for washing and a comb for my hair, but to me giving a sense of solidity and security wholly novel. Then there was the matter of my name. I had one, at last. It was given out that I was a kinsman of my guardian, and so I was James Crofts, and referred to in his household as Master Crofts. With the titles I bear now, it makes me smile to remember what satisfaction that gave me. Likewise my delight at being measured for new clothes, and the still greater joy of putting them on and beholding myself in Lady Crofts' looking-glass, while my guardian laughed and said I would be breaking hearts before I knew it. This was his way, of course, but his lady smiled too in a sad sort, and murmured that I was the prettiest boy she had ever seen.

This put me to some confusion, but for all my blushes I looked at my reflection with quickened interest. In my mind beauty was an attribute that belonged to my mother – exclusively, one might say – certainly not to such an unconsidered scrap of humanity as me. Indeed, the face I saw was changed: food, warmth, unbroken sleep had given me new flesh and colour already. But beauty was a new idea. I might have dismissed it, yet it was what my grandmother exclaimed at, when first she saw me.

Queen Henrietta Maria: my grandmother. Of course, she had always been so, as my father's mother. But that relation only truly began when my father took custody of me and sent me to Paris with Lord Crofts. I had my guardian's name, but it was well known who I was, and my grandmother wanted to see me. Now for the first time I was to come to know my family – a family that was royal.

Lord Crofts had long been attached to her household, as captain of her guards, such as they were. Indeed he was part of that particular circle of the exiles who had gathered around her little pensioned court, and were known for being mighty high and vengeful in their views about how the throne of England was to be won back from Cromwell. There were others who muttered that that throne would never have been lost in the first place if it were not for my grandmother's meddling. Certainly my father had long since detached himself from her influence, and turned a deaf ear to the counsels of her circle, as best he could, for my grandmother, alone and powerless as she was, still believed she knew best, and peppered him with letters of strong advice. But she had her faithful retainers like Lord Crofts, who very soon took me to the Louvre to pay my respects.

There was great respect in the way he saluted her, of course, but something more – a sort of idealized affection. She did inspire it, my grandmother – but I am afraid when I stood before her that day I was inwardly merciless, in the way of children, and thought how strange and ugly she was.

A poor return! – for she took my face in her lean hands, and exclaimed: 'But he is the most beautiful boy I ever saw!' And she would have stayed thus, I think, caressing and gazing into my face, if I had not grown restive and tugged away.

Queen Henrietta Maria did not like to be thwarted, and she might well have dismissed me for that. I have often thought since how different things might have been if she had.

Instead she was indulgent, and laughed.

'You have made him turn shy, ma'am,' Lord Crofts said, grinning.

It was not exactly that. It was my grandmother's eyes. They seemed the size of goose-eggs in her little bony face, their rims fretted with pink blood vessels. They had filled my view, and I had felt them about to swallow me up. There was a scent about her, not disagreeable but musty, like rose-water kept too long.

'Do you know me, my young fellow?' she said, seating herself and beckoning me near. 'I remember you, though you were merely a baby then, and your mother . . .' She made a curt gesture. 'Well, we need not speak of her. *Eh bien*, little Jemmy, do you know me?'

'I think you are my grandmother,' said I, and, on impulse, gave her a deep bow.

'I think you are right!' She gave a sort of delighted yelp, and took hold of my hand, pulling me to her. She was small, and as thin as anyone I had ever seen, and her long stringy arms made me think of a monkey, yet she was surprisingly strong. This time I tried not to flinch as she stared at me. 'Oh, there is no doubt of that. Here is my son's look, truly.' She ran her forefinger along my brows. 'Darkness – and yet fair too! There, you are *not* like your father. Do you know, when he was born I was quite shocked, for I never saw such an ugly monster of a child! What think you of that?'

Again some impulse worked on me. I kissed the hand that held me, and said, 'Ma'am, I honour you, and I honour my father.'

'Little courtier!' She laughed again in high glee, with a fizzing through her long teeth. 'My Lord Crofts, you have been schooling him well!'

'Not I, ma'am. He has your blood in his veins. That is the source of these graces.'

My grandmother sat back, fingering the silver cross at her narrow breast. Dressed in widow's black, her head veiled, she might have been a nun but for the clusters of faded curls about each ear. So quickly had my spirit moved beyond the shadows of strain and poverty that I actually felt sorry for her. The palace of the Louvre was as forbidding and dank as I remembered it from my first sight as an infant, and the apartments that my grandmother's French royal kin allowed her were, for all their lofty ceilings and booming great doors, frugal and ill-lit. She seemed a lonely figure here, almost like a prisoner; and the accoutrements of her Catholic faith, the crucifixes and reliquaries and prie-dieu chairs, made me think of the torture instruments my fearful fancy had pictured in the

Tower, with the priests I had seen in the corridors as her gaolers.

'You are happy with Lord Crofts, Jemmy?'

'Very happy, ma'am.' And I was; yet I stung with a moment's guilt, after all, and my mother's voice mourned in my ear.

'I hear he lacks learning. Not wit, though. I do not think he lacks that. What is to be done with him?'

'His Majesty charges me with engaging suitable tutors, ma'am,' Lord Crofts said. 'The lad has not even his letters, and—'

'And he will learn soon enough, will you not, my pretty? But what of the faith?' She pointed at the figure of Christ on a great crucifix that hung above the cold fireplace. I saw Lord Crofts shift uncomfortably. 'You know your Saviour, Jemmy, and the true Church He left to us, and the Holy Mother we remember in our prayers?'

'His mother was – was not of that faith, ma'am,' Lord Crofts said, 'and as for his father, of course—'

'His father has much to attend to. But now he has a grandmother to look after him, and see that he is raised in the right way. Trust me for that, my lord Crofts: I shall find teachers for him.' Both my hands were seized in hers, and I seemed to feel the stopped-up energy of the little queen throbbing through them, like the seething of a shaken cask. 'What say you, Jemmy? Will you be a credit to me, and brighten the life of a sad old woman?'

'I will try my best, ma'am,' I answered. 'I want to learn – all manner of things. Everything.'

She chuckled, pinching my cheek. 'You speak as if you know nothing, child.' And for the first time I detected a little scorn in her, and some instinct told me that when she was unhappy she could be cruel.

'I can dance,' I said proudly, and there and then I began to prance before my grandmother, using the steps that my father and his lady had taught me in the pretty house among the canals at Bruges.

She burst into laughter, in which Lord Crofts joined, and clapped her hands; and when I had run through the steps, she bid me begin again, and kept time with drummings of her little feet on the worn carpet, as if she were ready to spring up and dance herself. Well, I was new, of course, and bore the charm of childhood, and I was her grandchild, after all, even if I had entered the world under a cloud. I entertained her: no wonder in that, though I know her court dwarf, Hudson, disliked me for it, and in after times lost no opportunity to be spiteful to me. No wonder also if I was flattered, and began to think rather well of myself, as she loaded me with caresses and said that I had let the sun in on her darkness.

'And who taught you to dance so, my pretty fellow?'

'My father.'

'Ah! Yes, he dances neatly: everyone says so. In that, at least, he is like his father.' There was a sharpness in her smile. 'Oh, I could tell you some tales, child: your grandfather and I, when we were young, and before – before all was ruined. Such dancing! *Then*, then there was grace. Civility. No one could come into our presence in boots and spurs. No court in Europe was so refined. Everyone talked of our great masques. We presented visions of heaven, they said. Once I was Divine Beauty, descending in a golden chariot. My dress was embroidered with stars. I performed a dance with the spheres. Then your grandfather and I sat enthroned while Jove and Cupid flew above our heads and all the chorus sang our praises. There was never such a court . . . There was never a king so *loved*.'

Untaught as I was, I knew at least that that was not true. But I saw even then that my grandmother believed it, or needed to believe it. I think she had poured more and more of herself into that belief, through the years of exile, and it was that, quite as much as hardship, that had left her gaunt and shrunken beyond her fifty years.

'Ma'am,' I said, 'if you please, do you hear anything from my father?'

Praise had emboldened me, and I wanted to know whether he had sent any message for me. But I saw at once I had displeased my grandmother.

'He has no time for a little useless old woman like me,' she said, and all that uneasy sparkle left her face, and there was only a dead rancour.

'Oh, but you're not, you are a *queen*,' said I fervently, and pressed her hand. So quickly learned are the arts of flattery.

Yet I think my heart spoke too. And whatever share of the blame Henrietta Maria bore for the ruin that had come upon her royal House, I still think she merited some pity. Her fall had been great, and nobody wanted her. And this was the vivacious French princess who had gone as a bride to Charles I of England, her finchlike beauty celebrated in song and on canvas, her Court at Whitehall the admiration, as she said, of all Europe.

My grandmother pulled her hand away. But she softened.

'I am the queen of tears,' she said. 'That is all I am: the queen of tears.' And she made a dramatic gesture, head bowed, long fleshless arm sweeping out and down.

In truth, of course, she was queen of nothing. She had been Queen of England, until the Parliament-men had executed her husband and done away with monarchy, leaving her stranded here in the refuge furnished by her French royal kin. With the English crown passing to her son, my father, she had become officially the Queen Mother – and yet there was no English crown now, and my father was King only in name. What did that make her? A betwixt-and-between creature: the shadow of a personage.

Perhaps that was why she took to me. We had that in common.

My grandmother's hand was still extended, while she stared tremulously into space. Perhaps she was seeing herself at the conclusion of a masque, lit by a hundred candles, jewelled and plumed, viols in the gallery striking the final chord, applause about to break out. But then the bony hand pointed, and her great eyes fixed on something behind me, and she said with a note of throaty satisfaction: 'Ah! Now who, Jemmy, do you think this is?'

I turned, and found a girl in the room.

I knew she was beautiful. And yet for me the entire notion of beauty came from my mother. The girl who stood there, slender and tall, clad in a gown of silver-white, seemed to glow like a lit taper in that gloomy apartment; but it was not my mother's glow. My mother was wine and ripe peaches, rich colour and rounded flesh and bewitching scent. This girl wore no scent. She might have had no substance at all – certainly she had made not a sound in coming in. When my poor mother entered a room, I fear, everyone knew about it.

So, while I admired, I was bewildered also. My confusion must have made me appear quite crushed and tongue-tied, for my grandmother laughed and said: 'Why so shy, Jemmy? You were not shy with me. *Ma petite*, here is the little boy I spoke of: Master Jemmy Crofts.'

As the girl came forward, my guardian bowed low and said: 'Princess.'

'Ah, ah, you have given it away!' my grandmother said. 'Now he will know. Well, Jemmy, do you guess who this is now?'

I could not. My ideas of my father's family were still hazy. *My* family. That thought made me giddy.

'Well, well.' My grandmother took me by the shoulders, and pushed me like a chessman towards the girl. 'She is the Princess Henriette-Anne. She is my youngest child. And do you know what else? She is my *enfant de bénédiction.*'

Though I had picked up a little French, I did not know what that meant. But simply the passionate emphasis with which my grandmother spoke of her blessing-child gave me, I think, a sense of the girl as someone precious and remarkable.

'Hello, Jemmy.' The girl pronounced these words, and extended her hand, with much hesitation; yet it was charming too, and when I shook her hand, mighty gravely, I dare say, she laughed, and made me laugh. And in the same halting way she said: 'I hope you are happy.'

'Or well, perhaps,' my grandmother said with a smile.

For though my grandmother spoke English fluently, if with a strong French accent, the Princess Henriette-Anne had scarcely any English. This daughter of a King of England had been wholly raised in exile, as I was to learn, and in many ways was as French as Notre-Dame. Yet I found nothing amiss in her innocent mistake: happy I was, indeed.

I was nine years old. The Princess Henriette-Anne was fourteen, though so sparely and delicately made that she looked younger. So it must be understood on those terms when I say that I fell in love with her at once.

She was a vision: I had to stare at her. I wanted to do things that would impress her and make her think me a fine fellow. Most of all, perhaps, I did not want to appear childish to her. And thinking of how I had cut capers before my grandmother, I dreaded lest she ask me to repeat the performance for the Princess.

But my grandmother, her hard fingers pinching my shoulder, only urged me to make my bow. 'Come, Jemmy. Where are your manners? Have you nothing to say to your aunt?'

My aunt: so she was, of course. But that seemed quite unreal to me. And when the Princess repeated questioningly, 'Aunt?' and my grandmother said, '*Tante, ma petite. Voilà ton neveu,*' I could tell that it seemed strange to Henriette-Anne too. She laughed, shaking her head and repeating '*Tante!*', and again I laughed too. I can see her now, slight and brilliant amongst the mouldering tapestries and coffin-like panels of that forbidding place, with her chestnut hair rippling and a flush of merriment warming her white skin and her eyes like blue enamel catching and transfiguring all the light.

I can see now, also, that we should not have laughed at the idea of her being my aunt. But that is for by and by, and darker times.

'You do not know your aunts and uncles, I think,' my grandmother said. '*Eh bien*, it shall be your first lesson. Come.'

Bidding Lord Crofts to go find her chamberlain and refresh himself with a pint of wine, my grandmother took me into an adjoining room – her private closet, with a great desk covered in papers. 'My correspondence,' she said with an airy wave. 'I am always very busy in here, Jemmy, you may believe me – busy as the bee!' But I was glancing back also, to make sure the Princess followed us. My grandmother saw, and said with her dry laugh: 'Little Cavalier! Don't fear, she comes, she comes!'

Sitting down at the desk, my grandmother made me stand at her side, my hands on the carved arm of her chair. From a drawer she took a portrait miniature and held it up before me.

'Your grandfather,' she said. 'You know, of course, what they did to him. The men who took his kingdom from him – abominable sectaries and republicans. They put him on trial. They cut off his head. Oh, and they would have cut off mine too, you may be sure. But this best and truest of husbands had me sent here to safety before that could happen.' Her great eyes bulged as she flourished the miniature unsteadily before my face. 'Look, Jemmy. Look upon him.'

I have seen many other portraits of Charles I since then, and those dreamy heavy eyes and stubborn lips are as familiar as if I had known him in the flesh. Just then I saw only a solemn-looking man, and my chief thought was that he was not so agreeable as my father.

'Princes must not look for happiness when they marry. They must think first of all of the reasons of state. But sometimes a miracle happens, and there is perfect love as well as expedience. And so it was when a certain little young French princess' – my grandmother tapped her breast with a sudden girlishness – 'crossed the sea to marry a King of England. And then there were more blessings. Our children. There are five living now.' She took my hand and spread out the fingers. 'First there is Charles, the eldest, your father. He is . . .'

'The King,' I said.

My grandmother nodded a little irritably. 'He is twenty-eight. He is the thumb.' And she pinched it rather hard. 'Next comes Mary, your aunt. She is twenty-seven. She was wed to the Prince of Orange, and lives in Holland, and is very comfortable and has many jewels.' This with a sour smile as she pinched my forefinger.

'My mother knew her,' I said, unwisely perhaps, 'when we lived at The Hague.'

'But we do not talk of your mother. Next comes James, your uncle. He is twenty-five. He has learned to be a fine soldier with the army of France and makes us all proud.'

'He has the same name as me,' I said.

It was the first time I heard of my uncle James, and such was my only response. I am a deep believer in omens and foreshadowings (as few are in these times), but in truth I felt nothing just then – no note or tremor of warning. If anything, I was pleased at having an uncle.

'Next comes Henry, he is eighteen, your uncle likewise.' My grandmother spoke rapidly, frowning, and moved on to the last finger. Unwise again, I spoke up.

'Where is he?'

'Him we do not speak of,' my grandmother said; and I held my peace, for there was a look about her that made me think she was a little mad.

Henriette-Anne must have seen it and recognized it, for she came and put her hand on my grandmother's shoulder, and pointing to my little finger said, 'And that is me, yes?'

'So it is, my little bird! My youngest and truest,' my grandmother said, blindly clasping her hand. *'Mon enfant de bénédiction.* Would you know the story of how she came to me, Jemmy? It is most romantic. It begins in England, during the war that those devilish rebels made on my husband. Do you know, Jemmy, who was the best general he had?'

'Prince Rupert?'

'It was me! Is that not delicious? When the war began, I went to Holland to raise troops, I pawned my jewels, I sent over supplies and money. No one worked harder. And I went back to England myself with a fleet of ships. There was a great storm. All on the ships were sick and despairing. They counted themselves dead. *No,* I told them, you live. Courage is the easiest thing in the world, Jemmy: you just grasp it. When we landed at Bridlington, the rebels brought ships and fired on us from the bay. I hid in a ditch, with my little lapdog hidden in my mantle.

The cannonballs whistled over my head. I wasn't afraid. Even when a man was hit – quite near me, just *there*—'

I was so caught up in my grandmother's narration, that I actually looked to where she pointed in the corner of the room. But I saw only a dingy tapestry of leaping stags pierced with arrows, hounds and horses with rolling eyes.

'Just there – that close. The man blew apart. Do you think I was afraid? I rode south at the head of an army of three thousand men. I ate my meals with them in the hedgerows. They called me the little general. I brought those troops across the country to my husband.' My grandmother picked up a silver penknife from the desk and weighed it in her hand. 'This, Jemmy, is all the silver I have left: the last gold went long ago. All, all sacrificed: all given to my husband's cause.' Suddenly the penknife stood upright, quivering, embedded in the desk top. 'If I truly had been a general, we would not have lost. Bold strokes . . . No matter. I came to my husband at last, at Oxford. That was joyous. But he had a set of fools around him, and he listened to them too much. *Eh bien*, it was our last time together. But from that last meeting' – she pointed to the Princess, who stood behind her, luminous against her mother's fusty black – 'came *she*.'

Henriette-Anne smiled at me – to reassure me, I think, for my grandmother looked yet more mad.

'I went to Exeter, and there she was born, my last babe, in the midst of war. She made me very ill with her birth. I felt I would die afterwards. But I knew my husband would come to me in my affliction, and that he must not do just then. He must stay with his troops, fight, fight. So I left my poor pretty one in the care of her governess, and came away to France, for the rebels were advancing and would have seized me otherwise. Sick, mortal sick I arrived: people here were shocked to see me. I thought I would die – though I did not fear it. I do not, still.'

My grandmother's eyes were like the bolt eyes of the tapestry beasts in their ballet of death, but I could not look away.

'So. How comes she here, you say, Jemmy? There is the great miracle. Her governess brought her, when she was but two years old, through all the dangers of England as the devils had their triumph. She disguised herself as a poor woman, and she put a bundle of rags in the shoulder of her gown like an old hunchback, and she pretended that the child was her own boy called Pierre, returning home to France.'

'*Pas Pierre*,' put in the girl with a laugh, '*je suis princesse!*'

'So she did,' my grandmother chuckled. 'The little babe nearly gave all away, by saying she was not Pierre, she was a princess. Can you imagine it, Jemmy? But they made their escape, and got from Dover to Calais, and so to me here. Oh, there were such tears of joy. And she has been with me ever since, through all my trials and loneliness: she of all my children is . . . *mine*.' And the brilliant smile my grandmother gave was answered by the girl behind her; yet when she drew the Princess's hand down to her breast and enfolded it in both her own, I fancied in that squeeze imprisonment. 'She has shared my woes. We have been poor. We have lain in bed together to keep warm, when there was not a single block of wood for a fire. Ah! See, she feels the cold yet, *ma pauvre petite.*'

For Henriette-Anne had freed her hand, and turned to warm herself at the small fire in the grate. And as I saw her there, with her back to me, I felt my face flush.

Her right shoulder was noticeably higher than the left, and a little rounded. It was more imperfection than deformity. Plainly she had learned to carry herself in such a way as disguised it. But I beheld it with the tale of her escape from England fresh in my mind – most especially, the governess making herself up like a hunchback. And it was this which fused with my superstitious nature (as some have chosen to call it) and bred a thrill of horror. I can only say that I saw Henriette-Anne as bearing some mysterious mark of doom.

I nearly cried out. What prevented me was the swift melding of that horror into something that I know others felt, in after times, in the presence of that enchanting Princess – a kind of pitying tenderness, which they perhaps felt without knowing why. Certainly there was no condescension in it. I admired and loved her more, I think, than before.

My grandmother recovered my attention by rapping me across the knuckles, hard, with the silver penknife. She was always curiously unmindful of pain. She wanted me to repeat what I had learned, and so I counted the fingers off. My father; Princess Mary of Orange; James; Henry; Henriette-Anne. Pleased at her approval, on a whim I held up my left hand, crooking the little finger.

'And this one,' I said with a child's natural self-centredness, 'can be me.'

At first I was pleased at the low quaking of her laughter.

'The left hand. Oh, yes, the left hand,' my grandmother said. 'But of course. *Sinistre*. Oh, yes, that is you, my sweetling. *Sinistre* . . .' And as she rocked and hooted my own laughter died, and with it my breath. For the first time since I had thrashed those street urchins at Antwerp, I was seized by rage, the rage that came at me like a throttling footpad out of the dark and robbed me of my self.

It was not that I truly understood what she meant, as I do now. *Sinistre*: the left or sinister side in heraldry. The bar sinister, meaning bastardy. Oh, yes, I have reason to know all about that now. Perhaps even then I had some intuition of what the joke was about. But chiefly I felt myself excluded. My grandmother closed a door on me while she laughed at me. So I flew into a passion.

With its wailing and foot-stamping it looked I suppose like a childish tantrum of a sort I should have been too old for – even though inside it felt like the rending of the world. But then, as before, I entered a sort of oblivion. Without knowing how, I got hold of the penknife, and brandished it, and stabbed it again and again into the surface of the desk.

At last the mist cleared, and I saw my grandmother's face – snared by utter surprise. She was, as I came to know, prone to storms of fury herself. And I have found since that people of a fiery temper are always thus astonished when they see it in others. It paralyses them for a moment – like when we come upon a mirror unawares, and lock eyes with our startled self.

Sobbing and gasping I beheld the splintered constellation I had created on the desk top. And then my grandmother's arms enfolded me, and she murmured soothing words, and told me not to mind. I felt too, with a tingle, the cool hand of the Princess stroking my hair. I quieted – of course – and very happy I was to be caressed and cajoled, and made a great fuss of, as if I had hurt myself. Craving more approval, I counted out my family again on the fingers of my right hand.

'Good boy, good, good boy,' my grandmother cried, and kissed me. 'You have learned your lesson very well.'

Perhaps. But perhaps it was not a good lesson I learned that day.

Certainly I felt myself to be a person of some consequence when Lord Crofts took me away. I sat very straight before him on his horse, and wondered whether I should soon have a mount of my own.

'Well, my boy, what do you think of her?' Lord Crofts said over my shoulder. He had drunk freely of my grandmother's wine, and his hot breath stank of it. 'Ah, you don't see her as she was. She's a poor thing now, in truth. Like an almshouse widow. Oh, the Frenchies look after her well enough, I dare say – because they have to. She was a daughter of France, as they call it. The trouble is, when you marry your daughter off, you expect to be rid of her, not to have to take her back and play the parent all over again.' His chest bubbled laughter. 'Hey, well. I wish I could show you the old days, boy – before the wars. She was never, perhaps, a beauty. Abundance of life, though. Drew the eye. When the wars came, many of us drew the sword all the more readily to defend her.'

'She said she was like a little general.'

'Did she now? Well, in truth she showed more true spirit than ever the old King did . . . Pay me no heed, boy. Wine talking. She loved him true, I believe – whatever that means. Never been the same since she lost him. When the news came that the Roundheads had killed him, she was silent – silent for hours. Like marble. Curious thing, when His late Majesty first took her to wife, they didn't rub along at all. In fact for a year after they were married, I hear, he never bedded her at all. Well, there was bedding, probably, for form's sake, but precious little fucking. I shouldn't say this. Pay me no heed, boy. Pay no heed to any of us. We talk foul, and portion out blame, and fight over the old battles, because there's nothing else for us to do. Because we're finished.' He belched brutally.

Stirring, I said, 'But my father – the King—'

'Oh, yes, your father, of course. The fountain from which all blessings flow. He is going to set it all right, of course he is. D'you know, I wouldn't be him for a thousand pounds. God save His Majesty, though, and God help us all. So, did she talk of him?'

'No,' I admitted, with disappointment.

'Ah, they ain't on good terms presently. She wants to lead him, you see, like she did with her husband. No good. He won't be led, not he. Unless by his prick.' Lord Crofts swallowed laughter. 'Pay me no heed. Oh, I don't blame him. He doesn't wench and game because he's a fool;

he does it because he's not a fool. He knows. The Spaniards will drop him when it suits them, and the French are firm friends with Cromwell now, and the Royalist party in England adds up to two lame men and a donkey, and there's an end of it. Hope? Bugger hope. Eat, drink, and be merry.'

No one had spoken to me of my father in quite that way before. But I felt no anger towards Lord Crofts at that moment. Indeed, I rather pitied him for knowing so little about the world.

If a man cannot see the shapings of fate in his life, then he is blind, just as much as if he denies that he grows from a child, puts on flesh, finds grizzle in his hair, begins at last to stoop. These things, and the grave that succeeds them, are called with justice the common fate, and cannot be escaped. The same holds true of the individual fate. It is a man's path through the world, and he cannot step off it: it is as peculiarly his own as his face in the glass, which is like no other that ever was. So I believe, in my blood. And it was from this time, I think, that the belief entered me.

Lord Crofts, belching wine, dismissed my father's cause as lost. And yet, look what had happened to the boy who rode before him! From an unregarded brat little better than a street urchin, I had gone in a twinkling to royal state. Aye, royal – for was I not the son of a king, and petted by queens and princesses? So with my father: a vagabond about the courts of Europe, now pitied, now used, ever hopeless. Yet he too must emerge from travail into triumph. Why else should he pluck me from the weeds and rubbish of my former life, if not that we should bloom together in a brighter air?

EIGHT

'A sunflower,' my grandmother would say that summer and autumn, measuring me with her painful eyes, 'look at him. Up and up!'

I was pleased, but even newly vain as I was, I could take no credit for my physical growth. My father was tall, athletic, long-limbed: only deprivation had kept me stunted out of my inheritance. Now, day by day, my body was learning to speak its own language.

And mighty fluent I found it. Fencing, dancing, footracing, horse-riding – every species of exercise came easily to me, and I mean the opposite of a brag when I say so. They exacted no effort, then as now. When I set my horse at a fence or make a leaping reach across the tennis court, all I do is surrender myself. Discovering this prowess as a boy, I joyed and exulted – and yes, perhaps I was proud.

But in other areas I had cause enough for shame, for I was quite the stupidest pupil my masters had ever taught.

Lord Crofts it was who oversaw my instruction in the mindless accomplishments, but for true learning I was sent to the country house of a Monsieur de Bernieres outside Paris, Le Chesnay, where he kept a school for a small number of pupils. Most were French, but there were a couple of English boys, sons, perhaps illegitimate, of exiled courtiers. The eldest spoke in gruff new-broken voices, the youngest were scarcely breeched, piping, quick to weep when the fathers chastised them. I knew less than the littlest.

The masters put me in the lowest class, and laboured hard, with me and at me. That the teaching was conducted in a mixture of French and English made it more laborious, though fortunately I picked up French through my pores, as it were, living where I did. Reading was a dark thicket I penetrated slowly, with many a scratch and tangle, and I was the despair of my writing-master: the pen resisted my fingers like a live thing.

Willingness sustained me. I wanted to improve myself, and be a credit to my father; and I kept fresh in my mind the image of those street boys at Antwerp, with their eyes of cruel vacancy. I tried too – as I try still – not to be bitter about the early neglect of my education, which constrained me to a milk-diet of learning at Le Chesnay. For it was a remarkable place, offering rich nourishment to young minds sooner weaned than mine.

It was one of the schools founded by the religious solitaries of nearby Port-Royal, a convent outside Paris, who were already renowned for their learning as well as piety. Amongst their number was the famed Monsieur Pascal, of whom my own tutor spoke with solemn respect; and he also read to us a set of odes composed by one of his pupils who had just gone out into the world. The youth's name was Racine. I was to meet him many years later, when his tragedies were the talk of the French Court, and when I was stepping on to a grander stage myself. But I fear at the time I made nothing of those odes, celebrating in stately verses the beauty of the wooded hills about Port-Royal: I blinked and strained in my usual bafflement.

But I did appreciate the beauty of that spot: the sweet valley country, fresh and green above the smoky sink of Paris, about which the Little Schools of Port-Royal were dotted. I felt myself to be in a good place, even though much of the learning was beyond me. The murmurous sound of Latin and Greek recited in the higher classes entranced me. I was in awe of the masters, sober men who spoke melodiously and were gentle in their discipline. I took pains and made progress, and might have made more, were it not for the matter of religion.

When a man has enemies as I have, they will pick up any stone to throw at him. Lately I heard the nonsensical rumour that as a boy I was raised by Jesuits. Well, Port-Royal was the home of Jansenism, and my tutors Jansenist to a man. The worldliness and power of the Jesuits was the very thing their sect detested: in their way, they breathed the same austere air as Cromwell's Puritans. But yes, of course, they were Catholics, though of a special kind, and it was Catholic doctrine that I was taught.

And even that was not enough for my grandmother – for her hand was behind it all, restless, itching to mould me into her own shape. She set her own pet priests on me too. I loved to visit her at the Louvre, and her summons often granted me a holiday from schooling. There would be sweetmeats, and games at cards, and a flattering attention to my eager prattle, and of course there was the Princess Henriette-Anne with whom I remained doggedly in love. But there was a price to be paid, and that was being taken aside by my grandmother's confessor for an hour every time to be scrutinized and catechised until my head ached. I remember that I was always set upon a hard high chair too, and how I would fidget while the priest muttered in a voice like dead leaves about contrition and absolution, and I'd wonder what o'clock it was, and try not to look at the breadcrumbs in his beard.

My poor grandmother! Such was the depth of impression her faith made on me. She trusted to time, of course: water dripping upon a stone. I could have wished the time spent trying to make me a little Papist devoted to more profitable pursuits. But as it happened, her time was running out, because my father was soon to enter my life again, to decisive effect. The little scheming Queen who could not help spinning webs would find them torn asunder once more.

Rome would not claim me, in any event. And that was not because of my lineage. Born in exile, I knew little of England. I was but dimly aware that English liberty and English Protestantism went together, and that a Catholic monarch could only hold that throne with a despot's grip. And as for the notion that I could ever have anything directly to do with thrones and succession . . . well, in those days it would have seemed absurd, to me and to everyone. My enemies, who picture me ambitiously plotting from the very cradle, would do well to remember that. I was a child, and a soul; and the soul simply did not warm to the faith of my teachers.

All the same, something my tutor at Port-Royal said to me has stayed with me. I remember the occasion. I had stolen some pears from another boy – I know not why: because I was strong and greedy and he was timid, perhaps. The fruit was unripe, and my bellyache was punishment enough. But my tutor kept me behind after class to reprimand me. He was a grave and learned man, accustomed to conversing with Pascal; but he took trouble with the little rebellious whelp clutching his stomach and staring resentfully up at him. I wish I could remember his face.

'What made you do it? I think you are not ill-fed, or in want. Indeed, I am sure of it,' he said. I went by the name of James Crofts at the school, but the frequent holidays I was granted to attend my grandmother must have given the fathers a good notion of my real situation.

I could hear boys in the garden outside playing at single-stick. Itching to run and join them, I hurriedly gave the answer I supposed he wanted.

'I am truly sorry, sir. I was bad and I forgot my duty to God.'

'Duty to God.' He sighed in impatience. 'What is this formula that you repeat? Where is the meaning in it?' Suddenly he rapped, hard and delicate, on my breastbone. '*There.* That is how God comes to you. He is not a schoolmaster, marking your duty like a book exercise. Do you understand?'

I said yes, of course.

'And now, what made you do it?'

The shouts of the boys outside distracted me into honesty.

'I don't know, sir.'

'Better. It was your will that led you. When you peep at your neighbour's slate because you cannot do the work yourself – yes, I have seen you – that too is your will betraying you. What does this tell you?'

'My will is wrong.'

'Not wrong. Weak. And that is to say, human. Do you remember when you were a tiny boy, unsteady on your legs, trying and failing to reach up to the handle of the door? That is like the soul of man. For all our puny will, we cannot open the door. Only God can do that. When He chooses. We cannot conjure Him to do our bidding, by behaving in a certain way and repeating certain phrases. How could we? He is vast and beyond us, beyond our knowing. He is mystery.' He tapped my breast again, more lightly. 'You must pray for God's grace to enter in, here.'

He dismissed me; and I dismissed, I suppose, what he had said as I ran out to play. Yet there was lasting nourishment in it. God the stern arithmetician – no. My spirit recoiled at that. But God as mystery, even darkness – yes. I have never feared the dark. (As my father did. He never admitted it, but his bedchamber told its own tale – always a fire and tapers burning and clocks ticking. He feared being alone with mystery.)

As for me, I embrace it – mystery, darkness, all that is unknown. What do these words describe but the future, into which we must step blindly at each renewed moment? If we did not trust, we could not live. So my love said to me the other day, reading over these pages I have written.

And so I believe. Yet still I hesitate. My friends all urge me to action: each day come letters from England, trying to rouse and prick me. The hour is at hand, they say.

Perhaps what I am waiting for is that knock at the breastbone.

Certainly I feel, here in the watery light and cold peace of Gouda, that time almost stands still. Or rather, each day comes slowly into being, like a protracted labour and painful birth. But looking back at that summer of my boyhood, the days skim past and away. They are the dandelion seeds I idly blew as I lay in the sweet-smelling grass below Le Chesnay, or in the garden of my grandmother's house at Colombes.

The house was in a quiet village a few miles outside Paris, and was to be her summer retreat. Her sister-in-law, the Queen Mother of France, had taken pity on her and increased her pension so that she could buy it. She was busy fitting it out that summer, and often took me with her – going on a 'jaunt' as she called it, stressing the odd English word with mocking merriment.

I loved those jaunts, because Princess Henriette-Anne came too, and while my grandmother fussed about calicoes and gilt-leather, I could ramble with the Princess about the garden, presenting her, like the budding Cavalier I was, with the choicest flowers, and adoring her with all my might. There was a great swing, half-covered with rambling rose, that was her especial delight. I would push her, gently at first, but always she would urge me to push her higher. Like her mother in those cloud-machines, she had no fear. As she swooped heavenward, light-boned, skirts fluttering, I told her I would not be surprised to see her fly.

'I often dream of it,' she said smiling.

'Perhaps you will! Perhaps one day you will find—'

'No, no. There have been saints of the Church, I believe, who flew into the air by a miracle. It is not for us to think of such things.'

'But if you could fly, where would you go?'

'Nowhere. I am happy here,' she said, too promptly I thought. 'Where would you go, Jemmy?'

'To see my father.'

'Ah, yes. He was kind to me. For a long time I never knew him as my brother. It was just me and Maman. Then I remember him coming to

St-Germain. He said he had heard what a pretty dancer I was and asked me to dance with him. But he was so much taller than I. So he picked me up in his arms and danced me round the room with my feet off the floor.' She laughed happily. 'Yes, like flying again. And he said Henriette-Anne was a great big name for a little girl. He said he would call me Minette.'

'Minette!' Letting go the swing, I almost shouted it. It was so right for her.

The princess looked at me over her shoulder, and I thought for a moment she was displeased. Sometimes that happened: in the instant before she smiled, you could be utterly cast down, convinced you had offended. A sort of power: I think later she grew to realize it, perhaps to use it. But I cannot be objective about her, any more than I could then, when the transfiguring smile came and she said: 'You may call me that, if you like.'

I liked very much. Minette she became to me from then on, a name only my father and I used. It bound us together.

'There is a fountain at St-Germain made of shells and coral. You can see all the colours of the rainbow in it. He sat there with me and talked for a long time. He said I made him feel better. He was sad.'

'Why?' We had to talk in such simple French and bits of English as we could both understand, and that made us curiously direct.

'He had been quarrelling with Maman.'

'What about?'

'Oh . . . she wanted him to marry a lady of her choosing. *La Grande Mademoiselle.*'

'Who is that?' I said wonderingly – picturing, I think, some fearsome giantess.

'The Duchess of Montpensier. She is cousin to the French King and the richest woman in France. So Maman thought it would be a good idea if Charles married her. It would give him wealth and power to help him win back his kingdom. But Charles did not want to marry her and so . . .' I saw a flush creep over Minette's cheek and slender neck. It was as if even the thought of quarrelling pained her.

'I would not like to be told who to marry,' said I, stoutly, in my innocence.

'Soon after that he went away again. But before he went he asked me if I was a good girl. I was vain, and said yes, and he said, "One of us must be." '

'What did he mean?'

She seemed to shiver. 'I don't know. He was making merry, perhaps. But I shall try to be good, anyhow. For Maman's sake. She has no one but me.'

I would never scoff at Minette – but still I thought that untrue. My grandmother had her priests, and ladies from the French Court came to see her – now and then – and there was her adviser, Lord Jermyn, who stuck to her like a burr, and there were the nuns of the convent at Chaillot she had founded. (She retired there for religious holidays, dressing like a nun herself. Going to see her there once, I had to talk to her through a grille, and thought it foolery – like playing at being dead.) And then there were those memorable five fingers . . . Thinking of that, I said: 'Why won't she speak of your brother Henry?'

The flush bloomed again. 'That is not a happy story.' And she would have said no more, but I pressed her.

'Henry was held prisoner in England after the wars. But at last those wicked men let him go free when he was fourteen, and he came to join us here. Maman was overjoyed. People called him *le petit Cavalier*. He was so full of life. I liked him . . .'

'Did he die?'

'Oh, no, no. He is with Charles's army now. But Maman does not speak of him because he turned against her. Now that she had the charge of him, she wanted him instructed in the true religion of Holy Church. She sent him to the abbey of Pontoise to be taught. But he clung on to his Protestant belief very stubbornly, and when Charles found out what Maman was doing he wrote to her, quite furious, and ordered it to stop. And so there was more quarrelling . . . But you see, Maman was only trying to save Henry's soul. He would not give in, and he refused all the arguments of the priests, and so she sent him a message saying she would never see him again. Oh, she wept a good deal. And then she went off to Chaillot to pray. Henry met her carriage on the way, and he kneeled down in the road and asked for her blessing – but she would not speak to him. And when he came on to the Louvre, he found that his bed was bare and his horses sent away and the servants were not to give him a place at table. I was in my room. I could hear him cursing, but I think he was crying a little too.' The swing was still now, and Minette's head was bowed. 'He came to my door. He wanted to see me to say goodbye, but I would not let him in. I started screaming. I said he was not to come near me. There was a noise as if he had struck the door with his fist, and then he went away. I have not seen him since then.' Minette touched her hand briefly to her face. 'And we do not speak of him.'

'Why wouldn't you see him?'

'Because of Maman. Because I am of the true Holy Church and . . . because I must try to be good.'

I reached out – to comfort her, I suppose, but Minette gently shrank from me.

'Push me, Jemmy. Push me again – higher, higher.'

So I did, thinking meanwhile of my grandmother, who often seemed like a little brown wren brisking about her quiet retreat but could also be, apparently, a rapacious eagle.

She was wrong, of course, in her behaviour to her son Henry: selfish, cruel, and also desperately wrong-headed. The English had always mistrusted her for her Catholicism when she was Queen. It had not been their chief quarrel with King Charles I, but certainly it had made matters worse – the shadow of priests falling across the English throne. And now that throne was lost, and my father had somehow to regain it, with his cause hanging on the slenderest threads. For his own brother to turn Papist – how Cromwell's party would crow at that! Where one brother went, the other might follow . . . But my grandmother could not or would not see that.

I see it now, of course. I see also that, disastrous as her meddling was, her tyranny was more motherly than royal. She simply could not bear to see her children grow up and break free of her.

But at the time the story of my uncle Henry filled me with fear, a child's self-preserving fear. I dreaded my grandmother's turning against me too. Above all, I dreaded the thought of Minette screaming and barring her door against me. Therefore, I must hearken to the priests, and stay in favour.

I had one crucial doubt, of course. What would my father think? If he had been furious at his brother's being taught Popery, then what of his son?

All I could do was tuck that thought away like something stolen. For now, my father was not here. Minette was.

'Higher, Jemmy! Push me higher!'

She made it a command. I had not heard that sharpness in her voice before. Yet I was willing to be commanded by her, even when she swung so high that I began to be afraid for her, pictured her dropping to earth, broken . . .

'Higher, higher! Faster – faster!'

My arms ached and I grew hot and dizzy. Still she shrilled at me to push her higher, still her fluttering figure soared and blotted out the sun and plunged and soared again. There seemed punishment in the air, bewildering me, for I did not know who was being punished or why.

'Enough.'

Minette put her feet to the ground, hopped off the swing and faced me. She glowed and panted and smiled with a splintering sort of brilliance that I did not much like. For a moment I was afraid of her.

'Almost flying!' she said.

Then I heard a footstep behind me. Lord Jermyn had accompanied my grandmother to Colombes that day and now he stood frowning down at me with his arms folded above his paunch.

'What do you mean by it, sirrah? You push the swing too hard. Do you not see how dangerous it is? Would you see the Princess hurt, sirrah, would you?'

'No, sir.'

'Then have a care, boy.'

Minette did not speak up, did not explain, yet I felt no rancour. Such was my devotion.

'Princess, your mother is making ready to leave.' Turning, Lord Jermyn looked me up and down, clucked with distaste: mud on my shoes. 'You will soil the carriage.' He clucked again and waddled off.

Well, that fuss about the carriage was typical of the man who was my grandmother's master of horse, counsellor and confidant. He had the face of a pig and the mind of a milliner. But I knew Lord Jermyn did not like me and, by his lights, he had reason: I came between him and his star. There were rumours that he and my grandmother were lovers, even that they had secretly married. Nonsense, of course. She treated him as a favourite, but then he was just the sort of admirer she liked –

doing everything she told him to, agreeing with her every decision, bending to her rashest whim. I have no doubt that Lord Jermyn was in love with her, and was able, somehow, to love without hope. Lord Crofts, ever indiscreet in his cups, told me that Lord Jermyn had crept to Henrietta Maria's bedchamber once. 'And she just shooed him away, as if he were a lapdog begging for titbits. Ha! And so the oaf swallows his pride, and sighs on. What a jellyfish!' To Lord Jermyn's face, of course, he was always very civil.

'We had better go in,' I said to Minette.

She still had that glassy and feverish look about her, but quite suddenly she shook it off and, actually winking at me, followed Lord Jermyn up to the house with his own gait. It was a remarkable transformation. She planted her little feet on the turf as if they were his great flat gouty ones, and bent her spine as if supporting a fat belly, and turning to me she conjured from her delicate features his blubber-lipped grossness, half prim, half sottish. I could only gasp and laugh, and then cram down my laughter as on the path above Lord Jermyn began to turn his gingery head in suspicion.

No, she had not defended me, and perhaps if there had been a scolding then I would have come in for it again, and still I would not have minded. I loved the collusion: I loved that Minette made me privy to all these facets of herself, and I could fancy no completer jewel.

My grandmother was in good spirits, and said I should come home with them to the Louvre to sup that evening. And so I was there when she opened a letter that had been brought by a secretary from Cardinal Mazarin.

'From His Eminence himself,' my grandmother said, her eyebrows going up; and Minette, who had just sat down at the harpsichord, suspended her fingers above the keys. Then she jumped up with a cry and ran to her mother, who looked as if she were about to faint.

'What is it? Maman, please, speak!'

'Jemmy, give me your arm,' my grandmother said with a grunt.

I supported her to a chair, in some terror. Henrietta Maria was not the swooning kind.

'Well, well,' she said, fanning herself with the letter, and then gave a broken laugh. 'I don't know what to do. I want to thank God, but I fear it would be an impiety to do it, for this . . . He is dead. That demon is dead.' She laughed again, but with a bulging of tears. 'His Eminence has the pleasure to inform me that he has news, on the very best authority, that Cromwell is dead.'

Her ladies-in-waiting had hurried in at the commotion, and now they began to exclaim and gabble with joy. The monster, they said, is dead, and gathered about my grandmother to congratulate her, while she sat stiff and still with the letter crumpled in her hand.

I thought of that room in the Tower of London, and the man who had walked out of the light to measure me with his unrestful eyes.

'Who killed him?' I said.

'No one killed him,' my grandmother said, with a little twitch at her mouth. 'He took sick, and died in his bed.'

I had seen my grandmother, at her correspondence, work herself into a vindictive frenzy, smashing down the inkpots and growling that she would do the same to her enemies when England was retaken. But now, of all the people there – and Lord Jermyn had come in too and was shouting great huzzahs, and her dwarf, Hudson, had got up on a table to dance a jig – she seemed to exult the least. Perhaps she was thinking of her husband, executed on a public scaffold.

As for me, I could not help being infected by the excitement, and my thoughts flew at once to my father. Surely now there must be a great change. Surely now—

'Now my father can be King!' I cried.

My childish voice must have been piercing, for everyone fell silent for a moment, looking at me. Then someone clapped, and said 'Amen to that!' It was not Lord Jermyn: his smile was all malice. But my grandmother said quite coolly: 'We shall see, Jemmy. We shall see.'

'What more, ma'am? Where does Mazarin get his report? Are they rising for the King in England?'

'I know no more, my lord. Our greatest enemy is dead. For that let us have thankful hearts, and for the rest . . . we must trust in God.' She lifted her head and signalled briskly to her chamberlain. 'Let us not stay supper. No late retiring tonight. His Eminence says the Court begs leave to wait upon us tomorrow morning. Do you hear, *ma petite?*' She seized Minette's hand. 'Even *ton cousin*. Even he. We must be prepared. He will wish to congratulate you. A high occasion. We must omit nothing.'

Ton cousin. She meant the young King of France, Louis XIV, cousin to the exiled family, indeed, and their official host and protector here at the Louvre – but seldom to be found visiting my grandmother's pinched apartments. Here, then, was a sign of great changes afoot. Always when my grandmother spoke of him to Minette, she would say *'ton cousin'* in that special way, cooing and yet portentous. And over supper that evening – though my mind was occupied with delicious visions of my father taking ship to England with me at his side – I noticed how my grandmother kept mentioning Louis, and fixing Minette with her intense gaze as if she were memorizing her for a portrait.

When Lord Crofts took me home that night, though, my grandmother had grown grave again. I went into her closet to kiss her hand, and saw that the miniature of her husband lay on the desk before her; and her hand was limp and sadly cold.

'Our greatest enemy is dead, hey?' Lord Crofts said later, when I solemnly repeated what my grandmother had said. 'Well, let us hope so. Devoutly hope. Oh, I don't doubt the truth of the report. But *is* he our greatest enemy? There's your conundrum, my boy.'

'But he's the one who took my father's crown.'

'Well, yes and no. He took His Majesty's place, if you like. As a matter of fact they offered Cromwell the crown not long since, and he said no. Which is one blessing. But the Queen is quite right, we must wait and see. And then we will learn who is our greatest enemy. I think I know what she fears. That our greatest enemy is not Cromwell, or whoever takes power after him: it is the people.'

'Why wouldn't the people want my father?'

'Put it the other way, Jemmy. Why would they? They have done without a king. And if the country doesn't fall to pieces now that Cromwell is coffined, they will carry on doing without him. There was blood and fire across the land during the wars, Jemmy. For my part I like 'em because they stir my spirit, but there's many who don't want to taste them again. They want a quiet life. Ha! There's your greatest enemy, if you want my thinking: apathy. That's what stands in your father's way. Oh, maybe the tide will turn, but if he does come to sit his throne at last, he'll have to remember one thing – his people showed they could do without him. I had a mistress once who adored me, but I quarrelled with her and left her. When I came back to her, she was merry and thriving, where I thought she'd pine. She let me back into her bed, and mighty sweet it was, and yet . . .' He laughed softly. 'Well, I was the loser and she the victor, and I knew it. You'll understand that, when the time comes.'

It was by Lord Crofts' goodness that I was able to see the King of France when he made the promised visit to my grandmother the next day. She quite forget about me, in the fluster of preparing to receive the court – which was natural, I suppose. Melancholy comparisons must have occurred to her also: thoughts of when she was Queen at her own court, instead of a pensioner lurking in the shadow of kindly pity. But she had bestirred herself, at any rate, to make an impression; not in the matter of her own dress, which was nun-like as ever, but in Minette's. I hardly recognized the girl who rambled with me about the gardens at Colombes. Her gown was of silver satin, cut very low across her shoulders, with pearls all down the stomacher; there were pearls at her throat too, and at her ears garnets of a soft red that made me think of raspberries, while above her ears her hair was gathered in frizzed and curled bunches.

I did not much like the transformation. Minette looked thin, pale and cold. The gown had plainly been taken out in a hurry, and she moved stiffly in it. She did, however, look like a princess, and doubtless that was why my grandmother appeared so satisfied, presenting her to Louis of France with a clenching grip on Minette's goosefleshed arm.

Lord Crofts, in attendance as Captain of the Guards, had placed me beside him amongst the pages, and I had a better view than the ladies-in-waiting fluttering like a cage of birds in the anteroom behind us. Still, you will readily conclude how swiftly spoiled I had become, from the fact that I felt left out. I looked on sulky and cross, shuffling my feet, and wondering when these people would be done with their bowing and parading.

These people, of course, were the power of France, and so it is not too much to say that at that moment I stood at the centre of the world.

There was no mistaking the King. Louis XIV was then nineteen, and had yet to take the reins of government in his own hands, and Versailles was still only an obscure royal hunting lodge. But already he exuded grandeur. It was not that his looks were particularly impressive – he was nowhere near as tall as my father, for instance, and if the court panegyrists made a fuss about Louis's commanding height, it was because they only ever saw him from a bowing position. Nor would I call him handsome. That face, in its frame of swirling locks, had too much of the hawk about it, and he had little, grey, secret eyes. What made him so majestical was, I think, his thorough belief in himself. Not vanity – that is a froth that comes from deep springs of self-doubt. Louis in his plumed hat, ribbons, red stockings, and pointed shoes, stalking towards my grandmother amidst a murmurous surge of cringes and curtsies, was not vain. He was just receiving his due.

'You remember, of course, my daughter, Henriette-Anne,' my grandmother said. 'She has grown, I think, since you did her the honour of opening the ball with her at the visit of my daughter of Orange. Faith, it must be two years ago. Time flies away for an old woman like me. It seems only yesterday she first danced in the ballet. She was Erato and you, of course, were Apollo – she was quite a little child then, and now – now I behold a woman!'

'And a great credit to you, aunt,' the young King said. He had doffed his hat very graciously to my grandmother, and now he did the same to Minette.

'I remember it well. The *fête* was for the marriage of my niece. Everyone remarked on that charming little girl.' It was Cardinal Mazarin who spoke, in his soft Italian-scented French. Here was the power behind majesty. He looked, in his scarlet robes and skullcap, somehow theatrical: ever smiling, his many-ringed hands making delicate shapes in the air as he greeted and admired Minette. 'The promise is fulfilled.' He was courtly, even humble, but he could dispense with self-assertion. He was the great puppet-master of France. Louis had come to the throne as a boy of five and since then Mazarin had run things for him, in concert with the Queen Mother, Anne of Austria. She was a rosy, robust widow, healthy as a dairy-keeper, whose well-fed charms Mazarin was said to enjoy nightly. Rumour even had it that they were secretly married, but in public, as now, he kept a decorous distance from her. The gems on his clever fingers hinted at his wealth. Rumour called it vast, also corrupt and reprehensible. They said he even perfumed his pet monkey. Knowing the habits of monkeys, for Lady Crofts kept one, I thought the perfume a very good idea. Mazarin's domed head, lustrous even in the dingy light of my grandmother's apartments, suggested that he had many ideas, and his eyes, merry and crafty, seemed to see and measure and know everyone in the room, even me.

'*I* don't remember it. You're wrong to say *everyone*. Where was I? I must have been there. How provoking. What I do remember, sir, is you not wanting to dance with her after supper. You said you weren't interested in little girls – do you recall it? Tee-hee! Oh, but of course you were quite the soldier already, and that was why, you know.'

That was a curious long-nosed swarthy creature who, having got a tolerant laugh from the King – Louis laughed, as it were, officially, without smiling at all – proceeded to kiss Minette's hand. His gallantry, like his dress, was so extravagant that I could only suppose him to be some sort of court jester, like my grandmother's dwarf. He was small too, though not as small as Hudson, and delicately made: a youth, but painted and patched and powdered to a degree I had only seen in old ladies, his mouth a cherry pout, shallow almond eyes fringed with sooty lashes. As for his costume – well, men's clothes are soberer now than they were then, when even plain fellows went in for quantities of lace, but I had never seen such a fantastical peacock as this. He was so covered in embroidery and diamonds that to look long at him was to court a megrim.

'You are talking nonsense again, *mon frère*,' said the King, 'but if I have ever failed in etiquette to my sweet cousin, I crave forgiveness for it.'

'But no, no, sir,' the other squeaked, 'I never speak anything but the truth, you know. And so when I tell you, madam, that I am *enchanted* by you—' here he kissed Minette's hand again – 'you will have no *choice* but to believe me.' And he licked his lips, as if he relished the taste of her.

Yes, the creature was the King's younger brother. He was Philippe, Duke of Orléans, and styled the Monsieur of France – the second man in the kingdom. Extraordinary I, and many others, thought him, but that did not mean he was generally disapproved. The French Crown had often been troubled by younger brothers with great ambitions. A Monsieur whose chief ambition was to look prettier than all the ladies of the court was rather welcome than otherwise. Some said that his mother had kept him in skirts till he was ten with just that aim in mind. Hence this creature – frivolous, tolerated, harmless.

Well, so he appeared. In fact it might have been better if I had seized Lord Crofts' sword from its scabbard and run Philippe through there and then. At the time, though, I just wanted to laugh.

For Louis the sole *fauteuil* in my grandmother's apartments stood waiting, attendants poised to scuttle forward with it the moment his royal rear signalled imminent descent. It was part of the ceremonial that already surrounded this most aloof of kings, who sat in an armchair whilst others, even royal others, took the humble discomfort of tabouret stools. Nonsensical it might seem, but it was also serious: kingship was special and untouchable and no one was to forget it for a moment. No Cromwells for France. Very much at his ease, though, was Cardinal Mazarin on his lowly seat, leading the talk.

'Well, ma'am, I can vouch for that news I wrote you yesterday, beyond all doubt. You are to be congratulated.'

'Am I?' my grandmother said, deliberately awkward.

'Certainly. All Europe rejoices at the death of that viper. It is a day you must have eagerly awaited, ma'am – you who have suffered so much.'

'I wish I could rejoice, Your Eminence. Perhaps, as you say, I have suffered too much. For me, joys belong only to the dead past.' My grandmother was wearing, I saw, the locket bearing the miniature of her husband, and she touched it as she spoke. 'I do not say the news is unwelcome, not at all. But only for the sake of my younger generation – those for whom I live.' And she made her grand sorrowful sweep of the arm at Minette.

'Ah, yes, you have much to be proud of,' Mazarin purred, 'and much to look forward to, I'm sure.'

'It's natural that you should think of him,' the French Queen Mother said comfortably, nodding at the locket, 'quite natural, my dear, this news bringing it to mind and so on. But that will pass, you know.'

'Never a day goes by without my thinking of him,' said my grandmother, with violence. 'As I said, my own hopes are dead and buried with him. All I live for is to see my children rightly settled. Then I shall retire to Chaillot and close my eyes on the world.'

'Heavens above, you've many years yet!' the Queen Mother cried. 'Why, you're younger than me, sister-in-law, and I don't feel ready to go, not I. You should eat more. You should eat red meat. It invigorates the constitution, raises the animal spirits.'

My grandmother made a sickly waving-away gesture.

'Veal then. Veal is always wholesome.'

'There's something about veal,' put in Philippe, 'that always puts me in mind of babies. Isn't that the most curious thing?'

'It would be a curious thing if anyone else thought it, brother,' Louis said with his small smile, 'but not you.'

'Or chicken,' said the Queen Mother, who seemed ready to go on relentlessly recommending meats all day. 'Chicken in a good strong broth—'

'The pleasures of the table,' said my grandmother with her eyes tremulously closed, 'are the last things I am concerned with.'

'Digesting this news,' Mazarin said, 'that is perhaps our true task. Reports from England are scant, but it *seems* all is quiet thus far. The devil's passing has not been much mourned there, even among his party – that much I have heard.'

'Viper and devil,' my grandmother said, 'so he was. And yet not so much of either, it seems, that France declined to treat with him.'

Smiling still, Mazarin, born Mancini, gave a very Italian shrug. 'There is, I think, in English this expression: "It is needful sometimes to hold a candle to the devil." France has had a sore trial of arms, ma'am, and has needed to make alliances. Such is war. But the soul of France has always recoiled at these monstrous rebels. Troubled times. We must hope for better.'

'You put me in mind of another English expression, Your Eminence,' my grandmother said sweetly. ' "He who lives on hope dies fasting." '

Mazarin, who for wit could have run rings round everyone there, sketched an elegant pantomime of defeat. 'As you say. Yet I believe there is still a party friendly to the royal cause in England, is there not? Subdued, of course, hitherto, but surely growing. This fanatic regime – no feast-days, no theatres' – he gave a cultivated shudder – 'such barbarism cannot last. And a returning king who could lift that shadow – he would surely be welcomed with garlands as a blessed deliverer.' Mazarin smiled delightedly at the picture he had painted, though whether he believed in it was a different matter. 'What say you, sire?'

'Our cousin of England would do well, if he ever comes to the throne, to strengthen his power directly,' pronounced Louis, unhesitating. 'Surround himself with loyal arms – make himself feared. Only then can he rest, and rule.'

My grandmother quivered with agreement. 'So I have always believed, absolutely. But alas, before the King my son can think of such things, he must reach that throne. And for that there must be a *push* – a strong arm at his side.'

'Such,' said Mazarin, all pleasantness, 'as he has hoped to find with the Spanish.'

'I have always thought to find a true friend to our cause here,' my grandmother said, 'in the Crown of France.'

'Indeed, indeed, and the Crown of France' – Mazarin made a reflexive bow or cringe in Louis's direction – 'rejoices in the death of the usurper, and looks forward to better times for all.'

Philippe thrust his unmeaning titter into the ensuing silence. 'Well, the one pity of it is, that the wretch *didn't* take the crown. Oh, don't misunderstand me, I am the *severest* person when it comes to rebels. I would have their heads on spikes and no mercy. It's simply that if he *had*, one could wear royal mourning now, and nothing better suits me, you know, than a purple train. Monstrous vain of me, I know.' He laughed good-humouredly enough. 'Don't you think, cousin, that I'm monstrous vain?'

'You are proud of your appearance, Monsieur,' Minette answered him, 'as is fitting for a prince.'

'You know, cousin,' Philippe said, increasingly interested, 'you are so very much the Frenchwoman. What must you think of it all? I dare say you cannot even remember England – I dare say it is all . . . *pouf!*' And his own smokelike curls rippled as he giggled it.

'Oh, I am an Englishwoman at heart, sir, and Charles's cause is most passionately my own. But as for what I think – well, I think that before he can make himself feared, he must make himself loved. With respect, Your Majesty,' Minette added, inclining gracefully to Louis.

'That's because you are all tenderness and goodness, *mon enfant*,' my grandmother said, and turning ardently to Louis: 'So unspoilt – and yet sister to a king!'

Louis doled her a nod, and I saw how much my grandmother bored him.

'And this king,' said Mazarin cheerfully, 'whom we congratulate, as it were, by proxy – what are his plans now, ma'am?'

'Oh, you fish in the wrong pond, Your Eminence, asking me, an old retired widow quite out of the world. You surely know them better than I.'

'There is second sight in my family,' Mazarin chuckled, stroking his little beard, 'but alas, I didn't come in for it.'

'Oh, but what my aunt means is your *spies*, you know,' put in Philippe impatiently. 'They're everywhere. Lord, I believe even I am spied on in my closet, and I cannot *think* why.'

'His Eminence acts always for the security of the kingdom,' the French Queen Mother intoned. Were she and Mazarin lovers, as the gossips said? Probably: they had that conscious way of not looking at one another.

'And in times of war, of course . . .' Mazarin's fine hands made delicate shapes. Watching him, you half expected him to produce a posy from his sleeve. 'France has had to keep her eyes open all the time. Perhaps soon she may wink. Perhaps soon she may take stock of her true friends.'

'My son will be glad to hear that, if I may tell him it,' my grandmother said eagerly. 'That France is now ready to help—'

'Ah, ah, I fear, ma'am, I express myself badly. France is not ready for *anything* just yet. Alas. Is it not so. Your Majesty?'

'We have a war to win,' Louis said, cool and final.

'Oh, I adore war,' cried Philippe. I heard Lord Crofts give a disbelieving grunt beside me – but in truth there was something pantherish about the young man, despite the lace and absurdity. 'It is the most beautiful of the arts. Oh, but it is! There is colour, grandeur, pathos, the music of trumpet and drum—'

'But it is the only art in which men are killed,' Minette suggested gently.

'But no,' Philippe cried, with a kind of pounce of attention, 'no, cousin, for the art of love is very like it. A man can be slain by a glance from a pair of beautiful eyes, for example.'

'Philippe, you put your cousin quite out of countenance,' said the Queen Mother, fanning her red cheeks vigorously – I think the poor lady was at the change of life.

'Not at all,' Minette smiled, 'because I cannot believe I am worthy of compliment. As for killing with a look – well, if it were so, Monsieur, you could combine your favourite arts. Put an army of beautiful girls into the field, and who could stand against you?'

Philippe cocked his head at her, like a bright spoiled bird, then gave a shriek of laughter. 'I am just picturing it! It is so piquant! Brother, do you hear?' Minette was showing a new side to herself. My grandmother narrowed her eyes in approval.

'These pleasantries,' Mazarin said, his undulating hands expressing enjoyment of them, mild regret that they must end. 'We are all in high good humour, ma'am, because of your so encouraging news. You will convey our pleasure to your son—'

'My son the King. Indeed I will,' my grandmother said distinctly. 'I wish I might convey more . . .'

'We are happy,' said Louis in his metallic way, getting up. 'We are always happy to see you, aunt. And you, cousin.' He did not so much bow as momentarily unstiffen. The world knows Louis XIV now as a great profligate, laying out his millions on Versailles, but in truth he was always a man who knew the value of things, his nature resolutely frugal. He had given all he was going to give. My grandmother was plainly disappointed, but schemed on undaunted, prodding Minette forward as the royal party processed out. But Louis was now bestowing some crumbs of attention on her household, the ladies-in-waiting all dipping in a murmurous flurry of curtsies, the guards at attention. Lord Jermyn got a nod, Lord Crofts a little more, a nod with the plumed hat actually lifted, slightly, above the right ear, condescension indeed. And then I, prickling and fidgeting beside him, found a face staring into mine. Not the King, but Philippe, his black eyes like poisonous berries.

'Faith, but this is a pretty boy!'

'My ward, sir,' Lord Crofts said, 'Master James Crofts.'

Joli – pretty. I was used to that: it was still a while before I would be called handsome. But the way the Monsieur said it made me feel like shrugging the word off, as I wanted to shrug off his hand that grasped my chin, tilting my face to meet his eyes and receive his perfumed breath.

'Oh, do look, brother, look at this face! The prettiest sprig – quite the Ganymede.'

Louis, frowning, seemed about to pass on. But he did look, and so I had the experience of seeing Louis of France, that king of clockwork elegance, betrayed into surprise.

'Hm. A remarkable face indeed.' Louis glanced at Lord Crofts, then tapped his brother sharply on the arm, making him let go of me.

I, ever greedy for attention, for once did not want it. I was glad when they were gone, but already could feel Lord Jermyn's look of jealous disdain on me. He wasted no time.

'Well, well, my lord Crofts, singular attention for the little whelp. From the King, I mean. The *other* sort of attention we know all about. You had better watch out Monsieur don't steal him.'

The dwarf, Hudson, took hold of my chin and squeaked in imitation of Philippe: '*Si joli, O mon Dieu!*' Lord Crofts, smiling tolerantly, waved him away. 'His Majesty was very gracious,' he said.

'Oh, well, there's quite a resemblance. He must have known him for Charles's bastard,' Lord Jermyn said. He eyed me with bleary malice. 'That's all it was. Charles's bastard.'

That word. I had heard it before, of course. But Lord Jermyn, deliberately no doubt, made it burn like a brand.

I sought out my grandmother, to be fussed over. But she was distracted and irritable. 'Veal,' she grumbled. 'Faith, as if I care for . . . The King is not himself just now – did you not think so, *mon enfant*? He has had a fever, he is a little low. We must bear that in mind. You are so pale, you are not usually so pale, where are the roses?' She pinched Minette's cheeks, not kindly. 'Mazarin, of course, guides everything. And the great God only knows what he really thinks. Aye, Jemmy, aye, you were much honoured. Be thankful for it. Time was, *I* was the one who gave honour. No more . . .'

I felt annoyed by her self-pity, of which I sought the monopoly just then. I was the little bastard: I was different from everyone there, and that was not the same as feeling special, as I had felt special when Mr O'Neill had sought me out, when my father had taken charge of me, when my grandmother had petted me. I felt as if someone had put me before a mirror and pointed out, callously, a disfigurement.

'Never mind, Jemmy,' Lord Crofts said that evening. He had heard me sniffling in bed and came in, kindly enough but impatient, for he had company already loud and vinous downstairs. 'There are many worse things than bastardy, trust me. And *kings'* bastards always do pretty well, you know. Besides, I doubt you'll be the last, knowing His Majesty.'

'You mean he loves a lot of women,' said I, plainly: sex was no mystery to me.

'Well, I don't know about *love* . . .'

I did not like this notion of other children. Lord Crofts saw my pout, and said hastily, 'Look you here, Jemmy – whatever happens, you are his first-born. And after all, he has taken particular care of you, has he not? Which suggests he has particular plans for you – yes? Heyo, there's a bit of a smile coming. Now hark'ee, never pay any heed to old Jermyn. He's just wondering what's going to become of him in the new dispensation, if there is one, and it makes him fretful. So are we all.'

A little comforted, I went to bed, but the word still glowed coldly at the centre of my mind. An unanswered question hung over my life. Not so Lord Crofts' friends, who caroused noisily till dawn as if my father's throne were already regained. Well, after a decade of defeat and exile, that was understandable. But I could not help wondering why, if the Roundheads were weasels and cowardly scrimshankers as they said, they held the power in England while these men drank themselves blind in a foreign land.

And very soon the celebrations died down, and the hopes of the exiles stood as threadbare as their coats. My grandmother was grave over her correspondence. England had not risen from beneath the Protector's heel and cried out for its rightful king. England had not done anything. Cromwell's son Richard took his father's place. Tumbledown Dick they called him, for he had never distinguished himself. But nor did he have any obvious vices, and in that smooth passing of power from father to son there was much to alarm. Again, what need a king? Lord Crofts, it seemed, had been right about the greatest enemy. My father lingered on with his small forces at Brussels, his Spanish alliance souring, his resources draining away. My grandmother seldom spoke to me of her letters from him, and if I asked she was sharp with me – that was the greedy jealous side of her. But once she let slip something about his poverty that shocked me.

'He has not tasted meat for a week. All his plate is pawned. There is nowhere left to turn. And I can send him nothing. I have nothing.' She leaned her head tragically on her hand.

'What about the Princess's jewels?' I said.

'What?' It was as if she had forgotten I was there. 'What is this nonsense you talk?'

'She wore jewels – when the French King came.' I was trying to be helpful. I was sure Minette, who always spoke lovingly of my father and loyally of his cause, would give them up at once.

'They are not to go. No, no.' My grandmother was curt; then she softened. 'You would have her look her best, would you not, Jemmy?'

I thought Minette looked just as fine without them, and I said so.

My grandmother's smile was a little cruel. 'You will understand one day.'

How tired I was of being told that! I, who, as the year drew to an end, found myself taller than the other boys, stronger in the arm and surer in the saddle. I was even learning properly to fence. Every week Lord Crofts sent me to a fencing master in the Faubourg St-Germain, where I trained in a great bare room above a pastry-cook's, with the warm smell of dough in my nostrils and the harsh Breton commands of my master dinning in my ears. Dour and grim even when pleased with me, he would remind me, time and again, that rashness was my failing, that no amount of daring strokes would avail me if I neglected my guard. 'You are not in a street brawl, young sir. You rush in as if I stole your purse. Get rid of the heart. Use only this.' And his knuckled rap-rapped on my skull. I was perhaps putting my frustrations into the sword, likewise the vaulting horse that I would have raised to its highest level and leap across, before and after fencing, until the sweat coursed down my back and my dizzied eyes saw spots. Riding home with Lord Crofts' groom afterwards, I always felt calmer, for a time. There could never be complete peace, not since Lord Jermyn had spoken that word and I had taken it in. I wanted to know – or rather to *feel* – who I really was. In truth I wanted my father: like the exiles, I wanted him to resolve everything.

And resolution came on one of those afternoons as I returned from my fencing lesson. Not from my father, though.

From my mother.

NINE

We had crossed the Pont Neuf, where the mist of the Seine hung raw in the sombre November air, and were heading for my guardian's house by the Rue St-Denis. As always, we halted at an inn with the sign of a doe hanging from its worm-eaten gable, and Lord Crofts' groom, a flat-faced Fleming, got down and went in. He was in love with an ale-wife there, with what success I know not; but she gave him drink at least, and he would come out after half an hour pink in the face and chewing a clove. This weekly ritual was a secret between us. Lord Crofts, tyrannical to his servants, would have been furious, but I was flattered that the groom trusted me not to mention it. I didn't mind waiting, the bustle of the streets affording me entertainment enough. The great markets were nearby, and as the day died many poor folk made their way thither, to pick up such cheap leavings of bread as they could. I saw many hungry and even desperate faces. I was a lone boy, well-dressed, but I was never afraid. Fresh from my sword exercise, I felt equal to anything.

Yet what I was quite unequal to, that foggy November day, was the shock of hearing my mother's voice.

'Jemmy!'

I had been idly looking in at the window of a fan-maker's shop, and the gasp I let out took visible form, a sudden bloom of mist on the glass.

'Jemmy – Jemmy, no . . .'

That 'no' was because – and my face fires as I remember it – I made as if to run away from her.

The impulse was momentary, and I checked it. Still, she had seen it, and I could not deny what instinct had bid me do: get away from her. That came first, before any wonderment at what she was doing in Paris or how she had found me.

What did I fear? That she would take me back, I suppose; that this life, about which I had lately been so cross and discontented, would be lost to me. That I could not bear – understandable perhaps – but there was, shamefully, more to it. In that young peacock skulking away in a Paris street, I now see a boy who wished his mother did not exist. And though he did not perhaps know it, that was why he burst into passionate weeping.

'Jemmy, what is this? Are you not happy to see me? And you grown so tall and strong. Dear, dear.'

There she stood, she had hold of my hand now, and I must face her. She shook her head at my tears, but I think after all it did not displease her to see them.

'It has seemed so long – so long, my son. And you are changed.'

'I'm not,' said I – why, I cannot tell. I tried to get my hand away, but she had it fast. She bent – only a little – to bring her face to mine. There was wine on her breath, but something else too, a sweetness that was not sweet. I jerked my head back from it, and now I saw how changed she was.

Not altered, not really: here was the same rich hair and bold violet eyes, and though her dress was shabbier than I had known it and she wore no jewels, still that faded green velvet had, on her, a flaunting sort of grandeur. But she was thinner, and the paint could not disguise that she was as white as bone meal. The effect made her not less, but more herself, in a terrible way. That gaze of consuming intensity, that mouth all wilful sensuality and pride, were so pronounced that it was as if she were being reduced to a naked essence by her sickness.

Yes, it was plain that she was ill, her malady a gourmand eating away at her with a quickening appetite. The strength in the bony hand clutching mine was feverish, and when she straightened to gesture to a man across the street she swayed like a reed.

The sight of the man struck me with a new fear. He was a hulking wall-eyed fellow, booted and spurred, lounging in the doorway of a wine shop. Was he to be the agent of my abduction? But at my mother's gesture, he simply nodded and slouched away, picking his teeth with a little knife.

'Who is that?' I said, breathing again.

'Him? No one. A friend of a sort.' Her old disdainful grandeur was in her tone, and I was and am glad of it. But I knew that the brute must be her latest beau or protector, and that showed how far she had fallen from my father and Tom Howard, and even that wild Cavalier called Robbie. I did not like to think of her with such a man. But of course, I did not like to think of her at all: that was the trouble.

'How did you find me?' I asked.

'Why, do you think it such a hard task? What can stand in the way of a mother's love?' So bright, so harsh was her smile that I almost squinted in the glare of it. 'I could have come to you before, Jemmy, had I chose. You see, I accepted. What your father did – it was wrong, a great wrong to me, but I decided to abide by it. Do you see? Where and who you are now – you have *me* to thank for that. Remember it, Jemmy.' She put a hand on my shoulder, and I felt her weight press on me. 'Let us step over there. I want to sit down.'

She meant the wine shop. I began to protest that Lord Crofts' groom would miss me, that I could not stay from home . . .

'Nonsense. He always stays at the Chevrette for a good half-hour, that I know. Aye, Jemmy, you have been observed lately. Your father is not the only one who can play such tricks. No matter. All I want is to talk with you, Jemmy – my only sweet boy. Would you deny me that? Would you?' I could summon no answer; and she went on, pushing me forward, 'And I must sit down, you know, just for a space. I have been a touch liverish of late, and I soon grow tired. It is the most *vexing* thing – me of all people!'

Her old spirit shone out a moment in that, but it was a gleam soon quenched. My mother, whose vitality had been so uncrushable, was weak. It made me reel a little in turn to realize that this was she, leaning on me for support. I was used to sudden reversals – indeed, I could not conceive of life proceeding in any other way – but here was the greatest overturning yet.

In the wine shop she sat down heavily on a bench, pulling me close beside her. It was a shabby little place, ill lit by a couple of stinking tallow candles. Two men were dicing, watched by the proprietor, a dropsical fellow who came over and grunted something to my mother in a low Parisian French I could not understand. It was unfriendly, though, and I gathered she had been here before. When she gave him a few sous from her purse, he tried their goodness with his teeth before bringing her a cup of wine, slopping it down with a bang on the table before us.

She drank thirstily. I watched her, in growing trouble and wretched-ness and – yes – shame, seeing the scrawny sinews moving in her throat, noting the many patches she wore. The devil's freckles, Anne Hill always used to call them, and would bully my mother to be sparing with them.

'Where's Anne?' I burst out. 'Is she still with you?' I wanted, I suppose, to be told that everything was just as it was before – bad as that was – rather than to believe the evidence of my eyes, that things were much worse.

'Anne? There is no Anne. She took herself off, months ago. I made her go,' my mother said absently, licking her lips. Then I felt her attention snap towards me like the cracking of a whip. 'Why, what's she to you? Your own mother comes out of her way to find you, and you ask after the maid. Is that all you have to say to me, Jemmy? Is that my reward for birthing you and rearing you and – and for giving you up when I had to?'

I might have wept then, but the men playing dice inhibited me. They had already cast several speculative looks at my mother and I, boylike, dreaded more attention. Besides, how could something as simple as tears express my feelings at that moment?

My mother saw my confusion. Never very merciful, she drank it in for some moments, and then put her hand on my shoulder.

'Well, you should know, Jemmy, I have forgiven you. Aye, he had you stolen from me – but you *wanted* to go. Did you not? Come, you can't hide anything from me: I know it. Well, I have forgiven you that too. You have not regretted your choice, either, that's plain. You thrive.' She looked me up and down. 'You thrive, my son.'

'He is my father,' I said, pleading, 'and he has taken care of me, and I have new clothes, and I have been sent to school—'

'School!' she echoed, wryly, as if it were too absurd even for scorn. 'Aye, well, he has his own notions, I dare say. Not that he communicates them to *me*. No matter. That's all done with. I have . . . other friends now.'

'Good friends?' I ventured. 'Mother, are you . . . happy, and little Mary – does she do well? And are you safe, and—' The tears I could not shed choked me.

'Dear, dear! What can you learn at school, I wonder, that makes you such a goose? Safe, indeed. Have you quite forgot your own mother? I can very well look after myself, Jemmy, as you would remember if you ever thought of me.'

'I do,' I said miserably. 'But – but you are ill.'

She fixed me with a look, bleak and adult, then waved it away sharply, laughing. 'And now you are a little physician. I have been better. But I do very well, I thank you, Jemmy. If you do think of me – I shall take you at your word on that – then think of me among friends, and as gay as may be. I have stayed at Brussels, where there is plenty of company, and where there are still some of the King's party who have – who have not turned against me. But I have taken it into my head to come to Paris, because – well, because of important business.'

Because you are dying. I could not say it. Perhaps even my mind could only lightly cup the thought, like a thorny stem in the palm, which will tear and wound the grasp. But my burning face must have shown it. My mother patted at my shoulder blindly, turning away.

'Here, sirrah! More wine here!'

The wine shop keeper, thus summoned, came with sour looks, sourer still when my mother's purse yielded nothing. Lord Crofts always furnished me with a few sous. I took out my own purse and paid for another cup of wine. As my mother gulped it down I saw the dicing men watching us. One grinned his brown teeth at me and said: 'You're starting young.'

There was an exclamation of harsh laughter. My mother's eyes narrowed, but she was concentrating on her wine.

'Too young,' said another, rolling a cruel cockerel eye. 'Experience will teach him. You don't pick such a worn-out old piece as *that* until you're desperate.'

I leaped to my feet. My hands twitched, and if I had been allowed to wear my fencing sword I do not doubt I would have drawn it. That terrible boiling rage was upon me. Yet deep down perhaps I welcomed it this time, for I could put it at the service of my mother, whom I had abandoned and betrayed, to whom I needed to prove something. But I did not cry out that she was my mother and mortally sick. Other words sprang to my lips, loud and defiant.

'She is the wife of a king!'

They laughed, of course, after the first moment of surprise, and I, riding the swell of my rage, looked about me for something, I knew not what, something to strike with or throw . . . But my mother pulled me down. She, always so hot at the slightest insult, took no heed of those men. With a strangely wondering look she turned my face to hers and murmured: 'Jemmy, why did you say that?'

'Well . . .' In the ebbing fury I found courage – for in truth I had always been afraid of her – and looking her in the eye I said distinctly: 'It is true, isn't it, Mother?' I remembered the questioning in the Tower, with Cromwell hovering like an uneasy shadow; I remembered Lord Jermyn's piggish lips pronouncing 'bastard'. 'Is it true? Did he ever make you his wife, or are you—'

'It is true.' Shuddering she gasped the words out, like someone venting an oath in the grip of agony. 'Yes. Yes, Jemmy, and that is why I needed to find you and speak with you before I . . . while I may.' She drew out a thin smile. 'For who knows what may happen? That monster Cromwell is gone, and changes will surely come, and you are your father's ward now: your fate is his. So you must have this knowledge. Knowledge of yourself.'

I nodded earnestly. It was what I wanted, so badly.

'I have talked much lately with a good cleric here in Paris – an Englishman, a Protestant, of course. A rare good man. He listens in the true spirit of Christ, who did not judge. I have spoken to him of these matters, and – and he supports me. He has helped clear my mind, and my soul. I must set things in order while I can. You understand me?'

The bones in her face stood out. I looked at her and could not bear to look at her. 'Oh, Mother . . .' I moaned.

'Hush. I need you to listen, Jemmy, and master yourself: I command it. You must know that in giving you to your father I do not . . . I do not *surrender*.' The word pleased her, and she raised her wine to her pale lips as if toasting it. 'It's not that at all. I give you to him, not so that I can be forgotten, but so that I shall be rightly remembered . . . How fine you are!' She broke off to finger the lace at my cuffs, her look absent, a little envious. 'I suppose he is proud of you.'

'Yes. I think so . . .' A swarm of resentments I had only dimly apprehended now came suddenly upon me. 'But he does not keep me by him. And I go by Lord Crofts' name, and some people think—'

'Ah, do they? Well, well. You must not bear that, Jemmy. No, no. You must stand up for your rights, always, yours and mine, even when I am gone. Oh, I understand well enough the position he is in. I have seen how things stand at Brussels. His party have never been so low, for all that Cromwell is a corpse, and now even his foreign friends have no use for him. Hm – now he knows how it feels.' She put down her wine cup unsteadily. 'But the fact remains he is still dangling in the air, at the mercy of every wind that blows. He must still be so careful. And I have *always* understood that, for all the libels that are laid on my name. Dear God, if I had not, I would not be in this condition now. Remember this, Jemmy: the King's cause never had a better friend than me. Not that it was a *king* I first fell in love with. This is another thing you must remember: when we met he was only a poor dispossessed prince, and I saw no royal grandeur. I saw only him. And him I loved, at once, quite simply. That's something you will learn for yourself, I hope, when you are older. The lightning stroke from a clear sky, blasting into your heart – ah, there is nothing like it! It only comes once. So it was for me – and so it was for him. And that is something he won't admit, even to himself, and he's a fool for it. He has sealed off his heart, and thinks he will protect himself by it, and won't see that he has maimed himself instead. He is afraid of love, Jemmy. These women – these pretty creatures he entertains one after another – *that* is not love.' She laughed hoarsely. 'How blind folk are not to see it! That is a man singing at the top of his lungs to disguise how frightened he is. Love is going into the dark, love is faith and surrender and risk . . . and betrayal, sometimes, but then that's the risk. Your father went into the dark with me. That was love, beautiful and perilous, and he grew afraid, and now he only plays at it. I have done the same, perhaps – but I cannot be alone, and that's an end of it. Don't judge me for that.' She gave me a sharp look.

'I don't judge you, Mother,' I said with pain.

'Aye, aye, but you went away from me, my son, that you did . . .' She waved a hand, as if I had led her off the point. 'Well, we loved, as man and woman. Nothing else mattered. And so we . . .' She reached for her wine cup, but it was empty, and I had no more money. She banged it down. 'The circumstances of our marrying are not important. All you need to understand is that we were very young and passionate, and we acted accordingly – him most of all. Because he has never followed his heart like that again, and the memory of his folly burns him.'

'Then you were married to my father!'

'I say so, do I not?' my mother said, staring into space with a curious half-smile. 'Well. As I said, we were very young, and the times were turbulent. When we came to fall out, it was perhaps not surprising. He had duties, and they took him to Scotland – though I always warned him that would end in disaster – and I grew lonely, and . . . There is only one way for love to be born, Jemmy, but a thousand ways for it to die. I was partly to blame, perhaps, but he more so, because he retreated from love. So it ended. I never stopped loving, by the by. And that—' she gripped my wrist with all her old feline strength – 'that was the only claim on him that I kept. Another woman might have demanded a great deal – honours and influence. The empty name of queen.' She chuckled. 'People are very stupid if they fancy I was ever interested in that for myself. And I say again – I was a true friend to his cause. As his position grew worse, his difficulties greater, as his throne seemed further and further off, I clung to the one good that I could do in this world. I would not spoil his few chances by pressing my claim as his wife. You are old enough to understand this, I think, Jemmy. Royal marriages are a matter of power. All the more so for your father, whose powers have fallen away almost to nothing. He has no great armies or fleets or treasure chests. What he does have is his hand – his marriageable hand. With that, he might get the help he needed. Do you see?'

I nodded. 'There is someone called la Grande Mademoiselle, a cousin of King Louis. My grandmother – that is, the Queen Mother wanted him to marry her, because she is mighty rich.'

'Quite the little Frenchie!' my mother said, raising her eyebrows, for I suppose my pronunciation of the French words was very natural by now. 'Aye, I remember that creature. A great Amazon with cheeks like red apples. His mother was trying to push him into her brawny arms years ago. We used to laugh about it . . . Well, so you understand, my son. To make an alliance in marriage is one of the few hopes he has left. And I have chosen not to hinder that. The only claim I would make on your father is his love – and that he will not acknowledge. So be it. It is true, I have now and then made free with my title as his wife – when I have been in extremity, even threatened him a little with it. Those were slips. All in all I have clung to my good, and his. If he should make a good match while I – while I am able to hear of it, I shall still hold my peace. He knows that, I think. If he has found me troublesome, he knows how much more trouble I could have made. But, Jemmy, remember this. If in time he is restored to his kingdom, and takes some ugly royal bride who brings gold and horse-troops with her wedding clothes, you must be my witness. Swear it, now: on my hand.'

Her breath with its direful sweetness was hot on my face as she placed both my hands over her right. Part of me still wanted to fly from her – but the terrible gaze of those sick eyes tethered me there. Indeed, I have never escaped.

'I swear.'

'Very well. Remember that whatever happens, I was his true and first love and his true and only wife. And that means you are his trueborn first son. That is who you are, and no matter what shadows of doubt and confusion time may throw across your path, you must remember it, and stand up for it, and challenge any who would deny it. Because to deny it is to deny me. Now swear again.'

What was I to believe – I who had been surrounded from infancy by lies and disguise, who had put on different names and identities, knowing truth only as a shifting horizon? Here was my mother, whom I had run away from – and plainly she was a dying woman. She had made me swear, but the death in her feverish eyes was enough to put me on solemn oath.

And so I swore, with my lips, and with my soul, because I had no choice.

'If your father should deny it, and if it should ever come to a question of proof, then . . .' My mother frowned down at my hands. 'Well, there are papers. Marriage papers. I have lodged them with a certain person, who does not know what they are, but will keep them safe.'

Who? I didn't ask. Now, I would; but then I was a boy, and a boy whose heart was breaking. The phrase is common; this was not. It was as horribly physical as the slow splintering of a bone.

And besides, I had to believe. If I was to go on living, it must be in the certainty that I was no whorish by-blow, casually conceived and as casually raised. Seeing my mother again – for what I knew would be the last time – had made the burden of guilt I carried press on my back in a way there was no bearing otherwise. The guilt was for deserting her, and liking it, and not wanting to go back. I could only carry it by keeping faith with her, this last time.

'But never mind proof. It is belief that counts in this world, and passion and conviction. That is what you must have, Jemmy. Promise me you will keep that burning in your breast, and that you will defend my name and yours, if the time should come.'

Yes: I promised it, most earnestly, my hands over hers; and it is thus that we strike bargains with destiny.

She closed her eyes and sighed, as if in relief at a hard task done. For a moment it almost looked as if she could sleep where she sat. Then her eyes sprang open again, and in them was a startling glint of her old wilful mischief.

'He will never forget me then,' she said through her teeth, 'and I will always be with him.' Then she glanced at me as if she had forgotten me. 'So. I am content, Jemmy. Give me a kiss, for I must leave you. I won't tell you to be good: that's nonsense. Just be true to yourself. You needn't tell your father you have seen me. It will only cause trouble.'

Already she was on her feet. The brutish man was at the wine shop door, cocking his head for her to come to him. I clung to her, of course, clung and squeezed, until I heard her give a grunt in pained surprise, for her unregarded little boy was strong now, and she weak and ailing, yet I fancy she was not displeased either. And then she pulled away from me, and I whimpered or mumbled something. I hope that I said I loved her.

Then I watched her go. The man shoved her arm under his and tugged her along, as if he were pulling a stubborn ass. She turned her head once more, to look at me, but I could not read her expression: my tears, at last, came.

I was noisy and helpless with them for a while, and even the men dicing, who sneered at first, began to look discomfited. But finally I had done, and wiped my face, and went out to look for Lord Crofts' groom.

If he noticed anything, he remained true to our unspoken agreement, and made no mention of it. Nor did Lord Crofts press me that evening when he said I looked hippish, and asked if there was aught amiss. I was grateful.

And I was grateful some time later – not above a month – when Lord Crofts took me quietly aside, and told me that my mother was dead.

I had done my crying in that wine shop, and I hope my guardian did not think me cold-hearted. Perhaps he understood. At any rate, he carried me a couple of days after to a decent enough graveyard, though in a shabby dusty quarter of Paris, and I bared my head beside her little corner plot, with cold rank fog dripping from my hair and from the ivy that mantled the ancient wall beside me. One of my father's followers had seen to her burying – a Scots gentleman who had known her in better times – yes, known her in that way perhaps, not that it matters – and had told Lord Crofts about it. She had died of a consumption, Lord Crofts said.

There will be smirking at that as a misplaced gallantry, I know. The common word nowadays is that Lucy Walter died of the whore's pox. I know where the word came from – and as I shall soon be speaking of him, I shall name the begetter of these and other malign rumours: my uncle James. His hatred of me is such that he must traduce my mother, whom he never knew. The mixture of cowardice and moralizing is mighty typical of him.

Well, she is beyond hurt. I have never been back to her grave. My promise to her is of this world, not the next. Soon I must go out into that world, and make the promise good.

My love has just read over these last few pages, and they trouble her.

After long silence she came to me, looking both sorrowful and vexed. 'This matter of your mother, and what she told you . . .' she said, and then hesitated, bending to stir the fire. It has been a cold winter here at Gouda. The canals are frozen and every morning we find ice thick as goose-fat inside the bedchamber window. We are warm together at night, though, always. 'The way it is written . . . It makes your cause seem doubtful.'

'Does it?' said I. 'That's well, then, in a way. For you know I don't intend a tract, my love, I seek only to set down the truth.'

'But your enemies,' she said, her face a copper-gold vizard in the firelight, 'they would seize on it, twist it—'

'My enemies would do that even if I had the most indisputable claim. But I don't write for enemies either. I shall do nothing to oblige them, believe me. At any rate, if I should fail, they will have the last word.'

She stood, very straight, with a quiver about her that was not the heat of the fire. *If I should fail.* Yes: the matter was broached. It is always with us, of course, like a silent guest in our house, a spectral third. Not to be mentioned.

And I quail too inside – not, I hope, at the prospect of death itself, but because death would take me away from her, the beautiful elf-shape standing limned by fire, the companion and inspiration of my days and nights. Yet she believes in me – perhaps more than I do myself – and if I go, I know she will support me.

God, it is a hard place. I must return to my narration, and show how I came to it.

I must return to my father, who entered and altered my life again in the winter of 1659. He has appeared somewhat in the role of a hero thus far, I think, and the ardent boy that I was certainly saw him as such, and loved him. From the following time, I learned also to hate him; and often the two emotions were entwined, like grappling serpents, exquisite and poisonous.

TEN

It was Minette who told me that my father was coming to Colombes.

'Tomorrow,' she said, 'and he will stay till Christmas.'

She was seated at her harpsichord as she spoke, and punctuated her words with little twangs, as if we were in an opera. Minette was always full of such spontaneous games, and I might have laughed – were it not that I was furiously jealous in a moment.

'Grandmother didn't tell me! She must have known, and yet—'

'We heard last week.' Minette made it gentle, with a soothing chord, then put a hand on my wrist. 'Please, Jemmy. Maman has many cares. Also – she is perhaps a little afraid.'

'What? She says she's never afraid of anything,' I snorted.

'True . . . Call it anxious then.' Instant placation: that came from years of living with Henrietta Maria. 'You see, this is the first time they have met since the . . . the matter of my brother Henry. Charles was so very angry with her then, for what she did. She fears he has never forgiven her. Do you see? And so she is much distracted.'

I saw. But still I went and confronted my grandmother.

'Yes,' she said. 'Yes, he comes tomorrow, what more?'

'Can I see him?'

My grandmother sighed. 'I see no reason why not. But his time is not his own, Jemmy. We will have important things to talk about. These terrible times . . . He will want to know the mind of the French Court. Well, ha!' Snapping her fingers, she paced around. 'The mind of Mazarin, I should say. His hand is behind everything. Oh, a clever hand, but a trickster's. He might have done so much for us. Instead it is he regrets this, and he regrets that—'

'Then I may come here tomorrow, and see my father?' I would not be put off.

My grandmother fixed me with a stare, the stare that meant you were challenging her will. Perhaps that had been my uncle Henry's last sight of her, I thought.

'Very well, *bien bien*, yes. Do not bother me so.' Turning away, she stopped. 'Who told you?'

'Everyone knows.' I was shielding Minette, who stood in need of it that day, with the Queen Mother at her most fretful.

'We are used shabbily on all sides,' my grandmother grumbled, going to one of her waiting-women, snatching the needlework from her hands, and examining it critically. 'I cannot believe he got *nothing* from either party. Did he try? Did he really try? If only I had been there. The blessings of peace, he says. Pah!'

'Who says, Maman?' asked Minette, coming in.

'Mazarin, of course. Such blessings can be a curse.' My grandmother gave the needlework back, or rather tossed it in the waiting-woman's face.

'But peace is always better than war, isn't it?'

'You have much to learn, child. God forbid you should learn it in the same hard school that I did.' Yes, she was very bitter today, and bitter too against Minette, whom she seized by the arm and interrogated as if she were a stubborn child. 'Much to learn. Come, you have still not satisfied me. When you rode with him the other day – *ton cousin* – did he not address himself to you? Was he not attentive? Particular?'

'He was polite, Maman,' Minette answered, looking crushed. 'He is always very polite.'

'Polite.' My grandmother literally spat the word out: I saw the spittle freckling the silk collar of Minette's gown. 'I am surrounded by fools. You can get more than politeness, if you only try. Spirit, spirit! Everyone lacks it, I think, except me. Oh, well, it's probably too late now. Spain is everything now. Mazarin kisses the Spanish arse, and we – we are nothing, less than nothing, dust . . . Why do you look at me like that, child?'

Minette flinched, like a gentle dog suddenly smacked. Tell her, I thought. Tell her that she looks like a foolish, mad, sad, ugly old monkey.

But Minette said, with great tenderness, 'Poor Maman, I think you have a headache coming. You work so hard. Let me make you a draught of feverfew.'

My grandmother hunched, sighed. 'Yes, a headache.' After a moment her hand came out and patted Minette's arm. I saw Minette brighten. 'Good child. You are always a good child.'

A year had passed since the death of my mother. As my unabashed confidence against my grandmother shows, I had made great strides from the bemused boy who had first come to Paris. Such is the speed of change in youth, of course: we traverse mountains and cross leagues while our elders seem to stand still. Certainly there had been a sad stagnation in my family's affairs in that year. While England had remained quietly kingless, my father had clung to the shreds of hope from Spain – but now even the shreds fell away. He and his little force at Brussels had been a piece on the chessboard in the war between Spain and France – only a pawn, perhaps, but on the board none the less. Now France and Spain were making peace. The game was over, and he was superfluous. At last in desperation, and uninvited, he had taken ship to Fuenterrabia on the Spanish border, where the peace envoys were meeting. He hoped perhaps to persuade the Spanish, now their war was done, to lend their arms wholly to his cause; perhaps he just wanted to remind both sides of his existence. But no one was interested any more. The French had happily fought with Cromwell's doughty troops as allies, and happily they would rub along with Protectorate England now those troops had gone home. The Spanish, always weaker than their great pomp pretended, were just happy to have the war finished with. My father was irrelevant to the proceedings, which in traditional style involved the warring countries sealing the kiss of peace with – well, with a kiss. A marriage.

Louis of France and the King of Spain's daughter, the Infanta Marie-Thérèse, were both twenty years old, eminently marriageable, healthy, dutiful, neither disabled by those common royal inconveniences of insanity and idiocy. Nothing could have been more suitable as a symbol of the enduring amity of the two kingdoms. Marie-Thérèse of Spain had, it was said, a face like one of her own pug-dogs (not true – when I saw her, much later, she looked like a very pretty pug-dog) but that was a small matter compared with Spain's great empire. That was what Louis would really be getting into bed with. That was why Mazarin was busily working to bring the match about. All very sensible. Far more sensible than Louis's taking as his bride the Princess Henriette-Anne – that spare princess of nowhere, who lived, like a pensioned governess, on his charity, and who would bring nothing to the marriage bed but a needy hopeless family who were the embarrassment of Europe.

For that, of course, had been my grandmother's hope. Hence her disappointment: another of her webs destroyed. It would have been her greatest triumph, uniting the power of France to the broken-backed Stuart cause. The little general! And she didn't put the blame on the unreality of the hope. She blamed Minette for insufficiently fascinating Louis.

Minette, the child who had resolved to be good, took it to heart, that I know. Being human, she had vanity too – a good share of it, in truth – and that was wounded also. She was fifteen now, and though the gaiety still broke out her face wore more of a thoughtful look. There was no more of the swing in the garden. I saw a consciousness in her movements, and she took greater care to conceal that raised shoulder. But the truth was, Louis was never going to be fascinated out of common sense. He knew what he was doing. The young King was indeed mighty hard-headed, in a way my poor grandmother, who fancied herself a realist but lived in a cloud-machine of the mind, could never understand.

I think Minette began to understand, though, and to plan accordingly. She learned to calculate. I wish she had not. Perhaps I have more of my grandmother's romantic blood in me than I like to think – or would have liked to think just then, when I was angry with her. With my father due to arrive, I actually wished my grandmother was not there. I wanted it to be just him and me and Minette. That, I thought, would be perfection.

But I was disabused.

As ever, he arrived quietly, without ceremony, riding up to Colombes with a single manservant, and a couple of bags. (Even alone, Louis entered a room like a procession.) At my insistence, I had been at Colombes all day, but he was late and I, ever hungry, had gone to the kitchen to beg a slice of bread. It was vilely cold that winter, and as there was a good fire – indeed, it was the only place in that elegant house that was warm – I lingered long, talking with the cook-maid, and missed the sound of the horses. I came back up to the hall to find that my father was already there. He was embracing and kissing one of my grandmother's ladies-in-waiting.

A dismal proof of Lord Crofts' hints! – and already I picture the sneers of my father's detractors, who would paint him as a mere mechanism of lechery.

In fact he had mistaken the lady for his sister Minette, whom he had not seen in five years. The other ladies were giggling, and my father, when he saw his error, laughed readily at himself, as he always did.

'The true sister,' he said as Minette stepped forward. 'My dear, how could I have been such a booby? You had better salute my groom, and then we shall be equal.' He kissed Minette, studying her with surprise and pleasure, it seemed; then turned to my grandmother. 'And the true mother – the one, true, dear Mam. God, I am so happy to see you.'

So he met her again, after their bitter falling-out, passing it off so warmly and naturally that even my grandmother, all poker-backed and martyred and ready for histrionics, softened at once. There were others to be greeted, of course – Lord Jermyn especially obsequious, and laughing so much at a mild sally of my father's that he looked quite a lunatic – and even greedy as I was, I did not expect him to devote his attention to me at once.

And he did not; but he came to me at last, and shook my hand.

'Jemmy. I am glad to see you again, my boy. My, my!' He measured me with his eyes, and I him – with, I fear, a little perplexity. My father was then almost thirty years old, hale and strong. There was no touch of grey in the long black lustrous locks, nor surplus flesh on his body. Yet I thought him aged. Perhaps I had forgotten how very dark he was, for he seemed to move in his own pool of shadow, but had those eyes been so heavy-lidded before, the mouth so sharply incised with wry lines? Beside him I felt a sheer pink baby, untried, knowing nothing.

Not quite true, though, as he acknowledged with a sober commiserating look, patting my shoulder and saying quietly: 'I was much grieved to hear about your mother, Jemmy. Lord Crofts told me you went to see her resting-place, and have been a very stout-hearted fellow. I expected no less. We shall have some talk, my boy.'

'You look weary, Father,' I said.

'Weary, eh?' He chuckled. 'Well, at least it is no worse.'

After that he was claimed by my grandmother, of course, and there was a good deal of talk in her private closet. But by wheedling I had got a place at the dinner table – down at the far end, with Lord Jermyn's bulk beside me blocking most of my view, yet better than nothing. My father had Minette at his right hand, and was very attentive to her, as well as he could be with my grandmother peppering him with questions, which always turned into reflections on her own wrongs.

'Well, I am pleased for her, in faith.' They were talking of Princess Mary of Orange, my father's sister, of whom he gave a good account. 'I dare say she does thrive, when there is so very little to trouble her. The last time she came here, you know, I thought her blooming almost to the point of being fat, and I never saw anyone hung with quite so many diamonds and pearls. A very fine thing for her, no doubt, to be able to indulge herself so. Whether it troubles her that the rest of her family are so poor I know not – she has never been as confiding with me as a mother could expect.'

'We could never have survived without Mary as our moneylender, Mam,' my father said. 'She has done all she can. But she's not free, not really. The Dutch are not well affected towards the House of Orange at the moment. Some of those stubborn burghers would rather do without it altogether. And to see good Dutch gold being wasted on our cause makes them more stubborn than ever.'

'Wasted? How can you talk so—'

'I speak from their point of view. I have no love for the Dutch myself – any more than Mary does, though I fear she doesn't trouble to hide it.'

'And why should she, indeed?'

'Because you have to in this life, Mam. You have to.' He smiled at Minette. 'Is it not so, sister?'

'Oh, you do wrong to appeal to this sweet child,' my grandmother cried. 'She is quite as transparent as a piece of glass, no disguise at all.'

'Is that so? You had better cloud the glass, then, sister, upon my soul you had – else people will find out all your secrets.'

'Pooh, nonsense, she has no secrets.'

'Unless you have already clouded the glass, and we cannot see them,' my father said. He twinkled dark amusement at Minette, who flushed but seemed to like it – unlike my grandmother, who rapped on her plate with her knife and said again, 'Nonsense, you are talking nonsense, Charles. Come, what more of Mary? How does her little boy go on? He has been so sickly, I fear she won't raise him. That must be the father's strain in him – nothing of that on our side – though it is a wonder I am *not* sick, with all I have to bear.'

'William grows stronger, I hear, and is sent to Leiden at last to be schooled. Mary says he promises well, is very diligent and studious. Of course, how much power the Dutch will ever let him have is another matter. But at least he may call himself Prince of Orange, even if his people keep him on a tight lead.' My father grimaced and gestured for his wine cup to be filled.

'What is this?' my grandmother said. 'Are you despairing, my son? After all you have been through – and the arch-devil dead, and England crying for her king—'

'It must be exceedingly *quiet* crying,' my father said with a tight smile, 'for I really cannot hear it. But despairing, Mam? No. To despair is to see no good in life. And this wine is good – and the company of my dear ones is good – and there is much worth cherishing.'

My grandmother frowned. 'These are bad ideas. You have been mixing with the wrong sort of people. Your counsellors – you know I never approved them. I suppose Hyde still advises you. All *he* ever thought of was to oppose me in everything. I wish you had been guided by me . . .'

Even I wondered at my grandmother's going on like this. Here she was meeting her son after five years of estrangement, and supposedly reconciling; yet she was displaying the same meddlesome temper that had caused the breach. I heard Lord Jermyn – who was being very polite to me today – sigh deeply as he helped me to the fish. But my father looked untroubled, or at least unsurprised.

'Well, you are here, thank heaven, where there will be no defeatist counsels. No, no. I always strive to find hope,' my grandmother insisted. 'If France has not been friendly to you, you must remember that she is still in the toils of Mazarin, who is dead to feelings of honour. The *heart* of France beats with yours, my son.'

'It does no such thing, Mam,' my father said, gently but firmly enough. 'France doesn't have a heart, any more than England or Spain or any other country. That's a pretty sentiment and no more. A kingdom is a large number of human creatures ruled by a few, and those few look out for their own interests. That's all of it.'

My grandmother stared at him, baffled. 'Again this talk. The talk of the dice-box and the bagnio . . .'

'Oh, believe me, one does not talk politics there at all,' my father said with bland good humour; and I saw Minette suppress a smile.

'You would do well, my son, to heed the example of your cousin of France. He is always attentive to business.'

'I dare say, but then Louis has genuine business to attend to. I have to act the King's part on a bare stage and without even a pasteboard crown. I will say though,' he added with a wink at Minette, 'that I play the role indifferent well. I hear Monsieur Molière has set up his most excellent troupe at the Salle du petit Bourbon. You have seen them perform, sister? And what say you – would they take me as an extra player? Comedies only, mind: I am no man for tragedy.'

Minette shook her head. 'No. Monsieur Molière's comedies are about ordinary people – and that you could never be.'

'I appreciate the jest, Charles,' my grandmother said, not smiling, 'but you must consider that you may lower yourself in men's eyes even speaking in that way.'

'Indeed? Lord help Henry then. He speaks lately of becoming a tutor at tennis if things don't improve.'

There: the name of his brother was out, the one my grandmother had banished from her life for refusing to turn Catholic. The one she had still omitted to ask after, in fact, just as if he were dead.

The air seemed to sing shrilly. My grandmother was rendered speechless and my father, his black eyes glittering, allowed himself the small cruelty of dwelling on it for a little while. 'Another jest, perhaps. But he is excessively good at the game, and has had the beating of me. A healthy exercise. Henry's health is abundantly good: so I can assure you, Mam, as I know you did not part friends with him, and so are chary of enquiries. Of course, I know, as he does, that you think of him with the warmest love, even at a distance.'

'He . . . he is always in my prayers,' my grandmother said after a moment. Then, turning on Minette: 'My child, you are not eating. I've told you, you must feed yourself more. You're a shadow.'

I thought she had got off rather lightly; but my father smiled and turned the subject. 'Well, cousin Louis must be occupied with one particular piece of business just now. Everyone talks of this Spanish marriage. I wonder if it will happen.'

'If Mazarin wills it,' my grandmother grunted, knifing at her fish as if it were the Cardinal, 'then it will happen.'

'Perhaps. They do say that Louis is actually in love with a niece of Mazarin's – I forget which, he has so many. There are even whispers that Louis wants to marry her.'

'What? One of those Italian strumpets? God forbid,' my grandmother cried. 'Mazarin's family were no better than house-stewards. Those creatures would be in aprons making cheese if he had not crept his way into favour.'

'True. But Louis is master enough to do it, if he really insisted. But I don't think he is fool enough. Mazarin is already unpopular. There would be uproar if Louis took a queen from his family. Besides, Louis is too sensible to let love get the better of him. He knows that love and marriage are like sugar and onions – best kept in separate boxes.'

I don't know what made me pipe up just then – my father's eyes resting on me, perhaps, the lingering thought of my mother – but speak I did.

'I think the French King should marry the lady he loves.'

There was a general dismissive chuckle, but my father looked at me attentively.

'Ah. And do you have a lady-love, Jemmy?'

'La, Charles, he is not yet eleven,' my grandmother said.

'Well, it will come soon enough. And it can't be *too* soon, I believe. Get it over with early, like the smallpox, and then it need never trouble you any more.'

I was about to ask, quite seriously, whether that was what had happened to him. But already his attention was fixed on Minette again.

'Don't pay me any heed when I talk so, my dear,' he said to her. 'It doesn't mean anything. 'Tis as Mam says, the sort of talk idle fellows exchange over the wine.'

'But very sensible still, Your Majesty,' Minette said. 'Especially for princes. If cousin Louis married for love, I should think the worse of him.'

'Would you now?'

'I would.' Minette glanced, proudly I thought, at her mother. 'I understand very well how the world goes. Crowns must set themselves steadily, even more in these times.'

'Yes, yes,' put in my grandmother impatiently, 'but you know, my child, this Spanish match is not concluded, not yet, and the Infanta is not the only suitable princess—'

'She is the most suitable, I think.' Minette was firm; her mother blinked at her. It was my father, of course: he was giving her confidence. I wished I could have been happier about it. 'It is not for me to cherish any hopes in that direction. Indeed, I don't think of it. It is your crown, Your Majesty, that concerns me. To see you safely in possession of it – I have no room for any other hopes.'

'Bless you for that, sister,' my father said, smiling on her. 'But I pray you, whether I ever wear that elusive piece of smithery or not, don't call me Your Majesty. I have missed so much of your growing, alas – and now that I have found you, we must make up for lost time, and not be strangers.'

No, I could not be happy about it. My father and Minette – the two people I most loved, and wanted to love me – discovered each other afresh during his fortnight's stay at Colombes, and were much in each other's company, talking, laughing, reading together, trying over dances. And I hated it.

This was jealousy, of course. He had missed so much of her growing, and so on – did not that apply even more to me, his own son? So I reasoned to myself, sulking and watching. I fancy even then I understood something of the attraction between them. She was a delightful younger sister who admired without making demands, he a worldly elder brother who brought the dazzle of adventure and experience into her circumscribed life. And they were both clever, in a way my grandmother, fettered by her passions, could never be. (Nor, I know, can I. My mind cannot mount high and see with the hawk's conning eye: I am always too close to the earth, distracted by its scents, tugged by the heart.) As for whether either was aware of stronger feelings, or the possibility of them, shadowing their force-ripened affection – well, that is best left for another time. But certainly my own jealousy was loverlike in its intensity.

I did get a little of him alone that first evening after dinner. I did it by making a fuss when my grandmother was about to have me sent out, protesting so loudly that my father put aside his wine and took me to sit by him in a window seat.

'You like to be noticed, hey? So you were as a little infant. You would clutch at my pockets for sweetmeats and shout your name, as if I could forget you were there. Well, well, a long time ago.' He waved a hand, quickly divining that a boy of my age loathes to be reminded of such things. 'You grow apace. Lord Crofts tells me you have made good progress with your learning. You had much to do to catch up, I fear.'

'Oh, yes, but – I didn't mind.' In truth I was a little shy of him so close, seeing again how black and grim he was. But I began eagerly enough to tell him all I could do. I bragged, in short – chiefly about my fencing and riding and such, rather than my struggles as a scholar – and showed off my thrust and parry. He smiled tolerantly as I dispatched imaginary Roundheads. In Scotland he had seen the severed limbs of his father's loyal general Montrose nailed up on walls; at Worcester he had seen his followers blown to pieces with cannon-shot: he knew all about the glory of arms.

'Father, how long am I to stay with Lord Crofts?'

'That we will have to see. You are happy there, are you not?'

'Oh, yes. It's better than— I mean . . .'

My own treachery silenced me. But my father nodded his understanding.

'Jemmy, your mother would have been a better woman in better times.' Then he grimaced. 'Perhaps that excuses us all. But then, we make the times, do we not? Ah, well, Jemmy, you know there will be many claims on my attention. But remember, you will always be in my thoughts. I have so many unpleasant things to think of, that I know the value of the pleasant ones.'

Well, this was fine, but it was not enough. And each succeeding day at Colombes, I craved from him an attention I did not get, and that Minette did.

It made my eyes burn, particularly, to see the time he spent with Minette at the harpsichord, listening to her play, singing over songs with her in his rich dark voice. So often that had been my place. Thus there was a double twist to my jealousy. I felt miserably excluded, and boredom made it worse. Snow had fallen and frozen hard; there could be no rambling and tree-climbing in the gardens. All I could do was chew the dry bone of my resentment. I was not alone in this. My grandmother had quickly learned that he was deaf to her lecturing, yet still she lingered about, trying to nick him with darts of advice when he was unaware. Defeated, she would give up at last, but I hung on. One day I tormented myself by staying, sitting at a distance, until my father and Minette had quite forgotten I was there at all. This, I thought with furious satisfaction, was mighty revealing: I might as well not exist. Then I heard Minette saying what a pity it was that he would have to go away again, and my father answering thus:

'It is the greatest of pities, my dear. But be assured, you will always be in my thoughts wherever I go. I have so many unpleasant things to think of, that I know the value of the pleasant ones.'

The very same phrases. The stinging of jealousy was salted with betrayal. In stillness I raged. I was beyond reflection – which might have showed me that if I was betrayed, then surely Minette was too. And till now my father had been all hero to me: I had never seen this side of him, a side I was to come to know well, and judge less harshly.

For a time I felt paralysed. Then I rose from my seat, breathing hard, and making a great show, as I thought, of being there.

My father was occupied with looking in the harpsichord for a string that sounded dead, and did not notice me.

I took up the poker from the hearth, and began making fencing strokes about the room.

'A dead spider, I think,' my father was saying. 'Squashed against the string.'

'Oh, poor thing!' Minette said.

I thrust and cut more frantically, my shoes clattering on the floor.

'Well, there are worse deaths,' my father said. 'He expired in melody . . .'

I did it deliberately, I think. Though the rage was on me, I was not oblivious. Besides, it took some care and accuracy to swipe that Gobelin vase from its pedestal, and send it smashing into the fireplace.

Minette squealed and jumped up. My grandmother, hearing the crash, came running, already lamenting. I stood panting, seeking my father's eyes.

'*Oh, mon Dieu!* Jemmy – what the devil do you think you are doing?' My grandmother's hand instinctively bunched, as if to box my ears – but not of course while my father was present.

'I think he knows very well what the devil he is doing,' my father said coolly. 'Ring for the maid, Mam. We'll see if it can be mended. You shall have another if not, as soon as I can afford it. What have you to say, Jemmy?'

All heaving defiance, I said: 'Nothing.'

'No? Very well.' My father came and began to pick up the pieces himself. I stared at his bent head.

'He needs a whipping!' my grandmother cried.

'Why, no, I don't think so. For afterwards, we would have to feel sorry for him,' my father said.

'You would not!' I burst out. 'Because you care nothing for me!'

Looking faintly weary, my father said, 'What means this nonsense?'

'Just what I say. You care nothing for me – you give me no attention. I wish you had left me where I was!'

My father's brow twitched, but his voice was still smooth. 'Ah. My faults. I am interested, Jemmy. Do carry on.'

'Well – you should be a father to me!'

'As mine was to me? I see. You might not like it, Jemmy.'

'Anything would be better than this,' I spat.

He thought that, I could tell, very foolish: too foolish to be worth a reply. But my blood was up, and with a stamp of my foot I began to storm at him again, that he cared nothing for me . . .

And my father turned and walked out of the room.

I was stricken with surprise. Life with my mother, and my grandmother too, had steeped me in confrontation: with bared breasts you thrashed things out to the point of exhaustion. It had never occurred to me that you could do what my father had just done.

And that he had done it before was plain from my grandmother's look, which was miserably triumphant as she bent her face to mine and hissed: 'Now you know what it is like.'

But I was not chastened. That my grandmother thought I should be was plain from her sending her favourite priest, Father Cyprien, to speak to me. He came up to the attic bedroom that was mine during my father's stay and whither I had retreated to brood on my wrongs. The climb had made him out of breath and he could only sit for a while plucking at his grizzled whisker and gazing at me sorrowfully. He was wondering what to say, perhaps. A gentle creature, he had raised Minette in the Catholic faith and found her a willing pupil. With me, though he dutifully obeyed my grandmother's orders to top me up with piety whenever I was at Colombes, he was often timid and uncertain. Also, while my father was there he had been kept out of the way.

'The devil,' he said at last, 'the devil tempts men to anger, intemperance, and violence, my son.'

'Then it's not my fault,' I snapped, slouching to the window.

'Ah. There speaks pride. The fault, my son, lies in succumbing to the temptation. That is a matter of your free will, choosing evil. It is a choice, and that calls for repentance.'

'I'm sorry I did it,' I grumbled, 'because it did me no good.'

'Ah, but is that the right reason for repentance? We must be sorry for the sin, not for its effects,' Father Cyprien smiled, gathering his monk's habit round his meagre legs. He was at home now, ready to go on splitting hairs indefinitely – and might have, if my father had not tapped at the door and walked in.

Though plainly surprised at finding the priest there, he was courteous, and passed some civilities before asking to be left alone with me. I listened to Father Cyprien's groaning footsteps descending the stairs again while I stared out of the little window into whiteness, unable to look at my father, hating him, glad he had come.

'You are calmer, I hope, Jemmy.'

'Yes, sir.'

'Because I won't speak to you when you're in a passion. I do not single you out in this. I won't talk to anyone so. It is a waste of words.'

'I'm sorry I broke the vase,' I said.

'It was not well done. *I* am sorry I promised Mam another, as Lord knows where I shall find the money . . .' He seemed to catch himself softening, and frowned at me. 'It is not the vase, Jemmy. It is what you said to me.'

'But I only mean . . .' I heard my own voice whine. His eye was hard, but I could not stop myself. 'I want to go about with you, Father. I don't want to be hidden away. I want people to – to take account of me.'

'So. Out for what you can get, eh, Jemmy? Like all the rest.' He laughed: a wintry merriment, in which I could not join. I saw, or grasped for the first time, that he had changed, and I feared it.

'I'm not,' I cried. 'I'm not like all the rest.' That made him laugh harder, and with hurt I cried, 'You're my father. If you never get to be King at all, I shall still love you the same, I swear it!'

He quietened then, as abruptly as if some other voice had spectrally spoken in that little room; and I think it had. In that passionate, pressing sincerity my mother lived again.

'Hey, well.' He sat down on the bed, beckoning me beside him. 'Rot me if I don't believe you, Jemmy . . . It may be put to the test, you know. There are good chances that I never will be. It's all such an infernal mess. If I seem mistrustful, I have good reason. We have been cast out so long that we fall out among ourselves, as you must have seen. People fall to plotting for what of aught else to do. There are those who look to my brother James, for example, and fancy him as a better bet for the throne. He has been a good soldier; men like to follow him. It has surely crossed their minds—'

'I would fight anyone who challenged you,' I cried – I was the most absolute of Cavaliers then. 'I would spit them on a sword—'

'Would you? Don't be too hasty with the sword, Jemmy. Sometimes you can make people more obliged to you by keeping them alive . . . And besides, you needn't fear on that score. I can scheme as well as any – nay, better than any. What else have I had to do all these years?' Brightening, he studied me. 'Young sprig. Little vessel, drinking it all in – or sponge, really. Mam wouldn't approve these sentiments. She sent the priest, I presume, to instil good ones.'

'Oh, yes. He always does,' I said, then stopped. I remembered the story of my uncle Henry, and I thought I was getting my grandmother into trouble. To change the subject, I said quickly, 'How is that lady who was at Brussels?' As my father looked blank I said, 'When I first came to you. We danced together.'

'Oh! Yes, of course. Yes, she does very well. Thriving.'

I saw again that hard merriment as he said it, excluding me. It made me crude and bold. Remembering Lord Crofts' hints, I said: 'Did she have a baby?'

'Two, as a matter of fact,' my father said crisply. 'A girl who died an infant. A boy who does very well. You may as well know something about me, Jemmy. When people stand in judgement on me, and tell me what to do, my response is to do just the opposite.' I chewed my lip: I did not know what to say. More gently, but still distinctly, he went on: 'When I was a very little boy, I took a fancy to a billet of wood that was lying about the stable, and carried it everywhere with me. I even insisted on taking it into bed with me at night, and when my governors tried to wrest it from me I clung on: I would not have it. Some said it showed I would grow up a blockhead – or would surround myself with block-heads. Needless to say, once they took no notice, I threw it away. What I was really announcing, even then, was that I shall never, ever consent to be told what is good for me.'

'So,' I said, 'when I am told not to take unripe fruit, I should just go and do it?'

A moment's pause, and then he gave himself up to laughter, in which I could join at last.

'Well, well. If you must, then don't be found out. That's the best advice I can give you, Jemmy. Don't be found out.' And he made a mime of taking a key, and locking up his own breast.

'Father Cyprien says God sees into out hearts all the time.'

'Does he now? And what else does he teach you?'

'About the Church,' I said reluctantly.

'Which is where?' he smiled.

'The Church at Rome. He says – he tells me it is the one true Church that I must belong to, else I will not be saved. He says I should copy the Princess Henriette-Anne. She tried to make her governess be a Catholic, but her governess would not, and went back to England, and there she caught a fever and died. And that was a judgement, he says.'

'I see.'

'But – but it doesn't matter, Father. I mean – I just want to please my grandmother.'

Despite his frown, he gave me an understanding look. 'For a quiet life, eh? Odsfish, you really are my son.'

That filled my heart to bursting. I embraced him. Surprised, he patted me.

'I won't be jealous any more, Father,' I said ardently.

'Oh, you will, you will. No matter.' And with that kind, certain utterance he left me.

It was not the end of it. As far as the jealousy went, he was right: I smouldered and sulked again when he played cards with Minette that evening, though I held back from any more dramatic demonstrations. I had learned a sort of lesson. What I did not expect was that he would take up the matter of Father Cyprien and my religion that very night after the cards, when my grandmother came in from her own devotions. She was humming to herself as she went about trimming the candles, though the way she brushed past me as if I was not there showed that my delinquency was not forgiven.

'I think, Mam, it's time to look afresh at Jemmy's education,' my father said, casually.

'I'm glad you agree. He has been spoiled, I think. He lacks discipline,' my grandmother said.

'There is that. But I was thinking also of his religious education.'

Stiff-backed, my grandmother went round the candles again. 'You do not approve my arrangements? The Port-Royal schools have the highest reputation, you know. And with all I have to think of, it was generous in me, in truth, to take such trouble with him as I have – to such little reward,' she added, arrowing a glance at me.

'Generous indeed, and I should take the burden from you,' my father said easily. 'The Port-Royal schools are excellent, but I gather very Romish in their teaching. Also there is good Father Cyprien, whose zeal is perhaps a little too—'

'What? You would traduce my own confessor, a man of true learning and piety? What has he been saying?' 'He' meant me, whom my grandmother speared with another look.

'Your confessor is a good man, I do not doubt. And a good confessor. Which is the very point, Mam. I do not think the boy should have a Catholic instruction.'

My grandmother sat down tragically. (I cannot give a clear idea of tragical sitting-down, but my grandmother could manage it.) 'I see,' she said. 'You mean to reproach me with Henry. And this is your way of doing it.'

'If I meant to reproach you with Henry, I would have done so straight away,' my father said, with the faintest prickle of irritation. 'But I wanted us to be friends again, and set that in the past.'

'Yet you bring it up,' my grandmother said, untruthfully, trembling, her hand groping out. She wanted Minette, who came obediently to her. 'I would gladly forget, if I could, those cruel words you addressed to me then – but they are not to be forgotten—'

'I'm sorry if the truth seemed cruel. But the truth it remains, Mam. When you tried to convert Henry you endangered us all. He is third in line for the throne: that makes him a public mark. For my part I would prefer liberty of conscience for everyone. But the world doesn't wag that way, not yet. These are not private matters.'

'And your sweet sister?' my grandmother said, clutching Minette's hand to her. 'I raised her in the faith. Will you have nothing to do with her, then?'

My father shrugged. 'She has been here with you from a babe, and has grown up a Frenchwoman. And apparently my father gave you permission to rear her as you saw fit . . .'

'You doubt me? You doubt your father's words to me?'

'No, no. Let that be, Mam. I do not speak of Minette: it isn't her that the Roundheads are watching. But as for my father, you know his injunction to me before they killed him. I must maintain the Church of England as he left it. England is Protestant, Mam, and without England I am nothing. Besides, did you ever take it on yourself to convert Father? He was ever respectful of your faith, but he would have given you short shrift if you'd tried to force it on him.'

'Your father was a great king,' she said. 'It is different. This boy . . .' She snapped her fingers impatiently. 'This boy is nothing' was what I read into the gesture. I did not hate my grandmother for it, but I felt something like the breaking of moorings. From now on I would drift from her and she dwindle.

'Master James Crofts,' my father said, giving me an encouraging smile.

'Aye, aye, him – exactly. *He* is not in line for the throne!' My grandmother laughed, freezingly.

'Well, no.' My father looked at me thoughtfully. 'But then who knows what may happen? He may yet have his part to play. Whatever it may be, he will play it more securely in the Protestant faith. Pray indulge me in this, Mam.'

My grandmother threw up her hands. She loathed being thwarted – but at bottom she was not that interested in me.

I, meanwhile, was elated simply because my father was taking notice of me again. And in those words 'who knows what may happen', I tasted delicious possibility.

The next thing that did happen was a letter from Cardinal Mazarin, telling my father that he must leave France at once.

There were flowery compliments and regrets: it was not personal but a matter of statecraft. France stood at a delicate moment in her relations with the other powers of Europe, a moment of balance which His Majesty's mere presence might upset, and so on; nothing else would prevent the ordinary courtesies . . . My father said that he would remember all the courtesies he had received, and the injuries too. His smile was at its bleakest, and most unapproachable. It stayed so at his hasty leave-taking – except when he tenderly embraced Minette, and begged her to write to him very soon; and again my blood pounded with jealousy.

Yet I recognized, I think, that it would always be so. I was learning, as my poor mother never had, that my father was quicksilver. To grasp it hard was to lose it. I must not repeat her mistake. The trouble was, her blood was strong in me. When my father shook my hand on the steps of Colombes, with sleet slanting down and the waiting horses snorting vapour, I know that I gazed at him with all my mother's greedy yearning.

'Father, don't forget about me.'

'That I shan't, my boy. I shall write to Lord Crofts about your schooling directly. In the meantime, apply yourself. Not the fencing – *that*, I think, is advanced enough. You promise well. Let me see the promise kept. And remember, you—'

Was he about to repeat that formula? Had he caught himself out? Something stopped him, at any rate, leaving him wry and speechless. Then my cheek was touched, and he was gone.

And I, wretched at his going, sought out Minette. Because he was gone, she was no longer the envied rival. I supposed we could be as we were before.

'I wish I could help him. I wish I were not so useless.' Minette's eyes had a distant look as she sat turning over the pages of some French songs he had brought her. 'You're lucky – you're a man. Well, not a man. A boy.'

I was not used to such dismissiveness from her. 'I shall be a man soon,' I said. 'And I will help him.'

She shook her head. 'France. France should be his friend. All he has gone through . . . Did you know, when he was escaping from Worcester in disguise, he could get no shoes to fit him, and had to slit the toes, and when he got away his feet were all a mass of blood and sores?'

'Yes, I know.' He had told me the tale of his escape when I was with him at Brussels. The exiles often talked of it; I knew it so well I almost felt I had hidden up the oak tree myself, breathlessly listening to Cromwell's troopers beating the bushes below. But it was all fresh to Minette.

'He has suffered so much. If the people at the French court could only conceive . . .'

'Perhaps,' I ventured, 'if you married King Louis, then you'd be able to make him help—'

'Oh, hush.' Minette made a swatting motion with the rolled-up pages. 'You don't know what you're talking about.'

'I do. Grandmother talks of it. Why not? I'm sure King Louis admires you.'

'Louis,' Minette said distinctly, 'gave his opinion on me some time ago. There was a ball: he declined to dance with me. He said it would be like dancing with the bones of the Holy Innocents.' She sat up straight, as if defiantly to display her thinness. 'I heard about it afterwards.'

'But you're more beautiful than all the French ladies,' I said. It cost me a flaming face, but I was determined on it.

Minette smiled softly, though not for me. 'That's what Charles said . . . Well, no matter. Louis will take the Spanish princess as a bride. That is the game of kingdoms. Power, Jemmy.'

'Well,' I said, reasonably as I thought, 'if the Spanish princess has power, it shows you don't have to be a man.'

And at last, it seemed, I had pleased her. She smiled with all her old brilliancy. 'Perhaps so,' she said. 'Perhaps so.'

ELEVEN

My new tutor, or, properly, governor, was a youngish Scot named Thomas Ross. He was a foxy-coloured man with a tight mouth like a drawstring but eager untiring lashless eyes that I fancied no more capable of closing than those of a bust in bronze: a powerful scholar, a traveller who had enjoyed the exile, a glutton for experience who was abashed in no company and would study people in the street as if they were anatomical specimens. His was the task of undoing the religious work of Port-Royal and of Father Cyprien, in daily lessons at Lord Crofts' house, and spiritedly he undertook it; for his zeal was such that he could argue the Protestant cause for a day and a night without repeating himself. Mr Ross's only disappointment, I think, was in not finding me more corrupted by Rome – for I have said how generally impervious I was to my grandmother's covert campaign. He did not have to work hard to make me a Protestant. Making me a scholar was a harder job. But he never showed anything but relish for the work, and satisfaction with the decidedly middling results. I had a tutor who thought very well of me, and of the position my father had given him. He called me Master Crofts, but lost no opportunity, in company, of speaking of 'the King's son', or 'His Majesty's son', and would pronounce that 'son' with such resonance, and such tokens of respect, that he might have been referring to the sun in the sky, and showing himself dazzled by it.

I hardly need add that I liked Mr Ross greatly. But then I had never before had a truly sympathetic person always by me. Always I had picked up favour by dribs and drabs and perhaps that made me crave it all the more, and bask in it when I got it. And in truth I remained an insignificant creature – quietly living at Lord Crofts', learning my lessons, visiting my grandmother – even as I entered my twelfth year. That was when events vastly significant for my future, and that of the world, began to unfold. That was the year 1660.

My tutor was an excitable man. And when he burst into our reading room one cold spring morning, after talking with Lord Crofts downstairs for an uncommon time, and yelled at me what I thought was the word 'Monk', I was unperturbed.

'It is true. True, by God. What have I always told you, Jemmy? It has come to pass – or is coming to pass.' Mr Ross reeled into the room as if drunk, which he never was; and, just as unbelievably, slammed shut the book on our desk, breathing fiercely over me. 'Monk,' he seemed to mutter again.

I wriggled. I thought he was talking of some new enormity of the Papists; he was very severe on monks and nuns.

'London has welcomed him. He has entered in triumph. I thought there might still be shooting, from the last fanatics, but no. A pity. His regiments would have made hot work for them. It would have been a fine sight to see, fine and bloody.' Although, or perhaps because, Mr Ross had not fought in the Civil War, he was very martial. He enlivened our Latin lessons with descriptions of ancient battles, full of gore, and he loved to watch a cockfight and give me afterwards a Homeric account of the little slaughter. 'But London is his, that is certain; and what is now equally as certain, he has declared himself.'

'Who?' I said. 'Not my father?' I spoke quite without hope, for the notion that my father and his followers had somehow descended suddenly on London and taken it was too much even for my romantic temper.

'Of course not. Don't I tell you, Jemmy? General Monck. He marched from Scotland, and now the Rump is dissolved, and he has declared himself for a free Parliament. No, not your father. Not *yet*.' He showed his little feline teeth. 'I say, Jemmy, not *yet*.'

'But . . . but the Parliament are the ones who drove my father away.'

'That was the men of the Rump, the fanatics who have held England in their grip. Now their power is falling away. Without Cromwell at the helm they began to drift, and that son of his could not wield authority. He has washed his hands of the whole business and retired to the country. Those that are left yap at each other and cannot agree. The people cry out for order. But who is to give it to them? Well, now Monck has spoken. A free Parliament is to decide. Do you see? A Parliament without proscriptions. Where your father's friends may speak. Lord Crofts tells me His Majesty has already been in correspondence with General Monck – most cordially on both sides.' Mr Ross took a great breath and flung out his arms. 'The time is coming, Jemmy! Was there ever a more miraculous surprise? Though indeed, that is what I prophesied all the time.' My tutor always had to be right.

But in truth he would have needed clairvoyancy indeed to have foreseen what happened so swiftly that memorable spring. The death of Cromwell had not caused the republican state to collapse in a heap; but it had been the removal of a pillar, without which the edifice sagged, slumped, and crumbled at last. Amongst his legacies had been a firm control over Scotland, where one of his ablest servants, General George Monck, governed with a sturdy well-drilled army of three foot and two horse regiments. That winter Monck watched and waited while confusion in London deepened. The Rump Parliament and the leaders of Cromwell's army pulled in different directions, and no one could unite all the factions. Men woke to the fact that no one was governing. They spoke their discontent. Some few began to speak the name of the King, as they had not dared to for years. Hearing them, the waverers, who had held their peace from fear or prudence or apathy, found their voices. The air had changed.

Monck scented it. He knew well that his was the only disciplined force left in the island. But he was a close, cautious man, and kept his own counsel. He had worked for Cromwell as a professional servant of order, and it was the breakdown of order that concerned him, for he had no ambition of his own, and no stake in any system: he had not been one of the visionary men who had executed Charles I. When he finally made his decision no one knows. I knew him much later, and he never spoke of it. But decide he did. His army's pay was much in arrears, and going to confront the no-government in London about it gave him his pretext. In January he set off. His army went with him.

In London, cheered and fêted, he took a good look at the mess. There was the remnant of Parliament, consisting of those who had not been purged under the republic, and powerless without Cromwell's generals.

And there were the generals themselves, who could not agree on anything except a rule by the sword that none could enforce. In the streets people cried for a free Parliament. Monck heard, as he surely also heard the calls for the return of a king – but he was too shrewd to take those up directly. Instead he declared that the first and only step the tottering country could make was to call elections for a full and free Parliament. He was acting for the settlement of the country, not for any individual – not for the restoration of Charles Stuart, the exiled King.

But that was the result, and he had known it would be, and had decided it must be. The dramatic experiments that had begun nearly twenty years ago with a war against a king had run themselves out. A full free Parliament would be a Royalist one.

They would have the King back.

The exiles on the Continent watched each strange and sudden development with desperate hope, with delirious anxiety. Mr Ross, thrustful and inquisitive, seemed to find out everything as soon as it happened, and told me all about it – which was just as well, for I was seldom summoned to my grandmother's house during those feverish weeks. The proscription on Father Cyprien and Catholic doctrine had put her in a sulk with me. Remembering the rift between her and my uncle Henry, I hoped it was temporary.

Mr Ross it was who told me of the dissolution of the Rump and the calling of the new Parliament; of effigies and portraits of my father being put up in the streets of London; of my father's finally leaving Brussels and moving to the Dutch town of Breda.

'I hear Monck himself wrote privily to him, and advised the shift. No advantage in hanging upon the Spanish now: he must show himself independent. Also he will be nearer the ports.' Mr Ross tapped his nose. 'We are living through a great miracle, Jemmy!'

Well, I was not living it so much as hearing of it at one remove, in between conning dreary Latin. But a miracle certainly; and I rejoiced for my father, and half-feared, as he must have, that this was a dream from which there would be a wretched waking.

From Breda my father issued a Declaration, for the attention of the new Parliament in England. He promised a free pardon for anyone who asked it. All those who had fought against his late father and himself, and driven him into exile, were to be forgiven. The only exception was to be those men who had signed the warrant for Charles I's execution: they must expect a different fate. As for the religious differences that had destroyed the kingdom's peace, my father pronounced in favour of toleration, if the Parliament agreed; and Parliament was to settle the question of property, which had changed hands so rapidly during the late convulsions. And Monck's army was to be paid its arrears.

It was a most just and reasonable declaration. And though Mr Ross said my father's closest adviser, Hyde, had had a hand in it, I could hear my father's voice in it very clearly – especially when he deplored 'the passion and uncharitableness of the times'. I caught an echo of his baffled rationality when my mother would storm at him. And only someone as young and hot-headed as I could fault it, and say there should be more revenge.

'Nay, Jemmy, your father shows himself highly prudent in this above all,' Mr Ross said. 'Like a good physician, he has taken the fever of the patient, and finds it abated. Now is the time for a cooling and gentle treatment. Observe too that he leaves it to Parliament to decide the most vexing questions, which flatters them, by showing he trusts them. And meanwhile saves him a deal of trouble, and perhaps blame if the new arrangements go wrong. Oh, it is admirable altogether.'

'Still, it is a pity,' I said, little fool that I was, 'that he is not going to England at the head of a conquering army. That would be glorious.'

'Well, perhaps. But a king who has to conquer his own kingdom – how easily will he sit the throne? Of course, he will have the opposite problem. He will sit his throne only because his subjects said he could. Either way, kingly power is not what it was. Faith, it is all most interesting. I wonder what will happen.'

'He will go to England, and be crowned, won't he?'

'Aye, aye, it looks mighty like. But in the future, I mean – in the unguessable years.' And my governor looked at me thoughtfully, as he often did, and somehow measuringly – as if I were a bolt of cloth and he was wondering how many coats I would make.

What happened next was swift, again. Fresh wonders seemed to tumble over one another that spring. My father's declaration was read out to Parliament on the first of May – that old feast day of maypoles and May queens, of love and pleasure. With not a dissenting voice, Parliament approved it, and there and then resolved to invite my father back to the shores he had fled from in peril of his life, near ten years since, and to acclaim him in very truth, at last, King Charles II of England, Scotland and Ireland.

In Paris the exiles expressed their joy, true to type, with great debauches. I heard of one out-at-elbows Cavalier, who had patiently borne every reverse of his party's fortune, getting so drunk at the occasion that he picked a quarrel with a friend, fought a duel on the spot, and died of it, on the very threshold of the day he had awaited so long. (No wonder my father relished irony: even in victory it was never far from his cause.) Lord Crofts indulged himself in great gambling bouts, losing unthinkably, especially to Lord Jermyn – whom my father had rewarded for his loyalty with the Earldom of St Albans, and who was even more insufferable on account of it. Lord Crofts laughed off his losses. 'Ah, we shall all be provided for now,' he said; and Lady Crofts smiled wanly.

My father moved to The Hague, where his sister Mary, Princess of Orange was permitted to receive him at last. The Dutch welcomed as a king the man who as an exile had been a nuisance and a liability. Crowds cheered and cannons sounded as my father entered the Dutch capital in a great procession of seventy coaches. Mary's little son, the young Prince William of Orange, was fetched from his school to ride with his newly important uncle through the clamorous streets. I wished, when I heard of it, that it could have been me. But, of course, young William was a prince and heir, whereas I was – whatever I was. I held fast to my mother's own declaration: I steered my soul by its remote star. But for now, all depended on what my father chose to do with me. And as Mr Ross reminded me, my father had a thousand things to think of just now. 'All in good time, Master Crofts,' he said: for at this time he stopped calling me Jemmy. And I noticed he always took off his hat when we were out together.

So I heard of, and longingly imagined, the scenes at The Hague, where the commissioners of the Parliament had come to wait upon my father, and formally invite him to cross the water to his waiting throne. Even more welcome than the toasts, the loyal addresses and petitions, the bonfires and balls, must have been the great trunk of gold coin that the commissioners delivered to him. I heard afterwards that he laid it open in his room, and called Mary and James to look at it glistening there, as if he could hardly believe it was real.

Yes, it was a happy family occasion too: both his royal brothers with him. James was almost as much admired as my father: a man of twenty-seven now, seasoned as a soldier and sailor – which had kept him out of the Queen Mother's possessive clutches – his handsomeness everywhere remarked upon; and everyone had good words for the lively youngster Henry, saved now from the fate of becoming a tennis tutor. A fine brace of princes: and a fine king.

That was the universal report. Of course, England had resolved to have him now, fine or foul: of course, men bend to the wind that blows, and sow flattery where they hope to reap reward. Yet people truly were impressed with my father. That easiness and affability – how striking it must have seemed, after the chilly grandeur of his father – that sense he gave you of being the one person in the world he wanted to talk to at that moment. The commissioners of Parliament were, in a word, charmed. And I think my father, of all people, must have been amused: amused at speeches of loyalty spouting from the mouths of men who had called him the long black man two yards high, Charles Stuart, the enemy of the Commonwealth. And behind his genial smile, he must have been drawing some conclusions about men's nature.

My grandmother, relenting, had me back to Colombes at the end of May, when my father at last sailed for England. Express riders brought her all the latest news. She awaited them in agitation. The departure from the harbour at Scheveningen had gone off brilliantly, with thousands of people going by torchlight to the beach to see my father board the *Royal Charles*, and set sail for Dover. But my grandmother, naturally enough, was still haunted by the old warring times, and was full of fears. Some last fanatic might scupper the ship, or shoot at him when he landed. Only when she heard that he had set foot on the shore at Dover, to a unanimous welcome, did she calm herself.

She was a little sad too, but not in her loud queen-of-tears manner. She fell quiet, and fingered the cameo of her dead husband as we watched the celebratory bonfires going up on the hills near Paris. Later, when we went to her convent at Chaillot to hear a *Te Deum* sung in thanks for my father's restoration, I saw her weep a little. I felt I understood. I held her hand, and was not shaken off; and afterwards I was a little irritated by Mr Ross, who insisted on knowing all that had happened at the convent, and making sure I had taken no Popish infection from being there.

I recognized the next messenger who came to Colombes. Indeed, recognizing that plumply handsome face had been a matter of great importance two years ago. For it was Mr Prodgers of the Bedchamber – the agent who had spirited me away from my mother in the little park at Brussels.

He had come from my father, with a letter and a gift for Minette. The gift was a side-saddle, fringed with velvet and gold lace. Even in that dizzying time, he had thought of her. He had written the letter in a snatched moment at Canterbury, on his triumphant progress to the capital, and in it he said he hardly knew whether he was writing sense or not, his head was so dazed with the quantities of business, the acclamations of the people, the thunder of drums and guns and clanging of bells.

Everyone smiled at it. There was no resisting the joy of the news, and even I found no space for jealousy. Nor need I have, for a little later Mr Prodgers took me aside, saying very civilly he was glad to see me again, and presented me with my own gift from my father. It was a waist sash of scarlet silk. I put it on at once. It made me feel part of things, somehow. And Mr Prodgers, though fagged from travel, was kind and gave me his own account of the miraculous happenings across the Channel.

'Bonfires everywhere – on every hill and rise – as if the whole island were ablaze. And everywhere the royal arms hanging up. The noise – I can give you no notion of the noise – my head is still ringing with it, and His Majesty says he is half deaf. It started at Dover. His Majesty came ashore in Admiral Montagu's barge. Straightway he dropped to his knees on the sand and thanked God. His head was long bowed – one man I know says he saw him weep – but he was all cheerfulness when he went up to the town. General Monck received him, bowing low, but His Majesty lifted him up and embraced him. He will lift him up further, I'll warrant. At Canterbury he bestowed the Garter on him – a signal honour, but that old warrior has well deserved it. Oh, and the people lining the roads – shouting, strewing flowers before his coach. Every window lighted in the town. Well, every whole window.' He chuckled. 'Men went about and smashed any windows that refused to show a candle.'

And he chuckled again. I'm sure I laughed too. Now, I think it a pity; a little ominous too, perhaps.

But back then there was no shadow anywhere. On 29 May – his thirtieth birthday – my father entered London. He was not tucked away in a coach but on horseback, and bare-headed. His doublet was of silver; no one could miss him. He and his brothers formed the head of a vast procession, with heralds and attendants, with trumpeters and drummers and soldiers, that wound through London like a great slow iridescent serpent. Crowds crammed the streets to the very rooftops and chimney-pots, joining their voices to the booming ordnance and the endless peal of bells. That cloth-of-silver was far from my father's habitual style, even when he was in funds, and I marvelled to think of him, that familiar rangy easy figure, amidst such pomp. But then, he always understood the value of appearance – which Cromwell and his party never did. Theirs had been a sombre, even gloomy rule, forbidding all show and festival and public merry-making. In this they made a mistake and also, I think, did an injustice. Those prohibitions fell harder on the common people. A wealthy man under Cromwell might amuse himself privately, upon his own property, with music and games and sports. The ordinary folk could not: the village green was their ballroom, the travelling fiddler their orchestra. So when my father entered his capital with glitter and ceremony, making a brilliant theatre of the streets, it was no wonder that the ordinary people felt a breath of freedom.

And they turned out in such numbers that it was evening before my father got to the Palace of Whitehall. There, in the Banqueting Hall, the Speaker of the House of Commons delivered a windy welcome. At the end my father could do little more than thank him. He was weary and hoarse, and he told me long after that he felt like a child kept up late on a holiday. Perhaps also he was brushed by his own father's ghost, for it was from that very room that Charles I had gone out to his execution, stepping through a side-window direct on to the scaffold. But later, according to custom, my father dined there in public, and appeared very merry.

No shadow. My grandmother grew brisk again, receiving the congratulations of the French court loftily, and declaring herself much occupied with business. So she was, for there now came to Colombes a stream of visitors seeking her aid. They were, of course, exiles of various shades: soldiers maimed or half-starved, aged and decrepit gentry who had poured their fortunes down the well of the royal cause, even one or two of the poets who used to adorn her court before the verses ran out. And they wanted, of course, help, vindication, reward. She wrote on their behalf to my father in London, who was similarly besieged by those with a claim on his gratitude. Surprisingly, even suspiciously many. He was heard to comment that he wondered why he had stayed away so long, since everyone he met said they had wished for his return all the time.

Meanwhile I looked at myself in my new sash a dozen times a day.

'When will he send for me?'

'His Majesty,' Mr Ross said, 'has so many things to do, young sir. You must abide by that. Also, you must complete your education. You progress, but you are unpolished as yet. Remember he is no longer a poor exile, but a monarch with a court about him: a peculiar world of high civility and ceremony. You must be prepared for it.' He spoke patiently. He took time and pains with me – indeed, devoted himself to me, to the extent of minutely enquiring about all my past. There were many questions about my mother, which I answered with as much loyalty as I could both to her and my father, but her last words to me I kept to myself. Mr Ross was a shrewd interrogator, though, and had his own thoughts, which must have been stimulated when I clashed with Lord Jermyn again. Talking to one of those petitioners – a shrivelled turkey-cock of a man, half-blind from the pox, caught no doubt in His Majesty's service – Lord Jermyn saw me pass by, and explained my presence with the words, 'the little royal bastard'.

It was said good-humouredly for him. I was not good-humoured. With the old petitioner stretching wide his milky eyes in surprise, I said: 'When I'm grown, I'll kill any man who calls me that.'

Mr Ross bustled me away, but he seemed more intrigued than disapproving. Throughout our lesson that day he kept bestowing on me that speculative, tailor's-eye look. Only at the end did he say, quietly, 'I admire your spirit, Master Crofts. It is fiery and gallant.' Blinking at me, he held the closed book to his nose and sniffed it as if it were a posy. 'Perhaps a little misplaced as yet.'

'What do you mean?'

'Well, we do not know His Majesty's mind. He has shown you high favour, but not – not publicly. So I would counsel spirit with discretion, that's all. Of course,' he went on as if changing the subject, 'there will be great pressure upon His Majesty to make a good marriage once he is settled. To secure the succession, you know. In exile he has been to some degree a free man, in a way a king cannot. A king must be ever politic. Sometimes he may have to pretend certain things, or deny certain things, for the sake of statecraft. Consider that, Master Crofts, I humbly suggest.' He was looking so hard at me, or through me, that his eyes were glazed.

I considered. But I did not much like the idea of this marriage – firstly because, I suppose, it would be another claim on his attention. (I had reconciled myself to his frequent letters to Minette: at least she read them, partly, to me.) I knew, however, that it was what kings did. Louis of France did it, that summer, very soon after my father's restoration. As expected, the French King took as his bride the Infanta of Spain. More rejoicing, more bonfires. And if here at last there was a little shadow, it was unacknowledged – until my grandmother, unable to help herself, put it into words.

'Hey, well, bear up, *mon enfant!*' she cried, pinching Minette's cheek. The Princess and I were at cards. My grandmother had been closeted with some ladies who had seen the wedding at a little church down near the border. She sighed hugely. 'You must bear up, and try not to think of it.'

'I think of it much, Maman,' Minette said, 'and with great pleasure.' It seemed to me that only self-control had prevented her from pulling away from that pinch. 'France has made an excellent peace with Spain, and all must rejoice at that.'

'Aye, aye, the peace, that is very well. But to think—'

'A dowry of half a million écus, or the inheritance of the Spanish Netherlands if payment fails,' Minette said, judiciously studying her cards and laying one down. 'Now that is a very fine bargain. The cardinal arranged it brilliantly. Jemmy, it's your turn. How dull you are today!'

'Oh, Mazarin, yes, the infallible,' my grandmother said sourly. 'But, my sweetling, you are being very brave. You must have thought – as I have – if only Charles's restoration had come a little earlier. Just a little sooner, and what a difference to your prospects! Sister to the King of England! Oh, not that your own charms alone could not captivate Louis

– I'm sure they *did* – but you know he is quite in the thrall of Mazarin, and Mazarin is all policy. Well, it's done now, and you are brave not to think of it . . .' So she went on, like someone pitying a wound whilst poking at it. Or so it seemed.

Minette's face gave away nothing, and her voice was quite cool as she interrupted her: 'You must not think, Maman, that I am of the kind who sighs over what has never been – or could never be. I don't indeed. I look forward. Like,' she added, her voice kindling, 'like my brother Charles.'

My grandmother frowned and shrugged. 'La, well, yes, you could do worse than follow Charles's example. No one could deny he has a forgiving spirit,' she said, looking anything but forgiving. True to his word, my father had not commenced his reign with a welter of recriminations, though there were some. The bodies of Cromwell and his prime associates were dug up and hung at Tyburn, which was more messy than cruel. Those regicides who did not escape were taken for trial, and then execution – some, the most defiant. After a time my father did not press the business. He said he was sick of hanging. My grandmother would have preferred to see lots of heads rolling, of course. She had learned nothing.

The French royal Court came back to Paris ahead of the bridal pair, who were to make a state entry into the capital. Festivities had already begun. It was a brilliant, hot, hectic summer. I am still reminded of it if I smell cut meadow-grass and feel strong sun – that time when life seemed all poised upon a bright threshold. Minette had new clothes, and went out a good deal, to receptions and concerts and banquets. But she seemed to have drawn closer to me again. Instead of the swing, we played at archery under the trees at Colombes, in afternoons quivering with heat. She had a good eye and a firm grip. She would make me laugh, telling me as I drew to imagine Lord Jermyn's face over the target. She would act out speeches from the comedies of Monsieur Molière that she had seen at the Petit Bourbon. And she would make daisy chains for me to wear, no simple ones but great trains and intricate coronets, and I would sit absurdly and happily festooned, as much in love with her as ever.

And yet, and yet . . . I have ever been good at self-deception, but through that summery haze I felt the cutting breeze of reality. My love was a boy's love, and Minette was a young woman – besides being my aunt – and the time for such a fancy was ending. Even when I blurted out one afternoon that she was the most beautiful of all ladies, I knew it. I did not need her gently reproachful look, or her murmur of 'Nonsense, Jemmy, nonsense,' to tell me that this agreeable dream must fade.

She must have seen my face fall: she was quick to add, 'Of course it is very pleasant to be told so. And you do it very nicely. Soon enough, when you meet a girl who merits the compliment, she will be mighty pleased to hear you say it.'

'You must hear it a lot,' said I – crushed but still gallant.

'Oh, I don't know about that,' she said thoughtfully. Indeed, there were those who did not like her delicate looks. I wondered whether she was thinking of Louis's remark about the bones of the Holy Innocents, as I was. His new bride, people said, was forever eating. With decision Minette added: 'But where there *is* admiration, I hope I know how to appreciate it.'

She gazed into the distance, as if looking for something. I said, moved by some intuition I did not understand: 'I feel you are going away from me.'

Her smile was kind. But she did not deny it. 'Mr Ross is calling for you,' she said.

In fact he was not, but he pounced on me all the same when I went back up to the house, for as usual he had news.

'The Queen Mother of France is here. Did you not hear the coach? You must be more alert, Master Crofts, and you would learn things as I do. Aye, she came here half an hour since – discreetly, in no great state – and has gone into private audience with your grandmother. I wonder what it can mean.'

'They are gossiping, I should think.' A little lapdog of my grandmother's, shut out from the matronly conclave, snuffled at my boots. I picked it up and was promptly bitten.

'Ah, he is loyal to his mistress!' My grandmother had come out of her private room, and stood linking arms with Anne of Austria, laughing at me as I cursed and sucked. 'His teeth are sharp, Jemmy, are they not? Mr Ross, will you have the goodness to send the Princess to me?'

My governor went off like a hare. The Queen Mother of France, vigorously fanning her ham-coloured cheeks, was all good humour.

'Bloodwort will staunch it,' she puffed. 'And a dose of dog-fennel if it turns foul.'

'Dog-fennel for a dog bite,' my grandmother said, and both ladies shook with laughter – silly, I thought. 'Nay, he's of a strong constitution, this boy, are you not, my pretty fellow?' To my astonishment, she kissed me. Good humour all round: I was unnerved.

'The resemblance is really most remarkable,' Anne of Austria said, looking me benignly over. 'And I fancy he will have quite as fine a figure. Do you know how to dance, young sir?'

'Oh, you never saw a prettier dancer, in truth – that's in the blood, of course,' my grandmother said.

The Queen Mother of France invited me, by an encouraging smile, to speak for myself.

'I love dancing, if it please Your Highness,' said I. 'As long as it is lively – the galliard and the coranto.'

'Ah, youth! I was the same. Now all I am fit for is a pavane, if it be steady,' she said pleasantly. 'Well, my friend, I hope I shall see you dance at my ball. You know, my son returns with his bride tomorrow. There will be great festivities, and you shall be there, and have all the galliards you like.'

I was excited and flattered, and bowed low in thanks. When I rose up, neither lady was looking at me: they were beaming at Minette, who had noiselessly appeared. She looked composed but utterly pale.

'Well, well, *mon enfant*, here is news!' my grandmother cried, embracing her. 'Can you guess it? I feel sure you can. From what I hear, he has not been able to disguise it.'

'Oh, he is most thoroughly captured, believe me. I never saw a man so!' Anne of Austria exclaimed, fanning. More of that odd giggling. Minette, though, was very sober.

'Of course, of course he is, and he has not been the first, that I can vouch for, but never mind.' My grandmother was gabbling, pushing Minette bodily towards the other Queen Mother. Seeing her between them I had an image, unfair perhaps but vivid, of a coursed hare being pulled between two hounds. '*Mon enfant*, you behold your dear good aunt of France. You behold also – if God is willing – your mother-in-law.'

'I hope I shall still be dear and good!' chuckled Anne of Austria. 'My dear, I have been speaking with your mother of a proposal. A very *ardent* proposal, I may say. Whatever did you do to him? Well, whatever it is I am thankful for it. He is the best-natured creature in the world, of course, as you know, but he is perhaps not easy to suit. And you suit, my dear, so admirably well in every respect. I could hardly wait to come here and lay the proposal before you. I fear the poor horses are quite lathered—'

'Well, you must know it now, *mon enfant*. What do you say?' put in my grandmother impatiently. 'Is this not the most wonderful news? You may as well know that I have given my entire approval, because it is so very nearly everything I could wish for you. But we must hear what you have to say, of course. I hope I am not such a tyrant as to marry my children *quite* against their inclination.'

Marry . . . ? I, disregarded, gazed at Minette's marble face and tried to work out what it meant. It could not be Louis: he had definitely married the Spanish Princess, and they were on their way to Paris now; Anne of Austria's words confirmed it. Who else . . . ?

'My son Philippe asks the honour of your hand, my dear,' Anne of Austria said, taking the hand very warmly, 'and I hardly know how he shall bear it if you say no! Now this, of course, is a private proposal. Nothing is settled, no formalities of dowry or jointure. And there is the King your brother's consent to consider, naturally. All this will be attended to in due time. I am charged only with laying the proposal before you. But I may as well say that if you signify your willingness, it will make me very happy – and as for Philippe . . . !'

I was so shocked I actually reeled away, nearly tripping over the lapdog. It yelped bitterly – a fair representation of my own feelings.

Philippe! The little Monsieur – that absurd, painted, squeaking creature! Minette could not, would not marry him. I refused to believe it . . . But then I refused too to think of the Minette I had seen lately – grown, self-possessed, inscrutable. A young woman who was – I had said it myself – going away from me.

And so, though a black storm of emotions assailed me as Minette embraced the Queen Mother of France, there was no real surprise. Nor when she calmly gave her answer: 'I am honoured, ma'am. I am very willing to accept.'

I got away, leaving behind the congratulations and cooing. Mr Ross was unashamedly eavesdropping in the anteroom, and observed my stampings and snortings with his usual interest.

'You are moved, Master Crofts.'

'Mr Ross,' I said, trying to compose myself, 'have you *seen* Philippe?'

'Certainly. The Monsieur of France is a great personage. His title is Duc d'Orléans now, you know. Best remember it: I understand he is a great stickler for formality.'

I stared at him. 'You know – you surely heard—'

'Marriage to the Princess Henriette-Anne, yes indeed. A very suitable match, I think. Louis would not approve anything *too* grand. He doesn't want his brother growing overmighty. But then it must carry some honour too. The young sister of the King of England could hardly be bettered for the purpose, I think. She is loved by the French, and a Catholic. As for her, she does well by it too. I fancy her mother's hopes of hooking King Louis were always a little unrealistic. But this is a very good second-best.'

'How can you? How does she *do well* by this?'

'Come, Master Crofts, don't be obtuse. She will be Madame of France. In precedence ranking only after Louis and his queen – think of that! This is not like marrying some petty German princeling with nothing but a decaying castle and a pack of mangy wolfhounds. She will sit by the most powerful throne in Europe. Well, well, I wonder when it will be! You must congratulate her in due form, Master Crofts—'

'I cannot. I think it is horrible.' I remembered Philippe's small hard fingers grasping my chin.

'Oh, I see. Well, Philippe has not the noble presence of his brother, true enough. No fool, though, and has taste and culture. Certain eccentricities too . . . But I thought you had begun to learn better, my friend, and to understand the business of princes. Consider your father: he understands it very well.'

'My father,' I said, with a clench of hope. 'He has to give his consent, doesn't he? Well, that he will never do.'

'You think not? We shall see. I can only say I would be most surprised if His Majesty does not see the advantages of the match. He will want a friend at the French court. That she will be – and a permanent envoy – perhaps more besides. God's life, these are exceeding interesting times. I would not have missed them for the world!'

But I could not find the interest, or indifference, that he meant, and when I moped out to the garden, and found the daisy chains Minette had made earlier, my romantic fancy pictured them as fetters, with which she was to be bound and dragged to the altar.

And yet she had said yes to the proposal, without hesitation. I remembered her words about being appreciated, and how she valued it. I was uneasy, preferring to think of Minette as forced into the alliance against her will. But one thing I clung on to: the matter of my father's consent. I had seen how he was with Minette – almost adoringly affectionate. I had, God knows, taken plenty of notice of it. And he was no stranger to the French Court; he would know what manner of man this was who proposed to wed his sister. Yes, he was always at pains to show himself no sentimentalist – but this, surely, was different.

Yet my father's response would take time – even though my grandmother set about writing to him the minute Anne of Austria's coach had disappeared down the drive. And meanwhile, I could not rest without speaking to Minette. I found her in her chamber, gravely regarding herself in her looking-glass. Propitious, I thought: if she married Monsieur he would be forever hogging it.

'What do you want, Jemmy?'

That – the distant, unapproachable tone – was less propitious. But I plunged in.

'Minette,' I said, 'are you in love with Monsieur?' It was not quite the question I wanted to ask, which was 'How can you bear him?', but it would do.

Minette's eyes met mine in the looking-glass. I noticed then, for the first time perhaps, how different someone we know well looks in a reflection – somehow lopsided: yet beside them we look just ourselves. One must be wrong.

'Well,' she said, and to my surprise seemed to consider my passionate question carefully. 'He declares himself greatly in love with me, and is most flattering in his attentions. Our families are nearly related, we are much of an age, and both fond of music and the arts, and I have found much diversion in our talk. So I think he will suit me very well.'

'That's not the same.'

'Jemmy, I have never given you advice. That's not my place. But I will say this, because I am fond of you. You must grow up soon. I mean,' she said as I made a stormy motion of going away, 'you expect too much of people. And that is a sure way to get hurt.'

I stood glowering and irresolute, wanting to say more, but conscious already that I did not belong here. The sight of her hairbrushes and toilet bottles, patch boxes and pomatum pots, so intimate and alien, proclaimed my boyish intrusion.

'You are happy at what has happened to your father, are you not?'

'Yes, of course.'

'Well. Think of this as the same for me. Like Charles, I . . . I am coming into my own.'

So I left her, gazing into her reflection as if challenging it, as children will play at outstaring one another. Mr Ross, seeing me still disquiet, fetched out the Latin book and tried to nail my mind down to pluperfect tenses, but I was having none of it. Perhaps I felt I was learning lessons enough: that, for example, love was nonsense.

The very next day I watched the entry of Louis and his new queen into Paris. I was with my grandmother and Minette at a house in the Marais, with a balcony that gave a fine view of the procession. The house belonged to Anne of Austria's former waiting-woman, a garrulous lady said to have sexually initiated the young Louis when he was getting out of his bath one day. The Queen Mother herself was there too, and Cardinal Mazarin, and a big blonde high-coloured hard-breathing lady, gorgeously dressed, whom I soon realized was that Grande Mademoiselle of whom I had heard. I was glad my grandmother's scheme to marry her to my father had never succeeded. She was very grand and plainly rich, but seemed ill-tempered. She made a great fuss, when we arrived, at Minette's walking in front of her – the French Court was always fretted with these matters of precedence – and in the end I heard Anne of Austria, who could be very firm, snap at her that she was acting like a fool. The Grande Mademoiselle was disappointed, of course. She had fancied marrying Louis herself, or failing that, some other great catch, but she had been too choosy, and now, as I heard my grandmother remark, looked every day of her thirty-three years and more.

And of course, there had been a great change. My father, whom as a penniless exile she had thought beneath her, was now King of England. His relatives, whom she had never troubled to visit in their lowly apartments, had a new consequence. Minette especially, now. Nothing had been formally announced, but I'm sure the Grande Mademoiselle knew, and it made her puff and glare at Minette all the more. As for Minette, was that triumph in the erect, poised, and conscious way she greeted the court ladies, and took her place at the front of the balcony? If so she could be forgiven it. She had long been viewed with affection – but also pity; and she must have been glad to dispense with that.

I still felt it, mind, along with bafflement, for I could not get the grotesque image of Philippe out my head. The man himself came to join us, briefly, on the balcony. I was almost disappointed, finding him not quite so freakish as my superheated memory painted him. Grudgingly I even sought to find some good points: a spark of wit in the little black eyes, a genuine grace in the way he presented his compliments to the ladies. But handsome, never. If he wanted to be thought so, he should not have gone about with the young man accompanying him, who looked like a youthful Apollo, nor swathed his little body in so many ribbons and pearl-encrusted fleurs-de-lis.

I watched, lurkingly, as he bowed over Minette's hand.

'Princess, I know not what to say. And that, everyone will tell you, is practically a miracle!' There was a laugh. I saw Philippe's companion smile in a bored way. 'But we live in a time of miracle, do we not? Here is your brother of England most wonderfully restored – I declare it is like the most delicious fable – and here is my brother married, and actually, you know, quite taken with his little wife! The most entrancing creature. You must mind you don't stare, dear madam, as I did when you see her dress, for it is fearfully quaint in that most *Spanish* way. I thought myself whisked back fifty years at least! And then she has these parrots and little dogs like rats and capering dwarfs about her and altogether she is *quite* a fantasy. But the greatest miracle of all – well.' He licked his lips. 'It is not yet time, dear madam, to speak of it. I am the very last person to affront decorum. I shall only present you, again, with my *tenderest* compliments, and my assurance that I *thirst* for the day when it is not my brother, but myself, who is to be congratulated. Until then, I am only half alive!'

'Monsieur, you are all goodness,' Minette said, and then with a smile: 'The half of you that is alive, that is.'

Philippe, after a blank, tightly blinking moment, burst into a peal of laughter. 'What did I tell you?' he cried, tugging at his companion's sleeve. 'Is she not . . . ? Was there ever anything so enchanting? Ah, I wish I could stay. Alas, I must greet my brother.' He did some more exquisite bowing as he left, and I shrunk back as his eye lit on me for an instant, but he did not seem to remember me.

For the ladies there were chairs – the usual grand-looking, spine-torturing affairs covered in red velvet (my underlying memory of Louis's France is of everything being uncomfortable, and nobody admitting it), one of which was also reserved for Cardinal Mazarin. He needed it, being shockingly aged, yellow and sunken, his expressive hands all terrible veins, like anatomical diagrams of themselves. I had heard my grandmother murmur with satisfaction that he was not long for this world. But he must have been well pleased with his legacy: a country at peace, an advantageous marriage for a strong and undisputed king. He sat quietly as the trumpeting procession went by, while I leaned on the parapet and thrilled to the sight of the musketeers and pikemen in their neat ranks, the cuirassiers and dragoons with their breastplates flashing back the sun. I could only thrill so long, though: the procession seemed endless. I shuffled my aching feet and must have yawned, for I heard Mazarin say, 'You are weary, young sir.'

I hastened to deny it, for I had absorbed some notions of the cardinal as a capricious despot who threw people in dungeons when they displeased him. But he smiled and waved my protests away with one delicate terrible hand. 'It is long to be standing, even for one so young.' He spoke to me in English. There was a silver pomander in his lap which he lifted and sniffed, hooded eyes flicking. 'And a hot day. Still, the soldiers are fine, are they not?'

'Very fine, sir. I would dearly love to be one of them.'

'I was a soldier once. Captain of infantry. On a day such as this, yes, I would like to be so again. But when the guns are shooting at you, and not in the air,' he added, silky, humorous, 'then it is a little different. So. If those soldiers were yours to command, young sir, what would you do with them?'

'Go to war,' I said.

'Ah!' the cardinal sighed. 'I suppose there is very little else to be done with them . . . His Majesty, you know, when he was much younger than you are, would amuse himself always with toy soldiers of silver. He would marshal them and dispose of them most thoughtfully. Ah, yes. He will be a great king and a great warrior. France will glory in him. All

Europe will admire. You will remember this day, young sir, I think, and tell your children of it.'

Child of exile though I was, I was English enough to be a little tired of Louis's praises. 'Yes, sir. And my father will be a great king too.'

'Your father . . . ?' Mazarin said, sniffing. 'Ah . . . Yes, of course, forgive me.' No Jermyn-like smirking about little bastards: that was not Mazarin's way. 'Indeed, indeed, we rejoice at his restoration. He has travelled a hard road. Let us pray that it will be soft for him now – not the word, I think. Smooth.'

Yes, I thought, a hard road. Whilst Louis had been fawned on and cosseted and, as my father had said, even had a man to hold the pot while he pissed. I felt that the cardinal, though so pleasant, somehow put my father in a different class from the all-conquering Louis, and I said proudly, 'It is sure to be smooth. Because my father is much loved by the people. They wanted him back.'

Stifling his own yawn, Mazarin said: 'Oh, the people? Yes, to be sure. In every country, they love to shout, and drink free wine. We must not forget them.' And he made a sweeping gesture at the crowds below.

A tolerant gesture, one might say – no more. I still think pretty well of Mazarin, who at the time was much hated by the French, or rather the French who counted, because he was clever and foreign and powerful. He did garner great wealth, but he spent it on books and theatres, which he afterwards left to the nation. He had the training of the young Louis, but there is no doubt he trained him well. Yet the way he spoke of the people is dismally significant. It was a tone I heard often in France, and which I hoped even then never to hear from my father's lips. And if I love and venerate my father still now – as I do in spite of all that has happened – it is partly because I never did hear it.

At last came Louis and his new queen, riding through a hail of flowers. Marie-Thérèse, in a gilded carriage, very fair except for her rust-coloured teeth, looked pleased to be where she was. She did not look as if she would ever fly high in a swing, unless it was stoutly made. As she was – and here was the point, of course. Her sturdy hips promised reliable heirs. For the rest, the King was all, and none ever looked so kingly as the young Louis, deftly reining in his great high-strung mount and approaching the balcony to doff his plumed hat, first to his fondly waving mother, then to Mazarin. The cardinal inclined his foxy head. Some would disapprove of such favour, but it was one of Mazarin's legacies that the King of France could do without approval. He had only, like a deity, to be.

Of course, Louis was no god – but then he was no Philippe either. Rare as it was for me to agree with my grandmother on anything nowadays, I found myself sorely regretting that it was not Minette riding there. Anything, indeed, rather than the fate of marriage to Monsieur. But then my father would not allow it – would he?

I was taken, as promised, to the ball given by Anne of Austria at the Palais Royal, where I saw how attentive Philippe was to Minette. I saw too the strange manner of the new Queen's dress, which was of the old farthingale sort that stuck out straight at the sides as if she were sitting on a bench underneath her own skirts; and I marvelled at her bouquet, a gift from her groom, all entwined with emeralds and diamonds. There, I fear, my precise observation ends. Self took over, and I revelled in a luxury and gaiety unknown to me. Anne of Austria, kindly remembering me, called me to dance with one of her young ladies-in-waiting. She was dainty and I tall, and I felt no boy. I was well-versed in dancing, and indeed footing it came as naturally to me as riding or vaulting. The French music was the best – my father thought so too and had lately brought some of their musicians to England – and the lilt of the violins and hautboys seemed to transform and mingle my senses, so that those leaping phrases had the same taste as the Gascony wine on my tongue and the same colour as the Venetian glasses it came in. The music dazzled my eyes as did the jasper and gilt, the lacquer and lapis lazuli I saw when I roamed a corridor in search of a privy, and it shot my spirits upwards along with the fireworks that scintillated at the windows when the evening grew dark. I did not mind the heat and press of people, turning the air into a broth of pomade and chalk and sweat languidly stirred by the agitation of painted fans. It was like my own inner fever.

And besides, this was a world I joyed to enter. I belonged to it, even if that was not the same as it belonging to me. The shoeless brat dragged from lodging to lodging was gone now. And nothing but destiny, surely, could have made such a wonderful changeling of him. Destiny played the tune: I had only to follow the steps.

TWELVE

'The stubbornest horse,' Mr Ross said, 'bears the bit and bridle at last.'

This was his cautious approval of my reaction, when I learned that my grandmother and Minette were to visit England without me. I moderated my jealous rage, broke only one riding crop and no vases, and managed to restrict my sulking to a day and a half at most.

(I fear by the way that my reader may image me forth as the most dreadful brat. Well, perhaps. In extenuation I urge only my peculiar circumstances, in which I was at one moment spoiled and the next shut out. And I would suggest that you glance into the glass of memory, and see yourself as a child, and frankly consider how tolerable you were.)

It was to be Minette's first visit to England since she had been smuggled out in disguise as an infant, and she was a little apprehensive. No need, as Mr Ross assured me. England, he said, was Royalist to the very teeth – an oddly forbidding expression. They would love the charming Princess. My grandmother's reception would perhaps be cooler. I heard a friend of Lord Crofts say, to a general snigger, that there would be more flags and bonfires for the Queen Mother than for anyone – 'when she goes away again, that is.'

It has been said that ill luck is a ship belonging to the Stuart family: always it comes back to them. So it was that autumn, as my grandmother prepared to cross to England. She had found time, in amongst everything, to talk bitterly of Henry, the son who had defied her. He had written her some time ago, promising her a visit in Paris, but he had not come. He had preferred to stay in London, enjoying his share of adulation.

'Still trying to punish me for the past,' my grandmother muttered. 'I am disappointed: it shows he still has a contrary spirit. Hey, well, no doubt he is such a *grand seigneur* now, he has no time for a little nobody like me.' Then she would set her jaw and talk of the hard words she would have to say to him when she saw him in London. For his own good, as ever. Thus did she meditate on the reconciliation with a son she had driven from her in tears.

And then came the news from London. Henry, Duke of Gloucester, the uncle I had never seen, had caught smallpox and died of it in his twenty-first year. The doctors were blamed: they always are.

Ill luck indeed. My father scarce settled on his throne, the celebratory bonfires barely cold, and now royal mourning. Minette, I know, wept much. Her raw eyes told their tale, but she did all privately now, did not reveal her grief to me. As for my grandmother, she was, I suppose, very much herself. Of course she was no stranger to loss. There was not only her martyred husband but a daughter named Elizabeth, of whom one hardly heard, who had died young of consumption whilst in the custody of the Commonwealth. So, here was another such trial. Father Cyprien was much with her, droning of how there was no joy untainted by woe, or it might have been woe untainted by joy. She was, I think, truly affected. But whether she entertained any regrets on the way she treated her children is, I fear, a different matter. Her tears did not interrupt her packing, or her plans – which were all to do with arranging her remaining children's futures for them.

'I think Charles is not truly wedded to his kingdom until he is wedded to a wife,' she told Lord Jermyn, who nodded sagely, as he would have if she had told him herrings grew on fig trees. 'I hope he is looking about him, but even if he is, I can do the job better. And then there is my other son—' she sighed – 'and him I must not marry but *unmarry*.'

She meant my uncle James. For the first time there was a bad report of the man who had seemed everything a king's younger brother should be – loyal, upright, untroublesome, useful, and now, as Lord High Admiral, a sterling commander of the restored and royal fleet. (Hasty brushes had painted over the Parliamentary names of ships like *Naseby* and *Lord Protector*.) Now there was a change. James – the Duke of York, to give him his full title – had become involved with a most unsuitable woman. Rumour had it that he had even secretly married her.

The woman had been a lady-in-waiting to Princess Mary of Orange – that in itself not so bad – who was also visiting London. But her name was Anne Hyde, and that, God knew, could be held against her. She was the daughter of Edward Hyde, my father's constant counsellor in exile and now his Chancellor. My grandmother was incensed.

'Obviously the creature has entrapped him. He was always too trusting. And if she has done it to him, she will do it to another. Wiles, my Lord Jermyn, wiles' – she made a sort of verbal snake out of the word – 'and wiles taught her, you may depend upon it, by that father of hers. He is a *master* of them.'

I had never met Edward Hyde, but my father always spoke of him with respect; and general report had him as a steadfast and honest counsellor who had done much of the dull work of maintaining my father's affairs in exile, and had reaped a fitting reward of office now he was King. But to my grandmother Hyde was always an enemy, a corrupting influence on my father – meaning, I fear, that Hyde opposed his good advice to her bad. Her eager mind traced a conspiracy. This ambitious commoner sought to ally himself with the royal family, and strengthen his power, by means of his daughter. She must, of course, be a siren who had seduced the noble James with Delilah-like powers.

Lord Jermyn, demurring as far as he ever dared, said he had heard Miss Hyde was quite a plain lady.

'Oho, that sort are the worst,' my grandmother said, 'but no matter: she will have me to deal with.' And she rubbed her skinny hands together, relishing it.

Those were her plans for her sons. For Minette, she had another – but pleasanter, more a matter of formality. In London she would set about arranging a dowry for Minette's marriage to Philippe.

My father had learned of the proposal. He approved it.

'And why should he not?' my grandmother cried when I pressed her about it. 'It is an excellent match. How curious you are lately, Jemmy! I quite lose patience!'

I could only console myself with the thought that my father had agreed conditionally – that he meant to talk to Minette about it, properly and privately, when she came to London. With that in mind I sought her out alone, the day before they were due to leave, and with a little shuffling and stammering asked her if she would present to my father my love and humble duty.

'Of course, Jemmy. I'm sure he will be most happy to receive them.'

'Thank you. I know – I know you will have other things to speak of, naturally. More important things. I hope— That is, you know you can be quite frank with my father, don't you?'

'Oh, yes. He is my dearest and truest friend.' She stopped. 'But what *can* you mean, Jemmy?'

She faced me – and outfaced me. There were rose-cakes burning in a censer in her chamber, a cloying scent that always turned me giddy; and so did she just then, throwing at me this challenge that I could not take up, boy as I was, evident and self-possessed woman as she was.

The noise of horses spared my blushes. Minette hurriedly left me at the sound. It was Philippe himself come calling. His brother was hunting in the forest of Fontainebleau, but Philippe had cried off. He never hunted; it ruined, he said, the complexion. He never wore a hat either, because it disordered the hair.

I found him with Minette and my grandmother: very correct, he would not be seated but strutted about like a little bantam.

'No, madam, I thank you, but I have already trodden too hard upon the toes of etiquette by descending on you thus, in your sweet retreat. I confess, though, to a *thrill* upon seeing it – *ma tante*, you have the most enchanting taste that I feel myself quite in a *bower*. That cabinet is delicious, wherever did you get it? I see no such marquetry nowadays. And here is the pretty boy.' Philippe had the back of his head to me when he said this: I froze. 'But he does not like me to call him such, I think.' Looking at me, he laughed pleasantly.

My grandmother began, 'Master James—'

'Crofts, I remember. Well, Master James Crofts, you are a mighty fortunate young pup to be in this bower, are you not?' With a click of his high red heels, as if to say he had done with me, he turned to Minette. 'Madam, it is as I said: I come to feast my eyes upon my prize while I may. But I come with – yes, I confess it for before those bewitching eyes I am *naked* as a babe – another motive. I come to persuade you, madam, not to go at all!'

'But, sir,' Minette said laughing, 'it is all arranged. And His Majesty my brother—'

'Ah, His Majesty your brother – he has my profoundest respect but he lives on the other side of that *infernal* sea. And the crossing is, I hear, a most wretched undertaking even in the best weather, not that I have ever been or, my dear madam, intend to. I cannot conceive what there can be *outside* France that is even half worth seeing.'

'I have made the crossing several times, nephew,' my grandmother said, 'every time in bad weather – and believe me, it is nothing to fear.'

Philippe snapped her a deep bow. 'Before such an august queen as you, *ma tante*, the impudent waves should lower their heads, and Neptune himself smooth a path of homage. But you see my fear – and then there is the *place* you are going to. To think of my sweet princess going among those barbarous English – and none knows better than you, *ma tante*, what beasts they can be—'

'You forget, sir, that I am an Englishwoman myself,' Minette said firmly.

'But not very much,' Philippe chuckled absently, catching sight of himself in a polished silver dish, and inclining to get a better look.

'Very much,' Minette said. 'In my heart, entirely.'

Philippe pursed, or pursed more than usual, his lips, and gave his nose as violent a tweak as if it were someone else's. 'Well, I am of course a very foolish creature and do not *think* of these things. You do quite rightly, madam, to *remind* me of them. But I hope you will understand at least the *reason* behind my poor persuasions. I do not want you to go: my life will be insupportable until you return.'

'Sir, you are too good,' Minette said, shaking her head, smiling. 'All I can say—'

'Is that you will not go!' Philippe shrilled; and as she still shook her head, he threw up his hands. 'Very well, very well! I am defeated. I must retire from the field. But I declare that it is – oh, simply *not fair*.'

And he stamped his foot, tossed his head, and whirled about in a sort of parody of a temper, which made my grandmother and Minette laugh much. But I, watching, thought the performance so accurate that he must know very well how to do it in earnest.

'So eager a suitor!' my grandmother commented after he had gone. 'You are fortunate indeed, *mon enfant!*'

They left for Calais the next day. Colombes was shut up. Even Father Cyprien was going. I felt very alone. But I was fortunate at least in that indefatigable news-gatherer Mr Ross, who passed on to me every report that came back to Paris. There was the expected: my grandmother's welcome to England had been lukewarm at best, but everyone there was charmed by Minette. And the unexpected: my grandmother had not got her own way with her erring son, James, Duke of York.

Here was a scandalous tale. Lord Crofts and his gambling cronies, in their salacious way, were mighty merry over it. I only learned the worst parts of it later, but it was an unedifying story in any form.

James had not only fallen in love with the Chancellor's daughter, Anne Hyde, but had entered into a contract to marry her – a contract which that intelligent lady had made sure was binding. This was a year ago, before my father's restoration, in the dark days when James's only prospects had seemed the career of a professional soldier, and no grander match a possibility. The transformation of the royal cause had, it appeared, changed James's mind though not his appetites. Anne Hyde was pregnant by him, as soon became clear at the court in London: there was no wriggling out of it now. In September James was married to her, privately and even secretly, by his own chaplain. And only then, most incredibly, did he try to wriggle out of it.

The contract, he said, was unlawful. He sought to have the marriage annulled. Damnably, he tried to discredit his own bride. His court cronies helped, stepping forward in numbers to say that Anne Hyde was a whore, that they had all had her, and that the baby could be anyone's. That this was untrue was, to Lord Crofts' drinking friends, the funniest thing of all – the woman was the heaviest lump of suet pudding there ever was, they said – and must have been, to the lady, the most hurtful. Yet she was resolved to have him still, this husband who could deal so ill with her. Either powerful love or powerful ambition must have sustained her. Even her own father seemed chary of pressing her claim – as well he might. His daughter had hooked the King's brother, and he had enemies enough to accuse him of designing it. The only person to come out of the business well was my father. It was he who ordered his brother to stand by his word, who ensured that Anne Hyde should be received as befitted the Duchess of York, and who gave the tattling court a lead by visiting her during her confinement. (The baby was a boy – but the Stuart ill luck touched his cradle with the finger of smallpox, and he did not live long.)

My grandmother, meanwhile, threw her own pepper into the stew. Nothing would reconcile her to what she called James's 'base marriage', such was her loathing of Hyde and all his works, and she refused even to meet her new daughter-in-law. So things might have gone on, despite all my poor father's persuasions, but from France Cardinal Mazarin, dying but shrewd as ever, stretched out his hand. As my grandmother intended to continue residing in France, there was the question of her keep. The French Court had supported her during the time of trouble, but now, the cardinal signalled, that was over. Surely England would take up the burden. And it was Hyde who held the English purse-strings. Enmity with Hyde was not prudent. If she wanted to live out her days in comfort, she had better kiss and be friends. So she did, in the end, and I was tickled to hear of my all-conquering grandmother admitting defeat.

But there was one piece of news that Mr Ross could not give me, and I had been wrong to expect it. My father did not object to Minette's marrying Philippe. He was, it seemed, delighted with the proposal, and the match was to go ahead with all speed.

'Parliament have voted her a dowry of forty thousand pounds,' Mr Ross said. 'Munificence indeed! To be sure, it is a parliament of Cavaliers, and everyone is enthusiastic for the royal house just now. That may, indeed surely will, change as that first glow wears off. England and her king are on their honeymoon. Your father knows that well, Master Crofts, depend upon it. And so any alliance that secures him friends abroad is welcome.'

I did not believe that my father could be so coldly calculating. To marry his beloved sister off to a man like Philippe, just to make his throne more secure! No, I could only suppose that Minette had told him she desired the marriage – for whatever reason. Certainly she seemed set on it. And nothing, it seemed, could prevent it now, unless some fatal stroke fell upon Philippe. I am afraid I even prayed for such: could not the smallpox that was rife in London drift over to Saint-Cloud and snuff out Monsieur? Perhaps I tempted fate with such malign wishing – or at any rate, tempted the Stuart ill luck to return. For at Christmas there came news of another loss.

Princess Mary of Orange had been poorly through the winter, and could not take much part in the family celebrations, seldom stirring from Whitehall. Still, when she fell ill just before Christmas, the first report was that she had measles, and would do well. It was not measles: the Princess did not recover. While the kingdom prepared to celebrate its favourite festival, banned for the past decade, Mary of Orange lay dying of smallpox. My father stayed by her bedside throughout. On Christmas Eve she died. She was not yet thirty.

Those five siblings I had counted so proudly and carefully on my fingers – Charles, Mary, James, Henry, Minette – were now reduced to three. A melancholy time; but I remember acting as if it were not so. The manner of it was that I had been out riding with some youths, young sons and pages of Lord Crofts' set – it was a curious mild winter, with scarce even a fire lit – and came back to his house with them for a cup of Christmas ale, very pleased with myself. They were older, and rakes in the making; I wanted to impress them. (They spoke of me as 'Jemmy Crofts – His Majesty's bastard', and that I did not mind, for they made it sound somehow fine and dashing. Such is the absurdity of youth.) We were quaffing and talking big when Mr Ross brought me the news of Princess Mary's death.

'Why, 'fore God,' I found myself saying, 'I begin to think all my family will have died before I can meet 'em!'

My companions laughed. Lord Crofts, when he heard of it later, laughed too; and Mr Ross looked at me with even more interest than usual. I was trying, of course, for the tone of that set. My mother's lovers had used it, and I knew it well, and I was proud of my cheap little success. And if it did not come naturally to me – well, what youth wants to be natural? We want masks and stage voices to hide behind.

But later, alone, I was sorry. The Princess of Orange had been kind to my mother on our travels years ago, and always devoted to my father and his cause. She deserved a better tribute. She had been married off to the Prince of Orange when she was ten. She had lived among the Dutch in a state of mutual dislike. It was an unhappy life that had just ended amidst leeches and cupping-glasses in a darkened chamber of Whitehall, and I hope I had sense enough to feel it.

'A sad shade upon the festivities,' Mr Ross said cheerfully. 'And the Queen Mother burying another of her children! It would sink a lesser woman, I think. Well, well, the Princess died a good Protestant, which is a blessing. Also it is no bad thing if people begin to think of serious matters now. The position of the royal family is quite altered by these events, and though your father is so newly settled on his throne, it is not too soon to think of succession.'

'What do you mean?' I cried. 'Sir, you have not some news you dare not tell? My father has not taken the infection too?'

'No, no. He thrives. But succession, Master Crofts, is the thing that *must* be put upon a safe footing, after such years of trouble and tempest. A king must have a line. It is all the more urgent that he find a wife now.'

'Why?' I still did not like that notion.

'Well, as it stands, the heir to the throne is his brother, the Duke of York. But I fear people will begin to look askance at the duke after this queer business of his marriage. 'Twas strange poor judgement he showed from first to last. I also hear he is unsteady in the matter of religion – even looking with a kindly eye on Papism, they say. While young Henry lived, this did not matter so much: there was at least a firmly Protestant prince standing next in line. Now there is only James – and after him, Princess Mary's poor little boy in Holland. They do say on her deathbed she asked your father to stand guardian to the child: a Protestant, of course, and of Stuart blood, but still only a little boy, and much dependent on the favour of the Dutch, who are mighty republican at present. No, the succession is in sore need of settling. I wonder what will happen.'

Something terrible. Minette fell ill.

She and my grandmother had already set out for home, straight after Princess Mary's funeral, fearing the risk of infection. No one feared it more, it seemed, than Philippe, who had begun to shriek for his bride's safe return from pestilential England. (Perhaps he feared for her life: I heard that his chief anxiety was that Minette might catch smallpox and survive it with spoiled looks, for he could not bear anything ugly.) Embarking from Portsmouth, their ship ran into a storm and had to put back into port – where Minette collapsed in a fever. The rash soon appeared. Philippe, it was said, fainted away on hearing the news. My blasphemous prayer, it seemed, was bearing more terrible fruit.

This time the malady was measles, and not the smallpox. Minette resisted the doctors – who conceived that her brother and sister had not been bled *enough* – banished the leeches, and after a few weeks was well enough to resume the voyage home. Monsieur, they said, spent a full day on his knees in thankful prayer for her recovery. This looked, even I had to admit, like genuine attachment. Perhaps things would not be so bad.

Philippe, with the rest of the French royal family, met the returning travellers at the Abbey of Pontoise, and came back with them to Paris with much pomp. He could hardly stop kissing Minette's hand and gazing raptly at her, apparently – but I was spared that sight. I was not summoned to Colombes until my grandmother and Minette had been settled there some days, and by then Philippe had returned to the court.

Returned, though, in a fury – a perfect passion of wild jealousy.

'Aye, he actually stamped his little feet, which might have stirred a *very* nervous mouse, perhaps. And now he has gone, if you please, to complain to his mother. Maman, Maman, I declare it's not fair! Make it better!'

So, laughing and mimicking Monsieur's lisping petulance most accurately, said the man who was the cause of all the trouble: George Villiers, the Duke of Buckingham. He came to drink and gamble with Lord Crofts – 'Damn me if I'm welcome anywhere else just now!' he cried with good humour – and also, it seemed, to have a look at me. He had heard of me from my father, who was his old and close friend.

'We shared a nursery, His Majesty and I,' Buckingham boomed, standing me before him and studying me intently. 'I was his constant playmate when we were younger than you – still in coats. And damn my eyes if you're not the spit of him, boy! I swear it gave me quite a turn when you walked in. How long is he to bear your name, Lord Crofts, eh? For by my soul, it ain't a convincing fiction, with that face on the lad!'

'That is for His Majesty to determine, Your Grace,' Lord Crofts smiled, 'and you know his mind better than I.'

'That I do,' Buckingham said, as hotly as if someone had denied it, and threw up his great leonine head. Then a smile kindled, sweet and wry, and he added, 'If anyone knows it.'

Here was a fair summation of Buckingham, who, as I came to know him, seemed always bouncing like a tennis ball between extremes, and in whom one might fancy the cleverest man in the world, and the stupidest, had somehow been compressed into one body. At that time he was just past thirty, strongly handsome and blond as a Dane, though growing a little heavy, with wilful meaty lips and hard bright eyes. He wore an over-the-shoulder cloak and much lace, and to my eyes was the pure and perfect Cavalier; and his intimacy with my father enhanced his grand lustre. When he was in a room, everybody else seemed crowded out. At the same time I could not help but see the faint scribble of drinker's veins about his nose, and I noticed his smell. Beneath the perfume lurked something musty. There was a particular reason for it just then, as I shall tell. But in later times it was always faintly there, that scent: like an exotic animal that should never really have been made into a pet.

'So, Your Grace, Monsieur is complaining to his mother about you,' Lord Crofts said. 'And his mother, I fear, will pass his complaints to London.'

'Aye, doubtless.' Buckingham kept his hand on my shoulder, as if I were a stick or a shelf. 'Why, do you think I fear that? His Majesty has his quarrels with me, I don't deny it. God's body, we're like some prosy citizen and his fudgy wife after all our years together, bickering even when we're happy. But he's not apt to cut me off for falling in love with his sister, not he. Not for falling in love with anyone. When it comes to that, we have a most *indulgent* sovereign, my lord Crofts.' He laughed. 'Why, he *indulges* that pretty cousin of mine mightily. Twice nightly by all accounts.'

Lord Crofts laughed too, though with a little unquiet glance at me. 'You divert me out of conscience, Your Grace. Alas, I fear the alliance of the Princess and Monsieur is quite a settled thing—'

'I like to *unsettle*,' Buckingham sang out. 'I am medicinal, my lord Crofts, I am vigorous exercise and a change of air. I stir the phlegmatic and melancholic humours and brace the constitution. As for Monsieur, the man is naught but a joke, is he not? A great joke I would not mind, but a little joke . . . He is a sodomite, of course. No one gainsays that. You know, in London years ago a ranting Puritan reproached me in the street for my long hair. 'Twas, the pudding-faced one declared, an invitation to sodomy.' He glanced at me. 'Do you know what that is, my boy?'

My notions were biblically vague. 'Something very wicked.'

'Ho, is it now?' Buckingham laughed, and seemed to stop on the brink of saying something more. 'Hey, well, Monsieur is the King's brother, and may do as he likes, of course. And there, if you ask me, is the root of it. Monsieur has lived always in Louis's shadow and must be monstrous jealous of his brother. Louis has his rump-fed Spanish bride now, so Monsieur must have one. And damn me if she's not pretty and cultivated and altogether dazzling – even to Monsieur, whose tastes don't generally run in that direction. So he's proud as a peacock at getting her, mayhap even thinks to gall his brother a touch with it, for Louis will surely tire of that broody Spanish fowl, and begin to think on what he might have had instead. And so if any other man looks at her, Monsieur goes into these fits. Is that sack there, my lord Crofts? Give me a cup. It will serve for an opener. If we play deep, you must send out for Nantz brandy, naught else sustains me.'

'So rumour says, Your Grace,' my guardian said, pouring.

'Ah, you heard of our little affair or affray when we landed at Le Havre? The most absurd thing. I sat down to play that night with Lord Sandwich and old Jermyn – the old blubber-gut – not the freshest of company, but needs must. Out of the very dullness, I fear, I drank brandy until my wits were quite extinguished, and the next thing I remember is waking in my lodgings in a state of vilest crapulence. Now that, boy, is something truly wicked,' he added giving me a tap, 'as you'll find. And then comes Sandwich's servant with a letter asking if I remembered what I said last night, and if so would I stand by it with a sword and a second! Well, I was never less inclined to a duel in my life, but you know I do not refuse a challenge – ever. So I agreed, and we readied ourselves. But along comes the little Queen Mother with fat Jermyn at her heels as ever, and they beg us to compose our quarrel, and lay on the soothing words, and so at last Sandwich and I sheathe our swords and shake hands upon it. I was glad of it, upon my honour, for I truly do not remember what I said to my lord Sandwich – not for the life of me. And the piquant thing is, I can remember perfectly well what I said to Jermyn that night, and I insulted him roundly enough for a dozen challenges, by God! But the man's such a jelly,' he concluded, puffing out his cheeks in imitation of Lord Jermyn's grossness, while Lord Crofts laughed – and so did I.

'But what did you say to him?'

'Oh, my dear sir, don't make me repeat it in front of the boy. Sufficient to say I alluded to his new earldom, and said what a pity it was that there was no such title as the Queen Father, to reflect his true position. Though as to *position*, with his bulk and she so little, I fear there must be only one practicable. I conjecture her perching atop like a monkey riding a sty-boar . . . Well, is it not so, my lord Crofts? You blush to laugh, but come, it's common knowledge. I don't begrudge her: she has been long widowed, and with His late Majesty, you know, she went to it like a she-goat. I'll say this for Papists, they don't neglect lechery. They get the pleasure twice over – doing it, and then confessing it all to their priest. Who gets his pleasure in turn, you may be sure, listening with his hand in his breeches. You've seen that old driveller Father Cyprien?' Buckingham fell into a cruel imitation of my grandmother's priest, head nodding, lips wet. 'Oh – oh, *mon enfant*, your sin is grievous – oh – oh, grievous . . .' He turned suddenly to me. 'She has not made a little Papist of you, I hope, Master Crofts?'

'There were efforts that way,' Lord Crofts said. 'His Majesty stopped them, and brought in a Protestant governor.'

'Did he now? What did that mean, I wonder?' Buckingham looked narrowly at me, then took up a pack of cards. 'You shall see me build a house of cards, Master Crofts, while we wait for your guardian's friends. I flatter myself I can build 'em higher than any man – grander too, Gothic or Doric, whatever you please . . .'

So he could. He went about it as earnestly as if it were something important. I was still child enough to feel a pang of regret when, growing bored, he knocked the whole magnificent structure down with a flick of his hand.

Lord Crofts' friends soon arriving, they sat down to play. My guardian, far from strict on such matters, usually allowed me to stay at least until the deep drinking began. So I saw that the Duke of Buckingham, dominating presence as he was, did not command universal respect. There was talk of loyalty to His Majesty during the exile, and I saw some sour glances at the duke, for he was one of those who had made his peace with Cromwell, and had even married the daughter of Parliament's greatest general to regain his estates. But no one made any remark. Buckingham always wore his sword, and in its elaborate chased-silver scabbard it was forever flashing and clinking.

Not unlike its owner, perhaps. Mr Ross told me that night what brought the duke here, and why Monsieur was so angry. During her visit to London, Buckingham had continually danced attendance on Minette. In his theatrical way, he had declared himself madly in love with her. Knowing him, my father had not taken this seriously, and at his prompting neither had anyone else. Buckingham was full of such freaks and fancies, it was his way. But it was also his way to carry them to wearying extremes, as a child hitting upon a jest will repeat and repeat it until its parents despair. When my grandmother and Minette set out for France, he had attached himself to the party, still vowing that he would perish if separated from his angelic vision, and so on; and thus he had followed her to Paris.

Monsieur was suspicious at once, and very soon in a passion of jealousy. No matter that the nonsense was all on the duke's side, and Minette blameless. He had, as the duke said, protested to his mother, and the protests would reach Whitehall. As one of the greatest lords of the realm, Buckingham could get away with much, but my father, Mr Ross thought, would be as severe as he was able, and order him home. Meanwhile, the duke was parading his pretended grief in the wildest manner. He had been found sleeping in the grounds of Colombes, having camped there all night wailing his woe to the lute. He had had his servant publicly throw ash on him, and now he was going through a grotesque charade of not washing or changing his linen.

'He did the same, I hear, years ago at the time of your father's march on Worcester. The duke suddenly insisted that he should be General of the Scots army; His Majesty refused him. So he went into a prodigious sulk, and refused to be clean – a way, perhaps, of making sure he cannot be ignored.' Mr Ross made a smiling sipping noise, relishing his own tart humour. 'He is always in and out of favour; but your father is never less than fond of him.'

That would have prejudiced me towards him in any event; and when the next day Buckingham descended on our study, saying he wanted to take me off on a jaunt, I was glad enough. The jaunt was a tour of Paris, or such scenes of it as had for the duke either association or interest. He had been here with my father as a young man in the first days of exile. 'And here, I dare swear, is where he got a taste for it,' Buckingham said, greeting a fat-armed lady at the door of a sort of gilded eating-house, where I saw a billiard table with a man in his shirt lying full length and snoring on it. There was, in truth, nothing much in these places to shock me: Spanish-chocolate houses, common stews, even a flogging house with pictures on the wall of buttocks striped and smarting – places flaring sinfully enough by night, no doubt, but in the light of day looking only listless and shabby. The duke, though, seemed determined on an education I did not really need, and leaving one such establishment said, 'The baths raise a pretty sweat, I find; but it isn't the baths that men go there for, as a rule. You know why they go there, my boy?'

'To be with women, sir,' I said, more awkwardly than I would have liked.

'Aye, to be – but there are better verbs. To fuck, or be fucked. Or swyve or towse or poke.' He looked at me and then laughed as if I had made a great joke. 'Such a rich language. Did your father ever tell you of when we were in Scotland, before the march to Worcester? The Scots were the most abominable set of canting hypocrites. Four-hour sermons. Dismal manses where every room looked like a coffin. Even to swear a damn-me was a sin, damning you and no less. They wanted me sent away as a bad influence, but oh no: I clove to Charles. Even when we marched south, and it became clearer each day that we were doomed.'

'Why, sir?' I asked. 'Why didn't people rise and follow my father then?'

'And yet now they fall over their feet to welcome him – eh? Wise questioner, boy. Hey, well, he had an army of Scots with him then, and the English didn't care for that. But more to the point, he did not *look* as if he could win. Folk are slow to wager on a limping cock. They bend – they accommodate to power – as they must.' As he had, he might have said. 'Depend upon it, the point has not been lost on your father. Not long ago, we were talking of that Worcester time, and he said, "They should have had me then. I was young and full of hope and trust, and a better man, but they kicked me out. Now I have none of those things, and they cheer me." He smiled, but yet 'twasn't smiling. You know the look?'

'Yes.' I did.

That interested Buckingham – as indeed did everything to do with my father and me. Throughout our jaunt, which was not very jaunty, he kept drawing from me every detail of our association: of my past life, of my mother and how my father had got on with her, and of what my father intended for me now. What useful information he got out of me I don't know – none perhaps. It was simply the duke's nature to be always meddling. Then at last he seemed to grow suddenly tired of me: we should go home. But I felt I had earned a question or two of my own.

'Sir, who is your cousin?'

'I have many. You will not find a better-connected family in England.

Cock's life, they have stabled these horses abominably. I'd see that ostler whipped—'

'I mean your pretty cousin that you speak of.'

He stopped and curled his lip at me. 'What put that in your mind? Those bathhouses, perhaps.' Then he laughed. 'Apt enough. My cousin is called Barbara, my dear boy, as you would know if you lived in London. She is a close friend of your father – aye, close, close as that.' And he pulled on one of his kid riding gloves with a wriggling gesture.

'Is she the one my father's going to marry?'

'Eh? What's this, what do you know of his marrying?'

'Only – only that they say he must, now that he is King.'

'Ah. Aye, well, so he must. Barbara, though, is already married. Mind, she has a very understanding husband.' This amused the duke so much that his laughter frightened his own horse. 'You will meet her, perhaps, though not as Queen. Her title really belongs in French, for they have a tradition of such things here. A *maîtresse en titre*. The intimate friend of the King, who—'

'Fucks him,' I said, very bold. I suppose I wanted to pull the rug from under his feet: he was so sure of himself.

But the Duke of Buckingham was greatly amused, even ruffling my hair fondly. 'Aye, that, to be sure,' he said, mounting up. 'But does more than that, perhaps.' And he gathered the reins tightly in his soft-gloved hands.

My grandmother heard about the duke improving my acquaintance. I was summoned to Colombes the very next day. She told me to pay no heed to anything he said. Although Minette was inclined to laugh off his attentions, my grandmother was vexed at his presumption.

'It was the same when poor Mary was widowed,' she said. 'He fancied he had a chance there – ambition, or mischief, I know not. It is buffoonery, but it is in poor taste. Monsieur is right to be angry. I have written Charles myself about it. He must assert his authority.'

My grandmother looked worn and melancholy, as well she might. She had buried two of her children in England; and there had been some coldness between her and Mary too. I heard they had had to keep her away from Mary's deathbed. She would have gone in there exhorting the agonized lady to convert to Catholicism before it was too late.

Minette I found blooming again, and not marked by her illness. To my equal delight and envy, she talked confidentially to me, telling me of her time in England.

'The whole fleet came out from Dover to meet us. James was in command. Such a fine man as he has become, Jemmy – quite as regal as Charles. The ship captains adore him. And there was a great feast at Dover, and he had made sure there was fish out of tenderness for our religion, it being Friday, which was good in him. Father Cyprien even said Mass in public the next day, though I think the townspeople did not much like that. And then Charles came to take us to London – and oh, you should see how much he is loved, Jemmy. They cheer him wherever he goes. And when we went up the river to Whitehall – well, at first I said to Charles where is the river, because I couldn't see any water, only boats and ships and masts everywhere – and people, such numbers of people, I was almost half afraid. Then there were more crowds at Whitehall, which was – well, not quite as I thought it: not so grand as the palaces here, perhaps, but then it was all stripped by Cromwell, and Charles is setting about improving it. I think Maman was a little sad there' – she dropped her voice to a whisper – 'because that is where they killed my father. But then there was no time to be sad, there was such feasting and dancing. We dined in public with everyone crowding in to look, and I felt quite conscious and sure I must have sauce on my chin and look a fright. And when the Parliament voted me money, I gave them my thanks and said they came from a truly English heart. Charles said that was prettily done and smiled as he does – but I truly meant it so. General Monck – now he is so much the true Englishman – he entertained us to supper and a play and I didn't know what to make of him at first. He speaks so little and chews tobacco and looks quite like the stern Roundheads we frighted ourselves with. And yet underneath he bears a true and gentle heart, and that is what counts. That is what I shall remember.'

I might have asked, in that case, why she was going to marry Monsieur. But I had recognized my defeat.

So, presently, did the Duke of Buckingham. My father ordered him back to England. He had created, anyway, mischief, which was perhaps his intention. Jealousy had wrought Monsieur up to a frenzy. Until the duke was gone he daily dispatched to Minette little fragrant tortured notes telling how many fainting fits he had had. Once, I think, he accused her of encouraging the duke's attentions. There was a tearful conference with my grandmother, and later Anne of Austria herself came to Colombes and, closeted with them, spoke soothing words.

Plainly the wedding had better take place soon. Arrangements were hurried forward to placate the hysterical Philippe, but there was a papal dispensation to be got first, the bride and groom being first cousins, and then Cardinal Mazarin inconveniently died, so the French Court had to go into mourning. Some there were mourning another loss: they had expected the position of first minister to become vacant with the cardinal's death, and had plotted and jostled accordingly, but Louis announced that he was going to rule himself from now on – and, by God, did. I could imagine Mazarin's shade gracefully chuckling.

But it happened at last, in March. It was Lent, which meant a private wedding – also an unlucky one, I heard the waiting-women whisper; and Minette was still officially in mourning for her brother and sister. So there were no roses in my grandmother's little chapel at the Palais Royal, and only a modest array of love knots on Minette's gown. Monsieur, however, was tricked out gorgeously enough for ten brides; and he was trembling so hard that every last ribbon and pearl quivered. Seated beside Lord Crofts, I watched in a state of settled gloom as the Bishop of Valence turned my dearly loved Minette into the Duchesse d'Orléans and Madame of France. Monsieur squeaked his responses indignantly as if the bishop were accusing him of something; Minette spoke clearly but looked fearfully white under her veil. Anne of Austria, seated in front of me, seemed to notice it and put her head close to my grandmother's. I heard a whisper about an 'unlucky time', and so I think Minette must have had her menses that day.

Thus, she married Philippe bleeding. My father would always scoff at my propensity for omens, and true, she looked happy enough after the service, when heralds threw a shower of silver coins, and Monsieur, his shakes over, beamed and kissed her hand most gently and gallantly. But my father was not there to see her weep when the time came for Monsieur to bear his bride away to the Tuileries – weep, and cling to my grandmother and to Father Cyprien, and beg them not to forget her – just as if she were going to a place far away, from which she might never return.

THIRTEEN

'Ah, Jemmy, you at least have not deserted me,' my grandmother said, leaning on my arm as we walked in the garden at Colombes. 'You at least do not mind spending a little time with a pitiable useless old woman.'

Well, I did mind, in truth. I preferred to be riding or fencing or admiring my new suit in the mirror. But my grandmother was lonely without Minette, and had me much with her during the beautiful summer that followed. And there I could at least hear some news of Minette – even, at length, see her. There was news from England too. My father had had his coronation at last – the crown and regalia had been sold off during the Commonwealth and had to be new-made – and very grandly it went off. England, having shown Europe how to kill a king, now showed how to crown one. Soon afterwards came an announcement that the Thrones of England and Portugal were in accord over an even more joyful matter. A bride was chosen. A young Portuguese princess named Catharine of Braganza was to cross the sea, marry my father, and become his queen.

They had never seen each other, of course. It was a move in the game of kingdoms, as Mr Ross explained to me. The bride brought two thousand crowns, as well as the ports of Bombay and Tangier. That was the first consideration for my father and his cash-starved Court. In turn Portugal secured an ally that she sorely needed, forever shadowed as she was by her great neighbour, Spain. And France, always likely to come to blows again with the Spanish, approved the match for that reason. Only the Spanish, seeing themselves encircled, were displeased. My grandmother was as happy as if she had made the match herself; and I found I did not mind. My poor mother had said this would probably happen, and a marriage so coolly arranged did not threaten to take my father's heart away from me. There might be children of the marriage, of course. That was a different matter. But the negotiations were still going on, and that seemed a long way off.

I should have been satisfied too in discovering myself a poor prophet about Minette's marriage. For Minette, that golden summer, was happy. Everyone said so.

But that was the trouble.

I got the first hints of it quite early, though I did not understand them. One morning Lord Crofts, more drunk than usual, looked in on my dancing lesson, and began teasing the dancing master, who was French and very correct. He talked of English country dances, and how they were better than all your French posturing, and tried to demonstrate.

'Turn, so – no, I tell a lie, so – change partners, and down the line—'

'Change partners, *mon Dieu*, what is this barbarous stuff?' the dancing master cried, hands up in mock horror.

'Why, the French know about changing partners, I think,' Lord Crofts said grinning. 'Look at the royal house: *they* know all about it.' Then, realizing he had spoken out of turn, or perhaps just thirsty again, he literally reeled out.

What should have been plain to me then was made so only by my grandmother, whom I found looking gaunt and grave over a letter she had received from one of her friends at court. Father Cyprien was with her, offering consolation.

'Madame is young. Monsieur is young. His Majesty is young. The Queen is young. They are all, in fact, young.' This was, for Father Cyprien, quite concise. His vague eye lit on me; he seemed to refrain with regret from saying that I was young. 'And so we must make allowances, considering always that they are—'

'Young, aye, I know it,' snapped my grandmother, 'but that need not mean folly. And besides, *mon enfant* has always been wise beyond her years . . .'

'And yet you call her *mon enfant*,' Father Cyprien said, pleased with himself. He was not pleasing my grandmother, not today. She waved an irritable hand, then beckoned me to her. 'Jemmy. Pray walk with me.'

And so we walked in the garden, under a sun so high and strong that the stripes of light and shadow on the turf looked like bolts of cloth rolled out. My grandmother lamented her state, and then abruptly said to me: 'You must not hearken to any gossip you may hear about Madame your aunt.'

'What gossip?'

'Ah! I have just told you not to hearken to it, Jemmy,' she said, giving me a humorous tap. 'Oh, it will come to your ears, no doubt . . . You are fond of her, I think, Jemmy.'

'Oh, yes.'

'So you will not be ready to believe any ill of her. And that is good. You will be delighted as I am to hear what a success she is at court – what a fine figure she cuts there – and indeed, so elegant as she is, so sweet and accomplished, that is no surprise at all, is it, my boy?' Her great eyes probed my face.

'Not at all.'

'To be sure – you are quite in the right of it, Jemmy. And likewise if the King favours her with great attention, as his honoured sister-in-law, and shows himself much impressed with her, then that is no surprise either – is it? And if people put a bad construction upon it, then – then that is very wicked. And I know you will not pay them any attention.' She squeezed my arm. 'Because you are a good fellow. So, I feel better now.' But she did not look it.

The gossip soon came to my ears, and of course I paid attention: everyone did.

The royal party – Louis and his queen, Philippe and Minette – spent much of that summer at the country palace of Fontainebleau: a summer of ballets and *fêtes*, boating-parties on the river and hunting-parties in the forest, banquets in the open air and music under the stars. Yes, a beautiful fantasy it sounded, but no Eden without temptation. And gossip cast Minette as Eve.

Louis's dumpy queen played but an awkward part on that gracious stage. Her wit was as unequal as her French to that company, where people composed impromptu verses and recited from tragedies and sang to the guitar under the trees. She liked eating, going to church, and dressing puppies in bonnets, and she was pregnant. It was not she who was at Louis's side on that extravagant stage, but Minette. Everyone remarked how Minette blossomed there: her elegance, cleverness and taste made her the undisputed queen of the revels. She it was who planned the ballets and *fêtes*, and it was from this time, and under her influence, that Louis's court fostered that cultivation for which the world knows it; hers the guiding hand that elevated Monsieur Molière's theatre and the music of Monsieur Lully to the admiration of Europe. With this, I think, Philippe can only have been pleased. His wife was the admirable ornament he had wanted. But rumour whispered that she was not only queen of the revels. Louis was showing her such attention that she might as well have been the Queen herself. There were moonlight walks through the forest, there were little notes and verses exchanged on scented paper, there were hints and glances: there was everything, barring proof, to satisfy that scandal-ridden court that Louis and Minette were lovers, or going to be.

I have never been of a quick understanding. Probably I have too much of my mother's unruly heart ever to develop a nimble mind. I can sympathise with poor Marie-Thérèse, bewildered and shut out by wit. And yet while my grandmother sighed and shook her head over each new report of Minette's behaviour, I felt I understood entirely. Minette was so dutiful – had it not always been impressed on her that she must be good, a lone light in a dark world? – that people forgot she was human. There was vanity in her, and also pride. Louis had thought her not good enough to marry. If now he was looking at her with new eyes, eyes weary of the sight of his fudgy wife and surprised at this blooming brilliant creature whom he had thought would just do for his absurd brother – well, was it any wonder if she rather liked it? If she played upon it, and tantalized Louis with what he might have had?

Yes, I could understand it. I did not think badly of her. I did feel alarmed for her, though, when people talked of how jealous Monsieur was becoming. He must have complained again, to his mother, who wrote my grandmother a strong letter that made her sigh more than ever. For once, my grandmother was not relishing having to interfere.

Minette paid a visit, alone, to Colombes. Very grand she seemed, stepping from her carriage with its plumed horses. My grandmother could not forbear a few remarks about such high company calling on a poor insignificant old woman like herself, but her heart was not in them. She was troubled, and – unique, this – seemed daunted, almost fearful. And she only hinted that Minette looked tired, a little poorly (which she truly did not – I had never seen her so beautiful) before passing her burden to Father Cyprien. It was he who was closeted alone with her that afternoon, for a talk. Not strictly a confessional, though no doubt he and my grandmother would have liked some sort of confession – something to show she was still the biddable *enfant de bénédiction*.

I doubt they got it. Minette was wholly cool and self-possessed. Throughout the next two days she talked freely of life at Fontainebleau, of the Queen's pregnancy, of the grand outdoor ballet with herself as Diana that was being planned. My grandmother looked baffled. Meanwhile, I grew baffled in my turn, and then resentful. For this Minette with her rich dress and high-flown talk had no time for me. She greeted me amicably as if I were a favourite page, perhaps – no more. Her bright abstracted eyes seemed to look straight through me. When I asked her if she wanted to go on a ride, she waved me away as if I had proposed a game with dolls.

It is nonsense, of course, but I had an obscure feeling that I, who understood and sympathized while others made moral cluckings, deserved some better return. There was a look about her, complacent and secretive, that I came to see as a barrier that I must smash. On the second day a messenger in royal livery came, bearing a note for Minette. She took it away and read it privately, coming back with that look fixed ever more infuriatingly on her lovely face. I saw my grandmother itching, yet not daring, to speak out. I took a more direct path. I chose a moment that evening when they were at cards, and crept to Minette's chamber. There, after a short search I found the note under her pillow, and stole it away.

It was true about the perfume. And it was true, I realized as I conned the note with trembling guilty pleasure, that Minette was more to Louis than an honoured sister-in-law. I have forgot the exact words – and certainly there was nothing to shock. It was all florid compliments on Minette's beauty, and how much she was missed at Fontainebleau. 'The sun shines here, yet it does not shine' – that I remember: conventional enough gallantry. But there was a passionate conclusion. 'You know I scarcely live while you are away from me. I can only whisper my love for you to the stars. Hasten back to me, let me whisper it to your heart.' It was signed with a flourishing L that, poor penman as I was, I much admired, and even tried to reproduce in my copybook that night. Which was, of course, one way of distracting my mind from the knowledge that I had done a great wrong.

Oh, I knew it, but I can only say that possession of that note gave me a feeling of power, and I did not want to relinquish it. Perhaps also I can plead the inward turbulence of my age. I was approaching thirteen, and a prey to all manner of impulses and urges that I did not understand beyond that they made me unhappy.

Well, my theft had an effect, at any rate, in breaking that unnatural calm. I came in from riding the next morning to find Minette and my grandmother in a full-blown quarrel.

'. . . Now I know I have lived too long. I shall retire to Chaillot: I shall await my death there. That it should come to this – accused by my own daughter, the one child I loved best—'

'I did not accuse you, Maman. I asked you if you knew what had become of it. I was packing my things, and I missed it. Why will you not answer me?'

'You do wrong to throw these suspicions on me, child, very wrong. If we are to talk of suspicions, then I fancy I have as great a right as any. If you are so very concerned about this note, then I as your mother must be concerned too. About what is in it.'

'I have told you it is a note from the King to myself. There is no falsehood in that. If you cannot see—'

'And if you cannot see, you are blind!' My grandmother clapped her hands together fiercely. Minette blinked. 'Yes, I am a poor useless creature here in my retirement, no doubt, but I hear things, believe me, daughter, and I am not such a fool as you think me.'

'I don't think you a fool, Maman,' Minette said wretchedly. She was a poor quarreller: the old placating habit broke through. 'But I hope you would think well of me when there is no reason to think ill.'

'*Is* there no reason?' my grandmother demanded, with her most transfixing look. 'Is there, daughter?'

And Minette, her cheekbones slashed with red, did not answer. Turning, finding me there, she spoke more in relief than accusation. 'Jemmy, do you know anything of this note that I have lost?'

Apt little liar, I said with disgruntlement, 'No. What note? I don't understand – why are you shouting at each other?'

'I will ask the servants,' my grandmother said, tight-lipped. 'They should have been asked first, perhaps, instead of these accusations being thrown at *me*, but never mind. I shall ask them, and we shall see about this note.'

She stalked out of the room. Minette drew a long breath and then sat down, her back turned to me. I thought this was dismissal, until she said quietly: 'Jemmy, what is it that people are saying?'

'What about?'

She looked at me then, with faint impatience. 'About me, of course.'

No doubt my anger was excessive – it was primed with guilt, besides, but I was hurt that *now*, all of a sudden, she wanted to resurrect our old intimacy. 'Always you, you!' I cried. 'What does it matter? As long as they say *something*.'

But Minette was, on the surface at least, unflinching. 'What are they saying?'

Fresh from the wrong kind of company, I answered her: 'They say that you and Louis are fucking.'

And then the anger went out of me. I stood appalled, yet on Minette's face there was only a sincere puzzlement, and that was in her voice too as she said slowly, 'Well, that just isn't true.'

I shrugged helplessly. 'Things like that. I meant . . . well, you are so much with him, they say, and he treats you as if—'

'Now you are saying a different thing,' Minette said crisply. Her mind was logical, never woolly. 'That is different from the word you just said.'

'I know.' There was nothing for me now but abasement.

'Well. I am surprised, but I suppose I should not be. People will use such words, when they want to make something seem mean and dirty. It may be quite different, but that's precisely what they don't like. So they must pull it down and belittle it.' She got up. 'I don't expect you to understand, not now. Some day, though, you may, and you'll remember this.'

And so I have. When I show my love these pages, I know she will smile sadly and agree, reading Minette's words. I wish Minette were here, to know that she spoke true.

And I wish I could tell you that I at once ran to fetch the note and confess my crime. Alas, my conscience was not so prompt. Doubly ashamed, all I could do was skulk and brood. Minette was to return to

Fontainebleau that day. Even when I heard her carriage being brought round, I kept out of the way.

Only when she had gone did the misery of the parting – without goodbyes, and with on my side a sin unabsolved – hit me like a blow. I put the note in my pocket, saddled my mare myself, and set off after her.

But I never did return the note. A couple of miles down the Colombes road, where the trees opened into a glade with a ford – in high summer only a sparkle and trickle, and a haunt of swallows diving at gnats in the sultry air – I came upon her carriage, halted. Louis had ridden there to meet her. His two attendants had drawn themselves discreetly off with the horses, whilst Louis leaned it at the carriage window. He had a spray of flowers. Minette took them, and her hand lay gently upon his on the sill as they talked.

I had pulled up quickly, and the overhanging trees screened me. But I had been treacherous enough, it seemed to me, so I turned my mount about and did not stay to see more.

The life of the French Court was very public. No amount of discretion on the part of Minette and the King could have prevented the gossip spreading, as it did over the summer. My grandmother, I think, still wanted to close her ears to it. But there were further representations, sharp now, from Anne of Austria. Not only was Monsieur growing bitterly jealous, but the Queen, Marie-Thérèse, had looked up from her gorging, seen what was afoot, and protested her unhappiness. My grandmother was due to go to Fontainebleau, to attend the great *fête* that Minette had talked of, the Ballet of the Seasons, so she decided to go a couple of days early and, as she said, 'see if I may cure some young fools of their folly.'

She took me with her. I was all aglow, and resolved to comport myself most seemly; but as the coach drew near to Fontainebleau in its magical forest, she looked a little frowningly on me. She murmured that I had best not put myself forward, and once at the palace she consigned me to the care of a chamberlain, and told me to amuse myself quietly. She had come, after all, to preach morals, and perhaps she thought my presence would not have been a helpful illustration.

So, for now I was kept away from Minette and the court people, while my grandmother busied herself – and it might have been a dull enough couple of days at any spot but Fontainebleau. I loved the place at once, and I still prefer it to that fabulous Versailles which Louis was then planning and which has since risen in all its geometrical glory. Fontaine-bleau's rambling galleries caught my fancy more than any cold symmetry could, and all around it was the murmurous music of woods and running water. The chamberlain had a son of my age whom I roamed about with, even to the kitchens that were like steamy dungeons, and thus I got to hear the servants' gossip – always more pithy, and more accurate, than what passes above stairs.

For them, the scandal of Madame and the King was old news. When Madame and her ladies went down to the river to bathe, it was the King who would ride down to escort her back – that was his story, at any rate. And when the moon was up, they walked in the forest together – to discuss poetry, of course. The Queen Mother, they said, had already reproached him for it, and so he and Madame were looking for ways to veil their indiscretion. Madame had a pretty maid-of-honour named La Vallière: the King was now making a show of paying attention to her. It would not, they said, fool Monsieur. Not that Monsieur's heart was aching for love – for a woman it never would. He had flown into a violent temper with Madame on their wedding night because her courses prevented him fulfilling a husband's office, and within a fort-night he was openly telling his friends that he was bored with her. He still performed the nuptial business regularly – the laundry-maids could testify to that – but it was duty, not pleasure. If it was pleasure he wanted, he turned to the Comte de Guiche – or turned away from him. But Monsieur was a dog in the manger if ever there was one: he didn't want the hay, but no one else was to have it – least of all his brother.

This was disturbing talk, in many ways. Part of me wanted to shut it out; another part dwelled on it, with the same sort of fascination that took me back to the sumptuous decorated *galeries* to gaze up and up at the profusion of moulding – nymphs whose naked limbs seemed too soft to be made of mere stucco – and the painted panels with their languid tumble of mythological flesh.

I always made sure there was no one about, but once I was so rapt that I did not hear the man approach, and then his hand was on my shoulder. He laughed at my expression.

'I have broken in on your reverie. Unmannerly of me, young sir, I crave your pardon. You are a lover of art, I see.' His eyes twinkled from the nudes to me and back again. 'Armand de Guiche, at your service.'

I made my bow. This de Guiche was, I saw, that same very handsome young man who had accompanied Philippe on the day of the new Queen's entry into Paris. Despite the curtains of soft brown hair and dreaming eyes, there was something soldierlike about him, his stance sturdy, his voice deep-chested. The shyness that came over me was seasoned with a sharp and instant wish: when I grew I wanted to be like him.

'I am James—'

'Crofts, I know. Monsieur has spoken of you.'

I did not much like that, and my face must have shown it. He laughed again. 'Monsieur makes it his business to know everyone. Don't trouble about it. Ah, this smooth perfection, you know' – he waved an arm at the pictures – 'very misleading. The painters were, I think, Italian, which makes the hairlessness of the women all the more surprising. Have you ever been painted, Master Crofts? No? I think you will be. I have a – a presentiment.' He put his fingers to his temples, smiling, but serious too. 'A vision. But perhaps you do not believe in such things.'

'I believe in ghosts.' My mother had told me she saw them often, at the Pembroke castle of her childhood.

'Everyone does if they are sensible. Well, I'll leave you to your contemplation.' But he turned back, saying: 'Did you ever hear of Actaeon? He was out hunting one day, and came upon the goddess Diana bathing in a stream. He should not have looked. She turned him into a stag for his impertinence, and he was torn to pieces by his own hounds. Very cautionary. Still, I think I would have looked too.'

What success my grandmother had had in her project of talking sense into Minette I don't know – but I fancy little. Later that day there was an eating-party by the river, and for the first time she took me with her. 'I have need of company,' she sighed, and though there were many people there I saw what she meant. In her nun-like habit she looked sad and out of place, a disregarded little sparrow in that exotic aviary. Hers had been a chaste Court; here, for all the decorous manners, sex stirred in the air like the rustle of glistening satins and the ruffle of soft plumes on bare shoulders.

And this was a world of games too, subtle games – not to the taste of my grandmother, who for all her love of scheming had a most direct mind: games behind games, indeed, as if luxury must go on refining its pleasures until they were as delicate as lace and evanescent as perfume. On the surface there was nothing to show that there was trouble at that youthful court. They were all there beneath the trees, Louis and Minette and Philippe and the Comte de Guiche; Minette's maids-of-honour, including that talked-of La Vallière, who was not, I thought, very pretty at all; and as if in freakish parody, Philippe's own circle of minions, lolling, hard-eyed young men prompt to laugh at his every sally. Everyone was polite, and even when Louis made a point of refusing a dish of ortolans, rare delicacy (though to me always looking and tasting like little cage-birds cruelly betrayed), and sent the dish across to Minette with a flower laid on it, Monsieur looked no daggers. When they played word-games, there was the same outward accord – but even I could feel the dangerous currents swirling underneath.

It was Minette who began it – I was full of wonder at how naturally she took the lead in this company – proposing the old English game of 'I love my love with an A'. It was more difficult in French, I think, but Monsieur's quick wits were equal to it. The letter D coming to him, he said he loved his love with a D—

'—*parce qu'il est droit.*'

Because he is straight. The glowing look he bestowed on his friend de Guiche, standing close by, left no doubt about whom he meant. 'Well, is he not?' Philippe cried as there was a little teeming silence. 'See his martial form – like his father, the glory of our arms embodied.' The Comte de Guiche's father was the Marshal of France. Which carried it off, but as Monsieur repeated, with a purr, the word '*droit*', and looked across at Minette, I thought she hunched herself a little, as if conscious of that misshapen shoulder.

But she was composed again, when it came to her turn, and the letter K. That hardly occurs in French, so she spoke in English. I suppose that was the reason.

'I love my love with a K, because he is kin, and because he is kind.'

'No, no English!' cried Monsieur. 'That is not fair! Cheat, cheat! What was that you said? You said "king". I know that – I know what that means.' He began to look round in frenzied appeal – instinctively looking for his mother, perhaps.

But Minette said calmly, 'No, my dear sir, I said "kin". It means related by blood. And "kind" means gentle and good.'

'And it can also mean related by blood too,' put in de Guiche. 'I have read in the English bible. So, Madame, your riddle is all of a perfect piece. You must win the crown.'

'What crown?' Philippe said, giving his friend a displeased look.

'Well – the one I shall make now,' de Guiche said with a light laugh, and began busying himself with willow twigs.

'Kin,' Philippe muttered, and bit into a peach as if he were savaging it. 'Yes, it is very pretty, my dear madam. Still, English is not fair.'

For they were cousins, of course, as was Louis: it might have meant anything. It might even, I thought, have meant my father. The Comte de Guiche, sitting down by me to strip the willow twigs, said quietly to me: 'Also *Kind* in German. That means child. Perhaps she intended it for you. Of course, you are more young man than child, but still.' He was a good flatterer: as Philippe's friend, he had to be. I thought him kind, though.

'Armand!' Philippe's voice cut in sharply. 'Wake up. It is your turn. You have M. And no English, if you please.'

'I love my love with an M,' de Guiche said, eyes on his work, 'because it is a marriage. A marriage of all that is most admirable in either sex: the marriage of Monsieur and Madame.'

A nice piece of diplomacy I thought it, and others murmured in agreement. But Philippe stared long at his friend, before shrugging and saying: 'Everyone is being *so* clever today. I declare it is hardly a game at all and more like the schoolroom. Well, and what cleverness will *you* think up?' It was the turn of one of his young minions, but plainly it was not his brains the fellow was favoured for, and he came up with something acceptably foolish. So it proceeded till it was Louis's turn to love his love with an R. The King did not hesitate.

'*Parce qu'elle est la reine.*' Because she is the Queen. Very proper; and then he made it more so by doffing his hat gallantly to my grandmother, who was sitting so quietly that people had forgotten she was there.

I looked with new attention at the King. Was Minette dallying with him simply in revenge for the time when he had dismissed her as the bones of the Holy Innocents? Or was that merely the seed from which love had grown unbidden? If so, I feared even then the fruit would be bitter. Louis was certainly handsome, in a severe way – I thought de

Guiche's looks more enviable – and he was cool and self-possessed. Minette was a girl of seventeen; and there was no mistaking the glow on her face at this graciousness to her mother. Looking back, I think it would have been more remarkable if she had *not* fallen for him. But he, of course, had less to lose.

The crown was ready: now there must be judging. Louis, ever correct and, yes, kind, said they must defer to my grandmother. But Philippe grew shrill at that. His brother had complimented her, and she would be swayed by that; it was in any case a stupid game. He proposed instead a foot-race for the crown. No one was much disposed to argue with him; but drowsy with food and wine, not many fancied exercise either, and only Philippe and a few of his friends lined up at last at a spot between two lime trees, to run the distance to the riverbank and back.

While the others went to watch and cheer, I stayed gorging on the food. I had a boy's appetite, and the thrifty mark of my early life was still on me, for I could not bear the thought of its being thrown away. The Comte de Guiche stayed too, putting some finishing touches to his crown.

'You have been a soldier, sir?' I said shyly.

'Of a sort. That impresses you, eh?'

It did very much. All my dreams were of trumpets and battle – except the ones in which those marble-limbed nymphs appeared, and from which I would wake in discomfited guilt with an image of Father Cyprien sadly shaking his head.

'Well, this sword has seen service,' de Guiche said, drawing it out with a thrilling flash. 'Not against the English, though, Master Crofts. No, we must be the best of friends. Like Monsieur and Madame.' He sheathed the sword, his lips wry. 'Look, they are beginning. Ah, Monsieur is fleet: he is ahead at once. A graceful figure, is he not? What say you?'

Memory of those hard fingers grasping my chin stirred me to malice. 'I suppose,' I said, 'he is very *pretty*.'

De Guiche seemed delighted at that. 'Ah, truly! But would you say, now, that he is prettier than Madame?'

'My God, no.'

'Aha! She is exquisite. But that is precisely what you must not say, you know – that is precisely the trouble! Was there ever anything so diverting? Many men are pleased to see their wives complimented. But my dear Philippe is an utter original.' He laughed. 'Now look – is this not another scene straight from those classical paintings you admire? Atalanta racing her suitor. Do you know it? Atalanta refused to marry unless her suitor could defeat her in a foot-race, but he was cunning and threw down three golden apples, and she stopped to pick them up and so lost. I don't think Philippe will lose, though, do you? He does not like to lose. He is the most classical character though, you must confess. Look – isn't that a Roman profile? Can you not picture him as an emperor of old Rome?'

'Like Nero,' I said. For whatever reason, he was goading me into malice, and I was enjoying it as he was. And yet I felt a shudder. And when Philippe came back preening – he had won, naturally – and received the crown, I had a superstitious fear that he would know what I had been saying about him, and slunk away.

Minette sought me out alone that evening. Perhaps she felt she had neglected me. Certainly she sat by my side in quite the old way, and talked to me in English of her latest letter from my father, which could not fail to please me. But there was a distracted look about her, I thought. She seemed forever on the verge of saying something that never came out.

'Well, I ought to retire early,' she said at last. 'Tomorrow we present the ballet. You have never seen me dance, I think, Jemmy. It wouldn't do for me to be falling over . . . The Comte de Guiche has been very friendly to you, I see.'

'Yes, I like him.' Whether that was good or bad, in this world of games within games, I could not tell.

'Good. But don't pay too much heed to the things he says. Monsieur's friends have a – a certain way of talking.'

'He speaks very highly of you,' I said. I would not have liked him otherwise.

'Does he?' She looked interested; then she saw my expression. 'What's the matter?'

I had seen Monsieur standing in the doorway. Minette turned her head, paled, and got up. 'Well,' she said, 'I had better go. I shall make sure you have a good seat tomorrow, Jemmy—'

'English again!' Monsieur burst out. 'What is this, madam, forever talking English in front of me? Is it meant to insult me?'

'I was only having a word with Jemmy, Philippe, before—'

'A word in *English*, which makes it a great *secret*, though I cannot imagine what *secrets* you can have from your *husband*. Unless—' Monsieur struck his forehead and gave a mirthless giggle. 'Of course! But on my honour, madam, you are starting so *young* with this one.'

Minette, very straight-backed, walked past him into the corridor beyond. He gave me a look, black and empty, then followed her. A second or two later I heard the slap.

Well, I think he was not a wife-beater in the usual sense. The slap was the sort of thing one heard when spiteful children play – usually followed by a wail, but Minette was silent. Cruelty wears many guises. That sound spoke eloquently enough of their marriage, I think. Without it I might not have noticed other little things: as for instance the next day, when we were all walking in the fountain-court by the lake, and Minette turned away to wipe her face. Not spray from the fountain but from Philippe, who had spat at her – deftly, of course, discreetly. He was ever respectful of appearances.

In England nowadays the court ballet-masque, with royal persons playing parts on the stage, is a thing of the past as much as beards and ruffs; and to give a true notion of it as practised at Louis's court one must recall how great a separation exists there, between the life of the court and of the nation. One must fancy an enclosed world, in which all is ceremony and symbol, elevation and pomp; in which there is no absurdity in the King leaping across the stage, tricked out in green mantle and plumes, to be hailed by the chorus as the incarnation of spring. There, such a show made him more not less King; and in truth Louis, athletic and commanding, made a fine enough figure. But I could not help thinking of my father, and imagining his smile of high dry amusement at the idea of cutting such capers.

This *fête* was held outdoors. The night softened the garish splendour and made it beauty. Torchlight trawled the lake and gilded the canopy of trees. All the court was there. My grandmother sat me behind her in the royal box, where Anne of Austria slapped irritably at the gnats with her fan. She seemed quite as tetchy with my grandmother – because of the scandal, perhaps. I think she was missing Mazarin too. Young love is always more interesting, and we don't care to think of a fifty-year-old woman aching for her dead lover.

Minette was the undoubted glory of the ballet. Many of the court ladies took part, but how different they were – bosomy, prosy, so very much themselves. Minette's attendants, carrying her train and scattering blossoms, looked gawky – yet that was apt in a way, for they threw her into relief. She was gloriously separate as befitted a goddess. Diana, huntress of the moon. Watching her, I remembered my father telling me about the moon seen through a telescope, all crags and ugliness. I saw the moon, a peach wafer, above and in the lake. Which was it – beautiful goddess or pitted rock? Somehow, in my intoxication (the occasion partly, but I had been given wine also) I felt the question posed to me, demanding answer. Then I heard someone commend the dancing of the Comte de Guiche, and I stretched my neck to see. Yes, I had conceived a little boyish worship of the dashing comte; but I could not make him out amongst the elaborate costumes and masks.

Also, I was already tired. It was a long night, and at the *bal* in the gardens later my eyes grew mighty heavy after more wine, and the silken figures promenaded about me like the wraiths of dreams, their voices swelling and fading in my ears. I heard much praise of one of Minette's train-bearers – that same La Vallière of the kitchen gossip – though I had hardly noticed her. I saw Monsieur, one blaze of jewels, parading grandly with his young men following like lapdogs: I saw Minette, changed now out of her costume but still looking luminous, like some sylph got in amongst the chattering mortals. I heard my grandmother and Anne of Austria discussing her.

'Ah, *mon enfant*! She does bloom, indeed. Quite a special bloom. I wonder – could it be? I hope so. It will make things better. It will set a seal—'

'Yes, yes, no doubt.' Anne of Austria's voice, impatient. 'But things *will* be better, in any event. Because my son knows his duty. I have spoken with him, and be assured he knows it.'

'And my daughter knows hers, I hope.' Frost in my grandmother's tone, but anxiety too.

I saw the Comte de Guiche bowing over Minette's hand, speaking to her with what seemed, to my approval, warmth. I did not like him as Philippe's creature: I preferred this. It was my last vision before the pricking of my eyelids grew too much. I was hardly aware that I had curled up under a tree by the lake and gone to sleep, before the voices woke me.

The Comte de Guiche, and a friend: they were standing nearby, looking out over the water. De Guiche had a hangdog look, his shoulders slumped.

'What will you do?'

'Go and see the comtesse, I suppose.' De Guiche chuckled lightly. 'High time I did.'

'Philippe says these things. He doesn't always mean them—'

'Ah, that's exactly where people have Philippe wrong. Besides – well, damn it, I can't deny it.'

Blinking and stupid, I spoke. 'Who's the comtesse?'

De Guiche turned. 'Hello, little owl.' He looked unhappy and drunk. 'The comtesse? She is my wife, of course. You didn't think I had one? Oh, they married me to her when I was scarcely older than you. Appearances, my young friend: remember all is appearances in this world. She lives at our château in the country. Very dull. Time I visited her. Time for dullness.' He made an expansive gesture. 'Try if you can, my young friend, to marry for love. Contrary to opinion, it actually saves trouble. I shall leave tomorrow, I think.'

'Why?' I said.

'I suppose I . . .' De Guiche's fingers fluttered, as if he were trying to grasp something insubstantial. 'I suppose I complicate things. And they are already complicated enough.' He shrugged. 'We all have too much time, in truth. We need to do things. That's why we end up like this. That's the virtue of war. Mars not Venus.' He staggered a little, to my dismay: heroes should not booze. 'What did you think of the ballet? They should have chosen another subject. She is too good as Diana. Altogether too real.' He saluted me, and went away into the darkness.

The next day, while my grandmother readied herself to leave, I sought out the chamberlain's son. The new gossip was instructive. The King, they said, had showed marked attention to Mademoiselle La Vallière after the ballet. It was to disguise his affair with Madame, of course, with the Queen Mother watching – or was it? The King did seem mighty taken with La Vallière, and he surely wanted a mistress he could bed decently. As for Madame, *she* had been shown such attention by the

Comte de Guiche that Monsieur had flown into a jealous passion with his friend, and told him to get out of his sight. Monsieur had never intended for his catamites to take a fancy to his wife – but who could blame de Guiche if he preferred Madame's arse to Monsieur's for a change? The comte was to retire to the country until Monsieur's temper cooled. But then Madame was surely pregnant. Soon she would grow stout and lose her bloom along with her admirers, and that would suit Monsieur very well: he would be the prettiest again.

And so on. At the time I found all this bewildering, and almost feared growing up, if it meant I must learn to negotiate such labyrinths. Now I can see that these people were playing games; but I can see too that they were dangerous games, and the breaking of hearts their currency. They were all very well as long as no one brought genuine feeling to them. That, I think, was how Louis came off unscathed. He was canny and self-preserving: he would give no woman the power to make him happy or unhappy.

That sounds as if he only trifled with Minette, and I do not mean that. I believe he did fall in love with her that summer, as deep as his cool tidy mind would allow – that is, not so deep as to prevent his climbing easily out again. And I believe she did set out, at first, to captivate him, to show him what he had missed. That seems to me more natural than unnatural. And then, alas, she did fall in love with him.

I do not think it ever went further than vows and moonlight kisses. I think it was, for Minette at least, a truly romantic love, the sort we must all have: for some, with a happy issue – for more, perhaps, including Minette, not so. Still, I think no one can be whole without it. The gossip of the kitchen proved accurate. After the *fête* at Fontainebleau, my grandmother took me home, and I returned to the dullness of study. But court scandal was everywhere – urchins sang rude rhymes about it in the Paris streets – and soon it was a commonplace that Louis had taken Minette's maid-of-honour, La Vallière, as his mistress. If that truly had begun as a disguise for Louis and Minette's affair, as they said, there could hardly have been a more bitter result. Some said Madame was furious, and determined to bring La Vallière down, and that her new lover the Comte de Guiche was plotting with her.

Well, there was no doubt that when Minette came back to Paris in the autumn, de Guiche came too. Pregnant and in poor health as she was, she gave endless receptions and parties and de Guiche was always there. Was she playing with de Guiche in revenge for the straying of Louis? I cannot imagine her as so calculating. I have lately heard someone who knew her well say this of Minette: that one loved her without having to think about it. I thought it strange at first: isn't that a definition of love? But perhaps I see it, for in that world of intriguers and dissemblers, she had a unique effect, surprising people into feeling. It happened to the Comte de Guiche, I am sure, much to his own unease. He could not help himself: he was drawn to her in spite of Philippe's displeasure, which was no negligible thing. I am equally sure she did not love de Guiche. The wound of Louis went too deep. I doubt it ever faded.

She remained, of course, married to Philippe. If Philippe behaved more tolerably to her that winter, as seemed to be the case, it was because she was carrying his child, and pregnancy made her less attractive – thus flattering his vanity doubly. My grandmother, after much grumbling about grand ladies and how they forgot their own mothers, at last went to see her, and stayed to nurse her. She was low as her time came near and troubled with a cough and headaches. Taking charge cheered my grandmother; and now that Minette was about her proper duty of producing heirs, she was approved once more. The scandal of the summer could, perhaps, be forgotten.

Minette's first child was born in March of 1662. Soon afterwards my grandmother took me to the Tuileries to see her. I was eager – not only to see Minette, I confess, but because I hoped I might meet the Comte de Guiche there again. In truth I had reached the stage where hero-worship came to the fore, and the company of women irked me as belonging to childhood. But when I mentioned de Guiche to my grandmother, she hushed me and said I must not look to find him there, and I gathered that his infatuation with Minette had stirred up scandal again, and he was not to be mentioned.

The child, though premature, was alive – but I did not find much rejoicing. Louis's well-fed little queen had lately presented him with a healthy son and heir: Louis, it seemed, did everything right. Minette's child was a girl, and as far as Philippe was concerned, might just as well have miscarried.

'You have a daughter, Monsieur,' my grandmother chided him, 'and you are blessed. Don't you think I felt blessed, when I had my sweet Henriette-Anne?'

'You had sons first,' Philippe snapped. 'As my brother has, naturally. Always the heavens favour *him*.'

'My dear sir, it does not lie in woman's power to choose whether she will have a boy or a girl,' my grandmother said laughing.

'I don't know about that. I think there is no telling what this one is capable of.'

'This one' was Minette, who had received us in her chamber where she still lay abed. She looked pale and gaunt, as if she had delivered prodigies instead of the tiny waif whose hand feebly encircled my finger. Monsieur glowered at her in the mirror above her dressing table, then returned his attention to his eyelashes.

'Philippe,' Minette said, 'those jewels on your breast – aren't they—'

'Yes, yes, yours, my dear, of course,' Philippe said patting them complacently, 'but you are hardly going to wear them just now, are you? It's not as if you can go out. God knows when you will be on your feet again.'

'You men! It was a difficult birth,' my grandmother clucked. 'There would be a great squeaking from men if they had to suffer such things.'

'It is your lot, it is scriptural,' Philippe said primly. 'Besides, the Queen had a hard labour, and she was better soon enough. Not that her looks are improved. She is more fleshy than ever.' He shuddered and went to peer out of the window: there was the sound of horses in the courtyard. 'You must exert yourself, Madame, that is all. There is no pleasure in looking on a heap of bones . . . Ah! Company at last!'

'Who is it, Philippe?' Minette said, lifting her head.

'Friends. *My* friends,' Philippe pouted, already on his way out. 'Who were you expecting, my dear?'

'Eh, *mon enfant*, I had hopes that you two would rub along a little better now the child is born,' my grandmother sighed when he had gone.

'Philippe does not like girls,' Minette said, sitting up and motioning to the maidservant. 'A little water, if you please . . . When she was born, I said we might as well throw her in the Seine.'

'Henriette-Anne, for shame . . . !'

'I only meant it is a misfortune to be a girl. It's better to be a man in this world.'

'Ah, many women are hippish after the birth. It will pass . . . What is amiss with that clumsy creature?' My grandmother fussed over the bedclothes. The maidservant, a hulking hoyden, had spilled the water before trudging out.

'She is Philippe's choice,' Minette said dully. 'She carries tales to him.'

My grandmother stopped, frowning. 'Lord, this is a sad state of affairs! You know, my dear, Philippe has a good heart. I truly believe it. It is just a question of managing him. And I wonder—'

'Philippe hates me,' Minette said, quite calmly, 'and that is what I must manage. But I can tell you, Maman, that I have not given him cause. Indeed I have not.'

My grandmother would not meet her eyes. 'Why, I don't know what you speak of, *mon enfant*. This is just the melancholy talking—'

'Oh, Maman, of course you know,' Minette said, gently laughing and reaching out to stroke her hand. 'Even Jemmy knows – don't you, Jemmy? And do you believe it?'

'I believe you,' I said, stoutly, though I was a little embarrassed. Also – though I could not say so – I would not have blamed her at all. No one in that world thought much of fidelity in marriage; and as for being faithful to Philippe, even bearing him was heroism. But I did believe her, and still do. Minette had made her compact with herself. She was the good child: she had always been told so. Already, perhaps, she had decided to place her happiness elsewhere. Conspicuous by the bed were several letters from my father. He had written much to amuse her during her confinement. Here was a man of whom not even Philippe could reasonably be jealous. Here was a love that could not disappoint.

'Jemmy believes me,' Minette said, 'and he is my true friend. Ah, my little Marie-Louise thinks so too!' For the babe left off her fretfulness as I dandled her, and seemed to smile at me. 'Your little cousin likes you, Jemmy.'

'Cousin of a sort,' my grandmother put in promptly.

'Oh! Well, yes. But I have begun to wonder, you know, lying here and thinking – how much these things truly matter.'

'Now I know you are ill,' my grandmother said, 'because they matter a great deal.' And she took the baby from my arms. At once my little cousin began to cry again.

It would not be true to say that I cried inside at my grandmother's words – I was tougher than that – but my heart did ache, and when I returned to Lord Crofts' house I demanded of Mr Ross, impatiently, I dare say, what my father meant to do with me, and was I quite forgotten.

'Your father is preparing for his marriage, Master Crofts. That must greatly occupy a man's mind, you know: a king's mind doubly so.'

I thought bleakly, and said: 'His new wife will not want me about.'

For once, Mr Ross had no answer.

So I have no doubt that the following summer was for me a time of doubt and unhappiness. My father was married in May, and the little princess from Portugal, Catharine of Braganza, became his queen; and I remained shut out. Yet in memory I cannot conjure any gloom from that period: perhaps because I was young, and more than ever vigorous in body, unable to see a stile without leaping it; but more, I think, because what happened in July cast a retrospective glow over the whole time. It was almost as if I knew in my bones that this was going to come.

At Colombes I found my grandmother deep in preparations for a visit to England. She longed to see my father's bride for herself, and now he had invited her, most cordially and pressingly, and it was long since I had seen her in such good humour.

'God send a calmer voyage this time. It ought to be a fair crossing, in this season, but I put no trust in it. Neptune does not like me. I hope you are a good sailor, Jemmy. Lord Crofts, I know, has the feeblest stomach. You must not mind him if he falls to groaning and wailing.' She laughed merrily. 'I well remember a time—'

'Am I to go too?' I cried. My head began to spin. 'Am I to go to England – with Lord Crofts – with you . . . ?'

'Aye, aye, you are. Your father wishes it.' She looked me up and down, faintly smiling. 'I wonder whether to have you measured for a new suit . . . But there, your father will see to that in London, no doubt. Well, Jemmy, you are a good boy in the main, and I think he will be pleased with you – if you will but keep a curb on your spirits, and remember your duty. Your father's Court is the glass wherein England looks for her reflection. Let us have no specks or smears upon it.'

'London . . . When shall we go?'

'Soon. A fortnight, perhaps less, depending on the ship. There is much to do—'

'And Henriette-Anne?'

'No, no. She is Madame: she belongs to France now.'

I would miss her. The thought struck me without hurting me, for at that moment I was in the rarest of states – pure unmixed emotion. Joy, only joy, all joy.

'And Mr Ross?'

'He will continue your governor, I think. Again, your father will settle all these matters.'

'Where will I live?'

'Oh, Jemmy, Jemmy, these questions! Anyone might think you are not happy to be going.'

'But I am happy! Oh, Grandmother, I am!' And in the excess of it I seized her there and then and lifted her off her feet – Henrietta Maria, the Queen Mother – and whirled her little laughing protesting form round and round in my arms.

I had come a long way from the lonely urchin whom Mr O'Neill had found shivering in a fireless room. Now my last destination was at hand – the place where, my heart told me, I had always belonged, and from which I too had been exiled: the court of Charles II of England.

BOOK TWO

ONE

We did not have a fair crossing, and I spent much time bent spewing over the taffrail, where I was sometimes joined by a very fair young girl named Frances Stewart. She liked to be sick companionably; she liked also to comment upon our respective offerings.

'Oh, look there, Master Crofts! Little bits of orange. Yet I have eaten nothing orange today. Certainly not *an* orange, for there aren't any on the ship. Isn't it curious the words for the fruit and the colour should be the same? And isn't it curious I should bring up orange? I wonder what colour yours will be. We shall see in a minute, I dare say.'

The social voidings compensated her for the loss of her favourite amusement, which was to build houses of cards. The pitching of the ship made that impossible, though for a long time she kept trying, with superhuman patience. 'Oh dear,' she would say, as the cards toppled again. She had been a maid-of-honour to Minette, and was now coming over to England, with my grandmother's household, to do the same for my father's bride. Her beauty was entrancing and her mind tiny, or so it seemed. I will have occasion to speak of her later.

So, green but exulting, I came to England. As I had years ago with my mother, when Cromwell ruled, I sailed up the Thames; and as I had then, I staggered when we put ashore. To me it seemed as if my country was quaking and tilting at my setting my feet upon it.

Well, you know I am a believer in prophecy.

My grandmother and her train put up at Greenwich Palace for the time being, whilst Somerset House was made ready for her. Here was a place I joyed to explore, the moment my legs were solid, for here my father had been at work, having the park planted with lime trees, and steps

211

built up to the castle, where I viewed with leaping heart the coiling river vanishing into the smoke of London. This was my father's kingdom! Though he had sat his throne for two years now, I marvelled at the reality of it, and felt myself in a dream.

There was in me a certain awe too. My father, whom I had known threadbare, shaving himself, dancing to a ragged fiddler until the candles ran out, was now a man who could command a wood into being. Would he be changed – grand, lofty, even terrifying? When Mr Ross, who had accompanied me on my climb, said we should go down to await my father's coming, I even felt a little afraid.

Since their marriage in May, my father and his bride had been spending their honeymoon at Hampton Court. It was from there that they rode to Greenwich, for the new Queen's presentation to the old. Brilliant summer: people cheered the glittering progress of the Court. (The reign was still young, of course.) And I, with Lord Crofts and others, kicked my heels in an anteroom to the Presence Chamber.

My grandmother stood alone at the top of the palace stairs, a little figure in black, to receive her daughter-in-law. This was her natural propensity for drama, but also I think she had heard that there were already troubles in the marriage. And she was ever the one to deal with troubles.

Queen Catharine, I hear, kneeled at her feet, but my grandmother lifted her up and embraced her and called her *mon enfant*. There was policy in this – but I believe my grandmother, for all her misjudgements, also knew goodness when she saw it.

Then they were all there, in the Presence Chamber, and I looked on with anxious and greedy eyes.

There he was, my father, Charles the King in his own land. No worn and shiny patches now on that suit of velvet, but his dress was still plain compared to Louis's plumage; and I saw a touch of grey in the tumbling black locks. When I say I saw grey in his face too, I do not mean he looked ill or aged. He was tall and hale and altogether magnificent. But I could not tell what he was thinking. I had a sense of bars and shutters. And I wondered if I had been right, after all, to fear him. Folk always commented on the darkness of my father's complexion. In that room I thought I saw the darkness as something within him, like the negation of light.

But all that was dispelled when he spoke. 'Mam, this does my heart good,' he said, 'but I fear there's something amiss with my eyes, for on my soul you look no older than when we used to have our summers here as children. And that infernal sea-voyage don't seem to have discommoded you a hair! Where's your secret?'

'I put my trust in God,' my grandmother said smiling, 'and I thank Him that the journey is so short. You, my daughter, had a longer sailing from Portugal.'

'Oh, Biscay was kind enough to her, was it not, my dear?' my father said. 'Only a few storms. And they're to be expected.'

'Please?' Catharine said.

'Kind,' my grandmother said, pressing her hand. She had seated the young Queen in the place of honour on her right, while my father took a stool alongside. 'That means gentle – good. You will take up English soon enough, *mon enfant*. It was so with me when I came here: I found I was speaking it before I knew it.'

'Yes. I know what kind means,' Queen Catharine said. With her strong accent, it was hard to tell whether she put a certain emphasis on 'means'. Hard to tell too what signified the look she gave my father, under her long lashes.

But he beamed, all pleasantness. 'Aye, storms are to be expected, you know.'

I fear I was ungallant in my first reaction to Catharine of Braganza. I saw a small, sallow young lady, dressed like Louis's bride in that old-fashioned farthingale. Fresh from Fontainebleau, I fancied myself a connoisseur of beauty, and did not approve the smoky heavy-lidded almond eyes, the full out-thrust underlip. I even concluded her sulky – and that, in very truth, was the pot calling the kettle burned-arse.

If I had been more honest, I would have seen the fear in that quiet, immobile, crushed-looking figure. She had been raised in a convent at Lisbon, and knew nothing of the world. She had been sent across the sea to marry a man she had never seen, in a country that mistrusted foreigners and Catholic foreigners above all. People had gaped when she arrived with her quaint train of priests and black-clad duennas, and there was a tale that my father had groaned when he saw her and said, 'They have sent me a bat instead of a woman!'

I doubt that part – but there is no doubting that it had all been a tremendous uprooting for the little Portuguese Princess, and now, I confess, I wonder at her courage. At the time I was not disposed to like her. She stood in my mind as a rival for my father's attention.

And as someone who had taken my mother's place? Well, I must try to be exact on this; and truly I do not think I felt so, not then. My feelings were yet unfleshed and unformed, beyond a desire to be loved by my father as his son. Of course, it could not long be that simple, as I was to find. For Catharine was there to give my father, and the kingdom, an heir. And if I was to hold to the truth of what my mother had told me before she died, then this marriage stood in the way of my birthright. Yet she had told me also that something like this would happen. And that promise to my mother was all entangled with my own guilt and confusion. What was I to think? My father had brought me to England with a purpose, and all I could do was humbly trust him to reveal it.

So I avow that I did not look at Queen Catharine with anything more than mild jealousy spiced with curiosity. But when her eyes lit on me, there was surprise and trouble in them. She knew me for who I was, even before my grandmother beckoned me forward.

'Here is my young charge, my son, safely brought as you asked. He looks well, I think.'

Trembling a little, I kneeled before my father and asked his blessing. I felt his hand patting my shoulder.

'I am glad to see you, Jemmy. Come: greet your queen, my boy.' And as I kneeled before Catharine he said to her, 'Master James Crofts, my dear.'

So, that was who I still was, officially. But as I returned to Lord Crofts' side, having presented my duty to the other royal persons there, I heard my father say heartily, 'Well, and here we all are, a family at last!' And whether that was meant for me or not, I glowed at it.

The other royal persons – I must speak of them. One was that lady whom my uncle James had so scandalously married and then tried to unmarry – Anne Hyde, the Chancellor's daughter, now the Duchess of York, and liking it. My grandmother, all icy graciousness, allowed her to sit close by, but I could tell that at heart she was unreconciled from the way her eyes hooded whenever the duchess spoke – as if to say, I will attend as long as I don't have to look at you. It was hard to miss the lady, in truth, for she was big. A notable bosom: but the rest of her was fast catching up with it. Unlike the Queen, she spoke up with assurance. Indeed, you might have fancied her the Queen rather than mute, timid Catharine. I think the Duchess of York quite fancied it too. Firm-lipped, thick-browed, she had the air of someone standing their ground. Her husband had tried to discard her, but she was not to be discarded.

As for that husband, my uncle James, he stood behind my grandmother's chair. He never would sit down. Perhaps it was because he liked casting a shadow.

'And how does Madame go on?' the Duchess of York asked. 'She is often in my thoughts, believe me. She had a troublesome delivery, I think.'

Very proprietorial. My grandmother replied as if it were the Queen who had spoken. 'My daughter does very well. She has recovered her health – but I fear her poor infant is sickly.'

'Do you mean Philippe or the baby?' my father said, rumbling laughter. Then turning to Catharine: 'We speak of my sister Henriette-Anne, my dear. She is Madame of France now, and a great ornament to it. She has only the minor inconvenience of a husband who is not worth a fart.'

'What is that word, please?'

'Fart,' my father pronounced distinctly. 'Come, say it with me, my dear.'

Catharine did, to my father's evident amusement. My grandmother looked on, nostrils pinched.

'And how do you stand, my son?' she said with an impatient rap on the arm of her chair. 'Is all at peace? Are the fanatics still troublesome? You know they will never go away, even if they be quiet.'

'As long as they are quiet, they may go where they please, Mam. You know I am for all men being easy in their conscience. Cuckolds, though – they are troublesome. There's the real plague of the kingdom.' He spoke lightly, but the lightness was all edge. He had the fidgets and his eyes roamed the room as if looking for a bolt hole.

'I am glad to hear you talk of toleration. Now if only your Englishmen would tolerate the true Church! You have a queen of that faith, which is a joy to me. So—'

'All the Protestant princesses were ugly,' my father said with a shrug. 'Or poor.'

'The fanatics,' my uncle James said, 'are always with us, as you observe, Mam. But they can only sow discord if the Crown shows itself weak.'

He spoke heavily. He always did: eyes fixed on the middle distance, as if speaking to himself, and often a nod after, as if he found that he agreed with himself entirely. I remember I was surprised to find my uncle James such a fair and good-looking man – not a jot of my father's darkness: tall and slender, with an eagle's handsomeness, and arched lips that a woman might have been pleased to see in her glass. But at once I saw, or felt, something stony about him. When my grandmother reached back fondly to take his hand, he let it lie limp in hers, as a dog will. 'A house,' he said with the same deliberation, 'can only stand if it has a master.'

'I'd have thought bricks and mortar more important,' my father said, with a twitch of irritation.

'Men must have a master. And if they know it, it contents them.'

'Does it? It would not content me, I think.'

'But they must have one,' James said. His voice was not unpleasant; but he had a curious way of giving every word an equal emphasis. It was as jarring as a song sung on one note.

'Aye, to be sure, brother.' Restlessly my father got up and paced the floor; he could never sit for long. 'But it is better if they are not aware of it.'

'Our cousin of France makes himself master, Charles. And that is—'

'That is what I should do, eh?' He smiled at the Duchess of York. 'Between your husband and your father, my dear, I shall never lack for advice. Well, Louis has the advantage of me all ways. No Parliament to keep sweet. No differences of religion. No lack of money. What say you, Catharine? Would you not sooner have married Louis of France?'

'No,' the Queen said distinctly; and that seemed to arrest my father. 'Please – what is it you say of your sister – Madame? I not understand.'

My father sat down. 'Forgive me. I was making merry, that's all—'

'I know it. But what is bad with the husband? He is not kind to her?'

'Mostly. Not always, perhaps,' my grandmother sighed.

Catharine looked from her to my father. 'I am sorry for her,' she said.

'Oh, there is much to be sorry for in this world,' my father said breathing hard. 'There aren't enough hours in the day to weep for it all.

That's why it's better to laugh.' Not that he was laughing. 'My sister is a clever woman. She can very well manage a little gadfly like Philippe. There is, I think, altogether too much fuss made about these matters.' At the last he offered Catharine a smile. She refused it, looking away. She caught my eye.

I have spoken of the effect of beauty upon our lives: how it determined my poor mother's. It has determined mine too, in a way. I would have to be a fool not to know that people have found me handsome – and a fool, too, to deny my looks. They are just there; I did not make them. At this time, I believe I was coming into those looks (I was thirteen) and discovering what they could do.

I smiled at Queen Catharine. She was, I thought, lonely and bewildered and afflicted by a sense of not belonging. I knew well what that felt like, and with the smile I tried to say as much. To my intense satisfaction, her sombre face lit up. She even blushed. It was an exchange of gifts.

As I write this, I realize that I might look calculating. Not so. The simple truth was, I wanted desperately to love these people – all of them – and be loved in return. But if you see in me a designing flatterer already reeking of ambition, then so be it.

When the visitors got ready to leave, I hoped my father would come and talk with me. But he was all attentiveness to his queen, and instead it was my uncle James who came over with his slow stalking gait, exchanged a few leaden words with Lord Crofts, and then offered me his hand.

'Master Crofts. You have been long in France, I understand.'

Now here is the curious thing. If there be such a thing as love at first sight – and I strongly believe there is – then there must surely be its opposite: hate at first sight.

And yet my uncle James and I were quite friendly with each other, that day.

'Yes, Your Grace. I have been at school there.'

'Aye, have you now? I am well acquainted with France. I served there with Marshal Turenne. You've heard of him perhaps? A great warrior.'

'Oh, yes. I wish to be a cavalryman myself.'

'Indeed? You ride, young sir? We must ride together some time.'

'Thank you, Your Grace. I am so happy to meet you at last. I have long heard tell of you.'

'Have you?' He seemed to take everything with this same earnest sip of curiosity. 'I like to hunt. We must hunt together, perhaps, come the season. I have not heard of you, of course.'

'James! What do you do there? Come, the horses are ready.' That was his duchess: he went prompt as a dog. It was no wonder he liked to ride. It gave him a chance of holding the whip for a change.

'Attentive to the Queen, would you say? Or simply polite?' Mr Ross was eager to know all that had gone on. I was too loyal to mention my father's chained-up look, his flashes of irritation.

'He was very attentive. He showed her much . . . much courtesy.'

'Really!' Mr Ross's eyes popped. Uncomfortably, I felt that I had said something highly revealing.

'Why should he not?' said I. 'My father's manners are the most agreeable of any man's.'

'Oh, no disputing that, Master Crofts. I only wondered . . . Of course, they must put on an appearance for the Queen Mother. But her eye misses nothing. She was looking grave, I thought . . .'

Mr Ross, naturally, had already drunk deep of court gossip, and a potent brew it was. All was far from well with my father's marriage.

It had begun most promisingly. At Hampton Court my father and his bride had walked arm in arm together; had ridden together, she on a fine Arab mare that was his present to her; had bedded together, regularly. My father even developed a taste for Catharine's favourite drink, that exotic novelty tea. Spectators of the royal drama found themselves, quite unexpectedly, watching a story of love.

So it seemed. The name of Barbara Castlemaine, my father's mistress – that pretty cousin of his whom the Duke of Buckingham had mentioned – was still whispered, but it appeared she was put aside. Until my father one day handed his queen a list of names for her approval. They were to be her Ladies of the Bedchamber. One of them was Barbara Castlemaine.

Catharine had heard about her. Very firmly she scratched the name out. My father returned to her and wished to know why. I seek neither to accuse nor excuse him, but to give you a true notion of his character, when I say that I believe he was honestly puzzled by this – even though Lady Castlemaine was at that moment being brought to bed of his child, in an apartment in that very Hampton Court.

'She has a husband, of course, but there is not much beyond pretending there,' Mr Ross said.

'Roger Castlemaine,' put in Lord Crofts. 'Spiritless fellow. But there, he got his title from winking at His Majesty's poking his wife, so perhaps he's content. Not that His Majesty was the first. Even when she was Barbara Villiers, she had a reputation.'

'I know of the lady,' I said importantly. I did not want to appear an outsider. 'She is cousin to the Duke of Buckingham.'

'More than cousin sometimes, from what I hear,' Lord Crofts grunted.

Queen Catharine had remained obdurate, even against my father's persuasions. He, who had a genius for talking people round, must have been baffled again. The little Queen, apparently so gentle and biddable, had revealed a core of determination, even stubbornness. Did my father recognize himself in that? I think perhaps not. But he certainly seemed to assume that Catharine could keep her feelings on as tight a rein as he could. His next move was to have Lady Castlemaine presented, amidst others, to the Queen. A long line of curtsying ladies, a long recitation of strange English names . . . Thus he hoped to gild the pill. Catharine, once she realized whose hand she had just taken, broke down. Some said it was all but a fit: she wept, her nose began pouring blood, and at last she fainted. When she recovered, she said she would go back to Portugal.

This was serious. Shy, dutiful, convent-reared, Catharine was not a woman to whom dramatics came naturally. Faced with her refusal to countenance his mistress, my father did not draw what now seems to me the obvious conclusion: that his queen had fallen unroyally and genuinely in love with him. (I think, in a curious way, he lacked the vanity for that.) Instead he sent his chancellor to her, to seek a reconciliation.

Such had always been the job of Sir Edward Hyde, who was now become Lord Clarendon. The years of exile had schooled him well in it – balancing the claims of parties, patching up a compromise. But here he was not dealing with an embassy or a commission of Parliament. This was an unhappy woman, who answered his reasoned arguments with tears. Everyone saw how uncomfortable he was, and some were not displeased at that.

'He has been riding mighty high in the state,' Mr Ross explained it, 'and doubtless there are those who would joy to see him tumble. The Portuguese match was very much of his making, and he must stand or fall by it. Ah, the bigger a man grows, the more of a target he presents!'

Clarendon could not repair the damage. My father insisted that his intimacy with Lady Castlemaine was at an end, but that he owed her a place and favour, and that meant the Queen's Bedchamber. Through all this I can now see a frustrated longing on my father's part for the conveniences of Louis's court. He had brought many French fashions into England from his exile – from French music to little brushes for the teeth – and wished, perhaps, that he could import too the status of royal mistress, who at the Louvre was quite as official as the Master of the Robes.

But the battle went on. My father had Catharine's suite of Portuguese attendants sent home. She locked her bedchamber door against him. So matters stood when my grandmother came over to England. I am sure she had heard of these troubles, and arrived all the more readily on account of them. This was meat and drink to her, and perhaps my father had pressed her to come for the same reason, to use her influence, to work a reconciliation.

Or did he really want one? As a boy of twelve, when the Civil War broke out, my father was present at the field of Edgehill. His governor neglected to keep him away from the fighting, and at one point a troop of Parliamentary horse bore down on him. It is well attested that my father drew his pistol and, waving it at his enemies, cried, 'I fear them not!' It was the first instance of the physical courage that he was later to show in the march on Worcester and the flight after, and which I never knew him to lack.

And yet what happened during that honeymoon at Hampton Court made him, I think, afraid.

He had asked my mother once, in bafflement, what it was that she wanted from him. 'I want you, Charles', was her answer. And that he could not bear. So with the little Portuguese Princess, who had spent her young life in cloisters and never heard the sound of gunshot – but who, terrifyingly, wanted all of him.

This I believe now. At the time, passionately interested as I was in everything to do with my father, I still listened to Mr Ross's account with a fidgeting consciousness of myself. What was I here for? Where did I fit in?

And there we enter the shadowy question of whether my father wanted to be reconciled with his queen. The point of the marriage was to produce an heir to the throne. But what if a potential heir could be found elsewhere?

I did not think it, in so many words; nor did Mr Ross nor Lord Crofts say it. But I first scented it in the air, first glimpsed it in their faces, when I said that day: 'My lord, has my father spoken with you about me? Am I to live with you now, or . . . ?'

'I can't say, Jemmy,' Lord Crofts said, smoothing his moustache, exchanging a glance with Mr Ross. 'That is a matter for His Majesty's pleasure.' He smiled rather cruelly. 'Like so many things.'

'They are a strange people,' my grandmother said. 'I think I never understood them.'

She was going to Hampton Court to return the King and Queen's visit, and as she was taking Frances Stewart as well as myself, we were coaching it. Miss Stewart's stomach was unequal to going by river, and even the motion of the coach was making her turn pale. The strange people my grandmother referred to were the English, who stopped to goggle at the coach and even, when we slowed to take a slope, pressed up to the very windows to peer in. I was quite as curious, and not a little amazed at this familiarity. I was myself, I suppose, one of my father's Frenchified imports, and thought how different this was from the godlike eminence of Louis and his court. How different too the country, which even at summer's height had a rich damp pearliness about its greenery. The houses, rugged and ill-proportioned though they might be, seeming peculiarly solid upon the earth, as if they had put down roots like trees, the very horses and cattle looking sturdy, characterful, difficult.

'To call them cold, as some do, is to have them wrong – very wrong. They are the most excitable people in all Europe, once they are moved – pure tinder.' She looked thoughtful. 'I wish I had understood this before.'

As for me, I found I did not mind being looked at. Indeed, I liked it.

Just as well. Everyone was at Hampton Court, the vast palace by the river where once that fabulous brute Henry had entertained Anne Boleyn. The whole court joined in my father's honeymoon. There were water-parties and balls and plays and, most delicious entertainment of all, gossip. It rippled out as soon as my father greeted me in the great hall. You could see it, like the first signs of a coming storm that ruffle leaves and bend grasses. Curled heads inclined together and fans came up.

'We shall have some talk, Jemmy my boy,' my father said, his hand on my shoulder, while my grandmother embraced the Queen. 'Just as soon as may be. But I suspicion my mother has a fancy to read me a lecture first.'

My grandmother, who well understood the importance of show, made a great fuss of Catharine. She approved her, and was her ally, and the world must know it. More ripples. Then my father, all pleasant and inscrutable, pressed me forward to the dais where the Queen sat.

'My dear,' he said, 'may I present to you Master James Crofts?'

I made my bow, deep and respectful as possible.

'Please?' Catharine said. There was a devil of a noise in the crowded room, talk and laughter and the rapping of French heels. 'I do not hear quite.'

'May I,' my father said distinctly, 'present Master James Crofts?'

Catharine looked at me a moment, then squarely at him. 'Yes, you may,' she said, distinctly too. 'I will not faint this time, Charles.'

I had a dim gloomy sense of myself as trouble. For a moment I was back in the old unhappy days of my mother and those bitter wranglings in which I had been weapon and tool. Dear God, I did not want to go back to them! I tried to reach the Queen with a smile again; and said in my most ardent Cavalierish tones: 'I am ever Your Majesty's most dutiful servant.'

Well, she did not smile; but there was nothing hard in those sad, smoky southern eyes. There never was, poor lady. And when, as he had foreseen, my father was steered away by my grandmother for a private talk, I was left to make such conversation with Catharine as I could.

It was no easy work. She had little command of English yet, and there was the constant noise in the room; and she had, besides, such a fearful stiffness about her – someone said it was as if she were forever sitting for her portrait – that it made you gabble and run on to overcome the awkwardness, and then you would feel you had bored or offended her, and shattering silence would descend anew. I had grown cocky, of course, and had forgotten what it was like to be shy – the sheer paralysis of it.

Nor did I fully appreciate then the peculiar character of my father's Court. In truth, if Catharine looked about her like a lapdog set down in a wild-beast show, it was not without reason. This was a Court of restoration. Many of its luminaries had ruined themselves in the royal cause during the Civil War and the Commonwealth; others had bent with the republican wind, only to bend back again. Whichever way they had gone, truth and honour had been the casualties. Only cynicism seemed the apt response to this topsy-turvy world. The bleak years of lounging and quarrelling and dicing for a living in Continental backwaters were over – but I think no one, least of all my father, truly saw a glorious victory in that. The English experimenters had run out of ideas, and fallen back on the old idea of a king. All was royal triumph, then, but only for the present: anything that had happened once could happen again. The old moorings of faith had been cut, and could not be retied. The world was an uncertain place and nothing, from a man's word to a woman's virtue to a shopman's coin, was to be trusted – and least of all, the future.

Take, then, what you can get, while you can get it: drain the cup and the devil take the bill. It was this, I think, quite as much as the reaction against the Puritan drabness of Cromwell's rule, that gave my father's new-restored Court its feverish quality. The loose morals of that time are a by-word now, so I must beware of applying the lacquer of hindsight to the rough board of memory. But I do believe it was visible in the faces I saw at Hampton Court that day: greedy, sensual, observant, somehow less than happy even when creased with laughter. Above all, there was restlessness. No one was still. Ladies forever circulated, with a sound of satin and silk gowns that was like hearing an itch. The men prowled and paced and snapped their soft clutched gloves against their thighs and tossed back their long locks the better to see, behind or beside them, if there were someone more worth talking to, more profitable, more use.

And that made Queen Catharine, with her solemn stillness, so much more conspicuous. The Bible commends stillness, and now I am older I see why. But at the time I was glad of the chance to escape from her. The Duke of Buckingham, all lace and magnificence, appeared a little way off, and beckoned me to him.

'So, the young sprig o' the tree is here!' he cried, shaking my hand, and then not letting it go. 'You've sprouted since we met in Paris, Jemmy. Master Crofts, should I say – or what, indeed, should I say?' He rumbled a laugh, taking me into genial custody: his hand gripped my shoulder and steered me away. 'Come, instruct me, my dear, what think you of the Portugee? Shadowy sort of creature, ain't she? A flavour of nuns and incense – a sort of perpetual Ash Wednesday.'

'I think the Queen is a very gracious lady.'

'Oho! This is quickness! You have scarce been at court a day, and already you have it. Two faces, excellent – though I'd recommend three or four, if you can manage it. Then you will go far.' His laughter was a deep growl. There was much of the lion about Buckingham. But of course, I only know the Tower lions, which are a little seedy and untrustworthy, and will feed on lapdogs that cruel gentlemen throw them for sport.

'But was she gracious to *you*, Master Crofts?' he went on, still impelling me away from the crowd towards an anteroom. 'That's the question. Is the hen sparrow gracious to the cuckoo? She has to be, I suppose. To please the cock. Oh, yes, she must *please* the *cock*, you know, before everything, but I fear she ain't expert at that—'

'Cousin,' said a woman's voice, 'what is this nonsense you are talking to the young gentleman?'

'Ah!' With elaborate unsurprise Buckingham turned me about to face the lady, who was sitting in the window seat. 'Barbara, my sweet coz, can it really be you? Here? I had better wink at it. The hen's feathers, you know, would be most plaguily ruffled if she knew.'

'Hush, George: introduce me to the young gentleman.' With a smile that was all confiding warmth, the lady beckoned me to her. 'I have so wanted to meet you, young sir.'

'Well, Master Crofts, here is the cousin you have heard me mention,' Buckingham said, relinquishing me at last. 'I present to you Lady Castlemaine.'

From the gossip, I expected a harpy. But when I saw Barbara

Castlemaine I was overwhelmed, not only by her beauty, but by a feeling of recognition that made my heart ache. For it was as if my mother lived again.

There were as many differences as resemblances: this lady was taller and longer in the limb, her cheekbones stronger, and instead of my mother's brown colouring there was a waxy paleness to her skin that seemed to glow against the dense, voluminous russet of her hair. Yet to look on that skin was to feel the blood pulsing beneath it, as with my mother. She seemed, like my mother, a person cut out of richer and more exotic stuff than the common material. Even the pearls at her throat and ears, looking less like hard gems than some soft and molten part of her, brought the past back to me so vividly that I almost wanted to run into her arms.

And it must have shown, for Lady Castlemaine jumped up and embraced me, and it felt like the most natural thing in the world. Her scent was familiar too. Hugging her, I could almost have fancied that this was my mother as she might have been – if she had not been, God save her, so hopelessly herself.

'Now, Barbara, this isn't fair,' Buckingham was saying. 'I know you don't dispense *me* your sweets any more, but save 'em for His Majesty at least. Mind you, this is a piece of His Majesty, so—'

'Go away from us, George,' Lady Castlemaine said over my head. Buckingham only chuckled. 'My dear young sir, sit down by me, and let us be easy. It's peaceful here – your head is quite dazed with the noise, I dare swear. Now, what do I call you?'

'My name is James, ma'am. My father calls me Jemmy.'

'And as for the rest, we must wait and see. I understand entirely.' She gave a throaty laugh, then shook her head. 'But I think I have the wrong young gentleman. I understood you no more than thirteen.'

'So I am,' I said, blushing.

'Well!' Her catlike eyes, beautiful and distressing, explored me. 'Lord knows what you will be at sixteen! I tremble!'

'No, you don't,' Buckingham said, and indeed, like my mother, Lady Castlemaine looked as if she never did. Mighty fierce, though, was her snapped command to him – 'George, get you gone!' – in a way my poor mother could never manage; and this time he obeyed.

'Now we can be confidential. Which is quite natural for you and me,

James, because of what we have in common. I mean your father, of course, for whom I have the tenderest regard. You have heard it called by other names, perhaps, but it doesn't matter. People are always ready to cry down sincere feeling and call it calculation. Now you, I should think, must love your father a good deal – for all he's done for you, and all he might do.'

'I love him as my father,' I answered proudly, 'not for what I can get.'

Solemnly she seized both my hands. 'Oh, James, that is the kind of thing I love to hear, and never do. It gladdens my heart. We are so desperately worldly here – all that is true and honourable set at naught – it quite grieves me. Lord, you are strong!' she said, looking down at my hands, though in fact it was her grip that was the stronger. 'Well, I think it enchanting of Charles to bring you to court – and he surely, you know, means to do well by you.'

'Does he?' I said, wonderingly.

'What do you mean?' she said sharply, giving my hands a jerk. 'If you don't know, how should I?' I blinked. She laughed energetically, as if to wipe away that streak of temper. 'Oh, but I know Charles, and he is always honourable. That is why he is kind to me. You see, in being his – his friend, I have entrusted him with my reputation, and he would never be careless of that. Even if people wanted him to. You have met the Queen, of course.' She bent close to my face, so that I drank her cachou-scented breath. 'Do you know, I have loved her from the start! It is as simple as that. I would never hear a word said against her. I wish I could say I have had a generous return . . . Have you not met my lord Chancellor? You will. His finger is in every pie. It was he who arranged the marriage with Catharine, you know. He is no friend to me. If I am put out of the way, I know whom I have to thank. They do say' – she laid a dimpled hand on my knee – 'that my lord Chancellor says I should be *whipped*.' She made the word so much like the thing that I flinched. Then she laughed with tremendous good humour. 'Did you ever hear such a thing? What do you think of it? Now I ask you – would you whip me, James?'

'Really, Barbara, you shouldn't make such a request of the lad, not until he's of an age to oblige.' It was Buckingham, noiselessly returned and beadily watching us.

'Damn you, George, I am having the first pleasant talk in an age, and you keep springing up like a . . .'

'Like a what? Can't think of a decent figure, Barbara?'

'Ignore that brute, James,' she said, squeezing my knee. 'Or do you like Jemmy better?'

'Aye, we had better stick to Jemmy,' Buckingham said. 'We already have a royal James, you know. He has just been telling me of his last hunting at Windsor – *every* ditch and *every* fence. He is so prodigiously tedious that it becomes almost fascinating in itself. You wait in delirious suspense, thinking he must surely say something interesting if only by accident. Pity we can't swap one James for another, eh?' A glint seemed to pass between them, like light catching silver. 'No matter. I came to tell you Charles knows you're here, coz, and His Majesty—'

'Announcing me, eh, George?' It was my father, entering swift and smiling. 'If you'd a fancy to be my herald, you should have said. Barbara. I did not think to see you here. I had supposed—'

'Aye, Charles, it was very wrong of me, I know,' Lady Castlemaine said airily, 'but there, 'tis done now. I shall slip away again quiet as a mouse, believe me.'

'I can believe a lot of things, but not the impossible.'

'Well,' she said, not at all displeased, 'you like it when I surprise you, do you not? But let me congratulate you, at any rate.'

'On what?'

'On a fine son,' Lady Castlemaine said, taking my hand. 'He is a most perfect Cavalier, and I think we shall be the best of friends.'

'Thank you,' my father said, coolly regarding our linked hands. 'And let me congratulate you, Barbara – on your promptness. Jemmy: will you walk with me?'

Lady Castlemaine let me go with a caress, and a smiling wave. And I, God forgive me, thought how much nicer she was than the Queen.

'It seems best that my lady Castlemaine stay away from the court for now,' my father said as we walked in the gardens. 'I'm sure you understand why. Lord, everyone has been talking of it. Your grandmother amongst them.' He sighed: plainly the lecture had been a stern one. 'But Barbara is – an insistent woman.'

'She said people wanted her put out of the way.'

'Did she? Well, some do. They have fixed notions. Tell me, Jemmy, how much black do you see here?' He waved a hand. 'Look and tell me.

How much pure black, and how much pure white?'

I looked, seeing the fresh green of the lawns and the dense green of topiary, the tawny tints of the gravel walks, the honeyed stone of the palace walls. The topmost part of a sail was visible down towards the river, but that was as much yellow, I saw, as white. I looked among the people, and saw chestnut and copper in the darkest locks. The nearest thing to black, indeed, was my own father's hair, and even that in the sunlight had a crackle of blue about it like a raven's breast.

'Do you find any? A curious thing, isn't it? I have had some talk with men of science on this, as well as a painter – we must have you painted presently, Jemmy, by the by – and all agree that black and white do not exist in nature.'

'I see. And yet we all know what we mean by black and white,' said I.

'So there must be an ideal black and white that we have never actually seen – eh? But that is somehow lodged in our minds. I fancy this is something of Plato's reasoning, but I fear I was never a deedy enough scholar to be sure of it. Well, you take my meaning, Jemmy, I hope. Black and white don't perpend to morality any more than to nature. What think you, truly, of my sister and Philippe?'

I was yet unused to my father's swift skipping from subject to subject, and taken by surprise I could only blurt out: 'I think – I think she is unhappy with him.'

He grunted. 'Well, any woman would be.'

I did not know how much of the gossip of Paris reached him, and said tentatively: 'She has a good friend in King Louis, I believe.'

'Ah? Close to him, eh? That's well. That's excellent.'

'Some people – some didn't think so.'

'Black-and-whiters. Never tell me you're one of those, Jemmy?'

'No,' I said. 'But I wish she had married . . . someone else.'

'You mean Louis. Aye, that would have been better, perhaps. But it was not to be, and Minette knows that: she is no fool.'

'Well, someone she loved.'

'Hm. A fortnight of happiness, and then misery.'

I stopped. 'Is that how it was with you and the Queen, Father?'

His face was shadowed. For a moment I thought he would bark a reprimand at me. (Again, how little I knew him.) Then he smiled, and taking my arm urged me on. 'Jemmy, Jemmy, you take matters fearful serious! Mam's influence, perhaps. We must cure you of it, else I shall not be able to abide you near me, and you'll have to go and live in Scotland where they like being gloomy. Well, now what's amiss?' – looking into my face. 'You don't think I mean it?'

I shook my head. 'I just don't like to think of you unhappy, Father. Nor the Queen.'

'She will not be,' he said crisply. 'That I can answer for. As for how I feel . . . Well, I strongly feel, Jemmy, that there is naught on earth more tedious than listening to a man prate of his feelings. You remember I told you of the block of wood that I had as a child, and would not let go of? Well, there you have the matter of Lady Castlemaine in a nutshell.' He laughed. My father laughed as much as any man I have ever known, I think; yet I always found in his laughter something veiled and secret. Men make all sorts of wild noises when they laugh, and very seldom say 'ha ha'. My father did, though, distinctly: almost as if he mocked mirth itself. 'The lady would not take kindly to the comparison. Let's go and see the tennis court. I'm having it new fitted out. Have you played, Jemmy? No exercise like it. We shall have many a game. Odsfish, we shall have some fine times, you and I!'

He had drawn my arm closer to him as we went along, and all about the gardens heads were turning. 'People are staring at me, Father,' I said.

'No wonder in that. You have your mother's looks. And I hazard you'll be tall as me when you finish growing. For your sake I hope not, because it means you don't fit in this world. Coaches, chairs, beds, they all seem made for a race of dwarfs. Aye, they stare, Jemmy, and point and whisper: of course they do. Because you are walking with me. This is the court, Jemmy. How is your studying? Your Latin? When you con an unfamiliar page, do not certain words leap out at you, so that you think aha, and know where you are? Think of this Court as just such a page. Everyone is studying it for meaning. Now if I bestow a smile on that gentleman – observe, so – now folk think that means he is to be given a place or a favour. And in turn they will cultivate him. Now what if I bestow a smile on a man who everyone knows to be his enemy? Where's the meaning in that? It tickles me, I confess. I love to keep 'em guessing.'

If I was abashed at first, it did not last long. I swelled with pride at being seen thus with my father, here at Hampton where my royal ancestors whispered to me from the very stones. There were the tiltyards where Henry had played at old chivalry. His daughters had trod this turf. Mary the bloody with her grim bridegroom of Spain, and great Elizabeth who had scorned any husband but the realm. Here my great-grandfather James had gathered the scholars and divines who gave us our English Bible. Here the heart and spirit of England seemed to infuse my own. And the dark subtle man who possessed both paraded me on his arm before the eyes of his court: eyes watchful, wondering, and – as he said – greedy for meaning.

I was dizzy with it. What my father meant by it, of course, was a different matter.

TWO

A canopy of gold shielding them from the August sun, my father and his queen came into London in the royal barge, escorted by a vast flotilla that entirely hid the water, acclaimed by crowds lining the banks. Cannon coughed as they approached Whitehall Stairs. This was Queen Catharine's state entry into her capital: the honeymoon was formally ended.

Gossip had it that the honeymoon had ended long ago, of course. The presence of Lady Castlemaine on the terrace at Whitehall, awaiting the royal pair, seemed to confirm it.

Her husband was there also, for form's sake; but I, who was there with my grandmother, saw how they were like strangers to one another. Much warmer was Lady Castlemaine's smile when she saw me.

'How fine you look, Jemmy!' she said, coming over to embrace me: I had new clothes. She reached up to tidy her rich hair – it was breezy, and she wore no hat – and I could fancy its dark masses were as heavy as velvet in the hand. As for looking fine, I felt a mere shadow beside her. If Minette had wakened a first, innocent, boy's love in me, I know not what to call the fascination I found in Barbara Castlemaine. She was a woman who sheds sex as a candle sheds light, but I was young yet to know it as such. All I can say is that I wanted to be near her, and felt curiously anxious when I was.

'And how fine the King and Queen look – don't you think? When well dressed, you know, I believe our little Queen is as handsome as any woman in England.'

'I think she looks afraid,' I said. She had reason, in truth, for the noise of shouting and drums and guns was tremendous, and from her seat beneath the canopy it must have seemed the whole world was massing about to stare in at her. I could see my father, at his most gracious and friendly, holding her hand and talking to her, pointing out this and that; but Catharine sat so rigidly still that she might have been a captive in some Roman triumph, carried not to glory but humiliation.

'It is a pity she cannot show more animation,' Lady Castlemaine said lightly. 'People would take to her more kindly then . . . Oh, but when you know her, she is truly the most delightful creature. It is simply reserve.' She narrowed her eyes and added purringly, 'I hope people do not take against her for it.'

Well, the crisis of the Bedchamber was over. The Castlemaine, as her enemies had begun to call her, or the Lady, was to have her place at court – which meant her place in my father's life as before. This was her victory: yet won under a strange guise, for it was Queen Catharine, I heard, who mended matters by shifting her ground: supping with Lady Castlemaine, seeking her advice on English ways, and going out of her way to be friendly with her.

So I am not sure who was the victor, in truth. By accepting my father's mistress, Catharine made it unnecessary for him to choose between them. People had talked of Barbara Castlemaine as the uncrowned Queen, and that day as she looked down at the royal barge, and murmured again about its being a pity, she was I think less contented than she showed. A little later there was an accident down by the river-stairs, where a scaffold full of spectators fell down and a child took some hurt. It was Lady Castlemaine, to the sighs of her admirers, who ran down and petted the child, and I cannot help wondering now if she sought to show them how different she was from that stiff remote little doll of a queen.

At the time, of course, I sighed in admiration too. It was Lady Castlemaine who showed me the greatest attention of anybody, except my father, during that first autumn and winter I spent at the court of Whitehall.

Yes, this was to be my home. I had been lodged with my grandmother first at Greenwich and then at Somerset House, which was to be her palace for the duration of her stay in England: a long stay, it now seemed, as the people showed signs of loathing her less than before. The Earl of St Albans – bloated old Lord Jermyn as was – was with her, and she busied herself with improvements to the house; and when my father said that I was to be lodged at Whitehall, she made no demur. I noticed, though, that she gave me a cold careful look while I was excitedly packing my trunk.

'I trust you will bear yourself honourably and sensibly, Jemmy,' she said to me. 'And always remember who you are.' There could have been two meanings to that, and I was a little troubled. Not for long; I was going away from her into a new world. I promised faithfully, and kissed her.

Posterity may find the manner of living at Whitehall Palace, the seat of my father's court, as strange as I did at first, used as I was to the court of Louis of France; and it may be worth sketching it here. Picture first our great city of London, stretching – but no, the word suggests room and ease – huddling, rather, along Thames-side from St James's in the west to Wapping in the east: roof upon roof, countless, and endless chimneys smoking, and nowhere likeness to soothe the eye, for it is as if the builder of every house has looked at the house next door, and decided to make it as different as can be, and to crowd it out also, so that gable knocks against gable, like so many butting heads; and even the narrowest streets have bays thrust out into them, and rooms thrust out over them, as if to do away with the thoroughfare altogether. Steeples, many of them, stand amongst the smoke, but they too must rear themselves up in the general jostle, alongside taverns and tanneries, brew-houses and brothels. High as the steeples, see the masts of great ships downriver, seeming scarcely more able to move than the churches, such is the press of water-traffic. Now pass along the busy Strand – where the maypole lamented by my mother proudly stands again – past the great mansions of notables, to Charing Cross, and turn into King Street. Go through the Holbein Gate – you will not be alone: on foot, a-horse, in coaches, a continual stream of people pass this way, from the milkmaid with her pail atop her head to the Parliament-man in his carriage, for through the second gate up ahead is the way to Westminster, to the law courts and the Lords and Commons and the great Abbey. But do not follow them: pause here, and look around. You are already in Whitehall Palace, the mill of the state, and its wheels turn around you.

Yes – a public road runs through Whitehall: mighty strange I found it after Paris. Confusing also. I often got lost in those early days, for the palace buildings were a very warren, rambling and irregular, connected by curious passages and improbable staircases that seemed to go up six steps and then six down and yet still brought you to a different floor from where you started. It had grown up haphazardly over the years, of course, instead of being planned and devised from first principles. One did not need to have lived abroad to see it as a sad ill-proportioned place for the court of a great nation, and my father, who had known the courts of Europe at first hand, very soon expressed his dissatisfaction with it, and began improvements, whilst talking also of an entirely new palace that he would build when his purse allowed. And it was here, of course, that they had executed his father. He told me once, quietly, that he could never love the place for that reason alone.

That had happened in front of the Banqueting House, the newest and most regular portion of the whole, and the part that with its square pilastered façade struck the eye most forcibly – like a neat tea-chest amongst a lot of misshapen bottles, I always thought. It was the place for state and formality: nearby was the Council Chamber where the Privy Council met. But the true heart of my father's court was the range of buildings that overlooked the river. Here the Queen had her apartments, and likewise my uncle James; and, heart of hearts, my father's accommodations. Here was the Presence Chamber, the Privy Chamber, and the King's Bedchamber – supposedly the most private apartment of all, though my father had another room that led off it: the Closet, where he kept his collection of pictures, jewels, clocks, and mechanical devices, and where he took you when he wished to be confidential. And there were other secret rooms there, as well as the Privy Stairs going down to the river – a little world of locks and bolts patrolled by my father's servant of the Backstairs, a pursy narrow-eyed man named Chiffinch, forever rattling his great bunch of keys. If this sounds as if my father lived by enclosing secrecy within secrecy, like the skins of an onion, then that may well tell you something of his character.

However, he was far from inaccessible. I think there was never a king less remote – physically at least. Openness was the rule at Whitehall, as evinced by that road running through it. Anyone might go pretty much anywhere; the galleries that ran each side of the Privy Garden were always thronged with people – some upon business, others mere idlers and gogglers. The great ministers were lodged here too, and went about their work while others repaired to the bowling green or the tennis court: the navy lived, as it were, on the premises, in the person of Lord Sandwich, and likewise the army in General Monck. My father had paid his debt to the man who had set in train his restoration: Monck was made Duke of Albemarle now, though he never looked other than the plain buff-coated warrior. When Mr Ross first pointed him out to me, stumping along the Matted Gallery with his quid working in his weathered cheek, I realized that I had seen him before and supposed him to be a mere captain of the guard.

And so with my father: not that he ever looked less than a king to me, but his habits, so informal and approachable, always surprised the foreign ambassadors who came to Whitehall. Here were none of the grand attitudes of Louis XIV, who always looked as if he were in the process of turning into one of his own busts: my father never stopped moving. He loved to walk, and whether it was a turn about the Privy Garden or a ramble round St James's Park, he went so fast that only the hardiest courtiers could keep pace with him. He would return from the tennis court, where he played so hard a game that he drenched half a dozen towels in sweat, with the same loping speed that had taken him there. The spaniel dogs that he extravagantly loved, and that would follow at his heels even when he went to business, were in no peril of growing fat. Any man might approach and talk with him on these saunterings, as he called them, or watch him playing at bowls or pell-mell in the park. He dined regularly in public; he never forgot a name or a face, and never spoke, as the French have it, *de haut en bas*, from high to low.

He had learned, perhaps, from the doleful example of his own father, with whom no man was ever at ease. My father, I believe, loved ease better than riches. If ever there were awkwardness about him, shy stumbling or the grating of tempers, he was prompt with the balm of gracious words. It was his great skill but also, I think, his need. As for ease in its other sense – the indulgence of pleasure – there were already voices, when I first came to court, ready to accuse him of loving it too much.

A lazy king: content, now that the hardship and danger of exile was over, to while away his time with trifling pursuits and sensual appetites, with toys and women. It is a view of my father that has held fast in many quarters, and at that time there was one most influential voice to be heard stating it, often to his face.

The Chancellor, Sir Edward Hyde (the Earl of Clarendon as he now was – but one still thought of him as plain Hyde, which I dare say annoyed him) was as ubiquitous at that court as my father. He was ever to be seen waddling like a righteous duck about the corridors. I swear I saw him once go into the Presence Chamber and come out in no time at all at quite a different door – as if there were two of him. He was fat, like his daughter the Duchess of York. He had foxy-coloured hair, a round pink face, and a wisp of moustache that he seemed to have grown only at the expense of eyebrows, and he exuded a stale smell like a shut-up church. It was his habit to begin talking to you as if you were already in the middle of a conversation, and mighty strange I found it, the very first time he spoke to me. It was in the Privy Gallery, where he appeared suddenly at my side.

'And some there are who live pretty temperate all their lives,' he said, puffing, 'and yet are plagued with such hurts as if they had been the greatest of topers.'

He referred to his notorious gout, I supposed, after a startled moment, and I said that I hoped it was not very bad.

'Eh? Is what very bad?'

'Your infirmity, my lord.'

'You do me wrong, young sir, to accuse me of infirmity. A man who rises at five every day, and deals with a heap of business before breakfast, is not, I hope, to be reproached with weakness.' He had a chesty voice – a voice high as a woman's, really, which made him force it low. 'You are comfortable in your accommodation here, Master Crofts?'

I had been lodged in rooms above the Privy Gallery, and had just come from there, in a new suit of clothes – looking, no doubt, highly pleased with myself.

'I am most happily placed, I thank you, my lord.'

'Happily placed indeed,' Hyde said with a snort through his pointed nose. 'You are shown great honour, Master Crofts: uncommon honour. I hope you know it.'

All the time, as he toiled flat-footedly at my side, he did not look at me.

'Why should I not, my lord?'

'Men are apt to see as their due what is really a gift. Thus is pride born of ingratitude. This has been my observation, and I do not lack experience of the world. You have me wrong, Master Crofts, if you suppose me an innocent, quite wrong.'

Well, I did not suppose any of these things, but I found him dull, perplexing company: and seeing Mr Ross ahead, I said gladly enough, 'Pardon me, my lord, I must go to my governor.'

'So you must. Mr Ross, a man of parts, and a most active curiosity.' Hyde fluttered his doughy fingers, as if making a sketch of Mr Ross upon the air. 'And an excellent governor, no doubt. But he might govern his tongue better, Master Crofts. He might guard against irresponsible conjecture. There is not much,' he said, waddling away from me, 'that I do not hear, young sir.'

Mr Ross, typically, was unabashed when I told him what Hyde had said. His eyes gleamed. 'How very interesting! You see, of course, that my lord Hyde does not want anyone to *rise*, Master Crofts. Even to the eminence that is due to them.'

'Well, he said I should not think of things as due to me—'

'Oh, he would, he would!' Mr Ross rubbed his hands. 'Here is an excellent lesson in men's natures, my dear sir. For who has risen higher than he? The Hydes are no great family, and he was naught but a lawyer – yet by sticking fast to His Majesty, he is become Chancellor of the realm. And he has besides a family interest, he conceives, in the crown itself – with his very daughter wed to His Grace of York, and her children in line for the throne, until the Queen delivers an heir. Until – or unless.' He blinked brightly, assessingly at me. 'There are some who say – well, now, in this I only repeat the talk I have heard, Master Crofts. I hold no opinion one way or another: I am, you know, a mere observer, humankind my study. But they say how curious it is that this Queen whom Hyde chose for His Majesty should turn out to be . . . well, so unproductive. I have heard the word "barren" used, indeed. You are of an age, of course, to understand these things, Master Crofts.'

'Yes,' I said, blushing a little none the less, 'yes, I understand. But—'

'And 'tis not as if His Majesty has failed in his nuptial duties neither,' Mr Ross went on unstoppably. 'Never mind his other – association, shall we say, I have it on good authority that he has played a husband's part. Such is his admirable energy! And there can be no doubt of potency on his side. There is your honoured self as evidence of that – not to mention the Lady's late production – and then there are others—'

'I think, Mr Ross,' said I, my face hot, 'that I do not like to talk of this matter.'

'But you must get used to it, my dear young sir, assuredly you must. Because it is talked of, and will be more and more, if the Queen remains barren.'

I stared at him. I felt as though I were holding a door shut against some overwhelming power, which would soon force its way in. I shook my head. 'It is not the Queen's fault, poor lady. And I don't see how my lord Hyde can be blamed—'

'Why, he promoted the match. Now folk begin to say he deliberately chose a barren princess for His Majesty's bride. Do you see? If Queen Catharine cannot birth an heir, then the Duke of York stands next in succession for the throne. And who is the duke married to? Why, Hyde's own daughter. Most convenient. Not only has he garnered much of the power of the state, but he will be kin to monarchs. No limit to his ambition! Look at this business of Dunkirk. Protector Cromwell won it for us – whisper it, sir, but there is no doubt that under him we stood tall amongst the nations – and yet now we are selling it back to the French. Or rather, Hyde is, for it is his project. And where is the money to go? Into Hyde's purse, perhaps? Again I must remind you that I am only a sort of parrot, Master Crofts – I only voice the words.'

These were, indeed, common complaints against Edward Hyde. Now I see how absurd was the notion that Hyde could have known whether Catharine of Braganza was fertile or not. She had come virginal to our shores from a Portuguese convent; and no doctor can pronounce before the fact on whether a woman may bear children: the matter is all in the proving. Overmighty Hyde certainly was – but no magician, scrying in a glass like old Dr Dee.

Yet at the time I know my governor's words impressed my mind with a dreadful plausibility. I gazed at him as at a dark oracle. My life thus far at my father's court had been like a pageant in which I found myself wonderfully set down, and I had been content only to walk along beneath its dazzling banners. Now I glimpsed urgent and fateful workings behind the display. And the idea that they might concern me . . . That was the weight behind the door, pressing to be let in.

I said: 'Mr Ross, I should tell you that he was stern about you – the things you say—'

'To be sure he was!' exclaimed Mr Ross delightedly. 'Because I say what people are thinking!'

'You mean about me?'

'Well—' Mr Ross stopped, thinly smiling, seeming to nibble the words back. 'Let us have done with Hyde. A dull subject. Consider instead His Majesty – your father. I speak not as a parrot but in my own person when I say that he is no fool – dear me, anything but a fool. He has foresight. He does not intend, having come to his throne by such a hard road, to leave it without an heir. That I can answer for.'

Well, he was not the first nor last to make the mistake of thinking he knew my father's mind.

If I was not so certain, I was sure at least that he was fond of me, and proud of me, and meant to do well by me. And it was not simply a matter of my lodgings, where at first I could hardly bear to go to sleep because it meant closing my eyes on the damask and brocade, the gilding and carving and lacquer and ormolu; nor simply a matter of my many fine clothes, which I could not forbear changing half a dozen times a day so that my father laughed and said he must place a bet on how I would appear next; nor a matter of the beautiful bay mare I had to ride, with the queenliest neck you ever saw, and so quick to the spur you only had to think of a canter and she responded; nor the freedom with which I could come and go in the Privy Apartments, even the Bedchamber, where all but the princely few must wait on invitation. Yes, I appreciated all these things, but what truly mattered was that my father came quickly to love me as his son. And that I place above all in our relation: from that depended all, for good and ill, that happened after.

And there were people aplenty, then and since, who said he was wrong to do so. Perhaps. All I can say is that if he had not, I would have been lost. After the way I had been parted from my mother, after the wounds and tears and tangles of my passage into his care, it would have been fell destruction to have cast me aside. I had placed everything in him: this he knew, and so was kind and loving.

I know that I have turned out very imperfectly. I know I have fearful failings, and there are delinquencies in my life that I shall hardly be able to pen, as the time comes, without trembling in shame. And yet I think sometimes of how very much worse I might have been if my father had not inclined his heart to me and made me feel that I was loved.

Perhaps that is the perennial pleading of the spoiled: again, I must leave you to judge.

So I see us, in that golden time – my father and I, just as I had wanted it. I see us in his Physic Garden, where he would rub leaves between his fingers and break sappy stems, scrutinizing and sniffing, and discourse to me of the properties of seeds and herbs. This was his delight; and often he would fill my hands with his gleanings, to be taken up to his laboratory in the Privy Apartments, where he could pass hours in chymical experiments. I was always happy, of course, to join him there, but I could never quite share his eager interest in the experiments, the sulphurous flashes and gurgling retorts and slow-dripping residues. My mind, perhaps, has never been analytical. It seems to me that if you probe and probe, and divide and dissect, there will in the end be nothing left. But my father was all minute curiosity. He relished science, and the talk of men of science above all. He had given his patronage to the gentlemen of the Royal Society, and nothing pleased him better than to hear their disquisitions, or to send to their meetings his own inquiries.

'Consider, Jemmy, how curious is the case of the oyster and the pearl. Pliny, among other of the ancients, has it that the pearl is produced when raindrops fall into the oyster while it is open. Yet it is hard to see how something as pure as rain could precipitate the formation of a pearl – nor why every oyster does not therefore produce them. As for this tale of the Italian philosophers, that the shine of the pearl is made by doves pecking at it, it rests upon the same unlikelihood. 'Tis most likely, I hear, some foreign body intruding into the oyster flesh that begins the process – and so this gem we treasure is a sort of tumour or cancer to the creature that bears it. So here is a reflection for us. What is good? Is it not an entirely relative question, like a view that changes from wherever we stand?'

'I like the picture of the doves polishing the pearls, though, Father.'

'Aye, aye: fancy is always pleasing, and that is why we prefer it. But there is a savour to scientific truth, too – 'tis a sharp dry wine against a cloying sweet one. Now consider the account of Cleopatra and her pearl. You know the story? She gave Antony a great banquet, and to signify her extravagant love for him, took a pearl and dissolved it in a cup of vinegar, and drank off the draught as a pledge to her lover. Now I have consulted the learned gentlemen about this, and they are agreed that vinegar is not acid enough to dissolve something so hard as a pearl. Was it some more potent acid – and if so, how came Cleopatra to drink it without hurt? There is a tale that Sir Thomas Gresham, in old Elizabeth's time, melted a pearl and pledged it to his queen in a draught: perhaps we may come at what he used.' He chuckled. 'For my part, I would prefer any subject of mine to omit the vinegar, and just give me the pearl: Lord knows I have need of the money.'

'My mother used to say—' I stopped, for sometimes when I spoke of my mother I saw a hooded, watchful look come over his eyes; but he nodded encouragement. 'She would say that pearls lost their shine if you didn't wear them for a while. She called it growing sick – and if you put them away altogether, they died.'

'She was always a creature of imagination,' my father said after a moment. 'Well, there may be something in it: the touch of life. There is much in nature that we do not see – a whole teeming world – unless we equip ourselves with new eyes. I must show you Mr Hooke's apparatus, a most ingenious optical contrivance. Can you imagine the eye of a fly, Jemmy? Not as a mere speck like a poppy-seed, but magnified so vastly that you may behold its every facet like the pattern on a playing card? That is but one of his specimens. And I hear tell of a fellow in Holland who has studied the ignition of gunpowder under his lens, at the risk of blowing off his own head. There's the Dutch for you: damnable clever pushing set of people. They will outstrip us if we don't take care . . .'

Fascinating indeed was the realm of the tiny I saw through Mr Hooke's apparatus, and likewise the vastness that assailed the eye through my father's astronomical tube, of which he was as possessively fond as many men of a blood mare, yet I could not repress a thrill of horror also at what they seemed to tell me of the world. Again I suppose my baffled thought was, when we had viewed the delicate tracery of a frog's lungs and mapped the furthest stars, what then? What remained of joy and mystery? My mother in me, I surmise. I recalled my father telling us, years ago, of the great book anatomizing the surface of the moon, all jagged peaks and gouged caverns, and how my mother had said it sounded ugly. Now his great wish was to have a globe of the moon, exact in all its delineations as the terrestrial globe in his closet.

'We have grown used to calling the moon feminine – because the ancients called it so, I suppose: Diana and Cynthia and so forth. But the Danes and the Germans, I hear, have the moon as male. Perhaps northern women are of a different sort, for on my soul I always thought the moon female because it is so infernally changeable . . . And of course, it's none of these things, but a great mineral accretion, and it doesn't change at all. Only the way we see it changes. Knowledge has made fools of the ancients; and to be sure, it may make fools of us in future ages. 'Tis all in where you stand, Jemmy. Take a fixed position, and you will never see all round the matter.'

I thought of Minette dancing, light and unearthly, in the ballet of Diana; I thought of the Comte de Guiche with his sad beauty, telling me about the chaste goddess and the death of Actaeon; I thought of those scented nights of treacherous beauty by the lake at Fontainebleau, where it seemed the high-strung fancy needed only to be tuned up a very little more for dryads and nymphs to become visible in the encircling woods. Here was a division between me and my father: I preferred Diana to the lump of mineral. It is, I hold, not a lie but a different sort of truth.

But there was no discord in this division. My father was all for men holding their own opinions. He was as little of a dogmatist as it is possible for a king to be. The notion of men quarrelling because they held different ideas was to him a painful absurdity, and he was already mired in troubles with the Parliament over his liking for religious toleration. It may be that this was a lack in him: he could not conceive of anyone believing something very strongly, because he himself believed strongly in nothing. Others have gone further, and said he was so tolerant because he had no principles. All I can say is that my young soul was able to breathe and grow in that ample room he gave me. And I felt that room physically contract, like the slamming down of bars and shutters, whenever my uncle James joined us.

It seemed to happen increasingly often, when I was enjoying my father's company, whether in his laboratory or the Bedchamber or walking by the aviaries he had set up in the park. Whatever we were talking of, it was James's way to close the subject with a few heavy words. He did not so much nip talk in the bud as prune it, lop it, and seal the stump of it with tar. Not for him the pleasures of speculation.

'We have the authority of scripture on these matters, surely,' he would say. 'There is no further call for remark.'

'Ah, but there is naught in scripture to say we should not employ the brains God gave us,' my father answered. 'It is a curious question why the egg of the ant should be larger than the ant—'

'We gain nothing by these inquiries,' James said, 'unless they be of some practical purpose. And on that subject, Charles, I would speak with you on this matter of the West African trade. There are new reports.'

'Aye, by and by, brother. Come, never tell me you have no faculty of curiosity? Call it idle curiosity if you will, though I always mislike that phrase.'

'So I must call it, Charles, pardon me.'

'So? But what else could move you to such marked attention to Mistress Middleton last evening, James, if not curiosity?' My father clapped my uncle's arm, which gave such an unyielding effect that my father seemed to wince as if he had slapped a marble statue. 'Was that not the pure spirit of discovery? The adventurous mind, seeking to know whether she be as fair beneath the bodice as she appears above it? I should be interested, by the by, to know the results of your researches.'

'This is not a thing to speak of with the boy here,' James said with a glance at me; but his handsome head waggled also, as it did when he was pleased with himself, for he was getting a name at court as a great pursuer of women. At balls the Duchess of York would follow his wandering progress with her great fishy eyes. She was pained, I think, yet she knew he must come back to her, just as if she had him on the end of a long thread. She was strong, whereas he was only hard. He had besides a curious taste in conquest: it was said at court that no ugly or stupid woman was safe from him. 'Nor, in truth, is the West African business, sir, and so I crave we may speak alone.'

'Eh? What, d'you suppose Jemmy a Dutch spy?' my father said, laughing.

'No, brother, I don't suppose that at all,' said James solemnly: never was a man so slow to a jest. 'That is not what I mean. But I would speak with you, privately.'

Oh, I know what he meant: who was I to have aught to do with royal councils? At the time I felt only a slight chill and, being still desirous of pleasing everyone, was quite prepared to go out of the way.

'Well, it can wait, surely,' my father said.

'I think not. It is a pressing matter.'

'Everything is!' said my father with a laugh. 'If I were to attend to every pressing matter, I should be squeezed flat like a flower in a book. We shall talk of it in council, James.'

'Certainly. Yet I would speak with you now.' He was like a man hammering in a nail, and finding it going in crooked, hammering harder instead of plucking it out. And yet I never saw my father lose patience with him. Telling me once about the time the Scots had abortively crowned him at Scone, before Worcester and the flight, my father remarked that the most miserable touch to a miserable occasion had been a soldier parading about the stony church in sackcloth and ashes. 'Imagine it!' he laughed. 'If that is pleasing to God, then I must be a heathen.' Yet I wonder sometimes whether James was not my father's equivalent of sackcloth and ashes.

Well, no such penitential garb for me: I was a young popinjay, and loved it. I even had a man to wait on me, and help me into my clothes, though I was curiously shy of him at first, and would hurry to shift for myself rather than give him the trouble. Of appearing in public, however, I had no shyness, even when I knew every eye was on me. Such were my first visits to the theatre with my father. Everyone would peer up at the royal box, not only to get a glimpse of the sovereign, but to see how things went – for the theatre was, aptly enough, often the place Lady Castlemaine chose to stake her claim with my father. She would paint and dress herself most extravagantly, with a display of snowy bosom that made men transfixed and stupid. She would tap my father with her fan, commune with him behind it, loudly commend this player or that. Her great husky laugh was the first to ring out at a witty piece of business on the stage. She appeared, in a word, queenly. And never more so than when the real Queen was present. Not that that was frequent, for Queen Catharine was out of her element there, and though her English steadily improved, I could see that many of the speeches were lost on her.

But then I too was a little taken aback by what I found at the London theatre, which was the favourite resort of the town in those years. After my experience of Louis's France, I expected grandeur, loftiness, decorum upon the stage. There had been, of course, no plays at all during the time of Cromwell, who had laid a ban on all such entertainments, and one of my father's first acts on his restoration had been to give patents to theatre companies: one in his name, one in the Duke of York's. My father dearly loved a play – comedy chiefly: he said he did not want to go the theatre and be made miserable. Likewise he loved to see women acting, a thing he had grown accustomed to during the exile abroad, but which then was entirely new in England, where youths had always played the female parts. Here then was an added novelty to draw people to the playhouses, novel in themselves – my father's company, after making shift in a tennis court, moved to a building new-made for the purpose at Drury Lane, and nothing had been seen like it before.

After Fontainebleau, I could not call it impressive. Yet to step into the theatre was certainly to step into a vivid little world, by turns amusing, startling and alarming – and by that I do not mean only the traffic of the stage. That was colourful enough: the stately masques of Louis's court would never have done here, where vulgar jigs and comic songs mixed with thunderous declamation, daggers and sheep's blood with plumes and high heels, pretty sentiment with cold jests about cuckoldry and doses of pox. But you did not go just for the play. There was the theatre of the theatre, as it were; even more fascinating.

It always felt as if you had somehow moved outside time, for while the play began at three in the afternoon, there was a peculiar light in the theatre, a compound of daylight from the cupola and the glow of the chandeliers over the stage, which felt like no time of day that ever was. Then there was the noise, and the heat, and the smell, which seemed to unite into a single assault on the senses – something like a warm stinking roar, laced with the scent of orange-peel. No one was still, except perhaps the solider citizens in the galleries, stiffly determined not to turn their necks no matter how the gallants catcalled or the courtesans in the pit preened and fussed and broke into little tigerish fights – I remember seeing one pluck all the patches from her rival's face, chew them up in her mouth, and spit them back at her. There were others who wore vizard masks. It was court ladies who began it, I fancy, but the women of the town took it up also. It was remarked by wits and moralists alike that there was no telling the whores from the ladies any more. And that says much, I think, about that little world within the theatre walls. High and low, nobles in their boxes and orange-sellers prowling the aisles, looked at each other as in a glass. What they saw, perhaps, was the cheapness of their own urges and desires. Certainly that was the kind of reflection to amuse my father, whose taste was all for the wry. The stiff-necked citizens were in the right of it, of course: the theatre was the place for intrigue and assignation. The air was rank with it, unmistakably even to my boyish senses. Indeed, my rest was often troubled, as it had been by those naked Arcadians in the Fontainebleau salons, by images of the actresses at Drury Lane, which lingered long after the performance. Far more earthly and earthy, though, were these tantalizing visions. There was a fashion in the theatre for 'breeches parts' – in other words, the drama would often call upon the actress to disguise herself as a man, at least as far as donning drawers and stockings. Thus were shapely legs revealed, admired, whistled at. And as the rest of the costume was often a smock that showed every inch of bosom, nothing less masculine, or more titillating, could be imagined.

There were actresses who were virtuous, I am sure, but those one did not hear of. All the talk was of who was enjoying their favours. The young bucks in the pit hurried to the tiring rooms after the play. Sometimes they would loudly talk of their conquests during the play itself. I recall one who, in the midst of an affecting speech from a pretty tragedienne that had quieted even that audience, stood up and clapped his hands together once. 'I am returning a favour, my dear,' he cried to the girl. 'That is for the *clap* you gave me.'

Everyone yelled in delight, of course: this was nothing out of the common. It was the way things were then. Even if my father had been as solemn a figure as his own father, the manners of the time might still have exhibited such freedom – or licentiousness, whichever you prefer. Men's spirits were marked by the years of war and exile and religious ferment. Yet if he did not altogether set the tone, there is no doubt that he and the tone were one. There could be no fuller emblem of the times than my father coolly smiling in the gilded royal box above the seething playhouse, his beautiful mistress at his side.

And often at his side also were men active in the theatre itself. There was Thomas Killigrew, the licensee of Drury Lane. He had been a faithful companion to my father during the exile, and was now made Groom of the Bedchamber. He ate hugely, venerated the memory of

Charles I almost as much as my grandmother, and turned out plays by the yards. Sometimes he would try out the bawdiest lines on my father, and the pair of them would chuckle like schoolboys. There was William D'Avenant, who ran the Duke of York's Theatre at Lincoln's Inn, and always claimed to be the natural son of Shakespeare. He was forever falling into an attitude, finger pressed to forehead, as if posterity were taking his portrait. And then there was Buckingham, who was not only at the play every day – and, it was said, at the actresses likewise – but turned his hand to play-writing. Very naturally – for I think that capricious man acted his own life.

Others there were who dabbled in the theatre as they dabbled in satires and scandals, in verses and vices: young men and wild, whom my father liked to have about him for their wit. Chancellor Hyde was much displeased with this set, partly because he always sat a moral high horse, but more particularly because they formed a sort of frivolous fence about the King that made it hard for Hyde to get to him. And Hyde, of course, with his pompous airs and his stale whiff of parchment and sealing wax, was the perennial butt of their jests. My father himself came in for some, but never seemed to mind it – which I, with the holiness of youth, could not understand.

'I can forgive a man anything if he amuses me,' he said.

'But if they say sly things behind your back—'

'Odsfish, I should be mightily surprised if they didn't. Indeed, I would think something must be amiss. If a man shows his duplicity, I am obliged to him. He has saved me some trouble, for otherwise I would have had to look for it.'

Conspicuous among this circle were two youthful rakes, Lord Buck-hurst and Sir Charles Sedley, who were often partners in the most extravagant exploits that restless minds could devise. Lord Buckhurst was an idle, pretty, wenching fellow who took life more lightly than any man I have ever known. He smiled upon the world as if it were a dream or game, or anything but what it is. Sedley, short, button-eyed and pudgy, seemed little formed to be a rake, yet his nimble mind and tongue won him as many conquests as his crony, and they were reputed to share their mistresses occasionally. A famous frolic of theirs was at a tavern in Covent Garden called Oxford Kate's, where after prodigies of drinking they climbed to the balcony, stark naked, and preached a filthy mock sermon to the crowd who came to gape. One version has it that they concluded the service by pissing down upon their hearers. I know not if that part is true: the delight of the town in those days was not just the debauchery, but the recounting of it in tales that grew more fantastically embellished with each telling.

Then, as now, there were many who deplored my father's choice of companions such as these. Had he consorted with a different circle, they say, he would have had a better view of the world. What they forget is that my father at this time, though little past thirty, had had a comprehensive experience of the world. Every quadrant of fortune's wheel was known to him. And it had already given him a view – a fixed one, and a dark. I think he liked the company of rakehells and scurrilous wits because they confirmed what he believed about the human lot – and that, I avow, was as bleak as ever man held. Behind the raillery and laughter was the abyss, and I do not blame him if he chose not to send himself mad by staring into it.

Still, I did not feel comfortable with these men, and I think that was not just my youth. My mind has never been able to flit like that. There is something dogged about it and, I suppose, dull. I remember supping with my father and some of his friends after the theatre once, and hearing someone tell a jest of a citizen and his wife at the play. When they came out, the goodwife found that her purse had been stolen. Her husband, recollecting a fellow who had sat next to her, asked whether she had not felt a hand creeping into her skirts. 'Oh, yes!' answered she. 'But I didn't suppose it was that he sought.' This was a tale to tickle a boy's humour, and I laughed much, but Sedley pronounced it low and stale.

'Besides, no man of sense would venture thus upon a citizen's wife. He would come away with a handful of cobwebs, or else a trap would snap on his fingers. Your mercantile clods are as careful of their women as their money, and they would keep a cunt in a strongbox if they might.'

'Now there would be a challenge,' said Lord Buckhurst dreamily. ''Tis like Danae locked in her tower of brass. You know the tale, young Jemmy? Zeus came to her in a shower of gold.'

'And she got wonderfully wet. A pretty myth,' Sedley said, 'but the one that has always enchanted me is that of Leda and the swan. That was Zeus again, my boy, ravishing a lady in another of his curious disguises – and surely the most unlikely. Did the woman not find anything strange about a swan suddenly paying her such attentions? In truth this question has so exercised me that I resolved to try an experiment on it. Aye, sire, those learned chemists of yours are not the only ones with inquiring minds. Here then was my test. You recall our sweet Betty, my lord?'

'Ah!' Lord Buckhurst sighed. ' "Chestnut-maned Betty, whom all the town fucks." That was a mean verse, whoever penned it. I hope it wasn't me.'

'Well, Betty was reserving her favours for me at the time. And so I selected her as my Leda. Now as to procuring a swan, there I feared poaching on Your Majesty's preserves, and so I must needs make do with a live duck from the poulterer's. So, I came early to Betty's lodging, and let myself in as was my wont – come and go as you please was Betty's watchword, though in truth there was more coming than going. In I go to her chamber, where the nymph lies sleeping in sweet disarray. Gently I lift the bedclothes, thrust the duck under them, and stand by to make my observation. Will Betty wake all graceful unsurprise, like Leda in the pictures, or will she go into a screaming fit at her feathered bedmate? Ah, I was mistaken in my estimation of Betty. She did neither. I know you are a connoisseur of fowl, Your Majesty, so I will be delicate and not distress you. Suffice it to say that Betty, feeling the duck's agitations down below, reached down with her practised hand, still half-asleep, and murmured, "My dear one, don't dilly-dally; in, in at once," – and so it was: the wench had the duck by the neck and encompassed him in a trice. The poor creature was suffocated, though I vow 'twas an admirable way to die.'

'Admirable!' agreed Lord Buckhurst. 'But you surprise me, Sedley. I had always supposed Betty no great housewife, and yet you see she knew well how to stuff a bird.'

'Just so; and though she was a little mortified when she awoke to the true case, I hastened to assure her it was a pardonable error.'

'Aye – she had mistaken it for the morning cock, which always roused her.'

'You did not dine upon the duck after, I hope,' my father said.

'No, no: I gave him a decent burial – a hero's funeral, if you will; for where he died, after all, a hundred men will come after him.'

'Pay these wretches no heed, Jemmy,' my father said to me. 'They are idle, and must talk nonsense for want of occupation.'

'Aye, but loyal, sire,' Lord Buckhurst said, 'for do we not make the sovereign our model?'

'Do you likewise, young sir,' Sedley addressed me, 'and you'll not go far wrong.'

'I hope I shall be like my father in everything,' said I, very solemn, for I hazily felt that something of value was being mocked, though I could not have said what.

'In everything, eh? Fine sentiment, young sir, very fine.'

Obscurely I felt my words had been read as empty flattery, and I flared a little. 'It is not just sentiment – it is my aim, my one aim.' Looking back at my young self hotly protesting to those lolling too-clever men, I wonder, was this the beginning of a pattern that was to flourish later, with results that make me cringe with shame? For I know that later times were to see me, not without some justice, called a vain braggart, a man who would quarrel with his own shadow. (I have also been called, by the by, a cunning Machiavel ruled by ambition, a thoughtless straw-in-the-wind, and a congenital idiot. I leave it to the reader to determine, not whether I was any of these, but whether I could possibly be all of them at once.) But what made me insistent was simply the fact that I had to be. I had no fixed and secure place in that world; I had no place or title that would have made my words heeded; and in such a position, a man will shout to be heard.

And I see here too the beginning of a long joust of frustration with my baffling father. Witness his response to what Sedley said next.

'Your one aim, eh, young sir? Fine again. I'd be wary of airing it before the Duke of York, mind.'

'Why, what nonsense is this?' my father said, frowning, yet smiling.

'Only, sire, that your brother has similar aims. He wishes to be like you in all ways – even to the wearing of the crown.'

My father's smile was thin now, but he was quite in possession of himself. 'James has nothing to fear from anyone, as he well knows. All will proceed with due form. The Throne is not so secure that we can afford to play at musical chairs with it. But whoever is thinking or talking of these things, 'tis wholly unseasonable. I am young, and much may happen – of my choosing and out of it.'

'You mean there is happy news from the Queen, sire?' someone put in excitedly.

'No, no. But that may come to pass. Also other things. Who can foretell the future?' And his eyes dwelled on me with brooding affection – or speculation? Precisely what, I could not tell. Hence the frustration. And then he turned the subject, and proposed a game of cards. He was an expert player, my father, and no man ever held the cards closer to his chest.

Barbara Castlemaine enjoyed the company of the wits too – after all, her cousin and confidant, Buckingham, was their crown prince – but part of the reason I liked her was that she shielded me from them. If ever they turned their blades lightly on me, or teased my young brains with things I could not understand, she called them to order. 'Pay them no heed, Jemmy,' she would say, threading my arm through hers. 'I do not, any more than the chatter of magpies.' And I was glad of that, for I heard them say some wicked things about her behind her back.

When I say that I was much in Lady Castlemaine's company, and also in Queen Catharine's, you may swiftly conclude that I was in search of a mother. Perhaps – but I think in truth I simply wanted to be friends with everybody. And I had yet to learn the impossibility of that, at my father's court. For all the apparent friendliness between the Lady and the Queen, I was really passing between two armed camps.

Alas, I found the Queen's the duller of the two. From living with my grandmother, I was used to that doleful air, redolent of incense and priests' habits, that permeated Queen Catharine's chambers. More trying to my young spirits was that playing-card stiffness that the Queen had yet to lose. Aptly enough, it was to games at cards that she most frequently invited me. This was kind, and I was happy to accept. Probably I had some consciousness that she found it politic to befriend me, because my father loved me, but I didn't mind that. Nor did I mind the tea she always served: I got used to the strange beverage. But it was the dreariness of sitting there amidst her begowned waiting-women, as if we were caught in a palisade of choking velvet; the effort of penetrating her prickles of shyness and incomprehension and awkwardness. This last, especially, led me to the injustice of thinking her rude. For often I would find her gazing, or staring, straight at me, in such a way that even my burgeoning vanity could not find a reason for.

Stupid of me, of course. There was increasing talk of her barrenness; here was I, a living emblem of her failure. More, perhaps. She was there to produce an heir: that was her purpose. She may have already begun to wonder what my purpose was, and whether it was to render her superfluous.

But, unreflecting animal that I was, I cried: 'I wish the Queen would not stare so!' when Lady Castlemaine had me to sup in her apartments. These were much more to my taste, furnished with every luxury. The Lady moved amongst gilt and silk and saw her sultry beauty multiplied in a hundred silver reflections. This was my father's bounty: people were talking of that too.

'No wonder in that, my dear – Lord knows you're handsome enough,' Lady Castlemaine said, pouring me wine with her own hands. 'But come, I'm sure she doesn't spend all her time staring. What do you talk of?'

'Oh, nothing very much.'

'You don't want to tell me,' she said looking at me with a sad smile. 'I fear that means it is I who is talked of – and not kindly. But I don't mind it!'

'No, no—'

'Then you talk of His Majesty, perhaps, and being a loyal son, you don't wish to speak of it to me. Never mind again – drink your wine, Jemmy dear. Nay, it is true I am shut out from these things. I have enemies, as you know, who would see me shut out altogether. But I confess it seems unfair, when His Majesty's own new babe – your half-brother – sleeps in the nursery next door. I think I have a claim, you know, not to be treated as a stranger of no account. Some might say I am entitled to as much consideration as the Queen. But if you don't think so, Jemmy, then I say again, never mind.'

'Oh, but that's not what I think!' I cried anxiously and, of course, racked my brains to think of something the Queen had talked of. There was only the great frost, which was then beginning. She had seen people skating on the ice in St James's Park, a thing entirely new to her, and said she had a fancy to try it, though the King had warned her it was not safe . . .

'Safe, what does that mean?' Lady Castlemaine said pouncingly. 'Are you sure that was what was said? Safe for her particularly, now, what?'

'I don't know. I think the ice is only just formed, and not bearing, so—'

'Why, what should he care if she falls on her little fucking narrow dried-up nun's arse? Is she so important to him?' When Lady Castlemaine flashed into viciousness like this, it was so sudden, and so swiftly over, that only afterwards did the mind take it in, and wonder if it had really happened. ''Tis a treacherous sport, though: he's in the right of it. I would not venture till it is thoroughly hard – when the river freezes. That's a pretty sight – when they set a fair upon the Thames. Well, I take it kindly that you are frank with me, Jemmy. I know it is not easy. No doubt my lord Chancellor—' she gave me a droll, sly look, and puffed out her cheeks – 'warns you most direfully against me as an evil influence.'

'Oh, I don't think he likes me overmuch.'

Her violet eyes, slanted like a cat's, widened. 'I'm sure I cannot see why – so charming a youth. Oh, but of course I *can* see why. Charles loves you and would bring you on, and that don't suit Hyde's hand. All his desire is to raise up that fat milch-cow daughter of his, and he will bring down any who stand in his way. All very shocking, is it not? These designs. And you simply a handsome boy who loves his father – what should you have to do with them? But there is no one they will not make a tool or weapon of, Jemmy, trust me.'

I thought this kind of her. I was going to pursue the subject, when my father walked in.

He did not expect to see me there, and was not pleased. That was plain from his face even before he spoke. But when he did, it was with his usual temperance.

'Well, we are merrily met. Forgive my gaping a little – it must be my mistake. Not that I don't appreciate your showing Jemmy the attention, Barbara, but I could have sworn on my honour that it was I you asked to sup here tonight.'

'Oh, my dear, is it so?' The Lady said, tapping her lips with the prongs of a fork – she was prompt to follow all the new French fashions. 'Yet we were in such a disagreement, I truly supposed you would not care to come. And as I did not relish supping alone—'

'What disagreement is this?'

'Pretty in you to forget it, when I have not had a moment's easiness!

Well, let us not talk of it, as your mind is made up. Jemmy, I have syllabubs, made with the freshest of milk – will you have them brought in? Jellies too—'

'Oh, I have you.' My father came forward with a look on his face that I soon came to know: a sardonic absence of surprise. It was the look he wore when people behaved badly, like a man greeting an old disreputable friend. 'Now, let's see, what was the request? Something for you, or for one of your associates? Ah, yes, the Yorkshire heiress who must have a husband, and you know the very man.'

'So I do, Charles, and an excellent gentleman as I told you, but you would not listen. If you would just manage the matter, he would be entirely grateful, and ever ready to serve you—'

'And even more grateful to you, of course. The fact that he has already buried one wife, and spent her fortune, is by the by.'

'Oh, come, Charles, have you been dining with the Quakers that you should turn so moral? But there, if you don't choose to oblige me, there is naught I can do. Jemmy, did you ever try one of these? They are peaches, grown under glass. Most succulent. Here, my dear – we'll take turn about.' She bit into the tender fruit, smiling, and then held it towards me. Juice trickled down her white fingers.

'Well, well,' my father said, with a little impatient twitch in his cheek, 'let it be so, Barbara. I shall oblige you. But have a care, my dear. People will say I can refuse you nothing.'

'People!' she cried, with a gasp of laughter. 'Besides, why should you want to refuse me?' She put the moist peach to my lips. 'Do you mean to say you get nothing in return?'

Well, she was not long in packing me off after that, and my father, though he gave me some kind words, could not disguise that he wanted me gone also, so he might be alone with her. That was the point. Perhaps Barbara Castlemaine did play a mother's part to me after all, for she had used me as a means of influencing my father, though more skilfully than my poor mother ever knew how.

And yet I did not feel myself used. I was, God knows, sensitive enough to slights, but I remained warmly attached to Lady Castlemaine. Those who set her down as a greedy shameless virago are not perhaps inaccurate, but they diminish her. They leave out the vitality that came from her like the hot wave from an opened stove. And she was too passionate a creature to be forever calculating. At least sometimes, I am sure, she saw me as a boy as well as an instrument, and then she could be vastly entertaining. I remember her demonstrating to me, when no one was about, how to slide down a banister. She did it with the most regal grace, seated as if side-saddle, and with a book balanced on her head to show how little she wobbled.

I dare say it was this gamesome spirit, when I was in her apartments one evening, that made her hide me behind a curtain when my father came calling unexpectedly. We heard his voice call her name in the outer room, and springing up and laying her finger to my lips, she whispered that it would be a merry jest to conceal me, that I might jump out and surprise him.

Well, I dare say she meant no harm, and cannot have known the mood that would be on him. But he had been meeting with the Parliament that afternoon, as I knew, and I saw it writ upon his face as I peeped out at the side of the curtain. There was always a strained, strung-up look as of a dog that has had no run all day. Singly, my father could persuade any man to anything, but he hated to face people in the mass: somehow it dwindled him. When I first saw him address the Commons I was reminded of a candle in daylight.

So, with this oppression of spirit on him, he had come to see his beautiful mistress, and it was plain that he had no interest in the wine she offered him, nor food, nor talk. His impatience did not even permit a removal to the bedchamber. So I supposed, back then: now I think Lady Castlemaine, who did not lack will, might well have led him to another room if she had chosen. But she did not, and so in some strange sort she must have wanted me to witness that fierce coupling that had her yelping delighted curses in moments. Scarce breathing, my eyes round and burning, I beheld my father bare-rumped, her lifted skirts around him like the flower around the bee.

What should I have done? If I had stayed there behind the curtain, I must have been discovered at last, unless I were inhumanly still and silent. But I did not even think in such rational terms. I simply had to bolt – to be out of there, away from that sight that so disturbed me – or frightened me. Indeed, I had no name for the emotion I felt, which was what made it unbearable.

So, bolt I did. I ran to the door, meaning to keep my face averted. And yet I looked, and saw my father's flushed face turning startled, his body still thrusting as he met my eyes.

I took refuge in my own chambers, and there hid my face in pillows, and cursed softly, in a bottomless wretchedness. I wished I had never gone to Lady Castlemaine's apartments; I wished I had not seen. Of course I knew what went on, as did the whole Court. There was no revelation. Any of my father's cronies would have slapped my shoulder, laughed heartily, and said it would be a fine tale to tell when I was older. But I could not take it lightly. I was bewildered, most of all by my own sense of shame, as if I were a thief or miscreant hiding from his guilt.

I am not sure whether I expected my father to seek me out, nor what my reaction would have been if he had. But he did not come, and I soon found my own miserable company oppressive. I did not know who I wanted, though – not Mr Ross, not my grandmother, certainly not the young pages of the court with whom I fenced and rode, and who loved to talk smut. It came to me all at once who I wanted to see, and I did not seek for the reasons. I went straight to the Queen's apartments.

Catharine was having her hair dressed – she did her best to emulate court fashions, though simplicity suited her well – but she welcomed me kindly, and I was content to sit by her, and have such simple talk as her English would allow. It felt as if I was in the presence of healing, somehow. It was like her to notice that I was pale and distracted, and to ask in her sweet low voice if I was sick. I said no: she did not press, but she put up her gentle hand to push the sweat-damp hair from my brow, and said I must be sure and take care of myself.

I stayed long with her, but when one of her ladies came to say the King was on his way to pay his respects, I fled. I dreaded a summons to supper that evening, from Lady Castlemaine or my father, so I slipped out, and moped about St James's Park, all in the bright frost. I was alone in a world of silver, almost soundless but for the stealthy noises of nature, the faint grinding crackle of ice hardening on the canal, the scratchy communion of leafless twigs. Still I had a sensation of being watched, and traced it to the sky, where I met the slitted white gaze of the moon, the goddess, huntress, implacable.

The next day my father touched for the king's evil.

Urged by Mr Ross, I went to the Banqueting Hall to watch. Though one of my father's first acts on his restoration had been to resume this ancient ceremony, I had not yet seen it, and Mr Ross was eager that I witness so potent a demonstration of the mystery of monarchy.

I still could not banish the memory of that other potent demonstration, and Mr Ross chided me for my sulky humour. Still, nothing could have more effectively restored my father's majestical place in my esteem than the sight that met my eyes in the Banqueting Hall, where he sat in the chair of state beneath the royal arms, his chaplains standing beside with bibles open before them, and leading up to the dais a great murmurous shuffling line of the afflicted.

The belief that the touch of an anointed king may cure the disease of scrofula – the king's evil – goes back, they say, to Edward the Confessor, and it still holds much credit not only among simple people, but amongst physicians. Certainly I think no king ever maintained the custom so thoroughly as my father, who touched several times a year, receiving hundreds of sufferers on each occasion. It was no pretty task – the disease makes sad disfigurements upon the face and neck – and might have had a grim absurdity about it. Yet when I first saw it that day, I was moved – moved in such a profound sort, that I think the impression has never left my heart. The long patient file of people, all ages and conditions, ragged and fine, men hobbling on sticks and babes in arms; the kindly dignity with which my father laid his hands upon their faces, as they kneeled before him; the wondering look in their eyes as they came away, clutching the little coin, the touchpiece, that was given to them to close the ceremony.

This, I thought, was something important. It almost seemed as if my whole life, from the time Mr O'Neill had found me and told me of my father the King, had been gathering itself towards this moment, this scene. Coming as it did after that horrible farce in Lady Castlemaine's chambers, it made the tears stand in my eyes. I stood as if pierced and torn. It would be too simple to say that I had seen the worst of my father and now saw the best, but the emotion that shook me had something of poles and extremes about it – a presentiment that the world was altogether too much for me, and that I would be tossed to pieces on its dizzy seas unless he held and steadied me.

Yet I still shrank from speaking with him. After the touching was done, I would have crept away, but he sent a servant to say he wanted me to dine with him. 'It is His Majesty's command,' the servant said; and so I must obey.

It was one of his days for public dining, in that same Banqueting Hall. Now, instead of the solemn ranks of supplicants, there was the usual crowd of gapers in the gallery to watch the King at his meat. The Queen joined us at table, where, like everyone else, I stood with bowed head till she and my father were seated. The Duke of York was there also, and would have taken the chair by my father, I saw, if my father had not beckoned me thither first.

'Can I help you to some of this fish, Jemmy?' my father said to me. 'Don't fear – you may be sure I have washed my hands most thoroughly.'

And he smiled, but I would not or could not. Across the table I saw my uncle, having pinned me with a long pale-eyed look, begin eating in his methodical passionless way, as if everything from capers to sugar-plums tasted exactly alike to him.

'Some of those poor wretches had a long wait of it today,' my father said. 'There was one woman at the back so heavy with child I feared I would have to play midwife as well as quack-salver.' He looked at my face. 'You know the term? Hedge-doctor. Mountebank, charlatan, what you will.'

'Aye, I know.' I was surprised at how bitterly my voice was shaken from me. 'But what do you mean, Father? Don't you believe in touching for the evil?'

'Why, you have just seen me do it, Jemmy. And I make sure to do it as often as possible, and always will.'

'But that isn't—' My voice was shrill now: his eyebrows went up. 'I thought you must believe that it works – that it cures people.'

'Oh, as to that, there is no telling what secrets nature may hold. We can only judge by likelihood. If a man has an operation for the stone, and the stone is cut away, the strong likelihood is that the pain of the stone will be gone: 'tis evidential. If a king touches a child with scrofula, it may be that the scrofula will heal, but there is naught evidential about it.'

I stared at him. He looked blandly back. He did not believe in the touch, I was sure of it.

'If you have no faith in what you're doing,' I said, 'then that is – that is like cheating the people. You are a cheat.'

I had never used such disrespect before. But, of course, this was not just a matter of touching for the evil. This was the poison of yesterday coming out, as my father saw.

'Well, now we are getting to it,' he said with a faint sigh. 'Jemmy, do you recall what I said about black and white?'

'Yes, sir. I recall many things you have said – and they are very pretty – but I never know which you mean, or what to believe—'

'Oh Lord, then you are in the same boat with the rest of humankind. That is the world, Jemmy, and you had better get used to it. If you seek perfection, you will have a long looking.'

I was like my mother, I fear: hating it when he gave me this rationality, which felt like a cool handshake.

'The people expect me to touch for the evil,' he went on, 'for it is what they expect of a king. Therefore I make sure to do it. My feelings are naught pertaining to the matter. Nor, I think, are you much concerned with it, Jemmy: you are angry with me because of yesterday.'

My face flamed at once, but my father went on calmly eating as if he spoke only of a disputed game of cards.

'I may as well say that if there was mischief on my Lady Castlemaine's part, I disapprove it,' he said. 'Beyond that, I can only add that I am what I am, and no amount of sullens can change it. And also that twenty years ago, in this very land, you might have seen men blowing each other's limbs off with cannon-shot. I saw it. You would be surprised at how high the blood fountains, and how long a man can live, screaming, while it pumps out. If I could see that, and live with it, then consider how much easier is your case.'

His voice was sombre, even stern, but at the close he gave me such a smile as even my smarting stubbornness could not resist. It was his most relaxed, genial, crafty smile. When you saw it, it always seemed that the world altered a little: tragedy was dispelled, life like a dark garment was suddenly turned inside out to reveal a lighter hue. At last I was able to smile in return, for the first time, it seemed, in a horrible age.

'Brother,' came my uncle James's voice, 'what is the jest? Will you share the merriment?'

'Oh, it is a jest against myself, James,' my father said easily, 'and those, you know, I never share.'

My uncle grunted. Throughout the meal his eyes kept fixing on me, seated at my father's right hand. That he did not approve of this was plain, though in truth James's expression was always vaguely affronted, like that of a man who suspects someone close by him has let fly a fart.

But of course, everyone noticed these attentions of my father's, and had an opinion on them. I know that Chancellor Hyde did, because soon after I walked in upon them in the Privy Chambers, arguing about me.

'Jemmy may lack something in polish yet, but he promises well, and that pleases me. I do not see why I may not express my pleasure.'

My father's voice. Hearing my name from the anteroom, I froze.

'Because by raising him to such an eminence, you will turn the boy's head.' Hyde. 'Not to mention others.'

'Will I, my lord? And how do you know this?'

'Because it is palpable to any man of sense and reflection. Such, sire, I had supposed you on a fair road to becoming.'

'I thank you, my lord. If I have failed in my lesson, I am sure it is not for want of schoolmastering. But pray, who are these others you speak of?'

'Sire, if you paid more heed to business, and less to diversion, you would better understand the way the wind blows. Already men who should know better are looking at the lad, and the favour you show him, and allowing the wildest conjecture to flourish.'

'Indeed? I rather like wild conjectures. Name them, my lord, and the men.'

'It would ill become the first servant of the state to turn tattle-tale—'

'Humour me.' My father's voice was hard.

'Well, then, my lord of Buckingham has been heard to remark that you show the boy as proud an affection as if he were your legitimate issue. Even that he inclines to the rumour that you were secretly married to the boy's mother.'

There was a silence. I held my breath.

'Whence come these rumours, I wonder?' my father said at last, and his voice was light again.

'Who can say? The boy's governor has an overbusy tongue. But I would not be surprised if Buckingham himself were their author. The man is an intriguer.'

'Which means you do not love him and he does not love you. Oh, come, my lord, that is no secret. As for rumour, we may as easily banish that from the court as take the stink from a turd: they go together.'

Hyde gave a disdainful snort. 'Rumour is dangerous. It can take on a life of its own. Even rumour of an outrageous sort – which not all are. Some have grounds, however tenuous. I hope, sir, that if there were aught of that kind – a rumour with substance – you would see fit to tell me.'

I could hear a watchfulness in his tone, the words narrowing like eyes. But my father's gave nothing away – nothing.

'You may be sure, my lord, that you always have my entirest trust,' he said smoothly. 'And that is why I am dismayed to find you making much of this matter. I seek to honour my son, and there's an end on it.'

'It has not occurred to you that he won't thank you for it?'

A little laugh. 'It has not occurred to me, because Jemmy is a most affectionate and well-disposed lad.'

'Aye, aye, now he may be. But to heap honours on one so young and inexperienced is to spoil him for a surety. Once you've done it, he will want more, and more. And, at last, may want something you cannot give him.'

I was lucky in the Chancellor's gout, which made his rising from his chair a long and loudly audible process, and gave me time to hurry away, my heart pounding wildly, in concert with my thoughts.

Honours. Whatever they were, my father did not speak of them yet. And I did not press him. I knew him somewhat by now – as much as any man knew him. I knew that wilful dislike of being told what was good for him. If Hyde lectured him against promoting me, he might well say that he was going to simply out of devilment.

Still, simply for the Chancellor to be my enemy was significant. With shock, I found myself a piece on that crowded chessboard of court. Certainly no more than a pawn, though; and it did not occur to me that pawns may advance to the last square, and be transformed, and dominate the board. Not yet.

The Comte de Guiche's prophecy came true: I sat for my portrait. My grandmother came to view the work one day, and paled as she looked at the canvas. '*Ma foi*, it is just like Charles's picture at that age,' she murmured, and she fixed me with a hard look, as if I had tricked her somehow. Lady Castlemaine came too, and shook her head, and said I would soon be breaking hearts. 'Perhaps my own among them!' she said lightly. Since that terrible day in her apartments, she had been more circumspect with me, but not in the least embarrassed. And sometimes, at public occasions like the theatre, I would feel her hand gently caressing the back of my hair, or tickling my hand – even when she was not sitting very close to me – as if her arm were long and sinuous like a snake.

But I think I must go forward, and set before you the great ball held in the Banqueting Hall upon the last night of the year 1662. I remember that night vividly for several reasons.

First for its beauty. This was a youthful Court, and even its plainest members could look fine in the golden haze of candlelight, in their richest clothes and their hair new-dressed. Everything shone: silk, satin, jewels, glasses, silver, eyes. Even the music, of the best French viols, seemed to shine to the ear. For my part I could hardly resist its lilt from the moment I entered the room. My feet were forever twitching and skipping, though I had other reasons for that.

Beneath the beauty, darkness – yes; though perhaps that is always there. But I remember it, the seductive darkness of doubt, intrigue, speculation. In amongst the tripping twirling figures stalked a figure made of this darkness, touching a naked shoulder here, a ribboned lovelock there: call it Talk. It had no formal function at my father's court, it was no privy councilman or groom of the bedchamber, but there was no doubting that Talk had power there.

For the first dances, the stately ones, my father led out the Duchess of York. And Talk still made much of her, fat old Hyde's fat daughter who had snared the King's brother and aimed to see the issue of her ample loins wear crowns. I danced with Lady Castlemaine, to Talk's delight, for the Lady was Talk's especial favourite, of course, what with her diamonds, her temper, her delicious wickedness. She was intensely hated and also intensely admired. Men would buy copies of her portrait, hang them in their closets, and then – I suppose – daydream. Above all, Barbara Castlemaine was the victor, the woman who led my father by the nose or, as it was more frequently expressed, by the prick. Hers the paramount influence, she the one to approach if you sought place or favour. She had quite vanquished Queen Catharine – that quiet dignified lady, with her dusky look of always being half in shadow, who did not dance much. Talk wondered about that, briefly – could it be that she was pregnant at last? – for that was Talk's great concern with Catharine. Talk was forever counting her menses and assessing her belly. But in fact the Queen did not know the steps of these dances, least of all the English country dances that my father called for.

'Let us have that finest dance of old England,' he cried to the musicians, ' "Cuckolds All-a-row"!'

Much laughter at that: for was this not a court of cuckolds, as Talk well knew, and my father the king of cuckold-makers?

Three ambassadors of Russia had lately arrived at the court, bearing outlandish gifts of furs and hawks, their English rudimentary as their manners were formal; and I had heard the Duke of Buckingham talking to one of them of the customs we observed.

'It is usual here, sir, as a mark of polite attention, to commend a gentleman upon his whoring and fucking: a lady likewise, as long as she be married; and the customary greeting upon state occasions is "Good fucking".'

The Russian repeated gravely. 'For-king.'

'Aye, sir, just so. In truth we lay the emphasis on the first syllable – but I'm not sure yours isn't the better way after all. Yes, when you say fucking, emphasise the *king*.'

And Buckingham was at the ball too – everywhere at once, all restless wolfish charm; another favourite of Talk's, who had him intriguing with Lady Castlemaine against the Chancellor they both loathed. No dancing for Hyde, naturally: indeed, he was hardly able to stand this evening, his gouty foot propped on a stool, his pouchy eyes darting sourly about the room – like a man who must watch a doting relative's spoiled little children run rude riot about him, impotent to scold them. Here also, for a wonder, was Buckingham's duchess, a homely lady married for her money, and no doubt knowing it: helplessly in love with her faithless lord, perhaps – who knows what accommodations the soul may not come to? It was my uncle James who danced with her, but then, as Talk would have it, he was used to plain women. Did he see her at all, though? For James's gaze seemed always fixed on something in the middle distance. Not for him drink, finery, or gaming, or pictures, books, beauty. Even his infidelities seemed no more than the absent sniffings and piddlings of a plodding dog pursuing a trail. Talk had an answer, of course: my uncle's eyes were fixed on the crown, his thoughts on whether he would get it, and what he would make of it. He was a competent but curiously graceless dancer, my uncle: so handsome and well-made as he was, it was almost perplexing to see his clumsiness – as if nature had somehow not finished him.

Finished, though, most beautifully finished, was the young woman whom my father led out for the country dances. This was Frances Stewart, with whom I had shared the stormy passage to England, and compared vomitings. Her beauty had flowered, and now it dazzled. As her name suggested, she was distant kin to the royal family. She was as comfortable at court as if it were her own parlour, and serenely happy as long as she could build her card-houses, play with her kitten, and always locate at any moment a mirror to admire her elegant fairness in. Talk could not make up its mind about la Belle Stewart, as she came to be called. She was a star in the ascendant, but she seemed also to be the most stupid young lady ever to ply a fan. Seemed – for I have always wondered whether her apparent imbecility was not a cloak for the utmost cleverness. There was much merriment about her habit of showing her legs. They were reputed the shapeliest in England, and a man only had to dispute it for Frances to lift her silken skirts and reveal them, with an innocent cry of 'But are they not? Look well, I pray you, and judge.' Men were smitten by this, especially worldly men, like Buckingham who pursued her along with his other quarry, which ranged from whores to actors. And no one was more worldly than my father. Talk had it that Frances Stewart had dazzled his eyes to blindness – even that he was in love with her. But Talk could only say that with a sort of grimace. Love, and my father – could they ever go together? It was not long before I would begin to wonder about that.

And me – did that rippling shadow Talk hover about me on that enchanted night of year's dying? No doubt. I was too happy to notice it; but there is no doubt, Talk was as interested in me as anyone.

For my father had revealed to me, a little while before, some at least of his plans. I am conscious of setting many names before you, but I must trouble you with two more. One is James Scott, Duke of Monmouth, Earl of Buccleuch and Doncaster, Baron Tynedale (the mouthful is all one person). The other is Anna Scott, Countess of Buccleuch. She was present at that ball: a girl of only eleven, flame-haired and thin as a sapling, but trim and self-possessed withal. This girl was to be my wife. The Duke of Monmouth was to be me, or I was to be he. My father had told me so, shortly before, and of course Talk had got hold of it.

Marriage: a dukedom. No wonder that Talk, having swallowed and digested these, should begin nibbling at the question of what next, and whether my father was going to make me the heir to the throne.

THREE

I was married to Anna Scott on Tuesday the twentieth of April 1663. This was the first thing my father did for which I still cannot forgive him.

She was twelve; I fourteen. When he had first introduced me to her at court, I paid scant heed – what had I to do with little girls? And when he had told me that I was to marry her, I thought for a moment it was one of those gamey jests that he and his friends enjoyed.

The girl herself seemed much more comfortable with the whole business. I found out later that my father had first proposed the match two years since – even before I came to England. Anna Scott was used to the notion. And she was very practical.

'I have, I reckon, about four or five years' growing yet,' she said, looking up at me critically. 'You, perhaps two or three. So I shall catch up to a fair degree. Then we shall look better assorted.'

This talk of years perplexed me. Was this the end of my youth and hope – to be harnessed to this strange creature? That sounds ungallant, but she was freckly and gawky then, with a way of looking at me as if she were peeping round the edge of a screen. And she had a fantastical garrulous mother: the Countess of Wemyss, who was very Scottish, incomprehensibly so when excited, and had a red nose and the kind of raw bony elbows and knuckles that are like red noses transposed, and she would gabble her gratitude and loyalty to my father whenever he was within ten feet of her. Perhaps I had already imbibed that sour male wisdom about girls growing up like their mothers. In fact Anna grew up to be quite a beauty. Not that that mattered, in the end.

My father was amused at my reluctance.

'Anyone would think I was sending you to the galleys,' he said, 'instead of matching you with an excellent bride.'

'I don't think I want a bride, Father. I'm very well as I am.'

'Ah, but you're not, Jemmy. I am owning you as my son, and my son must have more in life than a set of chambers and a waiting-man.'

Here was the point of it. The marriage was to endow me. Anna Scott was heiress in her own right to the Scottish Earldom of Buccleuch. Marrying her would give me riches and estates, as well as her title. With mixed feelings I learned that I was to take her name, and become James Scott, though I dare say I minded that less than other men might, having had so many names. It was partly, I think to reconcile me to this, that my father insisted on a further title, one created for me alone – Duke of Monmouth. That did please me, as much as it displeased Chancellor Hyde.

A dukedom, he protested, was too much. It fixed me on the borders of royalty. It was unwarranted, imprudent, ill-judged, and so on. The trouble was, Hyde used this language so much that one ceased to hear it. He had made a profession, even a personality, out of being right. That was wearisome; I know my father found it so. And of course, in all such questions he was handicapped by his daughter's marriage to James. When he prated of the good of the state, people smirked, and whispered that what he really meant was his own interests.

'Of course he does not like to see you advanced,' Mr Ross told me. 'He would have his kin stand near the throne – no other.'

'But I am— ' I hesitated – 'I am not near the throne.'

'Are you not, my lord?' cried Mr Ross, all a-twinkle. (My ducal title had been conferred in February, but I am sure Mr Ross was my-lording me before then, to my great embarrassment – and when he used 'Your Grace', I could hardly bear it.) 'Well, not yet, perhaps. But His Majesty does naught without a reason, my lord, believe me. This Scottish business, now – folk should take more heed of that, for upon my soul there's meaning in it!'

I thought he meant my marrying, of which I could hardly speak without cringing, and would have dismissed the subject. But no: what he referred to was an investigation into the archives of Scottish law that my father had commanded, to see whether there was a precedent for a king legitimizing an illegitimate son.

English law did not allow of it, that was certain, and the Scottish quest proved fruitless. But the mere fact of its being undertaken was important, as Mr Ross hinted. How he had heard of it I'm not sure. He cultivated Edward Prodgers, the man who had spirited me away from my mother, and who was now a confidential agent of the Bedchamber, entrusted with many shadowy enterprises. (Some called him my father's pimp – as if he needed one.) It may have come from there. Certainly my father did not speak of it to me, and when I taxed him with it, he was cryptic.

'Hm, that? Call it a whim. Some of our statutes are most curiously framed, and one hardly knows what to make of them. Not all, mind. There is the statute of dear dreadful old Henry "against buggery". They minced no words when he was King.'

But I would not be put off. It was time, I decided, to be plain; time to raise that question that had haunted me ever since my last meeting with my mother in the Paris wine shop.

'Making a son legitimate,' I said. 'So that means the son must be illegitimate in the first place.'

'Aye, aye, so,' my father said absently. We were in the Privy Garden, where he had had a handsome sundial set up. He studied it, then his pocket-chronometer: always this fascination with time.

'Then am I?' I said. 'Am I not your legitimate son, Father?' My mouth was dry. The spring sun struck full in my eyes, giving me a headache. These great questions of our lives, I observe, seem never to be posed or settled with the proper preparation and ceremony. The world is awkward to them: our stomachs growl as we declare our love, and we make a great decision in between tying laces.

He frowned. 'Who has been talking to you?'

I shrugged in irritation. 'It needs no one to talk to me of these matters. Don't you see they are ever on my mind?'

'Dry stuff to be a-thinking on, Jemmy. You should be enjoying life at your age.'

I stared at him, and with a feeling of digging in my heels said: 'You and my mother were married. That is what she told me.'

He adjusted his pocket-chronometer, put it to his ear, and stowed it away.

'She told you so, eh? And did you believe her?'

I had to: there was no choice. It was the only way of keeping faith

with her memory . . . These thoughts went through me like a swift
lance, but I could not explain them to my father. And besides, his
coolness angered me.

'Why should I not believe her, Father? Why would she say such a
thing, if it were not true?'

His eyebrow lifted. 'You are passionate, Jemmy.'

'Yes – why is that always such a bad thing?'

'If you have to ask, you'll never know.' Then he sighed, and said, 'Ah,
Lucy, Lucy . . .' almost as if my mother stood by us in the flesh. 'Did you
believe everything she told you, Jemmy?'

I clenched my fists. 'Are you saying she lied?'

'I fear she did lie, quite often,' he said temperately.

'I mean' – I struggled to control myself, for I knew he might
simply walk away if I did not – 'I mean about you and she being
married.'

'Lucy and I were never married, Jemmy,' my father said, almost
casually. 'If she called herself my wife, she had no right to do so. And
now let that be the end of the matter.'

Well, she had said he might choose to deny it. I gazed at him, trying to
read him. I was not the first, or last, to try getting at the truth behind
that splendid mask, that benign darkness.

'You doubt my word?' he said.

I could not speak.

'Well, good,' he said with a soft laugh. 'Excellent. It's good you should
learn to doubt people.' He urged me to walk with him. 'Tell me, Jemmy,
why this should matter to you.'

'I do not like the title of bastard,' I said stiffly.

'Oh, there are worse. But if that's all it is, then I am pleased. If you
were so anxious after legitimacy from mere ambition – for the crown –
then I fear we should fall out.'

The crown? I did not think of the crown then. Believe me or not, as
you like.

'I only want to know where I stand, Father. I feel – I feel the ground is
ever moving beneath my feet—'

'So it is. The earth is turning. That is worth remembering: we talk of
solid ground, but in truth there is no such thing in existence. I love you
much, Jemmy.' He did not look at me. 'Better, I think, than anyone. I

have great hopes for you. And the greatest is, that my love will be enough.'

So, once again, I was left not knowing what to think. Mr Ross saw my confusion. If the rumour of my father and mother's being married had begun to float about the court, I fancy it may have come from him. But when I told him of my father's flat denial, he was unconcerned.

'His Majesty is sagacious. Ah, people see only that manner, that charming negligence – but there is a most admirable cunning mind!'

'You mean he is lying, sir?'

'Let us not talk in those terms. Let us look at the facts of the case. His Majesty has made a fine kingly marriage to Portugal – but a marriage that has hitherto failed of its prime purpose: to furnish an heir to the throne. If it continue so, the apparent heir must be His Majesty's brother, the Duke of York – a man not everywhere approved, and nowhere esteemed for his judgement. Now His Majesty publicly owns you as his son, and lifts you to an estate little short of princely. This is a careful husbandman, planting a tree or crop. Careful, aye, that's the word. For he still must consider Queen Catharine, Jemmy – my lord, I should say, I crave your pardon. The Queen may yet produce an heir, though it seems unlikely. To acknowledge *you* in that role so soon would be to demolish the Queen's position, and make enemies of her friends. His Majesty is both too gentle-spirited, and too wise, to do that. Be assured, my lord, your father knows what he is about.'

I was comforted, somewhat; and should not have been, perhaps. It is, I well know, my failing to be impressible – to believe what people tell me, in other words. My father once said I was like a pillow – always bearing the mark of the last person I was with. Perhaps it is because I have ever lacked confidence in my own judgement. Perhaps if my father had given me certainties, I would not have run to others in the hope of finding them.

Well, to my marriage. A strange day! I commenced it by being copiously sick. I was afraid. There had been sly jokes from some of my father's companions, about bedsheets and maidenheads and such. Seeing me green and shaking, my father was quick to reassure me that the wedding was a form: being so young, we would not have to do anything that belonged to a union of adults. I was to think nothing of it, he said cheerfully.

But this I could not do. He was wanting me to be, in essence, like him – able to seal off the feelings in a compartment. I tried, but still they spilled over. There was some pride and curiosity, as well as wretchedness and apprehension, but altogether the mixture made me thoroughly discomfited as I stood in my father's chapel at Whitehall in my wedding clothes, scarcely able to look at the little girl by my side.

She, though, was composed. Her responses, in her piping Scots lilt, fairly rang round the chapel, whilst mine could scarcely be heard. And at the end it seemed she darted at me, from behind her sidelong screen, a look of reproach that I had not borne myself better.

The marriage feast was held at the house of my bride's stepfather, Lord Wemyss, in the Strand. Very grand it was: my father and Queen Catharine there, and my grandmother, and my uncle James and his duchess, and Lady Castlemaine – most of the Court, indeed. And here pride did begin to vanquish discomfort. For while I had been present at court occasions, this was different: I was the occasion. As for my little wife, I still hardly knew what to say to her – not that it signified much, for she was quite at ease talking with everyone there, from the Duchess of York, whose bulbous eyes looked her up and down and up again while her lips pretended a smile, to my father himself, who delighted in her, saying she had more wit than all his Council put together. And then there was dancing. Here, I found, was something Anna and I both loved, and we exchanged our first tentative smiles as we footed it. Buckingham, roaring drunk, said that as we danced so well together, it boded well for other sports, and made a lewd mime, but Lady Castlemaine hushed him. She was most warm in her congratulations to me, and made sure to kiss me with everyone looking on, saying lightly to Anna that she would steal this last one while she might.

'Lady Castlemaine is very beautiful and fine,' Anna said to me as we walked out to dance again, 'and it is a pity she is so great a whore.'

I don't know why I was so shocked at something everyone said: that frosty precise Scots voice, perhaps; that level-headedness. If she had blushed and giggled, I would have been more at home.

'Lady Castlemaine has a high position at court,' I said with hazy gallantry.

'Aye, a whore's position.'

'You should not talk so.'

'Nonsense. Everyone knows this. I hope you are not silly, Jemmy. I am quite pleased to marry you, all in all. You are very handsome, and I think we will have a grand way of living, but I'd rather you were not silly.'

'Indeed, I am not silly,' said I – sounding, I fear, as silly as could be.

'Good. I hope so, for you and I are to lie abed together tonight, which will be queer, and it will make it worse if you are silly.'

Lie abed! All my murky fears returned. I looked at my father, who was dancing with Frances Stewart: had he misled me?

Going to a privy, I was sick again. Coming out, I found my grandmother there. She had been pained and pokerish all evening, but festivities always brought that out in her – as if, by enjoying themselves, people were cavorting on her martyred husband's grave – and she was sharp-eyed as ever. She demanded to know what was amiss with me. Scarlet, I told her.

'*Ma foi*, child, is that all? It is just a ceremony. Why, your aunt Mary, God have mercy on her soul, went through the same when she was younger than you – just nine she was, when Dutch William came over to marry her. Ha, I can see it now! We all crowded into the chamber, the Dutch ambassadors and all, to see them put abed together. All that was required was for their legs to touch – and here was a problem. Poor Mary's nightgown reached right to her ankles. And so my dwarf, Hudson, fetched some shears, and made a cut in it – how we laughed! And then they lay a quarter of an hour in the state bed, pretty dears, and then the prince came away.' She chuckled, as I could not – it seemed all grotesque and horrible – but there was always this flavour of old barbarous times about my grandmother. 'Hey, well! If you are to be this great personage, Jemmy, you must get used to such things, you know.'

All at once her tone and look were acid, and I said weakly, 'You wish me well, Grandmother – don't you?'

She made an open-handed gesture. 'I am fond of you, Jemmy, still. I think there is such a thing as being too fond, and I fear your father has it. Perhaps I am at fault too: I indulged you. Aye, I wish you well. You are my grandson, after all. But James is my son. I hope you will always remember your duty to him. And to the Queen.'

Well, here was a reminder – which perhaps I needed – that not everyone rejoiced at my promotion.

My uncle James, though, gave no sign of displeasure. He was as heavily correct as ever, shaking my hand and congratulating me in his mechanical way. Queen Catharine, while courteous, did not appear happy. Just how unhappy she was, I discovered later.

In the meantime there was the bedding to be got through. It was only about twice as excruciating as I thought.

In our nightshirts Anna and I lay side by side in a great bed, and at my father's urging – for he came in to witness it, along with my grandmother and my uncle and the Countess of Wemyss – I held my wife's thin cold hand, kissed her cheek, and then shifted my bare leg so that it touched hers. After a moment I felt, with surprising pain, her little sharp toenails dig into the flesh of my leg, but that might have been by accident. The Countess of Wemyss went into garbled raptures, my father was genial with everyone, and at last, to my intense relief, I could rise from the bed and go to a chamber of my own.

Such was my wedding night.

Three days after it came another ceremony: one that, boy as I still was, appealed much more to my taste.

I was installed as a Knight of the Garter at Windsor Castle. My hatchments, my banner and escutcheon, hung in the Chapel of St George, alongside those of great princes of Europe. In an atmosphere of ancient chivalry, dreadfully impressive to my young and romantic spirit, I swore my oath in a far firmer voice than I had conjured for my wedding vows. And here I was taken notice of, to my great pleasure, by my father's cousin, Prince Rupert of the Rhine.

To a little Cavalier such as I had been, Rupert's name was as fabled as that of Arthur or Lancelot. Of all who had fought for the royal cause in the Civil Wars, he wore the brightest sheen of glory and heroism – though there were many innocent countrymen who had stood in the way of his troops that had ample cause, I fear, to give him that other name of Prince Robber. He was a man of past forty now. The years of the exile, when he had sailed a privateer ship, had given him a sallow complexion and a hard glittering eye; the beautiful youth of story was gone, and I confess I was a little afraid of him. He loved war, and talked to me of it – though not of dashing cavalry charges, as I had hoped, but of mines and fortifications, in dry detail. It was as if he dreamed of a war without people, all science. My father, though courteous as ever, did not really care for Rupert. I flatter myself that he was a little jealous of his cousin's attention to me. And all of this, you may be sure, made my head mighty big.

After the ceremony came a great ball in the evening, and here something happened that, small in itself, like a pebble dropped into a pool, sent out ripples far beyond its scope, and soon had all the Court talking.

At the ball I was conscious that Queen Catharine looked low and out of sorts again. I had sense enough to realize that this was probably because of me – because of the honours that my father was heaping on me, child of a former love, and standing reproach to her barrenness. If there was a breach, I wanted to repair it, and was young and vain enough to suppose that with goodwill and charm I could do so.

Thus I went to the Queen, and with my prettiest gallantry invited her to the dance. And I was rewarded, just as when I had first sent her a smile at Greenwich. The cloud lifted from her brow as she took my hand and walked out to the floor with me.

'Now, you must not to make jealous your new wife, Jemmy,' she said, in her sweet fluting voice. I wished that my new wife had such a voice, though not as much as I wished I had no wife at all.

I danced with my hat in my hand – the correct form, for this was my queen, just as every subject must uncover his head in the King's presence. My father had a meeting with a Quaker once, whose religion forbade him to doff his hat to anyone, and so my father took off his own, saying with a laugh that it was the custom for one man to be uncovered in the presence of the sovereign. That is the essence of my father that I love to remember.

And yes, I love to remember what happened at Windsor as I danced with Queen Catharine, fateful though it was. For my father came up to me smiling, embraced me and kissed my cheek, and said, 'Come, my dear son, no need for that. Clap that hat upon your head, my boy.'

Beaming, he watched me do so. Everyone watched: movement stilled about the room, froze. There were gasps.

My father signalled to the musicians. I finished my dance with the Queen, my hat on my head, but now she would not meet my eyes, and when I gave my final bow she had already turned on her heel and was stalking away.

What did my father mean by it?

This question, on everyone's lips, troubled others more than me. I took it, joyfully, as an instance of his great love for me. Here I was perhaps foolish. As my father had said, the court was a page that people scrutinized for meaning. And to command me to go covered in the Queen's presence could only mean one thing – that my father saw me as a prince of the royal blood.

My uncle James, they said, was going around with a face like thunder. I did not notice that – in truth, I never saw any but gloomy weather on his face anyhow. But such was the talk, according to Mr Ross – that my father, whether meaning it or not, had administered a rap across James's knuckles. And there were some who said that was no bad thing: that the duke carried his authority very high, that he presumed too much upon his standing next in line to my father's throne. I had seen for myself how officious James was in telling my father how to manage his own business – and I knew how very little, of all things, my father liked to be told that. If they had any words on the matter, I did not hear of them, and my uncle showed no overt change towards me. But then the processes of his mind were always wintry-slow: he would not blaze into hatred so much as freeze into it.

What did flare up – and greatly I regret it still – was a quarrel between my father and the Queen. Lady Castlemaine told me of it.

'It is all a great pity,' she sighed, 'for I had hoped, indeed, that Her Majesty was learning to bear a better temper at last. For she can be passionate, poor creature. 'Tis her weakness. Lord knows, I've done my best to commend her to discretion, and I declare the King has used great patience with her. I cannot think he was pleased to hear her say such things, of you whom he dotes on so,'

'Why – what did she say?'

'Oh! I know not the whole of it. But I can swear that she told him if he owned you as his true son, she would never see his face more. She would go back to Portugal straightway.' Lady Castlemaine gave a hard laugh. 'Ah, never mind that, Jemmy dear! When first she came here, and was so set upon making an enemy of me, she was threatening that ten times a day. The jest was she kept a servant whose sole occupation was packing and unpacking her bags. I don't know as it might be better if she did go – being so mopish and unhappy here, and doing no one any good – but there, I for one should miss her fearfully. I would not, as some would, have her gone.'

There, I think, the Lady actually spoke true in spite of herself. For Catharine was after all the best sort of rival – one she could beat. The Queen could never hold sway over my father's passions as Barbara Castlemaine did. She lacked the flamboyance of sex; she was too genuine, perhaps. And so Lady Castlemaine had her victory there. But another force was entering the field, and the Lady could be seen arming herself to combat it, in ever richer jewels and silks and scents.

The new arrival was Frances Stewart, to whom my father was beginning to pay a marked attention. Not that Lady Castlemaine was at loggerheads with that delicious doll-eyed girl. Her strategy was to make friends with her. Rumour even had it that she invited Frances to her bed. No doubt I should have drawn some conclusions about Lady Castlemaine's friendliness to me from that – but I was still very green.

And my chief desire was to mend matters with Queen Catharine. I felt sick at the idea of her disliking and resenting me (I always do, still, with anyone – I know that is folly). I was desperate to speak to her privately, above all when her ladies were not by. So I sought her out at her chapel, where she took Mass every day.

I waited at the back. A priest came along, and said I should kneel, but I said I could not. All this – the Latin, the incense, the dramatic supplication – struck so alien to my heart here in England. Probably it made me stare. For when Queen Catharine came out, gliding in her swift shadowy way so that she was near me before I knew it, she looked bitterly into my face and said, 'Please, sir, this is my faith. Do not make mock of it as well as me.'

She was gone before I could answer.

It is a common enough error to suppose ourselves at the centre of the world.

Look in a mirror – even in a crowded room, does not your mind, like an apt painter, place your figure at the centre of the composition? Men resisted when Signor Galileo placed the sun, not the earth, at the centre of the universe – a matter my father loved to talk of. Their sense of self was affronted. In truth, we are told, the earth is one of many bodies circling the sun. We lie insignificant on the margins of vastness.

But who can be happy to know such things? Indeed, I am not sure the error is an error. We have only our own eyes to look out of, and can know none but our own soul, and the world only matters as it converges upon us, like the spokes closing upon the hub of a wheel.

Queen Catharine, in the summer that followed, spent much time at the spas of Tunbridge Wells and Bath, taking the waters, in the hope that they would help her to conceive. Hence what I have just said: it was surely natural to conclude that I was the occasion of this. Oh, there was pressure on her from all quarters, of course, to prove herself capable of bearing an heir. The whole country gossiped about the Queen's barrenness, and how the stability of the Crown was endangered by it. Then there was the contrasting fecundity of Lady Castlemaine, who was lately brought to bed again of a fine boy, her third child by my father. He loved to visit the babes in the Lady's nursery at night, and though he tried to be discreet about it, it surely came to the poor Queen's ears. Still, my presence must have been the great goad and spur to her. For here I was, an acknowledged son of the King, in everything his darling, lacking only one thing – legitimacy. And people were beginning to say that my father would not be making so much of me if he were not preparing to declare me of legitimate birth, or confer it on me – somehow.

All they waited for, as I did, was a clear sign. In vain.

And here I have a potent recollection of my father leaving his box at the theatre, and how people would look to him to see how he liked the play. How often they were mistaken! Seeing his narrowed eyes and curved lips, they would say they quite agreed with His Majesty, the play was a wretched worthless piece, and then find that he had delighted in it – or the other way about. There was never any telling. Did he even change what he thought, just to catch them out? That too is possible.

But I was sure that with me, at least, he was his true self: genial, open, tolerant – a man in whom I could repose my trust. I felt I was special in this. And so I found I could bear the uncertainty, the unknowing. He would – he must – do right by me in the end.

And whether that might mean making me the heir to the throne of England – well, I find it hard to pinpoint the moment when that shifted in my mind from a wild dream to a palpable possibility. You have heard much of my obscure beginnings – more than I have ever spoken to anyone: my humble days when a crown would have seemed to me the furthest reach of fantasy. I have been at pains to set those early days before you in detail, because they are little known, whereas much of my subsequent life was enacted in the eye of public fame. And it will surely seem to you that that shoeless wretch of the Brussels streets must have felt such a revolution in his heart and mind at this new prospect as can hardly have been accommodated without his head quite turning. I suppose it was so. Yet I have long remarked how incrementally our expectations grow. Luxury soon puts on the garb of necessity. A man may never have kept a saddle-horse in his life, but let him come to fortune, so that he keeps two, and you will soon hear him proclaim that he could not possibly manage with just one.

In the meantime, my easiness with my father, who was my constant and warmest friend and companion, was matched by my uneasiness with Queen Catharine. And I half wished that she might be delivered of a child, if that would make things better – though for me it might make things very different.

Then, when she came back to Whitehall after the spas, rumour began that the Queen was with child. She was sickly and kept to her apartments. Physicians went back and forth. That poor lady's womb was always so much the subject of common talk, that I do not know yet if she had conceived on that occasion, or whether the first signs of the fever she had contracted were mistook. If there was a child, she must have lost it early, as she began to sink. Soon it was known that the Queen was very low and weak, and could not leave her bed.

The first time I heard how serious it was, I was coming from playing at bowls with old General Monck's son, Christopher, with whom I had begun to be good friends, and as I went through the Matted Gallery, I fell to my usual temptation of leaping up to try to touch the arched rafters above. Today I heard a cough behind me, and found Chancellor Hyde, all pinched reproof.

'Aye, well might you leap,' he huffed. 'The Queen, young sir, is dying. And you leap. Well, 'tis apt. I am disappointed rather than surprised.'

Dying! This could not be. I sought out my father. He was in the Queen's Bedchamber with her, and not to be disturbed. There were long faces and doleful whispers. (Some cheerful faces too, of course, alight with speculation.) My uncle James was closely questioning one of the physicians. I hung about.

'Great pain, Your Grace, and high fever. The poisonous humours of the fever must be drawn out, that is the first task.'

'Pain where? Does she bleed?'

'There is, ahem, at present no bleeding.'

'But there has been?' That was the Duchess of York, who interposed her impatient bulk like a cow shoving open a gate.

'Ma'am, I was only called in this morning. My observations have not been exhaustive. Now, if you will pardon me . . .'

I touched my uncle's arm. 'Uncle,' I said, 'I have only just heard – how does the Queen?'

James faced me stiffly. I felt he would have turned with the same ponderous unsurprise if I had jumped at him in a dark alley.

'Jemmy, how d'you do? Yes, the Queen is in a poorly way. It is a most troublous circumstance. Everyone must feel it so. Our prayers—'

'We are talking, sir,' the duchess said to me with a glare, cutting him off, 'and you interrupt us.'

'Aye, best go out of the way, Jemmy,' my uncle said. 'You can do no good here.' And their stares followed me away.

My little wife had been made one of the Queen's Bedchamber ladies, and though she had been largely kept away for fear of infection, she was able to tell me a little more. The Queen was in a continual sweat of pain, she said, and lately had begun to ramble in delirium. The physicians had tried everything to draw off the fever, bleeding and blistering her and even setting to her feet the breasts of new-slaughtered pigeons, but she grew worse.

'His Majesty is always with her,' Anna told me, 'at least, until night-time. Then he goes to sup with Lady Castlemaine.' She gave me a bright, birdy look. 'He must have his rest, of course.'

That evening I went to Lady Castlemaine's apartments. The Duke of Buckingham was lounging there, his boots up, eating a dish of cream.

'I only say if she *should* die—'

'Enough, George. I'm tired of talking of it,' Lady Castlemaine said. 'Lord, anyone would think she was the first woman ever to take sick! Young sir, I hope *you* haven't come to talk to me of Her Majesty. If you have, I warn you, I shall have no patience.'

She looked as if she had none already. The whites of her eyes flashed, and the noise of her breathing seemed to fill the room. I hesitated, for I had indeed come looking for news.

'I only say, coz, that if she does die, there will be many to suggest that His Majesty take a new wife as soon as may be. The little Queen has not been a successful experiment. Folk will look for better results next time.' Buckingham winked. 'It may be a blessing.'

'You cold creature!' Lady Castlemaine said absently, which set him laughing.

'Oh, to be sure, and you are all warmth, Barbara, of course. What about when you said – now what was it? – if the Portuguese bitch should fall off a cliff, you would dance naked for joy on the palace roof?'

'I did not know Her Majesty then,' she said, looking evilly at him.

'And now you are all concern for her. Hey, well, let us just consider the painful prospect, Barbara. You know there will not be voices lacking to advance Mistress Stewart as a bride.'

'Your voice, you mean.'

'Ah, I have my duties, as Charles's true friend and counsellor, and I must point out her suitability – her youth and beauty, her good birth—'

'And her stupidity. Which is why she always listens to you. Come, George, you know you only seek to make a tool of her. And I fancy there is pique as well as ambition – because she would not have aught to do with *your* tool, ain't it, my dear?'

'Well, there is another thing in her favour,' Buckingham said, dabbing his moustache. 'She has proved most resolutely unfuckable. Charles has had his eye on her for months – yet I swear it has been no more than an eye, which is a wonder. Mistress Stewart is most damnably chaste – do you know that word, by the by, coz? And contrary to appearance, she's no fool. She values her maidenhead and means to get the best price for it. And that is a commodity you threw away ages ago, Barbara. Pity, isn't it? If the Queen dies, and throws the marriage market open, you'll be hard put to sell your damaged goods.'

Lady Castlemaine snatched up the cream dish and broke it over his head with a great swipe. Such violence often has something of farce about it – but she was dire and deft and meant to hurt. Buckingham tried to laugh, but he went out with black looks. I wondered if this was one of

Lady Castlemaine's famous rages, though I had seen nothing yet.

'Talk nicely to me, Jemmy, I pray you,' the Lady said when he had gone, smoothing her hands across her flushed cheeks, her eyes still roaming and flashing. 'That – that great booby has quite discommoded me with his nonsense. And he has taken that cream I meant for your father's supper. Dear, what a mess . . . !

Haltingly I tried to talk of other matters – of my late riding and hunting with my uncle James, of the entertainment I had been given by the University at Cambridge – but she seemed not listening, and when a servant-maid cleared up the mess of cream, she screamed at the girl to hurry, and give her no saucy looks. I grew more uneasy, and would have left, but for my hope that my father would soon come, so I could ask after the Queen. But as time passed, with Lady Castlemaine pacing and glaring at the clock, it became at last plain that my father was not coming here tonight.

'Curious!' she said, turning very still, and dully smiling at a spot above my head. 'Very curious, this!'

I said – most ill-advisedly – that he was surely staying with the Queen.

Then I saw the rage in earnest. It was in all ways extravagant – there must have been several hundred pounds worth of crystal glass scattered across the floor before she was done – and fabulously, even imaginatively obscene. My father could plant his faithless prick in that rotting Portuguese corpse all night if he liked, he would find it no different from when she was alive, if anything better, he might feel the worms stirring in her mildewy cunt and suppose the frigid bitch had warmed at last. And so on. The rage was also indiscriminate as a whirlwind. It caught me up. I was a little pert jackanapes who need not think to come here putting on my airs, as she knew my mother had been the greatest whore in Christendom, as my father was the greatest whoremaster . . .

Well, there you have a sample. There was more. I was as much bored as shocked by the time I escaped, though I came away with one interesting realization: what a hopeless amateur my poor mother had been.

I went back, without much hope, to the Queen's apartments. In the anteroom her chamberlain only shook his head and would have sent me away. But then I heard my father's voice.

'Is that Jemmy there?'

He had been weeping. He looked worn from it, his cheeks hollow. He seemed ill himself, and when he put his hand on my shoulder I had to steady him. But he waved away my concern.

'I do well enough. Not like she – dear God, the poor creature. Such a load of suffering. This is not a fair world, Jemmy.' He made me sit down by him in the empty audience chamber, and took out a handkerchief, but he only twisted it in his bony hands as if he had half a mind to tear it to shreds. 'Not a fair world. I have always felt it so. Here is proof. She has had plenty to bear, God knows. What needs this?'

'Is she . . . ?' My throat tightened. It alarmed me to see my father like this. 'Is she no better?'

'She is raving. She asked me how our little baby was. A little boy, she said. Was he not an ugly little fellow? No, I said, a pretty boy, a fine boy. Like his father, she said.' He covered his face with his hands. 'If it be like you, she said, it is a fine boy indeed. That is what she said.' There is always that lurching moment of disbelief when someone we love starts to cry – as if the world has rocked a little – and I felt it most horribly as my father sobbed through his fingers. 'To hear her say that . . . if she had called me a whoreson, well and good, right enough, but this . . . She loves me. God help her.' He drew a deep breath and wiped his eyes. 'She took a little rest then – seemed a little recovered. Then she was delirious again. She asked me how the children did. It seemed she thought we had had three. One a girl who looked like me. Poor girl, said I. A pretty place for a jest, eh, Jemmy?' he said, his smile gritted and mournful, his fist beating gently on my knee. 'I must ask the gentlemen at the Royal Society about laughter. What it is. Why the beasts don't have it. Is it like the baying of a dog who howls to stop himself going mad?'

'Father – the Queen's fever is talking—'

'And out of it comes truth, like wine.' He glared suddenly around him, as if challenged. 'Well, well. The physicians are useless, by the by. Cannot even agree on her malady. She – she says only I can help her get well.' His grin was savage. 'Like the king's touch. Very well. I shall not leave here until . . . I shall not leave here. Jemmy, I have but one conviction, and that is that no one gets what they deserve in this world. I hope, you know, that it does not all turn out to be a joke.'

'What, Father?'

He gestured broadly. 'All of it. You've heard of Sedley's latest freak? He invited some friends to a wenching party. Just as things were getting warm some watchmen, all shorn and fierce and Puritan-like, burst in and accused them of sodomy – just as the wenches revealed they were youths painted up. Of course, wenches and watchmen and all were actors that Sedley had paid to carry the jest. One fellow was near having a heart-stroke before the deception was revealed. So you see, I hope it is not like that, when we get to the end. Forgive me, Jemmy' – he looked at me, seeing me I think for the first time – 'I'm wearied – a little disordered myself, I fear.'

'Will you not sleep, Father?' There were, I saw, great tendrils of white in his black hair. Many people commented on them at this time, and it was soon after that he began to wear a black periwig instead. Well, scoffers say a man's hair cannot turn white overnight: I am not one. Especially when I remember his next words: 'She said she would not grieve to die – except for leaving me.' He gave a little grunt, as at a blow to the stomach. 'Well, she is sleeping now, thank heaven. I fancy – I fancy she did look a little easier: I don't know, I hardly know what to think . . . Come, take a look, Jemmy. Step in quietly, and tell me what you think of her. Your eyes are fresh.'

The Queen's Bedchamber was hot and stifling. With its dim paintings of saints on the walls, the vial of holy water on the night-stand, a cowled priest mumbling prayers in the corner, and the Queen's duenna, Donna Maria, hovering witchlike in her deathly black, it seemed to me quite a place of nightmare. Most horrible of all, the physicians had cut off Catharine's hair, the better to apply blisters, and it made her look tiny and childlike in the great bed – as well as throwing into relief the gauntness and pallor of her face.

But her brow, I saw after a moment, was dry. My father, seeing it too, seized a candle and drew near, his lips twitching. With infinite gentleness he laid his hand to her forehead and cheeks.

'Contessa,' he whispered to Donna Maria, 'she is no longer burning. That is good – that is surely good. Has she been lying still?'

Before the duenna could reply, Catharine's eyes opened. They were yellow and weary but not, I thought, feverish.

'I knew . . . your touch,' she said huskily, blinking up at my father.

'I didn't mean to wake you, my dear.'

'No matter. I have had – good sleep.' She shifted in the bed. 'I wonder—'

Then her eyes fell on me. I smiled, but the Queen looked stricken, and glancing from me to my father, with a most anguished bewilderment, murmured, 'Oh, Charles, why? Not him – not here. Why, how could you do so . . .' And she buried her shorn head in the pillows.

My father sought and found her hand, nodding at me over his shoulder. 'God bless you, Jemmy,' he said, 'but you had best go.'

Queen Catharine recovered. It was a slow process and she was long weak, but my father stayed at her bedside throughout.

And when she was better, he discreetly resumed his nocturnal visits to Barbara Castlemaine's apartments. If you are surprised at this, then I have not painted his portrait aright. Nor would it be true to say that nothing had changed. Beneath the surface there had been a most profound shift. Between my father and his queen a bond had been forged anew. It was not love – at least not the sort of love that poets extol, that we all hope to find once in our lives, and that was so noticeably absent at that court where only the word, much cheapened, was bandied about like bad coin amidst the lusting and groping. Yet it was, yes, love. What Catharine possessed of him, little as it might be (and I do not think Barbara, or any mistress of his, truly possessed any more), was hers for ever. In his way, he would never forsake her.

Lady Castlemaine was calmed. She even offered prayers of thanks for the Queen's recovery – she was turning Catholic about this time, drawn no doubt to the theatrical – and I do not doubt there was sincerity in those prayers, for the Queen was a known quantity. As for Frances Stewart, her face was too carefully empty to give away any disappointed hopes, but Buckingham chafed openly at the wreck of his plans. And some said that the Duchess of York could not leave the matter alone, that she kept questioning the Queen's physicians – was there a lasting malady? Would the Queen be unable, now, to bear children? For the fudgy duchess had seen the crown hover nearer to her husband and their line, and that she liked even better than pastries.

As for the duke, I seemed to notice his pale eyes increasingly on me, as if I were a card face down on the gaming table, and he were wondering whether I was a deuce or an ace.

★ ★ ★

I have hardly spoken of my wife, or rather of our married life. A nonsense, of course, as we were both so young. But a nonsense it always remained.

My father gave us a house at Hedge Lane, hard by Charing Cross. I kept my apartments at Whitehall, shifting them presently to a new building on the Old Tennis Court, where I could see the comings and goings at the Holbein Gate from my windows; and you may be sure there were murmurs at my thus getting some of the best accommodation in the palace. For my part I would have been happy to stay there all the time, but at Hedge Lane I must have my own establishment as befitted my status – and not alone, of course. My governor, Mr Ross, who had begun to be very fine in his dress, was lodged there. Often there was the Countess of Wemyss, cawing like an enthusiastic crow through the echoing rooms. There was a hallful of servants in my own livery, and there was a companion for Anna, some poor cousin, I fancy, who always had a streaming cold, and used sometimes to secrete food in her apron. And, of course, there was Anna, my wife.

The rooms, on which at first I used to close the doors in a kind of embarrassment at their gaping largeness, soon filled. Even at that age, Anna knew what was good and what was wanted. Cabinet-makers and upholsterers, dressmakers and picture-framers were in continual procession to our door. We were duke and duchess, and must live so. It was at Anna's insistence that, on the rare occasions we dined together, we be served on the knee. I was still awkward with servants, caught between trying to be friends with them and being scared of them. Anna showed me the way. She showed me lots of ways. She loved to instruct.

'Faith, Jemmy, you take too great a piece of meat upon your plate. D'you fear starving? Be served moderately, 'tis more elegant.'

'You need not have bowed so to Lady Chesterfield. You have the precedence there – only a gracious acknowledgement is required.'

'Fie, Jemmy, you laughed like a very donkey this evening. Don't throw your head back like that – it doesn't show you to your best advantage. Look at the way His Majesty laughs.'

I was highly conscious that I lacked that supreme ease of manner that characterized my father, and I did want to acquire polish. Little precise perpendicular Anna, a peeress in her own right – as she liked to remind me – was, I dare say, the right person to teach me. If only the lessons had not been doled out so drily, like so much oatcake; if only I had not been aware of her forever watching me with that sidelong look. Peeping behind a screen, I have called it, though that suggests shyness, and Anna was not shy. Rather it was as if, like a fly buzzing about the room, I was always in the corner of her eye.

Well, that is a fair description of how I saw her in turn: something to be put up with. We spent very little time together – sometimes at Whitehall I would come across her with some other ladies, and bow formally with utter forgetfulness that this was my wife – and the only taste we truly shared was for dancing. We set aside a chamber at our house for practising it. The account book that the house-steward brought me was full of payments to dancing masters and fiddlers; and in that room we would forget ourselves and smile and laugh. And then a sort of fear would come over me as it had on my wedding night, and I felt the future as a pit into which I must fall.

Meanwhile, my father was the centre of my world. At court, at the theatre, at games of pell-mell and tennis, at the Newmarket horse-matches, which were soon to become a great passion with him, I was his chosen companion. I basked in his favour: I adored him. We never alluded to that night of the Queen's sickness, but to me it was a golden link in the chain binding us. I felt that there I had seen the best of him. And innocently loyal as I was, I often had a bullish wish that others could see it – his critics.

His honeymoon with his kingdom, as he himself had foreseen, was coming to an end. There were general reproaches about his personal extravagance, especially when the name of Lady Castlemaine came up. She was very addicted to gaming, and when, as not infrequently happened, she lost thousands at the tables, he paid. That my father's Court was given over to luxury, pleasure and idleness was more the grumble of citizens in the coffee houses and at the Exchange than the men of the Parliament, which was still mighty Cavalier in its affections. Still, there was friction, for the Parliament must vote my father his expenses, and there never seemed to be enough. Nor was the matter of religion happily settled. My father's desire was still for religious toleration, which would not disable Puritans or Catholics from offices. He never forgot the valorous kindness of the Catholic families who had hidden him during the flight from Worcester, which gives, I fancy, a credible notion of how he viewed religious matters – personally, the man rather than the faith: he surely would have felt the same if they had been Mohammedans. But the settlement was all for the Anglican Church, of which Hyde especially saw himself as the protector, and my father's intentions went by the wayside. And increasingly there were mutterings against the Dutch, who were carrying all before them at sea. Was the lion of England to lurk tamely in its cage, or roar across the nations as it had under Cromwell?

Well, my father had come to a country broken by faction, with a healing promise to be all things to all men: no wonder that he failed of complete success at such a task. So I, in the flush of young loyalty, wanted to say to those who attacked him.

And at the same time, I developed spots of hate for my father, moments when he seemed a bad man – not what he should be somehow: I know not how to express it. But I say spots advisedly, for like spots on the skin I noticed them only singly, without a great deal of trouble at the time. Only later do we see a rash, and find ourselves sick.

One such spot was the first days of my marriage, when I would stare miserably at the girl I was tied to, feeling I must put away all dreams of love. I suppose this was a revelation of difference: I did not like to think I was unlike my father. There were other signs of this. A lady at court recommended an astrologer. Fired with curiosity I went to see him in a set of dark tallow-smelling rooms off Cheapside. Mr Ross, ever inquisitive, went with me. The astrologer was fat as a ham and a little drunk, which disappointed me, and when he offered divination by dreams, I was vexed to find I could not recall any. In truth there was a certain risk about a person such as me attending an astrologer. To have horoscopes cast for kings and princes was seen as tending to treason, and Buckingham was to get into one of his many scrapes by doing just that soon after. But it was not only the thrill of the forbidden that sent a tingle over my nape. Fatness and brandy notwithstanding, there was something about this man that I felt he was hardly aware of himself. That is the way of the gift of second sight, I fancy. It does not descend decorously upon a suitable person, or even on one who wants it: it is a thing beyond us.

He read my physiognomy and my palm, and spoke of riches and honours to come – specious enough. Then he frowned and said, 'There's blood here.'

'Ah! Blood royal!' Mr Ross breathed, indiscreetly, I suppose.

The man only wagged his head, not quite shaking it. 'Blood,' he repeated; and then went on to tell me of the many ladies who would love me.

Afterwards I felt I should tell my father that I had seen an astrologer, and was a little afeared he might be angered. I was not prepared for his burst of laughter.

'This is a quaint freak in you, Jemmy. And this man's lodging, was it a grand house or a mean? He could not foretell his way to riches, then. Hey, well, no matter, if it amuses you.' And my wife being by, he shared the jest with her, who laughed uncommonly.

A trivial thing, no doubt, but in such trivialities I felt the yawning of a terrible gulf. And so it was with my first true quarrel with my father. It came of little, but it set the echoes booming in that gulf, so that I hear them still.

FOUR

It happened upon Candlemas-night – February in the year 1665, a time which all remember for the bitter frost. The Thames was frozen over, the streets were like scoured glass, and there were icicles in the Whitehall privies.

Yet looking back at that time, I have an impression of feverish heat, hectic and perilous.

Partly that was the times, for war was in the air.

For months the English and Dutch had been coming to blows all about the globe. Over the rich pudding of commerce their knives clashed; in the Indies, the Guinea coast, America. This was a rivalry of long standing between the first sea powers in the world, who must live or die by trade. They had fought in Cromwell's time and there was long a lurking sense that they must inevitably fight again.

But there was a more active party, urging war as a desirable stroke, of whom my uncle James was the head. He longed, as Lord High Admiral, to lead the fleet out to glory. Moreover, he was a shareholder in the East Indian and Royal African Companies, and so had a curious alliance with the City merchants who sought profits behind the smoke of the guns. Already an expedition mounted in my uncle's name had seized Dutch outposts on the American seaboard, where the settlement of New Amsterdam had been renamed in tribute to him, as New York. All the dull force of his nature, that tepid stubbornness, was bent upon war. And it seemed to infect the whole country. New tales of Dutch infamy were ever circulating: Dutch sailors were ill-used in portside streets, and Danes also, because people thought they were Dutch, or thought it was the same thing. The shop-windows of Amsterdam and The Hague , they said, were full of libels and scurrilous prints attacking the King of England.

And as for that King, whose manifest duty was to draw the sword on the indignant nation's behalf, he seemed for a long time – as he wryly remarked to me – the only man in the kingdom who did not want war.

It was not that he had any great love for the Dutch. Like the Scots, they had the great sin, in his eyes, of being serious-minded. But there was much in the energy and ingenuity of that soaring little nation that he admired. Rather than fight them, he felt we should try to learn from them, match them, and outdo them. His mind was often occupied with matters like glass-blowing and the weaving of cloths, which he had demonstrated before him, and he would urge the taking up of Dutch innovations in such things. He sought to foster the Dutch manner of finance, its careful accounting and book-keeping, and if the Dutch seemed to be outbuilding us in ships, then we must look to our own tradition, and breathe life into it. This was a subject dear to his heart. He always loved to go upon the water, and had a yacht of the Dutch design built for him to sail the Thames. He was as happy inspecting dockyards and studying the plans of ships as in his laboratory. But as for war – ''Tis a brutal appetite,' he once said, 'and the worst of it is, it feeds on itself, and is seldom satisfied till there be ruin on all sides.' The cries of the petitioners for action against the Dutch seemed to him conceived in a blind passion – and he of all men mistrusted blind passions and where they might lead.

Yet he also knew how to bend with the wind. Indeed, all his success was founded upon that art, and in the end there could be no resisting such a gathering gale as this. I think his great love of and pride in our ships was what swayed him. Also he was still supposedly guardian to his late sister Mary's son, the young Dutch Prince William of Orange, yet the republican statesmen of Holland allowed him little say in the bringing up of his nephew. They seemed determined to slight the boy's Stuart heritage as they had his mother, and here old hurts rankled. Yes, he would go to war, but he feared ill-preparation, and was above all wary of baiting the French, who were tied in a defensive alliance, formally at least, with the Hollanders. But here he had one signal advantage: Minette.

My father's correspondence with Minette was faithful, constant and intimate. I never saw him on Sunday evening, for that was when he wrote to her, and was sacrosanct. He was forever dispatching presents to her. When the courtiers brought her own letters, he always rewarded them handsomely; and if her letter was late, he was high-strung all day. I felt, with jealousy, that a good deal of himself was contained in those exchanges across the Channel, a part that I perhaps could not reach. Still, I was always eager for news of her. It was naught striking – such as he cared to give me, anyway: just that she had had another child, that she rubbed along with Monsieur pretty well, and she was still the chief ornament of the French court. And that she still enjoyed the warm friendship of Louis, the King.

Here was something mighty important to my father. Through Minette he always had a private channel to his powerful cousin-monarch across the sea; he could always speak, as it were, directly in Louis's ear.

Had he heard the rumours about their intimacy? And did he see it, in his canny way, as useful to his purposes? I did not wonder then, but I did after. Certainly it was through Minette's good offices that he drew his reassurance about Louis's intentions: France would not leap to Holland's aid.

War, then, was part of the fever inflaming that icy winter. But memory tells me that was not all. The air was full of strange talk. A comet had appeared in the night skies, bringing from the fanatics and doom-sayers, who had been quiet since Cromwell's end, stern prophecies about sin and retribution. And at court there was a ferment of bitterness against Chancellor Hyde. Many stopped their coaches to stare sourly at the great mansion he was building at Piccadilly. Wits called it Dunkirk House, alluding to the belief that the old man had lined his own pockets from the sale of Dunkirk to the French. Buckingham's circle were quite wild in their libels against him, and the duke himself would even perform his celebrated impersonation of the Chancellor, puffing and waddling and quacking, in front of Hyde's face.

And this matter of pretending to be someone else came to a curious pitch, in the diversions of the Court. I heard of ladies pursuing such freaks as dressing themselves up as orange-girls at the theatre and seeing how long they could go without detection. One spark changed places, for a whole week, with his own footman, who was made to go to bed with his mistress. Everyone was acting. And that Candlemas-night at Whitehall, we had the apogee of frivolous disguise, a masquerade ball.

I went, of course, very gladly: the folly only appears in retrospect. I recall getting ready in my chambers in high excitement. I remember I put on my vizard mask, of blue velvet, while I was yet undressed, and regarding myself in the mirror with mingled thrill and trouble. So strange, the naked body and the clothed face. I was me and yet anyone.

In late years I have seen my children at play, and know the times when they are too elated, their spirits forced to a febrile height. This play, the wise parent knows, will end in tears. So I think it was at that masquerade, for me and perhaps others. Certainly as I strutted to the ballroom in my costume of Alexander the Great, I was less happy than I pretended, for a part of me was still gnawing at a set-down my wife had given me earlier that day. There was some contorted scandal about Lady Chesterfield that I did not comprehend, and at last Anna had snapped: 'Ach, you're like a mere babe in these matters, Jemmy!'

Well, she was at the ball, too. Masked, we bowed to each other: there you had our relationship perfectly portrayed in dumb-show.

My father was in Turkish garb, but without a mask. Perhaps I may say he hardly needed one. He hailed me at once.

'Why, I knew you in a moment, Jemmy,' he laughed, embracing me. 'No disguising those great brown eyes of yours.' It was here, perhaps, that I began to be vexed. I did not want to be open and obvious, like a friendly dog. I wanted to be subtle and clever and impressive.

My uncle James greeting me, I asked how the duchess did: was she not here?

'The duchess is near her time, Jemmy, and has her lying-in,' he said. 'Surely you knew.'

'Oh! Yes, to be sure.' I had known, but forgotten. Christopher Monck murmured to me, as my uncle stalked away: 'A forgivable error, Jemmy – such a great cow as she is, who's to tell when she's in calf?'

I gave a shout of laughter. My uncle turned and darted me a look. 'Aye, so – because she is so fat already,' I said – which was killing wit stone dead, I know. Such was the ass I played that night.

But I was not the only one. As the night wore on, I grew more and more irritated with my father's behaviour. He was, I felt, making a fool of himself – and how severe the young are upon their elders doing that!

The fuss was all over Frances Stewart, who, in an antique Tudor dress in white and silver, did look, true enough, most radiantly fair that night. His pursuit of her, and her virginal resistance to all his persuasions, was an old Court tale now, but somehow seeing him still dangling after her acted on me like the chafing of a sore.

I was not alone in this. Lady Castlemaine was now at open enmity with the girl. There had lately been a great to-do about a glass coach, gift of the French ambassador, and who was to ride in it first. La Belle Stewart had won, and the Castlemaine had gone into one of her most exhausting rages – but tonight she was all airy dismissal.

'Dear, dear, look at that poor fool!' she said to me, her hand on my shoulder, as Frances went through her trick of displaying her legs to a slavering gaggle of gentlemen. 'And never tires of it, that's the wonder!'

'Which fool do you mean?' I found myself saying. For there was my father amongst them. He had got a piece of string to measure the girth of Frances's thigh: they were taking bets on it, and a servant was sent for a rule.

'Why, Jemmy,' Lady Castlemaine said, looking at me with interest, 'you grow apace.'

'I wish others might see that.'

'Oh! Well, you must recollect that your father is not the young spark any more. He must cover his grey with a periwig and watch the younger men sprouting up around him, and that gives him pause, perhaps. And so he halloos after that infantile chit over there. Oh, it makes me laugh excessively!' But there was no mirth in the sound she made.

These were new thoughts, but they stirred in well with my mood, along with much wine. I joined the group around Frances. She was telling of a dream she had had last night.

'Yes – there I was, in bed with the ambassadors of France and Sweden and Holland, all in one great bed. Whatever can it mean?'

'Oh, not the Hollander,' someone said. 'You kicked him out, I hope!'

'No,' she said seriously, great eyes blinking, 'they were all very pleasant. But how curious dreams are!'

''Twas a treaty conference, perhaps,' said my father. 'Did they come to terms? But you know, my dear, a meeting of ambassadors without me – that won't do. I should have presided. Was I not there?'

'Oh, no,' Frances said. 'Not in this dream, sire.'

Presently she sat down and fell to her favourite occupation of building a card-house. My father kneeled at her side, handing her each card, his breath stirring the tress on her bare shoulder.

'Is it not curious,' she said, 'that cards should be made of card? I often think of these things, you know. I declare I am quite a thinker.'

My father laughed, delightedly.

'Oh! I must go to stool. But the house isn't finished. Your Majesty, pray watch over it for me while I'm gone. Don't let anyone spoil it, please.'

'Who would dare?' He bowed deeply as she tripped away; then seeing me, smiled. 'Ho, Jemmy. Shall we build another storey on here? Careful, though—'

'It's a stupid occupation, surely,' I said.

'Oh, I dare say it is.'

'And she is a stupid woman.'

He paused in surprise. 'Not very gallant, my boy.'

'Aye, Your Majesty, for one of your blood, this is strange indeed,' someone piped up.

'I don't know how you can bear her,' said I, stubbornly.

'Don't you now?' There was in my father a sharp stillness of displeasure. 'Well, that is your youth. The fact is, you know nothing of these matters, Jemmy. The fledgling don't instruct the cock-bird how to fly.'

There was much laughter, which I seemed to feel striking me like so many flung stones. I thought of Lady Castlemaine's words. Aye, I was growing: I was now nearly sixteen, tall and well-made, and in truth I had not lacked offers from young women at court: there had been whispers in corners, looks of invitation. Just then I hated myself for never having the courage to take them up – and there is nothing like self-hatred for making a man lash out.

'Perhaps I do know nothing, Father, as you say,' I said. 'Or perhaps I simply know better.'

As I walked away I heard, after a moment, my father's tolerant chuckle.

'You are in a passion, I think, Jemmy.' It was Lady Castlemaine. I turned my angry face to her, and she nodded at my expression as at an old friend. 'I like to see it. I adore spirit. Oh, we are a spiritless set altogether, now – it's *she* who sets the tone. I hope drivelling insipidity is not to be the new fashion, else we with red blood in our veins will be quite shut out. Come, take a glass with me. Pledge me.'

Before I could do so, my father came over to us. 'Barbara, my dear. You are helping Jemmy to a better humour, I hope.'

'Aye, Charles. I was telling him he must learn to simper and dimple and have milk-and-water in his veins, and then all will be well.'

'You will have naught but liquor in your veins at that rate, my son,' he said eyeing me.

'I may drink, surely?'

'Certainly.' He shrugged. 'I am not one to stand in judgement. Ah!' A man had taken up a guitar, another new fashion at court, and began singing some verses that I recognized. My father had written them.

> 'I pass all my hours in a shady old grove,
> But I live not the day when I see not my love;
> I survey every walk now my Phyllis is gone,
> And I sigh when I think we were there all alone.
> Oh, then 'tis I think there's no Hell
> Like loving too well.'

There was more. They were not very good verses. They were addressed, of course, to Frances Stewart. A peculiar grimace crossed my father's face.

'And now you are about to reprove me again,' he said.

'No,' I said, meaning yes. 'I only wonder how you think she can be worthy of . . .' Your love, I would have said, but somehow could not.

'Worth? Who is worth anything? These thing's don't matter, Jemmy. You are too much the romantic. You must grow up.'

Almost the very same thing Minette had said to me in her chamber at Colombes, when she was set on marrying Philippe! I hated it then; hated it more now.

'You used to be better than this, Father,' I said, distinct and harsh.

Then – for the first time – I saw my father touched by fury.

'I, I? I am this, I was that? Don't you dare be so impudent as to think you know me, boy. No one . . .' His voice, thick and choked, gave out. His look was like hate. What he really hated, perhaps, was being made to lose control, but I could not think of that as he glared, turned, left me.

He spent the rest of the evening at Frances Stewart's side. Some of Buckingham's cronies kept plying her with drink. There was, I knew, a mock-committee to get her into the King's bed, and running wagers on the outcome – such was the temper of the times. To be fair, my father kept quite out of this. He just doggedly adored.

Meanwhile I drank bitterly and danced, in a rage of flirtation, with every lady I could.

Most of all, though, with Barbara Castlemaine. We were natural allies in that room, in that time: brooding on similar resentments, looking to hatch them into vengefulness. Well, I have said I must set down some things that shame me. You have probably guessed the conclusion of that night. When the ball broke up, my father followed Frances Stewart to her apartments (a fruitless quest again, I may add), and I followed Lady Castlemaine to hers.

She did invite me. 'Let us drink a cup together, Jemmy, away from all this tedium,' she said, yawning, her eyes rather hard and absent. 'As for Charles, I wish him good fortune. Faith, he'll need it. Nothing short of a crown will satisfy that little wretch, as he should know by now. I would laugh – if it were not to slight the poor Queen. I pity Her Majesty, knowing that minx's eyes are ever on her, wishing her in her grave.'

'Aye – that's true – the poor Queen,' said I hotly. In truth I had not thought of the Queen, who had not been present at the ball; but I was in a mood to pile any fuel on my fire.

And so, still grimly meditating on my father's manifold wrongs, I drank with Lady Castlemaine in her chamber – from the same cup; and even as she put the cup aside, and I felt her soft lips on mine, my resentment fused with my lust. Yes, it cried, even this lady too, did she not deserve better treatment from him? Such cunning alchemists are our brains, that can convert sordid appetite into chivalry! We are strange creatures, mostly self-deceived. Even our frankest desires are apprehended through a mental fog.

Aye, desire, certainly. Barbara was as voluptuous, as hot to the act, as repute had it – not that I had any means of comparison. I will only mention that the hard, absent look remained in her eyes, even when she took me most fiercely to her. You will readily believe that I was not in her bed, or rather upon it, above a few minutes. And I mean no disrespect when I add that, to such a carnal gourmet as she was, I must have been the merest snack or titbit, consumed and forgot in a moment.

But then neither of us, after all, was thinking of the other, in that brief vinous toiling among the scents and silks. My father was not there, but in a sense he was, for it was all about him.

I dressed myself blindly, and Lady Castlemaine, scarcely concealing her yawns, murmured some commonplace endearments where she lay, and so I lurched out. In the dressing room beyond, I found her waiting-woman folding her cloak. Lady Castlemaine had not sent her out of the way. I bowed confusedly, supposing she must have forgot – which shows how innocent I was.

I felt weary, but also as if I would never sleep again, and with my head full of strange clanging thoughts, rambled to my own lodging in the Old Tennis Court, where the servant told me my wife had taken a coach home to Hedge Lane. Though this was quite our normal way of going on, I was all at once aggrieved at it. Was I not a man? (Deep down, I did not feel like one: I felt like a boy who has stolen something.) I kept my own saddle-horse in the palace stables, and I ordered it made ready. The ostler, roused from bed, grumbled – understandably. If I had been myself I would have said sorry for his trouble and given him a shilling. Instead I was curt. For, of course, I was not myself – though I rode home, in the freezing starlight, mentally blustering that I was – that this was me at last, a man, a grand fellow come into his own. And all filled with this sickly unnatural boldness, I decided it was time for my wife.

Were we not married? She had a woman's figure now. Was it not nonsense to live like brother and sister – not even that? Was I not a man?

I paused in our yard to sluice myself under the pump. Lady Castlemaine's scent clung: I felt a little sick.

Anna had not long gone to bed. She was lightly dozing when I entered her chamber, and a candle still burned. When I drew back the bed-curtain, she was alert at once, and seemed not particularly surprised.

'Aye, Jemmy? Oh – yes. I dare say you are right. Come, then. Tsk, have a care – take off those boots, they spoil the rug.'

Thus, very business-like, our consummation was concluded.

'What a peculiar thing it is!' Anna mused afterwards, neatly pulling down her nightgown. 'Oh, well.' And she slept.

★ ★ ★

Prince Rupert once told me of a man shipwrecked in the Indies, who subsisted on the beach of a deserted coast till his rescue. Some flotsam came ashore from the wreck, over time, which he would hunt for and put to such use as he could. The curious thing was that after his rescue, and return to England, he could not leave off collecting odds and ends even in the street, and wondering how he might use them.

Compare the life of my father's court, where everyone's thought upon each other was: 'How may I use this?'

It was, or should have been, no surprise that the rumour of my going to Lady Castlemaine's bed was soon about. The Lady's amours were so notorious (she even bedded a rope-dancer whose muscular thighs had pricked her fancy) that the report was less shocking than interesting. But if she had thought to rouse my father's jealousy by bedding his son, I doubt her success. As for me, I know not what blow I thought to have struck against him, such was my bitter confusion of heart and mind. If he knew the report, or believed it, he was much too subtle to show it. The next day he was coolly pleasant to me. The sharpest response came from an unexpected quarter: my uncle James.

A few days after the masquerade, the Duchess of York was brought to bed of a baby girl. I went with my father and the Queen to St James's Palace, where the Yorks had their household, to congratulate them and present a gift.

The sight of this growing family must have been a sadness to Queen Catharine, still childless. In addition to the new baby, fat as her mother, and named after her Anne, there were two elder children: Mary, a well-grown, pretty, serious girl of four, much petted by her father; and a boy of three, James, pretty too but inclined to be sickly. St James's had been new-fitted and decorated, and it seemed pleasant and airy after the warren of Whitehall, and life seemed to go on here rather more naturally. The duke would even have the children to dine at table with him, which was uncommon. I must in fairness call this true affection, for all that there was policy in it too. For while the Queen remained barren, this, after all, was the royal family in waiting. I am sure Catharine, who was as eager to hold the baby as the duchess was willing to relinquish it, must have felt that keenly. And I can think of no one who would have made a better mother than Queen

Catharine. An unfair world, as my father had said.

'Jemmy,' my uncle said, 'I have a handsome new courser in stable, just brought from Newmarket. Come and see her.'

Quite unwitting, I went along; admired the horse at length, finally running out of things to say. When I looked to my silent uncle, he was standing with his cumbrous arms by his sides, balefully watching me. But even this was not untypical of his manner, and so I was utterly surprised when he said: 'I wish to say something to you, Jemmy.'

'Sir?'

'You will take it, I am sure, in the friendly spirit with which I intend it. It comes from one who would gladly see you secure in all the advantages belonging to your situation, and shield you from the temptations that do not so belong, or appertain. Do you understand?'

I did not, but I was used to my uncle talking like an Act of Parliament, so I nodded.

'When my father was put upon the scaffold by the rebels,' James went on, 'he spoke to the people most wisely. He said that a subject and a sovereign are clear different things. It was when that difference was muddied over that the trouble began. Let each know their place and station: let each man know aright where he stands, and there is harmony. I hear things, Jemmy, that disturb me, for I would not have you fall into such errors.'

'I don't know what you mean, sir.'

'I mean,' James said, 'that it seems you would do all the offices of a king, Jemmy. Even in the bedchamber.'

I was embarrassed at once; but I also disliked being catechized thus, and I could not help remembering the talk that my uncle had sued without success to be Lady Castlemaine's lover.

'You have an excellent wife, Jemmy,' my uncle went on, with a most irritating complacency, 'who must I am sure do very well for you; you have many honours. Indeed, I think my brother is sufficiently indulgent. I cannot think you would wish to make him an ungrateful return for his excessive kindness, by seeking for more.'

'I am pleased to accept what is due to me,' I said. 'If anyone chooses to give me more, I do not see why I should refuse. And my father – my father, sir, is King. These matters are up to him. I was not aware that he had any master.'

I had spoken, as I thought, quite feebly for the tumult in my breast, but my uncle looked as if I had slapped him in the face.

And then he gave himself a little shake, and said in his most wooden way: 'Well. A fine courser, is it not? The stabling is not all it might be yet, but we have workmen coming. Well. Let us go in.'

Well, now I was a man – a fine thing! Now I possessed my wife, and my household knew it – aye, let them; very good, now they had a master. (What nonsense this possession is. At the highest moment of embraces, the creature we enfold may be a thousand miles off in truth, as unreachable as the Pleiades.) So I strutted. And if my other conquest was known, well and good too: this was a court of conquests, and now I wholly belonged to it.

Yes, I was a fine fellow. And if I could not meet Barbara Castlemaine's slanted eyes, fearing the mocking knowledge in them, and if in my father's presence I tingled as if there were some Cainish mark upon my brow, why, what then? I was still a fine fellow. Here, let me show it – pour another glass, for a man must drink, 'tis proper to his estate . . .

Thus I drifted in the turbid wake of my unboying. I made the bottle my best friend, because there was a voice within that said this was not how things should be, and the bottle was good at silencing it. At last, it was drink that sent me to Queen Catharine's chambers one day: not the drink I wanted, but the drink I didn't want any more. Without knowing it, I sought its opposite, in all ways. After my bow I stood drooping and fidgeting in confusion before her, until she said: 'Well, Jemmy, what is it I can do for you?'

'Your Majesty,' I burst out in a curious broken voice, 'may I have some tea with you?'

She looked surprised, but was obliging at once. 'Why, to be sure. Please, sit down, and be easy.'

Well, easy I certainly was not. Still fidgeting and sighing, I faced her across the tea table with my eyes on everything but her grave, gentle face. Still I drank the tea most gratefully. And I drank in, even more so, the peace and dignity that Catharine shed around her. And when at last I did meet her eyes, I saw that she looked at me with sadness. Aye, there was always that, for I was the child she could not have, but there was more: she was sad for me, this lady who had cause enough to be my enemy.

And that undid me quite, so that I began sobbing in front of her.

'Oh, Jemmy.' She shook her head: she was not embarrassed. 'This is not happy to see. All is not well with you?'

'Oh, yes, it is, it is,' I cried rather wildly, 'I crave your pardon, Your Majesty – I am quite a fool,' and I made a grab at the dish of tea, and tried to swallow it down.

'You will make yourself to choke . . . Have you had a quarrel with your father?'

'No. No – why – has he said anything?'

'Not to me. He would not.' There was the faintest trace of bitterness, soon gone. 'But I only wondered . . . I try not to listen to talk, but there was some talk lately.'

'I never know where I am with him,' I spluttered, 'and sometimes I almost wish— Oh, I'm sorry – I shouldn't talk so. It isn't fair to you—'

'No matter,' she said. 'I am glad to talk with you.'

'I am glad to talk with you, Your Majesty,' I said, mopping my eyes. 'You make me feel better.'

'Do I?' She smiled then, and I saw there was much humour in her, too seldom let out. 'It hardly looks like it, Jemmy, but if you say so.'

'Will you tell my father that I—'

'No, no. Not if you don't wish it, Jemmy. I think you love him, do you not?'

'Oh, yes.'

She gave a little sigh, and shyly patted my hand, looking away. 'That is perhaps the worst thing in the world to do. For anyone.'

I caught her hand a moment and held it. I understood much about her at that moment. I wish I could have kept that understanding always, but we never do.

'Perhaps I speak too strong. I mean that it is . . . not wise,' she said, giving my hand a squeeze and then gently withdrawing. 'But who can always be wise? You love him, and that makes a difference to everything. If it were only his crown you loved—'

'No!' I cried, indignant.

She nodded, her own eyes damp but clear. 'I believe you. And if I were wise perhaps I should not. I think perhaps I ought to hate you, Jemmy, but I cannot. Not where there is love.' She smiled. 'Now drink some more tea. It is a very good cure for the sickness of too much wine.'

'Oh, I think I shall never drink wine again.'

She smiled, though with a return of sadness. 'Oh, you will.'

Whether my uncle James complained to my father about me, or whether my father, who missed nothing, divined that there was disharmony between us, I know not. But it was my father's decision to throw us together when war broke out at last. In May James sailed out on the flagship *Royal Charles* at the head of a great fleet, and I was with him.

I had long been eager to prove myself in action, my prowess in riding and with the sword fitting me particularly, as I saw it, for the army. But this was a war of ships, and I was excited to be in it at any price. Besides, two of the three squadrons were commanded by military men, my uncle and Prince Rupert, with the third under Lord Sandwich. Grand names, and grand hopes.

And a grand sight was the fleet riding off Harwich: a hundred men-of-war, white sails brilliant in the sunshine, pennants flapping: smaller auxiliary ships around them, like courtiers to these fabulous creaking grandees. It seemed a marvel that such mighty constructions could be the work of men – and as for the men on the ships, there one saw, as so often, that we are lesser than what we create. For this was very mixed human material: of the twenty thousand that sailed, a good portion never wanted to go, for magistrates had set the press gangs to work to fill the ships, and even they had resorted to landsmen to fill the quotas, so that there were ragged beggars and thieves aplenty in the crews. Many of the captains had begun service in the Commonwealth, and were of the stern Cromwellian sort, ill-matched indeed with the ardent court Cavaliers who had clamoured to play a part in the expedition, and who came aboard with trunks full of fine clothes and wines, and men to dress their hair. I was such a one myself, I suppose. I saw the ship-master, a rugged fellow with a face like scarred leather, give me some thoroughly sceptical looks.

Partly because I was conscious of this, but also from a true fascination, I set myself in the days before we weighed anchor to learning all I could, from the intricacies of the rigging to the handling of the guns – eighty of them on the *Royal Charles* – and generally trying to make myself useful. My uncle noted this, and began to employ me to relay commands, often trifling things to do with victualling or with the daily water ration. I was willing enough, and whether it gave him pleasure to order me about, or whether my very willingness spoiled the pleasure, I could not tell: his feelings about having me there he kept well guarded.

But Prince Rupert, coming on board the flagship to dine the night before we sailed, could not help raising an eyebrow at the two of us together.

'Dog and cat in the same basket together,' he remarked to me, when my uncle was not by. 'Very cunning of His Majesty.'

'I don't understand, sir,' I said, priggishly enough, for I felt my father slighted.

'Then you had better, and soon,' Rupert said with his hard smile that did not reach his eyes. 'Don't you see, he plays you off, one against another? Hey, well, 'tis his way with all, and it's worked thus far. You've heard of the Gordian knot – whoever could untie it would rule Asia. Alexander cut it through with his sword. Charles, I fancy, would simply tie it even tighter. God send the Queen a child, I say, though you'll not like to hear it, no doubt. Are you firm in your religion, Jemmy? The Protestant religion?'

'I am, sir.'

He grunted. 'I wish everyone was . . . The Dutch are, of course, and we are going to fight them.'

'They threaten us, sir.'

'To be sure they do, and we shall have their hides, and then – what then? I wonder.'

Yes, even the princely commanders of that fleet were all too human. After Rupert's words, I could not help thinking of when my father had come to the Hope to see us off, and how, looking about him at the great ships, he had murmured: 'Gad, brother, but I envy you!' If the envy was in fact jealousy, for the renown that his brother would win while he stayed at home, then had he sent me along to be the stone in James's shoe, the gall in his cup of triumph?

These thoughts troubled me as we dined. But I was surprised to find my uncle, here upon the threshold of his great hour, troubling himself by musty memories that should have been laid to rest. He and Rupert fell to talking of the time of the exile, when a part of the Parliamentary fleet had come over to the Royalist side at Rotterdam: an unruly set of rogues, Rupert recalled laughing, but they came to heel when he threw a couple of the most mutinous overboard with his own hands. My uncle, solemn and flushed, began to talk over and over that time.

'Aye, and I was name High Admiral long before then—'

'Before we had any ships,' Rupert put in.

'So, so – but when the ships came to us, then it was surely my right, by my title, to take command of them, and so I did. I did no wrong there. I acted entirely upon my rights.'

'Aye, cousin, so you did, no man disputes it,' Rupert said, drinking, unlike my uncle, very deep. 'You were very young though – not even the age of Jemmy here.'

My uncle turned to look at me for a glowering moment: the comparison did not seem to please him. 'No matter for that. I speak of my right by title, as High Admiral. The command of those ships was rightly mine. Then along came Charles and took it from me. I was not, it appears, to be trusted with myself. I should have had the command of those ships. I still do not see why I was deprived in that fashion.'

'Charles was the elder, and heir. Were we not fighting for royal prerogative?' Rupert said, narrow-eyed. 'Besides, Cousin, this is long past.'

'I do not deny it is long past,' James said. 'But time does not alter the fact. That command was mine, and it was a very ill thing to take it from me.' And so he went on, like a man picking at a scab. It seemed strange that a man who now commanded a fleet of a hundred warships should be griping over this, and I could see it was on Rupert's lips to say so. But he restrained himself. It was, after all, the Dutch we were meant to be fighting.

And when the fight came, it was like nothing I had imagined. For a long time it seemed to me that I had the measure of a fleet action, and that it was mostly seasick tedium, and routines of swabbing and rope-tying, and awkward incompetences like the way the beer ran out and the victualling ships could not get to us, so that at last we must put back to Harwich to take on more stores.

And then the Dutch came out – a fleet as great as our own; and off Lowestoft, they clashed.

Noise, and blood, and smoke, and terror – these are my memories;

above all noise. Apparently the boom of the cannon could be heard in London, where people stood out in parks and on roofs to hearken to it. But that must have been a very different sound to the one I heard, in the midst of it: a continued pounding and roaring and shrieking, in which everything was hellishly not what you expected – the breached timbers of stricken ships giving forth great moans like dying monsters, while men, dying, squealed like pigs or sobbed like infants.

My uncle displayed prodigious courage. It was he who gave the order, after the fleets had passed in line pounding away at each other with inconclusive effect, to go about and close with the enemy. His own particular quarry was the flagship of the Dutch admiral, Opdam, right in the centre of the line; and so the ships closed into that terrible mêlée, thundering fire at each other at close quarters. I remember once catching a glimpse, beyond the confusion of smoke and flying timbers, of the open sea – how vast and blue and serene it looked, while here forty thousand men crammed together killing. Little time for such reflections, though, nor for any troubles about order or precedence. I ran hither and thither, doing whatever I could whenever I could, sending men from powder magazine to gun-decks to replace their fellows who had been hit, helping – with groans I could barely conceal – to shift the wounded out of the way and into the unmerciful hands of the surgeon, arranging a water-train to sluice the red-hot guns and their blood-slaked carriages, reporting casualties to my uncle, who stood throughout up on the quarter-deck, calm as a man watching a tennis match. This phlegmatic patience extended even to me. Once I went up to ask his orders, and found I could not speak – the air was full not only of smoke but of whirling fragments of shredded canvas, like hot chaff, that got into my throat.

'Take a moment, Jemmy,' he told me. 'Hawk, and spit well – that's it.'

As I did so, there was a whining of chain-shot in the air, and instinctively I flung myself down on the deck. A terrible yell rang out. Lifting my head, I saw my uncle still standing sturdy as a figurehead, but the three men around him had gone down, horribly. They were courtiers eager for action, and particular friends of his, especially Lord Falmouth, who had shared much of the exile. The chain-shot had cut them down like ninepins, quite mangling them. There was a spurting of arteries, like blown casks. The quarter-deck was like a butcher's floor, and Lord Falmouth's head lay shattered across the rail, long hair dangling. My uncle blinked, staggered: he put up a hand to wipe his face, and then moaned, for his cheeks were all jellied over with the brains of his friend.

I moved away to be sick then. I thought I heard a kind of keening or howling, like a dog in pain, but it was hard to tell with all the din; and when I climbed back to the quarter-deck, my uncle was composed again. He had wiped his face, though his coat was still drenched with blood. I would have fetched water, but he said no. His mind was all bent now upon the enemy flagship, which was having the worst of it, one mast broken clean away and several gun-ports out of action. God knows, though, how long it would have kept on pounding, for the Dutch fought as desperately as reputation said; but all at once the sea itself seemed to burst upwards, with a noise so frightful that it made silence of all the rest.

A fortunate shot had struck the powder magazine of Opdam's ship. When my ringing head cleared, and the black curtains of smoke parted, I saw the Dutch flagship a blazing hull upon blazing water, peppered with twisted men, dead and half dead.

All about us, such of the Dutch ships as could manage were turning about and withdrawing. The day was ours.

We came into port to a heroes' welcome. The evening before we dropped anchor, my uncle, for once in his life, celebrated with drink. He had remained grim and purposeful hitherto. There were the defeated Dutch to pursue, and refits to be made to our fleet, and prize commands to be appointed; and there was mourning. I think that horrid death upon the quarter-deck struck my uncle deep, though he was too reserved and formal to give anything away, least of all to me. But coming home, he allowed himself to unbend. Someone said they could hear the church bells from here. James shook his head, serious as ever. 'Nay, nay – it cannot carry so far. Nor would they ring at this hour.'

'Well, they shall ring, Your Grace, depend on it!'

'Aye, aye – so they will,' he said, faintly smiling. 'Aye – I think they will love me now.'

So they did. The bells rang and bonfires blazed for the great victory of Lowestoft. My father embraced his brother, and then me, and admired how brown we were from the sea, and seemed almost upon the point of tears. James gave a good account of my courage in the battle, which put me to a little shame, for though I hope I carried myself stoutly enough, I know that I was praying inside all the time for it to end. And so all seemed well – as it so often does, just before all turns dreadfully ill.

My father had also been firm friends with Lord Falmouth, and was greatly shocked and grieved at his dying. They say he locked himself away when he heard the news; and the impression of it did not leave him. He asked for several accounts of how it happened, picturing no doubt the way James had stood up on the quarter-deck, and how narrowly that chain-shot had missed smashing him to pieces as well. I am sure the Duchess of York, who had gone into faints at the news, spoke privily to my father too. The result was that my father told James he was not to go to sea again. The risks to his person were too great, and he must direct the war from the safety of shore.

What was James to make of this? Here was love and care and also that respect that he was forever claiming as his due, for, as people began to say, he was the apparent heir to the throne and so must be safeguarded. Yet might there not also be, to James's dully suspicious mind, a whiff of envy in my father's prohibition? Was he not being prevented from becoming too popular and powerful? Certainly his frustration at being confined to shore was plain, but those other darker sides to him were made plain to me, really for the first time, when I saw him in his Whitehall apartments soon after.

This was not a place I went to much, nor was it common for James to summon me as he did. I felt unwelcome at once, as the duchess, who sat reading a devotional book and gorging, gave me a cold unspeaking look. But my uncle took me into his closet, talking amiably enough of the unhealthy weather. And then: 'I craved a word, Jemmy, on this matter of the fleet's going forth again. Whenever it may be – there is much refitting yet. Still, the Hollanders are not beaten, and so . . .' He broke off, gazing balefully into space. 'What did you say, Jemmy?'

'Nothing, sir.'

'Hm.' He frowned as if I had interrupted him. 'Well, you know I am not to sail with them. This is a matter of prudent policy. As you surely know. But I just wanted to give you assurance that I have made favourable report of you to your father, and so if you should wish to join the fleet again, there is naught against it. No indeed.' He picked up his riding crop and began fussily to smooth the frayed leather. 'There is no such proscription on you, Jemmy. I must bow to my position, in line for the throne. But of course this does not apply to you, which is very happy for you, if you like to go to sea again.' There was a look of bitter pleasure slitting his lips, like a man supping on pickles. 'I wanted to be sure you knew this, and entertained no mistaken notions that what applies to me applies to you. For it does not.'

'I see, sir. But I have not been thinking—'

'Oh, I don't know about that. I am not sure about that at all. I regret extremely that I cannot go after the Dutch – but no matter, there is a good side to everything. And at least this has cleared up certain matters. We know where we stand, Jemmy, and I hope you have sense enough to rest content with that.'

'I was not aware, sir, that I had shown myself discontented.'

'Indeed? Then pray tell, sir, why you foment these stories about your birth, and your mother's being married, and all the rest of it? If you do not foment them, then I crave your pardon.'

Feeling stung and humiliated, I answered: 'It was my mother's assertion that she and my father were married, and in honour to my mother I must—'

'Charles denies it,' my uncle said hastily, 'Charles denies any such thing. I have his full assurance that my position, my rights stand unaltered, and none of this mischievous rumour may hurt them.' Breathing hard, he laid the crop down with a tremble. 'Really, Jemmy, I speak for your good. You would do well to put these notions of your mother from your mind. They are gallantry, of course, which is admirable – but the gallantry is misplaced. I knew of your mother. To place any confidence in that quarter—'

'I won't hear you speak ill of my mother,' I said hotly, 'and nor would my father, if you dared say it to him.'

'I say again,' James said through pursed lips, very pale, 'be content. Some would say you have had far above your deserts already, and that your father is deceived. Your mother's reputation was not of the best when he met her. Some would say he erred on the side of indulgence in claiming you as his child at all. Therefore—'

'Is that what you say, sir? Never mind *some*. I would know what *you* say.'

My uncle shifted, a little uncomfortable. 'Faith, Jemmy, there is no call for this passion. I seek only to have us talk truthfully. I know Charles is mighty fond of you, and that is very well. I only fear that you allow yourself to be misled by it.'

'So you would have me know that not only am I a bastard, but I am not even the King's bastard. Well, sir, you must be very maliciously affected towards me, or very afraid of me. I cannot think I merit either of these – but if I do, then so be it.'

My uncle had turned yet whiter, as if he were being slowly bled in front of my eyes. 'I see a rebellious spirit, Jemmy,' he said hoarsely. 'I am sorry for it. I hope you will not make your father sorry also.'

'My relation with my father is my own affair. What he chooses to say and do is his own affair. He is King, sir: no one else.' I was shaking with fury; and what I said next was, perhaps, better not said. But then, once we have an enemy, why pretend enmity is not there? 'As for his marrying my mother – well, who can say? Lesser men than he have contracted marriage, and then chosen to deny it.'

After a second's silence, my uncle breathed: 'But this is impudence,' just as if I had physically laid something horrid and incredible before him on the desk.

'No: from a subordinate it might be. But I am the King's son, and I know only his authority.' And so, with a sort of terrible elation, I left him.

It is hard to think of something so poisonous for the future as a victory, but victory I suppose it was – for pride and hardihood of self rather than ambition. This sense of self may be for other men a steady fire that they can leave unattended: for me it has not been so. I must ever feed it, and keep its flickering flame sheltered; and so I felt fiercely glad that I had not let my uncle quench it, and resolved that he never would.

There came soon another victory, unlooked for. My father talking of Lord Falmouth again one evening, his eye fell on me and he said suddenly: 'No more of that for you neither, Jemmy. You shall have other duties on shore.' And that got back to my uncle, no doubt. I was pleased, of course, at this proof of his regard – though I could not help remembering Prince Rupert's words.

But it was at this time that a shadow more ominous than that of Dutch arms fell across my father's kingdom, and ruled a black line beneath the palmy days of his restoration. I have spoken of a feverishness in the air: the figure is all too apt. The bells that rang for our sea victory were tolling soon in proclamation of a vaster triumph – that of Death itself, who descended upon us in ghastly conquest: in the plague.

FIVE

Everyone has their own plague story – often grisly and grotesque: whole families lying dead in one room with no mourners but gnawing rats, or victims thrown upon the burial carts still breathing. Mine is mild, perhaps, but none the less it is the single image of that time that haunts my mind still.

My half-sister Mary had been provided for at my father's charge, and taken into a family with estates in Ireland. She was visiting some connections of theirs in the City early that summer, and I set out one morning to visit her. For weeks now people had been talking of the sickness spreading round the town. In anxious hope they would say that there were no cases in their parish, or that some physician had assured them it was no great outbreak, but the true tale was told by the red crosses one saw painted upon the doors of shut-up houses, with the doleful words 'Lord have mercy on us' inscribed above. Some families, such as were able, had already taken coach or wagon and left London for the country. Many men had taken to wearing a pomander of herbs about the neck, or carrying tobacco to chew, as a ward against the infection – the suddenness of which was beginning to excite a growing fear in the breasts of even the most sanguine, for it seemed that you might be well one moment, and stricken half-blind and staggering the next.

This I could hardly credit. But I learned otherwise on going down to Whitehall Stairs, to take a boat downriver to the City. At the landing stage before me were a man of thirty with a little child not above three, just preparing to step down into the boat. I saw a curious hesitancy come over the man's face. He gave a shudder, and then lifted his little girl into the boat, and to the surprise of the watermen stepped away from the dock.

'Take her – take her to Blackfriars Stairs. Set her down there and – here, here's silver for you – pray you send up to Mr Price at Ludgate Hill – that is her uncle, a mercer, sign of the Maid's Head, he is well known—'

'Sir,' the waterman said, shaking his head, 'I can't carry the child alone – is that what you ask? She's too little. My guild would not allow—'

'Dear God, man, it is a simple request!' the man cried, seeming much agitated. 'Is it money? Here—' he fumbled, nearly dropping his purse – 'take more – whatever you will . . .' But the waterman, perturbed, still shaking his head, the man turned desperately about and, seeing me, entreated me to take the boat, at his expense, if I would but just see the child to her destination.

'I trust I know an honest face,' he said, 'and I am in – in somewhat of a difficulty.' The skin about his eyes was red, I saw, like raw flesh; and he squinted as if the sunlight hurt him. 'Pray, sir, if you will be so good . . .'

I assented, though troubled for my own part by the man's appearance. In the boat the child began calling 'Papa!' and reaching out her little arms. The man seemed to hold himself back, with a visible wrench, from embracing her.

'Go with the gentleman to Uncle's house. Good girl. I shall see you soon . . .'

We sculled on to the water. I patted the hand of the little girl, who pouted uncertainly. When I looked back, I saw that the man had dropped to his knees on the landing stage as if poleaxed.

The waterman presently divined, as I did, that the man had felt the plague-sickness growing on him as he stood at the dock, and so had sent his daughter away from him – surely never to see her again. But instead of being moved by this, his face darkened with mistrust, and he might have set her down earlier to be rid of her. I was firm, and said who I was, using my status for the first time. I lifted her ashore myself, for the waterman would not touch her, and carried her to her uncle in the City. I had the pain of telling the uncle what had happened, and seeing his face blench; but it was the face of the man on the dock that I would never forget, as he sank down into slow death, having relinquished what he most loved.

I understood the waterman's fear. As that burning airless summer progressed, and the red crosses on the street-doors multiplied, fear became the plague's twin, an invisible palpable presence stalking among us. Dread suspicion attached itself to the slightest matters. Had this parcel of linen come from a plague district? Was not that gentleman, who was normally so high-spirited, somewhat low and quiet last evening? At the same time, people continued to grasp at an equally elusive hope. The Mortality Bills were studied and passed around as eagerly as had been the news-sheets of prices in the taverns and coffee houses, and men would nod wisely at the figures for plague deaths, and say that though they were up, they were not up as much as might be expected, which meant the plague was surely on the wane. That line of reasoning ended when the weekly deaths went into the thousands – by which time the taverns and coffee houses were closed up anyhow, along with the theatres and gaming rooms. Still some would find other grounds for hope. Infallible remedies were everywhere, along with quacks and charlatans to puff them: charms and simples to wear next to the heart, decoctions of every exotic species, from brimstone and Venice-treacle to angelica and juniper to the powdered horn of a unicorn – a rare substance, one might suppose, though in fevered London that summer it seemed as common as sugar. I heard of one man who swallowed so many of these nostrums at once that he invited the death he strove to elude, and poisoned himself; another who died of starvation, because he feared that every food was tainted. No tobacconist ever caught the plague, rumour said, and so the price of tobacco soared as people rushed to chew and smoke; and rumour, unfailing even as all else fell apart, claimed that the syphilis prevented the plague, and men rushed to brothels to contract a medicinal dose. Later the Lord Mayor was persuaded that fire would purge the city of its contagion, and a night was appointed in which huge bonfires blazed, to no avail, on every street, so that London's sky showed fierce red from miles about. In this there might have been prophecy.

But prophecy was in the air too, wild and strange. This terrifying blight upon the land called forth all the most fanatical doomsayers, who scattered apocalyptic broadsheets and could even be seen, Baptist-like, roaming the streets naked but for a clout of sackcloth, declaring the plague a punishment for our sins and wailing for repentance. At first folk scoffed and boys shied mud; later they stood silently regarding, half-respectful. For who was to say they were not right? As soon listen to them as to the doctors, who secured themselves an unhappy reputation by being the first to leave the city. A few starveling apothecaries were left, while the physicians snapped down the blinds of their laden coaches and headed for the country.

But flight, which became a swelling exodus as the weeks went on, was a natural product of fear – and the fear, before God, was natural too, for a plague-death was singularly horrible. Men who had braved the guns of war dreaded it. Commonly it took three days, from the first shivers and headaches to the obscenities of the end, with its buboes erupting in the groin, tongue swelling out of the mouth, and skin purpling like spoiled fruit; and not a moment without rending pain. It did not permit of stoical silence. People moaned and screamed, though at one stage a terrible listlessness struck, and it was those sufferers that one saw most often about the streets, shambling about or lying down in doorways. Sometimes they were indistinguishable from corpses – aye, they were to be seen in the streets too, usually of the poor and friendless. Some sought their quietus in the river, or were heaved in by fearful neighbours, and the grey bodies would join the pitiable carrion on the banks, for there was a belief that cats and dogs spread the infection, and so household beasts were drowned by the hundred. I had lately got two dogs of my own, and would have spared them, but my house-steward at Hedge Lane had them hanged before I could contradict.

Such supposedly preventive measures were, of course, futile. And those that did work in at least containing the spread of the plague were of necessity stern, and sometimes unpopular. My father was much occupied, in concert with the Lord Mayor, in planning these measures. First was the requirement that any house in which a person had taken the plague be shut up for forty days, with none allowed to go in or out, which in turn required officers to enforce it, watchmen to be stationed at the doors, and a class of women, much maligned, called searchers, who, bearing a willow rod as a badge of their office, were charged with finding out and reporting plague cases. There were some who submitted bravely to this, others who tried to escape the closed houses, or bribed the searchers; and some even fomented riots against the rule, and went about breaking down the doors with red crosses on them, to let out the 'plague-prisoners'. Then there was the matter of the disposal of the dead – an overwhelming urgency in a city denuded of labour and stinking under the relentlessly beautiful sun. At first evenings were like one long obsequy, with church bells forever tolling and funeral processions passing, but death coming by wholesale put an end to all such formalities. Even burial in consecrated ground had to be put by, and the noble capital of the kingdom accustomed itself to the dead-carts trundling through the streets, heaped with corpses, with the handbell ringers pacing before them; and to the pitiful indignities of the plague-pits in fields beyond the walls, where burial gangs steeped in liquor raked the lolling and uncoffined bodies with long hooked poles into great trenches that with their tangle of beseeching limbs, and yellow faces staring up from wormy darkness, presented a nearer likeness to hell than any imagination could devise.

Nature exhibiting herself at her cruellest, it was perhaps not to be expected that the nature of man should reveal itself any better. There were those who, as if in defiance of the prophets, made a religion of tippling and whoring, and even went carousing wearing shrouds and paint in imitation of plague-haemorrhage. With so many houses deserted, there was much robbery. There were thieves hardy enough to set upon the sick in the street. Conversely, I heard of sufferers who thrust their heads into coach windows, breathing on the occupants or even setting a kiss upon their lips, and crying that they had given them the plague. Most notorious was a race of old women who set themselves up as plague-nurses, and who at the best seemed to be drunken, brutal and fee-greedy. The worst tales, which alas I cannot doubt, have them smothering or throttling their dying patients, stealing everything they could carry, and proceeding to their next engagement.

There were some in my father's circle who found a grisly amusement in these stories, and, loving sensation, would eagerly collect them. My father, who has been so much reproved for flippancy, would have none of this. He was sadly affected by this disaster descending on his people: ordered a thousand pounds a week to the relief of the poor, who were most afflicted; and was bleakly sensible of the wider consequences of the calamity, for trade had all but ceased, the Exchange standing empty and grass growing through the cobbles of the principal streets, while the Thames, normally a floating market, saw scarcely a craft, and even such of our merchant ships as were abroad could find no port that would receive them or touch their goods.

But what the tales of the thieves and murderous nurses did produce in him was a kind of grim assent.

'Why, people cannot be so,' Queen Catharine cried at one such account. 'It is against nature.'

'I fear, my dear, that is just what it isn't,' he said. 'These are the things that are in men's natures, as the plague lurks in the air. It only needs the right weather to fetch 'em out.'

Well, I think it brought out the better in him, though there are voices who will reprove him for leaving London himself. He did not go till the summer was well advanced, long after the clergy and doctors had fled, and at first hoped to remain only at the small distance of Hampton Court; but other counsels prevailed, and at last we were all to shift to Salisbury. By that time my grandmother, at Somerset House, had packed up too, and elected to return to France. There was nothing to be gained by the Court's remaining in London to die, with the Throne only so recently restored to security. And so we left the city behind, parched, silent and spectral. Old General Monck, sturdy and imperturbable, chose to remain and keep order. Years of chewing tobacco, he avowed, had made him impossible to infect. By that time all but a handful of a hundred parishes were plague-struck, and five thousand were dying every week.

At Salisbury my father fell sickly, and I remember a day of watching him in dread, but it was only the air he found disagreed with him, and soon we were looking for new accommodations.

It was during this time, though, that my father and I made a visit to a place called Wimborne St Giles that ought to resonate fatefully within my mind. I say ought to, because the man who lived there played a part in my destiny, the consequence of which are still not ended. Yet such is the caprice of fate, which so seldom trumpets itself, but steals into our lives on slippered feet while we look away.

I knew him from court. He was of my father's council, and at that time stood high in his favour, though he had once supported the Commonwealth, until he had seen tyranny in Cromwell and changed sides. He was Anthony Ashley-Cooper, Lord Ashley. Such a lot of names, as someone said, for such a little man; and insofar as I noted anything at all, I believe I rather pitied him, being myself young and strong and well-made, whilst Ashley was a man of shrunken and twisted form, with a great head of sandy hair and a sharp, clever, sickly face that seemed always to be brooding upon some past injury. Mostly I think I felt uncomfortable in his presence. I thought of the rumours about his poor health, which they said was due to some ghastly prolapse of the bowels that he had to keep strapped in under his clothes. Also I felt he was ever watching me – though in truth he seemed to watch everybody, like a man who suspects there is a thief in the room. He was vastly rich, and at his mansion we were grandly entertained. His pictures and books spoke his culture, but much of his talk just then was of the Dutch war, and fierce implacable talk it was. War to the knife, he said: the Dutch must be utterly crushed and destroyed if we were ever to sleep secure; and when my father with a chuckle said he never slept the worse for knowing there was such a place as Holland across the sea, Ashley fixed him with a quickened, half-smiling look, as if that thief had betrayed himself at last.

That war, however, was no longer going so well. Under De Ruyter the Dutch rallied bravely, and as time brought no new victory in its train, one felt another presence in that still-fevered air – a venomous spirit of blame. The Court, and the Parliament, shifted to Oxford, where our welcome was tepid. It was not only the inconvenience to the scholars of giving over the colleges to us – my wife and I were quartered at Corpus Christi – but something deeper, which I only dimly began to apprehend. We of the Court were different: a separate little world, self-enclosed – and, I fear it appeared, self-satisfied and self-indulgent also. The lewd gossip and intrigue, the casually licentious ways, stood out glaringly in those venerable cloisters: the wits, like gorgeous exotics, lost no opportunity of mocking the drab sparrows of the university. God help me, I laughed along with them – but with a lurking consciousness of how shallow my own learning was. Secretly I resolved that I must set myself to some studies. It was a resolve that I did not keep till much later. But what did stay with me after Oxford was this perception that the court was not England, and that it was perilous to forget it.

There was particular hostility to Lady Castlemaine, who was pregnant again. Someone pasted a libel upon the door of her chambers at Merton College: '*Hanc Caesare pressam a fluctu defendit onus*' or

> The reason why she is not duck'd?
> Because by Caesar she is fucked.

My father was angry at this – surprisingly perhaps: for God knows the talk at his Court was robust enough. But then he had come to his throne adored and praised on all sides, and for all his rooted mistrust of men's motives, I suspect he had fallen into the trap of taking that love for granted. Now he began to see differently: the crowds that had cheered his restoration could soon tune their throats to jeering instead. I remember at this time Buckingham snickering over a pamphlet, writ by some ranting preacher, which called the plague a judgement sent by God in retribution for the wickedness of the King's Court. My father for once was not amused, and threw the paper on the fire.

'If the Almighty has any quarrel with me,' he said darkly, 'then let Him say so plain.'

'Ah, sire, your sins,' Buckingham said, still mirthful, 'be sure your sins will find you out.'

'Sins? I cannot believe a merciful God would punish a set of poor creatures so barbarously just because a man takes his pleasures while he can. And if that is God's way, then—' He broke off, gnawing his lip. I met his eyes, and I seemed to see a deep terror in them, of where his words were leading him.

Yes, there was change now. Things were going wrong, and so his kingdom, like any jaded lover, might grow disaffected. It only needed one more thing to go awry, Mr Ross said to me, and matters might turn very ugly indeed.

'Against who?'

'Whom, my lord, whom. Ah, that remains to be seen. But there has been naught but rising thus far – and nature's laws do not allow of that. Someone, sooner or later, must fall.'

There is no greater impotence than that of childhood, and there could hardly be a more impotent childhood than mine, torn about between powerful people, and lacking even a true name.

And yet, in my passage to manhood, which saw me vested with consequence and grandeur such as few mortals can know, I seemed to *lose possession* of myself, in a way I never did as a boy.

(Two curious thoughts occur to me here. One is of a dream I have had intermittently all through my adult years. I meet an enchantress, who throws the world open before me, and says: 'What would you have?

Name it – it is yours!' And always I reply, 'I would be a child again!'

The other is a memory of a quarrel between my father and Hyde, soon after the plague-time, when Hyde was reproaching him again for neglecting business in favour of women and luxury. 'You lose yourself in these dissipations,' Hyde fumed, and my father with a queer look answered: 'I don't have a self to lose.')

This feeling, of losing or perhaps forfeiting possession of myself, was not apparent to me at the time. It was more like one of those processes we apprehend only at their completion – falling sick, falling in love; falling from grace also, perhaps, if such is the innocence of childhood – and I am almost sure it is. Most of the time, in the years that took me into man's estate, I was very happy in an intense and uneasy way – which suggests that I was actually unhappy.

My love has just come in, looked over my shoulder at these last words, and laughed ruefully, ruffling my hair. 'How were you unhappy, my dear?' says she. 'Unhappy to be made a prince?'

Aye, very well. Yet she knows, better than any other, what I mean.

I see my young image in memory's crystal, spending the Christmas season at Saxham Hall in Suffolk, the seat of my old guardian Lord Crofts, who declares that he hardly knows me – yet do I know myself? That is me, certainly, joining in the carouse with Lord Crofts' other guests, who include Buckingham and others of the Court circle; that is me throwing in my clumsy pennorth to the fund of coarse talk and prickly wit; that is certainly me receding into a doubtful cloud of my own, plucking my lip, wondering if that last jest was at my expense, and then being ever more loud and thrustful to make up for it. Yet what this 'me' is really thinking or feeling, I cannot tell.

And now I see myself returned to a London recovered, at last, from the plague, a long winter frost accomplishing what medicine could not, the city quiet, gaunt, and altered like a recuperating invalid. I am living now in high state, with a great household and even my own secretary; and I am living too at great expense, or in debt if you will. Every tradesman from shoemakers to silversmiths, periwig-makers to jewellers, values his account with the House of Monmouth, and would value it more if it were sooner paid. Yes, periwig-makers – I am the very fool of fashion, and must needs cut off my hair, thick and black, and replace it with a periwig that looks like it – and jewellers, for my wife dearly loved pearls and diamonds.

She dearly loves our life, too, for it has all the fashion and consequence for which her self-assured temper fits her. She does not love me, but is content to accept me as a necessary part of the bargain. And periodically, rather like a wife reminding her man to wind up the clock, she reminds me of my nuptial duties, and so we get them over with.

As for me, I reserve what I am silly enough to call my affections for mistresses. There is a dalliance at this time with a lady of the Queen's household. If I do not name her, or those that came after, it is not out of disrespect for them but rather its opposite; and also because to do so would be to burden with importance affairs too trifling to bear it. I mean explanation, not excuse, when I say I followed the tone of the court in this. If I seem, in my later narrative, to be hard upon my father, consider that I followed him into the dreariest extremes of appetite, and found nothing there that compelled me to linger as he did.

But the young popinjay in memory's glass still loves his father extravagantly, and is loved in return. Indeed, as the year 1666 wore on it seemed my father cherished my company more than ever – perhaps because it was at least a respite from my uncle James.

The unhappy progress of the war, in which the French had now joined with the Dutch, brought out all the most exasperating aspects of his character. If he had been allowed to maintain personal command, of course, we would not have been losing. Whether he truly believed that my father was so jealous of his prowess that he preferred to see England go to defeat rather than permit him to exhibit it I don't know. My uncle was certainly capable of believing some outlandish things. What he could never believe was that he might be wrong. Never mind that he had pressed and pressed for this war for which, as he must have known, our shipyards were ill-prepared: the blame must lie elsewhere. My father suppressed his irritation with James's continual nagging quite masterfully. But I saw it break out once at cards, when James laid a card out of turn, and then had to be laboriously persuaded that he had done so.

'Ah. Indeed – I see now. Yes, yes, I was mistook. Your pardon, brother. I was wrong,' he said.

'Great heaven!' cried my father, good-humoured enough, but with a cold glitter in his eye, 'I fear there's something amiss with my ears – I could have sworn, brother, I heard you say you were wrong. I'd best fetch the surgeon and have them looked at.'

'Nay, Charles, what do you mean – are you ill? It is— Oh! A jest, yes, I see. No, the way it happened was, I turned aside to give the dog a sweetmeat – you recall? – and that was what misled me. That was what it was.'

And even afterwards James would not leave it. 'I was mistook, you see,' he kept putting in, 'with my turn – the dog, and so forth – that was how it came about.' He was only silenced when my father said at last with a deep sigh, 'Pray, James, stifle this urge to *confession*. Believe me, you are shriven.'

Well, whatever spirit of calamity had brought the plague had not finished with us yet. I have spoken of a fevered time, and anyone who has suffered fever knows that at the height there is a terrible burning.

I was with my father at Whitehall on a peaceful Sunday of bright gold September weather, when there came word of a great fire in the City.

It was, I remember, a secretary of the navy, a bustling young man with the curious name of Mr Pepys, who came to the palace with such an account as set folk buzzing, and caused my father to invite him in after chapel, to hear the tale. The fire had begun in the small hours at a baker's house in Pudding Lane. It had seemed, at first, no great matter. There were always fires in the old quarters of London, especially after such hot dry weather as we had had, and the Lord Mayor going to view the scene at first light had declared it was only such a little blaze as a woman might piss out.

But a gusty east wind was blowing up, and had carried sparks into Thames Street, where the fire had found better eating on the wharfsides, in warehouses of oil and tallow and heaps of timber and straw; and it had fallen to with a quickening appetite. By the time the secretary brought his report, there was a great blaze on either side of London Bridge on the north bank, with whole streets afire, and the very houses on the bridge beginning to catch.

My father listened gravely, and consulted with my uncle and others what was best to be done, while Mr Pepys almost danced upon the spot in his agitation; and soon concluded that any houses standing in the path of the fire must be pulled down to stop it spreading.

'Tell my Lord Mayor, Mr Pepys, if you will be so good, that he is to order the demolishing of any building, and heed no protests – it is the King's command.'

'Is this wise?' my uncle said. 'Consider, brother, the rights of property. It may be held much amiss.'

'So it will if we do not act. We must have the gunpowder stores from the Tower— Stay, Mr Pepys, think you the Tower is threatened? We must have a care for that.'

'Soldiers,' said my uncle – that was his answer to everything. 'If my Lord Mayor needs more soldiers, Mr Pepys, he shall have them. If need be, we shall have the county militias in. There may be disturbance, and we must have order before anything. Is it not so, brother?'

'Aye, aye, very well,' my father said. James could have his soldiers, but my father was more concerned with securing people's lives than ordering them about.

From the windows of Whitehall, with the eastward bend of the river, we could not see the fire yet, but there was a rich glow upon the sky as the day went on, and I found on going up to the roof to look that there was a powdery film upon my hands from the railings, and a sulphurous taint in the air that reminded me of my father's laboratory. Soon after, I went with my father and uncle in the royal barge downriver as far as Queenhithe, where Mr Pepys joined us again, and gave a sad account of the Lord Mayor, who was almost in despair at the task. People took no heed of him. There was opposition from merchants, especially, at having their houses brought down, and there seemed something supernaturally malicious in the way the fire skipped on the wind, even across the spaces that were made to break it.

'What of soldiers, Mr Pepys?' my uncle said. 'You told him he can have more soldiers, I hope?'

'Yes, Your Grace. He says that isn't needed, but he hardly knows where to turn – everyone being most concerned to save their goods as they may, and no effort to stop the fire spreading.'

Such, indeed, was the melancholy evidence upon the river, where a multitude of boats, many overladen with everything from feather beds to harpsichords, were trying to make way to the Southwark side. People sat or clung atop the precarious loads, and shouted to other craft to get out of the way. Others were grimly silent, their faces in their hands, all streaked with tears and smoke and sweat, but none could forbear, as with an awed fascination, from turning their heads ever and again to the scene upon the north waterside. From here the fire could be seen as a great crescent of orange – no cheerful colour, but a thick diabolical orange that somehow had black in it, and that made exultant lunges upward as if it would consume the very clouds. Even from the river the noise assaulted the ear, a hollow rushing and gnashing that filled you with a peculiar dismay – something like a superstitious dread, as if a god were at large, and you hardly knew whether to flee or prostrate yourself. Upon the surface of the river itself there was a perpetual hissing, as sparks and burning motes rained upon the water with molten dimples, while the smoke, all hints of horrible flavour, seemed to reach to the depths of your lungs in a moment.

'Dear God,' my father said, spitting and staring; and for a time he appeared dumb and stricken, before he roused himself, and ordered that more houses be pulled down on either side of the bridge. 'And let there be no more of these damnable rumours,' he said, as we took ship back to Whitehall, for already people had begun to cry out that the fire had been started by a plot of Papists, or Frenchmen, or Dutchmen, or all three, and more than one foreigner had had his head broken.

I slept little that night. That fascinated dread took me out on the leads again to view the eastern sky, which was all aglow as if with some angry wrongful dawn. In the morning my father summoned his Privy Council, and heard the newest reports. Half a mile of the city was burning now, and no sign of the fire's being contained. The Lord Mayor could not demolish houses fast enough, and a strengthening wind was whisking the fire ever onward, the old timbers and plaster of the City streets furnishing it with such excellent kindling that it was stoked up to kiln heat, sufficient to consume the very stones of churches and melt the lead upon their roofs. People seemed to have given in to helplessness and despair rather than fortitude and, just as with the plague, there were dispiriting accounts of men's natures under the calamity: the old and sick, and pregnant women being refused places on carts bearing plate and silks and even cheeses; thieves looting houses that stood in the fire's path on pretence of helping the owners to shift; countrymen swarming into the city with their wagons and carts and offering them at exorbitant prices. This last I remain sceptical of. Plague had left trade everywhere depressed, and if poor struggling men could suddenly earn enough to feed their families for the winter, from men seeking to safeguard their riches, I do not see great harm in it.

Certainly, though, there was great confusion and ruin in hand, and none seemed to strive in concert for remedy, but each for himself. If my father has been often reproached for a negligent and indolent man, he surely answered the reproach at this time, for he was all energy and decision. He ordered the setting up of fire-posts all about the city, each to be supplied with bread and cheese and beer for the manning, and a shilling for any man who would volunteer service in fire-fighting. The sailors from the docks were enlisted to take a hand with the blowing up by gunpowder of any building that might make a firebreak. And he had the barge made ready again, and went to see for himself, I and my uncle and a handful of the guards with him.

How hideous it was to see that dense world of streets right at the City's heart all one mass of flames, with all their freight of human lives, their industrious doings and pleasures, caught in so merciless a crucible that would melt them all down to naught. Going ashore, we were soon in the thick of it, amidst sights horrible in their desolation and also, often, in an incongruity beyond the power of invention. Besides the smouldering and levelled ruins, where the eye made a leap of amaze at finding a great stretch of space where hitherto had been a busy huddle of buildings, there were burned houses that still stood as intact shells, incandescent and fragile. One church tower I recall standing crazed, delicately translucent, just as if it were a bottle of smoked-glass from the lips of a giant blower. In other places the heat had buckled walls and floors in such a way that they depended in long arrested drippings, like stupendous candles. I saw an old invalid man being borne away on a mattress held aloft, like some potentate on a litter; others digging holes to lay their valuables in, with servants making tents of sheets about them, so no one would see what they put there. There were hens and geese, scorched and frantic, running about the streets, and in a ruined outhouse an entire pig that had burned in sty, whereof a gang of men were trying to hack themselves joints of roast pork, though burning their own hands to meat in the process.

But if there was a heartening sight, it was my father, who was everywhere – cheering, chivvying, exhorting; looking into the best manner of laying the gunpowder, and standing so close to the explosions that his face was almost black, and the guards, of whom he had given me command, were in a ferment of anxiety for him: talking easily and kindly with the poor wretches who had lost their homes, some of them plodding about in a sort of daze and clutching the oddest and most pathetic remnants – a birdcage, a single pewter dish, a candle-snuffer. It was dismal to discover how inadequate were the means of fighting even the smallest fires: how the leathern buckets, ladders and iron fire-hooks that were supposed to be kept in every parish church, feeble as they would have been, were scarcely even in evidence, being lost, or stolen, or broken, while such fire-squirts as the City could provide were as ineffectual as their name suggested, and did not hold above a gallon of water. But after that first bleak stare upon the river, my father seemed by sheer will to banish discouragement, in himself and in others, and I saw many men that day visibly jogged out of despair by his example. The deeds of royalty are oft cried up too much, I know, and a king has only to stop a man from stumbling, for it to be said that he saved him from death. Still, even my father's enemies could not but commend him for his action during the Great Fire. Indeed, some people wondered whether this energetic man, darting amongst the collapsing timbers with a fire-axe in his hands, ordering provision for the houseless, quenching his thirst with a sip of ale from a watchman's mug, could be the same neglectful rake who wasted the nation's treasure on silken mistresses – and if so, why: why was he like that, when he could be like this?

The sky that night, to my wondering eyes atop Whitehall, was the colour of blood. When the sun rose, you could look straight at it, so dense was the column of smoke over the city, making it like a tarnished penny. The river swarmed with laden boats, and here and there dogs and cats desperately paddling. Cinders swirled in the air, among them, most painfully, fragments of molten silk, for the silk-weaving districts had burned down, which stuck to your hands and face like hot candle-wax. The news was grim: the fire had reached Guildhall and the Royal Exchange, and all Cheapside was ablaze; and the fingers of flame were touching St Paul's.

The fire progressing westward, I was seized with alarm for my own household at Hedge Lane, and sent early to have all the servants remove. My father likewise set men to removing the timber-work from Scotland Yard, at the north end of the palace, to make a firebreak. That done, we went into the City again, upon horseback. My father wore a pouch about his shoulder, with a hundred guineas in it, which he handed out as rewards to the workmen still labouring to halt the fire. Before that day was done, it was hard to tell him from them, for he worked right amongst them, often knee-deep in muddy water, lifting timbers, digging, passing buckets, and plying the fire-pumps. I knew the peculiar store of energy he possessed, which would make him play a furious game of tennis before breakfast and still send him striding about the lake all morning, but I had never seen it so demonstrated. It quite outpaced me, young though I was: I remember him at one point squeezing my shoulder and saying, 'Take a little rest, Jemmy,' and then darting off into the thick of it again, face blackened and hair straggling with sweat. My uncle James labouring doughtily, could hardly keep up with him likewise.

But for all everyone's efforts, it was a black day: the day when Merchant Taylor's Hall disappeared, and Blackfriars was swallowed up, and Cornhill; and then, with quickening violence and ferocity, so that the very cobbles beneath your feet seemed on the point of combustion, the fire whipped itself down Ludgate Hill and Fleet Street. There was burning at all points of the compass, and such a roaring and crashing and cracking that when there came a rare pocket of quiet your ears seemed to sing. And as evening came on – not with any real darkening in the sky, but rather a relinquishing of light, as if the fire had vanquished nature itself – the flames began to dance on the roof of St Paul's.

The great cathedral went to its death most horribly. It shed a lurid and brilliant light on the faces of the watchers, who broke out in strange dire groans, for this seemed indeed the very heart of London in its stricken throes; and like a living creature the building appeared to sweal and melt with ghastly peelings and sloughings, as if the stone were skin. I remember murmuring aloud, as many perhaps did, 'What have we done?' – for if this was not some vengeful visitation, it was hard to see what it was. Such is our need to make sense of things.

'Why, Jemmy,' my father said, putting a hand on my shoulder – I hadn't known he was by – 'we have sinned, that's what. Didn't you know?'

And with his face all dark with smuts, he smiled, his teeth and eyes showing very white – devilishly so, I may say: he never looked more cunning, wordly, and composed – even *at home*, somehow. And I think that was why he showed such fortitude during the fire: he did not need to ask that question that had sprung to my lips. The world was only behaving as he expected it to behave, and he was no more surprised at it than when he caught a man in a lie.

The fire ended at last: but it did not so much go out as seem to consume even itself with its own violence. The calm that fell upon the City, or rather the bare stony waste that had been the City, was in a way as dreadful as the conflagration. This was a different circle of hell, but hell still, with ruins yet smoking and settling with hoarse exhalations, and the air all stinking vapour and swirling ash, and the ground sending up waves of heat like an oven, so that it was impossible to walk long about those notional streets without tears streaming down your cheeks. Upward of thirteen thousand houses were gone, and churches, wharfs, warehouses, workshops, markets besides. How many had died I know not: some said not a soul had been lost, but I heard of charred bodies, or even the mere tarry shapes of them, being found for weeks after: poor beggarly people, I fear, with none to miss them.

Beyond the destruction, at Islington, Highgate, Moorfields, the home-less survivors huddled with their bundles, and the rain that extinguished the last patches of fire added to their wretchedness. My father had already sent army tents for shelters, and food rations with strict injunc-tions that they were not to be sold or dealt in; and presently he went in person to Moorfields to address the pitiful crowd there, and assure them, as he said, of his particular care. Above all he went to quash any notions of a plot behind the fire, for still the rumours ran about that the fire had been the work of Papists or foreigners.

'Men are hungry for blame,' Chancellor Hyde said. 'I fear they will not be content until they have a mouthful to chew on.'

'These "desperate daggers" that have been discovered in the ruins?' my father said with a smile. 'They must have been careless plotters to have left their own weapons in the way of the fire.'

'Aye, true' – Hyde himself could not forbear smiling – 'but men's minds have been sadly worked upon by these calamities, and I confess I do not see how the temper of the times is to be cooled.'

'By making new times,' my father said.

For he had a vision already before his mind: London as a phoenix rising new-made from its own ashes. Soon he was displaying to me a ground plan for the rebuilding of the city, most ingeniously and delicately drawn by the small, dry, dapper man at his elbow, Sir Christopher Wren. My father delighted in this gentleman, who was learned in astronomy and mathematics, as well as a most brilliant architect.

'See here, Jemmy, Sir Christopher is the man who gave me the moon,' my father said – for he had got his lunar globe as he had long desired, 'and I swear he is the man to give us a new London. Look here – streets wide and straight, after a rational plan. The old city grew up anyhow: this we may train like a vine. We must think above all of convenience and safety. A city well drained, well lit, airy – no street markets straggling across the thoroughfares, or noisome trades carried on amongst the houses. None of those courts and alleys where fevers and fires begin. And handsomeness as well as utility. A walkway all along the embankment, with the guildhalls ranged about it, to present the most pleasing view to the visitor.'

It was indeed a handsome plan, even if the straightness was a little too straight for my tastes, and I missed the romance of antique windings; but then my father and I always differed on such things.

'It remains to be seen whether all interests may be sufficiently squared,' Sir Christopher said, as precise as his drawings. 'There will be a multitude of landowners, each with his own notion; there will be jobbing speculators; then there is Parliament to consider.'

'Heyo! I wish there was not,' my father said. It was always difficult to tell whether or not he was joking.

While my father strove to summon a genie of hope out of the ruins – with, as Wren had foreseen, much impedance in the City and elsewhere – the time following the fire was a bitter one in many ways, some foreseen, others falling like a thunderbolt. And, indeed, it was at this time that one heard men say, quite as a matter of cool fact, that the kingdom was lost.

The crowning disaster, and one that still gives Englishmen a plunge of shame to think of, came in the summer of 1667; but something occurred earlier, in the spring, that I fancy had an even stronger effect upon my father, and subsequently the kingdom, though it appeared – to me at least – mighty trifling.

Frances Stewart, who had so long barred her virginity against my father's advances, eloped with the Duke of Richmond. Here was a new sort of scandal indeed – a lady choosing the respectability of marriage rather than the honour of being the King's mistress.

'Richmond – a poor whey-faced slubberdegullion with chalk for brains!' cried Lady Castlemaine. 'Hey, well, they're suited in that regard. By cock, imagine their children! They'll have to be knocked on the head – they'll be too stupid to live. Mind, I know what's behind it. The minx was after the Queen's place, and couldn't get it, and so has settled for second best – tenth best rather, or a hundredth . . . Oh, I'm sorry for her, I truly am!'

'Well, I am not sorry,' I said: I was glad the folly was over.

Nor, of course, was Lady Castlemaine sorry. 'It is given out,' she said, inspecting herself in the glass with dashing turns and tosses of her head, 'that the Stewart's going was a great surprise. Yet it was not *so* great. The truth of it was, the King tired of the siege, and resolving on a frontal attack, slipped to the vixen's chambers by night. Her waiting-woman tried to put him off, saying her mistress was in bed with a headache – but she has had quite enough of *those*, by God, as Charles no doubt thought. But when he got to the inner sanctum, he found the chit was indeed in bed – not with a headache, though, with Richmond. I won't say doing what, but suffice it to say she could not *speak* for a moment. But there – there are worse things than people going to bed together, eh?' She laughed, cocking me a look. 'And would you know the most *piquant* thing of all? Who do you suppose played Cupid for the Stewart and her lack-wit beau? Why, my lord Chancellor! Aye, he had a hand in the whole contriving. Not from sentiment, you may be sure, for he's a corpse below that fat belly – but he wants Charles's nose at the grindstone, not sniffing around the Stewart's skirts, and so he's up to his old trick of running His Majesty's life for him. Charles ain't pleased – by cock. I never saw him so out of humour, but he'll come round.' And she exchanged a smile with her reflection, as with a warm friend.

She spoke true, in that my father's displeasure was plain. But as for coming round, I saw no sign of it. Frances Stewart's desertion, as he saw it, cast him into a dark and resentful mood from which there was no rousing him. The new-wed couple were banned from the court, and it was a foolhardy man who dared to speak of her to him.

Well, I was that foolhardy man, presuming on his love for me. I did not like to see him brooding thus, not only for his own sake but because people were talking: he would make himself a laughing-stock. I spoke in his bedchamber one day, when one of his spaniels had just given pup, right there on the bed. He always indulged them thus, and the circumstance seemed promising, for a new litter of puppies was usually his delight, and he would quite beam with fondness.

Today, though, he looked on with a cold unmoved eye at the mother licking her blind squirmers. Still I plunged on.

'I fear you are still out of humour, Father.' As he did not answer I went on: 'It's this matter of Mistress Stewart, is it not?'

He glowered at me. 'Who has put you up to this?'

'No one. I wouldn't venture on it – only I don't like to see you making yourself so unhappy.'

'Making *myself* unhappy. Here is a sort of accusation.'

'Aye, if you like,' said I, rash now. 'Isn't that the way of it? I cannot think the occasion is so very grievous—'

'Well, well. I never thought to find *you* so cold-hearted, Jemmy, of all people.'

But it isn't, I thought but dare not say, about *hearts*.

'I don't expect you to understand,' he said. 'Though 'tis well known enough that no man cares to have his affections trifled with.'

I looked for some glint of humour, of self-mockery, but for once there was none.

'I do want to understand, though, Father. What I mean is – if I thought you loved the lady . . . then I would understand.'

He scowled. 'There is a great deal of stuff talked about love. And now, of course, you are going to say I am incapable of it.'

He was a step ahead of me. Quite spontaneously, I found myself changing tack.

'No,' I said, 'for I think you loved my mother.'

He turned his face away from me, and I heard a struggle in his voice. 'I never want to lose my temper with you, Jemmy – so I advise you to get gone.'

I did so, with the satisfaction at least of having spoken out – though no other satisfaction in truth, my father continuing bitter as before till I felt bafflement become impatience. If he had succeeded with Frances, I thought, then he would only have – well, not finished with her, for, as it was said, in card-playing parlance, the King never discarded, he only added to his hand; but she would have become just another mistress awaiting her turn like a harem concubine. Reflecting on this, I perceived in him something closer to weakness than vice. For if you put all your trust in one person, you gave them a great power to hurt you; distribute it amongst several, and the risk was lessened. If my father, who relished mathematics, reasoned thus, then he was no doubt prudent. But there are limits to the areas of life where reason and prudence apply, and I think it is as well to know them.

So I must record that when the crowning disaster fell upon the kingdom in the summer of 1667, my father was still preoccupied with the empty-headed girl who had rejected him. Thankfully for his reputation, he roused himself to action when the crisis came; nor was it his fault that things had come to such a pass. The root of it was, we were still engaged in that war with the Dutch that my uncle James had been so eager for, but we could not pay for it. The disruptions of plague and fire had so depleted the coffers that there was no question even of putting the fleet to sea. The ships had to be laid up in harbour, and such resources as we possessed put to strengthening the coastal defences. The Dutch had taken command of the sea, and all that spring we were torn between rumour and expectation. Admiral de Ruyter was out there somewhere with eighty Dutch men-of-war, and they would surely descend upon our coasts: but where?

With a captain's commission, I was dispatched by my father to Harwich to inspect the fortifications there, and to take command of a troop of horse against any invasion landing. This was gratifying: I wanted to be doing, and to be doing as a soldier most of all. I remember Mr Ross saying to me, as we rode by the sea wall, that I looked as if I had stepped out of the shadow at last. Harwich I found well prepared, and I wrote to my father that I doubted the Dutch would hazard anything here, and that if they did they could expect a hot welcome.

In truth, though, I was something pained by the spectacle of my companions-in-arms, young braggart lords of the court mostly, who swaggered about and seemed to think the great feathers in their hats would conquer the Dutch as they conquered the women of the town. I was conscious too that I must appear just like them. Indeed, report had it that I was debauching the local ladies, when I was busy learning the arts of naval battery and the science of ordnance. Well, there is no stopping the mouth of scandal, but I resolved at Harwich that if arms were to be my vocation, I would not be a graceful amateur. I took pains to consult with the ordinary seamen, the dockhands and engineers and labourers – finding shrewd and sensible men where the chatter of the Court would have only block-headed hinds; finding, moreover, to my peculiar satisfaction, that they readily entrusted their confidence to me, and that we stood upon an easy ground. The common man was no stranger to me, who had been in a way to becoming one myself, until my father owned me. Here I seemed to distil something vital to my identity, murky though it yet was.

Harwich was safe, but the Dutch fleet passed by Harwich. Thames mouth itself was their object. When news reached us that the Dutch were in Medway, with none to oppose them, I and my troop rode as hard as we could to muster at Gravesend. At every one of the fifty miles, it seemed, someone cried out a fresh report – that our fleet was smashed at anchor, that the Dutch had the forts, that they were up the Thames proper and training their guns on London itself.

The truth was mortifying enough. The Dutch fleet had entered the King's Channel and taken Canvey Island and Sheerness, burning our flag and hoisting their own over the fort, seizing sheep and stores at their leisure. All along the river there was panic. Monck, trying to organize resistance, found no boats and few men to serve, especially for nothing, as there was no money to pay them. The great chain that was meant to stretch across the river was all encumbered with mud, and in the event the Dutch just sailed through and broke it. The crew of the first English guard-ship deserted at the mere sound of cannon. In triumph, to the sound of drums and trumpets and the roar of flame, the Dutch advanced on Chatham, and had their way with our helpless fleet. Three great men-of-war burned at their berths, while the flagship *Royal Charles*, the same on which I had served at Lowestoft, the Dutch boarded and seized, and decided to tow away as a token of our humiliation, leaving their fire ships to destroy the rest. All Monck could do was order the surviving ships scuppered, and watch as the Dutch returned downriver with their great prize, raking the land with insolent salvoes of celebration.

This was, indeed, the sort of fabulous daring exploit that one thrilled to – if it was Englishmen doing it. As it was, the Medway raid threw London into a greater consternation than the fire. Men quite lost their heads, sending their families flying into the country, scrabbling to hide or realize their money, giving over the kingdom for lost. It was here, in the midst of terror that the enemy would venture on London, that my father leaped into an energy such as he had shown during the fire, supervising the sinking of boats along the Thames creeks so as to block them against invasion. The Dutch did not choose to penetrate further, but settled to blockade us instead, most effectively. Prices were soon dear, merchants cried that they were ruined again, and the poor, as ever, felt the pinch hardest.

There would have to be peace, which was in fact what the Dutch wanted, upon the best terms they could get. But in the meantime the war turned in upon men's hearts, in furies of reproach and blame.

Already the popular feeling against Chancellor Hyde, as helmsman of the wrecked state, had reached such a pitch that stones flew at the windows of his great mansion at Piccadilly, and someone nailed up a gibbet outside it. Monck's son Christopher told me that at the meetings of an agitated Privy Council Hyde had done nothing but proclaim that he had never approved the war from the beginning. My father, who could with truth have adopted the same defence, did not escape censure either. Rumour said that on the night of the fleet's burning, he had been supping with Lady Castlemaine, and joining in a mad hunt for a moth flittering about the candlelit room. Well, it makes an apt symbol, no doubt, whatever the truth; and we were entering upon a time in which truth was a sacrifice upon the pyre of men's passions.

The odour of sacrifice, indeed, was upon the air. Like fearful pagans, men sought to propitiate the vengeful gods of catastrophe. Hyde was to be the victim, and my father the high priest.

He would have preferred, I know, to do it as quietly as possible. If Hyde did not surrender his office, he would surely be attacked by the Parliament at the next session, perhaps impeached, so strong was the feeling against him. My father's temperament was such that he believed any sensible man must prefer discreetly slipping away to such a destructive confrontation – surely. But his first approach met with little success. He closeted himself with my uncle James one day, and must have asked James, as Hyde's son-in-law, to speak to the old man, and put the suggestion.

They emerged together, yet grimly apart.

'There is nothing more to say, I think, brother,' James said.

'There is much to say, James, but it is perhaps better not said – not until we have both cooled a little.'

'I crave your pardon, but you mistake me. I am quite cool – no reason to be otherwise,' my uncle said, going away at his most grand and ponderous: at such times he had the look of a man mentally wading through deep water.

'If you choose to remain at odds with me on this matter,' my father said after him, harshly, 'then you disoblige me, and you must pardon me, James, if I draw certain conclusions from that.'

James paused a moment, like a man fancying he hears his name called, before progressing stiffly on.

My father, seeing me, sighed, and placed an arm about my shoulders. I felt his fingers poke under my periwig.

'What are you doing, Father?'

'Checking for the family stiff neck. Ah – I feel it a little – not too bad. Beware of it, Jemmy.' And he laughed, but sorely.

The next morning, Hyde came at my father's summons to the Privy Apartments. His wife had lately died, and he was purple with gout. One might suppose him very ready to put off the burden of office – until one saw the stubborn, righteous knot of his lips.

The interview was long. When Hyde came out, though he looked weary, the stubbornness was still there. I thought he was going to walk right past me, but at the last moment he veered and, addressing me in his sudden, choking manner, said: 'You are happy, no doubt, young sir. No doubt you are one of those that exult.'

'Why so, my lord?'

He frowned, a schoolmaster with a dull pupil. 'You cannot suppose me a friend to your ambitions, *ergo*, you will rejoice at my going. In truth I might have been a better friend to you than you can conceive: better than those men who will seek to make a tool of you.'

'I shall be no man's instrument, believe me, my lord.'

'*Sancta simplicitas!* Believe you?' He snorted distressfully. 'No matter. I shall not be here to see it. But believe *this*, young sir: I was once as confident of the King's favour as you are now. When your time comes, remember this.'

Well, I dare say I tossed my head at that, and swaggered, but at heart I was perturbed. And that at least prevented me joining in the demonstrations of Lady Castlemaine, who seeing Hyde leaving by way of the Privy Garden, threw open her windows and stood waving, clapping, and calling mocking farewells. Being no early riser, she was still in her smock, displaying her white limbs and silken bosom. With her were some of her cronies, including Lord Arlington, who was to rise with the Chancellor's fall, and who were all grinning. Here, indeed, you had the living image of all that Hyde, dry and churchy and staid, had set himself against at my father's court; and here was its triumph.

I saw Hyde's shoulders twitch, just as if her were being physically pelted. Then he turned and cried up at Lady Castlemaine, his voice cracking and fluting: 'Pray remember – remember, ma'am, that if you live, you will grow old.' But she only laughed at that, as we do.

Hyde and the Lady, of course, were long antagonists. His prim distrust of her influence, his advocacy of the Queen, were well known, and those ambitious courtiers who sought Hyde's downfall had always gathered about her gilded apartments, and done their plotting at her well-stocked table. Buckingham was prime among these men, of course, and Ashley, pale and waspish, was often to be seen passing through her doors, as well as this Lord Arlington, who had long been a companion of my father's, and aimed high. He cultivated a dashing air, half grandee, half rake, and liked to hint at a prolific past during the exile – even, I heard, claiming intimate acquaintance with my mother, though I remember no such thing, and I believe she would have thought him silly. Similarly, he finished his dandyish dress with a piece of conspicuous black sticking plaster across the bridge of his nose – token of a wound from the Civil Wars, supposedly; in fact a mere scratch from a duel, I heard.

But affectation aside, he was a coming man. And certainly gossip was prompt to trace Hyde's downfall to Lady Castlemaine's chambers – which is to say my father was manoeuvred into dismissing his chancellor.

My father, though, did nothing he did not want to do. It may have suited his purposes to have it appear that he was gracefully giving in to public pressure. But in truth there was ruthlessness in him. In part it was a canny survivor's instinct: the ugly mood of the country must be appeased. Yet I am sure he also blamed Hyde for the loss of Frances Stewart, and that when he ordered the Chancellor to return the Seal of Office, that was in his mind quite as much as matters of state.

Before the Seal was given up, though, there was more wrangling. Hyde would not fade into private life as my father hoped: he would carry on making his voice heard in the Parliament. In all of this my uncle James supported him. Night and day I heard his deep passionless voice droning at my father. Only later when the Parliament convened, and the threat of impeachment and trial hung over Hyde, did the old man give in; and as my father had wanted him to all along, he quietly left the country for an exile in France.

By then, however, there was a settled coldness between my father and James, much remarked upon. My father was too mindful ever to quarrel in public; but when my uncle entered the room, or began to talk, I saw a sort of summoning-up look cross my father's face, like that of a man steeling himself to a wave of sickness or pain. Other men's view of my uncle changed too.

'It is not simply a matter of a man defending his wife's father,' Mr Ross said. 'It is a matter of power: the power the duke possessed while his father-in-law ruled the state, and the power he fears to lose without him. Some might say, what has the duke to do with power? That belongs to His Majesty. But I fear the duke looks to the day when His Majesty's power is his. Others look to that day also – and tremble at it. The late reverses have brought out the most inflexible elements in the duke's temper. He has been heard to say that only a strong manner of governance, with a standing army, will save us, and do more good than any Parliaments. I only repeat the talk, of course. And praise be, His Majesty continues in good health, and we need not think of such things just yet.'

My wife, who was growing quite the politician, was thinking of all these things. One night, after our customary duties, she stayed me from going to my own chamber as was my wont, and spoke of Hyde.

'Oh, I am not sorry he has gone,' I said carelessly.

'Are you not? Why?'

Shrugging, I said he was no friend to me.

'Because a friend to your uncle James. Aye: that's so.' She nibbled a comfit in the dark. I could almost hear her mind efficiently ticking away. 'Consider, though, Jemmy, this may not be a good thing – for you. Consider where the Queen stands.'

'Hm?'

'Tsk, attend, Jemmy. Without Hyde to stand by her, folk wonder whether the King will now divorce the Queen, or be otherwise rid of her, and so take a new bride who is not barren, and so have an heir.'

'My father will never divorce the Queen,' I found myself saying.

Alert, Anna said: 'What? How so – has he told you this?'

'No . . .' Like so many things to do with my father, it was difficult to put into words; but I felt in my bones that it was so. I remembered the time of her illness, and his tears; I remembered her sadly smiling words over the tea table. Catharine's great error had been to fall in love with my father. At first he might well have despised her for it, and perhaps in that too there had been fear: instead of a no-nonsense, biddable, official queen such as Louis of France had got, he found himself contracted to a woman who made demands upon his carefully hoarded feelings. Yet if he could not return them, I was sure he would, in compensation, never see her lose her royal position. I suspicioned he had made a bargain with himself in that – and I knew all about making such bargains. 'I am just certain of it,' I said at last. 'He will not abandon the Queen.'

'Interesting,' Anna said, chewing that over with another comfit. 'You know my lord Buckingham urges him to be rid of her. I fancy my lord Ashley is of that mind too. But they have both been heard to say also that he should declare you his legitimate heir.'

I stared into the dark, with a curious sensation as if my mind were prickling. 'If they are saying such things—'

'It simply means they're intriguing as usual, of course. Quite right, Jemmy: you are learning. But the wind is blowing that way – against your uncle. Take heed of it. Also, I have been talking with His Majesty, and you may as well know that he is going to do something for you. Tsk, don't look at me like that' – it was like Anna to be able to see in the dark – 'you know I often talk with your father. I am quite a pet of his, and we talk of lots of things. He is a most entertaining talker. I fear that is the trouble with your uncle: I try my best to converse with him, but he will insist on taking me over every fence of the hunting field. It's either that or religion, and I cannot follow him over those fences neither. If he means to make a convert of me, he is mistook.'

'A convert?'

'Aye, Jemmy. Your uncle is much affected towards the Catholics, as everyone knows; but I fancy it is more than that.'

'Oh, but it can't be. If he would wear the crown, he cannot turn Catholic. There would be another civil war . . .'

'Hey, well, he doesn't strike me as a man to fear that. I've heard your father say James wants to fight the old one over again.'

I sat up, searching in vain for tinder and flint to light a candle. My thoughts were much the same, groping in darkness. I knew that what I had just heard was significant, and that I must lay hands on and grasp it sooner or later. But for the moment vanity ruled me: I wanted to know what my father had planned for me.

'Hm? Oh, yes – well, he merely let this slip, and so you must remember to act surprised. He means you to have the Captaincy of the Guards. Quite an honour, Jemmy: I hope you know it.'

I was floating at once. 'This is fine!'

'Aye. I'm glad you do know it.' She turned on her side to sleep, which she could always do at will. 'You may be sure your uncle will know it too.'

My first office: Captain of my father's Guards. I remember going, newly sashed and gloved and bubbling with nervous pride, to inspect them; and how my uncle went out of his way to congratulate me, stepping before me in the Pebble Court. His words were leaden, his face stony, and as he stood there blinking at me it seemed for a strange moment that he was not going to move out of my path.

I remember too, soon afterwards, asking a favour of my father on behalf of a friend who had seen service against the Dutch, and was in sore need. My father at once ordered a grant of a prize ship to him; and at my thanks said distinctly, with my uncle looking on: 'Nay, my son, don't think of it. Anything, Jemmy – you have only to ask.'

Yes, everyone looked on, you may be sure. But how much they saw, and whether they read it aright, is a different matter. For it was from this time, I think, that the impenetrable mask my father presented to the world hardened and became fixed: here was the genial monarch who was apparently so open, and who was really so closed, locked, barred and guarded. I know that there was something gloomy and defensive in his spirits at this time – and no wonder. For all his unconcerned looks, he had suffered deep humiliations, from the bedchamber to the field of war. And after all the humble pie he had been forced to eat during the exile – that long travail of disillusion, never forgotten – humiliation was bane and gall to him. In future he would go any way to avoid it: never would he be dependent on the yea or nay of any man or woman; never set himself at the mercy of circumstance.

And already he had a design in mind to further this chill and narrow purpose. I was, unwitting at first, to further it. At last, it was to divide us fatally. The seeds were already present when, in the first cold days of January 1668, I set out for France – seeds of bitterness, betrayal, and death. If I was not aware of them, I did have a curious memory, as in grand state my father and my uncle saw me off, of the way we had all three laboured together in the mud and smoke of the Great Fire, together with a presentiment that we would never know, in family or kingdom, such unanimity again.

SIX

'See here,' Minette said, dancing away with the letter and evading my fingers, 'see where your father writes: "I believe you may easily guess that I am something concerned for this bearer James, and therefore I put him into your hands to be directed by you in all things" – Aha, you see? – "and pray use that authority over him, as you ought to do in kindness to me." That means, Jemmy, you must do as I say – and I say you must go to bed.'

'But I'm not tired!'

'You look as if you never are.' Her laughing eyes sobered a moment, in sorrowful admiration. 'I only wish I had your constitution.'

'Oh, I get it from my father, I think.'

'You do remind me of him . . . so very much.'

'What else does he say of me?' I made another grab for the letter, and we romped about that gilded chamber in the Palais Royal, as once we had played in my grandmother's garden.

'He says you are very bad boy – and cruel to your poor old aunt.'

And then we had to stop and laugh again. Aunt? The six years' difference in age between us had never seemed so insignificant. She kept looking at my height and breadth. As for Minette, was she changed? She had suffered ill health, and twice miscarried, and she was thin – like a light-boned bird, but lovelier, I thought, than ever.

'No, truly, Jemmy, you must be guided by me . . . Now what are you doing?'

'Following you. You are my guide. I shall follow you everywhere—'

'Nonsensical fellow! Hark now. Charles wants you to acquire a little polish, and so you must observe. Now there is no better place in the world than the court of France to learn the true arts of living—'

'*Mais oui, Madame! Bien sûr!*' I made her some extravagant bows. She laughed as one who has grown unused to laughter, in painful hiccoughs. '*Ma foi*, but you are – *adorable.*'

The laughter stopped. Unwittingly, I had produced an imitation of Philippe. And now with goblinlike promptness he appeared at the door.

'Madame, we must leave, the hour is late, quite unthinkably late. Your guest is comfortable with his accommodation, I am sure – you hardly need play the chamberlain.'

'Of course, Philippe.' It was like the dousing of a flame. 'It is just such a long time since I saw Jemmy—'

'Oh, time!' he said airily, as if she had mentioned something trifling and vulgar. But the look he gave me was narrow and assessing. Was he remembering the boy he had taken by the chin, years ago? Philippe himself was ageless: only a little more pinched in figure – corsets, no doubt – and in face too, from the habit of malice.

I had come to Paris in great state, and also wealth. My father had given me two thousands pounds for expenses, and my entourage had been greatly tickled at the way I had to keep opening the strongboxes and checking it all through the voyage across in my uncle James's yacht. I brought gifts from my father: for Louis, a string of horses; for Minette jewels and silks and reliquaries; and the letter, which I had strict instructions to deliver into her hands only. For all the jesting, she was firm in not letting me see it.

The purpose was, as Minette said, for me to learn a few graces, and the ways of foreign courts (as if I had never been there! – though, of course, only as a lowly observer). It was flattering that I was to go to Minette, whom my father so cherished. But then everything was flattering. My reception by King Louis, who was at the gorgeous height of his fortunes, fresh from military conquests, and treated like a god; my grand apartments in the Palais Royal; above all Minette's reaction to me, about which I had had some anxiety. When I had gone away from her, she had been Madame of France and I a gawkish boy. Now I returned princely – but with some fear that pomp might make us strangers. The bright melting look in her eyes as I first kissed her hand dispelled that. No doubt I brought my father to her mind, and England, and many fond associations, but I fancy also it was the warmth of the past that glowed there.

The past, before Philippe.

Everyone spoke of how capricious he was still, how jealous. Yet I thought that after some years of marriage, things might have settled down somewhat. He could at least no longer run crying to his mother: Anne of Austria had died of a cancer. Minette had nursed her.

'Left to himself, Philippe is not so very bad,' said my grandmother. She was back in permanent residence in France. I went to call on her at Colombes, where a rush of memory made my eyes moist. My grandmother noticed that, with her old faintly malicious smile. Her mind was quick as ever, but she looked sadly aged, shrunken. In strong light you could see a skull more than a face. 'But the trouble is, he is impressible. It is his choice of companions that is unfortunate. They – they act upon him in unhappy ways.'

'The Comte de Guiche?' I asked.

'Uff! No. Though that would not be so bad: de Guiche had qualities . . . But him we do not speak of, Jemmy.' This was not the first hint I had had of some scandal about de Guiche, but I could no longer learn the truth from servants as I used to. 'No – there is another young man just now. Philippe is very close with him. But it will pass, everything passes.' With sudden tetchiness she said: 'You young people, bah! You think you are the first to do everything. Love. The bed. It is all as old as creation. You will learn – not that I care.' My grandmother, with typical courage, was preparing for death. She spoke much of it, sharply, as if it were a neglectful visitor, a delinquent like poor lost Henry. I wished I could have been more sorry to go away from her.

I met Philippe's new favourite at a ball given by Monsieur and Madame at the Palais Royal. Most cultivated and elegant was the circle who gathered around Minette: poets, musicians, politicians, men of letters and women likewise, who rather frightened me with their prickly wit; and I was quite prepared to get little of her company. Yet she stayed by me. She wanted to talk; to know of all that had happened in England, and especially of my father.

'I much regretted the war,' she said sadly. 'As did Louis.'

'Ho, it didn't stop him joining against us.'

'That is over now. Louis would be a good friend to England, if he were allowed.' She saw my expression. 'Why, is France not trusted in England, Jemmy?'

'Well, all the shouting has been against the Dutch, of course. But they seem to want peace with us in the end, if it is to be had. It's not as if they could conquer us. But when folk hear of Louis's great armies sweeping across the Continent, they fear him.'

'Oh, so they should!' Minette said, with a shining look. 'For he is a great king – mighty. But generous too.'

'Hm. I don't think the English can ever be brought to love the French, in truth.'

'No? But I am something of both, you know. Perhaps I can set an example.'

'Also France is Catholic, and Louis is hard against the Protestant faith. England cannot love Popery.'

'But then again – I am Catholic. Now look at me – am I so very frightening?'

We laughed, and I do not know why a little part of me thought that she was, somehow.

'You had some Catholic teaching, Jemmy, did you not?'

'I did: but I did not believe it.'

'Ah, such a pity! Consider, Jemmy: such high state as you are come to now – quite princely. And yet you cling to the low religion of rebels and republicans!'

Her look was mischievous, but I could not help answering soberly: 'It is the religion of our country; and my father's. He could not have his throne else.'

'So? And yet a king is king by grace of God alone, not because the people allow him to be. Look at Louis. He answers only to God; and the French nation sees this, and glories in it.'

'Well – if so, they are no better than slaves.'

'Oh, fie, Jemmy, you are a Cromwellian!'

'No, no,' I said, laughing a little. 'I am my father's son.' Though again came a small questioning voice: what truly did that mean?

'I am glad to hear it. That is why I . . .' She did not finish. 'Well, you shall see how we go on in France, and what a true king Louis is. We shall change your mind about some things, Jemmy.'

'Aye – some.' We laughed: the wrangling was all in good humour, and we were quite at ease. Indeed, we made, I fancied, a handsome couple. It seemed quite natural to ask her: 'What became of the Comte de Guiche?'

A moment of stillness. 'Why do you ask that, Jemmy?'

'Because I remember him at Fontainebleau. He was kind to me. He told me my fortune.'

'What?'

'Oh, he said I would have my portrait made, that was all – and so I have. But when I left, he was – well, under a cloud. So I wondered. Also my grandmother wouldn't speak of him. Also I think he had fallen in love with you.'

'Oh, Jemmy . . .' Looking away, Minette took my hand in both hers, and mournfully beat it.

'That is surely not so strange. For you to be loved.'

'You are gallant!'

'No, only truthful.'

'You have heard some gossip, I presume.'

'No!' said I, a little hurt; but I reflected too what a small and airless world this Court was, seeing nothing beyond its own gossip. At least the public could saunter, gaping, through Whitehall, bringing breezes of reality with them.

'Well, there was a good deal of talk about it . . . De Guiche was – was foolish enough to conceive a certain affection for me. And I was foolish enough to like it. He was a fascinating companion, you see. He was clever and kind. If those two things could always go together, the world would be much better, you know. You gave me a start just now, Jemmy, when you said he told your fortune, for it was one of his whims to disguise himself as a fortune-teller to come and see me.' She smiled, reminiscent. 'It was all just a frolic and no harm . . . but of course it was not seen so, in some quarters. He went to the wars at last, and has been a great soldier. Once in Poland a shot struck him and would have reached his heart – but he wore my portrait there under his shirt, and that saved him . . . And so what a tale of nonsense it is, and now no more of it!'

I did not think so: a tale of beauty, I thought.

'Tell me your tales, Jemmy. Tell me of your pretty wife, and your new house, and what you mean to do in life.'

'Oh! My wife. I suppose she is. My wife, I mean. But it hardly seems so, for we did not choose each other.'

'That is not the way of things.'

'Aye, but – why? Why should we not spend this life we have, this one precious life, with whomever we love, and be damned to all else?'

'You have not changed so very much after all,' Minette said, shaking her head. But she did not sound superior or disdainful, not now. There was even a hint of reluctant admiration.

'As for what I mean to do – well, in a way I want to be like the Comte de Guiche.'

'Do you?' said she faintly. 'You are already rather like him.'

Pleased, I went on: 'Aye, to be a soldier – captain of horse, taking the field at the troop-head, you know, not creeping along with an artillery train. Leading your men, like Alexander did. I went dressed as Alexander to a masquerade, you know . . .' All at once I recalled how that evening had ended, with a shockingly vivid image of Barbara Castlemaine's strong white thighs gripping me. I faltered, half-choking, and took some wine.

'A soldier . . .' Minette shook her head thoughtfully. 'No, don't go soldiering, Jemmy. We should learn the arts of peace.'

'Aye – I suppose – but let me just learn the arts of war first. You know who I would wish to serve under? Marshal Turenne.' This was the great general of France, whose name I had come to venerate. 'There – a Frenchman – that should please you.'

'Well, well. As it happens, I know Turenne well, and he comes often to my salon. If I chose, I might introduce you. But I do not think I so choose.'

'Oh, why?'

'Because I like to have you here by me,' she said, squeezing my hand impulsively, 'and not talking horrid soldier's stuff with old Turenne – and you are to obey me in all things, Jemmy, remember—'

'Turenne? Who speaks of Turenne, what is this, pray?'

It was Philippe, descending on us in a cloud of sickly pomade.

'I was just saying, Philippe, that Turenne is often with us, for Jemmy admires the Marshal very much—'

'But it is a woman talking!' Philippe cried, appealing to the young man at his side with a kind of writhe of disbelief. 'About war! How curious! My dear sir' – he peered down his long nose at me – 'if you want to learn about war, you do wrong to address a *woman*. I was lately with the army in Flanders: you would do better to ask *me* about such things.'

'Sir,' I said bowing, 'I should be very happy to have the benefit of your knowledge.' Instinct told me to flatter him, so that he would not be cruel to Minette.

'To narrate my campaigns would take more time than I can spare, believe me,' Philippe said, and laid his arm around the young man's broad shoulders. 'We warriors, you know, have so many tales to tell.'

Minette said, quite calm, 'Jemmy, you have not been presented, I think. The Chevalier de Lorraine: His Grace the Duke of Monmouth.'

She said my title in English. Philippe screwed up his face like a petulant monkey. 'Oh, such affectation,' he said to his companion, 'it means *duc de*, my sweet friend, that is all, but she *will* do this English nonsense, even though there is no difference.'

'Madame is polite enough to accord me my English title,' I said in French, 'but as you say, Monsieur, there is no difference: we are dukes both.'

'How funny to hear him talk French!' Philippe cried to his companion.

'But I am a little confused, I think,' said the Chevalier de Lorraine, with a wondering half-smile which, I was to find, was his permanent expression. 'I understood you, sir, to be Madame's nephew.'

'As my father is the King of England, so I am.'

'Oh!' The chevalier studied me from the shoes up. 'Dear me – I had supposed there could be no near relation.'

'How so, sir?'

'Why, seeing the two of you' – he fluttered his fingers at Minette, as at a servant whose name escaped him – 'why, I supposed you a beau! But that is just my nonsense! Don't listen to me, I beg you!' He went into a shout of laughter, cuffing Philippe affectionately. 'You know me and my nonsense, Philippe, and you're good enough not to mind it, God bless you. Well! I have quite surpassed myself in folly tonight.'

'No, no, my friend,' Philippe said, patting his hand, his lips thin, 'your error is quite forgivable. The fact is, Madame does not know how to conduct herself. It is a thing she cannot help. It is a great pity.' He turned on his high heels. 'Come – let us go – there's that smell again.'

'Oh – you mean fish,' Lorraine said.

'Yes – fish,' Philippe said, glancing evilly back at Minette.

'Well, it's curious,' Lorraine said, rumbling with laughter, 'there is no fish around and yet – yes, I do know what you mean . . .'

'Pay no attention, Jemmy,' Minette said when they had gone; she wore a bright clenched smile. 'What were we talking of?'

'Minette,' I said, troubled, 'that man—'

'I said pay no attention!' Her voice was so sharp I flinched. She blinked, groped for my hand. 'It is the only way. Trust me, Jemmy, it is the only way.'

Philippe's new favourite was as handsome as Apollo; poor as Job, in spite of his nobility; and plainly as wicked as Lucifer, as everyone but Philippe saw. Philippe worshipped the beautiful, foxy, smiling young man most disgustingly.

It was not the matter of sodomy that I found so hateful. If I were truthful, my own youthful admiration of the Comte de Guiche had not been unmixed, though I was a lover of women now. No, Lorraine was hateful for himself. It is an attribute of the devil, I understand, that he can create nothing: only imitate, feign, inhabit, and possess. So with Lorraine, who was the completest toady to Philippe, echoing everything he said, even parroting his phrases. But that was his way to dominance: the man he fawned on became his puppet.

They had met at the French army's camp in Flanders – where, I heard, Philippe had soon tired of the spectacle of bloodshed and busied himself decorating his tent with mirrors and chandeliers – and since then had been inseparable. The chevalier was one of the household – even, people whispered, the master of it. Yet his ways were not at all domineering. I became aware of his influence through a series of little surprises. A gentleman of Monsieur's household with whom I would practise sword exercise of a morning was suddenly not there any more.

'He had a quarrel with the chevalier,' Minette told me lightly, 'and so Philippe dismissed him.'

Then there was a lady of whom I knew Minette was very fond. They had been closeted chatting for hours, but the next day, walking in the gardens with her, I found Minette bestowing only the coldest of looks on the lady, and passing by.

'Hush, Jemmy,' Minette urged when I mentioned it, 'she knows I mean no harm. It is necessary. Because of the chevalier. He is watching.'

'Aye, what then?'

'He does not like her,' she explained patiently. 'And if he sees me having a confidante, he will say to Philippe that we are conspiring against him, and Philippe will send her away.'

With bafflement I saw that there were two Minettes: the jewel of the Court, entertaining the most cultivated spirits of France at her salon, consulting with poets and ballet masters and scene painters over the plans for great masques and *fêtes*; and the wife who lived in a shadowy world of subterfuge and suspicion. All about her was taste and refinement – while her husband and his lover made sniggering remarks about fish. It was their code, I came to realize, for woman, or the supposed smell of her. There was more of it. Once the chevalier kept commenting, all smiling solicitude, on how pale Madame was, and wanting to know if she were ill, and could he not recommend a physician, and so on. At last Philippe said, 'Oh, she is not ill, except in the usual way – the time of the month. Can it be a month again? She seems to be forever bleeding; there must be something *wrong* up there. Hey, well, no matter. At least it means tonight I may forgo *business*' – he caressed a lock of the chevalier's hair – 'in favour of *pleasure*.'

And so on. It made me sick; also angry. But I lacked authority: there was only my revived intimacy with Minette, which I was still insufficiently sure of to approach her direct, and ask how she bore it. I could only say to her, when we were talking of the old days at Colombes, 'Minette, would you change anything, if you had the power?'

Gently she said, 'I would change many things in the world, if I had the power.'

'Well, I don't mean in the world. In your own life. Your – destiny.'

'Destiny? Tut, Jemmy, a heathen conception. God disposes, and whatever is, is His will.'

I knew her faith was sincere, but I felt it as a kind of nebulous vapour, masking truth. 'Still, we make choices,' I said.

'So we do. And abide by them. And perhaps, to be pagan for a moment, I do have a destiny. It was what brought me here to France as a child, and set me at the French court, and made me Madame. So that I could help Charles.'

'How?'

'Why, I have told you: to bring our two countries together in friendship. That is what I can do – my destiny, if you like. And so I would change nothing.' Her expression was both uplifted and severe, silencing me. 'Nothing, Jemmy.'

But this did not content me. And when, soon after, I was invited to be present at King Louis's morning reception, I tried another tack. The King speaking to me with his clipped graciousness, complimenting my father on the horses he had sent, and asking if I had everything to my liking, I said on impulse: 'I cannot praise my hostess too highly, Your Majesty. I would acknowledge my host likewise, but that I am in a little confusion as to who he may be.'

'Your host is Monsieur,' Louis said after a moment, giving me a sharp flinty look. But he was no fool: he knew what I meant. Indeed, I do not know if this intervention of mine had any effect on what happened next; Louis must have heard from many quarters what was going on in his brother's household. At any rate, the next day Philippe was summoned by Louis for a talk. Apparently there were such hideous squeals soon coming from Louis's private apartments that a guard went running, thinking the King must be murdering his brother – not that he ran *very* fast for that, they said. And then Philippe stormed out and went in search of Minette.

He found her with me at the Palais Royal. She had been teaching me the new fashionable dances, and now I was teaching her the country dances of England, which she pronounced barbarous, but really delighted in; we were both laughing and breathless.

'Pack your things.' Pushing the fiddler aside, slapping at him, Philippe seized Minette's arm, half dragging her away. 'Go, go pack your things, we are leaving.'

'Philippe, what is this . . . ?'

'You *know*! You *insult* me with this innocence!' He thrust his pink face into hers, spraying her with spittle. 'You love to humiliate me, Madame, but do not think I shall tolerate it much longer.'

'I don't understand—'

'Oh, get away from me! You make me sick!' He pushed her: she just kept her balance. 'Always my brother! Always you run to him with your little tales – always Louis, Louis! You show him your little fucking narrow cunt and he does whatever you ask!'

'Jemmy, I'm sorry, please leave us,' Minette said to me in English.

'Again, again you insult me! Always English – what have you to say to him that you must hide from me, eh? You invite him to fuck your stinking hole like my brother, eh, like all the rest? Well, we'll see. Go

pack, Madame, we go away, we go where you will have no one to tattle
to—'

'Sir,' I cried, 'I will not see you abuse my aunt so—'

'No, you will not see it, because we go, and you may do as you please.
What are you? Only Charles's bastard. I must be civil to *him*, but my
noble chevalier, my dearest and truest friend, oh no, he I am not to see.
So says my sainted brother, who is the greatest whoremaster in the
kingdom.' Philippe snatched up a glass and dashed it at the wall above
Minette's head. 'You will not rob me of my friend, Madame. I'll see you
thrown on a dung-hill first!'

'Jemmy,' Minette hissed, 'as you love me, no.' For she had seen my
hand, instinctively, go to my sword, and gathering herself up, she went
to the door. 'I will pack, Philippe: whatever you say. I am sorry if I have
done anything amiss.'

They were gone early next morning, Minette sending me a note
apologizing for failing in her duties as a hostess. Philippe's response to
being crossed – that is, to his brother's mildly reproaching him for his
behaviour with Lorraine – was to take his household off to his country
estate near Laon: a bleak prospect in the depth of winter; and bleaker for
the fact that the Chevalier de Lorraine went with them. This was
Minette's punishment.

Left to my own devices in Paris, I could not help thinking of her out
in the country, immured with a hating husband, and a devious favourite
who must now see her as an enemy, and I was at some pains to think my
covert appeal to Louis might have been responsible. But the authoress
Madame de la Fayette, Minette's especial friend, assured me that if it had
not been that, it would have been something else. She was good enough
to invite me to her salon, but I fear the conversation there was much
above my head, and I felt a poor booby. My mind still running on
military matters, I preferred to pass my time in talking with officers of
the army, and observing their methods of drilling and musketry; also
noting how very great this army of Louis's was, and wondering who it
might be turned against next.

The household of Monsieur and Madame returned to Paris after three
weeks. I suppose Philippe had achieved a satisfactory humiliation of
Minette, for he was in cheerful spirits, and the chevalier was still with
him. They came all three to call upon me. Minette seemed quite herself,

but I saw the shadows under her eyes. I could have wished to talk alone with her, but Philippe was soon urging her away.

'Madame, we must wait upon the Queen, you know. Come, you will have time enough for your young beau.' And though he gave that burbling giggle that was meant to convey what a harmless humorous creature he was, his black eyes shot me a look of bitter speculation.

For in that topsy-turvy world of Philippe's creation, here was the ultimate twist: even while he despised his wife and flaunted his catamite before her, Philippe was jealous to madness. Absurd of course, but I would have done well to remember that even in the absurd there may be danger.

Time enough, Philippe said – knowing full well that my visit was soon to end, and I saw little of Minette before my leave-taking in March. But on that occasion Louis, who never did anything casually, said that he hoped I would return soon. Philippe heard him: I was glad of that. Minette took her leave of me as tenderly as she dared. My heart ached at the parting, yet I was happy too to be returning to England, for there were things I must say to my father.

'Aye, I know she has her troubles with him,' my father said, throwing corn for the ducks, and chuckling as they nipped at his shoes. 'She often writes me of it: 'tis a great pity he has not come to more discretion with the years.'

'But does she truly tell what it is like?'

He frowned. 'I do not think my sister has any secrets from me, Jemmy.' He walked on, the ducks waddling after. 'I speak often to the French ambassador also, and they know I will not be pleased if Madame were not to be used with proper respect at the French court.'

'It is more what happens behind closed doors, Father.'

'All sorts of things go on behind closed doors,' he said with a sour smile, 'and we would fret ourselves into the grave if we thought of them all.'

'But this is Minette—'

'I know well who we are talking of,' my father snapped.

'Then don't you care?'

'I care more for her than for any woman in the world,' he said in a soft growl, studying me and then turning away. 'But I sent you to Paris so that you might learn the ways of the world, Jemmy. Surely you have not come back more romantic than before? Do you not suppose my sister, Madame of France, knows how to manage her life? She is not happily mated, I dare say; but that is a consequence of her condition, and you may be sure she knows that.'

'Not everyone . . .' I hesitated. 'Not everyone thinks like you, Father.'

'Oh? Now you have troubled me.' He smiled down at the ducks. 'Because that suggests people know what I am thinking. I must be more careful . . . Come, Jemmy, consider. Philippe is an unpleasant creature, no doubt, but there is only a minimum of mischief he can make: Louis has seen to that. Louis is wise enough to make himself master. And besides, he is still a good friend to Madame, is he not?'

'What do you mean?'

'Why, what I say,' my father said, blandly looking past me at the lake. 'From all I hear, she is always on excellent terms with Louis, who reposes great confidence in her. And this is very natural and pleasing. Consider, Jemmy: Minette is a princess of England, and a princess of France; and as such may well have a particular and delicate part to play upon a grander stage than the ballet of Versailles. That is a fine thing, surely?'

'Perhaps. But it would be a fine thing if she were happy.'

'I think you presume too much in claiming she is not. A stricter friendship between England and France is what we both desire: there she places her greatest happiness. As for Philippe, that is like having a cross-grained tiresome child, and I am sorry for it – not that I know,' he added with a fond pat of my shoulder, 'what that is like, thank heaven. Now speaking of that, Jemmy, when are you to have an heir, eh? You must wait upon your wife more – excellent creature that she is.'

Well, that was a reluctantly fulfilled duty – no more, though I was soon to have cause to regret that. In the meantime my thoughts were full of Minette – as well as this strict friendship of which my father spoke, and which was the talk of the coffee houses; not always with approval. The public mood was not a happy one, all in all. Though it had been appeased in some measure by the sacrifice of Hyde, still there was lament for a kingdom brought low, impoverished and alone. Thus far, at least, it seemed reasonable to look for powerful friends on the Continent – and what more powerful than the triumphant France of Louis XIV?

But it was not mere prejudice against the French that made men look askance at such notions. Louis's dominion over his subjects was absolute, while his ambitions for his armies, and for the Catholic religion he championed, were no less. English minds could not be quiet with that. But could my father's? People began to wonder. Whilst his impatience with the fractious Parliament who voted him funds grew, they in turn grumbled at the money that was spent on Lady Castlemaine's extravagances. Did he sigh for the freedom his grand cousin across the Channel enjoyed?

Certainly there was a change in the way he ran his affairs. With Hyde gone, it was as if he wanted no sobersides forever citing the constitution at him. The five counsellors he drew about him at this time were soon known, not affectionately, by the name of the Cabal – the initial letters of their names, Clifford, Arlington, Buckingham, Ashley and Lauderdale, most aptly forming that word. Yet the aptness was more seeming than real, for in truth they were an ill-assorted group. Clifford was an open, agreeable Cavalierish man, though with a fanatic's pout. Arlington, with his grandee's dress and his secret feline ways, reminded me of old Mazarin. Buckingham, now growing stout and flame-faced from debauch, was within the circle because he would only make more mischief out of it. Lord Ashley, small, sick and saturnine, brought the sharpest of brains and the most combative of temperaments to the group. He would soon be raised to that name by which posterity will know, and perhaps damn him – the Earl of Shaftesbury. Then there was old Lauderdale – a man of gross ogreish feature, with a single bristling eyebrow across his head, a pig's snout, and a slubber-tongue that protruded from his mouth when he talked, making his Scots accent even more impenetrable. It was he who ruled over Scotland for my father, who never warmed in his feelings for the northern kingdom. Lauderdale was in truth mighty learned. I remember chance once framed he and I in the same mirror in the Privy Chambers, and he cried: 'Look on that for a contrast! I fear me, sir, that you got my share of beauty – though assuredly I got your share of brains in return.' Of these men, indeed, only Ashley went out of his way to know me: he was always civil. But, of course, neither could any of them ignore me, while the question of the succession remained open.

Yet for all their power, they were far from a united group. Clifford and Arlington were rumoured to be friendly to Catholicism, for example, whilst Ashley was the firmest of Protestants. I think that no more than two of them were ever likely to agree with one another on anything. I dare say each also thought himself closest to the King. And that, I am sure, was how my father liked it. It was just as with women: to tie himself to one only was to leave himself vulnerable.

Still his critics claimed, with just enough justice to make it plausible, that my father had begun to rule through a secret clique, and that they were all of Lady Castlemaine's circle added fuel to the fire. For was this not, the moralists said, the most corrupt and debauched Court that ever was, and would we not all suffer for it?

Someone who did suffer that spring was my wife. The event was much talked of by the moralists, who found it peculiarly satisfying, and certainly no more ironic trick of fate could have been devised.

As for me, I was at Chatelain's, the French coffee house in Covent Garden, when it happened – so quickly Frenchified had my tastes become. I was roistering and bragging there with a set of young blades, all thinking ourselves fine fellows, when a servant came from Hedge Lane in search of me.

An accident: the mistress was in dreadful pain, and a surgeon was with her . . . My first thought was a riding accident, or carriage upset. But here was what made the moralists shake their heads. Anna had hurt herself dancing.

'I was trying over the new steps,' she said through gritted teeth as I stood staring by her bedside, 'that's all. I turned – and the boards must have been damp, and my feet went up and I fell – twisted—'

Her eyes rolled like an animal in pain. It was her right thigh: she kept beating at with her fist. Her forehead was wet with sweat. The surgeon said it should be set at once.

'I have your permission, Your Grace?'

'What? I – yes, whatever – whatever you must do.'

I must report that I could not bear the screams, and went downstairs to drink a glass of brandy. The surgeon came at last to say that the thigh had set very well, but Her Grace must be entirely still: he had some fear the hip was dislocated.

When I went back to her, Anna, courageous creature that she was, had pulled herself up on the pillows. Her grey eyes, distanced by pain, still pierced me.

Well, I kneeled and embraced her. It felt as utterly awkward as if I were on the stage of a theatre. Her thin arms clutched me, then half-pushed me away.

'You should have done this a long time ago,' she said, sniffing, bitter.

'You wouldn't have wanted me to.'

'Ach, Jemmy.' She shook her head. 'You don't understand women.'

I swallowed that. 'How does it feel now?'

'A little eased. Not much. I shall bear it,' said she, and I did not doubt that. 'When I fell – I couldn't move . . .'

I patted her hand. 'How did you get help?'

She looked at me. I meant, of course, *were you alone*? And really, once it was out, we needed to say no more. Doubtless she had had a man with her. I did not need to forgive, because I could not care that much. All I had to do was embrace her and say no more about it. Thus, in a few silent seconds, we came to a new accommodation. My father would have been proud of me, learning the ways of the world.

'You will soon be dancing again,' I said.

'Tsk, Jemmy.' That was too much for her accurate nature. 'Such nonsense you talk.'

Anna was right, as always. The thigh was not set properly, and a few days later she submitted to a resetting, with all the tortures of the damned. She walked with a limp ever after, and her dancing days were done.

In June I returned to France.

Again I carried confidential letters from my father to Minette, and he cautioned me to put them in no one's hands but hers. This I thought was merely his habitual secrecy. I did not suppose that anything more momentous was afoot, and I was simply eager to see Minette again. If I thought more of Minette than of my wife, who was convalescing at Bath, then – what then? If you think to find any saints in this narrative, then I have misled you.

And it was a golden time in France: I ache with the remembered sweetness of it. Minette welcomed me like a saviour. Louis granted me a long audience, talking much of his regard for my father. And I was to be an honoured guest at a great *fête*, at Versailles – my first sight of that fabulous palace with which Louis was monumentalizing his own living glory.

From my early life with my mother, I should have known that there is no beauty without some tincture of danger. And if there was Minette, there was also, of course, Philippe. But he had his beloved chevalier by him, and appeared besides all occupied with planning what he would wear for the *fête*, and I supposed his mood improved.

'I like you better without the periwig,' Minette said to me as we walked in the gardens at Versailles in the early morning. 'I am glad you have left it off. And there are many ladies, Jemmy, who agree with me.'

'Oh, indeed, who?' I swelled with vanity; though in truth I did not much care who. It was Minette's admiration I revelled in.

'I don't think I shall tell you. You might desert me for them . . . You were a long time with the King. What did you talk of?'

'Oh, my father, this matter of a stricter friendship, and so on. Minette, you know I would not desert you.'

'Well, good,' she said with a faint laugh. 'I have been – rather alone. So you will find me quite greedy for company, I fear, and will be glad to get away from my chatter—'

'Alone? What has happened? Philippe sending your friends away?'

'Oh . . . it is done now. I had a very kind friend, always full of good sense: the Bishop of Valence. It was he who married me to Philippe, you know – but I do not hold that against him,' she said with a droll sad smile. 'I came to rely on him too much, I dare say. He did not like the chevalier, and the chevalier knew it, and so he put it into Philippe's head that the bishop and I spent all our time plotting and having secrets. And so my poor friend is deprived of his office and sent away.' She bit at her thumbnail. 'As I said, it is done now. I think it was my fault. I should have been more careful—'

'But why should you have to be?' I cried. 'Why should you pretend not to have friends? And don't, I pray you, tell me that is the way of the world and all the rest of it. I hear sufficient of that from—' I didn't finish that. 'I know about the way of the world, and it don't excuse such things as this. Does it, Minette?'

She looked at me uncertainly, discomposed. 'Well . . . it is simply what must be.'

'If you were some kind of serf or chattel, perhaps. But you are Madame of France, you have influence—'

'Do I?'

'Yes,' I said firmly. 'What of Louis?'

Her cheeks reddened. 'What do you mean?'

I remembered, years ago, her hand at the carriage window, and Louis young and ardent, seizing it: and I very nearly spoke of it. 'Well,' I shrugged, 'surely he – for the esteem he bears you, for the love he—'

'You must not speak of that,' Minette said crisply, she meant it.

I knew of it, though. I wondered whether it had ever truly died on either side, though I suspected that even if it had not, Louis had the toughness to manage it. He was like my father in that. Minette was not tough, though, and a great tenderness moved me as I looked at her, and I longed to embrace her.

'Well,' I said, 'as you wish. But you know I would do anything for you – and it hurts because there is nothing I can do.'

'Nothing you can do,' she echoed, nodding. 'But you do do something, Jemmy, and for that I thank you. You make me feel of flesh and blood again. A woman.' She touched my arm, and then added hurriedly, 'Instead of a – what is the English word? Like wafer?'

'Waif? Or wraith?'

She seemed to shudder a little before she laughed. 'Wafer, waif, wraith. All of those.'

At Versailles, at any rate, she was truly in her element. All the Court was gathered there, all the luminaries of the salons: she introduced me to her friend the playwright Monsieur Racine, and I remembered him as the author of the verses they had read to us at the Port-Royal school. But when I mentioned this he only frowned, and I thought him a proud stiff fellow. I liked the comedian Monsieur Molière, whose troupe were to give their new piece at the *fête*, much better, with his lined melancholy clown's face. Though he was a great favourite of Louis's, there seemed a glint of satire in his eyes at the magnificent trappings of this place, Versailles – which, though the King had scarcely begun that unthinkable expenditure that was to make it the grandest palace and the greatest folly upon the earth, already appeared to my wondering eyes as the habitation of a demi-god. As, of course, it was meant to: for here, in the watercourses and fountains, the straight parterres and sculpted shrubs, the precisely symmetrical paths and avenues where every pebble of gravel was of exactly the same size, was nature tamed and ordered by princely decree. Here in the vast perspectives, teeming vaulted ceilings, and endless corridors a man was made to feel at once his own insignificance and the mighty importance of the monarch who could command such a place into being. And the formality, the bowing and processing and the torturous standing for hours at a time that had even the willingest courtiers yawning and wincing, was part of it too: it held mere mortal nature at a distance. It was for the common man to fall greedily upon his bowl of hot soup; great Louis would eat his meat cold, after it had made its long progress from the kitchens, bowed to all along the way as the King's Dinner.

And even the entertainments called for stamina – which I, young and eager and joying in Minette's company, had in full measure. Before the comedy there was a concert of music; the play was interspersed with a ballet by Monsieur Lully; then came a prodigious banquet, the hall lit by so many thousands of candles it was as bright as day. I dined at the King's table – not that I was near him: half a hundred ladies, like brilliantly plumed birds, separated me from Louis, and I only got a glimpse of the woman in whose honour this celebration was partly held. For while the official occasion of the *fête* was the signing of a peace treaty, it was also, everyone knew, for the instalment of Louis's new mistress, Madame de Montespan. Such was the way the French Court did things: even whoring was given a due formality.

'She is a woman of sense and taste,' was all Minette said, 'and will do very well.' But I thought a shadow crossed her face.

After the banquet fireworks lit up the terraces and tainted the soft summer night with sulphur. There was dancing then, and I took the floor with Minette.

We had never danced in public before. I was proud, but troubled too – the thought of Anna came to me. Minette sensed it, and asked what was wrong.

'It is a terrible pity,' she said when I told her. 'But then you are here as your father's representative, and this is a duty, you know.'

'Is it?' I breathed in her scent. 'Yet it cannot be – it is such a pleasurable one.'

Her smile glinted at me. 'And besides, it is not as if I can be a true rival, you know, Jemmy: she must know that. Because of our – our relation.'

'Yes . . .' Our eyes met, slid away. 'But you know there can be no question of rivalry. It is not . . . Well, I don't love her, and she doesn't love me: that's the whole of it.'

'Hush, Jemmy.'

'Why? It's the truth.'

'I am – sad for you.'

'You needn't be. I am very happy now.'

'Well . . .' Her voice was very low, felt as a throb more than heard. 'It is the same for me.'

As I bowed at the end of the dance I caught sight of the Chevalier de Lorraine among the spectators behind Minette. His face, with its wide-eyed smiling look, seemed to hover genie-like above her shoulder. But when I looked again, he was gone.

'Presently, presently,' Minette laughed when I pressed her to dance again. 'I am an old married woman, you know, Jemmy. I must sit and ply my fan sometimes.'

'Old? You look hardly older that when I used to push you in the swing at Colombes.'

'I wish that were true,' she said shaking her head but her eyes shone. 'And these are very pretty things you say, Jemmy, and now I order you to stop saying them. Your father writes me as before, you know – I am to be strict, and chide you when you misbehave—'

'Oh, I know,' I said, jesting, 'I opened the letter and looked.'

She turned white. 'You could not! You must not, Jemmy—'

'No, no, I didn't, I jest.' I studied her curiously. 'But what can be such a great secret?'

'It is not— You shouldn't be so inquisitive,' she said, her tongue stumbling. 'There is nothing . . . Well, only some matters that are going forward – quite dry stuff. But I may say that it is possible – only possible, that I may visit you in England at some time soon. Now, you are not to say a word of this, Jemmy, for it is only a notion. Promise me – I am quite in earnest – say nothing to anyone.'

'Yes, yes – but to England, that's wonderful!'

'Promise me, Jemmy.'

'Very well. Not a word to anyone.' I hesitated. 'Especially to Monsieur?'

She did not answer; only squeezed my hand.

Going to stool, I came upon Monsieur with a gaggle of ladies, shrieking in mirth and protest. I would have slipped by, but he called me.

'Let us ask him – he is English, and they are all frightful unbelievers and sceptics, you know. Sir! Your opinion, sir, what think you?'

He displayed his costume with a flourish. It was the usual ribboned and jewel-encrusted confection. I wondered what I was expected to say.

'Well?' Philippe snapped with a click of his high heel. 'What say you to the green? These *nonsensical* creatures say it is unlucky, which I say is the *basest* superstition and yet you know' – he tittered – 'I am a *little* frightened – is that not absurd of me?'

'Oh, my mother was very superstitious,' I said, 'but she often wore green and thought nothing of it.'

'But did she come to a bad end?'' came a purring voice that I thought was the chevalier's, though I could not see him anywhere.

'There! I am vindicated!' Philippe cried with a wave, and then to my surprise took my arm and urged me away. 'All the same, I do not think I shall wear green again. I am not easy in my mind, sir, not at all easy . . . Ah! Now there is the very man to enlighten us. You know that gentleman, sir?'

'No.' It was a swarthy full-lipped fellow in clerical garb, whom I would have taken for some village curé but for the strange show of respect that the people around accorded him; and but for his coal-black eyes, which, as he turned, seemed to transfix me to the root.

'The Abbé Pregnani,' Philippe said. 'He was a poor Italian monk, but he displayed these most extraordinary *talents*, and my brother brought him here and made him an *abbé* and now everyone beats a path to his door and he is getting *quite* a fortune, I hear. I am not sure my brother believes in him, but then, of course, Louis knows *everything*.' Philippe's mouth twisted.

'Talents?'

'Astrology, you know. It is quite the fashion. My good *abbé* – a moment, if you please – can you settle a question for me? Utterly trifling I know, but tell me – is it unlucky to wear green?'

The Abbé Pregnani, with a small smile, shook his head. 'Trust me,' he said in snarlingly accented French, 'our destinies are not subject to such things. You may wear what you will, Monsieur: it will never hurt you.'

'Well, that is a relief! Strike at my *wardrobe*, and you strike at *me*!' Philippe cried with his high titter. 'I am obliged to you, sir.'

Pregnani bowed. 'Monsieur.' And to me, in English: 'Your Highness.'

I was stunned. *Your Highness* . . . But before I could speak to the *abbé*, Philippe was steering me away.

'An interesting subject,' Philippe said. 'Though I hope I am a truly *pious* son of the Church, still I confess these matters entice me. What of you, sir? Tell me, do you believe in witchcraft?'

'I am not sure. I believe we do wrong to dismiss such things out of hand. The world is full of mystery.'

'Oh, so it is! Curious you should mention your mother,' Philippe said, looking at me sidelong from under his sooty lashes, 'for *women*, I am convinced, are deeper versed in these mysteries than ever men can be. You know, I have even heard that a woman, by subtle arts of her own, may stifle a child growing in her womb. I don't mean with powders and such: I mean through will. She *wills* the poor babe to wither and rot within her.'

'Why on earth would a woman do that?'

'Spite. Malice.' Philippe took a silver pot of salve from his pocket and dabbed it on his lips, making them shine. 'I think that's what *she* did.' He pointed to Minette, who was dancing with the King.

'I don't understand—'

'Oh, come, you must know that she miscarries repeatedly. I don't suppose she has any *shame* about talking of it. She knows I want a son, and so she denies me, on purpose. No natural woman would miscarry so much. I wonder I did not think it before.'

'Someone has put this notion in your head, sir,' I said coldly. 'And it is a very ill one: you do wrong to speak of it.'

'Do I indeed? And yet she is my wife! Mine, sir! Am I to be told how I may speak of my own wife? What is it to you, sir?'

'She is my kinswoman, and dear to me, and I will not hear her abused.'

'Oh!' Philippe pouted triumphantly. 'You betray yourself, sir, by this *warmth*.' All at once his expression was foul and vicious. 'You need not think I do not observe, sir; you need not think I am a fool. I am Monsieur of France and I *never* fail in etiquette and so I must bear your *distasteful* behaviour.'

'Oh, pray, Monsieur, don't consider yourself bound by anything. If you have aught to say to me—'

'Oh, but I am bound, God help me. We must entertain you because of who your father is, and if the King of England owns his bastards, then that is his right. Of course, I have heard it said that he errs on the generous side, and will own any whelp that a whore presents to him, even though it might be fathered by a footman. Instruct me, my dear sir, is it so?'

The old rage rose in me, then sank: blackly, I thought of a better way. 'As to that, Monsieur, I shall leave you to think on it. Though I cannot suppose you would find much comfort in such a notion. For if you suspect Madame is not my kin after all, where may not your deeper suspicions lead?'

So I left him, and returned to Minette; and we were together all evening.

The rest of my stay in France, too soon concluded, was all delight. Philippe was quiet. Doubtless I was wrong to feel in this any kind of victory: if his jealousy turned to smouldering watchfulness instead of firework tantrums, that boded no less ill. But I was glad to see Minette given a respite from that small purgatory of her marriage; to see her laughing and vivacious, her warmth unfettered. That the warmth was directed at me – well, I was glad of that too; again, no doubt I should not have been.

Still, though all was openness between us, she would not speak of these matters she was negotiating between my father and the Crown of France. So I felt the less trouble in concealing something from her – my visit to the Abbé Pregnani, of whom I had heard her speak dubiously. I asked him to cast my horoscope for me, which he readily agreed to; but when I asked him why he had addressed me as 'Your Highness', he was evasive.

'Ah, that is not your title? Forgive me, sir – I am not well instructed on the English forms of address. Perhaps I may visit your country soon, and there I will learn better.'

'It is the title of a prince,' I said.

Pregnani made an ambiguous motion of the head – neither shake nor nod. 'Just so. It must have seemed right at the time. But time, Your Grace – that is correct, no? – time goes oddly with me, I find: a curious consequence of my gift. Instead of apprehending only what is, my mind touches upon what was, and what will be, quite indifferently.'

'Do you mean I will be a prince?'

He gave a great shrug. 'This I cannot say. I must have leave to study your planets, sir, and even then . . . But I can tell you one thing,' he added casually, gathering up his papers, 'you will be a king.'

And then he was gone, leaving me dizzily unsure whether I had heard him say the words, or whether they had appeared like some verbal phantom in my mind.

I was all the more resolved to say nothing of my consultation, though on the night before my departure, when there was a banquet in my honour, Minette kept playfully pressing me.

'We had a pleasant talk, that's all,' I said as we sat listening to the consort of music. 'He spoke of visiting England. I wonder what my father would make of him.'

'He would be amused, I think – no more.'

'Aye – everything amuses him,' I said, with an odd sting of dissatisfaction. 'But when are you coming, Minette? I hate to leave you. And if I just had some notion—'

'Hush, Jemmy, I've told you not to speak of it.'

'Aye, but tomorrow I go, with no idea of when I will see you again. Do you care so little for me?'

'Care so little?' She looked wistful, almost pained. 'Oh, Jemmy, it is assuredly not that . . .'

'So, still talking English together, hm?' Philippe thrust his curly head between us. '*Monsieur le duc de Monmouth*, you must pardon me, it has been very pleasant having you and so on, but really I shall be glad when you are gone in *that* regard, for I shall no longer have to hear that *barbarous* tongue.'

'My native tongue, Philippe,' Minette said.

'Tut, nonsense, my dear.' Philippe kept his eyes fixed on me. 'You never speak it except with *him*. Now why would you do that? Little secrets, I suppose.' He laughed indulgently. 'Really you are like children. Oh, oh, here comes Philippe, let us talk in English and *shut – him – out*.'

'Sir,' I said in irritation, 'if you only learned a little English, then—'

'Pooh, why should I? Europe belongs to France.'

'Not yet,' I said.

Philippe shrugged. 'A tiresome subject. Like these prosy ambassadors – I don't know how you bear them, Madame: I cannot conceive even you would find them worth flirting with.' He touched Minette's hair, monkeyish, roguish. 'Still, you know, my dear, you had better not be keeping any secrets from me, because I would feel myself rather *crossed*.' Straightening, he gave the lock of hair a little tug: a strand came away in his fingers. Minette's lips tightened, but she made no sound. 'Ugh,' Philippe said, examining it dispassionately and then dropping it on the floor. 'Your hair's coming out.'

SEVEN

I was now nearly twenty-one. To the advantages of beauty that Nature, about her blind handiwork, had bestowed on me, I now added the affectations of a luxurious foreign Court; and I was silly enough to be proud of both, earning me as they did the candid admiration of several ladies about Whitehall and the town. Thus on my return to England I embarked upon more than one successful pursuit, and secured myself a reputation for amorous conquests, scarcely merited, and still less deserving of the vanity with which I invested it.

I was prouder, though, of the ceremony in Hyde Park, where my father formally appointed me Captain of his Life Guards of Horse: of the saddle and trappings, all in green velvet embroidered with gold, adorned with the initial 'M' and the ducal coronet; of the men all drawn up at muster before me, to take the salute; most of all the kiss my father bestowed on me.

Later there was a ball in my honour, at which I drank a little freely, and was soon in that familiar temper of loving all the world, and wishing them as happy as yourself. Thus I hailed my uncle James, who was stalking silently about.

'Uncle, I see you do not drink. Will you not take a cup, and pledge me?'

'Indeed, I do not drink, as you observe, Jemmy,' my uncle said. His hawkish face had of late grown more severe, the thin line of his lips contracting further, as if it were a wound about to heal away completely; and when, as now, he abruptly smiled, one could fancy a tearing of sutured flesh. 'Certainly, I shall pledge you – in a cup of bastard.' He paused for a cold instant. 'Or sherry-sack, or any Spanish wine – you know 'tis only the Spanish wine agrees with my stomach. But I do not see any here: never mind. Take the pledge as drunk, Jemmy: take the intention.'

'You may be sure I take the intention, sir,' I said, my face all flaming; but my uncle was already turning away.

My father, ever observant, came to me, and wanted to know what we had been saying to one another.

'Oh, nothing. Nothing of consequence.'

Coolly my father noted my shaking hands and heaving breast. I often felt that in another life he would have made an excellent physician. 'It has put you into a great passion, Jemmy, whatever it is.'

'No, it has not. I am quite in command of myself, Father.'

'So? I am glad to know it. For if you are to command men, Jemmy, the first person you must command is yourself. They will not follow otherwise.' His voice was pleasant, precise, and firm. 'I shall be glad to know, also, that you are excellent friends with James.'

I said I was. For I was learning, just a little, the arts of concealment. In truth I was bitter against James, and soon afterwards, I pursued all the more diligently a young woman of the court, whom I knew my uncle had his eye on also; and I had the victory. And I exulted to learn from her, during the confidences of the bed-curtain, that my uncle's chosen method of seduction was to narrate to the lady every detail of his day's hunting – perhaps on the supposition that boredom would at last render her horizontal.

I soon shared this with the cronies, beruffled and sword-wearing and fatuous, with whom I wasted my days, and we laughed much on it. Another confidence I kept to myself, because I found it faintly disturbing: the lady's account of the experiences of her friend, a wardrobe-mistress who had submitted to James's advances, and had been surprised to find him leaping up immediately the deed was done, scourging himself with cold water, and calling upon his partner to kneel at once with him by the bed, and earnestly beg forgiveness of their sin.

Well, well: the trivial malicious gossip of a corrupted court, you may say, and you might be right. But deeper and darker gulfs were to yawn between my uncle and me. And it was this matter of the succession, of course, that was to open them.

Speculation on that subject was ever simmering, but at this time occurred two events that gave the pot a stir. First Queen Catharine miscarried of a child.

Gossip was always having the poor lady pregnant, or thinking she was, but this was the only true occasion I can vouch for. Anna, who often attended on her, knew all about it. The Queen had begun to wear the white smock of an expectant mother, and a physician had confirmed it. But very early on, the babe was lost.

'It was never very promising, I fear,' Anna told me. 'Her courses never entirely stopped, and she still shed a little blood, in a manner that no woman who will bear a child to full term should ever do. I did not like to say so: she was so hopeful.'

'There is a rumour that it was her pet fox, jumping on the bed, that frighted her and made her miscarry.'

'Well, she says it wasn't – but that is from fear your father would be angry, and have the beast killed. But of course, he is no such thing, because he is no fool. He understands well that if she can be frighted out of a child by such a small matter, then 'tis as we have always feared – Queen Catharine can never bring a live child into this world. I think, now, he is resigned to it.'

The other event was the attempt of a peer, Lord Roos, to secure a civil divorce from his wife. Such a step required a special Act of Parliament, and the case occupied the debates of the House of Lords for some time. My father followed the proceedings with interest – and from that people concluded he was studying how the land lay, for his own purposes of divorcing his barren queen. When my father said, after attending the debates, that it was better than a play, some thought he was hiding his intention under his usual mask of joviality, but I knew better. I knew he would never divorce Catharine.

I said so casually, I recall, when I was at the tennis court with my lords Buckingham and Ashley, watching my father play his usual strenuous game. Buckingham snorted.

'If you have divined His Majesty's mind, sir, then you have the advantage of me – and I have known him a great deal longer than you.'

'I do not know my father's mind, perhaps,' I said, thinking how gross and pompous Buckingham had become. 'Who can ever know another's? But on this, I simply feel certain.'

'Hey, well, let her retire to a nunnery then,' Buckingham said shrugging, 'and if she won't choose to go, someone might spirit her away in the dead of night. That's what I told Charles: 'twould be simply done.' In his way he was quite serious: there was always a touch of madness about him.

Ashley, who was not at all mad, and very serious, was looking at me attentively. 'You interest me, Your Grace. Do you mean your father has spoke to you of his intentions?'

'He would not be my father if he had,' I said, which made Ashley smile in his wan shrewd way.

'Just so. Still, this is an important consideration, if 'tis as you intuit, Your Grace. It means we can expect no heir of His Majesty's loins.'

'That would please James, at any rate,' said Buckingham, who had no love for my uncle. 'He's been wearing a face like a collier's horse over this Roos business.'

'His Grace of York does not trouble, perhaps, to hide his expect-ations,' Ashley said in his sibilant voice, his narrow eyes still dwelling thoughtfully on me.

'Oh, a poor stroke,' Buckingham cried as my father, for once, let the ball by him. 'Charles is sluggish today. I fancy even you might have the beating of him, my lord.'

It was a crude slight upon Ashley's little crippled body; but Ashley only gave his curious smile, which was like a sort of sketch or abridge-ment of mirth. 'I hope I know better than to waste my strength in such a contest,' he said. 'I save it for those I can win.'

To know my father's mind – aye, that was the aim of many, but at this time one avenue to that mysterious region was closed off. The ambitious no longer cultivated Lady Castlemaine, for her influence was dwindling.

Rumour could hardly exaggerate the greed of a woman who insisted on borrowing the crown jewels to wear at the theatre. But I think it was her worsening temper that soured her relations with my father at last; and while he did not mind paying for the establishments of her children, I fancy he balked when the latest bore no resemblance to him. The tantrums grew more violent as their effect grew less. Also she had a new rival, who did what Barbara had long ceased to do: amuse my father greatly. This was a young actress from the King's Theatre, Nell Gwynn.

I had seen Madam Gwynn act upon the stage, and it was perhaps too soon forgot, in her greater fame as my father's mistress, what a superior performer she was: a pretty dancer, but above all a comedienne who could set the house roaring. There was nothing of simper about her, dainty though she was. She bounced on to the stage like a firecracker, and rapped out the most comical lines not as if they had been writ, but as if they sprang that moment to her lips. Above all you had the feeling that she might wink at you over the footlights – and this applied too, as it were, in real life, for she took the world as an amusing show, and to catch her eye when anyone said something even faintly ridiculous, was to risk an explosion of laughter which it would cost you some pains to explain.

It was Buckingham who introduced her to my father. He had fallen out with his cousin Barbara, and so sought, I suppose, to place another ally in my father's bed – not that Nell ever troubled herself with politicking, or was ever less than her own woman. Still, she was presented to him, of course, with but one purpose, which all knew. I remember her first coming to Whitehall, to give a song and jig before us, and how my father presently withdrew to sup with her alone: a sheer piece of pimpery, in short. Here was my father growing ever more secret, crafty, and self-sufficient. Even wooing was shorn of its hazards and chances, and set upon a rational business-like footing. There would be no more Frances Stewarts.

However, there was no doubting the true attraction between my father and Nell. That habit of hers, of viewing life as a mere parade of folly, assorted very well with him, though I am convinced that where her laughter was very sane, his had something darker in it, and contained a fearful contempt, as if he could never quite outface that midnight question: *is this it? Is this all there is?*

Nell's response would have been an energetic cry of 'Aye – and so let us enjoy it!' She was truly of the people. She had grown up in the dingy court of Cole Yard by Drury Lane, in a house kept by a termagant mother that was a bawdy-house in all but name, and where she had served Nantz brandy to lolling gentlemen when she was quite a little girl. She had begun her career in the theatres as an orange-seller, before the actor Charles Hart had lit upon her wit and beauty, and lifted her to the stage and, incidentally, his bed. She could read scarcely enough to learn her parts, and could not write her own name, and her tongue was ever apt to fall back on the language of the guttersnipe. But there was something ineffably cheerful about her. Even her beauty was not of the imperious sorceress sort that sets a man grovelling; she looked at her best in the plain light of day, with her merry brown eyes and peachlike complexion. And though she was less than five feet tall, somehow you always had the sense when talking with Nell that she was looking you straight in the eye.

You will have gathered that I liked Nell Gwynn: we got on famously from the beginning. Perhaps our backgrounds had something to do with it – for only I, at that court, had experienced an early life that was anything like hers, very like it, in some regards. Of course, at the time I did not care to think of that. I was peacock-proud, as Nell soon saw.

'Another duke and another James,' she said to me, when we first spoke alone at one of my father's suppers. 'You high folks are so niggardly with your names! Are you afraid they'll run out, that you have to keep using the same ones over again? I shall confuse you with t'other one.'

'My uncle? You could not confuse me with him, I hope.'

'What, Dismal Jimmy? Nay, I think not. He seems forever in need of a good purging of the bowels. Lord, I know the sort: need to shit but too proud to go. Well, I must find another name for you, Your Grace.'

'A kind one, I hope,' I said, still chuckling over Dismal Jimmy.

'I'm not sure. I must come to know you first. Mind, I do *know* you, of course, as everyone does.'

'Do you?'

'To be sure – you are the one who will save us. Didn't you know? They toast you in the taverns. You are all that stands between us and Popery, and Frenchmen, and worst of all, Dismal Jimmy. But perhaps, Your Grace, you don't like to think of folk in low alehouses making free with your name? Pray, don't mind it. You should hear what they call your uncle.'

'Tell me.'

'Ho, no, I shan't. They'll say I'm an intriguer, like Lady Castlemaine, who gets her uncles made bishops. Not me. There aren't churches enough in the kingdom for all my uncles, for every morning my mother would breakfast with a different gentleman, and tell me, "Say hello to your uncle, Nelly." '

I laughed, though a little constrainedly – remembering my own mother. Nell looked at me closely.

'What, have I offended? Never tell me you're of the Castlemaine party, Your Grace?'

'No, no,' I said, though blushing a little, for Nell seemed to see right through me. 'Why, if I were, I would not be here, would I? If I'm of any party, Mistress Gwynn, it is—'

'Oh Lord, don't start professing yourself my slave!' Nell cried, slapping my knee. 'I never know where to put my face when men say that. Mind, *they* usually have some notion where to put it . . . Such stuff! "I am your slave, madam!" "Aye? Then go do my laundry." Nay, waste no pretty speeches on me, Your Grace. You are too handsome a spark for me anyhow – I run to curious-looking men. My Charles the First was no Adonis, and my Charles the Second spoiled his looks with wine, and my Charles the Third is quite the oddest fish of all.'

So she was accustomed to call her lovers – Charles Hart the actor, Charles, Lord Buckhurst, her former beau, and now my father. He knew of it, and laughed at it. As for me, Nell always made me laugh – yet I suffered a little trepidation, wondering what name she would come up with for me.

Despite Nell, I still missed Minette, and felt that life was a little greyer since leaving her. I was hungry for news of her from my father, but my appetite went unsatisfied, even though the correspondence between them increased. At first this seemed no more than an aspect of the warmer climate developing between England and France, which included a new ambassador from Louis, as well as a sort of unofficial one – none other than the Abbé Pregnani, who came to present himself at my father's court.

I was eager to see him again, and to con the horoscope he had prepared for me. I was disappointed that it was not more specific, and when I reminded him of his startling prediction that I would be a king, he only smiled enigmatically and said in his soft snarl: 'Such is the possibility in your stars, Your Grace: it lies among other possibilities. A man may be king in many ways: a man may be king to some and not to others. If there be a crown, let us not forget that our Saviour wore a crown of thorns and blood. But consider, sir, the most propitious quarter of your chart. Here is Mars in your ascendant; it is Mars that beckons you to your greatest glory.'

The god of war. Everything seemed pointing me thither, as I said to my father who was richly sceptical when I mentioned Pregnani.

'Don't rush into battle because some hedge magician says so. Well, is he not? He may have impressed my cousin, but I shall require some proof of his powers. I put no faith in such cattle, Jemmy, and nor should you.'

For the proof, he invited the abbé to the horse-matches at Newmarket, which was becoming his favourite resort for his favourite sport. He had lately bought himself a house there, and delighted in inspecting the Royal Stables, observing the dawn training gallops, supping with his jockeys-in-ordinary, and even in riding races himself, with no small success. I went with the abbé, who was bemused to find my father inviting him to predict the winners of every race at the meet. Here I found my father irritated me. The abbé, who could do no less, made his choices, I backed them with wagers, and when all Pregnani's horses lost, my father and his friends amused themselves hugely at the expense of mountebank fortune-tellers.

'I am sorry you lose your money, Your Grace,' the abbé said to me, shrugging, 'but in truth, as I tried to tell His Majesty, it makes a mock of such powers as I possess to employ them thus.' Well, so I thought. It was not Pregnani's reputation I cared for so much – for I guessed that he had partly come to England to do a little spying for Louis – as this tendency of my father's to deflate everything, as if he could not bear that anything should remain of mystery and fascination in life. Perhaps that was the way the world would wag, in future: I thought it bleak. Afterwards my father clapped me on the shoulder, and said he hoped I had learned a lesson. If I had, it was not the one he meant. I had not thought to win when I backed the abbé's predictions, and I would do it again, and probably lose again; it was something to do with taking a stand.

As for my father's intentions for the kingdom, there seemed no pinning them to a point. A *rapprochement* with France was in hand, and our differences on commerce and the passage of the seas to be settled by treaty: all this was very well. As for how much further the friendship should go – well, some said it would be a good thing to clasp hands with the greatest power of the Continent. It would certainly be a good thing for Louis, whose eyes were forever turned in baffled hostility on that prickly little republic of Holland, so close to his borders, so determined to resist him. Louis would go far to secure our friendship so that he

might do what he would with the impudent Dutch, and did we not have
cause to hate those Hollanders who had humiliated us? Yet we were at
peace with them now, fastened by treaty, and there were many, especially
in Parliament, who thought we should remain so: that we would do
better to stand by that Protestant and freedom-loving republic than give
a free hand to Louis's France – Catholic, absolute, and hungry for ever
more conquests.

Well, there were some who whispered that my father did not think so;
that there was more to this French friendship than met the eye. Yet for
now the kingdom bore a lustre of peace and glory. My father, taking the
government into his own hands, seemed to be steering us into safe port
after the storms of the past few years. And if he had secrets – well, no
man ever knew better how to keep them.

As for me, I was no nearer to divining his mind. He contented me and
discontented me in equal measures. Old General Monck went to his rest
at last. My father gave a grand funeral to the man who more than any
other had restored him to his throne, and the very next day told me I
was to have the seat on the Privy Council he had vacated. I, scarce
twenty-one! This was dazzling. I stammered out my gratitude, and on
first taking my seat was so full of the honour – and so unsure of myself
– that I kept interrupting the assembled lords to babble any old nonsense, until Prince Rupert, who sat beside me, wrote upon a piece of
paper the words 'Don't fear, my friend – we all know you are here!' and
slid it across with his wolfish smile. Which was kind, and sobered me. I
sought out Rupert's company a good deal at this time. My father made
him Warden of Windsor Castle, where Rupert, ever warrior-like , hung a
fierce array of swords and halberds and muskets all over the walls.
Glory-struck, I mooned about him listening to his old campaign tales.
For such was still my longing.

But my father, in his frustrating way, did not appoint anyone to
Monck's office of Captain-General, nor present aught but an unmeaning smile to my talk of military command. I was growing weary of the
airless, labyrinthine ways of my father's Court. I sought a bracing air
where one did not have to wear a mask and speak with a double
tongue. I seemed even to be becoming a stranger to my own feelings:
I struggled with an earnest and passionate nature where no one was
earnest and passionate. In the spring of 1669, at Colombes, my

grandmother Henrietta Maria had died in her bed, peacefully and courageously, with her husband's portrait at her side. When I had the news, I did not know how to feel. Neither my father nor my uncle were much stricken. I knew Minette would grieve, but then she had always been much closer to her mother, for better or worse. And what of me? I had found my grandmother wearisome in later years, even malicious. Yet remembering when I had first been presented to her, a shrinking bewildered boy, and the way she had counted off her children on my fingers, I wanted to weep. And did not, because I feared it would look like affectation.

Only one thing could lift my spirits. Like an answered prayer, it came. Minette was coming to England.

'Aye – we shall have her here to visit us, Jemmy – brave news, is it not?' my father said. 'Lord, I'm trying to reckon the years since I saw her – more than I care for, anyhow. Mind, you have the advantage of me there, my boy.' He nodded at me – with the faintest glint of jealousy – but I hardly marked that in my joy, and asked him what the occasion was for her visit – a state matter?

'Occasion? It needs no occasion, I hope, to welcome my sister to these shores,' my father said quickly. 'The French Court is making a progress in Flanders, and so she will simply take a ship across to Dover, and pay us a family visit – nothing more natural.'

'Without Monsieur?'

My father grinned. 'Do you think I would be smiling else?'

But Monsieur was not to be so easily dismissed.

It was Louis himself who told his brother that Madame was to make a visit to her kin in England, and this was what baffled my father, when news came that Philippe refused downright to let his wife come. His brother and king wished it: how could Philippe behave so? I think my father failed to understand the nature of Philippe's jealousy, or its range: if Louis seconded a proposal, Philippe would be all the more suspicious. For weeks the issue hung in the balance. I am sure there was a fourth party in the wranglings – Philippe's minion, the Chevalier de Lorraine, who was doubtless prompt to put notions in Philippe's head that he was being excluded from secret matters. When news came that Philippe, after a strict command from Louis, had at last given his consent, we could still hardly rejoice, for Philippe's stipulation was that Minette could stay in England no longer than three days, and that she was to come no further than Dover.

'Dover? A wretched place! How am I to receive my sister properly there?' my father fumed, but even as he swallowed that, there were other difficulties to surmount. Monsieur now thought he might come too. After some groans, my father overcame that with a cunning appeal to Philippe's passion for etiquette. If the French King's brother was to come here, the English King's brother must visit France in return, and unfortunately James was already otherwise engaged . . .

Surely that must be the last of it? But no: Philippe conjured up one last objection.

'It is you, Jemmy,' my father said. He sat slumped at his desk in his private closet, amidst the thickly ticking clocks, like so many beating hearts. 'His last great objection is you.'

'Why?' said I, dry-mouthed.

'That is what I cannot conceive. If Madame is to be here, then you, he says, must not. He even suggests I send you away to Holland for the duration of her visit.' He looked broodingly over my figure from under his dusky eyelids. 'It is all very strange . . . But then, so is everything that fantastical creature does.'

'Father – I don't have to go, do I?' I cried.

And for a dark stifling second I thought he was going to say yes. Then he stirred and shrugged himself up and smiled, with an effect as if a window had been thrown open.

'No. Odsfish, no – send you out of the kingdom on the whim of that jackanapes? No, he must put up with it. There can be no rational reason why you should not see Madame. Can there?'

So at last she came, conveyed from Dunkirk to Dover on the flagship of our fleet.

It was a wretched spring: cold rain pocked the grey face of the Channel when we set out in the royal barge – my father, my uncle, Prince Rupert and I – to meet the ship off Dover. When first I saw Minette on the pitching deck, I was shocked. She looked not just thin but gaunt, spectral: her great eyes reminded me of my grandmother's.

My father had not seen her for nine years, and so perhaps did not mark the change as I did. If he did, he concealed it as adroitly as ever, and was all genial joy, embracing and kissing her, and remarking only that she must have had a rough crossing.

'The seas were kinder than the land,' she said, gasping a little at the strength of his embrace. 'We have had such rain in France – the roads were naught but mud, and the bridge at Landrecies was quite carried away and we had to spend the night on the floor of a barn – it was quite an adventure, was it not?' she added with a weakly smiling appeal to the ladies of her train, who looked indeed as if they had had adventures enough.

'Well, at least I need not apologize for the English rain,' my father said. 'But I'm troubled, my dear – shipboard is not the best place to recover from such an experience. My lord Sandwich has made you comfortable, I hope?'

'We have had the best of escorts,' Minette said, 'and all that is needed to complete my happiness is to set foot on English ground. And seeing you – how fine you look, Charles!'

'Pooh, an old grey fellow,' my father said. He was a few days away from his fortieth birthday.

'No – you are just as I remember you. It is as if we only met yesterday . . .' Blinking at what might have been salt spray, or tears perhaps, she turned. 'And such a handsome welcome! What a tall set we are – like a row of sunflowers! James, my dear brother, how do you do? I bring you a good report of your little girl. Her trouble is much improved, and she is quite the delight of our household.' This was my uncle's younger daughter, Anne, a placid plump little princess who had been sent to France, first in my grandmother's care and then Minette's, to be treated by an eminent French physician for an eye complaint. 'My dear cousin – I think you are scarcely changed either,' to Rupert, who pounced into a Cavalierish bow. 'And Jemmy.' She smiled with surpassing sweetness as she gave me her hand. 'Now you must return the favour, and coach me in the English ways.'

'Ho, no – this young rogue – he will teach you naught but dicing and drinking,' my father laughed, stealing her hand from me.

It was understandable, I suppose, that he should be greedy for the company of this adored sister he had not seen for so long. Over the next few days, while we were quartered at Dover Castle, I tried to still the protests of my heart as my father and Minette spent long hours closeted together. I was not the only one kicking my heels, as many of the court had descended on the little seaport also. Some few had audience with Minette, as did the French ambassador, but I supposed merely some civilities of state were going forward. Such is our nature, in which our private concerns always loom greater than public calamity: I recall a man during the plague lamenting: 'First this damnable sickness – and now my wife's brother will not give us his linen-chest as he promised!' If I was disquiet at Dover, it was not from any suspicion of what was going on behind the locked doors, but because I wanted to see more of Minette, and felt that my father was enviously preventing it.

But he had to relinquish her at last. The Queen and the Duchess of York were coming down to Dover, for the public celebrations marking his birthday and the tenth anniversary of his restoration. Happily, too, a message had come from Louis – not Monsieur – saying Minette might now stay a fortnight. Finally, as my father and uncle rode out to the gates to greet the Queen's party, I spoke with her alone.

'You look reproachful, Jemmy,' she said. 'I have neglected you – I know, but your father and I have had so much to talk of, and then there have been all the formal greetings and so on . . .'

'Oh! It doesn't signify. Who am I, after all?' I was all prepared for that selfish luxury of being chivvied and flattered out of ill-humour. But she only smiled wanly, and looked about her for a chair. I saw again how drawn and tired she looked, and repenting at once I fussed over her.

'Draw nearer to the fire – and let me get you a screen . . .' The dank castle chamber was full of draughts: in that stony grimness Minette reminded me of the princesses in the tales poor Anne Hill used to tell me as a boy, sad doomed creatures immured by enchanters.

'How kind you are! I do very well now, Jemmy – now I may take my ease a little.'

'Which was the more tiring?' I said, taking a low stool by her. 'The journey, or the battle with Monsieur to let you come?'

'Hush,' she said; and then burst out, with a kind of sick relief, 'Dear God, that was a horrible time. The journey – the journey was unlucky, to be sure, with such weather, but I wouldn't have minded it but for Philippe coming with us most of the way. Isn't that a terrible thing to say? He was in the worst of moods. Not just my going. His box was lost somewhere on the road – his box of face-paints and so on' – I made a noise of scorn, but she gestured me quiet – 'and so he was angry at that. And at my being sick. Philippe is actually rather sturdy, that is the curious thing; and he started to talk of an astrologer who had predicted he would marry more than once. "And I think he was right, you know, indeed I do – for you don't look long for this world, Madame, in faith, tee-hee!"'

This time I could hardly speak. What was almost more shocking was that I had never known Minette, a wicked mimic, ever imitate Philippe like that. And it was so horribly accurate I almost felt Philippe in the room with us.

Then she smiled, dispelling him. 'Well, this was a little too much even for him, and no one would speak to him for a time, which he didn't like, so he tried to be more agreeable. Still, I confess I was glad to be on board ship, no matter how the tea tossed . . . And now I am here. So—'

'But you will have to go back,' I cried. 'And if I can hardly bear that thought. I wonder how you can.'

'Well, there are some things that may be better,' she said hesitantly. 'There is one . . . annoyance that I think I may be free of.'

'The chevalier?'

'Perhaps . . . I hear the horns, Jemmy. The Queen must be here. Come, we should ready ourselves. I will tell you of it presently . . .'

This gathering at Dover was a rarity – a family party; and we were as ill-assorted, I dare say, as most families are. The Duchess of York welcomed Minette to England as grandly as if she were queen of it, pushing ahead of Queen Catharine. Indeed, she did everything but thrust Catharine aside with her elbows, or rather the places where her elbows had been, somewhere under the rippling fat. This was Minette's first meeting with Queen Catharine, and she exerted herself to be friends with her, even though the Queen, whose manner had grown easier over the years, seemed suddenly to have thrown up all her old fences of shyness. Perhaps she could not help but be aware that here was another rival for her husband's affections – indeed the most potent of all, for her charms could never be diminished by the satisfaction of appetite. So she seemed to hint to me, at any rate, at the birthday banquet, as we watched my father and Minette dancing.

'They match very well, do they not, Jemmy?' Catharine said. 'As if they had danced together all their lives.'

I grunted, a little jealously I suppose: I thought Minette and I made the handsomest couple.

Like most quiet people, Catharine saw much. She touched my arm gently. 'Your father,' she said, 'is a man who can have whatever he wants. Almost. What is left for such a man to desire?'

Again he was covetous of Minette's company all evening, but I managed some talk alone with her later, and asked her what she had meant about the chevalier.

'Well. There is hope. I do not want to count all my chickens in one basket,' she said seriously, holding up a finger – sometimes she mangled English like that, too delightfully for correction – 'but there is hope. The chevalier became so very absolute that I think he overreached himself. He wanted Philippe to grant him the livings of two abbeys in his gift, which Philippe was very ready to do. But his brother came to hear of it and would not have it. He told Philippe that it would be a scandal for a man like the chevalier to have Church revenues. There was a great quarrel between the King and Philippe. The Chevalier de Lorraine publicly said that Louis was a meddling fool and a whoremaster, and that he always crossed Philippe because Philippe's wife led him by the – well, you can supply the expression. So Louis had the chevalier arrested and thrown in prison.' Minette could not help that spark of vengeful triumph in her eyes, and God knew I did not blame her for it. 'Philippe went to beg at his brother's feet. Louis was firm. Then Philippe swore and raged at him and said he would never look at his face again – and so he dragged me off to his country place, and there we would remain, he said, for ever.' She gave an acid smile. 'Naturally, he grew bored at last, and we returned to court; but not before he had put me through the mill. That is the right expression?'

'I wish it were not . . . Minette, this cruelty of his—'

'I can bear. He does not beat me with a broomstick. That is not – not Philippe's way. Well! You know the rest – the difficulties he made at my coming here. He is very bitter against me. He blames me for the loss of his chevalier: for Louis has remained quite firm on his banishment. But Philippe also thinks I have it in my power to bring his friend back, if I chose, so I am doubly the villainess.' All at once, though she tried to smile, there were tears coursing down her face. Squeezing her hands, I wondered how long those tears had been pent up. 'But it is better,' she said breathlessly, 'for at least there is no chevalier about – and the things he had begun to say and do – so it is, it is better . . .'

'Let me come to France again,' I said wildly, 'and call the chevalier to a duel, and kill him, and then he will never—'

'Hush, hush, Jemmy, you mustn't talk so,' Minette said, wiping her cheeks. 'You are very gallant and I'm honoured, but truly I do very well. I have this, after all.' She made an embracing gesture – but it was at my father, receiving the congratulations of some courtiers, that she looked.

Later my father took me aside; his eyes were stony.

'I saw Madame weep,' he said. 'When you were talking with her, Jemmy: she wept. What pray, did you talk of?'

'She was talking of Monsieur, and how monstrous he has behaved,' I said, returning his sharpness, 'and quite naturally, she shed a tear. I'd shed them myself, if I were forced to be with him.'

'Oh, that . . .' My father frowned, then shrugged. 'Well, 'tis a subject best avoided, Jemmy. We want Madame to enjoy her time here. There's no profit in thinking on unpleasant things, trust me.'

The time slipped by, indeed, too swiftly. There were fireworks, and rides, and water-parties, my father at Minette's side all the while; and we went inland as far as Canterbury, where he had commanded the players of the Duke's Theatre to perform a comedy adapted from one of Monsieur Molière's. The adaptation was very free, and the comedians were dressed in the short laced coats that were the fashion at Louis's court. Indeed, the French were rather mocked, and I realized how little the innocently laughing Minette knew of this country she claimed to love. There was a ballet, too, in her honour – admittedly a poor thing beside the revels of Versailles, but when Minette and I began to speak of those, at the banquet in the hall after, my father soon changed the subject.

And then her time was up: we must relinquish her, to France and Monsieur. My father included a couple of gifts for Monsieur amongst the presents which he heaped on Minette at our leave-taking at Dover, but most were for her, and extravagant they were. I say 'our' leave-taking – but it was only mine. My father and my uncle were to sail in the yacht along with her ship as far as the roads of Calais, while I remained behind.

It was not my father's way to play the King – unlike his own father,

Charles I, of whom it was said he could not eat a morsel of bread without proclaiming his divine right to do so. My father made no lofty commands in the matter, rather he simply omitted to tell me about this until the last minute, and passed it off by saying that the Queen and the Duchess of York would need a proper escort back to London. Which buttered me up sufficiently to prevent my feeling my exclusion until it was too late.

So at blustery Dover, with her entourage all about, clutching at their skirts and periwigs, and my father waiting to hand her into the pilot boat, Minette embraced and kissed me. I seemed in a vivid instant to feel all the contours of her face against mine, brow and eyelashes and nose and lips and chin, like an impression in wax; and I whispered in her ear: 'Remember what I said. I shall come to France whenever you like, and do anything in my power—'

'I know it,' she murmured back, 'and I love you for it. God bless you.'

Then she went across the strand to the boat, the wind whipping up her gown around her rush-like slenderness and making her appear as she used to in the great swing at Colombes, like a creature of thistledown, scarcely touching the earth and liable at any moment to take to the air and fly. But on her face, as she turned to look back at the cliffs of England, there was quite another look: tired, hectically flushed, but with a certain secret satisfaction of conquest, like a mother successfully delivered of a child.

Before the yacht turned back at Calais, I heard later, my father tore himself from Minette's arms three times, and three times held her again, weeping. Perhaps there was more than a jealous possessiveness in his keeping me from that last leave-taking; perhaps he did not want me to see him thus – see him in the throes of feeling.

But that I was to see, quite soon, and in such circumstances as I have never forgotten – and after which, perhaps, we were never to be the same together again.

It was Queen Catharine who summoned me urgently to the Privy Apartments, one hot bright day a few weeks after Minette's return to France. I found her in the anteroom to the bedchamber, in great agitation, and I suspected at first some quarrel over a mistress of the sort that had blighted her early days here. For though she had long come to an accommodation with her faithless spouse, there had lately been an incident in which she had entered the bedchamber while my father was entertaining Nell Gwynn. Nell, in true comedienne style, hid behind the bed-curtains; but Catharine saw one of her slippers on the floor, and said she would go before the pretty fool who owned it took cold. So the tale went. I could believe it; that pained dignity sounded like the Queen.

But what I saw in the Queen's face then was a different pain – the pain of love. Wildly she seized my hands, and I became aware, not of a noise, but of a noise ceasing; as when the howling of a dog that has troubled our rest stops at last, and the silence startles us wakeful.

And howling, indeed, I realized as I faced the Queen in that terrible silence, was what it had resembled. Deep-throated, though: no such sound as my father's little spaniels could make.

'There is an envoy from France,' she said, trembling. 'He came post-haste with this news. I was here with your father, and – oh, I don't know what to do, Jemmy, I cannot . . .' She gestured to the bedchamber door. 'He will speak to no one. Perhaps you—'

'What news? Ma'am, I pray you, what is it?'

It was news from the château of St Cloud, the summer residence of Monsieur and Madame, where Minette had died in great agony three days ago.

'Damn Philippe.'

Those were the first words my father uttered, as I sat by him in his chamber. But that was only after the clocks had ticked away half an hour or more: half an hour in which my father had lain like a man cast up from drowning, prone upon the bed, with his grey face open-mouthed on his arm, his hair draggled in his eyes, which stared redly into nothing.

And I, wrenched by my own shock and grief, had babbled to him, begging him to tell me what had happened, to speak to me – anything. I wanted him perhaps to make sense of it for me, he who could always mould the wanton matter of life into rational shape, but most of all I wanted to conjure my father back from this disturbing stranger who had usurped him.

'Damn and curse Philippe,' my father said, unmoving, his voice hollow. 'Damn and curse him to hell. And damn the day that—'

But he did not say what day. He fell into silence again.

'Father, please, tell me what has happened. Do you mean Philippe—'

'What happened? She died. She took mortal sick and swiftly, so swiftly—' He broke off, his breath rattling almost as if he were dying too; then turned his head so I could not see his face. 'Go away, Jemmy. Go, go away from me.'

It may sound trifling, but the fact that my father's courtesy had deserted him was the most horrible thing of all, for it was his essence; just as if someone's familiar features should sweal and alter before your eyes. I started forward, to find his hands, to touch; but he had tucked them away.

'Damn everything,' he said, 'and everybody.'

I turned away, and saw one of his spaniels cowering beneath a chair, soft eyes wrinkling in alarm. Wiser than I. Picking up the dog, I left the room. My father did not leave it for two days.

On returning to France, Minette had been welcomed by the whole Court, and Louis had invited her to spend the summer at Versailles. But Monsieur would not have it. His temper had not improved in her absence. He took her off to their summer house at St Cloud, there to talk endlessly of the chevalier. Openly and acidly he spoke of her as this so-important, so-powerful personage whom all must bow to: she could surely get the chevalier back from exile if she chose, but she did not choose, which showed how spiteful and cruel she was, and so on. Going on a visit to Versailles, at Louis's strict command, Monsieur kept up this behaviour to Madame even before the King; and whenever Louis tried to ask her about her time in England, Philippe would shriek his interruptions, and generally make the conversation intolerable. It was here that Louis's plump queen, Marie-Thérèse, took Minette aside and asked if she were ill: she looked so pale and drawn.

Back at St Cloud, Minette's spirits were improved by some visitors, including the English ambassador and her good friend Madame de la Fayette. On the twenty-ninth of June, a Sunday, she spent the morning with her elder daughter, who was eight years old now, and having her first portrait made. The afternoon she spent with Madame de la Fayette, and saying at last she felt weary, she lay on some cushions on the floor and slept. Madame de la Fayette stayed by her, stroking her hair: she too thought Minette looked ill.

When Minette woke she complained of a pain in her stomach, and called for a glass of chicory water. As soon as she had drunk it, she fell to the floor crying out in agony. Madame de la Fayette helped her to bed, where her cries grew more terrible and she began to writhe and thrash about. A physician came: also Philippe, who stood by the bed and watched her.

The physician said it was colic. Minette began to cry out that she feared she was poisoned, and must take a purge. Philippe said, quite calmly, that if that was what she suspected, they should give some of the chicory water to a dog. Minette's serving-woman, who had mixed the draught, burst into tears and said that it could not be: she had drunk some of the chicory water herself. A purge was given, but Minette seemed unable to bring anything up, though her whole body bent double in her spasms. Two more physicians came, and conferred, but none seemed able to suggest a remedy. Meanwhile her sufferings, which made her ladies weep to watch, continued unabated. She soiled the bed, and they had to move her to a smaller one, where she was lying when Louis and the Queen came hurrying from Versailles.

She managed to say to Louis, in between her convulsions, 'You see the condition I am in.' Louis went white, and rounded on the doctors. Minette shook her head and said she knew she was going to die. Louis kneeled by the bed and, to the amazement of the onlookers, broke down in sobs. She whispered something to him: it seemed as if she were giving consolation.

It was now near midnight, and Minette had been in agony for six hours. Her hands and feet were cold and blue; she kept hiccoughing but could not be sick. She was lifted back to her own bed. The English ambassador came, and found her being given the sacraments by a priest. She told the ambassador that she did not fear dying; her only regret was leaving her brother, Charles, whom no one could love better than she had. When the ambassador, speaking in English, tried to ask her about the matter of poison, she hushed him and told him to say nothing of it. She was growing weak now, though with no diminishing of pain. Some who saw it said they could not believe any human creature could endure it. It was another two hours before, clutching a crucifix, Minette suffered a last convulsion and died.

She was twenty-six. The French Court was thrown into grief, and

Louis was inconsolable. Philippe's first act was to seize all her letters from England, and have them translated. His next, to summon his tailor, and begin looking over patterns for mourning. He always loved purple.

Such was the account that came to us, piecemeal, at Whitehall. I have asked about it in later years, and found nothing more to add. Of course, the rumour of poison was on everyone's lips, and that had indeed been my father's first frenzied cry when he heard the news – 'He has killed her' – before he broke down and took to his room.

Louis ordered her body to be opened and examined by a group of physicians, including two from England. They found no evidence of poison. Still, the physicians had been able to propose no remedy for her beyond a dose of senna; and there were many who remained convinced that that hellish death could not proceed from any natural cause. Philippe was suspected, though not alone. Rumour traced the hand of the exiled Chevalier de Lorraine behind the plot and the poison; he must have persuaded his lover to the murder, even procured the substance and sent it from Italy, where he was living and where, as everyone knew, poisons were ten a penny. Certainly Philippe showed no great sorrow; and rumour added that whatever Louis said, he could not act against his own brother. But nothing could be proved.

It was the arrival at Whitehall of a courtier from Versailles, on a formal visit of condolence, that roused my father at last from his trance of grief. The gentleman brought the findings of the post-mortem doctors; what was more, he had been present throughout these horrid events, and could give his own account of them, which my father was plainly anxious to hear; he was closeted with the gentleman for hours.

And afterwards he seemed, in some measure, more himself. He left his own chambers at last, and went to call upon the Queen in her apartments, and my uncle likewise; and later we all supped together. This in itself felt unnatural – there was no forgetting that the last time we had gathered thus had been at Dover with Minette – but rather than speak of it, my father doggedly avoided her name, in spite of all the efforts of the Duchess of York, who would as ever be talking, and whose voice of brass grew ever louder on the subject of death and providence as he grew more silent.

Something else he avoided also: my eye. I wondered if this was shame or embarrassment at my having seen him in his bedchamber, helpless and unmanned. But I thought it no occasion for shame, and intended saying so; and when he retired, I followed him.

He busied himself with winding the clocks, and fussing over the spaniels, as if I were not there, only grunting at last, with his back to me: 'You have something to say to me, Jemmy?'

'Only – only that I share your grief, Father,' said I tentatively, 'and that I wish—'

'Wishes are for children.' With fastidious care he began to trim a smoking candle. 'And you – you are not a child any more, Jemmy. Perhaps I was wrong not to take account of that. No matter. 'Tis done now.'

'I don't understand.'

He looked at me narrowly, disdainfully, like a man suspecting a pedlar of swindling him. Then he shrugged. 'God knows if I believe that. Perhaps I will: it can make no difference. But this daisy-eyed innocence, Jemmy, will not do for ever, you know. Come, it is already absurd. I know of your reputation with the women – and I don't wonder at it, or mind it. But these protestations—'

'I protest nothing,' I said hotly, 'except that I don't know what you're talking about. Is this aught to do with Minette? Because I cannot see—'

'Who gave you leave to use that name, sir?'

His fierce tone took me aback, but I answered straightly: 'She did. Long ago. You know that, Father.'

My father breathed heavily, glowering at me. 'You would know what the matter is, Jemmy? I have these reports from France. Of my sister's last days. At Versailles, when Louis asked about her stay on these shores, one of her party talked of her reception here. He kept talking of the *si beau Duc de Monmouth*, and what particular attentions you had paid to Madame, and how flattering this was from such a handsome young nobleman . . . Fine, is it not? When Philippe had made it so plain that he distrusted the intimacy between you. Well, Philippe seethed like a kettle and Madame ended up in tears. 'Twas very ill-chosen of this courtier of hers, no doubt: still he was only saying what had happened. He can scarcely be blamed—'

'What?' I cried. 'Do you mean, then, to blame me? You would hold her death against me . . . ?' I could not go on. To my shame, I felt tears choking me; it was as if my father had turned and without warning slapped my face.

He studied me. He seemed unmoved – though who could ever tell? 'We are assured,' he said after a moment, in a dull iron voice, 'that there was naught suspicious in Madame's death. So we must take that assurance and live with it. But I am sure of nothing in this world. And the more I think—'

'Philippe was always insanely jealous. Any man, who paid any attentions—'

'These were not just any attentions. I saw myself.'

'I loved Minette, and was happy to see her again,' I said. 'As she was me. These feelings—'

'Be damned to your feelings!' my father snapped. 'What is so fine about them that you must be forever parading them? You know your scripture, I hope: we are enjoined to put away childish things. Discretion, boy, forethought, calculation: do you suppose you can leave learning these things till doomsday? This I say for your good, Jemmy.'

'For *your* notion of good, perhaps,' I said.

He did not expect that: perhaps it was even a slap back. His head jerked up and his face darkened. 'I put the best case for you, Jemmy: reproaching you only with the idiocy and vanity of youth, in your intimacy with Madame. I should not like to think that there were more I should reproach you with.'

'What, Father? What is in your mind? For, before God, if Philippe had cause to be jealous of Minette with anyone, it was surely you more than me.'

In truth, hurt and bitter as I was, I hardly knew what I said, though as I spoke I had a flash of memory, of what Queen Catharine had said to me at Dover. But my father recoiled violently. For a moment he seemed actually to shrink before my eyes.

'Everything she did, she did for you only,' I went on in a passion. 'I don't know whether that is a cause of satisfaction or shame to you, for I don't know all that has gone one. There are whispers of state business that she undertook for you and Louis, and you may be sure Philippe misliked that also. But whichever it is, you do wrong to try and put it upon me.'

'You had better get out, Jemmy,' my father growled, 'else I may do something I shall rue.'

'Will you? If it be for once honest, and from the heart, then let it come.'

He gave a faint cold smile. 'You should have a care. You should recall that everything I have given you, I have the power to take away.'

'Recall it? When am I ever allowed to forget it? It is all on sufferance, so that I may never know where I stand. Am I your lawful-born son? Do you intend to declare me so? Or will you keep my uncle and me forever dangling on your strings, until we are worn away? Well, do as you will, Father. If you won't confirm my rights, then I will prove them.' I was shaking now. 'My only crime with Minette was to be loved. I'm sorry if you can't bear that, but I can't promise not to commit the crime again. It is all I have ever wanted from you, after all, Father. You give me the taste, and won't satisfy my appetite. I am not to be blamed, then, for the craving.'

'Ah, now we get to it. I congratulate you, Jemmy. This is a very ingenious pretty way of saying you aim for the crown.'

'I aim to be worthy of it,' I said, going out. 'That is the difference between us.'

BOOK THREE

ONE

It was in 1678, when I returned from the wars to an England gone mad, that the events began that have led me here: to exile, to estrangement from my father, and even enmity.

None of it was meant to happen. Looking back over these later times, I find it harder to think straight. The truth – of which I had hoped to make this narrative a repository, plain and unadorned and perhaps, in part, ugly – becomes elusive. For these were times of plots and counterplots, of rumour and innuendo; and of lies. As for what or who was to blame – well, that I can scarcely untangle. I know that I am not good at subtlety. Perhaps that in itself is the key to the whole business . . .

My love has just come in, and read these words, and she protests.

I make it sound, she says, as if my father and I were at odds all from the time of Minette's death, or at least, as if those intervening years saw no warmth between us. She knows this is not true, she says; and she would have me set down that when I came back from the wars in '78, I was a hero – and the apple of my father's eye.

Well, as to the hero, I am not sure of that, though there were people aplenty treating me as such, and I know I was weak and flattered enough to be braggarty about it. But the apple of my father's eye? Yes: so I was. And perhaps there is the master key that unlocks it all.

But I must give a notion of those years, before the souring, before the fall.

In our relations with those we love, there are few passages so squally that we cannot row ourselves back to calmer waters, with will and time. Bitter indeed were the words between my father and me after Minette's death: such venom was not easily to be drawn. But our hearts cannot be continually boiling with violent emotions, any more than we can spend all our lives running full pelt. Exhaustion will deputize for reason at last, and we lapse into kindness.

So it was with us. Yet for some time after Minette's death, my father was not himself; and I do not use that familiar expression lightly.

Outwardly he was the man and the King he had always been. Most characteristically, his grief did not take the form of a revulsion of the flesh: no ascetic he. Indeed, I would say he rather plunged into the gratification of appetite, and it was from this time that the most scurrilous tales and rhymes were coined about his amorous exploits. His own friends, a set of new-grown gallants who seemed determined to outdo the former generation in bawdry and outrage, would repeat them to his face, assured of no reproof beyond a tolerant laugh. Though Lady Castlemaine's day was over, he soon took another new mistress. But this one was different. She was, in a way, a piece of Minette.

She was a young Frenchwoman named Louise de Kéroüalle: dark, dimpled, ruby-lipped and buxom. When Minette had made her last fateful visit to England, Louise had been among her ladies-in-waiting, and had caught my father's eye: when Minette had asked what parting present she could make him, he had half-jestingly suggested this beauteous attendant of hers. Minette had put him off. But later King Louis had got to hear of his royal cousin's admiration for the girl, and so she was dispatched to the court at Whitehall, presently to be a Lady of the Queen's Bedchamber. Buckingham, who had gone to France to sponsor the treaty of commerce between our countries, was her escort hither, and introduced her. Doubtless he thought to place another ally in the King's bed; no doubt too that Louis saw her as a useful go-between, spy, and general agent of French interests.

It was a role that Louise, whom my father soon made Duchess of Portsmouth, was well equipped to play, for I think she was the chilliest little designing minx that ever breathed, who could not blink without a stratagem. But she liked herself too well to be only a tool. She had her own ends in view.

'Oh, Squintabella thinks to play Madam Stewart's game, and hold out for a wedding,' was how Nell Gwynn put it. 'But alack for her, the Queen obstinately refuses to die off, and so she'll have a long waiting. I fancy she'll give in, and learn that she must have the tumble without the bauble, like the rest of us.' Nell had christened her rival Squintabella, on account of the slanting look about the Frenchwoman's sloe eyes. My father had set Nell up in a house at Pall Mall, where she nursed her babies, dressed in gold and sky-blue, entertained callers to tea or canary wine but no more, and maintained her lucid good humour. But she did not like Louise, who, though she came here without a bean, had mincing refined ways and made much of her noble family. Nell found this absurd. 'I don't mind a lady,' she said. 'I don't mind a whore. What I can't abide is one pretending to be t'other.'

Well, Louise did give in, prompted no doubt both by the French ambassador and by self-interest. The occasion was marked, indeed, almost in the manner of a wedding. It took place at Lord Arlington's country mansion near Newmarket, where a week of junketings culminated in my father's bedding Louise – or her bedding him; with a stocking thrown after, as with a bride, and much congratulatory comment.

All very amusing – to the Court at any rate. Beyond the Court, people began to look differently on these things. One did not need to be an old alehouse republican, sighing for Oliver's time and saying that the King was squatting himself down in a nest of Frenchies, Papists, and spies, to share the disquiet. Between the King, who had been welcomed back to these shores with laurels and bays and loyal addresses, and the people who had put their trust in him, a slow sure division seemed to be opening up.

And at this time, I am afraid, there could be no doubting on which side of the gulf I stood. Two incidents illustrate this. They have been all filigreed over with lies and half-truths, but the facts beneath are grim enough.

From the reproach of the first, the attack upon Sir John Coventry, I entirely absolve myself. I set it down here as evidence that my father, as I said, was not himself after his sister died. The matter was simple: the Parliament was debating an entertainment tax, to be levied upon theatre tickets. A member opposed the motion on the grounds that the theatres were part of the King's pleasure: another member, Sir John Coventry, a man I knew well, could not resist the jest that came to his lips, and rose to ask whether His Majesty's pleasure lay most among the actors or the actresses.

A few nights later, Sir John was set upon in the street by above a dozen men as he walked home from dining at the Cock Tavern in Bow Street. Though he fought doughtily they pinned him down, cut him with swords, and slit his nose to the bone. This nose-slitting was a favoured revenge-stroke among the duelling and brawling young bloods of the town. But no fancied slur over the dice-box was behind this. The attackers were officers of the King's Guard, which I commanded. Two of them came later to my house to brag of the exploit – in the expectation, it seemed, that I approved it; or else to make sure of my being held to account.

I did not approve it nor order it, though rumour soon asserted that I had – and went further, claiming that I had acted on instructions from my father. A curious business. If I have portrayed my father aright, you will readily conclude that Sir John's jest was precisely of the sort he would have enjoyed. I have never been able to like jokes against myself – I think few men do, but my father was definitely one of those who did. And so I cannot believe he would wink at, still less press for, such an assault upon a Parliament-man, which had a most tyrannic flavour. The outraged Parliament put through a bill making nose-slitting a felony, and demanded the arrest of the malefactors, and my father promptly agreed to all of it. Yet still I feel a tingle of uncertainty as I recall his face at that time: more impenetrable than ever, and oddly expressionless, as if he simply did not care. And when I talked of it, he yawned and said, 'Odsfish, Jemmy, still harping on that string? Let it lie. The Parliament shall have their satisfaction, and then we shall have a general pardon. Perhaps,' he added with a shrug.

If he intended that, it never came. But it still makes me wonder if he had dropped a word to those officers – subtly, of course, being the man he was – with another word to the effect that he would square the account for them.

There is another possibility, scarcely more palatable. My uncle James went out of his way to deplore the assault. He kept speaking of it as insistently as if he had scribes on hand writing down his words. And I heard the Duchess of York, in one of her last ventures in public, loftily informing a friend: 'James did everything in his power, everything, to prevent it. He used every persuasion. La, well, 'twould be a better thing all round if his counsel were more heeded.'

Now I find it hard to believe that James, who grew more fiercely absolute with each year, and who made no bones about his belief in the unfettered privileges of the Crown, should care so much for the rights of Parliament-men. This heavy talk of his was, I think, a blind, and if behind that screen it was he who pressed the attack on Sir John, I should not be wholly surprised. The more so, as he knew it must throw some shadow of disgrace upon me.

But if you cannot follow me into such plottish speculation, no matter. The second incident was worse, and you may be sure that here I shall lay no blame except at my own door. A man lay dead at the end of it, and the best I can say of myself is that it was not my hand that killed him: though it may as well have been.

I was roaring drunk: so were we all. There were many such nights as this, nights of carousing about the town, swaggering and swearing and bandying stale jests; and ever drinking and again drinking. There is no overstating the sottishness of those times. One of my father's boon companions, that scandalous Earl of Rochester who blazed about the court with his witticisms so obscene and his adventures so freakish that old Buckingham looked staid beside him, claimed that he was never sober for five years. He once said to me that, though a man of thirty, he was in truth a youth of fifteen, because he could only remember half of his life. It was he, rumour said, who was behind another nocturnal savagery, when Mr Dryden, the Poet Laureate, was set upon in a Covent Garden alley and beaten half to death. Well, such were the times: more than a touch of madness in the air, I think; still, again, no excuses. That night of my shame my cronies and I were driven by nothing more mysterious than liquor and cock-on-a-dunghill vanity.

We were all young. There was the Cornet of my troop, who I remember kept having the hiccoughs, and the young Duke of Somerset, who could not stop laughing, and my friend Christopher Monck, who, with the death of his father, had inherited the Dukedom of Albemarle. Friend, I say, though we had been quarrelling of late. Christopher suspected me of having an eye to his wife, which I did not, and told him so, but I think he doubted me yet. And we were all going about the town masked, for such was the new fashion. I cannot remember who suggested that we conclude our carouse with a visit to Whetstone Park, though I recall young Somerset kept shrieking that he was so drunk he would not be able to perform. For Whetstone Park was the name given to a notorious resort of prostitutes, hard by Lincoln's Inn Fields. I fancy I made some bluster about not having to pay for such pleasures, at which Christopher made some cloaked remark that set us bickering again; but I went along.

It was a winter night, and dark as pitch, which made us grope and stagger all the more, and though Christopher swore that the house we came to was of the kind we sought, and hammered at the door bellowing for admittance, there were no lights, and, in truth, I think we were mistook. But when someone did throw open a shutter and cry us to be quiet, we were, of course, all the more clamorous. We shouted, and demanded to know where the wenches were, and the others began to chant that the King's own son was here. 'The King's son – d'you hear? Would you deny the King's son? Treason, damn you all, treason . . .' Like the ass I was, I was mightily puffed up by this. I shouted too, and rapped at windows. And then the watchmen came.

To get into a brawl with the watch was so traditional an ending to a buck's night upon the town, that the wonder is we did not fall to immediately. The strange thing is, we did not. We groaned and catcalled when the watchmen, dour old bodies in greatcoats and broad hats, reproved us for disturbing the peace and told us to go home. And one lifting up his lantern and staff, we seized hold of it, and said that would do very well to rouse our quarry, and began knocking at the upper windows with it.

That man had the prudence, seeing how wild and drunk we were, only to protest. The other watchman, a stout grizzled old fellow, was of different mettle. When we tried to seize his staff, he held on grimly, swearing he would have us in the round-house if we did not disperse. Inflamed by drink and self-consequence as we were, we yelped at that. A challenge! How dare he! Did he not know who we were?

He did not, of course. He might have known us, but for the masks. And I think the masks added another piece of mischief, for behind the mask, you were not yourself: you might do anything. That was the reason for the fashion, which lent extra spice to the intrigues of lust, and I have ever feared that lust and violence are steeds at the same harness.

The watchman lunged, cursing; I tried to wrench the staff from his grip.

'Ah, would you?' he growled. 'Would you, now, you young bastard?'

His staff struck my cheekbone. I recoiled and staggered down upon one knee. When I rose, with the name he had called me ringing in my ears, that terrible red fury was upon me, the passionate transport that I had first undergone with the street urchins at Antwerp, all those years ago. I wrenched the staff from him, and wildly swinging it, knocked him to the ground.

Yes: I thought I had killed him. And no, I had not. Groaning he tried to rise, his gnarled hands swatting out, but the others pitched into the sordid brawl now, as I stood panting and glaring in that red mist.

Blows rained down: not many. But one, instead of a soft thump, made a clear cracking sound. The watchman slumped motionless. I still do not know whose was the hand that dealt that blow, but I saw Christopher Monck's mask-ringed eyes meet mine, with a bright unholy look. The best I can report of myself, is that as the crimson rage drained, I stammered out that it was enough; but too late.

'You don't have to tell me, Jemmy,' my father said.

'But I want to. Father, what happened—'

'What happened is the talk of the town,' he said. 'Three drunken dukes and a dead watchman at the end of it. By next week they will say two dead watchmen, or five, or ten; and the week after it will be forgot. And now you conclude that I do not judge you hard. You conclude wrong.'

'I judge myself hard. But I meant no – I meant no killing. We were brawling and – and the truth is—'

'You delight me, Jemmy: you persist in believing that there is such a thing as the truth.' We were in the Physic Garden. My father plucked a herb and crushed it, sniffing. 'I have a new receipt for medicinal drops, but I cannot bring the liquid to clear. It does not obey me . . . You know I have extended a royal pardon to young Albemarle. I will say no more on that, except that I am clement for his father's sake. There will be no peace, I think, until I have extended the same to you.'

'I thank you,' I said miserably. 'But people will reprove you for it.'

'Probably. But then who wants to be always loved? 'Twould be mere tedium.'

I did, though I did not say it.

'I think,' my father said, walking calmly on, 'it is time you had something to do.'

My uncle James became a widower at this time. The Duchess of York died of a cancer, crying out to her husband: 'Death is terrible, very terrible!'

To a man who prayed for forgiveness after each act of adultery, this was surely a fearful thing to hear. But if he truly mourned, he gave no sign. Soon he was businesslike. The death of the duchess changed great matters. Their little boy had died in infancy: the surviving children were both girls, Mary and Anne. James was soon talking with my father of marrying again, so that he might beget a male heir. A male heir, of course, for the throne. For there was no expectation now that Queen Catharine would have a child. My father would not see a child of his own inherit the throne.

Unless, unless . . . Unless he did that which he gave no clear indications that he would do: acknowledge me as his true-born heir. He spoke publicly of James as his one apparent heir; he would countenance no talk of my legitimacy. And if that had been the only message he sent out to the world, things would have been different.

But he sent out another message during those years that followed, one that made me his most trusted servant, and the darling of the people, and the crown prince in all but name. Were we wrong, I and those who followed me, to think that the name itself must eventually come?

It began with my father, as he said, finding me something to do. And it was what I had long wanted. He placed me in command of the army, six-thousand strong, that crossed the Channel in the year '72. We were at war again.

This war was against our old rivals the Dutch, and accordingly men cheered it, at first, as revenge for the Medway. More problematical was the fact that we fought in concert with the great armies of Louis of France, who sought to lay low the impudent cheesemongers once and for all. I was enraptured enough by my first command to care little who we fought. I was slow to come to the realization that this was a war undertaken upon no principle whatever.

'The nub of the matter is that if we do not doff our drawers and lie abed with Louis, the Dutch will,' my father said. The choice of image is typical of him, no doubt, but also of the way the intrigues of those times were conducted.

It is no part of my purpose to make this narrative the record of my experiences in the wars. For they at least, I trust, will pass undistorted to posterity: full of horrors as the battlefield can be, it is a place of simplicity, plainness, and truth, as the court is not, and that is why I felt more at home there. Besides, I have heard my uncle James talk of setting down his military memoirs, and seen even his toadies roll their eyes at the tedious prospect.

Also, I fear we never like to hear a man prate of his happiness, and my first campaign was for me a time of happy discovery. First, that I was courageous, or rather not afraid – or, more simply, my body obeyed and did not betray me, just as on the fencing floor or the tennis court: it would go forward to the red belches of cannon, it would leap the parapet and scramble up the counterscarp, it would not flinch when the enemy sprang a mine that sent bodies flying like a charnel firework into the sky. The other discovery was that men would follow me.

I had felt the first thrill of this, I believe, when years ago in Brussels my poor mother, threatened with arrest, had persuaded the people in the streets to come to our aid. Now the thrill was renewed, though in more sober fashion, for the men under my command placed their lives in my hands, and I hope I was ever sensible of the responsibility. I know that I saw few captains who knew their men as I did – their names and their nicknames, and the villages of England they sprang from, and the families that depended on them. Of this last I tried to take particular care. Now that I was eminent, I employed my every influence to get provision for men maimed in service or cast off when they were no longer needed, or for widows and orphans left behind. It was not true that I had never forgotten the poverty and insecurity of my early years – for by God, I had, as a lounger about my father's court. No shadow of it could touch me there, and by now my wife and I had a country mansion, at Moor Park in Hertfordshire, to complete our rise to fortune. But soldiering reminded me of what it was like to be a mere mortal. It reminded me, indeed, that we are all such. Thus, lionized by kings, I found my heart inclining to the people.

I say kings, for it was not only my father who heaped praises on me for my exploits on the battlefield. King Louis, our ally, fêted me; and it would take a stronger head than mine not to be dazzled by Louis then, at the height of his magnificence, with his vast hosts sweeping across Europe. I remember drawing up my troops for him to review at Courtrai, when he made me Lieutenant-General, and the way the bray of the trumpets seemed to enter, like sound turned molten, into my very veins. I remember going before him at St-Germain, where he presented me with a sword encrusted with diamonds, that was like a sunburst to look upon. And I wondered, then, whether he ever thought of the insignificant boy I had been, standing among the attendants to have my chin squeezed by damnable Philippe – who kept, I may add, out of the way. And those thoughts, of course, brought the memory of Minette. I reflected how happy she would have been to see this near alliance between the two countries and the two men she loved and sought to bring together.

And I reflected, too, on whether she had played a greater part in this than anyone knew, on that visit to Dover. And at last, dimly, through the haze of glory, I began to wonder as others did, whether it was a good thing, or a very bad one.

This Holland, which the armies of France and England seemed to be on their way to crushing, was a peculiar state. It was a republic which retained a sort of king within its borders – the Prince of the House of Orange, to whom tradition gave the command of Dutch forces, and the allegiance of Dutch hearts, but no sovereignty. The young Prince who held this title was William.

He was the only child of my father's late sister Mary – hence, nephew to my father and cousin to me; though the relation had not thus far been a close one. William, the sickly child who had not been expected to live, had had a lonely and difficult growing-up at the court of Orange, surrounded by the powerful burghers of Holland who felt that he and his House were too Stuart, too royal, and too dangerous. The brothers De Witt, the ministers of Holland, were determined to keep him from his hereditary offices – as William, in his quiet way, was determined to have them. Then the war came; and as Louis's great forces massed on the Dutch borders, and destruction threatened, the people turned against the De Witts – a mob setting upon them in the streets, and literally tearing them to pieces.

That left William. Some said he had urged on the execution of the De Witts: certainly he did not press for the murderers' arrest. Characteristically, he kept clear of the whole matter. Thus he had more in common with that other great survivor, my father, than appeared. He had visited England shortly before his twenty-first birthday, and sat stony-faced and sober through the parade of banquets, horse-races and plays with which my bemused father had entertained him. 'A dry stick,' was my father's conclusion, 'and so *very* Dutch.' But no one knew much of William then – or expected much. But as he took upon himself the leadership of Holland, and rode at the head of their troops, we soon had cause to know him.

The Dutch opened the dykes, letting in, as the fen-men of our country say, Old Captain Flood. Under William they fought, as I saw for myself, with ten times the valour. The invaders advanced, and then advanced more slowly, and then stopped advancing. Louis, who had begun to expect victories like the rising of the morning sun, looked on in bafflement, while the Dutch began to call William the saviour of their country. Even amongst his foes there was respect – above all in my own troops. We battered against the Dutch for near a month at the siege of Maastricht, where in pouring rain and hellish confusion I won I suppose my greatest laurels leading the charge to capture the Brussels Gate. In truth I was lucky to live. I was saved from a fatal sword-thrust by the quick intervention of one of my comrades, one Captain John Churchill, whose name, if it survive not in other connections, I gratefully set down here for posterity.

Yes, this was a fine time for me, sealed by the birth of a son, of whom Anna was safely delivered in London. I was home from the wars, for a short while, to see her, and we were as kind together as we had ever managed. 'You need not study him so, Jemmy,' she said as I held the tiny, dark, goggling babe up to my face, 'you may be sure he is yours.'

'Aye, he is a handsome fellow, and so he must be.'

But all was not well beyond this charmed circle of mine. At sea, our ships had suffered reverses, and there were none of the great victories that my uncle James, as Lord High Admiral, had promised. And the French ships allied with us, it was said, struck sail as soon as they saw the enemy. Very swiftly, the mood of the people – and the Parliament above all – grew dark. Had we, they asked, been led into a war that was not of our making?

Here, it seemed, was the real fruit of that friendly union which Minette had so busily promoted on my father's behalf. The whisper was that we had been secretly entangled, more than we knew; that we were made the mere tool of Louis's ambitions. And what was Louis offering in return? My father seemed less concerned now about treating with Parliament to supply his finances – as if, some said, he were planning to do without them altogether. Certainly he seemed to have money enough, from somewhere, to lay out ten thousand a year on Louise – who was French likewise, of course, and whose apartments at Whitehall were so luxurious that a Swedish envoy, gone astray, thought he was in the Throne Room and made obeisance to Louise's dining chair.

Thus the whispers. If my father was lining his nest with French gold, I can understand, I think, without approving. I believe it was that same lynx-eyed fear that he showed in matters of love, the fear of dependence, of laying himself open. Others, of course, could not see it so. But these rumblings of discontent were as nothing to the thunder that was to shake the kingdom in that year of '73, and presaged a storm fiercer than any guns Dutch or French.

Ever since great Elizabeth had set our Church and our liberties secure against the tyrannous power of Spain, England had rested its freedom and its religion upon the same foundation. Now we were allied with a triumphant France, Catholic and determined that all of Europe should be so. At court a Catholic mistress held sway over the King; and rumour had long hinted that James, the heir to the throne, was unreliable in his religion. It was no great surprise that the Parliament should now pass the Test Act, which said, very simply, that a man holding offices of state in England must be of the English Church.

My uncle James promptly resigned all his offices, and confirmed what my wife had long divined: he was a Roman Catholic.

So, it transpired, had his duchess been. She may have had a hand in converting him: for as more than one wit remarked, the notion of James thinking anything for himself was too fantastical. But once he had taken something into that strange, intense, airless mind of his, he would never let it go. He was a convert of the most freezing and implacable zeal.

'He has been reading some damnable book, that's what it is,' I heard my father say to Lord Arlington. 'And that particular exercise is so rare with him it's flown to his head. If he'd happened on the Koran of the Turks, he'd be telling us we must all be Mohammedans.' He was angry with his brother, more indeed than he cared to show. He foresaw the trouble to come, and that it should come from a matter that a sensible man could surely keep to himself – well, that my father could not comprehend.

But here lay a great difference between him and James. More than once, when James was urging upon him some fearful high-handed course, my father said to him: 'You may do as you will, James. But as for me, you know I am resolved never to go on my travels again.' My father never forgot the miseries of the exile. Whatever happened, at whatever cost, he would not go back there. But my uncle seemed oblivious to that. Perhaps miseries meant nothing to him, as he never truly appeared to enjoy anything in life, except perhaps power. Perhaps he thought no one would ever again oppose the Crown. Certainly the frigid pride of his manner hardened from the time he declared his faith.

I mentioned Queen Elizabeth, and I should have guessed where my uncle's mind was tending from some extraordinary things he said about that queen to my wife, at our son's christening. We had named him Charles; and talk turning on the fashion in names, my wife remarked on Walter, and how it was not much heard now, for all that Walter Raleigh had been a favourite of the great Queen.

'A great queen?' James said pouncingly. 'A great impostor. A great disaster. There is her only greatness.'

'Fie, sir,' my wife cried, 'you must not make such jests, else people will believe you!'

'I do not jest,' my uncle said – which was very truth, God knows. 'I look upon her reign as a most wicked wrong-headed time. But then such is to be expected – from a bastard and a usurper.'

'Old times,' my father said quickly, 'old and stale. Here we have a pretty babe who belongs to the future – a sweeter theme. You must give him a little brother or sister soon, my dear . . .'

So he turned the talk. But my uncle's extraordinary pronouncement hung in the air. It was only Catholics of the most intolerant stamp who would disinter this old fiction of Queen Elizabeth's bastardy. Elizabeth was born to Henry the Eighth's second wife, Anne Bullen. To the stubbornest of Papists, that meant she was not legitimate, because Henry had divorced his first wife in defiance of the Pope. In carrying through the divorce, Henry rejected the dominance of Rome, and established our English Church independent of it. And this Elizabeth upheld, as well as our freedom from the invading Spanish, who set forth to crush the nation of heretics.

So it was not only his Catholic religion that my uncle hinted at in such a remark. There was a strange, grim flavour of a fanatic past: a most curious refusal to countenance the history that had made our country; most of all, an alarming ignorance of what the people of England loved and believed. But then he seemed to think of them, if at all, as a set of barbarians beyond the gates. He would say to my father sometimes that the Crown existed here in a state of siege.

And this was the man who waited – impatiently, it seemed – for the throne of England.

Great was the disquiet, but it was soothed in some measure by a consideration of James's daughters, Mary and Anne, who would come after him. For they, at my father's insistence, were raised in the Protestant faith: at least his line would not partake of his aberration. But then my uncle, having reviewed by proxy various princesses of Europe, fixed upon his new bride, and the dismay began afresh.

She was Mary of Modena, daughter of a petty Italian princedom. She was young – only seventeen to my uncle's forty – and had been intended for the cloister before my uncle's envoy arrived with his offer; and was, as it turned out, quite a beauty: tall and slender as a lily, rich and dark as a musk rose. But my uncle did not know that when he chose her, nor I think did that interest him. Most characteristic of what I can only call his granite silliness was his remark to his little daughters about their new stepmother: 'Well, my dears, I am bringing you a new playmate.' What made him choose her was her faith. And Mary of Modena, arriving veiled with her train of Italian confessors, could hardly have been more flagrantly Catholic. The jest was that James had first sent to assure himself that there was no chance the Pope might be a woman, and then resignedly settled for the next best thing.

I remember when I first met my uncle's bride, she could hardly lift her violet eyes. She murmured in broken English in a voice that seemed full of tears. But once the attention was not upon her, she looked about her with great quickness, and not a little haughtiness. I thought of a cat taken into a house, observing where the softest cushions are. And I noticed that when she turned to summon her attendants, they came with a fearful and wincing hurry, which suggested there was steel beneath the velvet.

Perhaps the most curious thing about my uncle then was his heedlessness. Though the Test Act forced him to put off his formal offices, he remained as high and imperious in the councils of state as ever. Nor did the opinion of a Protestant nation seem to trouble him. Such a man must collect enemies as a broadcloth coat collects burrs; and there had long been a mutual dislike between him and a man then at the height of his fortunes – Lord Ashley, now the Earl of Shaftesbury.

Shaftesbury had risen high in my father's circle, and at last was Lord Chancellor. He merited the position because he was clever, industrious, and fiercely determined. There seemed will enough in that small sickly body, with which Buckingham had mocked him, for ten men. My father respected clever men, more, perhaps, than honest ones – he was clever himself – and such was the relation between him and Shaftesbury. It was never quite ease. Perhaps in a way they were too well matched. My father once, seeing Shaftesbury approach, said in his light way, 'Here comes the greatest whoremaster in the kingdom.' To which Shaftesbury replied, with a little bow, 'Among the subjects, sire.' It was pretty, and almost too prompt. I wonder if my father, who prided himself on penetrating men's worse natures, was sometimes discomfited by the presence of one whose mind was even more of a surgeon's instrument than his own.

'Will you not trust it, Father?' I said to him once, when a frost had iced over the lake in the park, and I was venturing on it to try skating.

'I would trust it,' my father said with a faint smile, 'about as much as my lord Shaftesbury's principles.' It was the kind of remark he made more than once about Shaftesbury, and was, I think, a little revealing. For it was my father's habitual maxim that men were not to be trusted: he preferred them so, indeed, for then he knew where he stood. Why, then, this particular judgement upon Shaftesbury? I cannot tell, unless there simply be something between certain men, small and grating and unignorable like grit in the eye, that destines them to be at odds, or unless my father, looking at Shaftesbury, found himself looking in a sort of mirror and did not like it.

But in Shaftesbury he had, certainly, a man who could manage the Parliament most resourcefully, and that was much needed as feeling rose against the Dutch war and the path the kingdom was taking. The trouble was, Shaftesbury began to share that feeling. Afterwards, my father would say that the earl was disloyal all along. I think not. The crux of the matter was my uncle James. Between him and Shaftesbury there was a long-standing dislike and distrust. When James revealed his religion, and announced his intention of founding a Catholic line to the throne with his fertile new Italian princess, this smouldering enmity burst forth in dangerous flame.

My father dismissed Shaftesbury from the Chancellorship at the end of '73. It was because the Parliament was obstructive of the Dutch war and the French friendship, and Shaftesbury had either not stopped it being so, or secretly encouraged it: so went the reasoning. But everyone knew what was really behind it. Shaftesbury was on such bad terms with my uncle by now that they could not sit together at the same table. It was Shaftesbury who had spoken most violently against James's ill-advised marriage. My uncle did not forget: he was a man of slow settled vengefulness. I do not doubt that he pressed my father to dismiss the pugnacious little earl. There was always a weary hunted look about my father when James had been at him. Just as Lady Castlemaine used tantrums, and Louise babyish tears, my uncle worked on my father with his remorseless, passionless nagging.

Still, I doubt not that my father was glad to be rid of Shaftesbury – simply on the principle that there is not room for two foxes in one earth. But he never expected, I think, the direful result. As with his women, so with his ministers: he always made it plain that they did not possess his heart, and that the attachment was of temporary convenience. He surely supposed that Shaftesbury would retire to the country and fade out of sight, piqued certainly, but resigned to the common rise and fall of courtiers.

No: for the first time, my father miscalculated. Shaftesbury remained in London, busying himself, cultivating his supporters. He knew well who was responsible for his downfall; he knew my father could have stopped it. In place of a servant, the Crown now had a redoubtable opponent.

Occupied with soldiering as I was, I observed these events distantly. But there was something I could not help but notice, as I returned to England after campaign: at Deal, at the approaches to London, at the gates of the City itself, crowds of people gathered to cheer me. They shouted my name. They doffed their hats.

Some even kneeled.

TWO

Shaftesbury came to see me at Hedge Lane.

'To offer my congratulations, Your Grace,' he said, seating himself with a wince. 'My double congratulations – public and private, as it were.'

It was the summer of '74. I had been made Master of the Horse in place of Buckingham, who was duelling and debauching himself into middle age, and I had become a father for the second time. Only one babe sweetened our lofty chambers with prattle, though. Our first had died in the winter: a horrid time. I had been desperately afflicted – as had Anna, of course. But she held it better, and in the end had told me sharply to master myself.

'Thank you, my lord. But this is old news.'

Shaftesbury shrugged, peering around the room. 'I was prompted by this remarkable performance at Windsor the other day. It brought your exploits fresh to mind. You are a coming man, Your Grace.'

'But I did not see you there.' In a meadow below the terrace at Windsor, at my father's command, I had taken part in a representation of the siege of Maastricht, complete with guns and grenades and storming of trenches. All the Court had watched, applauding under a moonlit sky.

'Because I was not there,' Shaftesbury said. 'Of course. I might have been invited, perhaps, if it were sure that a stray cannon-shot would take off my head.'

'This breach,' I said uncertainly, 'if such it is, is much to be regretted—'

'Pooh, nonsense. Men disagree: great men disagree greatly; for great issues are at stake. No matter, I heard a whole account of it. Most entertaining. Curious, though, that the Duke of York should be the one making the charge beside you. 'Tis not as if *he* was there.'

'As you say, my lord.' I had certainly not been pleased about that, especially when, at the conclusion, my uncle had coolly said to me beneath the applause: 'And this, Jemmy, was a true representation of how you conducted the siege? Faith – it is a wonder you won.'

'I dare say there would have been trouble if he had been excluded,' Shaftesbury said casually. 'It is no secret how jealous the duke grows of you.'

'Indeed, it is not something I court or seek—'

'Why not?' Shaftesbury said, giving me a challenging look; and then wiping it away with a laugh. 'Hey, well, if only all our wars were play. 'Tis a thankful matter that this ill-conditioned enterprise against the Dutch looks to be ending.'

'Yet you promoted the war, my lord, did you not?'

'So I did.' Shaftesbury gave a faint tolerant smile, as at the powerless punch of an infant. 'When I was in favour – as you are too gracious to add. And now I am out, I make mischief by opposing all the Crown's policy. Oh, such is the talk, I know. I don't care for that. I do care, though, that those whom I might expect to sympathize with my aims should understand my reasons.'

'To sympathize . . . ?' I hesitated. 'I am certainly no enemy to you, my lord. But you cannot expect me to turn against my father.'

'I do not think I said any such thing.' The earl rose, wincing again, and took a limping turn about the room. 'I expressed myself poorly, perhaps. I supported the war while I saw it as necessary to defend the interests of this kingdom. But now it has been revealed in quite another light, not only to me but to many true-thinking Englishmen. This is no joust with our rival in trade. There is a grand design behind it. A grand and ill design. I am still unsure of its extent, but it may be traced, I think, to the visit of Madame to Dover.'

I jumped. There was such a strong flavour of the inquisitor in Shaftesbury's tone that it was as if I saw Minette placed in the dock. 'My lord,' I said, 'if you mean to defame my late aunt, I cannot hear you—'

'You sound priggish,' Shaftesbury said mildly, with interest, 'and really that is not like you, Your Grace. It is what everyone marvels at: you are all openness and charm, but it does not cloy. It is a great gift, sir. As for defaming Madame, I mean no such thing. A woman of much wit and sense. And devoted to His Majesty. But devoted also to her adopted country and its religion. There lies the mischief. Whatever the intentions, this friendship, this alliance, does us no good. It bids fair to make us slaves.'

'We have partnered France,' I said, 'and I confess to some misgivings. But it is not as if we have submitted to her—'

'Nor shall we,' Shaftesbury said with a fierce fresh look. 'Not while there are Englishmen who are certain of what they believe in. Come, sir, you have been in France. You have seen the power, the ambition of the French King. He is the declared enemy of the Protestant religion. His appetite will not stop at reducing the Dutch republic. Nor is there any to say him nay: you know he is absolute in his kingdom. There are those here who would see the English Crown absolute likewise, and fetter us to Louis's Catholic designs.'

'I hope . . . I hope you do not speak of my father.'

'I hope so too, Your Grace, most devoutly!' Shaftesbury said, with a grey smile. 'And I may as well say, I shall be your father's enemy from the moment I suspect it. But in truth I see nothing so naked in His Majesty's subtle mind. The plainest aims are to be seen in the man who expects to succeed him. I do not imagine there is much fondness between you and your uncle of York. All the same you may reprove me for saying this. He is a traitor.'

'My lord,' I said in perplexity, 'if you make free with such words—'

'Nothing will happen to me. Not as it stands, with the power of the Crown restrained, just, by Parliament. But if James had the power he craves, no, I could not say such things. Nor could many men exercise the liberties we have hardly won. There would be full gaols, and royal troops marching on every road. I should more strictly call him a traitor in embryo: caterpillar before butterfly. But he makes no secret of his aims, as he makes no secret of his Catholicism. His religion, Your Grace, makes him traitorous; his character makes him a despot. He would be a Louis – even now.'

'But my uncle's profession of his faith has diminished his influence, surely.'

'Superficially. But while your father – excuse me – chooses to beguile his time with the pleasures of the *boudoir*, a great vacancy is left at the heart of our affairs, and James fills it. Believe me, I am no Puritan. Your father is a man who enjoys his pleasures: very well. But even there the peril lurks. It is at the least an unhappy coincidence that the woman who most engages his attention is a Frenchwoman and a Papist, who seeks at every turn to advance her master's cause.'

'I dare say the lady is an intriguer,' I said, 'though in truth she has shown only friendly attention to me.' This was true. Louise in her mincing way had rather cultivated me of late, though I always had the feeling that she began talking about me the moment I left the room.

'Why, so she would, Your Grace. So she would.' Shaftesbury paused in his roaming before a portrait newly framed. I had just been painted again, and I freely confess that I liked it. It gave me a sense of assurance to look upon my picture: yes, there I truly was, fixed in the world, undeniable. Sometimes, if I slept ill, I still had dreams in which I was the patched boy dragging from lodging to lodging with my mother and Anne Hill. 'A handsome likeness. Though I do not think any picture I have seen has quite caught you. Your late mother must have been a great beauty, sir. No, no, I mean no court flattery, merely the truth. And I, you know, may comment fairly on such matters, as I' – he gestured humorously at his own lean ugly face – 'am quite shut out from them.'

'My mother was certainly very handsome.'

'I had not the honour of knowing her. I have heard about her, of course.'

'You surprise me, my lord,' I said, surprising myself with my own sudden flare of bitterness, 'as her memory is so often traduced by gentlemen saying they had that honour, who never saw her in their lives.'

'Ah?' Shaftesbury said gently. It was characteristic of him that you never had to explain yourself: he was with you in a moment. 'Yes, one hears these calumnies. One knows, of course, whence they come. Forgive me, you will suppose me quite obsessed by your uncle of York, but surely here he is again. I have heard him with my own ears cast doubt upon your paternity. No baser revelation of his envy could be imagined, for any man with eyes can see you are your father's son – leaving aside that His Majesty claims you so whole-heartedly. One wonders indeed why he is not more severe on his brother for such talk. There is family affection, of course. The bond.'

'My father is certainly loyal to his brother,' I said, with reluctance. 'I fancy the years they had in exile have planted these loyalties deep—'

'Admirable,' Shaftesbury said, turning away from the portrait at last, as if he had been fixing it in his memory. 'And regrettable. He never, I think, speaks of your mother?'

'Very seldom.'

'Now you see, I find that curious. We speak freely of the things that do not greatly touch our heart: it is deeper matters that tie our tongues. One might suppose, indeed, that there is truth to these rumours.' He passed close to me, and – most unusually, for he was not a man for touching – laid his hand briefly on my arm. 'Of there being a marriage, and so forth.'

'My lord, on that score I hardly know what to say—'

'Don't you? Yet I have heard it said, Your Grace, that you threaten to kill any man who will call you bastard.'

I hesitated. 'I might have governed my tongue better, perhaps. But these are, as you say, deep matters. I have a belief – a sacred belief . . .' Vividly came the memory of my dying mother in the wine shop, her great sick eyes exacting my faith. 'But it is a private matter between my father and I—'

'That is exactly what it is not,' Shaftesbury said, so sharply that I flinched. 'Your pardon, Your Grace. You do right to remind me of the delicacy of these matters, as they regard a father you love and a memory you honour. Still, you must be aware that they are of great moment also for the kingdom. Monmouth is a name everywhere spoken with warmth and admiration. How much louder the acclamations would be, if to the name were added the title of legitimate heir to the throne of England, I leave you to determine, though I think your natural modesty balks at the dazzling prospect.'

'I – I would be a liar if I said I had not thought of it. But my lord, it is still a matter of the love I bear my father, and he me. That has been – the making of my life. And where there is love, there is trust; and in that trust, I suppose I have expected my father will always – make everything right in the end.'

'Perhaps he may,' Shaftesbury said, after a brooding moment. 'We must hope so. But we cannot forget that there are other voices ever whispering in his ear. Voices meaning no good . . . And such, people will say, is mine,' he added, with a grim kind of cheer. 'Oh, yes! I am a villain, you know. A fearful snake, or wolf, or fox – any ravening beast: chiefly fox, of course. Such is the curse of red hair. Red hair, fox, cunning. It saves people thinking. Would you know what I am in truth? I am a man of fixed belief. Already I hear the sniggers. The great turncoat! Aye, I served under the Commonwealth, when there was good government; and when Cromwell grew too mighty I withdrew my support. When your father was restored, and offered good government, I served then. And what would I see? Good government, in the realm and the Church that Elizabeth bequeathed us, and its Parliament. Any king who would ride roughshod over it, and play the tyrant, I count the enemy of my country. These are the dangers I see, and would avert. To those who say I am ambitious, I would only reply that I am not strong. I am a cripple, as anyone may see, and do not expect a long life. So I shall not live to see the disasters I want to avert, nor that happier issue I hope for. Is that ambition?' He shrugged, and moved towards the door. 'I have already, perhaps, offended you: you are of royal blood, after all. But 'tis as well you know my mind, Your Grace, for I have a great interest in you, and if it be an unwelcome one, at least I shall know it, and embarrass neither of us further.'

'No,' I said hesitating, 'truly, my lord, you needn't think that. I know . . . I know that if I were to be a king, I should wish to rule for the people, not over them.'

'The people,' repeated Shaftesbury, after a strange blank moment, as if I had said peacocks or water-voles. 'Aye: to be sure. The Parliament, of course, stands to protect them, securing property and law. To be sure.'

'And is not the truest king,' I mused, 'one who is king because the people want him to be so?'

''Tis an agreeable speculation,' Shaftesbury said with a tight smile. 'A people's king. Well! Be that as may, Your Grace, let me only add to my congratulations the assurance that you are certainly on the road to becoming the people's prince.'

Leaving, he bowed quickly, and for a moment if gave him a scuttling look. I did not like it. But after all, he could not help his infirmity.

My wars were not ended, but for now I put away sword and musket. We disentangled ourselves from the war against Holland, as we must: feeling ran too high.

It was my uncle's profession of his Catholicism, and his new marriage, that made the difference. England must not be dragged into a Catholic crusade. My father's feelings over the whole business were as impenetrable as ever. I know that he was angry with James for his tactlessness, but he was ever courteous to Mary of Modena – who very soon, by the by, overcame her shyness, and took such tributes as her due. My uncle had managed to find another wife who already fancied herself Queen.

Underneath, my father may have felt himself bitterly thwarted. The French alliance had been close to Minette's heart – perhaps, as Shaftesbury hinted, closer than we knew; and my father had embraced it. Perhaps he, who believed in so little, had not expected his own people to react so violently on a matter of belief. But so it was, and he found himself at odds with them. They would not follow him down that path, and that awoke all his canny caution.

Such victory as there was belonged to William of Orange, who had emerged from shadows to save his country. This disregarded nephew, of whom my father had sometimes spoken with a trace of contempt, could not be ignored, any more than the mutinous feeling running through the country. There must be a change, of course. So, quite soon, William was to come amongst us – and I was to find in him, quite unexpectedly, and after an unpromising beginning, a good friend.

Before that I must mention – my love *insists* that I mention – an occasion quite trifling in itself. Our first meeting.

It was at a court masque given at Whitehall, called *Callisto* or *The Chaste Nymph*. Aye – you may be sure there was smirking at that: where at my father's court was such a thing as a chaste nymph to be found? And in truth the masque, though prettily done, was a poor thing. Minette would have frowned. I fear we had grown too rational for such fantasies. I danced the part of a shepherd, but the point of the affair was to honour my uncle's daughters, the young princesses Mary and Anne. They were well-grown now: Mary notably tall and graceful for a girl of twelve: ten-year-old Anne grown a little the wrong way, and turning plump, but pleasant withal. They were grown too in consequence, as they neared woman's estate, and as all hope disappeared of the Queen giving my father an heir. Mary and Anne stood next in succession to their father James, and there were many who wished they stood even nearer, as they had been kept free of his religion and his temper. So Mr Dryden's epilogue verses at the masque, addressed to my father, made clear:

> Two glorious Nymphs of your own godlike line
> Whose morning rays like noontide strike and shine
> Whom you to suppliant Monarchs shall dispose
> To bind your friends and disarm your foes.

Poor Anne was yawning by then, for it had been a long evening. Mary was still lively, though, and would have danced a last galliard with me, if she had not turned red and cried off. I was not sure whether she was shy of me, or disliked me as her father did, or was even half in love with me. Who can say with a maid of that age?

And I have to record – my love still insists on it – that I was not in the least struck by a girl only a few years older, who danced a shepherdess at that Masque, quite in the background. Yes, that was she who now shares my life and owns my heart. She insists that the indifference was not mutual: that she gazed worshipfully on me from afar, and resolved there and then that I was to be the man she would for ever love.

But destiny only fenced with us then. The killing stroke was left for another occasion. My eyes were elsewhere. I had a mistress – yes, my love insists I say that too, and laughs, though she frowns too, as she need not. For the lady was very pretty and obliging, and I kept her in a comfortable establishment, and we were fond enough of each other – which is to say, that each supplied something that the other wanted, for the time being. There was a little weary scandal at court, when Anna found out. She was not surprised, or even I think angry, but she was mortified that I had not kept the business more discreet as a gentleman should. We had a grim little scene in which I felt, as so often with my wife, as if I stood with muddied boots upon a clean new carpet.

'You are still a child, Jemmy,' she said disdainfully. 'I despair: I think you will never grow.'

Well, she was right, as always. In feelings, I was a mere child, even as I disported with my mistress like any rake. It was only when I properly met with my love that I got a man's heart instead of a boy's.

Ah, now my love, who has superintended this portion of my narrative most deedily, blushes smiling, and withdraws to the fire. So beautiful she looks, and I would fain feast my eyes . . . But I must return to those years before the fall, and above all to William.

'I do not care for it.'

These were William's words, delivered in a broken and guttural English that suggested a fist thumping into flesh, when I asked him how he liked the music of the viols.

It was at the great banquet at Guildhall, given by the City in his honour, where, being seated by him, I tried to improve his acquaintance, as I had had small chance to do since his arrival in England. All had been close talk and negotiating. Now the business was settled, perhaps we might be easy.

But William, who was not so much eating as methodically feeding himself like a man keeping a fire going, was not easy. He was silent. He kept his eyes fixed on the distance. I dare say I am not the only person in such awkward circumstances to try too hard and make blunders. Thus I went on about the viols, saying they were much commended, and the players the best of their kind, coming from France . . .

'Your pardon, sir,' I said hastily, realizing that while Louis's armies still stood menacing Dutch gates, this would not be a recommendation to William. 'I meant only that the musicians—'

'Are French. I do not mind that. I do not care for the musics.' William stoked the fire again.

'The trumpet, perhaps, better pleases your ear,' I said, going nonsensically on, 'as you are so renowned a warrior—'

'What is that words?'

'Warrior. The art of war, which you so well—'

'War? I do not care for it.' He sipped his wine as if it were vinegar. 'I have to do it. King Louis will not let us live else.'

'Ah. To be sure. Still, your exploits are much talked of, Your Highness. Witness the great welcome you have had here.'

'Hm.' For just a moment there was a curiously shy look on William's unprepossessing face with its narrow beak of a nose. 'Hm. But I do not come to talk of exploits. I come, sir, to take a wifes.' And he began fuelling himself again.

'A wifes, eh?' murmured my father, who sat on my other side, and who had observed my struggles with his most twinkling amusement. 'Suggests a hybrid creature – two women in one. Odsfish, what a deal of problems that might solve!'

The wife William had come to take was Princess Mary.

This was at the end of '77: Mary was turned fifteen now, and there had long been talk of her marrying; and the temper of the times pointed to William as the most suitable candidate. Above all, it would reassure a country increasingly anxious over French influence and a Catholic succession. None saw more clearly than my father the advantage of allying the princess with William, the Protestant hero. Louis would not be pleased, of course, at the King of England's taking into his family that impudent Hollander who troubled his vainglorious dreams. And my father, if no one else, still cared for Louis's friendship. But then my father still believed it was possible to please everybody – which if it be, he was certainly the man to do it. A closer relation with William, at any rate, might secure my father more influence over him, and over Dutch policy. The snarling war still dragging on in Flanders might be composed at last, with my father as peacemaker between France and Holland, loved on all sides. The politics of the boudoir, perhaps, but it had always worked there.

As for my uncle James – well, it was not to be expected that he would like giving his elder daughter and heir to a Protestant heretic. Even though he had little choice, he was a stubborn enough man to dig his heels in over it, and I know there were bitter wranglings at first. But he gave in, not because it made sense – that would have been utterly unlike him – but because his eyes began to turn elsewhere. For did he not have a beautiful young bride, who might produce a clutch of children – above all, a son, whose claim to the throne would be set above Mary's? A son who would be brought up in the Papist faith of his parents, and endow benighted England with a holy Catholic line of kings?

He was certainly busy, conjugally. Rumour came from St James's that he had a servant wake him at intervals throughout the night, so that he might set to work upon his wife again. And by the time of William's visit to England, my uncle's toils had been crowned with success. Modena was pregnant. James exulted. The loss of his daughter could be borne. A new world was in the womb.

417

And Princess Mary herself? How did she face the prospect of her marrying?

Well, with tears. So everyone said, after her first meeting with William. I did not see the tears, but the marks of them were plain on Mary's gentle face when I went to call on her at St James's. We had become, by now, good friends, though her shyness would still sometimes fall suddenly on her, like the stopping of a clock; and if I say that she was a little in love with me, I mean only that she was a girl with all the ardour of her years and inexperience. She had lived retired, and her notions of the male sex had been formed by her father, a man who never laughed and whose chief interest in his children was whether he could claim them for Rome.

'You haven't come to persuade me to my duty, I hope, James,' she said to me as we walked in the garden. That she called me James instead of Jemmy was characteristic of her: there was always this charming touch of gravity about her – gravity and yet lightness. I cannot account for the combination except to say that was the essence of Mary. There was frost on the grass that day, but Mary, sunflower-tall and elegant, seemed scarcely to bend the silvery filaments of turf as she walked.

'No, only to inquire after you.'

'Then I am very well. But I am not, of course. It is not true, by the by, that I wept two days together after Father told me I was to marry Prince William. It was only a day and a half.'

'Dear, dear.' This was before I had seen much of William. He had arrived when we were all at Newmarket and, resisting my father's entreaties to settle down and enjoy the races, had insisted on coming to court, seeing his prospective bride, and talking business. But his mere appearance, on top of this peremptory behaviour, was not encouraging. He was slight, thin, and sallow. Asthma had given him hunched shoulders and a habit of breathing loud through his long nose. And as for fashion, the ladies gaped – and we men, princcocks that we were, gaped harder: for William wore no periwig, and what made the omission more unthinkable, had only lank brown locks to show, falling coarse and uncurled on his snuff-coloured coat. 'But it cannot have come as such a great surprise – the marrying, I mean.'

'No. I hope I am not silly enough to ignore the realities of my position,' she said seriously. 'I have always known . . . But James, he is twenty-seven! And seems so much older! And he is so very gruff and grim!'

'Well – there may be shyness in that, you know. After all, he did not know what to expect of you, and it must have startled him in turn, to find his bride so extremely lovely.'

She looked miserably at me. 'I wish you would not talk so.'

'I'm sorry. I meant only that William may be feeling—'

'I don't care what he's feeling! At least – no, I do not want him to be uneasy. I entirely wish him well. And I wish I did not have to marry him.'

'Twenty-seven is not such a great age, Mary. Why, what does that make me, at twenty-eight?'

'If it were you, it would be different, I wish—' she said; then suffered one of her sudden shy extinguishings.

'Oh, well, you know I have a wife,' I said with deliberate lightness.

'Yes – but what I mean is – I wish everything were different. I know that is a very vain wish. And I am not, I hope I am not vain and giddy. But I feel rather alone. I should not: my stepmother has been most sweet and kind. Oh, I know why she does it – to please my father, of course. This is why they get along so famously. Father is a most easy man, you know. As long as you worship him with your entire soul, all is well. If not, then—' She made a mime of a slamming door: then gave me a guilty glance. 'Still, she is kind, and I'm glad of it. My mama— Mama's time was always very much occupied . . . I am sounding horribly discontented.'

'You sound entirely natural,' said I. 'As for your marrying, I wish I could say something that would ease your mind. If William seems to lack graces, you know, it may be simply that he has been so much pressed with the business of war, and keeping the French at bay . . .'

Her smile was sad. 'Now you are doing it too, James – persuading me that it is all for the best.'

'Well – simply as policy, I think it is. I have seen the power of France. I believe we must choose, if we would keep our English freedom and our English Church. For that we must stand upon the same ground as the Dutch. And in this matter, Mary, you have a mighty importance. Some day you may be Queen.'

'I hope not.'

'Do you?' I studied her. 'For if not, that means—'

'I know. It means Father having a son, and passing the crown to him. And part of me wishes, most desperately, for that to happen. Because then there will be no more responsibility. And I do know' – she bit her lip – 'I do know that is precisely what many people dread. Yes, I have been sheltered, but I hear these things. Indeed, I quite understand their feeling. That is horribly disloyal, isn't it? My own father. But I am devoutly attached to our religion. It is quite a part of me. And when my father sneers . . . No, that is not the right word. He simply treats me as if, by holding on to my faith, I am doing something silly – incomprehensible – like keeping a doll by me once I am grown. He has washed his hands of me now. I am to marry a Protestant, and go and live amongst a set of Protestants, who are all knavish rebels and would see Crowns brought low. A great pity, says he, but there, if I will be a heretic . . .'

She swallowed hard, and I know would have wept but for my presence. I looked away, pretending to pull a rose-stem from my coat-skirts. When I had done, I found her composed again, but looking very soberly at me.

'Father would frown to hear me say such things,' she said. 'But most of all, saying them to you.'

'Aye, well, we have our differences,' I said uncomfortably.

'Oh, more than that. I know well he is jealous of you, and fears you.'

'Nay – surely not—'

'Lest you come between him and the crown,' Mary went on implacably. 'Everyone knows it, though 'tis not spoken. If he knew I'd said to you I don't want the crown, he'd be angry. He would say I only encourage your ambition by such talk . . . Are you ambitious, James?'

'I'm not entirely sure what it means. I know that I would have my rights, and that is – that is a more difficult matter for me than any of you. Because I am not acknowledged a lawful prince,' I said with difficulty. 'And so where others have only to speak, sometimes I have to shout. Thus I am vain and ambitious and all the rest of it.'

'Yes, I see,' Mary said thoughtfully. 'That is what I mean about wishing everything were different. Many people, you know, want you to be the lawful prince. They talk of the King being secretly married to your mother, and not daring to say so. Or not choosing to say so yet.'

'I cannot talk of this, Mary.'

'I suppose not. But 'tis not so improbable, I think, though Father pretends to scoff at it. After all, everyone knows he secretly married Mama, and then tried to cover it up. That's a thought, isn't it?' She gazed across the grey lake with a clear hard look. 'At bottom, if he had had his way Anne and I would not be here . . . I do love him. But that is a different thing from being able to forgive him.'

William pronounced himself, as well he might, delighted with his future bride, but then came the hard bargaining – William seeking England's full support for his beleaguered country, my father urging William to make his peace with France. Wearily my father said to me in his bedchamber one evening: ''Tis a strange thing – his mother, rest her soul, was English to the root, and yet he is the veriest Dutchman!'

'That is what the Dutch like about him, I think,' I said.

'Oh, they would . . . What about you, Jemmy? What think you of this marriage?'

'The people are eager for it. It would be a sign that you are – well, that you are not in Louis's pocket.'

'Indeed, indeed.' My father looked calm, but his breathing quickened and his voice became a growl. 'In Louis's pocket. Great God, as if I would be in anyone's pocket – as if there were anything I could hate more. I had a full taste of that on my travels. That is partly why . . . But come, Jemmy, I asked your own view, not what people think. You must not let others place their notions in your head.'

'Very well. I am not of the French party. I agree with the Parliament-men, that our interests lie upon William's side.'

My father inclined his head – a gesture peculiar to him, neither shake nor nod. 'Plain enough. But the fact is I must balance betwixt the two. William tells me that we can either be the greatest of friends or the greatest of enemies. You may be sure Louis would say the same. So. I try not to whine of my woes, but in truth it is an infernal difficult game I must play, and no one realizes it.'

'I do, Father.'

'Do you, Jemmy? Well, I am glad of it. You grow friendly with those who oppose me, and I thought you inclining away from me.'

'Never from you, Father. And I do understand how careful you must tread,' I hesitated. 'I understand better than any, perhaps – situated as I am.'

'And how is that, my son?' he said, with his wariest look.

'I mean that whatever you intend for me – well, you must be cautious with that too. So I do not press you. I think I must wait and – and prove myself.'

My father bent and stirred the fire, which he always kept roaring with Scotch coal even in mild weather. 'You are talking of the succession,' he said in a colourless tone.

'I am trying not to talk about it,' I said, 'because I know it is such a ticklish matter. But others are talking of it: 'tis on everyone's lips. Other things too—'

'Pray name them.'

'Well . . . my uncle James tried to deny his first marriage. And so – people say – it may be with you and my mother.'

'Interesting,' my father said, his eyes on the fire. 'And why – again as a matter of interest – would I do that?'

The old evasiveness! My heart pounded, and I could feel my anger like distant thunder. But I kept it at bay, for it was worse than useless with him. Instead I was trying to speak in my father's own oblique language.

'Because, as you say, you have a difficult game. And not the least difficult part of it is my uncle.'

'James is as he is. I cannot change him, or make him any less my brother. People – I presume we are still talking about "people" – must not expect that I ever will.'

'You are loyal to James, Father. I understand that too. But how loyal do you suppose he is in return?'

My father's heavy brows went up. 'I am King; and if there is one thing James believes in, it is that kings must be obeyed.'

'*Absolutely* obeyed,' I said. 'But there is one thing he believes in more – the Romish Church; and he will stamp it upon us.'

'Not while I live, Jemmy.'

'No – so I believe: but you know he is only waiting for—'

'For me to die?' My father smiled the words coldly. 'Dear, dear. But is he the only one waiting for that doleful opportunity, Jemmy?'

For a moment I did not understand. Then I burst out: 'Father . . . !'

'Nay. Pardon me, Jemmy, that was not well said, for I do truly believe you love me. As for James . . .' He chuckled. 'He was talking the other day of rogues and rebels, and how I walked about too free and unguarded, and risked the assassin's knife. I could not help telling him that I did not fear assassination, for no one would kill me to make *him* king.'

I should have laughed, but I was too tight-wound. 'This you know,' I said. 'And yet you do not act.'

'There is something amiss with your memory, Jemmy, else you would remember how greatly I dislike being *reproached*, and *told* what I should do. If my hand were in this fire, and someone *told* me to take it out, I believe I would bear the burning rather than submit.' All at once he fetched up a great sigh. 'Jemmy, I ask you in a spirit of honest inquiry, why would you want this damnable crown? You have wealth and honours, and the affections of men – aye, I know how folk cheer you wherever you go, and I am glad of it. But the title of king would hardly bring you any more of these.'

'I would want it,' I said, 'simply to forestall my uncle's getting it – because he will bring the kingdom to disaster.'

'And you will save it, eh?' my father said, petting his moustache.

'Father, I am not the only one to talk so. Many men are of this mind.'

'Oh, indeed. And they are all, of course, concerned purely for the good of the kingdom, and have no ambitions of their own. Does it not occur to you, Jemmy, that you may be made a tool of designing men?'

'I – I know there is that peril. But one must believe that some men are true and honest and sincere, or else—'

'Or else one becomes like me,' my father said, with a beaming smile, 'who believes none of that.' He rose. 'Well, it has been a most interesting talk, Jemmy; but I am engaged to sup with Louise, and must pay my compliments to the Queen before—'

'You can give me no answer, then, Father?'

'I was not aware there was a question. You have put the case yourself. You said that you must wait, and prove yourself – weren't those your words? You seem to know very well what you are about, Jemmy, so there is naught for me to say.'

'Wait and prove myself – and trust you,' I said, holding his eyes.

But they would not be held for long. 'Again,' he said, patting my shoulder as he went out, 'that is up to you.'

There was a wedding, at last – two weddings, in a sense.

For the marriage of the Princess Mary to William of Orange was an event much liked and celebrated across the country, with bonfires and toasts and pealing bells. There you had the public face, as it were, and it was joyous.

Then there was the private ceremony, performed at St James's by the Bishop of London; and that was rather different. I had made several attempts, after that awkward City banquet, to get upon cordial terms with William, but to little avail. He remained stiff and gruff, a man who seemed all angles and no roundness; and such was his bearing at the wedding, where he appeared itching to take off his bridal suit and have done with the business. As for Mary, she was nothing if not dutiful, but tears stood in her eyes the whole time – not falling – as if she blinked gems. I knew she felt alone, and she looked it indeed. Her sister, Anne, had a fever, and was kept at home, while her father, James, stalked about as if he were merely lending his presence to the honouring of some country knight he had never heard of. Such attention as he could spare from looking insufferable was all for his pregnant duchess – who was very near her time. And that in itself cast a curious shadow. For here was a Protestant succession being secured – or was it? What would be the issue of that great belly? A boy, who would take precedence?

Everyone was thinking of it. It was my father who said it.

'Make haste, my lord Bishop,' he said, 'else the duchess may be delivered of a son before we are done, and then the marriage will be disappointed.' And he gave William a sly smile – which the Prince was the last man in the world to return.

In that gloomy company, my father was the brightest: mightily brisk indeed, chattering and chaffing. Some said they had not seen him so merry for years. To me, there was something of jangling nerves about his high humour. Perhaps he was yet fearful that James's fanatic temper would get the better of him, and that he would whisk Mary away from the arms of her heretic groom, and throw her in a nunnery. Perhaps it was simply his love of ease that made him breeze through an occasion that everyone found doleful. At the part of the service in which the groom endows his bride with his worldly goods, William laid the customary offering of gold coins upon the prayer-book; whereupon my father nudged Mary and said to her: 'Put it up in your pocket, my dear, for 'tis all clear gain.' He meant perhaps to make her feel better: I hope with success.

We had but a small feast, with sweetmeats and sack posset. It was an evening wedding, and the ceremonies of the bride-night very soon began, with my wife, Queen Catharine, and waddling Modena conveying poor Mary to bed to undress her, while my father and uncle and I supported William. When we squired him into the bedchamber, he looked as pale as a man going to his execution, and Mary was in no better case; and once again my father strove to carry it off, closing the bed-curtains with a great flourish, and crying: 'Now, nephew, to your work! Hey, St George for England!'

Well, William's habitual formula – 'I do not care for it' – certainly did not seem to apply to the pleasures of the marriage bed. The pages were soon putting it about that the marriage had been consummated four times over, and William found no fault, in beauty or temper, with his bride. But Mary remained quiet and subdued throughout the time that remained to them in England, before their departure for the court of Orange. And meanwhile, my uncle James's hopes were, it seemed, fulfilled most brilliantly. Two days after the wedding, Modena gave birth to a son.

My uncle could hardly conceal his delight: others, their trouble and unease.

'So we are not to have the Oranges come to the throne after all, and must look to a long line of Dismal Jimmies all muttering their rosaries,' said Nell Gwynn to me at her house in Pall Mall. 'What a way your uncle has of spoiling things! Have you seen the babe?'

'Aye – a pretty, sprightly fellow,' I said.

She eyed me. 'And you are too good-natured to wish he was not. Well, 'tis no pretty prospect. The Court will be naught but priests and soldiers, and my profession will be out in the cold. But there's cheer here, surely, Your Grace, especially for you. Now that Madam Wimple is breeding, folk will turn all the more to you, to get between Jimmy's brood and the crown before it's too late. If Dutch William is knocked down the line of succession, why, there's still hope: there's still our own Prince Perkin!'

Yes, Nell had her name for me. I was much vexed when I first heard it: Perkin Warbeck being a pretender to the throne at the time of the wars of the Tudors, long ago, who claimed to be the son of Edward the

Fourth – and was generally agreed an ambitious impostor. There was a play about him, which I think Nell had acted in. Of course there was no being angry with Nell's good nature – but still the name grated; and she saw it.

'What, d'you think I mean to put you out of your claim, calling you such? Don't think it, Your Grace: I'm no great politician – I leave that to Squintabella, who's ever boasting of what great men she can make and unmake. Still, I would back you against Dismal Jimmy, if it came to a contest.'

'Would you, Nell? Why?'

'Oh, because Jimmy's too high; and he's fonder even of the French than the King, and come his day we may as well bow our heads towards Paris and learn to parley-voo, for we'll have no country of our own worth a candle. And because I like you: how will that do? Don't, I pray you, set too low a worth on that: 'tis the strongest card in your hand. You sort well with the people, and there's but few royalties can say that. I tell the King so, believe me. You may always count upon me to be a friend to you.'

'Thank you, Nell. 'Tis the same for me.'

'That I'm glad to hear, for next time you have His Majesty's ear, put in a word for me, or rather my babes. He don't stint with his purse, but it takes more than that to set a child up in this world, as you well know. Squintabella soon got a title for her bratling, and all I ask is the same treatment, for, after all, we both do the same job – though she won't see it. "Why, Nelly," she simpers to me t'other day, all honey and vinegar, "how grand you are dressed. Why, you are fine enough to be a queen." "Aye, madam", says I, "and I am whore enough to be a duchess." Well, she may keep her own consequence, but I would see my boy treated fair. The King came to see us lately: I fetched my boy in from the garden. "Come here, little bastard, and greet your father," I said – which put His Majesty in a pother. But I have no other name to call him, says I, as you will not give him one.'

She laughed uproariously. Still, there was truth in what she said. Nell, who was of the people, was not treated at court in the same way as mistresses like Lady Castlemaine, or the reigning favourite, Louise, Duchess of Portsmouth. Such was the way of things, but I felt the injustice.

Well, the time came for Mary to take ship, and cross to Holland with her new husband, and embrace her new country. She appeared something brighter on her last night, dancing at Queen Catharine's birthday ball all decked in the jewels of William's bride-gift. But then came a delay that must have tried her nerves, as there was fearful weather, and even when the ship sailed, it was forced by the storm to put in at Sheerness and wait there. Being about business with my troop, I had missed her departure, and tried now to get a boat down to Sheerness and snatch a goodbye, but William was impatient, and would sail despite the weather, and so I was too late. But my wife was at the leave-taking, and she told me that Mary wept sorely. Queen Catharine, always kind, tried to comfort her, talking of her own first voyage to England from Portugal, to marry a man she had never even seen. 'But, Madam,' Mary sobbed, 'you were coming into England – and I am going out of England.'

So they went; a storm-lashed passage, and a landing that I heard was no easier, with ice-floes blocking Rotterdam so that they must put ashore amongst the dunes, and struggle up on foot. I can hardly guess at Mary's feelings.

And what could scarcely have been guessed also, from this inauspicious beginning, was that Mary and William's marriage should turn out to be a love-match.

Smallpox and the Stuart family have an unhappily intimate history. Soon after Mary left for Holland, her sister, the Princess Anne, was known to have it. For a wonder, Anne not only recovered but her face was left unmarked. There would soon be talk of matching her with a husband in turn. My uncle James, though, could not rejoice. For the disease that spared Anne took away his infant son a month into his life.

THREE

I called at St James's after a decent interval, to offer my commiserations. My own similar loss was a wound that still smarted, and prompted a fellow-feeling that must, I thought, overcome ill will. And I was welcomed readily enough by Mary of Modena, who was all tears, and seemed glad of someone to weep at. Indeed, as long as I sighed with her and did not say much, all was well. When I tried, however, to say I understood the pain of losing an infant, she seemed put out.

'But you have still a child living, I thought.'

'Yes, thank God for him: but—'

'Then it is not the same,' Modena said, sending her maid scurrying for a fresh handkerchief. 'I have none.' And then she repeated in an undertone, as if to some third party, or familiar spirit: 'He has a child living!'

'Well, he is, to be sure, a comfort. Still the loss is great. My wife was much perturbed. You may believe, her heart went out to you when she heard the news. I wish we might offer some consolation. People always talk of time, but 'tis, I fear, a small solvent to sorrow—'

'Your wife is a Scotswoman. Yes? They are hard people, I think, and do not feel much.'

'Anna is a Scot, certainly, but has all a woman's feelings, that I can vouch for. It is perhaps a difference in showing—'

'Yes, it is different,' Modena said, applying a fresh handkerchief to her inky-lashed eyes; and then, to her invisible confidante, 'He can vouch for her feelings!' At first I had thought this habit of hers came from her weak grasp of English – a way of trying words over to make sure she understood them, but she was fluent enough now, and it was impossible not to be irritated.

428

Just then my uncle came in from hunting, hard-breathing and noisy, with a great stamp and creak of muddied boots. Somehow it typified him that when he wore boots they creaked and when he wore shoes they squeaked.

'Jemmy. I did not think to see you here.'

'Uncle. I came to offer my condolences, and Anna's—'

'Aye, did you? We are obliged. It is all a great pity. Of course, there is naught to be gained, and much perilled, by protesting at Providence. Madam,' he said bending over his duchess and examining her eyes as one would a sickly hound, 'I observe you have been weeping again. Dear, dear. This will never do: you must collect yourself. We shall have more, you know.'

'I do try, James—'

'That's well. I repeat, madam, we shall have more, you may be sure of it, and so there is no need of weeping. Now, I pray you, be so good as to leave us: I would speak alone with my nephew.'

Obedient, Mary of Modena made her swan-necked way out of the room, and I faced my uncle.

'I fear, Jemmy, you have upset her, going over this old ground. I had hopes of her growing firmer.'

'Indeed, I'm sorry. I meant only to commiserate. 'Tis surely best to let the feelings out—'

'No,' James said. 'But that's by the by. I thank you for your intention, Jemmy; and I will take it as sincere.'

Did he really think I could exult over the death of a child? 'Uncle, this is a harsh reflection upon me—'

'Nay, not so. I have said I will believe your sincerity. Enough of that matter, at any rate. It is, I repeat, providential, and even to repine is impiety. It is something else that I wish I might acquit you of.' He paced, beating his thigh with his riding crop, as if even that great chamber were too small for him. 'I hear you have it in mind to be Captain-General of the army.'

I was surprised, though perhaps I should not have been. My father, observing me restless, had lately asked my will. I had said I would be with our troops in Flanders. 'Aye, and who can I set over you, Jemmy?' he had said indulgently. 'With such a reputation as you have gained?' And I had promptly answered, 'Let me have the whole command,

Father, and you will see that reputation soar!'

'I hope for it,' I said now to my uncle. 'I know there is my youth, but—'

'Your youth?' He stared as if I were mad, then went on his heavy creaking prowl again, shaking his head. 'He talks of his youth.' Curious how couples pick up each other's habits. 'Well, Jemmy, if you cannot recognize the headstrong folly of this notion, so be it. I had hopes of your own discretion. Instead I must say it. I ask you, in deference to me, to abandon it.'

I was still more surprised than angry. 'The generalship is in my father's gift,' I said, 'and so it is to him I must defer, Uncle.'

'The King, as I have oft told him, would be ill-advised to appoint anyone to such a rank. After General Monck died, the post was left in abeyance, and wisely. 'Tis too great a power for any one man.' His eyes glittered. 'It is a temptation to adventurers.'

'I know not how you conceive the title of general, Uncle. But I see it as leading the kingdom's forces against the kingdom's enemies – no more nor less.'

My uncle looked down at me: I had not stood. 'You will oblige me, sir, by relinquishing this dream. For I must warn you, you will never find a friend in me, if you take the command.'

'It is, I say again, my father's decision. Would you set yourself against that, Uncle?'

'I fear you are grown swell-headed and impudent,' James said colourlessly. 'My brother has been indulgent to you. Such is his amiable weakness. You might at least show some conscience, sir, of how very much above your deserts you are treated.'

'Why, what should the King's own son deserve?'

My uncle made a prim mouth. 'He has claimed you: very well, one accepts it. But this is taking the fiction to unconscionable lengths—'

'Fiction?'

'Your claim, Jemmy, rests only upon the King's generosity. Being liberal with his favours, he is accordingly easy in recognizing those who are presented to him as his offspring. And talking of liberal favours – you force me, Jemmy, to allude to your mother's reputation, of which more unhappy stories have come to my ears. When she first went out of England, it was a matter of procurement – a gentleman named Robert

Sidney was to have her, you know. I lay no blame upon her. She was young and friendless, and it is all a sad pity, but the fact remains that Sidney spoke of having got her with child, and the matter is extremely doubtful . . .'

A sad pity! Indeed, it was almost pathetic to see my uncle grubbing about amongst these old rags of rumour: almost.

'I never realized before,' I said, 'how very jealous you are of my father.'

My uncle went white. For a second I thought he would strike me.

'A most horrible jealousy,' I went on with savage relish, 'and it must be a torment to you. But you are afraid to make any move against him, so you turn on me instead.'

'You dare accuse me of disloyalty to the Crown?'

'That depends on what you mean by the Crown. You have your own notion of it, I think – but it is not one the people of England would recognize. It is not what they wanted when my father was restored.'

'The Crown has naught to do with the will of the people. A king rules of his own unassailable right.' My uncle snapped his fingers. 'You reveal, Jemmy, how little you know of these matters.'

'I know my father could not come back to his throne until England invited him, and he does not forget that. Nor should any man who thinks to be King in this island.'

'But this is pure rebellion!' my uncle said – with simple astonishment, as if he had opened a bottle of wine and found it honey. 'You talk like a Cromwell, Jemmy. Curious, indeed, from one who would claim royal blood. Mighty interesting.' He bent to pat one of his dogs that had come frisking in. When he straightened his face had resumed all its old stony composure. 'But we stray from the point. And it is a plain one. If you take the generalship you do me an injury that I will not forget. If any man in the kingdom should have that office, it is I. This you must know well. Yet you set yourself up against me. I do not understand.'

I sprang up in anger irrepressible. 'You said just now, Uncle, that no one should have that office. But now we get to the truth – no one but *you* should have it. Well, I may or may not be fit for it. But if I have it, sir, at least no one will fear what I might do with it. Put the army in your hands, and the ports will be blocked with people quitting their own country in fear and despair.' At the door I added, 'I would not be one of

431

them, though, Uncle – trust me for that.'

'What shall we do about the generalship?' my father said.

He took me by surprise, for he was showing me over the fittings of his new yacht at Greenwich, and talking only of damask and gilt leather, when he casually slid the question in.

'That is your choice to make, Father,' I said, stiffly enough. For I had deliberately refrained from appealing to him, since my uncle's challenge. Pride, I suppose.

'So it is. Well, the command is a great responsibility, and will need broad shoulders. I have been in two minds . . . I think to call her *Fubbs*, by the by. Why, the boat, of course,' he added at my stare. 'Not a grand name, but she has an easy touch and a comfortable look, so it's fitting.'

Fubbs was the pet name he bestowed upon Louise. I liked it about as much as I liked her.

'Some might say the Duchess of Portsmouth has honours enough, Father,' I said. 'There is Mistress Gwynn, who is quite as deserving. Yet it is a matter of remark that she is not so well set up as Portsmouth—'

'And it is Nelly herself who remarks it most frequently, eh? Nay, my boy, I don't mind it if she sets you to plead her case. But I must think how to square all these calls upon my purse. I have a Parliament more fractious and demanding than any mistress. Before they will yield their favours, I must flatter and please them: I must make war on Louis, I must do this and that . . .' He sighed and sat down heavily. 'I greatly, *greatly*, dislike being told my business. And as you say, Jemmy, the choice is mine.'

In that moment I knew that my uncle had been at him. In the watery, splintery light coming through the leaded panes of the stateroom my father's face looked worn and grey.

'I will not be told,' he murmured, as if to himself, 'I will not . . . Well, Jemmy!' Suddenly the spark was back, as he looked up at me. 'You shall have the command, and there's an end on it. Mind! There is no seesaw, with you and James upon either end – don't conceive it. You rise at no one's expense. I do this out of my trust in you, and my love for you as my son.'

Well, my love was in the right of it, when she said I should show how my father loved me in these years before the fall. Here it is in very truth, in the affectionate embrace he gives me: his pride in me; my pride meeting his. I am almost undone, viewing the memory, knowing the wound that was to come.

My uncle's bolt was not shot, not yet.

True to his word, my father ordered the warrant to be made out for my commission as Captain-General of the armed forces of England. In vain James nagged and upbraided him: the King had made his decision.

So my uncle took matters into his own hands.

It was for the Attorney-General to draw up the document of commission. My uncle went to see him, and inspected the document; and seeing that it referred to 'James, Duke of Monmouth, son of His Majesty King Charles the Second', flew into a passion – or as near to a passion as his frosty nature would allow. He ordered that the word 'natural' be inserted before the word 'son' throughout the commission.

You may well ask what right he had to dictate in this way. Yes, it was mighty revealing of a man so impatient for the crown that he had begun to act as if it were already his. But what struck deepest upon me, when I heard of it through my secretary, was the insult.

By making no reference to illegitimacy, the commission did not confer legitimacy. No one could have supposed it did: that was a nonsense. But to James's suspicious mind – I was going to say maddened by jealousy, yet that is not right, for a wild ungovernable impulse I could at least understand. This was much more deliberate. His suspicious mind saw plots, and he responded by most carefully, insultingly insisting upon my bastardy.

Still he was not satisfied. He badgered the Secretary of State, whose duty it was to present the document for signature to my father, not to do so without showing it to him first. Perhaps the Secretary of State did not much like being threatened. Certainly he placed the commission before my father, with some others, at the end of a meeting of the Privy Council, and my father quickly signed it, without my uncle's interference. Then my father stepped out to the Privy Garden to take the air – whereupon my uncle seized the papers and hunted amongst them for my commission.

'Aye, he pursued your father in quite a fury, waving the wretched paper under his nose, if you please,' Prince Rupert told me after. I was already about my business of raising troops, and was not at the Council that day. 'His Majesty looked quite ready to leap over the wall, and run away.'

My uncle's complaint was that everywhere in the document the word 'natural' had been scratched out. Now you will guess whom he accused of doing so. If he could not lay it to me, then it was my secretary, or some other servant of mine. It is interesting that he should suppose others should be as free with their interference in a king's commission as he had been. I do not know who scratched out the word 'natural'. I can only assert that I had friends to my cause at court as well as enemies. I have even had occasion to wonder whether my father did it himself – and then, unable to bear his brother's endless upbraiding, backed down.

For, as Rupert told me, my father at last tore the paper in two, and ordered it to be drawn up again, with the word 'natural' throughout. He was exasperated, it seemed, with the whole business, and afterwards would not speak much of it to me, saying curtly, 'The warrant is made, and the command is yours, Jemmy, and let that be the last of it.' He only added, with a look of veiled reproach: 'The seesaw, Jemmy, remember: do not think of it.'

And I tried to obey. But it was hard, as the needling enmity grew between my uncle and me. And like the first nape-caressing chill of a coming sickness, I looked at my father and wondered whether he had not placed me, purposefully, upon that seesaw; set me there to balance his troublesome brother, now up, now down: whether he had not used me, all along, as he used others, to secure himself upon his remote, heartfree and sufficient island of self.

I had always thought myself the exception, with him. If it were not so, then I had nothing left – nothing but a new, horrible freedom.

'Well, sir, and how do you do? But you had better not answer, for you know I am not to speak to you. My father-in-law forbids it.'

So said Prince William of Orange, as we sat down together to a plain dinner in his campaign quarters at the fortress of Mons, following up his remarks with a snort and a wheeze which, I realized after a startled moment, was the dour young Dutchman laughing.

'Yes, curious, is it not?' William said, waving the servant away and pouring our wine himself. 'He is not my own father. He is not even the King of his own country. But he writes me the letters as if he were the two. The each.'

'Both.'

'That is the words. I show the letters to Mary. What is this? I say. Is it I am not understanding the English right? No, she say, that is how her father talks.' William frowned as the tallow candles guttered, and settled the flannel scarf more closely around his neck. 'This place is full of draughts. I must take care against chills. I have not your bigness. I wish I had.' He looked me up and down, without rancour. 'I cannot afford to go ill. It is all on me.'

'You have help now,' I said. I had come to take command of the English troops in Flanders, and to reinforce William, still locked in his exhausting struggle with France. Louis was refusing to give up his Flemish conquests, and at home there was furious agitation that we were allowing the French King's devouring ambitions to go unchecked. Hence my presence as Lord General – with all the folderol, very agreeable to me I confess, of liveried trumpeters and drummers. Though seeing William's position, with the French army occupying two fortified positions in front of Mons, I could only wish we had more troops, livery or no livery.

'Help, yes,' William said, stabbing at his cold mutton. 'It is good: it is not great. Your father should make war upon France, real war. There is no one safe till he does. But this he does not, even though your Parliament want it. Mary says he knows what he does. I hope so.'

'And how is Mary?' I swallowed the greasy mutton with difficulty. In the field William lived quite spartan, though all neat and cleanly in the Dutch manner; and I could not help reflecting on my own partiality for richness in my tent – even, God help me, Turkey carpets on the ground. 'I was grieved for her loss.'

'She does pretty well,' William grunted, then fixed me with his small shrewd eyes. To look straight at William, as when one looks close at a hawk or falcon, was always to feel oneself going a little cross-eyed. 'That is what we say, yes? But she does not do pretty well. She suffered when she miscarried. She suffers now, because she fears I will come back dead one day from these battles. And I suffer too, because I must be here and cannot be the husband she deserves.'

These were, I thought, warm words for William, and my surprise must have shown.

'Yes,' William said, flushing and bending over his food. 'Mary is – is all goodness. And I am fortunate. I cannot say it. Perhaps even to her. But that does not mean I cannot feel it.'

' "I cannot heave my heart into my mouth",' said I. 'That is in one of our English plays – Shakespeare—'

'I do not know English plays. I do not know any plays. I have never had time. Still, a good way to say it, yes. And I believe it is a gift *you* have. Is it not? You talk well to the men. You make a good figure. You stir love.' He tapped his own narrow chest untenderly. 'Look at me: this I do not have.'

'I don't know if that's true,' I said uncomfortably, 'but I should not like to think you had any jealousy of me—'

'No. Have I the occasion?' William coughed drily into his scarf, studying me. 'But no. You are here, sir; and you understand why we must be here. That is the pity of Mary's position. She has married a man who – loves her. A man who I think she – loves also now.' It was touching to see him gathering himself, like a rider at a fence, to get over that treacherous word. 'I know this is not usual in marriages of princes. And I am glad of it. Yet we cannot be together as we should – because of this.' He touched his sword, which he had laid naked on the rough deal table. 'We may have treaties and truces. But there will be no peace until Louis is beat to his knees. This you understand.'

'Yes,' I said, 'I do understand . . .'

'But, but. You are loyal to your father, that is natural. And he would keep friends with Louis. The King of France is rich, of course, and there is no blame in looking to those riches. But does not your father see? If he ties England to France, which is so great here, England must forever drag in France's train. And will not be free. Tie England to Holland, which is smaller, and together they will keep France down, and remain free.' He shrugged. 'So I do not understand him.'

'That's what my father likes. If you understood him, he would run a mile from you.'

William did not smile. 'A strange family. Your father seems to care for nothing! Very different from his brother of York – but him I do not understand either. You know what his private opinion of me was, when I came to marry his daughter? I have my spies, you know. "A very ill-brought-up young man." ' William gave a single bark of laughter. 'He means I am not Catholic and I am not afraid of him.' He raised his glass to mine. 'In this, my friend, you and I are alike – the two – the pair – *both*. Are we not?'

'So we are,' I said, clinking glasses. 'I must claim the advantage, though – for I believe I am the one my uncle hates most.'

'So?' William grinned like a dog. 'Well, you know best. But he would gladly see us *both* – ha, I am getting used to this word – put out of the way of his precious crown, I think. So perhaps he would not be displeased, after all, at you and I dining together like this. He is hoping, perhaps, that a cannon will blow us both up together – boom!'

Well, if such was my uncle's wish – and I do not think it too fanciful – it was close to coming true in that campaign. Bitter and bloody it was: I thought I would never get the screaming of men and horses, the leaping fountains of mined earth, the slippery pools of copper-smelling gore out of my mind after, though at the time I knew only reckless exhilaration sharpened by admiration of William's fierce courage at my side. We had the victory. We broke out of Mons and took the French camp at St Denis, and paid a blood-price of several thousand men; and William was for going doggedly on.

But the French had had enough – for now; and the burghers of Amsterdam wanted peace at any price. 'They fear that if I win too much, I will be too strong, and play the King to them,' William chafed. 'Fools! Would they rather have Louis, who declares he will destroy the Protestant religion like a weed? For before God, if it were not for me, it would be Louis's foot on their necks now. Fools!'

But there was nothing more William could do. At last the peace was signed between Holland and France – 'It will last,' William prophesied bitterly, 'just until Louis gets hungry again' – and I struck camp and prepared to go home.

And it was thus that I began this last portion of my narrative – with myself returning from the wars to an England gone mad. I was near thirty: a seasoned soldier, with the aches and the sword-cuts to prove it; a man of high estate and fame. I had aims, longings – naught fixed. I was not more discontented, I think, than the next man.

And then my life ran out of control.

FOUR

Those strange events that came to be known as the Popish Plot are quite recent. I speak now of times only a handful of years past, yet already they seem wrapped in mist, as a vivid dream fast-fading in the hour of waking.

What the Plot set in train concerned me nearly. Indeed, I still live in its shadow. But back then I was not very much at the centre of things. You may well hear from my enemies that I seized at once on the Plot to foster my own ambitious designs. Well, I wish that I were so thrustful, so sharp! My chief emotion at the outset was bewilderment.

I shall tell simply how it was.

It was a most feverish hot and fly-droning summer when a man named Titus Oates revealed to the Council the existence of a plot amongst the Catholics to assassinate my father and place my uncle James on the throne.

The great plague had been bred in just such a hot season, and you may well say that a plague of plot, of accusation and counteraccusation, was brewed up to similarly dreadful effect in the summer and autumn of '78. Certainly it brought forth a strange prodigy in Titus Oates.

Picture a man not yet thirty, yet ageless in ugliness, with the girth of a barrel, and splayed legs like the hinder end of a bull; and a face set low between the shoulder blades – a great doughy face, the tiny eyes dabbed in it like currants, and the jaw so large that the little pursy mouth is where the nose should be. He is half-shabby, half-dandy. His pudgy hands flutter in the air, and when he speaks there issues from his bisected visage a high wailing voice, like a strangulated prophet.

This was the man who brought the news of the Plot. He had been an

Anglican clergyman, and then was converted by the Jesuits, before returning to the English fold, bringing with him his evidences of plots among the Catholics at home and abroad to do away with my father. This was the man whom my father, reluctantly enough, returned from Windsor to examine at Whitehall, and whom he heard tell in that eldritch sing-song of deep-laid plans to poison him at dinner, stab him with daggers, and shoot him with silver bullets. My father was sceptical. He ordered Oates's testimony to be duly noted, and went off to Newmarket little troubled.

And then came two events that were, I fear, a little lost to sight in the tumult that was to follow. The time of the Plot became, indeed, a time of madness at last: that peculiar frenzy people still remember, when everyone suspected everyone else, and ladies went about with pistols hidden in their mantles to defend themselves against Popish insurgents, and a talking bird was put upon a bonfire because it could repeat the Mass. By that time, sober men had begun to talk of the Plot as a sort of brain-fever which must, like the plague, exhaust itself at last. Thus one could dismiss the whole thing as so much trumpery. But for me these two events still stand out, even now that heads have cooled: they will not go away.

First, there was the cache of letters found behind the fireplace of one Edward Coleman – who was my uncle James's secretary.

Well might Coleman hide this correspondence. It was directed to, among others, King Louis's confessor, the papal nuncio at the Spanish court, and the English cardinal in Rome; and its matter was startling. The future set out by Coleman, for which he and his correspondents must work, was a future belonging entirely to my uncle. Parliament was to be got rid of altogether, with French gold or arms: my father was to be left to enjoy his pleasures while my uncle governed both him and the kingdom. Catholics were to displace all the present holders of office, as the first step to reclaiming the country for Rome, by force if necessary.

This was treason plain enough, if seasoned with folly; and there were none to defend Coleman when he was gaoled, questioned, and condemned. The deep question was how much my uncle had known of what his secretary was about.

I believe he must have known, very well. James was from the beginning most insistent on having a thorough inquiry made into Titus

Oates's claims. He would make sure, he said, that his name was entirely cleared. But he was in a perpetual prickliness at that time. He would wince at the lightest shutting of a door or scratch of tinder; and I noticed on the face of this man who had always seemed too little human to perspire, even after a morning's hard hunting, a continual sheen of sweat that clung to his brow and lip. He had always cleaved close to Coleman: I cannot believe the secretary conceived these grand designs alone. And though Coleman went bravely to his execution without having pointed his finger at his master, for me the mark could hardly have stood out more glaringly.

Whether he dared actively plan for it or not, this was what my uncle James wanted for us. To want it he must either be a dangerous villain or a dangerous fool. Neither prospect was reassuring.

The second event was more mysterious, and I think more sinister.

Having presented his evidence to the Council, Titus Oates swore his testimony before a magistrate of the city, Sir Edmund Berry Godfrey.

Five days later, the body of the magistrate was found upon Primrose Hill, with a sword thrust right through his body.

Murky times: with each day, the fog of suspicion seemed to thicken, and it gathered even around the body of poor Godfrey, for the physicians could not or would not agree. Some said the bruising around his neck showed that he had been hanged – and so perhaps a suicide, but whence then the sword, and who had taken his body and laid it on Primrose Hill?

It fell to me, at my father's command and as Lord General, to investigate the matter. Chiefly, I had to question a man who was accused of involvement in the murder by an informer. (Such was the turn those anxious times was taking: men had to be either informer or accused, and would hurry to be the first, for fear of becoming the second.) The rogue was called, I remember, Miles Prance – most curiously named were all the actors in this strange drama! – and he had a story of three men who had lured the magistrate into the courtyard at Somerset House, strangled him, and then carried the body into the building, there to stow it until it could be safely disposed.

This Prance was certainly talkative – so much so, that he seemed able to say three things at once, all different. But he found it less easy to locate the room where the body had supposedly lain, when I accompanied him about Somerset House; and when I reported to the Council, I hardly knew what credit to give his account. Soon, examined by my father himself, Prance retracted it, only to return later to his original confession. All of which served, at least, to muddy the waters, and throw the solution to the magistrate's murder further off.

I am convinced of one certain thing – he *was* murdered. By whom, we shall perhaps never know. I can only say that if you wish to stop a man's mouth, strangling and stabbing him is an effective way. Others came to that conclusion, of course; and some ran away with it. So began the panic as the autumn nights drew in, with rumours of fire and gunpowder. Smiths did a good trade in 'Godfrey daggers', to be carried as a protection against cloaked assailants; others preferred a flail. And so absurdity at last cast its capering shadow over all – obscuring what I still believe was a foul mischief.

Titus Oates, whose accusations now seemed to have more substance, was at the request of Parliament lodged at Whitehall, and it was I who was recommended by the House of Lords as guardian of his safety. After my late experience in Flanders, here was a singular duty, and not one I much relished. Each day I went to his apartments, to hear the report of the bodyguard stationed at his door, and to ask him if he had all he needed. I confess to an uneasy fascination as I stood before this uncouth creature, slurping over his breakfast, his squinting eyes measuring me – measuring me too closely, indeed. There were rumours of sodomy in his past, and he gave me some looks that I was more accustomed to bestowing on a pretty woman. Yet what this man knew, or professed to know, the power he had come so swiftly to wield, disliked and mistrusted as he was, the great ferment he had set off in the kingdom – these things there was no ignoring.

And though I had scarcely begun yet to grasp it, and though Oates certainly made no hero of me, or anyone but himself, and advanced no plans of his own, still the mere fact of this man was to change my life. Amidst the fervent rumours of a Catholic plot, and in the certain presence of a Catholic heir to the throne, I who had had so many names found myself with another.

'The Protestant Duke!'

They shouted it in the streets, they gathered around my carriage and at my door. They hailed me like a saviour.

'It is as I have told you before, my lord – my father will always stand by Queen Catharine,' I said to Shaftesbury. 'And I honour him for it. 'Tis knavish indeed of Oates to begin tangling her name in the Plot. She is a most blameless lady—'

'Chivalry,' Shaftesbury said, smiling, blinking, pale. 'Gallantry – you do it well, Your Grace, it is charming. Nevertheless, I cannot conceive why the Queen should matter to you. She is after all of the Romish faith, even if she makes less noise about it than your uncle, and thus cannot be *relied* upon at such a time of danger as this.'

'But this is nonsense.'

Shaftesbury's lips went thin as he considered me. Then he gave a chuckle. 'Forgive me, Your Grace. I am accustomed to talking with such a politicking set, and I forget what plain speaking is, or else take it for the subtlest form of indirection. Dear me, I think you are in earnest, and that is very well – it is what people love in you, to be sure. Only consider, my dear sir, that in such a crisis as we face, it may be necessary to *say* certain things without meaning them.'

'That I cannot do. And I cannot countenance any attack on the Queen. I have no doubt of my uncle's ill intentions, and would not see him take the throne my father so hardly won, but as for the Queen—'

'The Queen is a small matter,' Shaftesbury said snappishly. 'This is straining at a gnat.' Always pale, he turned all at once as white as bled veal, and hugged himself.

'Your malady, my lord,' I said uncertainly, 'does it grow worse?'

'The pain is eating me,' Shaftesbury said, bright and fierce through clenched teeth. 'And I eat the pain. It is like a race, a contest. Yes – thank you, if you will be so good . . .'

We were at the King's Head tavern, on the corner of Chancery Lane. I summoned a waiter to bring brandy. The King's Head was the meeting place of the Green Ribbon Club, of which Shaftesbury and Buckingham were leading lights – an informal private association as yet: only later would it become known as the home of the Whig party. Still, there was no doubt as to what united the various men who met there – from nobles and Parliament-men to lawyers and scribblers. They were the opposition. Doubtless there were government spies there too, and my father would soon hear of my presence. But for me opposition meant only opposing my uncle and his influence at court. I would not set myself against my father, as I continually insisted to Shaftesbury. And the little earl would nod, and smile, and say certainly, certainly; and I was never quite reassured.

Now Shaftesbury gulped brandy, gripping the glass with both papery hands, and said with a wry look, 'I have heard you express doubts too, Your Grace, on the guilt of the Catholic peers in the Tower.'

'I don't know . . . If they have plotted against my father, I would not spare them. But as Mr Oates makes more accusations, and they grow wilder, one begins to wonder—'

'Oh, but of course,' Shaftesbury said dismissively, 'he must carry on. What is there for him else? That should not blind us to the real danger. Dig amongst the muck, some of which is certainly no use, and still we come to the Duke of York. There is the worm and canker that this whole business has exposed to the light. Now never tell me, Your Grace, that you are disabled by any tender feeling *there*. You are of a frank, manly and generous spirit I know, but a man who has so deedily set himself to be your enemy—'

'You know my feelings for my uncle,' I said, aware I was growing a little stormy. 'That is quite another matter from the Queen.'

'You are firm on this point,' Shaftesbury said, glowering at Buckingham, who was noisily entertaining some cronies with his imitation of my uncle at confession. 'Hey, well. I fancy there may be some tincture of a son's feeling towards a mother – no? Of course there is no blood tie, but she has long been your father's queen. And your true mother, alas, long dead. Tell me, Your Grace, what were the circumstances of her death? I speak only out of concern for the injured lady and her reputation.'

'She died in Paris,' said I, reaching for the brandy, for now I had an inward wince of my own. 'And was buried there. She was ailing a while. She did not die of – of—'

'Of what certain malicious persons put it about that she died of,' Shaftesbury said, nodding. ' "A disease incident to her profession" are the words I heard him use.'

I clenched my fists, and could not speak.

'Your father does not talk of her. He is never, of course, ungallant in his expressions. Indeed, one must allow, he is ever courteous in his dealings with the sex. Still this reticence is curious.' He placed a bony finger on my arm. 'Tell me, Your Grace, what is your belief?'

'My – belief . . .'

The finger held me, like a pin through my whole body. 'About your mother. About her relation with your father. Far-off, long-lost days: who knows what secrets they may hold?'

I could not speak of that last meeting in the Paris wine shop – not here, amongst the politicking gentlemen, amongst the smoky talk of bills and ministers and offices, though I knew well that the two things were now, at last, fatefully related.

I said, almost desperately, so as to be rid of that transfixing finger, yet from the heart too: 'I believe that I am my father's true and legitimate son.'

'Very well!' Shaftesbury said, releasing me, with an airy look – I was reminded of my old lessons with Mr Ross, when I gave an answer and was unsure whether it was right or fantastically wrong. 'Very well! And now as to evidences.'

'If there were such, we would hardly be sitting here now,' I said, a little irritably.

'You misunderstand me. I mean *possible* evidences. Now I have heard, for instance, that the late Bishop of Lincoln spoke of having solemnized the marriage of your father and mother in the year 'forty-eight, at a house in Flanders.'

'Indeed? I confess I never heard such.'

'Never mind: you need not say that,' Shaftesbury said rapidly. 'The bishop is dead, alas. But a dead bishop is better than none at all, do you see? The thought is there. A thought can go a long way . . . Unless your mother ever spoke of some other person witnessing the marriage?'

'She . . . she talked of having seen a clergyman, in her last days – I think because she grew devout. And she spoke of papers, that were lodged with a certain person—'

'Ah!'

'But I know nothing of the person,' I concluded gloomily. 'I was quite a child, and – and grieving; and I was never able to know more.'

'That is of no account. Forgive me – a great pity, of course, I sympathize. But these are evidences, good enough for many a man. There remains only the question of your father – and whether he will give in to them.'

'He will not if he feels himself forced to it,' I said. 'That I can engage for. Nor, my lord, would I see him forced to anything—'

'He will give ground, though,' Shaftesbury said. 'The country is troubled: the country is fearful. He must give ground.'

I had spoken truly. As Shaftesbury and his party beat the drum louder against my uncle's right to the succession, and began to talk of my legitimacy as the answer, my father felt himself hurried – and that, I knew, was no good.

'Your friends, Jemmy, would seem to delight in rumours,' he said to me, quite pleasant and cool, as we crossed Pebble Court to the Council Chamber. 'Do they think we are deficient in rumour, in God's name? Is the market not glutted with such trashy goods?'

'These rumours will flourish, Father,' I said, 'until you use your power to end them.'

'Oho, never fear for that,' my father said, with a grim look; and then, more gently, 'I spoke of your friends, and you did not contradict. So be it. I only urge you to consider whether they *are* your true friends.'

And then I felt myself patronized, and my blood rose. I thought of my father as I had seen him at supper last night, making up to Louise, who had had one of her weeping fits over some fancied wrong and must be cozened out of it with baby-talk and jewels: I thought of myself with cousin William on the blood-churned battlefield at Mons, with my men watching my face in loyal anxious hope. And I thought that my father treated me as a boy, and that it comforted and flattered him to do so. Perhaps everyone comes to such a moment with their parents. It is at once bleak and refreshing: an end and a beginning.

'I must get what friends I can, Father,' I said. 'That's the way of it, for a man who doesn't know where he stands.'

He said nothing. But in Council that day, he spoke plainly enough. He made a declaration, and ordered that it be placed in the Council record.

'There being a false and malicious report industriously spread abroad by some who are neither friends to me nor the Duke of Monmouth, as if I should have been contracted or married to his mother; and though I am most confident that this idle story cannot have any effect in this age, yet I thought it my duty in relation to the succession of the Crown, and that future ages may not have any pretence to give disturbance upon that score or any other of this nature, to declare, as I do here declare, in the presence of Almighty God, that I never was married, nor gave contract to any woman whatsoever, but to my wife, Queen Catharine, to whom I am now married.'

Well, he was never, as I have remarked, a good speaker in public. He made the declaration in the shuffling awkward manner that always came over him when he faced Parliament; and afterwards some said that was significant. I thought, indeed, he looked miserable and full of suppressed fury. But those words about friends struck home to me. I felt the private rebuke. I felt it quite as much as the public blow to my hopes of legitimacy.

And yet afterwards – such was his unpredictable nature – he embraced me, and said quietly: "Tis no time to fan the flames, Jemmy. All is too tindery at the moment. I want the fire put out.'

'The declaration is mere policy,' Shaftesbury said. 'The phrases have not even His Majesty's stamp. This is your uncle's work. The effrontery of the man is remarkable. 'Tis as if a thief discovered in the pantry should go on calmly putting silver in his sack.'

'You think so?' I was still gnawing inside. Policy, aye: there was no greater master of that than my father, who could serve lies and truth on the same platter. But I kept thinking of my poor mother – she was quite haunting me, indeed, so that I seemed to smell her perfume on my clothes – and wondering what she would want me to do. The time may come, she had said, when I must stand up for my rights . . .

'You know, Your Grace,' said Shaftesbury, who seemed as so often to read my thoughts, 'His Majesty has said to me in the past that he would wish to do well by you. But he is hindered because he would not do ill to his brother: there's the rub. You must trust that we shall lead him to see where his true interests lie. That is difficult while your uncle remains at court, forever *advising* in His Majesty's ear.' He made it sound rather obscene, as it were pissing in it. 'Depend upon it, the King knows – none better – where his interests lie. After all, what is the choice? A bigot and despot to succeed him – or a Protestant prince, beloved of the people, with His Majesty's own stamp plain upon him!'

'I am not a prince.'

Shaftesbury shrugged. 'That is not beyond remedy.'

'My lord, I must be clear on this. You would champion me – you do not propose my father divorce, and get another heir – you champion me alone to be the heir to the throne?'

'Aye, I do! And I can name a dozen lords and many more Commonsmen who will do likewise!' Shaftesbury spoke with great cheer, but a sort of impatience too, which he often betrayed with me – I know my mind was much slower than his.

'If I am to seek this, then I must declare my aim. And so declare myself against my uncle.'

'Aye, aye – a hard world, is it not?'

'Not against my father, though.'

The earl thought for a moment. 'Well, now, your father is a man of sense, that's beyond doubt. If he will only send James out of the way – as is surely sensible at such a time – then we may yet do more. The new Parliament will urge it – I shall see to that. And then we have our brisk boys, Your Grace, who may make their voices heard.'

Shaftesbury had much approval in the City, and could count upon bands of fiery young men taking to the streets in support of his policies: the foot-soldiers of the Green Ribbon Club, if you like. I have heard them called a mob – that curious magical word, which allows us to forget the existence of the people. Still, I never quite liked the relish with which he named his 'brisk boys' – which he, naturally, perceived.

'I speak only of precautions, Your Grace. But let us remember, that in James we face a man who is all for a standing army; who has unashamedly urged the King to bring troops of Irishmen over to keep us down. 'Tis as well to be prepared.'

'To be sure,' I said. 'But I would rather rise by love than force.'

'Oh, my dear sir!' Shaftesbury was seldom more than thinly amused, and I know that I of all people was no wit, but he burst into a shout of laughter as if I had made the finest joke he had ever heard.

James sent out of the way! I did not think it could come to pass. But my father, as Shaftesbury said, did not lack sense. My uncle was oil and pitch in that flammable air, and there could be no peace while he was about. No peace, indeed, in all ways: I am not sure that the prime reason for my father's sending James abroad to visit Mary and William, and thence to a sojourn in Brussels, was to be free of his nagging. Not that that entirely stopped it, for every packet-boat that landed brought a thick letter from James, instructing my father on how to run the country. I saw them heaped on my father's desk, some with the seal unbroken.

But feeling still ran high. My uncle's baleful presence was temporarily removed, but his shadow was not. The new Parliament was much affected against him, and against the Catholic and French interest he represented: Louise, the Frenchwoman, diamond-bedecked, who loved to boast of her power to make men and break them, was bitterly unpopular. A jeering crowd gathered once about a carriage thinking it to be Louise's, but it was Nell Gwynn who put her head out, crying: 'Good people, be calm! This is the *Protestant* whore!'

My lord Shaftesbury, at any rate, could congratulate himself on a partial victory; and what was more, he was brought back to the Privy Council, where my father would watch him across the table rather as a caged bird watches a cat – or was it the other way round? Certainly Shaftesbury perceived his star to be on the rise, and was full of business. He had one clear aim, to which he directed all the deceptive energy of his wasted little body, all his talents of exhortation and persuasion. He sought to have my uncle James excluded from inheriting the throne, so that a Protestant succession could be guaranteed. His means was an act of Parliament – an exclusive bill, it was called – and he was prepared to move heaven and earth to get it.

And this was to be the pattern of the following years – ever the swelling momentum, in Parliament and country, to have Exclusion made law: ever the arguments, the objections, the stubborn rocks in the current. My father was one such stubborn rock, but he did make some apparent concessions, saying he would be willing to set some limitation upon my uncle's power if he took the throne. There was even a suggestion of Mary and William acting as regents over him. But of course, my uncle was the last man in the world to accept limitations upon his power. When he got the crown, it would be more, not less power he would seize. It would not do. Shaftesbury and his party would not have James. But here was the rock: James was the due legal successor, and to that point my father stuck tenaciously.

And there was another difficulty, to be sure: if not James, then who? You know for whom Shaftesbury declared: me. Nameless Jemmy, the obscure boy who had trembled before Cromwell, who had had his chin insolently squeezed by Philippe d'Orléans, who had felt delighted to be given the name Master Crofts along with a suit of clothes. And it was not just Shaftesbury. There were many – many – people who wanted me to inherit the throne of England.

And yet even some of those could not countenance it.

'I talked to a gentleman today who spoke for, I think, a whole half-hour on my uncle James, and how he dreaded him taking the throne,' I grumbled to Anna. 'And at the conclusion, he said he could not vote for Exclusion. What am I to make of this?'

'Why, 'tis perfectly plain,' said Anna. Aye, what of this wife of mine? What did she, who grew more proud and straight-backed and absolute with the years, think of the prospect of becoming Queen one day? Well, she did not speak of it: she was too careful for that. But she had no love for my uncle, and I noticed she had instructed our little boy to show me a formal respect I hardly looked for. I felt embarrassed when he kneeled and kissed my hand, though I had to laugh when he first wiped the sugar-plum from his lips with a regretful sigh.

''Tis plain that he fears, as others do, what he may set in motion by voting for Exclusion,' Anna said in her precise way. 'For if people may refuse a king, and set up another, it is as much to say they may choose their kings – or do without them altogether.'

'Well, then let it be so,' said I. 'Let the King reign by consent of the people.'

Anna snapped a look at me – the muddy-boots look. 'Ach, Jemmy!'

'Why, is that so very bad? Anything must be better than my uncle. Even my father seems to acknowledge that, in his heart.'

'Oh, he does indeed. He said to me just the other day that if his brother took the crown, he doubted he would keep it above two years.'

I heard this with interest, and pique: he did not say such things to me.

But I was soon to be free, for a time, from the tortuous politicking that came so awkwardly to me. There had long been trouble and discontent in Scotland, where gross old Lauderdale ruled with an iron hand. Now there was rebellion. The freedom sought by these Covenanters who had taken up arms was a freedom of worship – this was a stirring of the old sturdy spirit of the kirk, and that showed how little of a threat they truly were.

But these were nervous times, and my father would have order restored in his northern kingdom. He sent me, as Captain-General, to put the Covenanters down.

I was eager for action. Gathering my own troop about me, I rode full tilt for Scotland, ahead of my supply train. The sun was high, the roads dry and hard, and there was hay-making in the fields. I remember wishing that I might exist thus for ever, riding onward under a summer sky, feeling the glad quickness of blood in my veins, horizons ever unrolling under my horse's hoofs.

In three days we were in Edinburgh, mustering. We had three thousand men; the Covenanters, roughly encamped in the field at Bothwell Bridge, twice that number. But when we came to battle, their numbers did not avail them. Before we fell to, there were reports from scouts that the Covenanter camp was a strange place, full of disputation: crop-haired, homespun men falling upon their knees in long prayer-fests, some denouncing others as insufficiently godly, others questioning the right of fighting a worldly sovereign. Divided and irresolute as they were, they fell like thistles to the scythe when we charged them.

I pressed home the victory, that we might make an end, and not have to do it again. But I gave a strict command to the dragoons – at which they chafed a little – that there was to be no hunting down and killing the defeated. These were not our foes: we did not stand as conquerors. I promised quarter and full assurance of life on their laying down arms, and we took twelve hundred prisoners: honest, troubled, awkward men, one of whom informed me, as he delivered himself to my Cornet, that he hoped I was a man of my word, else his God would sweal me to crackling. Well, I have a different notion of the Almighty, but if the Scotsman's be the true one, then I have naught to fear in that regard at least, for I made sure the prisoners were decently lodged at Greyfriars, and sent my surgeon to their wounded. Before I came away from Scotland – having been feasted to bursting by the Scots lords, who amply justified their reputation for hospitality, the Earl of Selkirk even suggesting, as I staggered from the table, that *one* more roast duck would do me no harm – I issued orders for the clement treatment of the Covenanters, and the orderly withdrawal of the militia. I hoped I had left peace, and no bitterness. After all, our Civil Wars began with a heavy hand north of the border.

Yes, the bells rang for me on my entry into London: yes, the people cheered me, calling me 'Your Highness'. Never fear, if you tire of me vaunting upon these pages: my fall will come soon enough.

At Windsor my father received me with warm embraces, and concern for a slash upon my wrist; and gouty old Prince Rupert came to shake my hand – which, he said in his growling way, was something he had not done for any man in five years.

'Mind,' he said before limping away, 'you were too lenient, sir. It will smack of weakness.'

'Aye, Jemmy, you were mighty tender to these fellows,' said my father, half-smiling. 'What means it, eh? Why should we have all this trouble of prisoners?'

'I cannot kill men in cold blood, Father,' I said after a surprised moment. 'That's work only for a butcher.'

He only made his characteristic motion of the head, betwixt nod and shake.

'Hey, well, they rain blessings on your name, no doubt. 'Tis certainly the straightest way to win popularity. Not that you were thinking of that, I know,' he said, clapping my shoulder and laughing.

What did he mean by it – the way he spoke to me that day? As I went to salute the Queen, I was all tumult, where a little before I had been all happiness. Was he simply sounding me out for the ring of sincerity? Or was it the ruthless influence of my uncle that had got into his blood like a venom? As ever, just when I should have been closest to him, he evaded me. A man might fish with his bare hands with more success, I thought, than get an honest answer from my father.

But I had another thought. It entered my head from nowhere, full-formed, as if a voice had spoken. *It is because they cheer you, where they used to cheer him.*

Yes, they cheered me, and not just in the streets. Parliament-men, men of the law, men with a great stake in the country waited upon me with their congratulations. To be sure, some who gathered about me were flatterers and intriguers, out for what they could get: it would be more surprising if they were not. And I was more pleased than vexed to hear of my uncle's thunderings from his Flanders exile, told to anyone who would listen, that my acts in Scotland were those of a schemer – that I spared prisoners to win hearts. For this showed, after all, that he was afraid of me.

And then – sudden, unexpected, direful – my father fell gravely ill.

FIVE

We were still at Windsor when it happened.

My father played his usual vigorous game of tennis in the morning. Then, his energy unquenched, took his saunter, as he called it, by the river. It was muggy weather: the air full of noxious humours, the physicians said sagely after – much good they were. When he complained of aches and shivers that night, the sawbones promptly purged and bled him – taking above sixteen ounces of blood. When he grew weaker, they nodded their heads and said that was very good.

The next day he lay in a raging fever. He moaned and plucked at the bedcovers; his breath rattled and bubbled like a stew-pot. People gaped in amazement, for my father was simply never ill. I was not the only one to feel that the earth had shaken.

The bedchamber, with its banked fires and drawn curtains and smell of burning pastiles, was made all the more stifling by the press of bodies. For practically every man of the Council squeezed in there to stare in perplexity, to urge courage upon the patient – and to talk. While my father tossed on the billows of fever, another fever seized the Court.

Would the King die? And what would happen if he did?

So the mutter went. Heads turned to look at me: with caution, speculation, wonder – also hostility. For my uncle's toadies were amongst them. And they did not forbear to press my father, in his lucid intervals, to send for James from his exile.

'They talk as if he is going to die,' I lamented to Anna, who had been waiting on the Queen. 'He cannot. He cannot die.'

'He can,' Anna said. 'As we all can, and will. What do the doctors say now?'

'Oh, that it will turn into a tertian ague. If it does not, of course, they will say they thought so. Damn them—'

'You must master yourself, Jemmy,' Anna said soberly. 'Many eyes are upon you.'

Towards evening the fever seemed to remit a little. My father's eyes, from staring into vaults and abysses, cleared and saw the bedchamber instead: saw me. He called me to him, smacking his dry lips.

'Jemmy. An inconvenience, this.'

'Do you feel a little better, Father?'

'I will feel worse again, I fear. They will – they will not try the Peruvian bark. 'Tis the best, I swear – I have seen its operations. There is a quantity in my chemical room, yet the doctors will not . . .' He lolled back against the pillows. 'Try your persuasions . . . ?'

'I will, Father. I will take care of everything.'

'To be sure . . .' He contemplated the ceiling with yellow eyes. 'Yet I wonder – I wonder if I should bring James back.'

'No, Father!' I clutched his hand. 'Don't say that. Let him be.'

'Why?'

'Because it would seem as if . . .' *As if you are going to die.* I could not say those words. 'There is no need. I am here. If James comes, people will think—'

'Aye, boy.' He disengaged his hand, turning his matted head away. 'I understand you.'

I had meant that to summon James would suggest this bed was a deathbed, and that I could not bear to think of. But the story was soon about that I begged my father to keep James in exile so that, if he did die, I might seize the crown. This, if you please, was what I was coolly planning as I sat by the sickbed of the man who had been my whole world. Perhaps you believe it: if so, I dare say we can go no further together.

But I fear my father, lowered and vulnerable as he was, did believe it in part. As he lay there, with James's henchmen whispering at him, I think he began to believe ill of me.

Certainly I did not want my uncle fetched home, for another reason – I disliked and mistrusted him, and hated the thought of his smug satisfaction at the summons. Yes, to bring him back was to suggest that he would take the crown, should death relieve my father of it. And I did not like that either. I liked none of it.

But if my father had died – would I have rallied the army to me as Lord General, and called upon the Lord Mayor of London to proclaim me as his successor? I can believe many bad things of myself. But I cannot believe I could have done that – with prompt calculation – without grieving.

The doctors, after turning a deaf ear to my pleas and trying every other remedy their idiocy could devise, at last tried the Peruvian bark – the *cinchona* – as my father urged. I have said that he would have made a fine physician: certainly, when I saw him beginning to rally, I knew that he had pretty well cured himself.

'I want to go to Newmarket,' he was saying soon, laying aside the broth bowl. ''Tis dreary here. I want to be up.'

'Oh, not yet, Your Majesty – it is too soon yet,' the physician – unabashed – said soothingly. 'Presently, presently. His Grace of Monmouth agrees, I am sure . . . ?'

'Ah.' My father's eyes drilled me. 'Indeed – what does His Grace of Monmouth say?'

I should have realized then that he thought the worst of me. But I was so relieved that I laughed and said he would be riding against me for the Plate, and beating me again, soon enough.'

'I wonder.'

He passed a good night; and I, in the exhilaration of relief, took a gallop about Windsor Park. When I came laughing and glowing to the stables I found my secretary, long-faced, awaiting me – to tell me that my uncle was here.

'Come, Jemmy. Pay your respects to your uncle.'

I am not good, I know, at disguising my feelings. My face must have fallen, seeing James standing by my father's bed, looking the picture of stiff-necked pride and complacency. No doubt my uncle saw it too – well, be damned to him. But my father was watching me closely too.

'Well, Jemmy?' my father said, an edge in his voice, ''Tis not like you to fail in courtesy.'

I advanced, made my bow, and greeted my uncle awkwardly enough.

'That's well,' my father said in a soft growl. 'Now is all as it should be.'

'I only regret that I could have not been with you sooner, Brother,' my uncle said, as if I were not there.

'It could not be helped,' my father said likewise. 'But you're here now.'

'This may be but a feint on His Majesty's part,' Shaftesbury said. 'He is capable of playing a deep game.'

'James does not take it so. He is all triumph. He struts,' I said. 'He has had the clearest possible signal. The crown is his.'

'Is it now?' Shaftesbury said. 'Do you think my bolt shot, then, sir?'

'Oh . . . I don't care any more.'

'You should not be down-hearted, Your Grace. Observe these bonfires, these loyal toasts for His Majesty's recovery – what do you hear? Do they not couple their cheers with your name – "and long live the Duke of Monmouth"?'

'Aye, but – it's what my father thinks of me. He grows cool. He supposes me a schemer.'

'Your association with me, I fear, will confirm him in that opinion.' Shaftesbury gave a regretful shrug. 'Sever our friendship, Your Grace, by all means. I would not blame you.'

'No,' I said, sharply. 'I do not drop my friends so easily. Oh, my father would like that, no doubt, so that I would have to be entirely dependent on him.'

'Ah. You grow wise, Your Grace.' Shaftesbury's voice made melancholy music. 'And in wisdom, alas, is sadness.'

On his feet again, my father summoned me. I should not have been surprised, perhaps, to find my uncle lingering about the anteroom.

'This is surely not possible,' he said. He was standing before a painting – a beautiful rendering of the myth of Cupid and Psyche. 'Observe the turn of this foliage. Now observe the way this person's draperies are blown about. The wind would seem to be blowing in two different directions, which is, of course, an impossibility. Dear, dear.' Having disposed of the picture to his deadly satisfaction, he turned his attention to me. 'The King makes an excellent recovery. It is a matter for rejoicing, is it not?'

'Yes,' I said, moving past him.

'Where do you go, sir?'

'I am summoned by my father.'

'You are summoned by the King.' James said, heavily and distinctly.

'To be sure. A word first, Jemmy, so that we are not mistook. You may suppose me to be a fool. I am not, sir. I know well that you tried to have the news of the King's illness kept from me. As a piece of ambitious mischief, this does not surprise me, I'm afraid – not any more. But I confess to a little surprise that you would flirt so with treason.'

'A man may only be treasonable to the crown, Uncle. And you do not wear it.'

'Oh, but I shall, sir. Depend upon it. And those rebels you consort with shall not stop me. The day will come when they will rue, sir; and so will you.'

'Your stay abroad seems to have benefited you,' I said, stepping back to look over him. 'What did you do there? Promise England to Louis for his hunting park?'

Stormily, I brushed past him and went in to my father.

He was at his most serene, calmly looking over some building plans. I, glowering and flushed, was at a disadvantage at once.

'You saw James without?'

'Aye, I saw him.'

'I was going to ask if you were civil to him. A waste of breath.'

'Well, I suppose I must learn to be so. If he is to remain. Is he?'

'I don't have to account for my actions to you, I think,' my father said, rolling up the plans. 'It is not decided yet. James has no wish to return to Flanders—'

'Of course not. He would be here, where he can pull the puppet-strings—'

'You had better say no more in that strain, Jemmy.'

'Why not? 'Tis what everyone says. Have you forgot the Plot, Father? Coleman's letters?'

'The Plot was nine-tenths nonsense. As you would know, if you thought for yourself, instead of surrendering your mind to rogues like Shaftesbury.'

'You would have me without friends, then, Father? Waiting only on your pleasure?'

'Shaftesbury is no friend to you, Jemmy. Nor any of these other malcontents. I hear things, my boy. The Earl of Oxford tells me he has had half a dozen men calling on him, urging him to vote to have the succession settled on you.'

'If people want that, I can't help it.'

My father sighed, then looked at me through the rolled-up plans, as through a telescope. But his mouth did not smile. 'I used to believe you loved me, Jemmy. Not my crown.'

Oh, how bitter that was to hear! 'And now you doubt it?'

'I wish I did not. But what am I to suppose? When I lay sick, you urged me to keep James away – James, the true legal successor to the throne of these kingdoms. Call this rebellion, ambition, folly – it has a very ill flavour, whatever it may be. And now I hear of your mixing with a set of men who would strip me of my every prerogative. It was not for this I lifted you from the pit, Jemmy—'

'What was it for, then, Father? Why did you take me up, and give me everything I could desire – and then stop?' I know I spoke, or meant to speak, beseechingly, for I was moved and desperate. I hear now the crack and flute in my voice; and I fear it must have sounded merely petulant, shrill, demanding. Dear, damnable hindsight. 'Is it as with your women – toy with them, lie with them, and then drop them if they make the claim of love upon you?'

'You make this no better for yourself, boy.'

'I doubt it. I doubt it can be worse – not after James has been at you. What has he said? No matter – you will do it, of course.'

'Consider this, Jemmy.' My father's voice was level, but the paper in his hand was screwed to a ball. 'I am at odds with my brother on many points. But I trust him. I trust his loyalty to me. And when I lay ill last week' – he caught his breath – 'I did not feel that I could trust you. You grow too great, and cannot be yourself again till you are cut down a little. I mean this as a kindness as much as a punishment. I was wrong. I confess, to give you so much power, without seeing if you could manage it. I do not think you can.' He looked down at the ball of paper in his hand as if someone had just put it there. 'So – so you are no longer Captain-General. Your command is taken from you.'

I stared miserably; and he would not look at me. 'I see. And it is given to my uncle, no doubt.'

'I give it to no one. I do this for the peace of the realm. And for the same reason, you must go abroad for a space, Jemmy. James has been kept out of the way, in these troubled times; and now I must be even-handed, and do the same with you.'

'You order me to go?'

'I prefer to request it,' he said. 'First.'

'Very well. Very well, then you must find a new Commander for your Guards too. Aye, take that from me – I resign it. After all, I am not to be trusted, is it not so? Well, well. If I am not to be trusted, Father, then think how that came about. For as you said yourself, it was you who made me. Like God, you made me in your own image.'

So I went – bitter, heavy-hearted, mutinous – to Whitehall, to my lodgings in the Cockpit, and there told my servants: 'Pack everything up: I am banished.'

All very dramatic. But such is the way of it, alas, when we feel desperately and intensely. We can only draw on this language, which is a currency much traded in, and soiled. So we sound absurd, even when we weep inside, as I did.

A few days later, before I took ship, I went to see Shaftesbury at his town house in Aldersgate Street. I wanted to see someone who believed in me. Again, absurd, I suppose.

'Oh, people talk of nothing else, Your Grace. There were bonfires lit in the City the other day just upon a rumour that the King had changed his mind.' Shaftesbury was being shaved; he paused while his barber applied the razor to his sardonic lip. 'There are many who cry shame upon it, and urge you not to go.'

'Defy him? I cannot do that,' I said, but I felt a voice murmur, *Not yet*.

'Well, I believe you are in the right of it. The people will be all the more for you, seeing you banished abroad: 'twill stir them. And you may believe, sir, that when Parliament is recalled, we shall demand justice for you. Aye, justice for a prince whose only crime is his attachment to the Protestant religion and the liberties of his country.' Shaftesbury gave it out in an orator's voice, right into the face of his barber, who shrugged impassively. 'Of course, it is your uncle's party behind it all.'

'You think so? For I – I still cannot think ill of my father – not to lay the blame upon him.'

'You may have to, some day, Your Grace,' Shaftesbury said. 'We all turn against our fathers, sooner or later.' Patting his new-shaven cheeks, he beamed, as if he described some delicious treat.

'Well, yes, England is at peace,' I said, sitting back, digesting the good Dutch cooking. 'But there is no peace there, not truly. Whereas here . . .' I looked around me in sorrowful admiration. The dining hall of the Prince and Princess of Orange, at the Palace of Honselaersdijck just outside The Hague, was all ease, taste and comfort – by which I mean it was more like a room in a house than a combination of church and bear pit. The Dutch have this way of making domesticity elegant: we have missed it. Everything was clean too. There was no need for that quick inspection of the knives on the table to find the least dirty; and there was assuredly no brimming chamber-pot behind that tapestry screen all riotous with fruits and flowers. The arrangements were quite otherwise, as I had already found in an astonishing room that was all white marble and running water. The fruits and flowers and trees and birds appeared everywhere, in tiles and lacquer and marquetry and in the China-ware on the table: at Honselaersdijck, you were in a garden even when you were indoors.

Domestically elegant: that well described my cousin Mary – but add the grave intelligence of those dark eyes that looked at me and saw much. 'What you mean, James,' she said, not unkindly, 'is that there is no peace for you in England. Which is why you are here.'

'Aye, I suppose so.' Moodily I added, 'You'll have heard your father's side of the story, of course.'

'I have heard many sides, and I shall make up my own mind,' Mary said. 'But there – we should not be talking of these things.'

'We may talk as we please in our own houses, I think,' William grunted. 'There are no spies here. You are not, are you, sir, hey?' He meant the English ambassador to Holland, with whom I was staying, and who had been invited to dine here also. He was a great toper and already half-asleep. 'Of course not. But true, true, my dear, we should not talk of it. No state matters when we are at leisure – no business – that is our rule. Thus we make our harmony.'

Harmony indeed. Here was another contrast with the England that I had left: of all the unthinkable prodigies, a happily married couple! Anna, of course, had not come with me into this exile. She said it was my fault. I envied William and Mary. When I had first presented myself to them, I had had an indifferent welcome. I supposed they thought it imprudent to have much to do with me, what with my father and above all my uncle's disapproval, and I had been about to go away from The Hague when William's invitation came. On reflection I wondered if that first coolness had simply been the flinching of a contented couple – who comes to break our circle?

'Well, how goes it with Anne?' I asked Mary now. 'I hear there are plans to find her a husband. I hope they will not marry her against her inclination.'

'She is a princess,' William said shrugging.

'Also,' Mary said, 'love may come, even from a marriage of policy.'

'Or it may not,' I said, thinking of Anna.

'What shall you find to do here, James?' Mary said. 'You must be quite at a loss.'

'Oh, I shall find something. Visit the soldiers' hospital at Amsterdam perhaps. There are some of my old troop there. I might go to Hamburg, see if I can employ myself there. I hope it will not be long. Oh, pray, don't think I mean— That is, I am most happy to see you, and I thank you for receiving me. They will not be pleased at Whitehall, you know,' I said uncontrollably, 'you entertaining the wicked scapegrace.'

'I do not live to please,' William said. 'Don't go to Hamburg, James. Stay in Holland – fight at my side again. Aye, I know you have no command now. Be my captain, or whatever you please. We'll tweak Louis's long nose together.'

'But you are not at war with Louis,' I laughed.

'I am always at war with Louis,' William said, grinning but not laughing, 'declared or not. Just now he nibbles.' He demonstrated with a piece of cheese. 'This town, that town. A little more, Your glorious Majesty? Will you taste Luxembourg? Ach, but I can do nothing. The Amsterdammers will not stir from their counting-houses. As for England, who might make all the difference . . .' He glanced at Mary, then swallowed the cheese down. 'But you are right, my dear. No business.'

After dinner I asked William if he would take a turn with me in the gardens. It was autumn: in the pretty gardens of Honselaersdijck, a graceful gentle autumn without foreboding. It was as if no chill wind could blow through these avenues, and the linden-leaves fell straight down, decorously twirling. William talked for a while of gardening, of parterres and exotics, then took my arm and said, 'Now, sir, you can speak freely, I think. It is all to do with my honoured father-in-law, yes?'

'Oh, naturally. But it was my father's doing to send me away – there's the bitterness of it.' I took from my pocket the letter from my father that had arrived that day. 'Well, there is *some* hope. See – he writes that I always have his friendship, and that I will not have to stay away long.'

William peered short-sightedly at my father's looping script. 'Hm. Still I detect my father-in-law behind it. They say he would not consent to go out of England again unless you were exiled also. Is it so?'

'Probably. I fancy Louise – my father's mistress – had a say in it too.'

'The Frenchwoman. You have formidable enemies. Have you friends too?'

'In England? Yes. Yes, I have friends.' I hesitated. 'Here too, I hope.'

'Oh, my dear sir, the Dutch? But you are a Stuart. How can you be friends with the – what is it? – the set of dreary cheesemongers?'

'Very easily. I am in a way half a Dutchman myself. I was born here, you know, at Rotterdam.'

'Ah, yes, your birth. That is a matter much talked of. Tell me about it.'

'Alas, I can't remember it.'

'It is no use making jokes with me, James. I do not understand them. Mrs Barlow. That is how your mother was called, yes?'

'Yes,' I said, stiffly. 'And she knew your mother quite well – the late Princess of Orange. She was very kind once to my mother, who was a lady of good family—'

'Pah, I don't care about that. Did she marry your father? Yes or no?'

'She maintained so. And – and if it should be proven so—'

'Then you become heir to England's crown, so, so. But I think this will not happen. Your father denies any marriage.'

'Yes. But then so did my uncle, when he married Mary's mother. Or tried to. And besides, who can ever get at the truth with my father?'

William grunted. 'You know, when the ambassador told me you were staying with him, Mary and I had a, what is it, a talk like big—'

'Long, deep?'

'Long and deep and big. About how we should – treat you.'

'Aye, well, I am unwelcome everywhere, I know that.'

'My dear man, don't go to pitying the self, please. You know what I mean. I must consider my wife's rights. She stands next after my father-in-law for the Crown of England, unless the Modena woman manages a son. So I must tell you that if you pretend to that crown—'

'I do not like that word.'

'Words words. If you aim for the crown, you cannot count me among your friends.'

'I didn't come here for that. Is that what you thought? That I came looking for an ally, simply—'

'Tsk, you are too passionate!' William said, shaking his head. 'It never does good, you know.'

'I came,' I said, 'because I did count you and Mary among my friends. *True* friends – not friends to my cause.'

William gave me a long, judicious look. 'Very well. As long as we understand each other.' He swished his cane at an errant weed on the scrubbed path. 'Of course, there is one very good reason why I would always give you a welcome, James, come what may.' William made the snorting, coughing noise, which I remembered after a moment was his laughter. 'And that is – to displease my father-in-law.'

Well, William's father-in-law, my uncle James, would seem to have little cause for displeasure just then. Was he not triumphantly restored to favour?

Partly. But he was still sufficiently mistrusted for my father to see the wisdom of removing him from the court. So James was soon dispatched to Scotland, to rule there in Lauderdale's stead; and there he soon outdid the old slobberer's tyranny, especially over the Covenanters. There was in the northern kingdom an instrument of torture called the boot, which James greatly took to; and watching its operations consoled him for the loss of his favourite stag-hunting, which he lamented was impossible in the boggy country, for his hounds came to hurt.

As for me, I lingered about The Hague, hoping for a summons from my father. I thought much of the past, and especially of my mother. The Dutch scenes brought it all back, and her shade was a pricking presence. I thought of Louise, Duchess of Portsmouth, with her grand apartments and her little Negro pages offering her almonds on silver dishes; and of my mother's poor grave in Paris. I felt we were wronged. And among the Dutch, a well-informed and politic people, I gained a new and disturbing perspective on my father. They pitied England with its luxurious and debauched court, presided over by an untrustworthy monarch forever groping after French gold.

Did I begin to hate my father? Perhaps – a part of me. Think of someone you have profoundly loved. Is there not hate there also – at some time, in some regard – a hate that is part of the love, like the dark face of the shining moon? Is the hate, indeed, because of the love: because of the power it gives that person over us?

I looked at myself in the glass. I was thirty years old. I had, as was always being remarked, my father's face. But I had my own too.

Shaftesbury wrote me a letter. The new Parliament was to meet; there were great demonstrations in the streets against my uncle: the time was critical. Would I not return to the country that was crying out for me?

'Without your father's permission?' William said, at our leave-taking.

'When Louis brought his armies to your gates, did you wait for permission to shoot at him?'

'That was war.'

'There's more than one kind of war.'

We were riding in the forest behind Honselaersdijck. Smoke from a woodman's fire had got on William's chest, and he reined in to cough and spit.

'You are crossing the Rubicon, my friend,' he said, dabbing his mouth. 'So is it *aut Caesar, aut nihil?*'

'My Latin is rusty. But that means, I think, I will be Caesar or nothing.'

'Just so. And you do not have to answer my question, James. Indeed, perhaps it is best you do not, if we are to remain—'

'Friends. Yes, I know. Well, never mind Caesar for now. What is the Latin for a man?'

'*Vir.*'

'Well, that is what I must be – or nothing.'

'I see.' There was melancholy in William's hawkish eyes, or it might have been the smoke. 'I may as well say I think you are being a fool.'

'Oh, I know that.'

London greeted me with a hundred bonfires. Between Temple Bar and Charing Cross the night was brighter than day; and watchmen crying the hours called that all was well, for the Duke of Monmouth was home. At Hedge Lane I could hardly get to my door for the people acclaiming me, nor had I much rest, for the church bells began pealing before dawn.

Anna greeted me with vinegar lips.

'You should not be here.'

'Where else should I be, at a time like this?'

''Tis your duty to submit to the King.'

'The King is not always right. After all, he married us,' I said bleakly, going up to see the children.

My father greeted me with silence. He very soon heard, of course, of my return; and sent a courtier to Hedge Lane to say that I was forbidden the court.

I proceeded to my lodgings in the Cockpit at Whitehall. I found that they had not, at least, been given to anyone else. Emboldened, I wrote a letter to my father, asking that he excuse my return. I had felt it necessary. There were more rumours of plots, on the Protestant side this time, and if I should be accused I could not acquit myself if I were cooling my heels in Holland.

In reply he sent another courtier, with the curt message that I was to return overseas, as I had been ordered in the General Post.

'General Post? But that suggests I was sent upon some mission of state, when everyone knows I was merely shuffled out of the way because His Grace of York desired it. Who rules here now, sir – my father the King, or his brother?'

Very intemperate. I dare say I raged and stamped, and the messenger – it was the Earl of Macclesfield, I recall, who later came over to my side – looked alarmed, and hurried off without an answer. But in truth I was sorely disappointed. I had thought – yes, I had thought my father would indulge me, when it came to it. The pique of one who has been spoiled, no doubt.

But there was no turning back now. I slept at the Cockpit that night, or rather sought sleep vainly, lying on a bare bed, watching morning give shape to the diamond panes at the window, and thinking of the days here with my father. The days of companionship: the tennis and pell-mell, the laboratory, the lake and the waterfowl. They seemed things of another world, lost.

Shaftesbury came to see me at Hedge Lane.

'You are downcast, sir.'

'Cast down, rather.'

'A pretty quibble. I am pleased, it shows you have spirits yet.'

'You are the first man to visit me, my lord. And for that I thank you.'
I seized his hand, which soon slid softly from my grasp.

'My dear sir, what did you expect?' The little earl sat, gathering his
coat about his meagre body. 'They all fear the King's displeasure. Once
that would not have been the case – but he grows absolute in his temper,
Your Grace; I'm afraid there is no denying it.'

'That's my uncle's influence.'

'I hope it is only that . . . But no matter: I am free to visit you, sir, for
I am shut out of favour too. Yes, I am dismissed from the Council again.
Why? I pressed too hard. Business was being dispatched without being
laid before the Council, and I protested, and that was the end of me.' He
snapped his fingers, with a crack so loud I jumped. 'Never mind. I was
never like to stay in His Majesty's favour for long, that I knew. He had to
tolerate me. Now he thinks himself free of me. Did you know he will
not allow Parliament to meet till next year?'

'He does not like being told what to do,' I said dully. 'Which of us
does?'

'It was malicious in him to strip you of all your offices, Your Grace.
The Generalship, perhaps, can be excused – too much power for one
man, and what-naught: but the Lord Lieutenancy of the East Riding?
Where is the danger in that? Is this not mere malice? And as for the
Captaincy of the Guards—'

'That was me. I told him he could—' I went to stir the fire, feeling the
earl's pale eyes on me. 'He could do as he would with that.'

'Ah. Well, he has given it to Albemarle. You knew that, perhaps.'

Albemarle – my old friend Christopher Monck. No friend now, of
course.

'My dear sir, you quite destroy the blaze,' Shaftesbury said, watching
me stab at the fire. 'But take from this an illustration. If you would have
your rights, we must make a blaze in the hearts of the people. There is
most tindery flammable stuff there, Your Grace, depend upon it: let us
stir it to roaring!'

I did not answer: Anna had appeared at the door, silent, deathly pale,
and reproachful.

'Pray send for a doctor, James,' she said. 'Little Charles is took sick.'

'I hope your . . . I hope the other boys thrive,' Nell Gwynn said awkwardly. She was not comfortable with unhappiness.

'Young James does well. Little Henry has a sickly tendency. But then there is never any telling. Charles seemed such a robust little fellow . . .'

It was a month since Anna and I had buried our eldest child. I say Anna and I, for we had both been at the funeral, but that was as far as our union went. Such fitful rays of warmth as had flickered through our marriage were gone now. A cold courtesy reigned. Behind it, a festering of hurts. My wife was the least superstitious creature that ever lived, but I knew she connected our loss with my behaviour. I had rebelled, I had wilfully upset the balance of life, and then our son had died; it was all of a piece. Blame is a glove that fits any hand.

Nell darted to her parlour window, which looked out on Pall Mall. A carriage was jolting by, a veiled lady within. 'Now that one is a conundrum,' Nell cried. 'She is ever at church, and repulses every beau, and carries herself like she's made of chiney-clay. Yet 'tis well knows she was delivered of a dead child at a ball, and laid it by in her handkerchief, and called for another country dance. Was there ever such a . . .' She met my eyes miserably. 'Oh, shite take it, Your Grace, I've blundered again. Indeed, I don't mean it – but the more I try to be mournful . . .'

'No matter, Nell,' I said. 'Why should you be mournful? You cannot bring the boy back.'

'No. But you have another trouble on your shoulders, my poor Prince Perkin – don't you? And there perhaps I *can* help you. Lord, I hate to see you like this.' She took up a silver mirror and held it before me. 'See? You're as lean as a shotten herring. I can keep feeding you my pastries, but I know it ain't the stomach that ails you. 'Tis this breach with the King.'

I nodded at myself in the mirror. 'You can help, Nell? I don't see how.'

'Why, I'll speak for you. I already have, mind – and he hushed me; but I'll not be hushed. 'Tis too bad, and time His Majesty saw it so. I'll melt him, Your Grace, if anyone can.'

'I fear it isn't as simple as that, Nell.'

'Why, how so? You've quarrelled with your father.' She took up a tortoiseshell comb and began tugging it through my hair. 'Even your

locks are turned doleful, look here ... Quarrelling with your father –
what could be simpler than that? Or more common? I dare swear I'd
have quarrelled with mine, if I knew who he was.'

'You don't understand, Nell. There are other matters at stake—'

'Oh, don't I?' She gave a deliberately hard tug. 'What, because I am a
simple whore, and know nothing beyond towsing and fucking?'

'Don't talk so,' I said irritably, my head smarting, ''tis ill-bred.'

Nell gave a shout of laughter. 'Now I know you are not yourself. Was
Mrs Barlow better bred than I? Ah, ah' – she pointed at my reflection,
which was flushed and thundery – 'now see – you fire up so. Why do it?
It don't help a jot.'

I swallowed. 'My cousin William said the same thing.'

'Good for Dutch Billy: he's right. I don't know – things are parcelled
out wrong in your family. If we could just find a way of spreading a little
of your fire to Dismal Jimmy, and a little of your father's good sense to
you ... Now you're going to flare up again.'

'No, I'm not. I dare say you're in the right of it. But we are as we are.'

'Aye – and there's the pity! I'm going to speak serious now, Your Grace
– not my habit I know, so hark. If you were our true Prince of Wales,
there would be none of this trouble in the kingdom – that I swear. And
that I shall tell His Majesty, quite plain. By keeping you estranged, he
does us all injury, and himself.'

'He will think you one of my partisans.'

'Well, so I am. Aye, let us hear it – Monmouth for King! No York!' She
held up the mirror again. 'There – now that's a better face.'

Nell did her best to persuade my father to reconciliation, but in vain.
Sourly I wondered whether it would have been the same had I had the
Duchess of Portsmouth on my side.

Yet Nell reminded me that I did have friends to my cause. Yes, I
thought of it as my cause, now. In the churches, in the playhouses,
people blessed the Duke of Monmouth. And everywhere ran rumour
about my birth, and about my father and mother's secret marriage, and
about the Black Box that was supposed to contain the documents
proving it.

About the Black Box I could not help feeling a little embarrassed. For
my poor mother had spoken so vaguely of these matters, and privately I

admitted to myself that I could not know there was such a thing, or where it was. Nor could I think who, from those dark far-off days of the exile on the Continent, might lead the way to it. But those who scoffed at the notion were most cleverly answered by a man named Robert Ferguson, who was of Shaftesbury's party. Ferguson was a gaunt gangling Scot, with eyes like cold pebbles and a voice that grated like fingernails on a slate, but with his pen he was a vigorous persuader, and he turned it to the service of my cause. Of the many pamphlets he wrote, the one that caused the greatest stir was on the matter of the Black Box – not for it, but against it. Might it not be, he suggested, that the Black Box was a fiction put about by enemies, seeking to discredit my claim to the crown by shrouding it in absurdity? And who stood to gain from this, but the Duke of York?

In truth this was all too subtle for me. I seemed caught up in a game of mirrors, in which I could hardly tell what I believed any more. But then was that not a fair description of how my father lived?

Certainly he remained obdurate. I had disobeyed and defied him, and he would not see me. And again he made a public disavowal of ever being married to my mother. He even placed an official notice in the *London Gazette.* 'I am confident,' he wrote, 'that this Idle Story cannot have any effect in this Age.'

An idle story. I found the words began to haunt me. It was not exactly that I began to wonder if it were so. Perhaps what I heard in them, and feared, was an epitaph: a weary, courtly, gently smiling comment on my life.

When my father fell ill again, I was dining at a tavern with some of my supporters – gentlemen of the Whig party, or rebellious malcontents, as you prefer. It was Shaftesbury's servant who brought the news, with a note from the little earl urging me to come to his house at once.

There, all was agitation. Shaftesbury greeted me hurriedly, absently: he kept darting to the door for messages from his supporters in the City. Meanwhile the Whig lords – Grey, Russell, others – shouted and disputed and drank Shaftesbury's brandy. At last I had perforce to seize the earl by his bony shoulders and make him still.

'My lord, tell me. What is the report on my father? Is it reliable?'

'He has taken an ague. He is feverish – those river-walks of his.

Careless of his health, is he not? The physicians are with him and he is put to bed. Now the point of the matter is—'

'I must go and see him,' I said, snatching up my hat.

'Oh, come, sir, do you suppose he will give you admittance? Or rather – those about him?'

'No . . .' I sat down heavily. 'Then I must send him a message—'

'Tsk, nothing of the shape, my dear sir!' Shaftesbury said. 'Apply your mind – be cool. Is this not an opportunity? Is this not a time to be in *readiness*?'

'You – you talk as if he may die. My lord, do you know more than you are telling me?'

Shaftesbury waved an irritable hand. 'I know only that it seems like his malady as before. No better, no worse. But men are mortal, sir – even the King. And if it *should* happen, then this time—'

'Oh God. God, no. If he were to die now – with this quarrel between us . . .'

Shaftesbury frowned, seemed about to say something, then changed it. He sighed. 'Ah, indeed, indeed. 'Twould be sad indeed. A sad reward of his stubbornness, his wrong-headedness – his *injustice* to you, Your Grace. But how better to redress that injustice, and secure your rights, than by taking swift steps now.' He clapped his hands once: the room was still. 'The City is ready to declare for you. So are you, my lords, are you not?' A confused babble. 'To be sure – this is all dependent, Your Grace, upon *your* declaring yourself. Put yourself at the head of the brisk boys. Unfurl your banner.'

'While my father yet lives? No, no, this is – this is too—'

'We must be prepared!' Shaftesbury snapped. 'That is, you must be prepared, Your Grace.'

'But – you know I must hope and pray for my father's recovery—'

'As do we all,' Shaftesbury said, turning and yawning as he signalled for the brandy.

'And should he recover, as I hope and believe he will – what then? If I am seen to be raising forces to claim the crown while he lies ill . . .'

'Oh, well,' Shaftesbury said, with a shrug. 'If you are afraid . . .'

I had no consciousness of it, but I must have come close to striking the little earl then: I remember his eyes widening in alarm, and someone grabbing my coat, and more vinous shouting.

Then Shaftesbury was going over to the brandy on the table, mopping his brow. He poured a glass, and brought it to me, and put it into my trembling hand.

'You are heated, Your Grace. We are all heated. Anxious times. I did not mean to suggest—'

'Good.' I took the glass. 'Then we need say no more.'

'You know, I fancy I am quite mistook,' Shaftesbury said consideringly, his head on one side, then tapped his brow. 'Tony, thou art a fool! The matter is, Your Grace, that you still care for your father's good opinion of you – do you not? Which is delightful. If not helpful.'

'Yes. That is the way of it, my lord. I admit it: I wish for esteem and love. Some men can bear to be hated; seem even to relish it. I cannot.'

'Just so.' This seemed to amuse him, rather as if a wobbling kitten had spat at him. 'I think what we have here is a divergency of means rather than ends. Your hope, I conceive, is to yet see your father acknowledge you of his own free accord: legitimize you; name you as his true and worthy successor, with pride and goodwill on all sides. Is it not so?'

'Yes – yes, it is.' I seized on that, indeed. It made things clearer in my mind. I could even live with the estrangement now. 'Yes, my lord, you have it.'

Shaftesbury's smile slowly left his face, like breath evaporating from glass. 'A pity. Oh, very laudable, to be sure. But he who lives upon hope . . . You are prompt and daring in the field of battle, Your Grace. Is this not – surely – the same?'

'I do not think it is the time, my lord. Will you give me pen and ink? I shall write my father. I must know how he does.'

'Of course I cannot dictate to you,' Shaftesbury said, bowing, all regret.

'Your dutiful son, Monmouth.' So I signed my letter. I meant it.

My father, making sure to dose himself with *cinchona*, soon recovered; and he sent me a reply. If I was dutiful, he said, then I should show it by obeying his orders and severing myself from Shaftesbury and the Whigs.

And this I would not do. But if I was stubborn, it was not from a sulky sense of being wronged, but from a conviction of my right. It was not Shaftesbury or any of his party who helped me to leap the last ditch of self-belief.

It was my love.

She has appeared plentifully in these pages, I think, though no figure in my narrative. Indeed, I would say she has been present in every line I have writ, for what I am, is she: I am made of her. And now I can give her a name, for it was at this time that we came together. Out of the court as I was, little employed in state affairs, I had a dreary excess of leisure that winter of '80. I flitted about the town, and supped and played cards and yawned and fretted at the routs and balls of such lords as were of my party, and felt ready to die of boredom. And then a friend presented me to Lady Henrietta Wentworth, and we danced. And my life changed.

'We have danced together before, Your Grace.'

'Have we? I cannot recall . . .' I should have said something gallant, to the effect that I would surely bear such an encounter engraved upon memory's golden pages, and so on . . . But already, as I took that lady's hand, things were different: the time for gallantry and nonsense was over. There was, in fact, no need for it any more.

'Yes – it was at Court, years ago – the masque of *Callisto* – you were a shepherd and I was a little handmaiden, a little nothing at the back. But you were kind enough to commend me after, and you picked up a ribbon I had dropped.'

'Indeed, I . . . your memory is remarkable.'

'It was a remarkable event, Your Grace. As is this. My dancing with you now.'

'Is it?' I said, and I found myself laughing. It was not the laugh of social chatter, but something else, that seemed to lift my spirit perilously high. Anne Hill used to tell tales of fairy enchanters who set people laughing till they died of exhaustion, and I have heard of saints and mystics expressing through laughter their religious ecstasy. '*Is* it? I believe it is. How strange . . .' Shot through with sudden seriousness, I added, 'You must not call me "Your Grace".'

'I know.'

And so we looked upon one another, and laughed, and turned silent, and talked madly, and danced. The clocks stopped: the world drew away like a painted screen.

The very next day, when she told me her mother would be absent from their town house, I went to her, and she took me to her bed. And at last, I knew – I understood – I was home.

Lady Henrietta Wentworth: then twenty years old, only daughter and heiress of the late Lord Wentworth of Toddington in Bedfordshire. But away with that: she liked to be known, she likes to be known, as Harriet. It is with my sweet Harriet that I have been consumedly in love ever since that night. And she, the heavens be praised, with me. If you be out of love, reader, I pray your patience. I do not crow. Only consider the love you have had – lost, perhaps, or perhaps only dreamed: be sure it is yet one of the great things of the world, and has added to that imperishable store of beauty, which will remain when all the kings and kingdoms are gone to wrack.

It was not easy, at first. Though fatherless, Harriet had a mother eager to hawk her about the marriage market, who was mightily displeased to discover our relation, and whisked Harriet back to the country. I know Harriet will not mind when I say her mother could be a termagant. 'My mother's ideal daughter,' she said once, 'would combine the intellectual development of a babe, the obligingness of a whore, and the obedience of a Negro slave.'

Needless to say, Harriet is not so. How then to describe her? She is fair – a fairness of old gold, not buttercups; of a willowy, flexuous height; in her neck are marvellous impossibilities, for there is the beauty of a marble column and the delicacy of the swan; she has a rich red lip; her brows are slanting and ironical while her eyes are all grey lucid candour, and even when she puts out their light, they dazzle, for they exhibit their beautiful shape when the lids are closed. Then there is her voice, which is low, rapid, and vivacious – but already I am disgusted with my pen. It is not equal to her, though in truth no pen could be.

We continued together in spite of her mother. As a baroness in her own right, Harriet insisted upon her freedoms – a circumstance that made a strong impression on me. Also, that sense of clocks stopping and the world making for us persisted. A family sickness called her mother away from Toddington, when I was already on my way there, to call and be turned away, if need be – just so I could glimpse her. Instead we had a whole week together.

'Our obstacles are most wonderfully removed,' I said as we lay curled in her bed.

'Well, of course they are. You know this is destiny.' She spoke quite matter-of-fact, as of a birthday or a frost. 'You believe that, Jemmy: I know you do.'

'How?'

She traced my brow with her finger. 'Because it is written upon you.'

'The belief, or the destiny?'

'Both, both, my darling one!' she cried laughing. 'And my destiny is to be with you. 'Tis in the stars – and how free people make with that expression but not I – I speak advisedly – I went to Mr Ashmole for my planetary wheel and he drew it up, and there you were.'

'Floating among the spheres.' I laughed, but my heart moved too.

'Aye – pretty much! Move your leg a little, dearest, it's heavy. There – now look upon us. Are we not matched?'

Firelight rendered our twined nakedness crescents of glowing skin, crevices of shadow. It was true: we seemed one creature. At such times I almost felt afraid, as if I stood on the threshold of tremendous revelation.

'What else do the stars foretell?' I said.

'Glory. Honour. Greatness,' my love said dreamily.

'Past, or to come, I wonder.'

'Never think that, my darling! The greatest is to come.' She seized my hand. 'I feel it here. No, bad man, here!'

'Do you truly, love?'

'Everything I feel,' she said with her lovely, sudden solemnity, 'I feel truly. Is that not the only way?'

I was warmed to hear this. Indeed, before Harriet it seemed the world had always made me shiver a little. This was so very different from the talk of my father's Court – that scoffing, worldly, sceptical talk that made everything small. The talk, indeed, of my father.

'Have you never seen a play, Jemmy?' Harriet said, sitting up and facing me. Snakes of golden hair uncoiled down her rich white breasts. 'Never mind those, sir – they are nothing pertaining – attend. Of course you have seen a play. Now when it comes to the fourth act, the desperate point of the characters' fortunes, would we not groan if the curtain came down, and declare ourselves cheated? Well, so it is with your life, my love. You are at the fourth act, and soon the curtain will rise upon the glorious resolution.'

Plays, indeed, were one of our diversions at Toddington. Harriet was a great lover of books, and together we would read play-books, acting out the parts between us – mostly the old dramas, like Shakespeare's and Ford's, that had gone out of fashion, for they were full of passion and excess, which your townish audience finds absurd now, preferring a cold wit; but we loved them. With Harriet, I found many new doors thrown open, for she was musical also, and conquered my shyness to sing at the harpsichord with her, and taught me something of how the notes are pricked out, and harmonies made. Above all, I learned through her of poetry. She would declaim it in the meadows and woods, to the birds, the skies; and I was moved even to pen verses of my own, to her, about her. The best I can say for them is that they were heartfelt: you need not fear I shall inflict them on you.

Again, obstacles removed: her mother gave in: she no longer prevented us. Beneath the shrewish ways, there may have been a feeling heart, for I think what she feared was that I had casually taken Harriet up as a mistress, in the way of my father's Court; that I meant to sate my ardour long enough to destroy her reputation, and depart; and it must have been plain that this was very different. So, Toddington became my retreat – and a beautiful one it was: a noble and venerable manor, with a great hall in the old style, complete with minstrels' gallery, and a park planted with great oaks and beeches. The estate was not extensive, but it was well kept, and all her tenants spoke warmly of Harriet, who took a care for their troubles, and would talk with them most frankly, with nothing of stateliness. Our retreat: so it must be, of course, for while I was in disgrace, she must share it, and be shut out of society. And that did trouble me.

'My dear, what do you mean? Should I be sad because I cannot circulate in the same stuffy rooms, with the same set of groping dullards, and whispering she-cats, day after weary day? What think you? Do I look as if I pine?' We were riding in the park. She turned her brilliant smiling face to me, then reined in and jumped lightly down. 'Besides – hearken now, Jemmy – they are wrong: they are all wrong.'

'You are wonderfully certain.' I got down, into her arms.

'So I am; so must you be. You are the champion of the true England and her liberties. Before I knew you, I always believed it. Now I know it in my blood. And if the Court is too busy counting French gold and grovelling to your uncle, then very well: they are wrong; and right will prevail in the end. *Your* right.' She pointed to the round towers of the manor, beyond the trees. 'Queen Elizabeth stayed here on her progresses. I hope there is a touch of her spirit still about. Think of her, Jemmy – not when she was Queen, but when she was yet a princess, and a doubtful one, branded a bastard under Bloody Mary's tyranny, and ever fearful her jealous sister might have her put out of the way. Did she ever doubt her right, think you?'

'And she was alone,' I said, embracing her, 'while I have you.'

'I don't miss the Court – the town – any of it,' she said, kissing my lips and chin. 'But mind, the Court will have you back – on your own terms. Depend upon that. Do you miss it, Jemmy?'

'Not the Court.'

'You miss your father.' She spoke, as so often, my precise thought. 'But he loves you – that is certain, is it not? Then he must be reconciled, sooner or later. It is very simple.'

And with Harriet, it seemed so. Yet I had an unspoken doubt. Love did not do for my father what it did for others. Somehow, it did not master him.

Not so me: I was entirely conquered, and gloried in it, and would proclaim it before the world. And yes, I was a married man. But Anna and I had nothing to say to one another any more, and the marriage revealed itself to be what it had always been – a sham. I remember going about the estate with Harriet once, and a pretty cottage girl giggling and asking for a kiss, so that she might tell her friends she had kissed a Monmouth; and Harriet saying in mock affront, 'Claim a kiss from my husband, indeed! Whatever next!' Yes, that seemed quite natural: we thought of ourselves as husband and wife before God, joined with our true hearts' consent; we even pledged it so, I recall, in a glade amongst the autumn woods. If you think this specious nonsense, never mind: many others did.

I remember Buckingham, at the Green Ribbon Club, clapping his great paw on my shoulder and saying, 'Now you are the man to tell me this, sir – you're pretty familiar with the Wentworth heiress, shall we say – what is this rumour of a suitor? Feversham, some say. He's always talking of making a good marriage. Is it true?'

'I hardly think so. The lady is united with me, and seeks no alteration.'

'United – cock's life, that's a pretty new word for whoring,'

Buckingham rumbled. He looked quite a ruin now, raspberry-cheeked, swollen, with wooden teeth where he had lost his own. 'What I don't understand is why you don't keep her in town, where 'twould all be more convenient.'

'No, you do not understand: I consider myself married to that lady.'

'But you have a wife!'

'In name only. We were made to marry when we were children, and hardly knew what we did. Neither of us would have made such a choice. But Harriet and I choose each other, and so we live as married people should.'

'Oh, my dear sir!' Buckingham laughed showily. 'Oh, 'tis a most absurd and airy pretence!'

Well, there you have a sample. And yet to keep a mistress like a whore, whilst maintaining a miserable genteel fiction of marriage, was quite acceptable. I had never felt so very separate from my father's Court before – a separation more than physical.

Our appetite tends to stories of love unrequited, doomed, star-crossed. Love fulfilled, golden and continuing is a less piquant subject, I know. I shall not vex you with an account of our every loving day. Suffice to say that we were each both lock and key. Harriet was freed from a narrowness and dullness that had made her gasp for air; I from perplexity. For now my sense of self became whole.

And while my father still clung to my uncle James as his due successor, I became newly aware of support for my claim – not merely in London. Letters and pledges came from all over the kingdom: lords and gentry from the shires invited me to visit them. So, I set out in the summer of '80 to see for myself. I toured the western counties, where my supporters were most numerous: my Progress in the West, as it was soon called.

The progress of a prince. Yes, I would show myself so, for my love had made me feel it.

SIX

It was a beautiful summer, and there could have been no more beautiful place to pass it in than the West of England. My progress took me from Wiltshire, where I stayed with my firm friends the Thynnes at magnificent Longleat, through Somerset, Devon, and Dorset. I remember hills that made me feel I had never truly seen the colour green before; fat valleys drowsy with the murmurous bleat of sheep; misty levels where the light was the hue of pearl and the turf succulent with dew. I remember the people: pretty maids strewing their village streets with flowers to welcome me, and old fierce smiling men coming forth from taverns and thrusting at me brimming mugs of ale, and mothers lifting their children to be kissed. I remember a group of Quakers watching me go by, their hats firmly on their heads, and how I made them smile by promptly doffing my own. I remember entering Exeter, proud and rich from its wool, and being almost alarmed at the great crowd of young men who swarmed upon me at the city gate, until I saw they were all dressed in gloves and ribbons of white, and heard them cry 'God bless the Duke of Monmouth!' as they escorted me. The people of the West have long been known for their independence, their sturdiness, and their attachment to liberty – or their rebelliousness, if you will. Certainly I felt myself among friends the whole time. Indeed, they did not shrink from the strongest avowals. 'We will have you for King, and devil take York and all his works!' one of those fierce old men cried, shaking my hand with such a grip that I could not feel my fingers after.

And I remember at a little hamlet near Yeovil, a young girl rushed up as I rode by, reaching out to touch my wrist. It was the lightest pressure, but somehow I felt it as much as if it were a burn. I looked down, and saw her poor disfigured face gazing up at me.

'God bless your goodness!' she said; and the reply was out of my mouth before I knew it: 'God bless you.'

It was the king's evil that marked her face. And I heard later that she said she was cured. I don't know about that. But I know that here was a great turning point. If I was to embrace my destiny, and invest it with my entire belief, then this was no small matter; though Lord Shaftesbury made light of it, when I came at last to his mansion at Wimborne St Giles.

'Aye, the common people are much affected by these tricks,' he said. 'And no harm in them, I dare say, if they win you some hearts. Well, would you know the news from Court, sir? 'Tis only this: His Majesty is mighty displeased with your ramble, as he calls it, and urges his friends to have no commerce with you. You are not surprised, of course.'

'No.' Though I felt a little foolish disappointment that my father could not joy in my popularity. For the people loved me as his son. Would he rather they loathed me as they did James?

'It is also reported that the Duke of York returns to Scotland in a poor suspicious humour. He has been heard to say he believes the King is abandoning him. Interesting. His Majesty has shown no sign of it. But we shall see when the Parliament opens.'

Well, at least my father could not ignore me. And nor could he when, at last, that autumn, the Exclusion Bill came before Parliament.

The Commons passed the bill, to exclude my uncle from inheriting the throne, without a division. With wild tumult in the streets about Westminster, the bill was carried, by my own supporters, to the Lords. In that chamber I sat as of right: my father could not prevent me. And there I looked at him across the floor, as I rose to support the bill.

Strange: a packed, noisy, fretful gathering – yet it was as if there were only me and my father in that chamber. He took the throne at the start of the debate, but soon prowled over to the fireplace, where he stood rubbing his haunches and cocking his head at each new speaker. I could see naught but him: somehow I felt he watched me also. And with his mere presence, though he made no intervention, there came over me a terrible, half-admiring, half-hating feeling. A voice within me sighed, *He is cleverer than all of us! We can never win, any of us!*

And so when I stood to speak, it was to him alone; and I faltered and rambled, I fear.

'I know – I know not how others may think – but I know of no other expedient but this bill, to preserve His Majesty the King from the malice of the Duke of York . . .'

To save you from your brother – was that what I meant? I suppose I did. We all needed saving from the Duke of York. Yet secretly I felt, again, that my father, king of foxes, was beyond us all; that never was a man in less need of saving.

As I sat down, I saw my father stir at last, and speak. He leaned over to his neighbour and murmured, 'The kiss of Judas.'

The chamber was so noisy I could hardly hear my own raised voice. Did I see his lips shape the words, then? It seemed more as if they winged straight to my heart. I was sad, vexed, and wretched; but all I could do with these feelings was turn them into pride, and swagger. And ignore the curious sensation of being defeated without knowing how, or at what contest.

But the bill itself could not be defeated – could it? So men thought. The great Whig lords were for it – and, of course, they had Shaftesbury. The little earl was a great speaker, and a great mover of men's minds. When he rose, you could see him summoning that self-consuming fire. This would be his greatest hour.

And admirable he was: his eloquence lit up with passion, wit, and scorn. But he met his match that day.

My father always seemed to find such men. Lord Halifax, who rose to oppose Shaftesbury, and traded verbal blows with him for hours, was not of my uncle's party: if anything, he had been with the opposition. But he did not agree with Exclusion. And as that was the one rock on which my father placed his feet, he had taken Halifax into his counsels, and found in him an able servant. What was more, he had found a counter-weight to Shaftesbury: a man who could fence with the little earl's own sharp weapons. Indeed, to see them facing each other across the chamber was to mark a curious resemblance: Halifax too was spare and sharp-featured. They seemed like fighting-cocks, ugly and lean and deadly. Yet it is often the way at a cock-fight, that the bird with the impetuous attack is the weaker in the end. And so it was with Halifax, who with lawyerlike precision answered Shaftesbury's every charge, while my father warmed his hands and looked calmly on.

The vote was against the Exclusion Bill.

There was great heat. I recall Lord Peterborough, one of my uncle's cronies, actually clapping his hand to his sword-hilt at one moment. If it did not come to blows, I think that was because of my father's still, serene, cool presence. He did not exult at the result: he did not need to. Nor, as he walked out of the chamber, did he look at me.

'Fools,' Shaftesbury hissed, when I saw him at his house that night. 'They caress the noose being made for their necks.'

'You argued eloquently, my lord,' I said dispiritedly.

'Aye – and I shall, still. Tomorrow we shall have one more throw. If they will not exclude York, then let us have the King divorced – aye, let's see them answer this – and get a new queen who can bear children, as soon as may be, and we shall have an heir that way—'

'You said you would not attack the Queen. This—'

'This is a matter of vital importance for the realm,' Shaftesbury rapped out, and gave me a sour look. 'But, of course, that would cut you out – yes? That is why you look so? You must ask yourself, sir, do you care more for your country, or your own pride and ambition?'

'That is exactly the question that is being asked about you, my lord,' said I, and I saw that shaft strike home. Not that that was any satisfaction. With renewed gloom I said, 'No matter. I fear – I fear we cannot win this way.'

Shaftesbury plucked at his lip. His face looked raw and bruised, as if it were truly a fight he had lost. 'It is not the end.'

No, but the end was not long in coming, at least of my hopes from Parliament and the Whigs. Yet the way that end came about made a deep impression on me. I learned from it, even as I lost by it.

The next Parliament, by my father's command, was to meet not at Westminster but at firmly loyal Oxford. Here, he reasoned, there would be no great crowds of citizens clamouring for Exclusion. To Oxford, then, we must repair; and a strange scene was made of the old town, with my father's Court dispersed about the colleges. Nell Gwynn, of all people, was amongst them – how the clerics stared! – and troops of soldiers lined the High Street. There was another army, of sorts – the opposition party, my own supporters, wearing ribbons woven with the words 'No popery, no slavery'. There was a hardness of mutual defiance in the air. Men muttered of the Civil War time returning; and I, though I got cheers enough as I passed down the street to my lodgings with a Whig alderman of the town, could not help but hear jeers too. And for the first time I felt a little fear of what we might be coming to.

Shaftesbury was undaunted. He looked more dreadfully sick than ever, but as if he drew his energy from his health, like capital reserves, he went freshly into the attack. He had abandoned the notion of divorce. He raised a new standard, unequivocal, flagrant. If James could not be excluded then, the earl argued, there was one other remedy: I must be made my father's legitimate son by Act of Parliament. Parchment and sealing wax, then, would unbastardize me.

Gratifying, to be sure: here was the most powerful support Shaftesbury had yet shown me. Alas, once he had come out and stated that he wanted me to inherit the crown, the doubts and divisions began, even among my uncle's enemies. There were those who preferred the claim of Mary and William of Orange, my uncle's heirs; others who murmured that if legitimacy could be conferred by a stroke of the pen, then all the laws of property and inheritance might go to wrack. Everyone could agree that they did not want James on the throne, but when it came to the question, 'Who, then?' the chorus became a babble.

Which, I believe, was just what my father expected.

So while we wrangled, my father watched in his lazy amiable way, and at last invited the Commons, who were awkwardly quartered in the Sheldonian Theatre, to come over and meet with him and the Lords, at the Hall of Christ Church. I suspected nothing. My father seemed merely in good spirits, which I had observed across the Hall with mingled resentment and longing, and my astonishment was as great as any when he withdrew into an anteroom for a few minutes, and then returned to us in full regalia.

Yes, he stood before us, and before the Commons who had just come grumbling and cramming in down the narrow steps that led to the Hall, in the robes of a king, with crown and sceptre – all the trappings of majesty. Whence comes that word 'trappings', which has such a trivializing sound? For it was full majesty, lionlike and magnificently self-confident, that I saw in my father then. And others did too. There were gasps even before he spoke.

'All the world may see to what a point we are come. We are not like to have a good end when the divisions at the beginning are such. My lord Chancellor, this Parliament stands dissolved.'

And so he did it. He marched out of the Hall, to his waiting coach; and presently, on a road discreetly guarded, set out for Windsor, leaving dismay and disarray behind him. For that was his power. He wore it lightly, but he knew how to use it. And though this was the destruction of my hopes from Shaftesbury and his party – and indeed it was their destruction also – I could not help but stand in amaze, and an admiration plucked from my heart against my inclination. For what were bills, and debates, and remonstrances and abhorrences – what were all these but so much dusty finicking, when put beside my father's grand stroke? What else was needed, but the King's touch?

You have heard me talk of plots, and how one all but sickened of the word in those times. We even had the Meal Tub Plot and the Pumpkin Plot – let the names stand witness to their absurdity. But the last one I shall trouble you with is the Rye House Plot – and here, apparently, is something much more serious. Put aside all thoughts of mealtubs and pumpkins. The plot at Rye House had as its end the assassination, not just of my uncle James, but of my father himself.

And I was privy to it.

There! I shock, perhaps. My love has looked at these words, and cries out. Never mind: I am giving you, for the moment, the version of events my enemies would promote. In truth I was never party to any plot against my father's life. Yet the Rye House affair had, curiously, an unexpected result, and that was my father clasping me in his arms again.

I perceive you struggle. I must disentangle it for you.

How came it, in the first place, that the opposition that had gathered such powerful forces, should end up grubbing about in the murk of assassinations? Well, because of that kingly victory of my father's, at Oxford. He lost no time in moving against Shaftesbury, who had defied him once too often. He had him arrested and placed in the Tower on charges of treason.

Whether he thought to make the charges stick I don't know. Perhaps so; there was a most personal bitterness between him and Shaftesbury by then. I stood bail for the little earl. Here my wife protested: this was flouting my father beyond reason, she said; she feared for our estates.

She need not. Such punishments as my father chose to inflict on me were symbolic. My portrait at the University of Cambridge, of which I had been Chancellor before my disgrace, was taken down and thrown on the fire: things like that. Certainly they hurt.

I well knew that Shaftesbury, who was bent double from an ague caught in the draughty Tower, could and did speak slightingly of me. He could not understand my irresolution: why had I still avoided a direct rebellion against my father? No matter. I felt a loyalty to the sickly earl who, so different from my father, had yet given to me what he would not – his belief in me. And I know pretty well what sort of a king Shaftesbury would have sought to make me – a king without prerogative, at the service of Parliament. Well, I had begun to think that not such a bad notion. I carried memories of Holland, where the people remained independent of William, the Stadtholder. Perhaps it was time to have a different sort of king: a different England.

Shaftesbury was acquitted. He was still a hero to the City: no London jury would condemn him. But he was without power now, and there was no sign that my father would call another Parliament. Some whispered that he meant to rule without it altogether, as my uncle had long recommended. And there was no power now to prevent my uncle's triumphant return to court from his Scots banishment. He came, though only after an eventful journey by sea. His ship foundered off Yarmouth. In the wreck he hurried to save his priests and his dogs, and then his duchess. They were fortunate: many people drowned. 'But none of quality,' was his remark. And indeed his henchmen had made sure of that, beating the drowning rabble away from the rescue-boat with swords.

I knew that the matter of my standing bail for Shaftesbury had not warmed my father towards me. How much, I discovered when I let it be known that I was prepared to ask the King's pardon for any offences against him. Not my uncle, mind; and I must have said, at a tavern or bowling-green somewhere, that I would rather die than submit to the Duke of York. There were spies everywhere, of course, and swiftly the remark was passed on to my father. Somehow it pricked him to his severest wrath, and he made a declaration that no servant of the Crown should hold any commerce with me.

Shaftesbury detected the hand of Halifax behind that. He was still smarting from his defeat, of course, but there was no doubt that my lord Halifax was now the great minister of the state, and of all men had my father's ear. And then one Sunday, at the church of St Martin-in-the-Fields where I habitually worshipped, I saw Halifax there.

'My lord,' I said as we came out. Halifax turned his long austere face to me. He always seemed to carry his own climate about him, for in a close room with a banked fire he would still look pinched, crabbed, high-shouldered, lean-chapped, and as it were frost-bit: so he did now, though it was a warm spring day. And this made me suppose him, perhaps, more hostile to me than he was.

'I have been told,' said I, 'that I have your lordship to thank for advising the King to publish this proclamation, forbidding his servants to have aught to do with me. Well, I can assure your lordship there's no need of a proclamation to forbid me keeping your company.'

People about us paused to stare and smirk. But Halifax's grey face bore no expression.

'Very well, Your Grace,' he said. 'Since you choose to treat me in such a fashion, then I am under no obligation to tell you what lately passed in Council.'

I gave a laugh – callow-sounding, I fear. 'I had not supposed you would. I did not think to find a friend in you, my lord, believe me.'

'Certainly, I believe you,' Halifax said, unmoved. 'Be careful of what *you* believe, Your Grace. Look for greater evidences before you pronounce.'

'I need no advice from you, I think,' I said. He was fifty-odd to my thirty-odd; but he made me feel hideously young.

'If you say so,' Halifax said, with a frugal bow, and walked away.

He left me chafing and gnawing, and I remained so for some time. But I decided not to tell Shaftesbury about it.

'You must show yourself.' So Harriet urged me.

My heart gave a ready echo. Aye, I would. At Oxford my father had played his part with flourishing conviction: if I would be like him, I should do no less. So I set out upon another progress.

Cheshire, Shropshire, Staffordshire, Lancashire – these places were, as the Court spies had it, very rotten and stuffed with Whigs. I was not lacking in invitations from great lords who were friends to my cause, nor were the people backward in coming out upon the streets, lighting bonfires and pledging toasts, and making demonstrations in support of me. But there was, I knew, a different feeling abroad than when I had travelled in the West. As the countryside was of a bleaker, stonier aspect, so there was something bullish in the welcome afforded me. There was a raw and desperate edge in some of the shouts of acclamation: some-times, in the larger towns, scuffles would break out in the streets, for the partisans of my uncle had begun to stir themselves. And increasingly there were spies of the Court about, ready to post letters to London, eager to place the worst construction on all I did.

It was no part of my design to cause disorders – and yes, I confess this was lamentably innocent of me, with the kingdom so bitterly divided as it was. But I did no rabble-rousing, as the courtiers would call it. I did not speechify, or provoke my opponents, or make declarations. I rode in horse-matches, I played with children, I ran foot-races with sporting gentlemen. I thought, indeed, of my father's coming to England on his restoration, and how he had calmed a still anxious country with his geniality, his instinct (had he lost it?) for harmony. That was what I sought. Strange paradox, perhaps, that as I defied my father, I strove to prove myself his true son.

And yes, I was staking my claim to the crown of this land, of which every joyful shout proclaimed me the chosen prince. The memory of my mother was much with me, all through my journeying. I felt she almost rode beside me. I felt she watched when, upon a high road towards the port of Liverpool, destiny presented its final warrant, and I put my signature to it.

I remember a straggle of moss-grown cottages, and a dried-up pond, and a couple of dogs barking; and a little knot of people, from which a woman detached herself, timidly it seemed, and drew near to me. In her arms she held – quite easily, for he was thin enough – a boy of three or thereabouts, with the largest, most compelling eyes I ever saw in my life: eyes that in their blue brilliance made a sad contrast with his poor scarred face. And still timidly, but with a sort of gathered determin-ation, the woman held the boy up to me.

He had the king's evil, so she murmured to me, and then fell silent. The two of them gazing up at me quietly, hardly even expectantly – simply waiting.

And when I reached out and laid my hand upon the boy's face, and spoke the words 'God bless you', it was not only the presence of my mother I felt, inspiriting the curious void that seemed to surround me, but the presence of the past itself – my past. I reached, not just across a few feet of space, but across time. Touching that ragged boy for the evil, I touched another: myself. And thus the old bargain with destiny was sealed.

I know that reports of the tumults attending my progress reached my father in London. Whether he also heard of my making this, the ultimate gesture of kingship, I do not know. But altogether I was not at all surprised when, as I made my return through Stafford, a serjeant-at-arms came with a warrant from the King to arrest me.

I did not protest. My thoughts ran still on my mother. I remembered Brussels, where she had managed to cause a riot in the streets. Well, truly, I thought, I was my mother's son as well as my father's, and I could not forbear laughing. It was touching for the evil that had left me with this feeling of lightness, perhaps; that, and a feeling that destiny was now a fast coach, in which I had not the reins, and must travel where it took me.

'This is troubling, Your Grace. I have had no rest in thinking of it,' said Shaftesbury.

He looked dreadfully gaunt, as if he had no rest for a year.

'I'm sorry for it, my lord. There's no need, I think. I doubt I am in any real danger.'

My friends in the City had secured me a writ of habeas corpus: the serjeant-at-arms had installed me civilly at his own house in the Strand, prior to my going before the Privy Council to explain myself, and here Shaftesbury visited me.

Friendly in him – though his look was not friendly.

'You misunderstand me. What troubles me is this.' He made an irritable gesture where I sat, like a father with a lazy hind of a son. 'This passivity. You disappoint me, sir.'

'Because I do not have at the serjeant with my sword? That would be a poor return for his courtesy.'

'The flippancy is worthy of your father. And I do not mean a compliment. Great God, sir, do you not see what an opportunity this was? And how many must you be presented with, before you recognize them, and seize the day? Your being taken into custody like this is monstrous – a monstrous affront to the people who earnestly place their hopes of a Protestant succession in you . . .'

His voice had risen to his oratorical pitch: I think sometimes he was hardly aware of doing it. 'You do not really think it monstrous,' I said. 'Isn't this party talk? What could I truly have done, but submit?'

'Not submit. Then the country would rise and resist with you.'

'Some would. Many would not. It would be folly, and bloody folly. And besides, who is such an insurrection against? The King: my father. Not my uncle, who would be King? 'Tis an essential distinction.'

'York is grown so great now, and takes so much of the government in his hands, that it is a distinction without a difference.'

'Nevertheless, the distinction is essential to me, my lord. And now, alas, you look at me as if you fear you have backed the wrong horse.'

Sighing, nearly smiling, Shaftesbury shook his head. 'There are no other horses,' he said.

They let me go. The Secretary of State interrogated me, and I went before a justice of the King's Bench, and I denied that I had breached the King's peace, or meant to. I was forced, like Shaftesbury, to put up sureties for my bail – twenty thousand pounds: I managed half, and my friends and supporters made up the rest. A mixture of severity and leniency: I was sure my father was behind one of the two. I could not tell which, for from him came only a curt message, suggesting that I return myself to the country for a time. So I betook myself to Moor Park, for I had a feeling I should be with my little boys, James and Henry, for a time of quietness, to play at country sports and hear their lessons.

'Oh – and to be with your wife, of course!' Harriet said, in London the day before I departed; and she turned furiously from me. Though she did not move away.

'Aye, she will be there. And so will the house-steward, and the grooms, and the buttery-maid – and I am as likely to love any of them as her. Anna and I are long gone past that – as you well know, my love.'

'I know nothing!' she cried, whipping round, and kissed me passionately, weeping. She was – is – of a most jealous temper. Perhaps you will understand when I say I loved her the more for it.

I fancy Anna had had a secret talk with my father, for at Moor Park she talked much to me of reconciliation with him.

'He is willing to forgive, if you are willing to submit.' She made it sound like a sum in arithmetic.

'That means I must confess myself a villain, in sort, and I am not.'

'He does love you still, you know.' Anna spoke as if carefully stepping around her own distaste. 'I have – people ·have heard him say that he hungers for his Jemmy.'

My eyes misted at that, but not to blindness. 'Then let him show it,' I said.

Anna looked me full in the face, which was mighty rare now. 'I am at a loss,' she said, in a tone of pure surprised confession.

At a loss: such was the mood, I think, that led to the Rye House Plot.

I did share it. Back in London that summer, entirely shut out from the court and with nothing to occupy me, seeing all my late places and honours heaped on those who bent to the King's will, my own thoughts turned dark and vengeful. It seemed perverse, at the very least, that my father who had never acted upon principle should now cleave to this one principle – the succession of his brother to the crown, and it was a wrong one.

And this we debated, Shaftesbury and the Whig lords and such others as remained of the opposition, long and wearily, in smoky rooms over wine, with all the nonsense of secret knocks and passwords. Some liked that, of course. Inevitably, as Parliament's opposition failed and melted, other men came to the fore – men who plotted for a living: old republicans from Cromwell's time; spies, informers, double-agents; men who loved the taste of conspiracy as others love fine brandy.

Shaftesbury's mind still ran on insurrection.

'Ten thousand brisk boys can secure London.' He had begun to repeat it like a charm. 'Ten thousand brisk boys.'

'And then what?' I said.

'Why, we prevail upon the King to redress our grievances, remove the counsellors who prick him to absolute and tyrannical policies, and for ever banish the Duke of York,' someone piped up excitedly, as if they were addressing a crowd.

I said: 'Where are these ten thousand? I do not see them.' The tobacco-smoke stung my eyes.

'They are there. They only wonder that their natural leader does not act,' Shaftesbury said. 'That he seems to care more tenderly for the King than for their liberties.'

'You reproach me with weakness.'

'I believe – that you think your father a better man than he is.' Shaftesbury drew a sketch with his finger in the spilled wine on the table top: it looked like a hangman's noose.

'Is that not as much to say I am human?'

Through his teeth Shaftesbury said, 'No one talks of harm to the King. We are not—'

'Some do.' That was the cadaverous Scot, Ferguson, who was ever present at these conferences.

'Fanatics,' Shaftesbury said dismissively.

'To be sure. But we must have a care against misunderstanding. Now suppose an attempt were made to secure the King's person—'

'How's that?' I said sharply.

'Detain him,' Ferguson said, squinting at me through the smoke like a genie. 'Only detain him, while we present our remonstrances. In fine, we must separate him from the Duke of York. The duke is ever at his side nowadays. Naught can be done with him about. Secure the King, then give the signal for the City to rise. Then His Majesty will see our strength, and hear our grievances, and the reform the country longs for will be effected. Putting yourself at our head, Your Grace, will reassure everyone, for His Majesty's own son stands guarantor of his safety. 'Tis no rebellion when the true prince leads it: 'tis only a setting to rights.'

I felt a little dazed and dizzy: the wine, the smoke, and the piping drone of Ferguson's voice. 'But you also said – you spoke of some wishing harm to the King—'

'Wilder spirits, aye, who say there is no ridding the realm of James without his death. And the brothers being so closely conjoined now, some say that both must fall, before—'

'Never,' I cried, jumping up, 'never. You know I will never suffer that.'

'Of course.' Ferguson stroked his hollow cheek. 'There are some who follow us on that condition, mind.'

'Then tell them we want none of them.' I turned to Shaftesbury. 'You do not approve this, my lord?'

'This talk of assassination? No. The promptness and fire I see in you now – yes, I approve that. If only you would show it in action!'

Well, round and round went the talk. I withdrew myself from it, in a brooding temper. And when at last the circle broke up, I found myself saying to Shaftesbury, at the door: 'When did you begin to be disappointed in me?'

He seemed on the verge of saying many things. But instead his last words, delivered with a sort of arid resignation, were: 'I did not say I was.' And then he went limping into the night.

His last words, to me. Soon after that the news came that a fresh warrant was being made out for his arrest. He must have known that his luck was running out. Also, perhaps, that he did not have the bodily strength for another bout with the Crown. Accompanied by Ferguson, he slipped out of England in the disguise of a Presbyterian minister. He went by ship from Harwich, through such stormy seas as would have turned the healthiest man sick, and arrived at Amsterdam more dead than alive. It took only a couple of months of exile, and of unrelenting pain, to complete the work. In the bitter January of '83, I heard that the Earl of Shaftesbury had died in Holland, attended by a single servant.

There were many who said that England was rid of a curse. But I knew Shaftesbury would not have approved the Rye House Plot that came after. Indeed, I think it was the loss of his commanding presence that turned the opposition into such desperate and shadowy courses. I accept my share of blame. I was still such a combustible brew of resentment, hurt, simplicity and vanity that I took what I wanted from those murky discussions – a vague project of my father's being secured by loyal me, my uncle got out of the way, and King and People at last coming together in a great reconciliation. The favourite notion was to stop the royal coach on its return from Newmarket, and order a general rising. My father's coach, of course, would be surrounded by armed guards; and having been a soldier, I could only see the folly in such a plan, and said so. But even to talk of it was, in some sort, to consent to it. And down the tangled chain of agents and conspirators, the word must have passed that the Duke of Monmouth approved even the wildest schemes.

And such was the wild scheme – the plot of Rye House – that at last saw an end to those candlelit conferences, the muttering and bickering and back-stabbing: and saw, also, my arrest for High Treason against the Crown.

Rye House was an old maltster's dwelling that stood at a lonely and narrow spot on the road from Newmarket to London. It belonged to an old republican of Cromwell's time, and from this house, which had a strong tower commanding a view of the road, the conspirators were to issue when the royal coach came along, overturning a cart to cause an obstruction, and then pitching in with guns. The end was to be the shooting of my uncle and my father.

And then what? I know not whether they even had a firm plan for afterwards. To proclaim me King? They surely knew how I felt about any threat to my father's life. If the plot had succeeded, I see the most likely result as their putting a pistol to my head also, and declaring a republic.

Of course it did not succeed. There was a great fire at Newmarket, as a result of which my father came back to London earlier than the conspirators expected. So it was put off – and in the meanwhile, one of the conspirators turned his coat, and betrayed the plot to the authorities. That suggests to me that he was perhaps a double agent all along. But no matter: once word was out, others of that murky conspiracy tumbled over themselves to name names. The greater the names, of course, the better.

Of those detected, some fled abroad. Some of the great Whig lords – Russell, Grey, Essex – were pounced on as they dined. Russell sent me a note, warning me that my name was sure to come up, even though I was no party to the Rye House scheme. I pondered whether I should give myself up, but he said no.

I hardly knew what to do. I was in great anguish to think my father supposed me a party to his assassination, for there was a bill against me for treason, and a reward of five hundred pounds for my apprehension. I seemed to move in the slow, treacly suspension of nightmares, waiting for the jolt of waking. And yet – no one came for me.

Even now I hardly dared suppose that I did have a friend at court. All I could imagine was my uncle, with his stony stare, wagging his finger in my father's face, and intoning 'I told you, Brother, I told you, Brother . . .' Yet still no one came. And so I betook myself to love, and to wait.

I went with Harriet to Toddington. My love was ardent to shelter and protect me. It brought out all her romantic courage. I had to dissuade her from shouldering a musket, and mounting guard at the manor gate. Instead, we must settle to enjoy what we could of our being together. Very beautiful it was, in a declining, wistful, autumnal fashion: the taste of those days is of crisp apples from the Toddington orchards, turned to faerie plantations by the spangle of spider-webs and dew in the mellow mornings; the colour is old gold, shining in the massy leaf of beech and oak, and in my love's hair as we walked the sun-dappled bridle paths between the great trees. In the bole of one of those oaks I carved our initials and my love watched me with a rapt, serious attention, and when I had done, gave a great sigh and closed her eyes a moment.

'I am imagining,' she said, 'that you have carved upon my heart. I feel it there: I feel it well.'

'I would touch your heart,' I said, moved, but troubled. 'Not score it, I hope.'

'No,' she said in her decided way. 'I want it scored deep. Then you will know – you must know, Jemmy – that whatever happens, I do not change.' She seized my hands, and gripped them till the blood stood still. 'Whatever happens.'

And at last, something happened. A letter came from London – from none other than Halifax – telling me my hiding-place was known, and summoning me to the court. My chief emotion – as when some perplexing feeling of indisposition resolves itself into an identifiable malady – was one of relief.

SEVEN

Such is the contrariness of fortune, that I had a house new-built in London at this time, at Soho Square, which had been begun before my disgrace. So, here I secretly repaired, and walked about in the smell of fresh paint, and looked with a turbulent mixture of feelings at my coat of arms, the varnish still sticky, mounted above the mantel. I had ordered that the bar-sinister, the mark of bastardy, be omitted. Thus do we seek to change the world, when we cannot change ourselves.

At eleven that night, a carriage rattled into my empty echoing courtyard. My manservant went out with a lantern. I stayed gazing into the empty fireplace – there was no wood or coal laid in – until he returned with my visitor, and then I jumped up in surprise.

'My lord Halifax . . . I don't know what to say.'

'That, Your Grace,' he said crisply, 'is one of the things we must remedy.'

I talked long with Halifax, in that chill bare parlour. And yes, the chillness and bareness suited him, in a way. But in truth I had misjudged him.

'You know that Shaftesbury's body was brought back to be buried at Wimborne? 'Twas fitting, I think. I marvel that he kept going for so long.'

'He was a courageous man,' I said.

'My lord Shaftesbury and I agreed on some things,' Halifax said. 'Many things, once.'

'Aye – you were once of a mind to oppose my uncle, I recall,' I said. 'But then you turned . . .'

'Turned my coat, you were about to say.' Thin-lipped, composed,

Halifax held up his hand. 'Shaftesbury's policy was mischief, and must have led to destruction and chaos. Those I abhor. I abhor all extremes. The anarchy of a commonwealth; the tyranny of an absolute monarchy. That is where I stand. I say this, sir, because you still look at me as if I were your enemy.'

'Well, are you not? I think of my friends and supporters – hounded, clapped up, tried for treason. Are you not the State's right hand in this?'

'This . . .' Halifax's long forefinger hovered, lawyerlike. 'This is an ending. See it that way, Your Grace. At the time of the Popish Plot, did you believe all of it? Truly?'

'No.'

'Just so. No more did I. But there were real evils that came to light amidst the nonsense, and we took heed, for the sake of that. So it is with this Rye House matter. There are, without doubt, most violent and disaffected men who would like nothing better than the overthrow and death of the King. This fact enables him to finish that victory begun with the defeat of Exclusion. Some old scores may be settled along the way: that is the nature of high affairs. You must accept that, sir. An ending, but also a beginning. I may say that this wild business has hindered those who are reasonably troubled about the future behaviour of the Duke of York, as regards the throne. I mean sober responsible men: the fanatic rogues have silenced their debate. And that, you must see, rather helps the duke's case than otherwise. But if we may close this whole tumultuous account, rational councils may prevail again.'

His long grey face gave away so little that for a moment I was unsure what I was hearing. 'You mean – you mean that you too mistrust—'

'Tut – tut – no more of that, if you please. You should be aware, Your Grace, that sometimes only a *word* is needed. Not a shout.' He allowed himself a wintry smile.

I sat back, digesting this. 'My lord . . . do you believe I was a party to this plot?'

'I would not be sitting here now if I did. But I believe you entangled yourself with foolish men. You cannot touch pitch, sir, without being blackened. And you must work hard now to make yourself clean. But it is what His Majesty believes that is important. And he does not believe you knew of it: not at all.' Awkwardly he added, 'His Majesty loves his son yet, sir. Extravagantly, I would say.'

I shaded my face. Ridiculously, I wanted to weep.

'Hum! 'Tis a curious matter,' Halifax went on, studying his finger-nails. 'The King is reputed for his *amours* – but as for a hold upon his heart, there is no woman who has achieved it, I believe; no one, indeed, but yourself. I sometimes think that if he loved you less, you and he would both have lived easier . . . But to the point, sir. The King believes you innocent. Yet for certain weighty reasons, he must act as if he believed your guilt. Do you understand me?'

I tried, under Halifax's piercing eye, to rein in my ever-impetuous feelings. 'I . . . I am not sure . . .'

'Certain parties will insist upon you making confession and showing penitence. There will be no peace else. This His Majesty knows. I wish you to know it, sir, and act accordingly.'

Certain parties. My uncle, of course – but Halifax's raised eyebrow bid me not say it.

'I'm obliged to you for speaking to me in this way, sir,' I said, trying to imitate his own composure. 'But I must be frank about my great fear – and that is that I shall be called upon to betray my friends.'

I thought he winced for a moment, but his tone was brisk. 'Come, put aside such thoughts. The task, sir, first the task. You must write the King a letter, a full, candid letter. I shall call here tomorrow, and collect it, and carry it to the King himself.'

I could not quite keep down the old mutiny. 'Must I make the first approach?'

'Your father is expecting the letter, sir.' Halifax said. 'Indeed, I may say, at the risk of violating discretion, that he awaits it – eagerly.'

I wrote the letter that night. I wrote with feverish speed, my heart brimming, my hand trembling. I was filled with a pure, uncomplicated excitement at the thought of seeing my father again, just as when I was a boy in Paris with my grandmother. My love will forgive me if I say that I had never – in spite of anger, bitterness, even hate – felt quite whole since our estrangement.

Halifax returned on the morrow as he had promised. He read the letter over thoroughly, with some murmurs – for he was a learned man, and eloquent with his pen as his tongue. And my letter had more passion than craft about it. 'I wish I may die this moment I am writing if it ever entered into my head, or I ever said the least thing to anybody that could make them think I could wish such a thing,' I had written, of the assassination plot. There was much more of it, all very clumsy. But Halifax at last pronounced himself satisfied, and took the letter away, saying only: 'We shall see.'

I waited. I loitered about my grand empty house, looking out at the windows for the return of that dry old courtier as impatiently as a man trysting with a lover.

'Very well,' Halifax said when at last he came again. He nodded judiciously, motioning me to sit down. 'Very well so far. The King looks favourably upon your submission. As favourably as he *may* at the court. You understand, of course. Oh, and the Queen speaks for you – that is another advantage.'

I blessed her silently.

'What is needed, Your Grace, is another letter. The initial approach has been made: now a fuller explanation is required. I have taken the liberty of making a few notes . . .'

A fuller explanation. In sum, I had not said enough in apology to my uncle; I had insufficiently grovelled to the man I loathed. Halifax had some suggestions ready-phrased.

'This goes hard with me, sir,' I said to him, as he stood beside me at the writing desk.

'No doubt. But I cannot overstate the importance, sir, of *seeming*. You must seem to submit yourself entirely to the Duke of York's interest.' He paused, and then said distinctly, 'You are not alone in that deception, sir, believe me.'

Well, that gave me heart. I think the second letter had as much of Lord Halifax in it as me. But it did its work. Halifax came with a note from my father, ordering me to render myself up to him tomorrow.

'Play your part,' Halifax urged me. 'Try to avoid questions where you can. Remember that His Majesty must play a part too, to some degree, to please certain parties. And remember, if there are words that *seem* harsh – yes? – bear them. 'Tis to your advantage, I assure you.'

So, to Whitehall: the rambling old palace unchanged, but impressing me as strangely and forcibly as when I had first come here as a boy. I went to the office of the Secretary of State, formally to surrender myself, then to the Presence Chamber, where my father waited.

He looked older – of course; grander, with the deep lines of his face looking carved and forbidding; also melancholy. All I wanted to do was throw my arms about him – such the unthinking, blank impulse of my heart. And I believe I saw his hands twitch, as if he would do the same. But I heard a little cough from Halifax, and recollected myself, and went down on my knees before my father's chair.

'My son.' For a moment, it seemed, my father could not go on, but the disguise of gravity covered it. 'Do you know how displeased I am with you? Do you, Jemmy?'

I met his sad, pouched, yet deeply twinkling eyes, and after a moment lowered mine, and bowed my head again. 'I do, sir. And I crave your pardon.'

'For what, Jemmy? We must hear it.'

'For my becoming embroiled in the late conspiracies, sir.'

'Embroiled. A quaint word. It suggests that you were pulled down, or dragged – something quite against your will.' His voice thickened to a growl. 'I thought you had come to make confession, Jemmy.'

'So I do, Father. I confess to being party to plots subversive of the throne – plots ill-conceived and destructive to the peace of the realm. And I heartily beg your forgiveness.'

'That forgiveness,' he said, 'is not mine alone to grant.'

A door opened, and my uncle came in.

You may be sure he liked very much to see me on my knees. Indeed, I think I never knew him so happy. He was long past being able to smile, but his nostrils flared and his colour rose, which in him was the equivalent of another man's greatest mirth. I got through it, though, somehow. I was mindful not only of Halifax, but of something emanating from my father himself, like a hum or note on the edge of hearing, urging me to do it. An ending, remember: remember, a beginning.

'I confess my guilt, Uncle, and I humbly ask your forgiveness.'

My father's eyes flicked sharply to his brother.

'This is very well,' James said. 'And now the rest of it.'

I looked at my father – which my uncle did not like.

'Names, sir, names,' my uncle snapped, as if the King were not there. 'Let us have names, and dates, and times. 'Tis mere trifling without.'

'I think there can be none you do not know,' I said. 'They are fled or taken in the main, I hear—'

'Who are?'

'The lords with whom I had commerce – the lords accused of the conspiracy?'

'Which conspiracy?' James said, pacing, beating his own leg. He was in his element. Indeed, he was only at ease in two places: the saddle, and the cell of interrogation.

'A conspiracy of insurrection,' I said dully.

'At which you would place yourself the head?'

'I . . . I was the one men would follow. But I sought more moderate courses—'

'You call murder moderation?' James said.

Halifax coughed again: he must have detected the rage rising in me. I swallowed. 'Of the Rye House matter, I am entirely innocent. I was not a party to that scheme. If I had known of it, I would have done all in my power to prevent it.' I turned in appeal to my father. 'There is no folly of which I have not been guilty; but of these violent malicious courses, against you, I am guiltless. It would make a mock of my confession to say otherwise.'

'Against me?' my father said pointedly.

'And His Grace of York likewise.' Well, it was the truth. Yes, I had wished my uncle dead many a time: but if we are to be judged on that alone, who amongst us is not a murderer?

My uncle said in his dogged way, 'Those who supported you: I return to this question.'

'You will know them, I am sure,' I said. 'I make no secret of who they are – but I would not stand witness against them: that's different.'

'Aha!' my uncle cried.

'I submit myself to your mercy,' I said, looking up at my father. 'But that is not the same as agreeing to condemn others.'

'Now we come to it,' my uncle said, shaking his shoulders and striding about. 'Now, you see, we come to it—'

'James – enough.' My father's tone was sharp. He drew a deep breath, then took my hand, and lifted me up. Just as he had lifted me, from the shoeless boy without name or future. 'I am satisfied, Jemmy. This is as it should be. Mr Secretary, I shall need your services presently. For now . . . Well, till tomorrow. I am still very displeased, Jemmy. There is hard talk ahead of us.' But he squeezed my hand as he let it go.

'Yes, sir. But I – do ask a boon from you.'

He frowned. 'Do you now?'

'Only this. Before I go, may I pay my respects to the Queen?'

Had we been alone, I think my father would have smiled.

'Very well.'

I bowed my way out. I had just reached the anteroom when I heard my uncle's remorseless voice saying: 'Brother – a word, if you please.'

'You only come to drink my tea when you are in trouble, Jemmy,' Queen Catharine said, passing me a cup.

'Because it always puts me in a better frame of mind, Your Majesty.'

'Then I think you should drink much more of it.' She smiled sadly. 'No, I shall not read you a lecture, Jemmy. I am only concerned for you.'

My hand shook, and I had to lay the tea-cup down. 'I remember once before,' I said, 'sitting with you like this – and I wept of a sudden. And now I almost want to weep again. But I am not unhappy – not that. Just – seeing him again . . .'

'I know,' the Queen said gently. 'You may be sure he feels the same.'

The hard talk came the next day. Though it was a cold morning, my father insisted we go for a walk down by the lake – perhaps to be away from my uncle.

'We have had to be severe,' my father said. 'Even vengeful. You must understand this.'

'We?'

'Ah, don't touch on that, Jemmy – stop there. I want an end to this feud. Would you know why? Because I grow old—'

'Never! I can still barely keep pace with you.'

'Very well, I feel old,' he said with a reluctant smile. 'I wish to be easy: I wish an end to disputation. I wish everyone were wise. Ha! That at least is one wish I shall not get . . . I have ordered your full pardon, Jemmy.'

'I thank you, Father. From the bottom of my heart, I—'

'Wait before you say that. For if I am not to be called seven kinds of fool, ass, gull and weakling, it must be generally known that you have confessed and repented.'

'Why, so I have. And more than—'

'Hush. I know. But in writing, my son, in writing. Come, 'tis no great matter, surely – after those eloquent letters you wrote me? They were quite a wonder – especially the second, where your style seemed to change . . .'

'Those were – not entirely my own words.'

He chuckled and patted my arm. 'I liked the first one best. I heard . . . well, I heard your voice. And that was like stepping into the past . . . Well, no more of that: let us think of the future. Now, it's a pity you missed the wedding of the Princess Anne. You must meet her new husband soon, and – well, tell me what you think.'

'Prince George of Denmark. I confess I have heard nothing of him beyond the name.'

'That's apt enough. For myself, I've tried him drunk and I've tried him sober, and there's nothing in him. But there, 'tis a decent pretty match. I've lodged them in the Cockpit: you shall be neighbours when you come back to Court.'

'When I come back . . . !' My heart leaped.

'There are conditions, Jemmy. Your confession must be made public.'

'But then – such a confession may be used by the law against my friends. I know the way of these things. I will be seen to betray them—'

'Oh, no, no. Trust me, Jemmy, we will find another way.'

I nearly said again: 'We?' But I held my peace.

So began my last time with my father – a time that, like those autumnal days at Toddington, had a rich gold harmony about it. In all our old easy ways, I was at his side. Again, I saw the eyes of the Court conning us and conjuring conclusions. The one who watched most, of course, was my uncle, though he kept at a distance from me. But I noticed he would always hasten to my father when we had been together for any length of time, as if to check that he had caught no contagion from my poisonous presence.

And it was Lord Halifax, who had done so much for me, who brought me the news that laid the killing frost upon that sweet Indian summer.

My confession was to be printed in the official *Gazette*.

He must be mistaken: so I said at first, with airy confidence. But Halifax shook his head. He did not make mistakes.

'My father said this would not happen,' I cried. 'I told him my fears, and he said it would not be needed—'

'There is no help for it, Your Grace. I fear it is decided. I do not think it is entirely your father's wish, but – consider, sir – consider . . . !'

Thus he called after me: I was already on my way to my uncle's chambers.

'You seek to destroy me, Uncle.'

The bang of the door behind me still resounded. His lurcher dog, startled, was barking frantically. James bent down and patted its flanks.

'Hush, now. Hush.' He straightened. 'You will address me, sir, properly, as Your Grace. I acknowledge no kinship. Now what have you to say to me?'

'That you seek to destroy me, and I know it.'

'I might with more justice say those words.' He spoke so loftily, that his very voice seemed to come from a great height: I could swear there was an echo to it.

'Well, we both know, then, where we stand.'

'You know, Jemmy' – and now the echo had a ghostly softness, as from a tomb – 'there can only be one winner here.'

I clenched my fists. The dog growled at me, sensing very well, perhaps, what was in my mind. 'I know that now,' I said.

I barged out, and almost collided with my father coming in. His face was grim.

'Jemmy, what is this I hear? You are going to deny your confession after all?'

'I made my confession to you. I did not agree to any publication of it. That was the one condition I made—'

'But you are not in any position to make *conditions*,' my father said. 'Now are you? Think a moment, sir.'

'It is thinking on it that has decided me. If this is printed, it will make me appear a betrayer. It will look as if I sold my friends for a pardon. It will be used – no, no, Father, I will not let it stand.' I gestured savagely at my uncle's chambers, where the lurcher was still barking furiously. 'You may let him dictate to you, but I will not suffer it.'

'I will say this once, Jemmy.' A cold, profound anger was on my father now. 'You will submit. You will see your written confession made public, and then you will hold your tongue. I *will* have peace.' He walked past me. 'With you or without you.'

★ ★ ★

503

I feel sorry for my lord Halifax. When he had won over the House of Lords with ten hours of intricate debate, he must have had no harder task than he found in trying to win me round accepting the *Gazette*.

'Plot. Do you balk at that word, Your Grace? But people have heard it so often, they scarcely pay any heed to it any more. And it is besides a general word – plot. Why, it may signify as much or as little as a man pleases.'

'Aye, that I do not deny – you are in the right of it, my lord, I know. But it is the way I am being forced to this—'

'These are hard terms, I concur. But they *are* the terms, and it is your plain duty to abide by them. Now, have you pen and ink there, Your Grace? Very good. Let us consider how we may phrase it . . .'

So, led by the indefatigable Halifax, I put my name at last to a document making confession of my sins. The subtle contriving of the phrases was Halifax's; my father, presented with the letter in his bedchamber, studied it and made corrections in how own hand; and with my signature at the foot of it, there the matter might have rested.

And then the doubts began. No more than seeds at first: little specks of suspicion that I had acted a coward's part, that I had been overper-suaded by cleverer men than I – above all, that I had played into my uncle's hands. Then two events watered the seeds, and forced them to a bitter flowering.

First, I received a letter from one of my supporters who had gone to exile in Holland. He assured me of his continued loyalty – and congratulated me that I had done no betrayal.

And then, I went to pay my call upon the Princess Anne and her new husband at the Cockpit. The servant who admitted me was a very young fellow, who looked unsure of himself, and instead of announcing me, left me in the antechamber while he went in search of the steward. Probably he was troubled about what to do, because my uncle James was there, visiting his daughter and son-in-law. But I did not know that – until a familiar toneless voice caught my ear, and I stole forward to the connecting door.

'. . . Well, daughter, you are too indulgent. I maintain that it is a great pity – a great shame, indeed.' It was James, holding forth. 'I much regret my brother's folly in allowing him back, even if I am not wholly surprised. But there – 'tis not all bad. Indeed, I am pretty sanguine, for Monmouth has made such a confession as can be used tae hang his cronies – and who will love him after that?'

If the servant came back, he must have been very surprised to find the anteroom empty. For I was already on my way to my father.

Even in growing older, which makes most men conservative, my father was ever the innovator. There was a new design of chair called a sleeping-chair, with a high back that could be let down at an angle. He had one set up in his closet, covered in his favourite red velvet: typically, too, I found him neatly peeling away the upholstery to examine the way the mechanism worked.

And yet he does not know how I work, I thought: he cannot.

'Father, I must ask you for that document back.'

He did not look up for a minute. 'Ah. Being Jemmy, I suppose you must. D'you know you are more changeable than any woman ever born? How long will it take to persuade you again? Can you give me an estimate? Only I have been receiving the envoy from Spain, you know – an unconscionably wordy man, round and round – and I am quite fatigued with talk.' He straightened, wiping his hands on a handkerchief. 'So is there a short cut to your better self? The sensible Jemmy. The one who knows when he is well off.' He seemed playful, but that was always deceptive.

'I must have the document back. I cannot subscribe to that confession.'

Sighing, he said: 'What do you care for these men? They only sought their own advancement.'

'It is' – I had a grim presentiment as I chose the word – 'a matter of honour.'

'Oh. Oh, I see. So, you allow yourself to hobnob with rogues and assassins, and you parade yourself to the people as a prince, and generally act the fool or knave or both – and now you turn all martyrish virtue.' His laugh was hard. 'Come, no more of it. You are not posturing at the Whig club now. We are friends again, Jemmy; we should be open. Away with the cant, please.'

'Father, I could not live with myself—'

'Oh, you'd be surprised. Better men that you have had to sue for peace on hard terms, Jemmy, and see their comrades go hang. 'Tis a fact of great affairs.'

'Not for me. I can't think like that.' I hesitated. 'We are different, Father.'

He sat in the chair, inclining it only slightly. He looked sardonic and inquisitorial, also detached, the King in the theatre-box. But again, that could be deceptive.

'You think yourself the exception to the general run of men, is that so? Well, come, tell me why.'

After a moment I said: 'I do think myself exceptional.'

'Ah.' His hand made an undulant motion: paying out rope.

'Yes, I do, and you have made me think so.'

My father groaned. 'You have the black box in your mind again. Jemmy, it is others who have made you think so – flatterers and toadies, turning your head—'

'No. No, Father, you won't slip by me that way, not this time. I want – I ask you to be honest with me. Do you not remember my wedding ball at Windsor – when I danced with the Queen, and you came up and kissed me, and in front of the whole company bade me put on my hat? And everyone marvelled. Everyone asked why you should do that, if you did not mean to claim me as your royal son. It was you who told me the Court was a page full of meaning. What was I to read there – and in a hundred other places – but this text? Yes, I say I am exceptional. You would not have raised me so high otherwise. My mother would not have spoken as she did, before she died, if it were not so.'

My father yawned discreetly. 'I have treated you well, certainly. And you have rewarded me by bad behaviour. So you must make your penance. This, Jemmy, this you try to slip by *me* – but I will not be put aside by such talk. The matter is the confession. Which I insist upon.'

'If I were Prince of Wales, you would not treat me so. Is this not correct?'

My father, half-smiling, made a gesture of appeal to the faces of his clocks. 'Would you have behaved so, if you were the true prince?'

'I would not have been forced to, for I would have had my rights.'

'And so we go on,' my father said laughing wearily. 'Try this. Don't you think I would sign that letter, if it were me?'

'No. Because I think better of you than that.'

'A pretty piece of flattery, and it won't work.'

'Not really. I simply mean I will not do something that you would be ashamed to do.'

That seemed to anger him, all at once. He flushed. 'Let the damned letter stand, Jemmy. Stop being such a blockhead. I order you to.'

'No, you want me to. You want me to betray my friends. Isn't that so? I must be clear on this.'

'Blockhead and prig.' He put an absently gentle hand down to one of his spaniels that came sniffing to the chair, but his eyes were elsewhere, and hard. 'You are not strutting upon any public stage now, Jemmy. What need these heroics? I know you have a lady-love. Is this for her? Never fear, she will not turn cold because you have acted with prudence. No woman wants to see a man make a fool of himself, trust me. Confess, have done. I'm tired of it.'

I still don't know what made me say it. Perhaps there are some things that are going to be said, even if they lie dormant for years. 'Minette,' I said. 'Minette would not have wanted me to sign.'

My father's eyelids drooped: a sudden ageing. 'This is poor in you. Dear God.' His tongue grew thick with disgust. 'I can forgive much. But if you make free with my sister's name, you trespass upon . . .' He jerked up out of the chair. 'Have done, sir. I warn you. You would do well—'

'She loved me,' I persisted. 'She was not blind to my faults, God knows, and I hardly think I was worthy of that love. Indeed, I think none of us was.' I saw him blink at that. 'But she cared for me. And she would not have seem me treated this way.'

Now I had galled him – how much, I knew only when his voice rose to a roar I had never heard. 'You prate to me of Minette – you, of all men! When, by your vain folly, you played such an ill part in her end! How dare you, boy, how dare you do it?'

Stunned, I said: 'You still believe that? But you can't . . . At the time, your grief . . . But to blame me for her death—'

'I do not talk of that time.' He paced away, shoulders hunched. 'I do not ever speak of it.'

'Well. It would explain a good deal. Why you have lifted me up only to knock me down again. Why you play this game . . . Is it because of Minette, Father? Do I suffer because she loved me?'

'Again you prattle of this love. You know nothing. Minette – my sister was quite beyond you, Jemmy, in all ways. If you must spout your vain fancies, leave her name out of them—'

'Beyond me? Or beyond you?' I thought of Dover Castle, and what Queen Catharine had said there. 'Wasn't that it, Father, in truth? Did you look at me and Minette, and see there your own longings?' I hesitated – though I did not, really. 'Your desires? When Philippe threw his jealous fit because of me, did your conscience prick you? Knowing that he might well have done the same over you, if he could only read your heart?'

'Get out.' He said it in a sort of inward grunt, as if to some possessing spirit.

'I'm not talking of . . . I don't accuse. We are all human, and fallible and contrary. ' I could hear my own voice, broken and uncontrollable, as separately as if someone else spoke. 'But I will take no blame that is really for you. Yes, I loved her more than I should have: so did everyone who knew her. But I was not the one who put her in the place where she died. I did not sacrifice her to make myself easy with Louis's favour and Louis's gold – yes, that rumour has long been about – why not let it out? If I loved Minette unwisely, I at least did not make her my tool—'

'Get out. Go.' My father was hunched, gasping: I thought of a soldier clutching a wound.

'Where? Am I banished the court again for the truth?'

'You are banished the kingdom. You won't stay – on pain of your life, you won't stay. Go where?' He drew himself up. 'Go to hell. For what you have said to me, go to hell.'

'Perhaps I will, in the end. For I know I have not been good. But I know of a worse place than hell, Father – the place you have made me live in. Limbo.'

'My last mercy – go, before I have you in irons.'

'I don't ask your mercy.' My tears burned my eyes. 'All I ever wanted from you was an honest love. But somewhere – somehow, you have forgotten how to give it. And there is my last mercy, if you like.' I walked to the door. 'Saying "forgotten". Not saying that you never knew how.'

I left the country soon after. With a single manservant I boarded a fishing boat at Harwich, at the bitter turning of the year. Ice came stinging from a gun-metal sky, blinding me: I had no last sight of England. Last, final – an end: so I felt it must be. This was surely an exile without return.

EIGHT

'Disturbing the peace of the realm! This is shocking, James. And entirely believable,' my cousin Mary said. 'After all, you come here to disturb our peace again, do you not?'

'Do I? I would go away if I thought that. But William has given me such a welcome. The lodging at the Old Court – there is a very old stiff chamberlain who proudly tells me it is only ever used for royal guests. If William did not want us to be here . . .' I looked questioningly into her face. Mary's seriousness had ripened into dignity; and she had learned not to give much away. 'Would he? I doubt that William does aught he does not want to do.'

She smiled. 'I was only teasing. William knows very well what he is about. But do you?'

'I have nothing to be about. I can only wait, and hope.'

'What is the hope? Of reconciliation?'

I grimaced. 'I mean a hopeless hope.'

'Is the breach so great, then? I can only judge by what we hear. You would not submit to your father over this matter of the confession, and he is monstrous angry with you. Surely . . .' It was her turn to scrutinize me. 'Or is there something you are not telling us?'

'You are quite the lawyer, cousin,' I said uncomfortably.

She laughed, seeming to like that. 'Well. The fact is, I can speak to you like this, James, because I am not in love with you any more.'

We were walking together in the Voorhout, the public promenade at The Hague. Other strollers were about in the watery spring sunshine. I coughed and glanced about me. 'Cousin . . .'

'It doesn't signify. Yes, I was, in a girl's way, back in England. Now I am not, and I can talk plainly to you as your friend. This is good, for you will hear sense from me, and not nonsense.'

There was a touch of William in those phrases: I could not help but smile. 'Does love make us talk only nonsense, then?'

'Not only nonsense,' Mary said in her thoughtful way. 'But love makes us different. That is the frightening thing about it. I like Harriet, by the by. I remember her from court when we were girls. She was just as spirited. I used to think she would do very well for herself.'

'Which I suppose has not happened. Scandalous exile with a scapegrace.'

'Fie, James. You know she is proud, and glories in you. As for the scandal . . . yes, I have heard some harsh words. About the way you live together.'

I frowned. 'The Dutch have given me a welcome. I would not wish to offend them. But – well, it makes me think. Lie with a dozen women, manage it discreetly, and 'tis very well. Love and be loved by one woman who isn't your wife, and you are a disgrace.'

'I'm afraid you are romantic in your notions. I did not say that was wrong,' she added quickly, as I bridled. 'Only . . .' Her tone freshened, as if she were changing the subject. 'William has had an affair.'

'No.' I was rocked. 'That can't be true.'

'That is quite a man's answer,' she said calmly. 'It is true. I don't know why I said it. Because truth is always good, perhaps.'

'But – Mary, this is terrible. I don't understand. You and William are so – so close and loving, I thought—'

'Oh, yes, we are. Still. I love him, and he loves me, and – that love had an illness. That's what happens with illnesses: we die, or we get better. Sometimes there are lasting marks . . . sometimes not.' She inclined her head to someone, faintly smiling. 'There – they are very surprised. Usually I walk only in our private gardens. That must be you again, James – stirring things up. Why did I tell you? Because gossip will, otherwise. And perhaps to show you that there is nothing we cannot survive, if love and faith be there.'

I squeezed her arm, but could not help saying sourly, 'They have to be there on both sides.'

She did not answer that directly. 'Do you dine with us this even, James? William will want to see you. There is a letter come for him from England. Oh, not from my father. We always get those.' She laughed a little sorely. 'William talks of using them to ballast his yacht . . . No, it is a letter from your father.'

And a harsh one it was. William had received several such since my coming to The Hague: letters bitterly complaining that he and Mary should so disoblige the King of England by giving me a welcome, and treating me as a guest of honour instead of a pariah. I burned at hearing it, but William, shrugging, said a letter was only a letter.

'It is not like a cannon-shot,' he said, putting it aside and reaching for the bread. 'It cannot hurt anyone.' But Mary's watchful eyes, across the table, could see otherwise.

I had not gone to them at first. Aimless, hopeless, I had taken a house at Brussels on my first coming abroad, and there my love had joined me. And there, presently, I had been visited by English exiles of my party. They were numerous in Holland, and they brought secret word that my cousins of Orange would not be loath to receive me. So we had moved to The Hague, and found it so: William courteously receiving me, even, it seemed, to the point of defiance.

'Yes, you are my friend,' he said. 'What of it? This is private matters. I may choose my friends.'

'But it isn't private. By receiving me, you – you put up a flag.'

'I know that. I am not a fool,' he said in his grumbling way. He had taken me to his hunting lodge at Dieren: a neat modest place, where he kept only the smallest of households, and he had left even those behind, leading me on a long ride into the woods of Gelderland. Now he reined in his mount, his breath whistling with asthma. 'Let us get down, now I have you alone.'

'A pretty place for an assassination,' I said with an awkward laugh.

'To be sure. And I might have the same fear of you.' William gave his hound's grin. 'But I do not. This is what I mean by friends. For there is much to make us enemies. My reverend father-in-law puts it plain, in his last late letter. What is it?'

'Latest.'

'Yes, that. I wish it was the last. He drives me to madness . . . Mary too. You know what he says to her? That everyone is shocked at the civility we show you. That she should know what good loyal people are saying about her – people who are – now what is his word? – monarchical.' He made a gargle of the word. 'I have it wrong?'

'No, no. God help us, that is the sort of word my uncle would use.'

'Hm. He wishes to warn me also that I should not flatter myself about your intentions. After the King is gone, and he is gone, he says you mean to have a push with me for the crown of England, and I will regret the favour I have shown you.'

'I see. You know he is—'

'I know he hates you, and he hates me, and he hates us doubly together, and would have us apart, yes, yes. Still, I must think of this.'

'I do not mean to fight you for the crown,' I said.

'But you would fight my father-in-law.'

'That is what I have been doing.' I kicked irritably at the leaf-mould, feeling stupid and boyish. 'And have lost.'

'Well.' William tweaked his beaked nose. 'That is the great question. Have you?'

'I am so far out of favour with my father,' I said, filled with bleak memory, 'that I may as well be in the Indies, for all the chance of my getting back.'

'So it would seem. Now I will tell you something. When I was latest in England – last, damn, whatever – your father took me aside and showed me his special seal. Whenever he wrote me, he said, I was to look out for that seal. If I did not see it, then I was to know the letter did not come from his heart. That it was a letter he had to give in and write, for the sake of policy.' He patted his horse's neck with a tenderness he seldom showed to people. 'It was there, mind. 'The letters he has writ me, so furious against you, do not have that seal.'

I took it in, or tried to. When I thought of my father, I had an image of marble blackness, like a great stone door forever closed against me. After what had happened, I could not conceive chinks, cracks, rays of light.

'Do you suppose . . . ?'

'I suppose nothing. Nor do I think you should suppose. But I tell you. Now we go.' His foot in the stirrup, William paused. 'But let us say, my father-in-law is premature if he calls himself the winner.'

'I wish I could believe that,' I said, mounting up, trying to suppress the faint glow of hope.

'Wish wish. I wish he would not write me ten times a week with his advice. Most of all, these letters talking of when he is dead.' William gathered up the reins. 'He should not distract me with such happy thoughts.'

Letters. I did not hope for, or receive, any from my father, as I lingered through the summer at The Hague. But the English ambassador did: letters conveying to me drafts of money. So I was not to starve.

Letters from my lord Halifax, who was still at court, and who began with the vaguest and most general regrets about the whole unhappy turn of affairs; but presently wrote in another style, which baffled my slow brain at first until I gathered that he was using a coded language, and used it to evade the spies of my uncle. And from him I learned things that perplexed me, and heartened me, and wrought to an almost intolerable pitch those clanging memories of my last meeting with my father.

For I was still a name not to be spoken at court. Yet if anyone did so, disparaging me to my father, no doubt thinking to curry favour with him, he angrily silenced them; as if, though he might think ill of me, he would not hear it from others. This even happened with my uncle James. There was talk of sending him to Scotland again. At times it appeared my father could not bear James near him.

Did I hope? Did I even want to hope, after that last meeting in which all the fermenting resentment, the disappointment, the anguish of a love tortured out of shape, had come bursting out to such a blasting effect that I could see only a scarred waste in the pleasant places where my father and I had once walked? I can hardly tell. But there was another letter: one that revealed to me, slowly, unexpectedly, how much stronger love can be than we can ever guess.

It came from an associate of Shaftesbury's, who had been entrusted with some of his papers before his death. Amongst them was something that seemed to be a note or letter to me, unfinished. It told me what had really happened when Minette had come on her memorable visit to Dover, to cement the friendship of England.

'I cannot tell whence this new information comes,' Shaftesbury had written, 'nor the exact truth of which this is the shape approximately rendered. But it confirms what I had long suspected, by hints and indirection. Clifford knew: also, I think, Arlington: Buckingham assuredly not. But then I fancy we were all more or less deceived.'

There had been more than gestures of friendship and commerce at Dover. Minette had been the proud and willing envoy of a secret treaty between my father and Louis of France. The treaty promised to help Louis destroy Holland: so much had been suspected when my father was pursuing his policy of French friendship. But there was another design. My father was to declare himself a Roman Catholic, and begin the conversion of England to the Romish faith. Louis would supply French troops to put down the expected resistance. And for the whole bargain Louis would supply my father with money – millions of livres: money to make him independent of Parliament, and free to do as he would.

'How much of this design was carried out, or intended to be, I leave Your Grace to determine: it may never be known: likewise how much gold the French King has disgorg'd over the years,' Shaftesbury wrote. 'But the religious design was close to the heart of the late Madame, for a certainty. If your father agreed to it—'

There was no more. Shaftesbury's illness had defeated his pen, perhaps; or perhaps he had decided not to send me the letter. No matter: I knew now.

I staggered at it. Wondering, brooding, I shut myself away, even from my love, though she will read this now, and know. So let me set down at once what cost me a long travail of tortured thought to arrive at: my understanding.

Yes, much became clearer now. Not only my father's cool, steady withdrawing of himself from the Parliament, as Louis's gold made him surer of standing alone. Certainly that made sense. It fitted with all I had divined of him: his fearful determination never to be beholden to anyone, in love or state; his lonely, self-preserving coolness. Of course, it made him beholden to Louis – but there was the crux of the matter. For I do not believe for a moment that he intended to fulfil his promises. From the war on Holland he would take what he could – as he did; and get out when he could – as he did; and at the end, form a friendship with the Dutch, sighing and saying to Louis that his awkward Parliament had forced him to it. As for the Catholic conversion, the most breathtaking proposal of all, he must have well known, from his brother's example, that nothing was more likely to stir a civil war, topple his throne, and send him on his travels again.

No, whatever God he served – I think I may dare add, if any – he would never set that service above reason and prudence. But Louis, the scourge of Protestantism, must be pleased by such a promise. And above all, Minette, the ardent child of the faith, would be overjoyed. She must have worked all the harder to bring the treaty about, knowing she obliged not only the brother she worshipped, and the King of France who had held her heart, but the religion in which her mother had shaped her. So, seeing all these things quite well, my father had made the pact, and taken the money . . . And laughed up his sleeve? That I could not decide. But I kept thinking of a word that the rakes of the court used much. 'Prick-tease.' My father, always gallant, reproved it. I remember him saying it only signified a woman who knew her own worth. Was he privately amused, knowing he had played the prick-tease of Europe, and got away with it unravished?

So my thoughts. As for my feelings – well, he had shown himself to be everything to which I was passionately opposed. And yet I could not help but admire. Perhaps we always admire what we lack; and I knew then that I could never be like him. His subtlety, his cunning, his nose for survival – besides these I knew I was a fanciful child hunting fairies in the wood. He belonged to a newer world, in which the fairies were dwindling, and must fade.

And I thought of what I had said to him of Minette, at our last quarrel; and I saw that I had grasped at a truth greater than I knew. Yes, he had used her: he had used her love, and lost her because of it. I could not see that as a good thing. I was not even sure it was a forgivable thing. But I was sure he had never forgiven himself for it. And I understood now the roar of fury at our last meeting: I heard the fearful self-loathing in it. For it was the betrayal of my friends that I had set myself against. And I had stood before a man who knew betrayal's acid flavour as well as he knew his own kingly name.

Letters. There were more from Lord Halifax, as the leaves turned in the Voorhout, and Holland, the place where my destiny began and where it seemed tailing to a meaningless end, drew on the russet-coat of autumn. They were cautiously encouraging, monotonously so. I ceased to believe in them, looked about me for occupation, talked with William of commanding his horse or taking a commission in Germany.

Then a letter from Halifax changed everything.

It must appear to be entirely my own idea: I must come secretly and incognito: there was no undertaking that the King would see me at all. I could visit only briefly, and could not linger. These were the negatives.

Set against this, I was going to England, to see my father.

'Like a Second Murderer in a play,' I said to Harriet. I had donned cloak and broad hat, and muffled up my face with a scarf before leaving her house at Stepney, where we were staying.

'Like a prince,' said she, kissing such of my face as she could find, and then laughing anxiously.

'I don't think we shall talk of such things,' I said.

'No?' She was a little indignant: such was her constant pride in me. 'Of what then?'

I thought. 'Family matters, perhaps.'

It was strange to go upriver cloaked and furtive, into the City where I had grown used to a tribute of bonfires and bells; to pass through the foggy twilight streets, amongst people trudging dour and rheumy and inexcitable, heedless of who was in their midst. Halifax had given me a password to present at the Privy Stairs, and as I mounted there, mist-drenched, my heart dully pounding, I had a momentary fear that it might not be recognized – that it was all a jest, and I would be turned away. And I knew then that I could not bear that: I would go mad.

My father was waiting for me in the bedchamber, surrounded by the busy clocks, seated before a vast coal fire. Even at the door I could feel the heat. It made my eyes sting. My father made an irresolute motion, half-rising, abandoning it. That was unlike him.

'Well, Jemmy. That is you under there, isn't it?' A chuckle, then he signed to his Groom of the Bedchamber who stood by. 'Leave us, Bruce.' Now he did stand, his joints cracking. 'Don't worry. He's on our side.' Still he went to the door after the man had gone, and laid his ear to it, and tested the handle. 'Odsfish, you see what you have done, Jemmy. You have even made a conspirator of me.'

'Father . . .' I said. I did not know how to go on – how to breach the brimming dam at my heart. But perhaps that word was enough, for now.

'Hush. Give me your hand first.' He came loping forward, then seized my hand and gripped it at a little distance, as wrestlers do. 'There. Now if we fall to quarrelling, at least we have clasped to begin with.'

'We won't quarrel. We cannot – can we?'

'After all that has happened – after last time – what ground is there left for a quarrel?' he said, very wry. 'Like two armies making a desert of the land they fight for. Or two men cudgelling each other over who shall ride a dead horse.'

I laughed a little, distressfully. 'That sounds horrible.'

'The figure is a thought gruesome . . . You should not be here, of course.'

'But it is by your leave?'

'But it is by my leave. And wish. Come, doff that cloak. Sit, sit, be easy.' But he was not easy: he looked at me and could not look at me. 'Jemmy, Jemmy, what are we to do?'

'Why – clasp again,' I said earnestly, gripping his hand. 'I've thought so much, Father – of you, of our parting, the things that were said—'

'Aye, aye, so have I.' He looked down at our clasped hands. 'And this makes it all right, do you think?'

'No, but—'

'As a general rule, I mean. Does it? Simple, direct, undisguised – are these always best? Is that the answer to it all? I ask seriously.'

'I think so. But I know you do not. You have your reasons. Deep reasons sometimes, deeper than men guess.'

He gave me a long searching look then; and said at last, 'Jemmy, what *do* you know?'

'I know that when I spoke of Minette' – I ignored the warning flash of his eyes – 'I spoke of great matters. Greater than I suspected. And that I touched on – a great pain.'

There came a silence that seemed to stretch till it filled the world. And at last, when my father spoke, it was as if he threw down his spear and shield.

'Yes,' he said huskily. 'Greater than you can imagine.' He went to his chair, stealing there as if to a refuge, and stared into the blaze. 'Do you – do you think she was happy?'

'Not with Philippe. But I don't think she would have been happy with Louis either, entirely. He is too cold.'

'Too like me?' he grunted, as if interrogating the fire.

'Happy . . . Her happiness was in you, I believe. Serving you, helping you. She saw it as being good. And Grandmother always—'

'Always told her to be good,' he said, in a chiming voice, like one of his own clocks. He leaned his head on his hand. 'Strange days. I never thought to be talking of these things with you.'

I had a feeling of moving across stepping stones. They were slippery, and I could not be sure they would not run out halfway across. 'Nor I. But – it's well. It is clearing away secrets. And that must be to the good.'

'I still misdoubt whether they should be cleared away. Veils and drapes – I have spent my life with them. Or behind them. Too old to change, perhaps.'

'You're not old.'

'I feel it. I feel like – a very little butter that has been spread miserably thin. I can remember the taste of that.' He made a face. 'On my travels. A very little butter. A very little grudging help. And God, they made sure you were thankful for it . . . People commend my manners, don't they?'

'Always.'

'I'll tell you something. When you see a person with good manners, know that they got them from spending a fair portion of their life in fear of being kicked out of the room . . .' Abruptly he sat straight. 'And so, you have been busy cultivating William. You cannot conspire at home, so you go about it abroad.'

'Is that what you believe?'

'Yes, I think so.' He clenched his fist, then opened it as if expecting, like a conjuror at a fair, to see a coin there. I would not have been surprised at it. 'It is very astute of you, Jemmy. You and William have a common cause, of a sort. You are mastering your face very well, but I can see you are smarting because I reprove you again. Wrong. At least, if I reprove you, it is only in reproving myself.' He huddled closer to the fire. 'Draw near, Jemmy – are you not cold? I feel cold . . . I have too much time lately. I have always been a lazy fellow with business – Hyde was right. And James – takes much of it on himself now . . . Would you know the new gossip? It is that I am impotent. Well, well. I share a jest with Nell; I have a hand of cards with the Queen; I sup with Louise, for I am comfortable with her, and she has the best cook in London. Such is the tenor of my life now, and it suits me. So the gossip.' He uttered a dry laugh. 'If only they knew how little I care about that one way or t'other! What I think about most – what I am ever aware of – is time.'

'I don't wonder at that,' I said, waving my hand at the clocks.

'Oh, those . . . Well, I would not be surprised to see those clock hands turning backwards one of these days, for I move so much in the past . . . Damn you.'

'Me?'

'Aye, I think you made me turn this way after that last time.' He made a scrubbing-out motion. 'Again, I don't mean a reproof. It would have come anyway, I don't doubt, this – this looking back at myself all the time, as if there is ever a mirror just behind my shoulder. Yes, I was displeased at you and William putting your heads together, and the prospect of more mischief. But the displeasure – it was like the striking of a clock, perhaps. Moving on a spring. And if I peer into the workings . . . why, then, I cannot be surprised, Jemmy. Nor can I condemn. You have intrigued for the crown – don't trouble to deny it. You have planned, and paraded, and cultivated men and made them promises, and sought every advantage.' He gave a ghostly smile. 'You have, in short, done everything I taught you.'

'Father, that's not—'

'Oh, I didn't do it wittingly, perhaps. Yet is that another piece of self-deception – if I say I never meant you to learn such lessons? Didn't I? Again, I look in that mirror, and there is another mirror within it.'

'I've learned much from you, Father,' I said, slow to understand. 'From the beginning, you have been—'

'Ah, don't reproach me, Jemmy. No need. I reproach myself amply – abundantly. Hm, when have you ever heard me say that before? I am a great dodger of blame. Hyde knew that: poor Catharine too . . .' Suddenly he fixed me with a sharp forensic look. 'Tell me, what principles of conduct have you ever learned here, Jemmy? Self-interest. Disguise. Deceit. Subterfuge. Are those principles at all, or their reverse? No matter. They are all you have had to learn from. And so the wonder is not that you have ended up scheming for the crown. The wonder is that you have not turned out worse.'

'This is hard on you,' I said after a moment. 'Hard on me also.' I struggled for an absolute candour. 'I don't scheme: I am not really clever enough for that. I – I *feel* it. I feel it as my destiny. I cannot call it any other name.'

'Because of what your mother told you?' he said, not unkindly.

'When my mother told me I was your true son – and bade me hold on to it – then, as I was then, I had no choice but to believe. And so it has remained. If I let it go – I will break apart.'

'Yet Lucy and I were never married, Jemmy. I say it to you now – quiet and private: there is only you and me, Jemmy, there are no kingdoms or councils, no succession, no policy. Lucy and I loved, and we made you; but we did not marry. I think she wanted it – but not so very badly: for you know, what she wanted was me, me.' He seemed to shiver. 'I told her plainly I could not marry her. The war was lost, and my father went to his execution, and the whole royal cause was at its last breath – all but hopeless. I was exiled, and had nothing – nothing but this marriageable hand. With that, I might get a bride who brought money, troops, influence. And yet' – the firelight seemed to dance in his eyes for a moment – 'I was tempted. Oh, yes. For devilment – the devilment of despair. I remember thinking, let us do it: find a minister quickly, and marry. All was in ruins: all had been taken from me, father, crown, country, name, dignity, hope; why not dispose what little I had of my own free will, instead of waiting to have it taken from me like all the rest? At least, marrying Lucy, I would be a free man. Ah, I came so near to it.'

'But you did not,' I said. I took it in: cautiously I breathed it. And I found I could breathe, strangely enough: I did not gasp like a landed fish in this new alien air.

'I did not. But came close. The thing you long to be, Jemmy, you very nearly were. And now I wish . . .'

He did not finish it. Nor did I say it: *now you wish I were?* To know was enough.

'There. It is told,' he said. 'But I get no satisfaction. Because I am very much afraid you will not believe me. I have given you – and others too – cause enough to mistrust everything I say. I know that, and I can't undo it . . . But did you not know in your heart, Jemmy, that this claim of your mother's was false?'

After a moment I said: 'I don't know things in my heart, Father. I feel them. It's different.' I offered a faint smile. 'Again the difference.'

'Again the difference,' he agreed. 'And you feel you should still be the heir, yes? Well, God knows you are not the only one who feels it . . . People do not understand because they forget. The exile: that made us what we are, James and I, our generation. Folk cannot see why I insist upon the due legal succession – when James is the man he is. They forget I know what it is to have a crown snatched from me: to have my world pulled like a carpet clean out from under my feet, leaving me tumbling, lost. I would not see another man go through that as I did.' He stirred, frowning. 'Yes, even James. I know what you are thinking. And I am – I am troubled about him of late. Like me he grows older and harps on the past – but for him it is different. A different lesson. He fights the old battles of the civil wars again; in his mind he wins them all, by being yet more severe, instead of seeing that we should never have come to war at all . . .' He slapped the arm of his chair. 'What can I say to him? What can I do? He won't change now . . .'

'No. He won't change now.'

'You left Mary well, I hope, Jemmy? She is an admirable sensible creature. Anne too, if a little dull. I have always contented myself with thinking of them coming after James, and so he— There will not be too much harm done. But now I begin to think, what if James's duchess should breed a boy at long last – stranger things have happened – and give him an heir to cut them out? I should have thought more of it before, but it all seemed far off yet . . . Not a word of this talk to anyone, Jemmy, by the by.' With a glint of dark humour he added, 'Conspiracy is cursed by loose tongues.'

'Why do you tell me all this, Father?'

'Because I am being frank. And because I know you see yourself as the answer, still. Jemmy, if I were to give you the crown, there would be – for all that the people love you – a great upheaval. And such never comes without grief and strife. You know that.'

'And if the crown goes to my uncle? Do you think that will bring no strife?'

For answer he gave only a grey smile; then rose and fetched a decanter and glasses. 'Sherry-sack. A mite congestive in these raw nights, but never mind. Let us drink together . . . I would not say much of myself, you know. But what I would say is that I have always found a way. My gift, if you like. I wonder if it is gone.' He raised his glass. 'Your lady-love accompanies you, I think, Jemmy? We should toast her. And yet I think it a pity, as far as your wife goes. I have always thought well of her. I shall always be a friend to her, you know.'

'I know. But you see – I can't rule my heart.'

'Ho, there is no surprise. Lady Henrietta is an impulsive creature, I hear; speaks most passionate on your behalf. I detect a touch of your mother there. Tell me, do you long for her – hunger for her? Does she sweep aside all else in your mind when you see her?'

'Yes. Oh, yes. She – well, I cannot put it into words.'

He looked sadly at the floor. 'You are fortunate. Blessed. I have always, alas, been very easily able to put it into words, very ordinary words. Well, Jemmy, is that not enough for you? I ask in earnest. Consider this prospect: that you and I may – only may – come together again, as we once were: father and son, no more nor less. And you will have money, and ease; and above all you will have your true love at your side. Is that not enough? For by God, it is what I have never had – the most important part.'

'Not even with my mother?'

He blinked at the fire, and did not answer.

'It is a beautiful picture,' I admitted. 'But there is something missing—'

'Your uncle, I know. If you were ever to return to Court, he would have to be – kept out of the way.'

'Father – you mean I may return? Soon?'

'You sound shocked. May you return after what you said last time, eh? Well, don't think I liked it, Jemmy – any of it.'

'I'm sorry. My feelings ran away with me—'

'What does that feel like?' he said, almost tremulous. 'Another thing that can't be put into words, perhaps. Well, Jemmy, don't overestimate the effect of it – what you said. I have survived many worse things than that in my life. Indeed as I look back, it seems one long exercise in surviving. And I fancy not many of my family have that gift . . . And I must love you still, Jemmy: that I know now. Because I see that survival is not enough. A man who hides in a cave all his life is safe – but has he lived?' He gave a great shrug, as if to shake off something hideously clinging, and went to a cabinet. Jewels flashed in his long bony hands.

'Oh, Father, I don't—'

'Nay, take them. You will need money. I can't say how long it will be, Jemmy. Now you must go, my son. Your hand again.'

'What shall I do?'

'Wait for word. And make amends to me.' Now he was stern and kingly once again. 'Be sober, and careful; keep away from your flattering friends; fight down that wildness in you. Will you do it?'

'I will.'

'Very well. And I . . .' He gazed over his shoulder, as if instead of the crowded overheated room he saw into vast distances: or perhaps a mirror. 'Perhaps I in turn may make amends to you.'

NINE

The Hague in winter: beginnings and endings. Here as a boy I had skated with my mother and Tom Howard, her beau. It was with that time that I began this narrative. And here as a man – a man scarcely less confused, sore-hearted, and baffled by the world than that boy – I skated again, in the winter of '85, with my cousin Princess Mary.

Still cloaked and secret, I had returned from my visit to my father in England, and on his instructions I had spoken to no one of what had passed there. Not even William, my ally: but he did not press. Again he welcomed me, settling me with Harriet at the Mauritshuis. There were firework-parties, plays, balls, fairs: the Dutch have tamed winter and made a feast of it. Sometimes William would even dance at the balls – unheard of before.

'Pah, that is you. You have turned me into a – there is a word like fop?'

'There is fop,' I said laughing, 'also rake, princock, popinjay.'

I remember too my first ride in a sledge, my arm around my love, and how the air cuffed our cheeks and made us laugh aloud like children. We rode behind William and Mary to the most delightful of their houses, the House in the Wood; and there in the Orang-Zaal, with its glorious paintings, I teased Harriet by admiring the abundant flesh of the women in Master Rubens' pictures, until she chased me into the gardens and thrust snowballs down my neck – Mary laughing in her reserved way, and William huffing like an excited dog.

And skating, of course. Mary was timid of such sports, but I enticed her to try it. With her petticoats tucked up and iron pattens on her feet she clung to my arm with a fierce terrified stiffness.

'I can't do it, I can't!'

'You are doing it – see. Now bend the knees, so.'

'Mine don't bend!' she wailed, though she persevered.

'Don't think about it,' I said. 'That's the trick of it.'

We drank a hot posset after, at the Mauritshuis. Mary's observant eyes conned me through the steam.

'Is that what you do, James?' she said. 'Not think about it? England. Your father.'

'Not quite,' I said. 'But I am content. I have to be.'

Content to wait: so I had to be, though it went hard with me. I lack patience. Halifax wrote me, cautiously. There were hopes, he said, that I might return to the Court in February – always depending. We must wait on my uncle's being posted away – to Scotland perhaps, or Flanders. And the right time must be chosen for that move. Everything was delicate, like Halifax's precise penmanship.

My father knew Halifax was writing to me. This is beyond doubt. For one letter bore a postscript in my father's hand. 'Bide where you are for now, Jemmy. Patience.' This is important, for what follows, and for my sanity – to assert that my father was working for my return, that white winter, the turning of 'eighty-five.

The snow still lay thick on the fretted roofs and spires of The Hague when I sat with Mary and Harriet and the Princess's ladies-in-waiting, yawning over a game of cards, a little blown and sleepy after dinner. We were staying at Honselaersdijck: all my thoughts were of the excellent bed upstairs. William had been called away by his secretary a while since, and I was just wondering whether I could make my excuses. I remember turning over the king of hearts. The room was candlelight, and soft patches of talk, and snow ruffling at the windowpanes. My eyelids prickled.

And then everything changed, for ever, as a servant came and coughed and said the Prince wanted to see the princess and me in his closet downstairs.

Down. I remember Mary took my arm as we entered. Did I sway, stagger, with premonition?

William sat at his desk. His cheeks were hollow and he looked yellow as wax in the frugal candlelight. Perhaps he was ill. Perhaps that was it. A letter was before him, the fresh ink shining like blood. The sand-box was in his hand, but his hand shook and the box dropped. The sand scattered everywhere. He stared down at it, almost appalled, as if it were the breaching of a dyke.

'There is news from England.' He cleared his throat. 'I have just writ a reply to it. It is very grave news. The King is no more. King Charles – I am sorry, Jemmy – your father died at Whitehall three days ago.'

I heard Mary softly weeping, somewhere: far-off, it seemed. The world had changed its dimensions. I turned, blundering through the door, banging and hurting myself. Somehow I wanted to run, even as I knew there was nowhere to run to.

My love came to me in our bedchamber. There was nothing she could do but listen to my howls. These were loud, embarrassing to hear, I dare say, much talked of afterwards. I think it was said that I wept for myself, and what was to be my future without him. Very well: so be it. He was my future, and my present, and my past.

The world had not ended. It was simply become a world lacking the sun. Only the moon left: only that light, chill and empty, to live by.

William came to my chamber after midnight, in his nightshirt. We sat in my dressing room, talking in low voices. It was cold; he rubbed fretfully at his bony bare shins.

'We know only that he had a troubled night's rest on the Sunday – woke apparently well, but then when he was being shaved, fell in a violent fit of apoplexy. He was put to bed, and did not rise again, though he lived till the early hours of Friday. The doctors tried every means. He was brave and uncomplaining throughout. His brother was with him, of course.' William shivered, hugging his slightness. 'Also the Queen came to him before his end, and was much affected. Also his – his other children were brought to his bedside for the farewell.'

'Also not me,' I said, with a hiccough of laughter, for I had spoken English like William's.

'He went into a sleep on Friday morning, and was past speech, and so he quietly went at last about midday. I know not if there was any – any message. It seems not.' He glanced at me for a fleeting moment, as if I were a searingly bright light. 'I am sorry for you, my friend. It is sudden. A great grief. Mary weeps. She was very fond of her uncle.'

'I am trying to remember,' I said, 'how old he was. And I know it, but

I cannot – cannot get at it. Fifty-four, or fifty-five? It is . . . Why can't I get at it?'

'I think fifty-four. Jemmy, what I now say – you are going to think me hard.'

'Why? Are you going to talk of Providence?'

'I talk of this world.' William made a sketch of holding out a comforting hand, abandoned it. 'You must know that your uncle of York is now proclaimed King. There has been no difficulty. Lords and Commons all agree. It is a settled thing. You see it, Jemmy? Your uncle – my father-in-law – is now King of England.'

'Well,' I said dully: my voice croaked from weeping. 'Then he is happy at last. What of it? What do I care for him? I only care for—'

'You do not understand,' William said harshly. 'You are dazed, I think. Better perhaps I talk tomorrow – but in truth it will not wait. You cannot stay here any longer, my friend. Everything is altered. While your father lived – well, he and I might squabble, but I knew I did not offend. With His new Majesty' – he grimaced – 'it is different. He was already angry with me for entertaining you. Now I face his anger as a king. He has power now. He is Popish, and much affected to France. We both know he will embrace Louis like a needy whore.' William was moved, after all: he never used such language. 'I cannot afford to turn England and France together against me. Holland would be crushed. I must – oblige him, for now. And that means you must go.'

'Yes, very well.'

I sprang up, and began throwing clothes into my trunk.

'You are angry with me,' William said. 'I'm sorry. It is the way it must be. It does not alter—'

'I'm not angry. I am only – only, all – empty.' Like William again: English words had become foreign to me; I could not command them. 'Where shall I go? Out of The Hague, of course. England, well, that is closed to me likewise—'

'It is. Very much. Your uncle closed the ports as soon as your father was dead, lest you try to come.'

I gazed at the shirt in my hands: somehow I had torn it. 'Where, then?'

'I am not your keeper. You have mentioned Germany. Why not? Sweden perhaps. Quiet, out of the way. Allow time for – well, a change.

You have friends, yes? Your wife, did you not say James thinks well of her? So. They might make a sort of peace for you. You might perhaps write your uncle a letter – offering your loyal submission.'

'I might.' The shirt was already torn. So I began to tear it more, until it was all in strips.

Watching me, William said: 'Think on it. Think wisely.' He got up. 'Don't go in dead of night – not like that.' Hesitatingly he touched my arm. His hand felt small as a young lady's. 'Mary will want to take leave of you. I shall give you money – a safe-conduct—'

'Thank you.' I did not look at him.

'The crown is settled on his head. That is sure. We have yet to see how it fits.'

'This need not have happened, you know,' I said. 'Many men sought to stop it. My father – I believe my father would have stopped it. If he had lived. I believe that.'

'My father died a week before I was born,' William said, in a remote voice: then, sighing, 'Sometimes, Jemmy, it is better not to believe anything.'

Beginnings: endings.

Here is where I have been, physically, all through this narrative. Now, I am come to now. This house at Gouda, where my love and I have settled, after a wretched straggle about Flanders – here I have written my story, and here I conclude it. It is three months since William told me of my father's death. I have gathered a little more about that event, here and there. Chiefly, that the doctors, with their purges and cuppings and red-hot blisters, put my father through the tortures of the damned in trying to stave off the death to which he went so bravely; and that a Catholic priest was brought in the day before he slipped away, so that he should be given the last rites, and die as a Catholic. Well, well. My uncle was there, exhorting him to it, no doubt. What conclusion about his soul my father came to in that crowded Whitehall bedchamber, amongst the agony and indignity, I know not, and it is not my place to know. But I can imagine him giving in, just to have an end at last to his brother's urgings – James nagging in his ear right to the brink of the grave; and I cannot conceive any God of any Church receiving his soul less warmly because of it.

We should not be here, in Holland. My uncle, enthroned and triumphant, has nagged William in turn, demanding to know where I am, and ordering the Prince to expel me from his domains. I know this because William has secretly written me so. He winks at my presence. We live quietly, for now: we share love, and that love has salved my grief, somewhat. Grief never goes. The hard lump of it remains, like the pearl in the oyster, the shiny canker, and we simply shape ourselves around it.

And England is quiescent under her vaunting new sovereign, for now. He only stretches his sinews as yet; and those who oppose him are crushed, or exiled. They come here, many of them, to talk to me. They pepper me with letters. They urge me to action.

And this has been all my action, thus far: this journey through the winding tunnels of the past. Now I emerge into the light, and ponder what I have learned upon the way, whilst my supporters rap urgently at the door, and talk of ships and funds, and remind me of destiny.

Beyond, the clouds show their faces in the canals, till the water-fowl shatter them into silvered ripples. The evening spreads like a slow sweet stain across the neat levels, and makes the lines of pollards stark and significant. Spring is about, skittishly, in fresh eddies of wind and sudden doses of green scent. And though I feel the promise of a new season, I feel the past yet – though not clinging. No, it is somehow as if my father, of whom I still think until thought itself wearies and sleeps, is alive yet, and not laid in his tomb in the abbey: as if he walks yet beside me, unchanged, unreadable, irreplaceable: my own father, King Charles the Second of England. If the past has shape, it is in his indelible presence. And it is his touch that I feel now upon my shoulder, and his touch that makes my decision for me, and tells me I must go.

Gouda, 1685

The End of the Duke of Monmouth's Narrative

Addendum Written by Lady Henrietta Wentworth, 1686

I add this account of subsequent events – in brief – for I cannot dwell upon it without superadding to the agony that has already shaken my frame to the edge of dissolution. It is a dissolution that I cannot, I fear, be long postponed – yet I do not fear but long for it – if it is the means as I hope and pray of reuniting me with my love. My beloved husband – not in name but before God – James Scott, Duke of Monmouth, whose narrative I conclude here.

After that period of indecision described above, in our retirement at Gouda, where he wrote this memoir, and pondered on the life and death of his father, King Charles the Second – afterward, his friends and partisans, who were many – and many alas more selfish than wise – urged my love to act, as the true heir of the late King. True inasmuch as His Majesty would have installed him as such, if he had not been cut off untimely – true also, in that the hearts of the people summoned him. Indeed, I have the greatest suspicions about the late King's dying so suddenly – a man hale and strong, and not in decline, stricken all at once, and just when 'twas in the wind that he meditated a change in his affairs – especially in regard to the Duke of York, a man ever impatient for the crown. Well – no more. My love was doubtful when I communicated these suspicions. But I urged him, as his friends did, to consider his certain destiny, and the wishes of the people already beginning to murmur under the tyranny of the new King – James the Second as he styled himself, though recognized as such by none of true English heart. We reminded him also that history itself cried out for him – through the bones of great Elizabeth and the martyred ashes of Bloody Mary's fires – cried out for a Protestant champion to redeem her favoured isle from the bonds of absolutism and Popery, and subjugation to rapacious France.

So I urged – and so all men and women of fiery spirit urged – and that lit at last the noble touchwood of the Duke of Monmouth's nature – and so he resolved upon his course. Thus: to gather forces, and make a landing in England, and stir the people to his side, and bring down that pious tyrant James, King as I must call him.

So 'twas planned, swiftly – too swiftly perhaps – but no more of that. My love renewed his correspondence with those great lords and gentry of the North and West who had supported him upon his progresses there, and received favourable returns, that they would rise upon his landing – the West especially, where the people were most warmly affected to him – and so the West was resolved upon as the likeliest place, as well as being the nearer sailing. There were hopes also of Scotland, whither the Earl of Argyle was to make an expedition to raise that country against the so-called King. We set about raising money. My love pawned his jewels and plate, and I likewise, and others of his party added their moiety, till he was able to engage with a Dutch merchant at Amsterdam, for the fitting out of a force of ships, a frigate and two smaller vessels, together with arms and stores. And in all of this I may mention the part played by Prince William of Orange – 'twas not an active one – no, he presented no countenance to such an expedition – yet he knew for a surety of my love's design, and if he did not further it, neither did he hinder it. That we were able to equip the ships unmolested at Amsterdam, I trace to the influence of William. Alas, I begin to think it was no desire on William's part for my love's success, that made him wink at these preparations: that he divined instead that he would be rid of a rival for the English throne, should the expedition fail.

But we thought not of failure, when the time came for sailing – at least I am sure I did not. 'Twas a most agonizing parting – yet with the sweetness of the grand and heroic moment – as of a tale of knightly antiquity – the more as I presented him, my love and champion, with a girdle embroidered in silver, to wear as his lady's favour as of old. And a token of me – to be with him in his enterprise – whatever passed.

They sailed. The balmy winds of June filled the sails of the little fleet. I stood upon the quay long after the horizon had swallowed them – turned at last to weep and pray in solitude.

I did not see my love again.

Those events that followed I was no witness of – but their sequence is most tragically straight and plain, and I have pictured them a thousand hideous times. The Duke of Monmouth landed at Lyme Bay – unopposed. He led his men, in number scarce above eighty, over the cliff, and into the town. And now began the welcome – the people swarming about him in most tumultuous exultation, crying out that he was come as the saviour of the kingdom. At Lyme he made his Declaration, for delivering the kingdom from the tyranny of James of York: 'twas an intemperate document perhaps, and had been writ by that sharp Scot, Ferguson, whom my love had begun to suspect was not the wisest of counsellors – yet 'twas a firm assertion of the dangers our country stood under, from the rule of James, and the wrongs done it – and of the resolve of the Duke of Monmouth to right them – and once that tyrant was brought low, to lay the question of governance and succession before the Parliament of the realm.

At Lyme he recruited: 'twas no matter of impressment: within two days a thousand men had volunteered to join him. And 'twas thus as he marched on to Taunton and beyond – everywhere passionate cries in his support, and men flocking to his side – more than he could well equip with arms in truth. And here he declared himself King.

Some urged against it – for many who followed him were of the sternest sort, from Cromwell's time, and republican – yet I think he must have contended that men's hearts would beat faster to the call of a king. And I for my part glory in it, and I honour those who kneeled before him and called him such – many there were in the West – and acknowledge him still, the only King in my heart.

Leaving Taunton he had above seven thousand men under his command; and if Bristol might fall to him, his prospects would be yet brighter. Yet James of York of course had not been idle. He had dispatched troops of royal dragoons, of foot and horse, who were descending momently upon the West. These troops entering Bristol, it was proclaimed to the citizens, many affected towards the Duke of Monmouth's cause, that if they sought to admit him to the town, it would be burned down around their ears. And my love, hearing this, resolved against such destruction. I hear that he was discommended for this by some among his party, who would have him more ruthless. I would not have had him so – God knows – even with the lamentable event – I would not have had my love so.

There came the first skirmish at a place called Norton St Philip, in which he had the victory – but now fate began to turn her unluckier cards – rain falling in torrents, to the misery of his encamped men – loss of stores to the enemy, and cowardly answers from those great ones he expected to support him. James of York promised a pardon to those who would desert my love's cause and come over to him. There were some few desirous of this course, who urged a return to the ships for those who were under attaint of High Treason, as my love was. Uncertainty – doubt – it was my love who overcame them. He would not abandon the men who had followed him. I think he cannot have trusted James of York's promise of a pardon would ever be redeemed, knowing the cold vindictiveness of that man's nature. He resolved to press on – planned I believed to turn north to rally his supporters there – but before that, it came at last to battle, at a place called Sedgemoor.

The enemy army coming in sight of his camp, he decided upon a night attack. His force moved off – in necessary silence – but they were betrayed by a man letting off his pistol, to give the alert to the enemy, and riding off at once to their lines. It was a foggy night – my love's troops courageous but raw and unseasoned – the heavy fire from the Yorkist troops did horrid work against them. I know my love fought bravely, pike in hand, at the head of his men – and they sold their lives mighty dearly, especially the foot, who would not break rank even as the night wore on to dawn, and revealed the hopelessness of the bloody field.

For all was lost. The troops of York had the victory, and my love's gallant force was shattered. There was nothing left for him but to fly as best he might – such friends as remained urged him this way and that, towards the Bristol Channel or the New Forest. He elected the latter – made the best way he could through the countryside, keeping to the remotest paths – once disguising himself in shepherd's garments – hidden and succoured by kind-disposed men and women, notwithstanding the five thousand pounds' price upon his head. I wonder if, in that desperate flight, he thought of his father, who had been hunted through his kingdom in just the same way, in borrowed garments, ever fearful of betrayal.

But for my love there was no Boscobel oak-tree – no ship's captain whisking him to safety ahead of the enemy troopers. For the romance of escape was submitted the tragedy of capture. Hungry, bearded, ragged, he was discovered at last, where he had fallen asleep in a ditch from exhaustion, by some militiamen: a cottage woman living nearby had spied him, and betrayed him. She got some money, I dare say.

He was taken to London by coach – his guard heavy, pistols drawn – and then brought by barge to Whitehall, and landed at the Privy Stairs.

And why there? Why not the Tower at once, as he was now an attainted traitor? So, knowing what came after, did many people ask – with trouble and bitterness: for what James of York did then was of a cruelty hardly to be expected even of his nature. He had the Duke of Monmouth brought before him to the Privy Apartments. And the one thing above all I cannot bear is the thought of my love, his hands tied, walking thither with what must surely have been a lifting heart.

For 'tis a well-established royal usage, that if a king agree to see a man accused thus, it is to pardon him: he will not see him else. So all present must have thought; so my love must have thought, as he went before his uncle. Instead, James spoke with him for half an hour, during which my love pleaded for his life, and then sent him to the Tower to await his execution.

The Duchess of Monmouth came to see him there. Her chief concern was to exact from him an assertion that she was not involved in his rebellion, as she termed it. She was shaking him off. He very readily assured her that he had no charges to make against her, and that she need not fear his fate. Such was all the tender cheer that could come to him, as he waited in the condemned cell – this most practical leave-taking from the wife who loved him not, and was anxious for her estates – and I – I who loved him – could not come to him – and still I incline almost to cry out upon Almighty God that He could let it happen so.

My love had writ to his late father's Queen Catharine, asking her to intercede for him – as I am assured she did – but what impression that gentle lady's persuasions might make upon the flint heart of James, I leave you to imagine.

Two bishops came to him the following morning, to inform him that he was to die the very next day. One day: such was the time that pious prince, James of York, allowed his nephew to make his preparations for the step into the eternal.

At ten o'clock in the morning of 15 July 1685, my love was taken by the Lieutenant of the Tower to the scaffold upon Tower Hill, where there was a great crowd, groaning and weeping sorely, and yet inclined to tumult also, for the man they loved – so that there were a great many soldiery to keep them back. The bishops preaching at him as he mounted the scaffold, he would say only that he acknowledged the doctrine of the Church of England. The sheriffs most insolently urged him to confess himself a rebel, which he composedly would not – nor would he make any speeches – yet he did speak of me. He gave to his servant a ring to be conveyed to me (I have it – my love, I have it upon my finger now!) – and said that there was a scandal raised upon him about a woman. He declared that woman was a lady of virtue and honour, and that what had passed between us was honest and innocent in the sight of God. Oh, they cried out at that, the bishops and the sheriffs, but my love was unmoved: he was firm.

He spoke to the executioner, and gave him six guineas to do his work well. He refused to be bound, and declined the blindfold, and laid his head upon the block.

The executioner served him very ill – I must write it – striking two most bungling and mangling blows, after which my love still lived – and the man would fain have thrown down the axe, complaining his heart failed him, but the sheriffs made him go on – for the crowd was in a howling state now – ready to surge up and tear him for his butchery – and so he finished his work, with a knife. And thus was my love's life extinguished in his thirty-sixth year – thus also my own.

I heard of it in Holland, at last. There was my death, inside. I came to London presently – James of York had me questioned, but 'twas plain I was nothing, and I was let be. I wanted only to see my love's tomb at the Tower chapel, but they would not allow it.

The death, inside: now I wait only for completion. And then, all griefs amended, I shall feel his touch again.

Author's Note

Lady Henrietta Wentworth died in 1686, at the age of twenty-six.

The survivors of Monmouth's Rebellion in the West Country were rounded up and tried at the Bloody Assizes, presided over by Judge Jeffreys, James II's Lord Chief Justice. Three hundred were hanged, drawn and quartered, and a further thousand transported to the West Indies.

James II was deposed from the English throne three years later, in the 'Glorious Revolution' of 1688. Seven members of the English ruling class submitted an appeal to William of Orange to come and take the throne. William and his army landed at Torbay and advanced on London virtually unopposed. James fled the country and died in exile in 1701, a pensioner of France. William and Mary reigned as joint sovereigns, and William devoted his energies, successfully, to the containment of the European ambitions of Louis XIV.

Anna Scott, Duchess of Monmouth, married again three years after her husband's execution, and lived to the age of eighty-two. She always refused to speak of the Duke of Monmouth.

Philippe, Duc d'Orléans, married a second time: his wife, a niece of Prince Rupert, outlived him.

Queen Catharine of Braganza returned to Portugal in 1692, and acted as Regent for her brother.

Barbara Castlemaine outlived Charles II and made a bigamous marriage at the age of sixty-five. Louise de Kéroüalle, Duchess of Portsmouth, retired to France. Nell Gwynn died of a stroke two years after Charles II, at the age of thirty-five.

You can buy any of these other **Review** titles from your bookshop or *direct from the publisher*.

FREE P&P AND UK DELIVERY
(Overseas and Ireland £3.50 per book)

The Seventh Son	Reay Tannahill	£6.99
Virgin	Robin Maxwell	£6.99
Bone House	Betsy Tobin	£6.99
Girl in Hyacinth Blue	Susan Vreeland	£6.99
A History of Insects	Yvonne Roberts	£6.99
The Long Afternoon	Giles Waterfield	£6.99
The Journal of Mrs Pepys	Sara George	£6.99
Still She Haunts Me	Katie Roiphe	£6.99
Vienna Passion	Lilian Faschinger	£6.99
Earth and Heaven	Sue Gee	£6.99
Stolen Marches	David Crackanthorpe	£6.99
The Last Great Dance on Earth	Sandra Gulland	£6.99
Scheherazade	Anthony O'Neill	£6.99

TO ORDER SIMPLY CALL THIS NUMBER

01235 400 414

or visit our website: www.madaboutbooks.com

Prices and availability subject to change without notice.